USA TODAY BESTSELLING AUTHOR

KASEY MICHAELS

how to
Wed a
Baron

"Michaels does it again...delectable."
—*Publishers Weekly* (starred review) on *The Butler Did It*

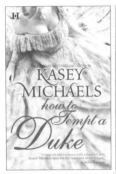

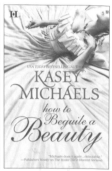

KASEY MICHAELS

how to
Wed a
Baron

HQN™

Recycling programs
for this product may
not exist in your area.

ISBN-13: 978-0-373-77463-0

HOW TO WED A BARON

Copyright © 2010 by Kathryn Seidick

This edition published by arrangement with Harlequin Books S.A.

For questions and comments about the quality of this book
please contact us at Customer_eCare@Harlequin.ca.

® and TM are trademarks of the publisher. Trademarks indicated with ® are registered in the United States Patent and Trademark Office, the Canadian Trade Marks Office and in other countries.

www.HQNBooks.com

Printed in U.S.A.

Dear Reader,

Baron Justin Wilde presents himself to the world as witty, urbane and decidedly harmless. Yet for years during the war with Bonaparte, the baron served as the Crown's most successful assassin. Outlawed for killing his man in a duel, Justin took on this soul-killing mission only in the hope of an eventual pardon and a return to his beloved England. But that royal pardon arrived with several strings attached to it—including an arranged marriage to one Lady Magdalèna Evinka Nadeja Valentin.

Lady Alina is no more thrilled with this arrangement than is the baron, but from the moment they meet their attraction is undeniable. But with secrets of both the past and present to overcome, will either of them live long enough to find the love that might be theirs?

How to Wed a Baron brings together the characters from my previous books, *How to Tempt a Duke*, *How to Tame a Lady* and *How to Beguile a Beauty*. It is the story of two people, yes, but it is also a tribute to friendship, trust and a belief in the power of love, forgiveness and new beginnings.

Please visit my website at kaseymichaels.com and let me know if you've enjoyed these four very special stories, and for information about all of my books.

Warmest regards,

Kasey Michaels

To Carol Carpenter and memories of a great day
of brainstorming ideas for this book while
seeing the sights in Williamsburg.

All vacations should be that much fun!

how to Wed a Baron

PROLOGUE

A QUARTER MILE FROM THE manor house located five miles outside the ancient city of Prague, and hidden amid mighty oak trees that swallowed up much of the September sunshine, a lone figure sat on the grassy bank of a meandering stream. Her knees were tucked up beneath her chin as she intently watched the progress of an early fallen leaf until it became caught up in a tangle of water lilies and disappeared below the surface.

The young woman's sigh was audible as she turned her head and seemed to pick out another leaf floating downstream, ready to follow its progress toward capture and oblivion, powerless to change its fate.

So, the man watching her thought. *She's been told.*

Luka Prochazka remained concealed behind a tree trunk as he cursed the Fates that had denied him any skill with the paintbrush, for surely this was a moment worthy of being captured on canvas for the ages. Her slim woman's body clad in a worn gown, her marvelous tumble of thick dark curls that seemed almost too heavy to be supported by the fragile column of her throat, the downcast eyes, the complexion of purest ivory…

She sighed once more, her shoulders rising and falling in dramatic fashion. Dearest Lady Alina. At not quite her nineteenth birthday, she was so very accomplished at drama.

Yes, this would be how he would have titled his portrait: *Lady Magdaléna Evinka Nadeja Valentin, In Despair.* Lesser hearts than his would break to see her this way. Her aunt, Lady Mimi Valentin, would give ten years of her life, perhaps twenty, to be half so beautiful, which was probably why she'd been so eager to do as the king had requested. Indeed, knowing the woman, she had most certainly delighted in the prospect of attending court with Lady Alina no longer in her train, capturing the eye of any man between the ages of twelve and three-days-dead.

Poor, beautiful Lady Alina. How very hard she had tried to be who and what she was not. Wild, free, unfettered. But an English mother and a half-Romany father, both long dead, did not a Romany make. In the end, it was the English blood that counted to those in power. Those in control. And to those in control, a young woman of marriageable age was nothing more than a pawn.

She would make a beautiful bride once Luka delivered her to her fate. Her groom, this unknown

Englishman she was being sent to in six weeks' time, would be a lucky man, indeed.

He turned away to silently retrace his steps, give Alina some privacy until the worst of her sulk was over. As he did, he thought to himself, *In the end, she'll make the best of it. She'll find a way, her own way. She is her father's daughter, and there is no defeat in her....*

CHAPTER ONE

JUSTIN WILDE MOUNTED the curving right-hand staircase of Carleton House with all the joy of a condemned man being marched to the scaffold, one of his royal majesty's flunkies on either side of him. At least the execution would be formal, not slapdash in appearance.

As his well-polished Hessians confidently struck each marble stair, his alert green eyes saw everything, his exemplary brain cataloguing and recording each detail of his surroundings. One might say the baron lived his life in a state of the highest readiness, prepared to fight or flee, should either necessity present itself.

Not that the pair of ridiculous liveried footmen, matching in their height and build and coloring as well, just as if they had been specifically chosen as a matched set—which they no doubt had been—would have entertained the slightest notion that, with little effort on his part, the baron could have dispatched them both to their final reward before they could blink.

And not that the servants could be faulted for their lack of perception. They saw, the world saw, what Baron Wilde wished them to see, and nothing more: a handsome, well-set-up gentleman who appeared to be as harmless as a morning in May.

Only those who knew Justin Wilde well—and these numbered less than a half dozen—saw more than the exquisite lace at his neck and cuffs, the fashionably fine cut of his coat, the perfection that was his longish, carefully casual black hair that matched in color a pair of wonderfully winged eyebrows.

Most impressive of all was his ready smile, which could be mocking, ironic, amused, open, disarmingly friendly and, as those privileged half dozen knew, very rarely genuine.

There was no smile on his lean face at the moment, real or subtly perfected. To receive the Prince Regent's summons at some point in time had not been unexpected. The man had warned of the eventuality at their last meeting. But now, scant months after their agreement, the sure knowledge that he was to consider himself at the man's beck and call for the remainder of one of their lives had been brought home in all of its unpleasantness.

"That chandelier is new since my last visit, isn't it?" he inquired of the footmen, pointing to a crystal-and-gilt monstrosity that hung at the top of the stairs. "I probably paid for it, you know. My God, is that a crystal dove at the center of it?"

The younger of the two servants looked up at the chandelier, nearly losing his step on the marble stairs, so that Justin quickly reached out to steady him.

"Coo, that was a close-run thing, weren't it? Thank you, milord."

"Nonsense. I apologize for distracting you, knowing the danger. My late wife perished on these same stairs some years ago."

"Is that a fact, milord? Took herself a fall, did she?"

"She didn't drown," Justin agreed pleasantly.

"Silas, stifle yourself," the older footman warned, clearly aghast at both the question and his lordship's answer. "This way, my lord, if you please," he then added quickly, gesturing to the left—away from the ornate public rooms and toward the private area of the residence.

Wonderful. The only thing more off-putting than Prinny at noon would be Prinny at noon and still in his nightcap. Less than five minutes later, Justin's worst fears were confirmed.

Once he was announced, the footmen retreated amid a flurry of deep bows. Justin advanced across an expanse of priceless carpets and parquet flooring, stopping at the foot of a bed so high, so wide, so lavishly hung with velvet draperies that even the Prince of *Whales* appeared small as he sat propped against pillows in the middle of it, munching on coddled eggs.

Justin smartly clapped his booted feet together and inclined his head and shoulders only enough to be civil. "Your obedient servant appearing at your command, Your Royal Highness."

"Wilde," the Prince of Wales said, sighing as he put down his fork. "You're the only man I know who can turn an expression of respect into an insult. Did you see it?"

Justin racked his brain for a moment, and then nodded. "The dove may have been taking ostentation too far, even for you. What next, sir, pink waistcoats?"

"Ha! Nobody has dared to speak so freely around me since George. How I miss that rascal."

"As do his many creditors, or so I've heard," Justin said, remembering the evening not so long ago he'd spent doing his part in spiriting George "Beau" Brummell out of the city and on his way to safety in Calais. "Is that why I'm here, sir? To somehow assist in raising fond memories of the fellow who was once bosom chum? I'm flattered, yet devastated to admit that my man Wigglesworth doesn't quite possess the man's clever way with boot black."

The prince swept out his arm, sending the silver tray loaded down with chocolate pots and plates and pastries crashing to the floor. "Damn you! Who are you to speak to me that— What do you want? *Get out!*"

This last was directed at the guardsmen who had entered at the sound of crashing silver and crockery, their swords drawn.

Justin stood his ground. And waited.

"For all of George's faults, it's true, I do miss him," the prince said at last, almost wistfully, his well-known mercurial mood having shifted yet again. "He was well when you last saw him?"

"Alas, I cannot answer that question, sir, as I fear I've never actually met the man," Justin lied smoothly.

"Yes, of course," Prinny said, apparently remembering that he should show no interest in the Beau, or the fact that he'd cared enough to have ferreted out Justin's participation in the scheme to extract the fellow from the clutches of the duns and even incarceration in debtor's prison. "Let us move on to other things."

"As you wish, sir. I am yours to command."

"Good, you remember who I am. There are times I find that difficult to believe. Then you recall our private agreement as well, Wilde?"

Justin inclined his head yet again. "I believe I've committed it to memory, yes. If I might paraphrase for you?"

"Yes, yes, go on. I want to be assured you remember it."

Justin's smile was brilliant. "As I would a badly throbbing tooth, sir. In exchange for a sum of money numbering somewhere in the vicinity of what could in some twisted way be termed a king's ransom, all of it deposited directly into Your Royal Highness's private purse—"

"*That* is never to be mentioned."

"I stand corrected. Although it was fifty thousand pounds, to be precise," Justin said, actually beginning to enjoy himself. "Your Royal Highness, known to his intimates as George the Kind, I might venture, acting purely out of a generosity of spirit acknowledged throughout the realm and without thought to personal enrichment, pardoned my sorry self for the crime of firing in self-defense when the fool I'd been forced to challenge to a duel turned and discharged his pistol on *two*. A mistake that proved fatal to him and disastrous to me, as I then had to flee England or else be arrested and summarily hanged."

"Better, although you fail to mention that dueling itself has long been outlawed, no matter the result of the meeting," the prince pointed out smugly.

"How remiss of me. Shall we dig up Robbie Farber and charge him for his crime, do you think?"

"You're impertinent. Go on, finish it."

Justin really would rather not, so that the insult wrapped in his answer came to him easily. "In return for this grand and noble gesture, I, Baron Wilde, grateful to be once more standing on the ground first trod by my illustrious ancestors long before yours, sir, had ever heard of England and were still happily speaking German and feeding on cabbages, after eight long and painful years of exile, and once again in possession of both my estates and my fortune—most of the latter, at any rate—am the eager and obedient servant of Your Royal Highness, ready at all times to assist him whenever the need arises. That is our agreement, until such time as Your Royal Highness believes sufficient penance has been served."

"I can't abide cabbages, so your paltry attempt at yet another insult will be ignored. But I would be remiss if I weren't to point out that you're running perilously close to the limits of my forbearance." Prinny wagged a finger in Justin's direction. "You actually did quite well, Wilde, until the last. Handsome devil, I'll give you that, but your jaw went rather hard there for a few moments. You aren't eager and obedient?"

"I'm here," Justin said, taking out his snuffbox. He wasn't having fun anymore. In fact, he was very nearly bored, which was always dangerous. He deftly opened the chased-gold thing with one hand and then, delicately holding an infinitesimal pinch to his left nostril, sniffed. "For eager and obedient, I suggest His Royal Highness might accept my gift of the pick of my favorite bitch's recent litter."

"Damn, that was brilliant. Such understated flair,

Wilde. You have to show me how you do it. Didn't even sneeze."

"Sneezing is so déclassé," Justin said, returning the snuffbox to his pocket. "It's all in the measure, sir. That, and I've had my blacksmith line my nostrils with lead."

"I'd almost believe you. But enough banter. I'm due at the palace at three, to present myself to mine father, who please God isn't ranting or drooling today. I'm about to make you a very happy man, Wilde."

"How interesting, Your Royal Highness. And here I am, under the impression that I am already happy. Perhaps you plan to make me ecstatic?"

Prinny readjusted the covers around his ample belly. "There are times I think I'd rather make you mute. A pity we're all now so modern and civilized. A well-maintained torture chamber was often a king's only friend. How does one eat without a tongue, do you know?"

"In very small bites, I'd imagine," Justin said, mistrusting the gleam in the prince's vivid blue eyes, and therefore prudently not pointing out that the man was still one live if hopelessly mad father away from the throne.

"Your wife is dead these eight years or more, yes?"

"I believe so, yes." Now Justin was all attention, at least inwardly. "A date you might remember with more clarity than I, as I was already escaped to the Continent. But I've always wondered, sir. How does one go about disposing of a dead body at the bottom of the stairs? A terrible inconvenience at best, I would suppose. Did you have her hauled away, or just fold her up inside a cabinet while the party went on without her?"

"You're cold, Wilde. She was your wife. Granted, a little too free with her favors, but very beautiful. Exquisite, actually."

Justin remained silent. Yes, Sheila had been beautiful. On the outside. And he'd been young, and beauty had mattered to him very much. Even after Sheila had no longer mattered, he'd found himself involved in a duel to protect her nonexistent honor.

"You don't agree?"

"I scarcely remember her face, sir. There may be a miniature somewhere. Would you like it?"

"Cold. Cold. You make me almost regret what I am about to offer. A single service to put a period to your…accessibility. An end to your indebtedness. You'd like that, wouldn't you?"

Wilde lifted a hand to his face. And yawned. It was amazing what one could dare when one had moved beyond the ability to *care*.

"I've found you a wife," the Prince Regent stated baldly, his tone clearly implying that he was no longer amused by Justin's antics.

"Oh, I think not, sir. I'm not in the market for a wife."

"You're also not in a cell, awaiting the hangman. Which one of those two alternatives do you choose?"

Justin wouldn't give the man the satisfaction of his answer. Even though they both knew that answer.

"Yes, quite. I will go on now. She is said to be the daughter of a war hero, unfortunately deceased. Allow it to be known only to you that this union is very important to the fellow who still most favors the ancient title of Holy Roman Emperor to that of—"

"Francis of Austria," Justin supplied tersely. "Father of Marie Louise, who was wife to Napoleon, until Francis convinced her to betray him. Nephew of the doomed Marie Antoinette, whom he refused to save from the guillotine because he saw no personal profit in it. The man turned his coat so often since ascending the throne it is something of a marvel that he didn't end up hanged and gibbeted by Bonaparte—or us. So, this female I'm not going to marry is German? Austrian?"

The prince shook his head. "Bohemian, although I'm assured that her mother, also unfortunately deceased, was English, and her late father a favorite at the court until his death on some battlefield."

Justin was careful to keep his expression blank, even as an event in his life he'd hoped long banished returned to slap at his composure. "I once visited a city in the region. Trebon. I did not enjoy my time there."

"No one but a fool enjoys being anywhere but England. Oh, but I know what you're saying. You think perhaps she's a Gypsy? Certainly not."

"They prefer *Romany,* sir. Never Gypsy. At any rate, if you were told the lady is Bohemian, even if only less than half of her, I believe I'd prefer being hanged in the morning, thank you."

"They're a dirty people?" The prince's face had taken on a rather haunted look, most probably thanks to a memory of his first sight of his now-estranged wife, Princess Caroline. It had been said that she harbored a decided dislike of soap and regular bathing.

"No, sir. And I'm certain the female in question is thoroughly civilized. I momentarily overreacted to an unpleasant memory, no more than that."

"Please, don't apologize. I believe I enjoy seeing the unflappable Justin Wilde even slightly discommoded. Trebon, was it? Nasty place? At any rate, this young woman, this—one moment." He extracted a slip of paper from the pocket of his nightshirt, then read carefully: "'Lady Magdaléna Evinka Nadeja Valentin.' Foreign names are all so needlessly complicated, aren't they? Give me a good Mary, or Elizabeth, or Anne. At any rate, this woman is in need of a husband."

"Disdainful as I am of repetition, I am not in need of a wife, sir."

"You'll pardon me my rudeness, Wilde, but I cannot find it within me to be concerned in the slightest with what you believe *you* might need. *I* need—no, strike that. *England* needs a suitable, well-born husband for the woman, for reasons of trade and all of that nonsense. You are to consider this marriage a foregone conclusion. Any and all information you might need will be provided to you as you leave. And one more thing—marry her and we're finished. You will no longer be obligated to me in any way. And, yes, before you are so bad-mannered as to ask, you will also find a signed letter from me stating that fact, along with all those pesky details such as the time of her arrival at Portsmouth, which I believe to be fairly imminent. Now, see if you can find your way out without saying something that makes me rethink my generosity. And send in somebody to clean up this mess."

Justin bowed, his jaw tight, and backed up three paces before turning to exit the overheated chamber. He might banter with the prince, he might even insult him, but there existed no way he could disobey him, not at the end of day, when such things mattered. And they both knew it.

He had his hand resting on the latch before the prince spoke again. Justin didn't know what the man would say, but he had known he would say something. There was, with the Prince Regent, always something else.

"By the way, Wilde."

"Yes, sir?" he asked, not bothering to turn around. Christ, the man was so woefully predictable.

"I may have forgotten to mention one other thing. Slipped my mind, I suppose. But, then, why else would I overlook your proven shortcomings as a husband for the lady in favor of your rather unique talents? You see, it would seem that someone wants your affianced bride dead. If any misfortune were to come to her, King Francis and I—indeed, England— would be quite displeased. You amuse me, Wilde, God only knows why. But my amusement has its limits. *Now* you may go."

THE HUSTLE AND BUSTLE of the Portsmouth seaport and the array of tall masts Justin could see from his bedchamber window had not altered considerably in the time it had taken him to bathe and dress; which, for a gentleman of the first stare like the Baron Wilde, was, coincidentally, considerable.

He'd arrived in the town late the previous evening, having delayed departing London until he could be assured word had gotten back to the Prince Regent that it appeared Baron Wilde was flouting His Royal Majesty's orders.

After all, why should Prinny be allowed a peaceful slumber if he, the victim in this sad farce, was to be denied his?

"Petty," Justin muttered beneath his breath. "You are a petty, petty man. With a sore backside from being in the saddle for two full days."

"My lord? You wish something?"

"No, Wigglesworth, thank you. I was only chastising myself for being seven kinds of fool."

"Somebody should," the valet answered, nodding his periwig-topped head. "It will take me days to brush all the road dirt from your buckskins, if they are to have so much as a prayer of ever being again presentable, which, sadly, I very much doubt. I'll continue in my duties, then, my lord, if you don't need me."

"I would no doubt perish without you, Wigglesworth," Justin assured the man. "Carry on."

Justin was only half teasing, and both men knew it. Not that Justin needed his valet to survive. Not literally, and not since Bonaparte had been caged a second time and the world was again free to muck itself up without him. But it was Wigglesworth who still kept the facade of Lord Justin Wilde intact, and for a man like Justin, who'd felt himself in need of concealment and for so many years and so many reasons, the foppish, overdressed, fussy little fellow remained the perfect foil.

Plus, Wigglesworth understood the complete

necessity of never overstarching one's shirts. One should never undervalue such talent.

"Still no sign of an Austrian or Czech flag in the harbor, Wigglesworth. I shudder to think we might be forced to endure another day in this dreary hovel before the lady arrives. The prince's man assured me he'd had word her journey was proceeding according to plan as of two days ago."

"A man of your sensibilities, my lord, could not but be rendered maudlin by such a thought. If the lady's ship does not appear by three, I shall make it a point to prepare your supper myself. You must not be made to endure both this inadequate chamber and a less than excellent repast."

"Be sure to take our good friend and personal protector Brutus with you again if that unhappy event should become mandatory," Justin warned, as Wigglesworth remained the only man in all of Creation to believe it was his consequence, and not the hulking Brutus's mountainous physique (and fearsome expression) that opened the doors to sanctuaries like inn kitchens. Bless Brutus, he was an army unto himself, and invaluable to Justin.

"Yes, my lord." Wigglesworth brushed some imaginary lint from the foaming lace jabot at his throat. He was a man who believed in his heart of hearts that Mr. Brummell should have been horse-whipped for convincing the gentlemen to give up their silks and satins and laces in favor of looking as if they were all a flock of penguins heading off to some perpetual funeral.

He fluttered about the inn bedchamber now like a small exotic bird himself, uncertain where to land.

Poor Wigglesworth. The man had a mind alive with bees....

Wringing his delicate hands, the valet finally flitted to the dressing table, counting for only the fourth time the number of brushes, combs and other silver-backed necessities of the well-groomed English gentleman to be sure none had slipped into the swift and crafty hands of the inn servants who had visited the chamber to light the fire or deliver his lordship's breakfast, the fine repast Wigglesworth himself had overseen being created in the kitchens.

"Will you be climbing down from your usual worrywart alts anytime soon, Wigglesworth?" Justin at last inquired lazily from the chair beside the window before the man could suffer some injury to himself for lack of anything to do. "Or will I be forced to find a bootjack in this decrepit establishment in order to remove my boots? You did notice this spot on the left toe, did you not?"

Wigglesworth threw up his hands in horror and joy at the same time. How he needed to be needed. "*Merde!* A spot? A *smudge?* Say it is not so!"

Justin rubbed lightly beneath his nose, as it wouldn't do to allow his valet to see him so amused at his expense. "Wigglesworth? Do you have any idea what you're saying, have been saying ever since you broke bread in the common room last night with the chevalier's valet?"

"Your pardon, my lord?" Wigglesworth asked as he ripped through the contents of one of the many pieces of luggage the baron required for an overnight stay on the road, at last coming out with a fresh white cloth and a tin of boot black. "And what is it I would have been saying?"

"*Merde,* Wigglesworth. You have been almost constantly parroting the word *merde* all the morning long."

Wigglesworth dropped a small rug fashioned just for the purpose in front of his lordship's chair before carefully placing his mauve satin-clad knee to it and motioning for his lordship to, if he pleased, lift the leg currently bearing the offending footwear.

"Yes, I have, haven't I? Frenchmen are by nature a filthy people, but their language is quite melodious, don't you think? So much better to say *merde* than *mercy,* which sounds so…plebian."

Justin allowed his good angel and his naughty angel a few moments of debate before deciding he should be a better man. "*Merde* is not French for *mercy,* Wigglesworth. It is, in point of fact—and forgive my blushes—the word employed most often by the French in referring to…excrement."

Wigglesworth, who prided himself on having risen from the depths of being put out as a chimney sweep in Piccadilly forty years previously to the heights of caring for arguably the most exquisite gentleman in this or any realm, looked up at the baron with tears in his eyes. "I am devastated, my lord. Ashamed. Aghast. Humiliated."

"Yes, I should think you would be. Shall I give you the sack?" Justin asked him as Wigglesworth applied boot black and began rubbing an invisible mar with everything that was in his pitifully thin body.

"If it would be your wish, my lord."

Damn. It was difficult to joke with Wigglesworth. The man was much too committed, too serious. "No, I shan't dismiss you. After all, if you left you'd probably take Brutus with you. I would miss his conversation."

"Brutus doesn't speak, my lord," the literal-minded Wigglesworth pointed out as he gave one last swipe at the boot and stood up once more.

"Precisely. Which puts him head and shoulders above most people. He can be counted on to never say anything boring. Ah, much better, thank you. I shall now not be ashamed to show myself in public." He looked toward the window once more, and frowned to see a new flag blowing in the breeze. "Wigglesworth, it would seem the lady's ship has just dropped anchor. Promise me you will not flee screaming from the docks if she should not be all you believe necessary in my wife."

"I will do my utmost to contain myself," the valet promised. "It remains to be known what *you* will do, my lord."

Justin accepted his hat from the valet and headed for the door. "Prinny took refuge in cherry brandy, as I've heard it told, when he first espied his affianced bride. I think I'd rather face my potential demon fully sober. Although, if our worst fears are confirmed, I suppose a blindfold as I enter the bedchamber for the first time wouldn't come amiss."

"We shall hope for the best, then, my lord. It's important that she's presentable, if she is to bear our name, if you are to have her hand on your arm as you go about Society. Pleasing to the eye."

Justin hesitated at the door, and Wigglesworth ran forward to throw it open. "Physical beauty is overrated, you know. As long as she is passably intelligent and well-spoken, and does not eat little children or frighten the horses, I believe we'll term the thing a success. Not that we have a choice. We must also remember that this marriage is not the lady's fault. Why, she may take me in complete dislike."

"Never, my lord," Wigglesworth said, bristling. "She is the most fortunate of women."

"Oh, hardly that. I fear I am not an easy man."

"You are a very good man, my lord," the valet said, following the baron into the hallway.

"Why, Wigglesworth, I don't believe, in our

nearly half-dozen years of acquaintance, you have ever before so insulted me."

Brutus, stepping out from the shadows to make one of his own with his considerable height and breadth, made that snuffling noise that passed for laughter, anger, bemusement and most any other emotion, and fell into step behind them before taking the lead once they were on the street in front of the inn.

Brutus never touched another human as they made their way to the docks. There was nary a shove, a push. But, as was always the case, the bustling tradesmen and loitering sailors and importuning streetwalkers all melted away in front of him, clearing a wide path for his employer and his employer's valet to follow. Brutus, Justin often thought, was more effective in parting the crowds than a fanfare of trumpets.

The whispers followed, too: *Who is that fine set-up Lunnon gentleman? He must be very important. Did you see the cut of his jacket? Coo, ain't he grand? I'd let him tup me for free, no lie! And look at the little fellow, all dressed up like a Christmas pudding. Let's follow, see what he's up to....*

Justin liked to think of this recurring phenomenon as hiding in plain sight, a ploy that had worked well in his years of service to the Crown. Or, as someone once said (on quite a different subject, but no matter), there are none so blind as those who will not see.

Why sneak in and out of cities under the cover of darkness? Why skulk about in alleyways if there are well-lighted streets to be had? And who suspects someone so determinedly visible of any skullduggery, when it is so much easier to write him off as a fool, a fop, a man concerned only with his own consequence and the tailoring of his waistcoat?

Who? Not the trail of dead men he had left behind him over the course of those years and in a half-dozen countries, that much was certain.

Justin had wearied of the game long before the war, and the necessity for it, was over. But he had held on to the facade, one he felt he needed now more than ever. If people, and most especially his few real friends, could be allowed to see past the silliness, the banter, the supposed fascination for show and fashion, they might be able to glimpse the darkness inside of him, the assassin he had been, the deeds he had done... the mistakes he had made. The one most terrible, unforgivable mistake he had made.

He was alone now, for the most part. Letting anyone in, truly *in,* was no longer in the realm of his possibilities. That's probably why he had so easily brought himself around to the idea of marrying at the Prince Regent's request. Better a stranger than someone he might care for. Better someone who had no interest in really knowing him, someone he had no interest in cultivating. An ancient title, a fine estate, a generous allowance, a blind eye turned to any discreet romantic peccadilloes once the heir was assured and an entrée into Society at the highest level. These were more than sufficient for any wife.

Bringing his mind back to attention, he realized that Brutus had halted at last, halfway along the dock, and stepped aside to give a clear view of the ship and those now in the process of disembarking down a—- Was that a red carpet rolled out over the gangplank and onto the dock? By God, it was. And there were ribbons tied to the rope railings. With streamers.

Justin, Wigglesworth, Brutus and the crowd that had followed after them all watched as a full squad of hulking guardsmen in dress uniforms, peaked metal helmets and carrying long, lethal-looking halberds made their way down the gangplank to stand at attention on either side of it for the length of the crimson carpet.

The crowd craned its collective neck when the parade of soldiers came to an end, waiting to see who next might descend.

First came two no-longer-young women, similarly dressed in not quite the first stare, but more in the sedate look of paid companions. They took their place at either side of the carpet directly in front of the gangplank.

Next to disembark was a tall man, probably

halfway into his thirties, although with those huge mustachios and sideburns favored in Francis's court it was difficult to know for certain. The man was also in uniform, the amount of braid and the size of his helmet denoting his elevated rank. His alert blue eyes seemed to be everywhere at once as he surveyed the crowd, before his intense gaze met, and held, Justin's.

"My, my, my, Wigglesworth, there's a specimen for you. Should I be cowering, do you think?"

Deftly flipping one side of his short, gold-braid-befrogged cape over his shoulder, and with a hand holding the sword hilt steady at his waist, the man headed sure-footedly toward Justin, removing the ceremonial helmet as he did. "Baron Wilde?"

Justin acknowledged the correctness of the question with a very slight inclination of his head.

"Very good, my lord. We were told you had been warned to be prompt. I am Major Luka Prochazka, emissary of His Highness Francis of Austria, I. Fernec, Apostolic King of Hungary, Franjo the Second, King of—"

"Yes, thank you, Major Prochazka, I am aware of the titles and their implications, as well as my geography." Stifling a yawn, covering his mouth with a lace-edged silken square he extracted from his sleeve cuff, Justin allowed his heavily lidded eyes to glide along the view of armed soldiers. "Tell me, and I make this inquiry only out of idle curiosity,

Major, are you by any chance expecting an imminent assault? Should I be sending Wigglesworth here hotfooting back to my coach to procure my sword?"

The major's neatly manicured yet hairy face reassembled itself into a bit of a scowl. He stepped closer, speaking softly yet forcefully. "You were not informed? I was told you would be informed, and respond accordingly. Her ladyship is in some danger. Where is your contingent of guards?"

Lord save him from serious men. Justin indicated Brutus with a languid wave of his handkerchief. "Behold. My army." He turned his head to reassure Wigglesworth. "No offense, my friend. You possess your own unique talents."

The major clearly was not pleased. "One man? You bring one man to protect your betrothed?"

"One very *large* man, you'll agree," Justin drawled. "There is also myself."

Luka Prochazka's lip curled as he ran his gaze up and down Justin's fashionably dressed form. Or at least the baron thought the man's lip curled; again, with those elaborate mustachios, it was impossible to say for certain. "You leave me no choice but to ignore my orders to dismiss the guard once her ladyship has been passed into your protection. They will accompany us to London."

"Oh, hardly, sir. A contingent of foreign soldiers, armed and appearing quite lethal, parading about the English countryside? Many would consider such a thing an act of war. That cannot possibly have been your king's intent."

"I will have her safe."

"I will have her to wife," Justin countered, a hint of steel creeping into his lowered voice, although the smile never left his face. "What is mine, I protect. Better that we were friends, Major. A fool judges by appearances only. You would not like me as your enemy."

The major didn't even blink. "I have heard stories…"

"No, Major. You haven't. When it comes to Baron Wilde, should anyone dare to inquire, your knowledge of him resembles nothing more than it would a blank slate. Now, if this no-longer-amusing pissing contest has reached its limits, shall we see the lady we have surely kept waiting long enough?"

At last, Luka smiled. "On the contrary, my lord. It is the lady who keeps us waiting."

"Cowering in her cabin, is she?"

"Hardly, my lord."

"Justin. As I was informed you are to remain in England for the foreseeable future, we either become informal, Luka, or we kill one another."

"Justin it is, then. I've killed enough men."

They set off down the length of the dock, their heights similar, their long strides matching perfectly, yet looking as outwardly dissimilar as any two men could be. "That's the spirit. Always believe you'll be the winner, even when it is painfully obvious that the outcome will not be in your favor."

"Oh? We'd duel with handkerchiefs?"

"Only if you fancy mine stuffed halfway down your gullet," Justin quipped with a smile as he gave the handkerchief one last flourish before it disappeared up his sleeve.

As they approached the ridiculous red carpet, one of the two females turned toward the gangplank, hiked up her skirts and returned to the ship, only to reappear moments later, her eyes downcast as she once more took her place.

Justin halted at the edge of the carpet and removed his hat, his dark hair immediately being blown about in a rather stiff breeze coming off the Channel. Behind him, Wigglesworth sighed.

"I sense her ladyship enjoys making an entrance?"

"Lady Alina is her own person," Luka said, and this time Justin knew the man was smiling beneath that great mass of mustache.

"Does it itch?" he asked impulsively.

Luka turned to look at him, a question in his eyes for a moment, before he nodded. "And acts as a poor strainer for my food, yes. But all officers are required to be so adorned. When this commission is successfully completed, I plan to resign from the army. Just so that I might shave the damn thing off."

Justin threw back his head, laughing, feeling that he and this fierce-looking soldier would have no problems now that they had survived their initial introduction. But the smile faded abruptly as a small figure appeared at the head of the gangplank.

She was cloaked in emerald velvet from head to foot, the hood edged with ermine, ermine tails scattered here and there as decorative tassels. Interesting. Queen Elizabeth had favored ermine at her coronation, to symbolize her virginity.

Her ladyship was more than a smidge of a thing, but much less than a tall, stately figure. The hand that reached for the rope railing was ungloved, the fingers long and slender. The face, however, remained in shadow. Teasingly, tantalizingly.

Justin's thoughts about his prospective wife, and they had been few and far between, if truth be told, had conjured up a meek and obedient woman who could give him an heir and then retire to her knitting while he went about his own pursuits. Now he felt his first stirrings of concern.

Her left hand lifted to the hood and drew it back, slowly at first, and then with a flourish, revealing a mass of shining black curls and a face that drew astonished and admiring gasps from the multitude of interested observers.

Every notion of feminine beauty Justin had ever considered paled into nothingness as Lady Magdaléna Evinka Nadeja Valentin raised her perfect, softly rounded chin and surveyed all the conquered who stood below her on the wooden dock.

Her skin was the finest cream, her brows like delicate ravens' wings above enormous, tip-tilted eyes the color of old gold coins. The nose, regal, the mouth, wide and softly curving, the cheekbones, high, turning all of her beauty slightly yet wonderfully exotic.

In the suddenly quiet crowd, and without the slightest idea who this creature could be, several of the women curtsied, many men bowed or touched their forelocks. The lady acknowledged this homage with an infinitesimal nod of her head, accepting the gestures as her due.

"Merde," Wigglesworth breathed, staggering where he stood, his eyes filling with tears of thanks and delight.

Luka's voice seemed to come to Justin from a distance. "Lady Alina, my lord. Your affianced bride."

"Sweet Jesus," Justin murmured under his breath, "the impertinent chit has upstaged me."

Worse, and for the first time in his memory, Baron Wilde realized that he might actually be experiencing some uneasiness—and a small modicum of anxiety for his own well-being.

CHAPTER TWO

HER HEART RACED SO RAPIDLY Alina feared it might stumble over itself and stop.

Tatiana moments earlier had whispered into her ear that the Baron Wilde was not an ancient ogre, but young, and a near-god, and that her ladyship had once more stuck her thumb into the pie only to emerge with a most glorious plum.

But that was the problem. Alina had not stuck her thumb into a pie. None of what had already happened had been at her desire or volition. His Majesty had stuck all of her into the pie, and she would have to find her own way out.

Except there was no way out. Luka had convinced her of that. Her mother dead these past three years, her father perishing at Waterloo, she'd had no one but her aunt Mimi to represent her wishes at court. Which was the same as to say she had no one to protect her, to fight for her, to convince His Majesty that his sometimes troublesome ward should not be sacrificed in some ridiculous gesture to help cement relations between her country and that of the greedy English.

Aunt Mimi had called the betrothal an honor, even as she could not hide her triumphant smile at the prospect of being rid of the now grown-up niece whose beauty was on the rise just as her own was teetering toward a slippery slide into middle age.

Once Alina had resigned herself to her fate, she had demanded only two things, one of which she received.

Her insistence on knowing everything there was to know about this Baron Wilde fell on deaf ears. She knew no more about the man today than she had two months previously, except for Tatiana's silliness just now.

Her second demand had been not only met, but exceeded, as the ermine-adorned cloak well demonstrated. If she was to represent the court, the king, then she must be of the first stare, her wardrobe and retinue worthy of the emissary of His Majesty.

Gone were the childlike gowns her aunt had insisted she be limited to, replaced by only the finest silks, the most elegant designs, the most fashionable of accessories—including the full jewelry boxes that had once belonged to her mother but for the past years had somehow become the possessions of her aunt.

Alina had gifted the woman with the set of garnets and a pretty speech filled with gratitude for her loving care of her, and done so in the presence of the king, so that Mimi could not throw the nearly worthless stones back in her face.

Small victories, few and far between, but Alina took pleasure in them just the same.

She had been delighted to learn that Luka would accompany her, remain with her as long as deemed necessary, and that Tatiana had declared she would rather die than be left behind.

She had been flattered when Danica had been added to her retinue, as she had never before had her own dresser, but only shared her aunt's. It was only proper that those closest to her be people with whom she could be comfortable, and not cold English strangers.

But the guardsmen? They had been a surprise to her.

Those guardsmen now stood at attention, clearly awaiting Alina's descent to the dock. Very well, she had done as she'd planned; her first steps on the island of her mother's birth would be taken with all the accompanying pomp and ceremony she could have wanted.

All she had to do now was face her betrothed, look into his eyes, allow him to take her offered hand, perform her necessary curtsy that indicated her subservience and willingness to obey.

And pray she did not throw up on his feet.

For the space of a full minute (she knew, because

she had counted out the seconds in her head), Alina had cast her gaze about the dock without really seeing anything or anyone. But now she had no choice but to look to the bottom of the gangplank, where Luka and the "near-god" waited.

She drew in a quick, silent breath. This was her affianced husband? This tall, disturbingly beautiful man whose heavy-lidded green eyes smiled at her and mocked her all at the same time? She'd expected older, jaded, even a paunch and a cane. She'd prayed for amenable, stupid, easily led.

What in the name of the Virgin was she supposed to do with *this*?

The self-assured creature approached the gangplank, planting one gleaming black Hessian boot on it as if this somehow claimed not only her as his own, but this ship as well, and held out his hand to her, openly daring her to take it.

"Your servant, my lady," he said, his eyes still mocking her. "On behalf of His Royal Highness, the Prince Regent, I, Baron Justin Wilde, your delighted betrothed, welcome you to the homeland of your mother. Her passing was England's loss, yet her daughter is clearly England's gain."

Very prettily said, she supposed. It was only as she opened her mouth to parrot the words she had learned by rote that must be spoken on this occasion, that she realized the baron had addressed her

in flawless German, now the official language of
Austria.

Alina supposed he'd wish to be complimented on
his expertise.

She'd rather poke hot sticks under her fingernails. Although how silly of him to let her know
she could not speak German in front of him and
think he would not understand. Should she thank
him for forewarning her? No, probably not.

Instead, she answered him in English as flawless
as his German, putting her hand in his open palm
and then watching rather intently as he bent his dark
head to within a whisper of placing a kiss on her bare
skin.

She ignored the tingle that ran up her arm, all the
way to her shoulder.

"You've met my secretary, Major Prochazka?"

The baron had not released her hand, but had
deftly drawn her arm through his, leading her back
to where Luka and an odd-looking periwigged creature stood waiting, the latter beaming at her as if
personally responsible for some wonderful occurrence. Then they both bowed—the little man with
much more élan than poor Luka, who had to contend
with his sword—turned and began leading the way
off the crowded dock.

"Your secretary, my lady? Ah, yes, of course he
is. And, in turn, I am the King of Siam."

Alina stopped in her tracks, which made the baron do likewise. "What are you suggesting, my lord?"

"Suggesting? I? Nothing more, my dear, than that we begin as we plan to go on. All that faradiddle you spouted about improving trade relations? Very nicely said, but we both know the truth. Or do you wish that we *go on* with you pretending that you're a pretty yet brainless twit, and that I…well, dear me, didn't I just paint myself into a corner with my tongue? Very well, that I also continue pretending that I am a pretty yet brainless twit."

Alina looked him up and down, amazed to hear a man call himself pretty; besides, he was much too much the male to be termed pretty, even in his fashionable clothes. But what did he mean? *Pretending*. Pretending what? Had she been betrothed to a lunatic?

"You're saying that you're not a brainless twit? Are you quite certain of that?"

"At this precise moment? No." His smile reached all the way to his eyes, but then stopped, as if something barred the way. "Very well, then. We shall for the moment allow the definition of secretary to stand."

"I don't recall granting it permission to sit down," Alina said, with just the sort of offhand sarcasm that had landed her in trouble so often, had called her to the king's attention in ways that probably had hastened her banishment to an English marriage. *She behaves as if she's queen,* her aunt had told anyone who would listen. *Queen of the Romany, I suppose, for all her thin Englisher blood.*

Alina walked forward once more, her gaze on the major's militarily straight spine. "He'd die for me, you know."

"Commendable of the major, I suppose. Allow me, please, to point out Brutus, my, um, *secretary,* lumbering along just ahead of yours. He'd kill for me. Of the two choices, I much prefer the latter. The major is fearful for your safety. But you're aware of that, of course."

Alina had been so busy trying to keep up with this verbal sparring that it took her a moment to understand what the baron was implying. "My safety? No, that can't be correct. You've misunderstood his mission, one for which he volunteered. Luka is concerned for my welfare. He was my father's aide-de-camp, and therefore feels responsible for me. Unless you're telling me that England is an unsafe place?"

The baron looked at her for a long moment, and then smiled, another smile that did not quite reach those unsettling green eyes. "Forgive me, my lady, clearly I mistook his purpose. And I assure you, England for you is as safe as houses. Indeed, you will have the entire kingdom at your feet the moment you first appear in Society."

"That is my intention, yes," she told him, not

understanding why she dared this impertinence, but enjoying herself all the same. He seemed to like teasing her, surprising her, for what reason she didn't know. Why not return the favor?

Begin as you plan to go on. That's what he'd said. As a good wife, she shouldn't disappoint him. And what a shame that they must marry, be bound to each other by duty. He would be so much more fun to flirt with, wouldn't he? As a husband, however, he might be more trouble than even his handsome face and enticing smile could overcome.

The baron cocked an eyebrow. "You're quite the honest little thing, aren't you? Some would consider that a failing."

"Would you be one of those people?"

"Ah, and inquisitive, as well."

"Inquisitive enough to have noticed that you have carefully sidestepped my question, my lord," Alina said, her heart beating faster yet again. Goodness, but the man made her feel delightfully alive! "I shall have to be exceedingly careful around you, won't I?"

He looked down into her face, his expression suddenly too intense, so that she looked away. "On the contrary. I believe it is I who will have to be exceptionally careful around you. I hadn't expected to like you."

She kept her eyes on the street at her feet, pretending polite indifference even as she felt ridiculously pleased that he'd said—admitted, really, as if it was some sort of failing of his own—that he liked her. "Oh. And…and is that so terrible?"

"It could be, yes," he said, the teasing note back in his voice. "A good wife would have had the decency to be staid and boring and completely ignorable."

"And I'm—"

"Hardly ignorable," he said, patting the hand that rested on his forearm.

Alina swallowed around the sudden lump in her throat. "I see. And…and is that a compliment?"

"Possibly," he answered in that already familiar, maddeningly light tone as they mounted the steps to an ancient inn. "That, or a warning…"

"YOU SUMMONED ME?" The clipped tone of voice revealed that Major Luka Prochazka was not at all pleased to be in the position of taking orders from an Englishman.

Which wasn't Justin's problem, was it? No. He had problems enough of his own, thank you.

The baron had spent the past several hours reading and rereading the contents of the packet he'd been handed by the Prince Regent's secretary, this time reading as much between the lines as he had the actual words. And it was those words *not* written that told him he'd been a fool to sign the agreement. The marriage, and "his silence on matters known to the Prince Regent and himself concerning a private arrangement," in exchange for the termination of his indebtedness to the Prince Regent.

It had all been too easy, even with the added responsibility of keeping his unwanted bride safe until Francis had dealt with the man who wished her harm. Justin should have known nothing with the Prince Regent, or any royalty for that matter, was ever that simple, or that straightforward.

He looked toward the door to the private dining room of the inn and the man standing there, no longer clad in his uniform, but in a rather drab brown jacket and tan buckskins, his cravat a pure horror that would have crumpled Wigglesworth to his knees at the abomination of the thing.

"She doesn't know," he said now, flatly, looking Luka full in the eye.

Luka Prochazka merely blinked, and did not answer.

"Cat got your tongue? Very well, Major, we have the whole evening ahead of us. You wouldn't care for a small side wager as to which one of us outlasts the other?"

"I…that is, you…your statement took me by surprise, and was not a question at all. To what exactly was I supposed to respond?"

"Ah, now you wish to play the fool? Too late for that, *Major*. Yet, much as such exercises pain me, I'll repeat myself. *She doesn't know.* She's dancing about somewhere above our heads, delighted in her performance on the dock earlier, happy in her ignorance, and with absolutely no idea her life is at stake at the moment," Justin said, even as he motioned Luka to take up a chair and avail himself of the bottle of wine that sat on the table between them. "No, don't look at me as if you still don't understand what I'm saying. She thinks this is all some political union we're going to be entering into, an advance of trade between our countries, or some showpiece of how Francis and our George have cried friends and allies yet again. She recited an entire speech on the thing while we were at the docks, just like a good little idiot. But she's not an idiot, is she, which is why you haven't told her the truth."

"But it is all of that," Luka said, pouring himself a glass of finest burgundy, as Justin never traveled without his own wines any more than he would see it as civilized to travel without his own bed linens.

"Continue to evade my questions, Major, and you and I will go to war. It's enough that the rain delays our departure to London until the morning and a man of my sensibilities must pass another night beneath this probably leaky roof. The girl is having herself a determined lark, even as it's clear she loathes the idea of a marriage between us. Ermine tips, enough baggage coming off that ship this afternoon to raise it a two full inches above its previous waterline, a baldly stated intention to take London by storm. She's beautiful, magnificently so, and she is clearly aware of that fact. As long as she must bow to the king's wishes, she has come to conquer England, and she very well might. God knows I'd wager on it. If she isn't put to bed with a shovel within days of her first conquest."

"She doesn't need to know that."

Justin slammed the side of his fist on the tabletop, rocking the bottle of wine. "Bloody hell, she doesn't!" He sat back, amazed at his outburst—he, who was always so cool, so controlled, so in charge of his emotions. He didn't much care for the notion he could be concerned with someone else's welfare, especially some impudent chit who seemed to have taken up instant residence in his head. He'd never been so attracted to a female, and he didn't much care for the feeling.

His eyes closed, he rubbed at his forehead, willing himself back to his usual composure. "Why? Why hasn't she been told?"

"It…it was decided that she might…balk at any strictures put on her movements if she were to know our concerns. The Lady Alina is young and…somewhat headstrong. If she can be made to believe that English customs are to be much more strict with the comings and goings of its females, more protective as it were, she would accept that as fact and not chafe at the restrictions quite so much. But if she were to learn that she is being guarded, that she is in fact more a prisoner within invisible walls than she is a young woman on an adventure, a young bride out to make her way in Society..."

Luka sighed and took a long drink from his glass. "A rather superior vintage for a simple inn, even to my admittedly unsophisticated palate. Clearly your economy is not so lowered as ours by the recent war."

Justin's mouth lifted in a rueful, one-sided smile. "Yes. And the streets of London are paved in golden cobblestones." He leaned forward once more, his elbows on the tabletop. "You're telling me that my soon-to-be wife is completely unaware that her life is in danger. That you or some other idiot has decided it is best she not know—because she might otherwise *chafe* at her restrictions? My God, man, you speak as if you and your countrymen are *afraid* of the chit."

"In my defense, Justin—if I might retain the honor of addressing you informally now that I have so disappointed you—you've only just met the lady. She has a decidedly strong will. The only reason she agreed to the marriage, in the end, was that she saw it as a way to become her own woman, out from under her aunt's thumb. I believe the words she used went something along the lines of *once I have put this husband I am burdened with in his place.*"

"Hmm," Justin mused, sitting back once more. "There was nothing in the packet given to me as to why she's in such danger, but just that I'm to guard her safety until such time I am notified that the danger is past. Now I'm wondering—did she step on someone's tail?"

Luka took another sip of wine, clearly a cautious man and obviously mentally measuring both Justin and the depth of information he was prepared to share. "Lately? Only her aunt's, I suppose. But then those two got along like chalk and cheese even before General Valentin met his end at Waterloo. Ever since Lady Alina's mother died, as a matter of fact. You mention a packet. Might I see its contents?"

"You may not. I am, however, reasonably comfortable with its contents as they pertain to Lady— you call her Alina. Does she prefer that?"

"Magdaléna is her given name, in honor of her paternal great-grandmother, but I've been told that her mother loathed it, pointing out that her daughter has more English than any other blood in her veins, and that she would have been fine with Mary, but Magdaléna was unacceptable. Her ladyship has been called Alina from the cradle, a compromise of sorts, I suppose. But to answer your question, if Lady Alina did not like the name, she wouldn't allow it."

"You're trying very hard, and quite heavy-handedly I might add, to have me take my affianced bride in dislike. Is there a reason for that? Perhaps you had seen yourself as her husband until our two royal meddlers decided to gift the lady and me with each other?"

The major's complexion—what could be seen of it behind the mustachios and ridiculous mutton-chops—colored. "Lady Alina is the daughter of a nobleman. I am the son of a farmer. I would never presume…"

God, the man was in love with her. Or doing his best to give the impression that he was in love with her. And why, Justin wondered, did he always doubt the motives of others? Of course, the simple answer was that it was this doubt, this hesitancy to trust, that had kept him alive all of those long years on the Continent. Yet he had accepted Alina immediately, seeing no ulterior motives, no undercurrents—only her honesty. Did that make him incredibly insightful, or a fool?

"No, of course you wouldn't, Major. Forgive me. But you would die for her, wouldn't you?"

"Without question or hesitation," Luka responded at once, drawing his body to attention—not an easy feat, as he was still seated at the table.

Justin sighed, becoming bored by this grand show of devotion. "Heaven preserve me from martyrs and heroes—they always seem to end up doing something destined to prove their glorious assertions. Let us pray then that the lady never calls on you to make such a sacrifice, as you begin to alarm me with your fatalistic fervor."

Luka chuckled softly. "I would I die for her,

should the situation call for that death. That doesn't mean I *plan* on any such event."

"How you ease my mind. And now I remember, you want to live long enough to shave off all that ghastly hair and discover whether or not you possess an upper lip." Justin put down his wineglass, and then asked the question that most troubled him. "Tell me more about this Jarmil Novak I see mentioned in passing in my packet, if you please, beginning with why he would want Lady Alina to be reunited with her deceased parents?"

Luka nodded. "Yes, Jarmil Novak. You were informed about him? *Inhaber* Novak."

"*Inhaber?* So he is a colonel-in-chief?"

Luka couldn't hide his surprise. "You know what that means?"

"I know the rank, but not the man. *Inhabers* raise and finance battalions during time of war, correct? But that doesn't tell me whether this Novak fellow rode out in front of those battalions, brandishing his sword, gallantly shouting 'forward, men,' or if he used his money for political gain and doesn't know which end of a sword to hold. In other words, is he dangerous?"

"Ah, *Inhaber* Novak is familiar with swords and their uses. But, yes, he only buys them, along with those who employ them for him. Otherwise, he does not dirty his hands to do what he can easily hire others to do for him. The Romany loathe him for the way he treated his hired soldiers. And, yes, he can be...dangerous."

"Ah, yes, the...Romany." Justin had nearly uttered the word *Gypsies,* but prudently corrected himself before he could make that particular blunder. He tucked away the information that the Romany hated Novak, as his concern now was more with Alina's safety. "Is there anyone who can abide the man?"

"Our king," Luka said, sighing. "Except when he doesn't. I think they each have uses for the other. You're a man of the world, Justin. You understand the fragility of political alliances."

"More than I wish to, yes. Alliances and long memories, old feuds. Boundaries that shift position with seemingly every decade and each new war. Where your grandfather had worshipped, what language his great-grandfather had spoken. People seem to fight new wars over six-hundred-year-old arguments all the time, both in your country and here."

"Then you do understand."

Justin nodded. If he had learned nothing else during his eight years of exile, years spent making himself as valuable to England as possible, in any way possible, in hopes of being granted a pardon, he'd learned that those in power or in pursuit of power didn't need a reason for anything they did. If they didn't have a valid argument, they'd stitch one up out of whole cloth. If no enemy was available, they'd manufacture one. With Bonaparte caged only a year, was somebody already looking for another argument?

"But what does Novak and any of that have to do with Lady Alina, other than supposedly wanting her dead?"

"She is part Romany."

Justin raised one well-sculpted eyebrow, gave a thought—not his first of the day—to the girl's astonishing mass of ebony curls...and how they might look unbound, cascading across his pillow. "Really. And what part might that be?"

"The part that matters, at least to the Romany. Her paternal grandmother's blood flows in her veins. Diluted as it is, what with her foreign mother and half-Austrian father, I'm told she is seen in some quarters to be the rightful owner of land suddenly returned to our country since the war. Even with the edicts of the Congress of Vienna, boundaries are still vague and shifting all over Europe, and arguments abound. There is for us even now some difficulty with France."

Justin dismissed the subject of border disputes with France as unnecessary information. "I thought the Romany prefer the nomadic life. There are many here in England, at least for much of the year. They prefer to be citizens of the world and not of one country."

"They prefer, Justin, not being scorned as outlaws and branded and murdered and betrayed. Always betrayed. In any event, there are murmurings of claims to this certain large tract of land, of some ancestral deed. With their own territory, no matter how small, how mountainous and mostly uninhabitable, they could begin to dream of becoming their own city-state within the kingdom. The Romany see such a thing as their refuge, their—"

"Yes, I believe I can take it from here." Justin held up a hand to stop Luka as more pieces had begun to fall into place for him. "Let me finish for you, if you don't mind. This expanse of land is now claimed by *Inhaber* Novak, while this supposed ancestral deed goes back any number of centuries, and then forward again to the sole surviving Romany Valentin, Lady Alina."

"Exactly, and that land, or rather the ownership of it in the absence of any formal deed, has been disputed for at least those myriad centuries, long before the Congress of Vienna took a carving knife to half of Europe. The king himself took me into his confidence and told me as much. The Romany don't have queens, per se, and power is traditionally limited to the men in any group, so that I was much surprised to hear what the king had to say. But as the saying goes, any port in a storm. Lady Alina is that port for the local Romany. Without her, the dream ends once and for all time, the possibility of one safe haven for the Romany people in the region. Not that it is more than a nebulous dream in any case."

Luka sighed. "Lady Alina is inordinately proud of her few drops of Romany blood. She would see herself as their savior, at the very least, were she to know. Truly, it will be easier for everyone if she is never told, and if she is bound to England, never returning to her homeland. I was sworn to secrecy by the king himself, forbidden to tell you this, but it seems only fair you should understand the danger, and take the proper precautions until the king decides what to do with *Inhaber* Novak, as your lightheartedness earlier causes me some concern. Perhaps, once Lady Alina is married to you, Novak will no longer see her as a threat to him."

There was a knock at the door and Wigglesworth entered, carrying a plate of bread and cheese. Justin waved a hand over the plate, inviting the major to eat, which gave Justin time to think.

He shook his head at his gullibility; how could he have been so blind? No wonder the Prince Regent had been so willing to allow his insults. The man had his fifty thousand pounds all safely tucked up in his purse, making Justin no longer necessary and, if he were to speak out of turn, potentially embarrassing. A nice, clean assassination of the pesky baron would not come amiss as far as the Prince Regent was concerned, and would rid him of that potential embarrassment. No wonder the man had been so eager to assist King Francis in his request.

It was time for another small chat with the Prince

Regent. But first, he'd ask a few more questions of the wonderfully forthcoming major.

"Tell me, if the king knows Novak wants her dead, why didn't he already do something about it, have Novak arrested? Why bother with this farce of a marriage?"

"Isn't it obvious? The king is playing for time, and some sort of amicable solution. He doesn't want to have his hand forced by making a decision on this land, the disputed deed, because either way he decided would gain him enemies. The Romany are an unavoidable nuisance, while *Inhaber* Novak has many who are loyal to him, and he is a great asset to the court."

Justin was beginning to see more of the spiderweb. He kept his tone conversational, even as he felt the slumbering beast inside him straining at its leash. "A king with many problems, your Francis. If Lady Alina is murdered, he must make a show of investigating her death, because she is his ward and because otherwise the Romany will make things difficult for him. To arrest or kill Novak would bring him trouble from factions loyal to the *Inhaber*. How much more convenient to have it all play out far away in England. Francis didn't apply to his ally the Prince Regent for a bridegroom. He applied to him for an assassin, and dear Prinny knew just the man to approach, a man who couldn't refuse. The moment I wed the fair lady what was hers is mine, and there will be a target painted on my back, so that it will be kill or be killed."

Luka had the good grace to blush, which probably served to save him, or at least preserve his teeth and jaw so that he could chew his bread and cheese.

Justin pressed him further. "And Lady Alina, she of the ermine-tipped cloak and plans to take London by storm? Does it matter to any of them what happens to her?"

"But you'll keep her safe."

"That is not your concern, Major. You concern, and that of our two plotting sovereigns, is better directed at what I will do to you all if Lady Alina so much as stubs her toe before I can find some way out of this damned farce. Now, if you'll excuse me, I believe I will pay my betrothed a small visit before she turns in for the night."

Luka leapt to his feet. "You're not going to tell her anything, are you?"

Justin looked at the major without saying a word until the man had the good sense to subside back into his chair. "Don't do that again, Major. Question me. And never stand against me unless you're willing to suffer the consequences. Are we clear?"

The major nodded.

"Oh, how wonderful," Justin drawled affably, smiling as if nothing had happened, as if there had been no threat of violence. "Now we can cry friends again, understanding each other so much better. Why, I might even be persuaded to convince Wigglesworth to give you a few pointers on how to tie your cravat so it less resembles a noose. Good night, Major."

Justin walked out of the room in his usual, unhurried stroll, softly closing the door behind him. It was only when he got as far as the narrow hallway leading to the stairs that he pressed his palms against the sides of his neck and pushed hard, forcing his breathing and his heartbeat back into their usual rhythms.

He was angry that he had allowed any of this to happen to him. Unworried that he would not succeed in ridding Alina of any threat from the *Inhaber* Novak.

But damned if he could understand how he, a man who prided himself on his lack of emotional involvement with the rest of the world, could have suddenly become so intensely concerned for the welfare of one small female.

I don't recall granting it permission to sit down.

At last he smiled with real amusement…and not a little bemusement. Yes, that was it. From the moment she'd uttered those words, he had become as wax in her hands.

God help him.…

CHAPTER THREE

ALINA SAT CROSS-LEGGED in the middle of the hard tester bed, her sketchbook across her knees. She'd been so certain the baron would come knocking on her door to inquire as to why she had refused to join him downstairs for dinner. But when the clock had struck the hour of nine, she had at last given up on her fetching outfit of palest lilac silk in favor of a comfortable night rail she'd worn to the brink of shabbiness.

She only wished she hadn't used the excuse that she wasn't hungry in order to avoid him, for now her stomach had begun grumbling at her, pointing out that, if she was going to lie, she should first consider the consequences. Citing a headache from the excitement of seeing England for the first time? That would have been much better.

Except that the baron might have interpreted that as excitement upon seeing him for the first time.

That eventuality was not to be contemplated. The man was already entirely too pleased with himself just on general principles—that was obvious.

"And much too intelligent for my own good," she muttered, her charcoal stick moving rapidly as she colored in the man's hair, which was nearly as dark as her own. His skin was darker than hers; he was clearly a man who spent considerable time in the sun—she'd noticed as much when he'd taken her hand in his and bowed over her fingertips. He had hard hands, strong and even slightly callused, which had surprised her, for he certainly dressed (and behaved!) as a man who never so much as brushed his own hair without assistance.

She could still close her eyes and see her pale skin against his darker tones, her fragile bones no match for his strength if he were to squeeze her fingers between his. And she most certainly could still see those laughing, mocking green eyes.

He really did upset her sense of being up to any challenges her new circumstances could toss at her. She'd been so sure of her plans, back in the safety of her own bedchamber. And all it had taken was one look, one too-intimate touch of this man's flesh against hers, to knock all of her confident pins out from beneath her. Oh, yes, he was going to be trouble....

Just to think—if she had worn gloves, as Danica had told her was proper, she would still not know that her betrothed had such an unsettling effect on her. Why, she might have gone down to dinner, prattled on in some inane way, all unaware that Baron Justin

Wilde was anything more than a pretty fellow with an impertinent mouth.

Now what was she supposed to do? If there existed a way to control him, she had to find it. Quickly.

Strange how she had not thought about the marriage itself as anything more than a minor inconvenience, a necessary detail. At first, she'd been too angry to do more than think about being bartered away by the king, being forced to leave her home. But once her aunt had explained that a marriage of mutual convenience was all she could look forward to in any event, thanks to her birth and station— and had pointed across the king's drawing room to where Count Josef Eberharter stood picking at his yellowed teeth with a penknife and declared the man to be Alina's only alternative—the idea of traveling to England, to the birthplace of her mother, had begun to seem a reasonable alternative.

Her mother had told so many stories about her homeland, and always with such a wistful look in her eyes. Now she, her mother's daughter, would see all the glorious sights herself. First London, of course, as everyone with any sense wished to visit this great metropolis. But then she would travel to Kent, and to her mother's childhood home. Wouldn't they all be surprised and delighted to welcome the daughter of their beloved and lost Anne Louise?

She cocked her head to one side and contemplated the now-completed sketch. Had she captured the correct degree of astonishment in his lordship's entirely too-wise eyes as he looked cross-eyed at the fat fish tail sticking out of his wide-open mouth?

"Oh, my lady," Tatiana said, leaning across the mattress to goggle at the sketch. "That's even better than the last one. Danica, come see."

"Humph," the older woman snorted, staying where she was, busying herself with laying out Alina's freshly pressed traveling outfit for the morning, a lovely thing of midnight-blue and military gold frogging, and a shako hat that was made to tilt forward above the lady's right eye just so. "Horns and a tail? I see nothing so amusing in poking fun at one's betrothed. You should only be thanking the Virgin for his handsome face and body. He could have been sixty, and fat and filthy into the bargain."

"I'd rather he was eighty, and with one foot teetering over the grave, too crippled with gout and dissipated by drink to worry about such things as his new wife," Alina said truthfully, for she saw nothing wrong with wishful thinking. "What am I supposed to do with a man no older than Luka? What will he want from me?"

Tatiana giggled, putting her pudgy hands to her mouth. "Should we tell her, Danica?"

"That is the job of the husband, and not for us to say. It is proper for a lady of breeding not to know—"

"About breeding?" Tatiana quipped, and then covered her smile with her hand.

"You have never been amusing, Tatiana Klammer," the dresser said, turning her back to the woman, who promptly stuck her tongue out at her.

Alina sighed. It had been thus ever since they'd begun their journey, the two women always jabbing at each other, the dresser believing her position to be higher than that of mere paid companion, the companion believing the dresser was altogether too full of herself. She had begun to wish Danica had not accompanied them to England, for the woman was stiff, humorless and full of rules.

Plus, she clearly didn't like her new mistress, something Alina couldn't understand, because everyone liked her. Well, perhaps not Aunt Mimi, definitely not Aunt Mimi. But everyone else.

She closed the sketchbook and put it to one side. "That is not what I meant, Danica," she said testily. "I don't know if he will want my company and conversation, or if he will ignore me for the most part, as I hope, and allow me to go my own way. I already know he will kiss me and give me babies. My mama explained that to me years ago. It's the only way to get babies. I asked her, and she told me. I am…resigned to that."

As her mother had been dead these past three years, it could be wondered just how specific the lady had been with her explanations.

The way Danica rolled her eyes as she turned about once more, Alina now wondered exactly that herself.

"What? What did I say that is so impossible that you made that terrible face?"

"Danica means nothing, my lady," Tatiana said quickly, and the dresser returned to her duties, laying out a pair of fine stockings with a flourish before dropping a rather insulting curtsy and leaving the room, muttering darkly under her breath.

"I don't like her," Alina told her companion, not for the first time. "And I don't think she really wished to come here. I shall have her sent home immediately."

"The *Entschlossen* sailed on the evening tide, my lady, along with all those handsome guardsmen. I saw it leave from this very window. You were sleeping, and I didn't think to wake you. I would have, had I known you were planning to send Miss Pickles and Sour Cider packing."

Alina slid off the side of the bed, her bare feet encountering the cool wooden planks. "Yes, well, there's no use for it then, is there? She was Aunt Mimi's choice, and she'd only have replaced her with someone even worse. We'll have to make the best of things. You don't suppose I could take a quick trip outside and find a nice fat toad to put in her bed?"

"Oh, my lady, you are such a joy to me," Tatiana said, dropping to her knees and helping to fit a pair of satin slippers on Alina's slender feet. "But so very young, for all your fine ways and wonderful ideas. Now I think you should tell me more about what it was your dear mother told you about kisses and giving babies."

Alina sighed. "Then Danica didn't pull that monkey face of hers simply to vex me, did she? What else do I need to know, Tatiana? I shouldn't wish to have to ask the baron the time of day, so I most certainly don't want him to be telling me anything else. He should believe I am a woman of the world."

The companion, old enough to be Alina's mother, but not accustomed to speaking frankly on a subject she knew about but, in her spinster state these past forty years, had no personal knowledge of, struggled to her feet once more.

"Husbands do not care to think of their brides as women of the world, my lady," she said, avoiding Alina's eyes. "They get really put out about it, as I've heard the thing. Best you should do as Danica says, I suppose, since your mother didn't see fit to explain the way of the world to you, and let his lordship tell you. Not that Miss Uppity knows any more than me, for there was never a man eager enough to brave that one's embrace. Be like bedding a board."

Tatiana, an earthy woman for all she had been serving in the manor house for most of her life, ran her hands down over her own considerable curves, then hefted her massive breasts one at a time, so that they fit more comfortably above her corset. "Not that these things don't get in the way, from time to time. Still, better a handful of these than those sorry pimples of Danica's."

Alina giggled. "You've got considerably more than a handful, Tatiana," she said, and then sobered. Swallowed. Looked down at her own muslin-covered breasts that were somewhere between Danica's pimples and Tatiana's impressive largesse. "Why should that matter?"

"No reason, my lady," the maid said hurriedly, pulling a handkerchief from between her bosoms and dabbing at her suddenly damp upper lip. "No reason at all, and I meant nothing by it, truly I didn't. I could go to the kitchens and beg something for you to eat. You nary had a thing but some watered wine and dry biscuits pass your lips since this morning. The crossing was a mite choppy, and I didn't eat anything, either, but I surely made up for that lack earlier. English food isn't so terrible, my lady. Just let me nip off downstairs and—"

"Tatiana," Alina intoned severely, hiding her apprehension. "I asked you a question. Why should it matter if a woman…if she has pimples or handfuls?"

"It's…um…the thing is, my lady—your mother said kisses give you babies?"

Alina was beginning to feel very silly. "I saw

Jurgen in the hallway behind the silver room one day, and he was kissing Astrid."

"Astrid, is it? The girl is a round-heeled fool, tipping over for any who ask her."

Round-heeled? And what did *that* mean? Silly was rapidly escalating to uncomfortable. "That's neither here nor there, Tatiana. We're much of the same age, and I thought I should know what she was doing, as it was…she seemed quite distressed. Moan…moaning and everything, and saying in this absurd voice, 'Oh, yes, Jurgen, my stallion.' Um…so I asked my mother, and she told me that Astrid was a very reckless and uncouth girl, and that kisses lead to babies, and that was why I should have nothing to do with kisses until I was married and my husband kissed me, as she had done with my father, and as good and chaste people have always done."

Tatiana pulled a face, the more round-cheeked version of the same expression Danica had displayed a few minutes earlier. "And now Astrid has two babies and no husband. A stallion, indeed! Jurgen? But, see, my lady, your dear mother was correct in what she told you." The maid turned companion sighed. "And that's *all* she told you? Truly?"

"You know how ill she was, Tatiana. I could see that the subject distressed her, so I thanked her and left her to her prayer book. And…and then she was gone, and I had never dared to trouble her with more questions. I suppose I could have applied to Aunt

Mimi, but I didn't want her to...to know that I didn't know. I...I'm supposing there's more than just kisses, and I've *heard* things a time or two at court." She shook her head in denial. "But they can't possibly be true. Nobody would do that."

Tatiana looked about the room, spying out the small table with a decanter of wine that had been sent up by the baron, whose man said that it was safer by far to sip wine than to get within ten feet of the inn's supply of water unless it was for one's bath. She hesitated only a moment before pouring herself a full glass and drinking the contents in three nearly desperate gulps.

Wiping the back of her hand across her mouth, she then sighed, replaced the wineglass and sat her bulk down on a chair without asking permission.

"Ah, that's better," she said, rubbing her palms together and looking at Alina expectantly. "Now, my dear, sheltered little girl, you tell your Tatiana— nobody would do what?"

THE SMALL GILT CLOCK that had been a parting gift from the king chimed out the hour of ten o'clock from a small table beside Lady Alina's bed. She sighed, supposing she would hear the lovely thing chime out every hour until dawn, her eyes still as wide and shocked as they were now, and staring up at the cracked ceiling.

Tatiana had left her after an hour. Alina would

have given anything to have their discussion forever erased from her memory.

That's what Jurgen and Astrid had been doing? Her *parents* had done this? The whole *world* did this?

Why? Why would *anyone* do this?

Yes, her mother had explained her monthly bleed when Alina had first experienced it. But she'd called it Eve's curse, which hadn't meant much, even when Alina had gone to the Bible in the study and searched it thoroughly. The snake, the apple, she knew all of that. But she hadn't found anything about a monthly bleed, and had to content herself with her mother's assertion that it made her a woman, and no longer a little girl.

That had seemed a fair enough trade. After all, men like Jurgen and Luka and Papa had to shave every day because they were men. She only had to bleed once a month.

Oh, if only she had known! She would never have agreed to the marriage had she known. Removing herself from her aunt Mimi's jurisdiction, her constant disapproval, had weighed heavily in her decision, as had Count Josef Eberharter's teeth. Pleasing the king had, of course, been paramount…even if displeasing the king by refusing probably hadn't been a serious option in any case.

The prospect of fine gowns, of moving in English society, of having a home of her own, these had all finally brought her around to the notion that, if she was not the luckiest girl in the world, she at least wasn't cleaning out fireplace grates or living in some damp cave, worrying when next she'd have something to eat.

But *this?* She hadn't known about *this.* The so disgusting, so crudely violating, so intensely intimate *this.*

She'd made Tatiana swear on her prayer book that she was telling the truth. She'd demanded the companion then swear on that same prayer book that people actually *liked* it. Tatiana wasn't sure enough to put her immortal soul in jeopardy by swearing to the latter. But she was fairly certain men liked it. Men liked the oddest things.

The soft knock on the door to her bedchamber all but had Alina jumping out of her skin.

"Lady Alina? It is I, Justin Wilde. I see a spill of light under the door and feel impelled to disturb you. I believe we should have ourselves a small conversation."

Her wide eyes popped open even wider. It was him…God and all His saints help her…her *stallion.*

"Forgive me, my lord," she called out, wishing her voice didn't seem to be a full octave too high, and piteously thin. Wishing she had dared to blow out her candle and face the dark, and the disturbing images Tatiana's words had planted in her brain. "I am abed."

"Ah, but not asleep," came the assured voice. "One could hardly expect you to be, if your bed is half so uncomfortable as mine. Please. We really do need to talk."

The disturbing images disappeared as her temper came to her rescue. Was the man always going to prove such a pest?

"Oh, all right, if you're otherwise going to stand out there making a fuss," she groused mean-spiritedly, throwing back the covers and slipping to her feet. "One moment."

She located her dressing gown, not caring that it was old—why had she purchased so many pretty things, and completely neglected to refurbish her nightwear? She should probably add that question to the list of Things Nobody Had Told Her, praying it would not be a long list. She could only be grateful that the thing buttoned from her throat to her toes, rather like muslin armor.

But her parents had not shared a bedchamber. It had never occurred to Alina that her husband would share hers, that he would ever see her in her nightwear. There was no avoiding the thing—she was stupidest person in creation!

Not bothering to locate her slippers, she padded to the door, slipped back the latch and stepped back a half-dozen very large paces. "It's open, my lord."

He stepped inside and closed the door behind him.

Alina crossed her arms protectively over her breasts. Just in case he became "maddened by lust," as Tatiana had said men were prone to do at the drop of a hat.

"My, aren't you a picture," the baron said, bowing to her before advancing toward her, daring to lift the single thick braid that hung down over her crossed arms. "I had a mare once whose tail was so long and fine that my groom enjoyed braiding it this way. It looks better on you," he added as he dropped the braid, so that she quickly gave her head a flip, sending the thing flying behind her back.

"I'm not a mare, my lord," Alina told him, knowing that, in many ways, she was. A broodmare...with an ermine-tipped velvet cloak.

He tilted his head to one side and looked at her more closely. "No, of course you're not. Is there something amiss, my lady? Have I made you nervous? I promise you, that was not my intent in coming here."

"Then what is your intent, my lord?"

Something was happening to her. He was looking at her in the strangest and most intense way, and something was happening to her. She was becoming curiously aware of her body, parts of it that had never before bothered to bring themselves to her attention. And hadn't they taken a fine time to wake up and say hello!

Alina hastened to the chair Tatiana had been sitting in an hour earlier. The wineglass she'd refilled three times during the course of their discussion was still on the table beside it, still with half its contents. She picked it up and drained it, suppressing a shiver as her first taste of unwatered wine served to make her feel warm from her tongue straight down to the bottom of her belly.

Tatiana had said that wine helped when one was nervous, and if taken in enough quantity could even make the unthinkable, thinkable.

But nothing happened. Clearly it would take considerably more wine for that! Alina sat down with a thump, crossed her arms once more over her breasts that were neither more than a handful nor pimples.

She looked up at Lord Wilde; so tall, so very handsome, she supposed. But the unthinkable remained unthinkable. Mostly. Those parts of her body that had heretofore slumbered happily seemed to be coming even more awake, aware in some strange, unsettling way. She clamped her knees together tightly, even as she forced herself to lower her arms, clasp her fingers in her lap.

Do not think about his strong, callused hands, she warned herself. Do not think of where he will touch you, how he will touch you with his hands... and with his...with that other thing.

She couldn't help herself. Her eyes strayed to the slight bulge at the juncture of his thighs.

She shivered and quickly looked away.

"Comfortable?" he asked, both his smile and his tone telling her he knew she was not.

"I am not accustomed to having gentlemen see me in my…when I am not dressed."

"I should most certainly hope not," he said affably. "But you are all that is modest. Almost aggressively so, one might say. Alina—may I please have the pleasure of addressing you so informally? I find it a delightful affectation."

What did he mean, aggressively so? Was he making fun of her? Oh, he was such a man of the world, wasn't he? The insufferable snot. "Alina is my mother's name for me. There is nothing pretentious about it. My cloak is pretentious."

His smile was different this time than it had been earlier. She could see this one in his eyes as well as on his lips. "Yes, it certainly is. You're going to bankrupt me, aren't you, minx? At least I've been forewarned. Please feel free to augment your wardrobe in any way you wish. I suggest you begin with your nightwear."

She drew the dressing gown more closely about her. He had already made his point. She did need new nightwear. Preferably fashioned out of chain mail.

"Ah, now I've insulted you." He pulled a straight-back chair away from the wall and turned it about, straddling it as he sat down. "I apologize, and can only put it down to something I learned earlier this evening."

At least he wasn't so big, now that he'd sat down. "The something you believe we must speak of tonight? Does it have anything to do with that nonsense you were spouting this afternoon? Because you very nearly frightened me. I thought I'd been betrothed to a lunatic."

"Yes, I suppose you did. I'd like to apologize for that, Alina. I was under the mistaken impression that your king had informed you of—well, how do I put this?"

Her bare feet were beginning to feel chilled against the cold floor. "I would suggest, my lord, that you put it quickly. I would like to return to my bed."

He stood up, replacing the chair against the wall, and held out his hand to her. "Much to my shock and even, yes, my consternation, I believe the devil is in it for me no matter where you deposit yourself, so why don't you do that? Tuck the covers up under your chin, and perhaps I'll be able to twist my mind around what I have to say."

Now, what did he mean by that curious statement? Really, if it weren't for the yellowed teeth, Count Eberharter was beginning to seem like the lesser of two evils. At least he was supposedly sane.

Alina scurried across the room and climbed onto the high bed, not unaware that she was, even if just for a moment, all but aiming her backside at her betrothed. Thinking about uncontrollable lust and dropping hats, she slid herself beneath the covers with alacrity. Then she quickly pulled the covers up and under her chin. "Back where I began," she said, looking at him. "But you're still here."

Not only was he still there, but he had managed to pour himself a glass of wine, using the same glass she and Tatiana had used, as it was the only one on the tray. The thought passed through her mind that she and the companion had employed the wine for courage. Had he felt a similar need?

"I had a long and rather interesting chat with your secretary, Alina. He tells me that you believe this marriage of ours has been concocted solely to display friendship between your king and my Prince Regent, and to be an outward show of a new era of trade cooperation between our two countries now that Europe is once more at peace. Is that true?"

"No," she said quietly, because she was, at heart, an honest person, and because her toes were curling beneath the covers at the way he kept *looking* at her and she would probably trip over her tongue if she dared a lie. "Not *solely,* my lord."

"Justin," he said, cocking his head very slightly. "Go on."

"Justin," she repeated, trying out his name, wishing her heart would kindly stop racing as if she'd just run up the long, curving flight of stairs at home.

"Those were the king's reasons, and your king's, as well, I suppose. But I could have refused, you know."

"How fortunate for you."

She heard something in his voice, something that pulled all of her attention to him. "You had no choice?"

"Well, we all have choices, I suppose. Mine, however, were not acceptable to me."

"Neither were mine," Alina said, pushing up the pillows behind her so that she could sit back against them. She felt ridiculous, just lying there, while he stood over her like some...some...*stallion.* "Aunt Mimi made it very clear that if I refused this grand honor the king was gifting me with, I would be married off to someone of her choosing. She seemed entirely too delighted to have that power, so here I am."

"I've been many things in my life, Alina, but I believe this may be the first time I am being seen as the lesser of two evils. I'm flattered."

"You probably shouldn't be, you know. I really never considered you. I've always wanted to travel to England. I want to meet the rest of my family, now that my parents are gone. It isn't pleasant, you understand, to think that your single remaining relative is Aunt Mimi."

Justin chuckled softly. "We must be thankful, then, that she didn't decide to escort you here herself."

Alina nodded, actually beginning to relax. Which was ridiculous. She was in bed, and he was standing there, and these newly awakened parts of her body were becoming more and more interested in having him continue to stand there. "She's convinced Englishmen are all barbarians, so she refused to accompany me. She may even now be rubbing her hands together in glee, believing some great bear has already eaten me, or something."

"There are no bears in England, Alina. At least not of the four-legged variety. I was told your mother was English, but I hadn't given that fact very much thought. What's your family name?"

"You'll allow me to go see them?"

Justin shrugged. "I see no reason not to, do you?"

"No, I don't. But Luka told me that English husbands are very strict, and that I will not be allowed to walk out alone, most especially in London, and that, as a wife, I will no longer have a mind of my own, but only my husband's will and permission."

He sat down on the edge of the bed, which for some unknown reason suddenly seemed quite a natural thing for him to do. "God's teeth! No wonder you don't like me. He told you all of that? Did he tell you that we lock wives in the cellars if they dare to disobey, and keep them there on a diet of stale bread and ditch water for a month?"

Alina's eyes widened at this, but then she noticed the tiniest bit of crinkling around the outside of Justin's eyes. "You said that you and he had a long talk this evening. Did he tell you that I'm a very good shot and that I have a very bad temper?"

"He said you are prone to do whatever people tell you not to do. He didn't mention any proficiency with firearms."

"Oh. Then perhaps I shouldn't have mentioned it, either. And not just with firearms. I am also extremely proficient at archery, and I know how to throw a knife so that it actually sticks in whatever it hits. That isn't easy, you know, getting the handle not to hit first."

"Now I'm intrigued," Justin said, and she believed him, because he was looking at her with some interest. "Many Englishwomen are proficient at archery. Some enjoy shooting, although not many. But I don't believe I've ever met a female who knows how to throw a knife without the handle hitting the target first. Why would you want to learn such a thing?"

Alina lowered her eyes for a moment, and then looked at him again. "Your English ladies were safe here, on your island, while Bonaparte seemed to go where he willed all across Europe. My father said that when the fox threatens the chicken house, even the hens must know how to defend themselves."

"Luka told me your father died at Waterloo. I'm sorry."

"So am I," Alina said, sighing. "But he didn't mean to die. If he did, he wouldn't have left me with Aunt Mimi. He would have been certain to leave instructions that I be sent to England, I'm sure of it. But Luka isn't so sure, as Papa never said anything to him."

"Ah, yes, your mother's family."

"My family," she clarified. She hadn't really thought seriously about her mother's family, not until her father was gone, but she'd daydreamed about how they would be. How they'd love her. "They live in Kent. I looked at a map, and it isn't all that far away from London. It's all down here the way Portsmouth is, at the fat end of the island, and not up near Scotland."

"Yes, I am familiar with Kent. My own estate is located in Hampshire, also in the...fat part of the island. What's your mother's family name?"

"Farber," Alina told him proudly. "My mother was Lady Anne Louise Farber, daughter of the Earl of—"

"Birling. Yes, I know the family title."

She watched as Justin stood once more, his handsome features suddenly cold, hard. She sat up straighter, sensing that the ease they'd seemed to have found with each other these past minutes was just that, a thing of the past. "What's wrong?"

His expression softened, but only with some effort, she was sure. "Wrong? Why, nothing, my dear, nothing at all is wrong. I just thought of something else I must discuss with the Prince Regent when next I see him. I must tell him how very clever, no, how fiendishly clever he is."

"I don't understand."

"You will, unfortunately. But not right now. It's time you slept. Good night."

"But…but you said we had to talk, that there was something you needed to tell me."

His hand on the door latch, Justin turned, looked at her in the near darkness. She couldn't see his eyes now, and she had the strangest feeling that this was because he didn't want her to see them.

"Yes, it had to do with our destination. I'm afraid we won't be traveling to London tomorrow. Instead, you'll be heading off to West Sussex, and the estate of my friend Rafe, the Duke of Ashurst. And his wife, Charlotte," he added almost immediately, as if he felt he should. "You'll travel quickly, I'm afraid, with only a single night spent on the road and two full days in the coach."

"And then we'll go to London?"

"I will," he said, and opened the door. "I most assuredly will be traveling to London. I'm convinced there is someone there who can barely contain his glee as he awaits my arrival."

She threw back the covers and got out of bed.

"But I won't be going with you to see this happy person? Is that what you're saying? You're going to take me to this Ashurst, and this Duke, and leave me there?"

"You'll remain with my friends until I return for you, yes."

"But—why?"

He didn't answer her. Instead, he closed the door and walked to where she was standing barefoot on the chilly wooden floor, and put a hand to her cheek, which made her feel very strange indeed. Not frightened. Not at all frightened. She fought to keep herself from tipping her head, so that she could press her skin more closely against his, feel the strength of his hand, the slight roughness of his skin.

"You've been badly used. I'm sorry, pet," he whispered softly. "I'm so very, very sorry. But I'll fix it, as best I can. I promise."

"You make precious little sense, Justin," she told him, caught between anger and fear...and a hint of something she felt fairly certain, after her instructional talk, Tatiana would have termed *interest*. Mostly, she knew she didn't want him to leave. "How can you fix something I don't even know is broken? How would I even know when you'd fixed it?"

He smiled, but it was one of those smiles that didn't quite reach his eyes. "Aren't your feet cold?"

"Never mind my feet," she shot back, deciding anger was perhaps the best option at the moment.

"Ah, but I find them adorable. Small and slim. Have you ever heard the expression *I kiss your hands and feet?*"

Alina curled her toes and clenched her fingers, and those parts of her that had been so happily slumbering shot out warnings that she might soon be in significant trouble if she didn't apply some maidenly common sense and put a halt to this strange conversation, and that those previously slumbering parts weren't all that averse to a little adventure.

"Once again you're not answering my questions," she pointed out, striving to regather her scattered wits. "We were speaking about my family, and suddenly you ran for the door."

"I beg your pardon. I do not *run* for doors."

"Very well, then, why did you come back?" she asked, believing the answer to that might be more important.

"Perhaps for this?" he offered, moving his hand so that now he was tipping up her chin. "One more look, and perhaps even a small taste."

"Oh. I…that is…you shouldn't have to answer *every* quest—"

Her eyelids fluttered closed as he brought his lips to hers, and then retreated before she could react at all.

"Innocence," he said softly. "You taste like innocence. And I should be shot."

And then he was gone, and Alina crawled back into bed, holding a hand to her mouth, knowing she wouldn't sleep a single wink for the remainder of what was going to be a very long night.

CHAPTER FOUR

WIGGLESWORTH DEPOSITED the coddled eggs in front of his master with all the trepidation of the servant charged with delivering the head of John the Baptist to Salome; he thought it might be what the baron wanted, but could not be sure of its reception now that it was a done thing.

The porridge had been looked upon, but not eaten. The kippers—done to a turn!—had been waved away without so much as a "ye gods, Wigglesworth, not those horrid things." Even the inn's own country ham, purely a desperate move by the servant who put little trust in any cooking save his own, had been met with a fairly blank stare and a short shake of the head.

"Wigglesworth, I said I wasn't— Oh, damn. Here, let me force these down. I wouldn't want to put you into a sulk."

"Thank you, sir," the servant said, sighing. And then he dared more. "Is there…something amiss, my lord?"

"Your solicitude becomes tiresome. A man can't

forgo a single breakfast out of thousands without something being wrong?"

Wigglesworth wrung his hands even as Brutus, standing in a corner—hulking in a corner—shook his massive head sorrowfully, either for worry over his employer or the fact that he now, after being passed the porridge and the kippers for his own consumption, would be denied the coddled eggs.

"Your bed wasn't slept in, my lord," Wigglesworth pointed out quietly. "There was nary a hint of reproach when I nicked you that small—infinitesimal, I assure you—cut with the razor. And you did not even a single time remonstrate with me when I informed you that your second-best Hessians seemed to have suffered a fatal crack to the heel on the cobblestones yesterday."

"My, what a litany of abuses you've laid before me, Wigglesworth. Very well, consider your sorry self run up and down by the rough side of my tongue. *Now* may I be left alone? Wait—a *fatal* crack?"

"Possibly. Perhaps. I may have overstated. I will deliver them personally to Mr. Hoby when we are returned to London."

Justin put down his fork, what little appetite he may have had, either for the eggs or soothing Wigglesworth's feelings, now gone. "An event that is to be somewhat delayed," he said as the major entered the breakfast room. "Ah, Luka, there you are," he went on, no trace of anything but happiness at the appearance of the man in his voice. "Would you like my man here to prepare you something with which to break your fast? He has quite taken over the kitchen, you understand."

"Thank you, no. I've been up for hours, and have already eaten," the major said, a note of recrimination in his tone, as if anyone who remained abed past dawn was a sluggard not worth considering. "Pardon me, but I could not help but overhear. We are not immediately setting out for London? It was my understanding that Lady Alina was to be presented to your Prince Regent, and then you and she were to immediately exchange your vows, sealing the…the, um, bargain."

"Just what I tarried here to speak to you about. Such haste is unseemly, don't you think? Her ladyship is fatigued from her travels. It would be unconscionable to force her to continue her journey without some small respite, which is why I sent off one of my outriders at first light to the estate of my dear friend the Duke of Ashurst, to alert him that Lady Alina will be his guest for a few days. The duke will be dispatching outriders to meet you along the road and escort you the remainder of the journey. They'll be with you by the time you arrive at your first night's lodging, I'm sure. Rooms will be waiting for you."

Luka narrowed his eyes. His moustachios may have twitched as well, but it was a close-run thing to know if this was a natural occurrence or a remarkable aberration caused by the man's consternation at the position he had been forced into by his king. If it was the latter, Luka had Justin's full sympathy. And empathy, if it came to that.

"Lady Alina will be the duke's guest? And *you* will be…?"

"Elsewhere. I see no need to provide you with a listing of my comings and goings, I'm afraid, as I've been my own master for quite some years now. Until recently, that is, which is a circumstance that is about to change. You've protected her thus far, and Brutus and my own trusted and quite prodigiously well-armed outriders will be with you. I imagine you're up to getting her safely to Ashurst Hall. Well, Brutus is," Justin qualified, getting to his feet, quitting the room and leaving the major to follow or not, whatever his inclination. Not that he was surprised to have the man hot on his heels as he strode out to the inn yard.

"I beg your pardon? Have you forgotten that you are charged with protecting Lady Alina?"

"She has her prepared-to-die-for-her secretary," Justin said, turning to his left and heading for the stables. "Anyone approaches with a nefarious look in his eye, and you just be a good fellow and attack him with your quill. You—yes, you. Saddle the bay now, my fine young fellow, and there's a guinea in it for you."

The eager ostler hastened to do Justin's bidding, but not quickly enough to save the baron from the major's fury.

"You're leaving? Just like this? I can't allow you to do that." To give credence to his words, he roughly took hold of Justin's arm above the elbow.

Justin turned slowly to face the irate man. "Allow? You cannot allow? Worse, you're putting a crease in my jacket."

The major loosed his grip. "The devil with your jacket. Last night you looked like a man who was going to tell her about the threat to her life. Did you?"

"I allowed my mind to be changed on that head," Justin told him, taking the gloves and hat and riding crop Wigglesworth, who had materialized seemingly from out of nowhere, pressed into his hands. "Thank you, Wigglesworth. You remain, as always, a treasure."

"You're welcome, my lord. I would have been here sooner, had you but told me you were about to depart. You will be careful, won't you, sir?"

"Am I not always careful, Wigglesworth?" Justin asked, putting on his curly brimmed beaver and lightly tapping it into place.

"No, sir, you're not." The servant turned to address the major. "He's not, you know. But he always triumphs. If his lordship says that everything will be fine, then it will be fine, because he wouldn't have it any other way. But perhaps not always immediately."

"I'm touched, Wigglesworth. Such damning praise." The ostler brought out the saddled horse. "And now, adieu. Major, please deliver my felicitations to the lady, and my promise to join her at Ashurst Hall within the week with, I most sincerely hope, news that will please her."

Along with information that will devastate her, Justin added silently as he put his booted foot in the stirrup and gracefully mounted the bay.

Once again Luka was proving meddlesome. He grabbed onto the bay's bridle and stepped close. "If any harm comes to her, there will be no place safe for you to hide. Leaving her like this, knowing the danger? You're nothing but an overdressed, pompous coward."

"And now I am desolated. Are you telling me you are not up to protecting the lady by yourself for two more days, after getting her safely halfway across Europe and onto these shores? Have I so badly misjudged my man?" Justin asked him quietly.

"No harm will come to her," Luka said firmly.

"Good." Justin smiled, even as his eyes remained hard, cold chips of green ice. "Because, my new friend, if any does, you'll have left me no choice but to kill you."

The two men stared at each other for long moments until, as Justin had expected, the major released his grip on the bridle. Poor fellow; men who lived by the rules had so many problems to beset them. That's why he'd given up on being bound by such pesky things a long time ago.

He was almost safely gone. But just as he was about to turn his mount and exit the yard, out of the corner of his eye he spied the Lady Alina in the doorway of the inn.

She had been an enchanting, provocative vision in her ermine-tipped cloak. She presented a heartbreakingly beautiful picture now, framed in the doorway, her midnight-blue traveling ensemble turning her exotic and yet still so very English—a mix of blood that had mingled to create a masterpiece.

Either he left right now, or he'd never find the strength to go.

He lifted his hat to her, bowed his head slightly, and without a word put his heels into his mount's flanks, causing the obedient horse to break into an immediate gallop.

All the way to London, the vision that haunted the corners of his mind was not of Alina in her ermine-tipped cloak, nor of Alina in her dashing traveling ensemble and that silly shako hat tipped down over one eye.

No, the picture he could not get out of his head was of Alina in that disastrous and wildly appealing nightwear, her golden eyes wide and innocent as she proudly told him the name of her mother…and sent his soul crashing straight to hell.

ALINA HAD NEVER SEEN Luka so angry as he'd been today and all of yesterday. Not that he'd paid her much attention, concentrating most of his time and effort on positioning the baron's outriders ahead of and behind the coach, and then, when the Duke of Ashurst's men joined them last night at the inn, giving each of them instructions on how he wished them to fit in with the existing ranks.

As if he expected the French to attack at any moment, or some such nonsense. He'd even donned his uniform once more, and he'd told her he wouldn't be wearing it while he was in England, so as to not insult the English government in any way.

When she'd attempted to question him about why the baron had left them, and why they were being sent to this Ashurst Hall and this good friend, Luka had only muttered and said something about having to supervise tying down the luggage so that neither of the two coaches might overturn if there was a need for speed at any time during their journey.

As to his impressions of the baron himself, Luka said even less. But when he left her at the inn doorway and promptly spit into the dirt, she'd gotten a fairly good idea of what her friend thought of her intended husband.

Why, anyone would think it had been his betrothed

who had gone racing out of the inn yard as if the hounds of hell were after him.

"Her," she corrected herself. "As if the hounds of hell were after *her*." She didn't know much about marriage, a fact that had been brought home to her with disturbing clarity by Tatiana, but she did know that women married men, and men married women.

Otherwise, her terrible, base, unable-to-beat-down but logical mind told her, the pieces wouldn't fit.

"So good to see you smile, my lady, even if you're only talking to yourself," Tatiana said from the facing seat in the coach. "So good to know somebody can bear these terrible English roads without wondering if she's soon to see her luncheon for a second time."

"I told you, Tatiana. It's silly for you to ride backward when there is certainly ample room next to me. Riding backward is sure to make you ill."

"We're not at home anymore, my lady, where we can do what we want because it is what we want. Danica told me as much. We can only be happy that she knows her place is with the second coach and the luggage. God never takes but what He gives, I suppose."

"I suppose," Alina said, her mind already off the subject of traveling arrangements and back on to the subject of, well, traveling arrangements.

Why wasn't his lordship—Justin; he'd asked her

to address him as Justin, so she may as well begin thinking of him as Justin—why wasn't he riding with them? Where had he gone, why had he gone, and would he really come back, or had he just said as much in order to get away without Luka shooting him or some such thing?

Had her night rail and dressing gown been *that* off-putting? And that kiss? Did innocence taste so terrible?

Or did he love someone, some sweet, biddable English miss with huge blue eyes and soft blond hair? Had he thought he could sacrifice himself for king and country, but one sight of Alina had been enough to make him feel the sacrifice was too much, even for a loyal subject?

Or it could have been something she'd said to him. What had she said? She'd told him the truth, she'd told him about Aunt Mimi and Count Eberharter's yellow teeth. Had that been *too* honest? How had he answered her? Oh, yes. He'd never before been considered the lesser of two evils.

Had he been laughing at her? Of course he had. Count Eberharter's *teeth?* Who said such things to one's betrothed?

Oh, she was such a child! Clearly Justin Wilde was a man of the world, and just as clearly she was an ignorant infant who possessed the understanding of a gnat.

And it was all Aunt Mimi's fault. Mama had gone

to heaven while her daughter was still a child—more a child than she was now, at least—and Aunt Mimi had abdicated her responsibilities to her niece. There was more to education than learning the globe and her sums. There was also…those other things. The least, the very least the woman could have done was to instruct her niece to expand her selection of nightwear.

But Alina should have asked questions. Especially the one about being kissed and getting babies, because that had always seemed an incomplete answer to her. Not that she'd known what questions to ask in the first place, but also because no one could possibly ask questions that personal of a woman who always loved to look down her nose at you and snicker as if there were some Huge Secret she knew but wasn't about to share with her annoying little niece.

Still, much as she wanted to lay any and all blame at her aunt's feet, Alina knew she had only thought of this marriage from her own perspective. But now that she'd met the baron, and most especially since Tatiana's lesson in the Way Of The World, it was impossible not to consider his part in the equation.

How selfish of her! To consider only herself, and not the man who would make up the other half of this arranged marriage. Men had feelings. She'd watched her father cry as her mother's body had been carried off to the cemetery. Men loved.

As did women. Women loved.

But what was love? She understood the love of a child for her parents, but did she understand the love of parents for each other?

No.

She understood love of country. She'd loved the many pets she'd had over the years. She loved her ermine-tipped cloak, which was doubtless horribly shallow of her, but she did love it.

Alina winced, shivered. How many meanings to that single word: *love*.

She and Justin had not come together through love, but that hadn't seemed important. According to Aunt Mimi, rarely did anyone of her station, her class, marry for love. They married to meld fortunes, to join lands, to improve trade relations, to beget heirs.

But her parents had married for love. Alina was certain of that. Her mother had left her home country for her father. She'd told her only child several times that she had never regretted that decision. Never for a single moment. She'd spoken fondly of memories of her childhood at Birling, but that was all.

Oh, how much easier to marry for love!

And how humiliating to be kissed, however briefly, by her prospective husband, only to have the man then bolt and run at the first chance he got, leaving her without so much as bidding her farewell.

That had been rude of him. Exceedingly rude. Possibly bordering on boorish.

Why should she be feeling ashamed? She hadn't taken one look at him and called for a horse and raced off into the countryside.

Alina, after nearly two full days spent rehashing the same things over and over again in her head, variously feeling frightened and sorry for herself, began to feel the first stirrings of real anger.

Yes, none of this could be easy for him. But how dare he think this was some whopping lovely large slice of plum pudding for *her?* Had he given her a moment's thought before he'd climbed on his big bay horse and raced out of the inn yard, leaving instructions that she be shunted off to some complete strangers? Oh, no, she doubted that. She doubted that highly.

"I think I shall be exceptionally cool to the baron when next we meet, Tatiana," she announced with rapidly rising conviction. "I was much too honest and open with him the other night. I should never have allowed him entry to my chamber, for one thing, and I never should have confided in him about—about anything at all. I did so well on the dock. Just as I'd planned it all, exactly as I had seen it all in my head. Truly, it was a thing of beauty, you'll admit. But I have had no practice at conversation with gentlemen other than Luka and those few gentlemen Aunt Mimi allowed to dance with me at court, and they were all my father's friends in any case. Lord Wilde is a wholly new experience for me."

The companion nodded. "Yes, I already supposed as much. I was waiting for you to stop worrying so much about the Englishman and realize you've been deserted. Will you also be out hunting for toads to put in his bed?"

Surprising herself, Alina bit her bottom lip in embarrassment. "No, I think that my years of childish mischief are well and truly over. He called me *pet,* you know. I am not a pet. I am not a child. I have learned the ways of a woman now, and must prepare myself for my new…position in life. But I will find a way to punish him, most definitely. After all, he did say to begin as we plan to go on. And I will not *go on* being left in the middle of nowhere whenever some whim takes the man."

"About…what we spoke of the other night, my lady?"

"Yes, Tatiana?" Alina's heart skipped in sudden trepidation. "Don't tell me there's more?"

Tatiana's plump face screwed up in thought as she raised her eyes to the roof of the coach and considered the question. She made a few hand motions— one of them fairly disconcerting, as if she might be stuffing a handkerchief inside her clenched fist— before finally sighing audibly and saying, "No, I think I had the right of it, my lady. Having not personally experienced…"

"Yes, thank you, Tatiana. In any event, I was not at my best when the baron came to see me, but that will not happen again."

"Yes, my lady, that was what I was about to say. *If* he comes back."

Alina skewered the companion with those golden eyes of hers. "Luka said that the baron said that he will be joining us within the week. Luka doesn't lie."

"Ah, but does the baron tell the truth?" Tatiana asked, and then, too late, realized she might have been better served to keep her thoughts to herself. "Which I am sure he does. Truly. And…and he is very pretty."

Alina rolled her eyes. "Yes, he mentioned that himself, I believe, on the off chance I hadn't noticed on my own, I suppose. What a strange man. He seems to poke fun at himself so that nobody else has to go to the bother of doing it for him. I wonder why. Drat! Haven't I had to learn enough these past few days? The last thing I want is to feel obliged to understand the man."

And then, thanks to both her rather precarious position on the cushioned seat and the quick sawing on the reins by the coachman, Alina found herself deposited on the floor, attempting to push the bulk of her companion off her with both hands as the coach lurched to a halt.

"This could be a trick. Eyes alert and weapons at

the ready, men!" she heard Luka shout as Tatiana slowly boosted herself back onto her seat, the companion muttering a few words of her own, none of them complimentary to the mother of the coachman. "I'll personally see to the lady."

Alina moved to open the door, to see what on earth was going on. But just as her hand settled on the latch, the door opened and Luka appeared, his stern face more immobile than usual.

"Nothing to worry about, my lady. Seems there's a tree fallen across the roadway. The baron's men are moving it now, and we'll be on our way shortly."

"May I come out and watch?" she asked him, as she was more than ready to be out of the coach for a while.

"It's nearly dark, my lady. Nothing to see."

"May I be the judge of that, please, Luka?" she asked, pushing the door open just as he was attempting to push it closed. "Honestly! Don't you think you're taking this business of being responsible for me just a little too— *Luka!*"

The shot had come from the greenery bordering the roadway. Alina knew that because she had seen the flash from the muzzle in the fading light. Luka looked at her strangely for a moment, surprise in his eyes, and then pitched headfirst onto her lap.

"Luka!"

There was suddenly ear-piercing screaming— courtesy of Tatiana—the sounds of more shots from both pistols and larger weapons, the shouts of men issuing orders, the nervous cries of horses, those locked in the traces and those being turned and wheeled to face some unseen enemy.

"My lady..."

She bent her head close to Luka, who was struggling to raise himself, although it seemed his right arm wasn't cooperating. "Yes, I'm here. Don't die."

"Not...not planning on it. Just get down...lie down on the seat where you will be safe."

"And what would that serve?" she asked him, already reaching into the pocket at the side of the cushioned seat, as an earlier inspection of the coach had unearthed the fact that the baron traveled with flasks of wine, lovely crystal glasses, a tin of sugar biscuits, and two braces of very pretty and also quite deadly pistols. Loaded pistols. "Somebody shot you, Luka," she said with typical Alina logic, "now I'm going to shoot him back!"

Luka didn't protest, assuredly not because he agreed with her plan, but because he seemed to once more have lapsed into unconsciousness as what sounded very much like a pitched battle continued outside on the roadway.

"My lady..."

"Tend to Luka, Tatiana. See the blood on his coat? He took a ball in the shoulder. We're short one man, with Luka down, so I must help. Oh, and do please keep your head down, like he said."

With Tatiana grabbing at her skirt in an attempt to stop her, with a heavy pistol in each hand, and what with having to maneuver her way over Luka's inert body, Alina's exit from the coach turned into a near somersault, landing her ignominiously in a puddle caused by the earlier rain, her nose an inch deep into the muddy water. One of the pistols went flying out of her hand.

Not that anyone outside the coach noticed, as they all seemed to be occupied either in shooting wildly into the trees or attempting to tie a stout rope to the fallen tree trunk in order to shift it off the roadway.

Alina was struggling to get to her feet when she felt what seemed to be a band of iron clamp around her waist from behind, and she was ignominiously hauled upright—hauled a good foot or more off the ground, actually. Kicking her feet impotently, she was unceremoniously shoved back into the coach, where she landed on Luka's back. The major, who was not dead, groaned at her added weight and muttered a word Alina had never before heard, but one she was fairly certain he shouldn't have uttered in her presence.

She righted herself, aimed her feet toward the door as she began to struggle to exit the coach once more, only to be faced with a wall of solid Brutus,

Justin's so-called secretary. Justin's mountain was more like it.

Wiping at her muddy face with her sleeve, Alina demanded she be allowed to pass.

The mountain only grunted.

"I am reluctant to shoot you, Brutus, but the highwaymen have shot my friend. They can't be allowed to get away with that, now, can they?"

The mountain rolled his eyes at this clear impossibility.

"I mean it, Brutus," Alina said, pointing the uncocked pistol at him. "I know how to fight."

The mountain, using only two fingers, plucked the pistol from her as if picking a bit of lint from a jacket. The weapon looked small in his hamlike hand. She wouldn't, in fact, have been surprised if he were now to bend the barrel in half, just to prove his point. Whatever his point—and she wasn't at all certain she wanted to know what it was.

Another male face appeared, insinuating itself in the small amount of space left over after Brutus had blocked the doorway. "We're clear, Major Prochazka. We're ready to move again. Two wounded, but they're fit enough, and able to ride."

"Then let's do that," Luka said, crawling out from under Alina, who was beginning to feel very much like a muddy cork being tossed about on a sea of unyielding angles and, *ouch,* it would seem that Luka was wearing spurs.

The looming Brutus stepped back, shut the door. Opened it again, tossed in Alina's lovely shako hat— now covered with mud—and closed the door once more, before she could send it sailing back at him.

By this time Luka had managed to sit himself down on the cushions, and even to hold out a hand to Alina so that she could join him. "If you wish," he said, looking angry and amused at the same time. But mostly amused, which was not nice of him at all.

With the back of her hand she swiped at the tip of her nose because it tickled, catching a rivulet of muddy water just as it was about to drip and ruin her— Oh! Her new traveling costume! Look at it! It was ruined. "My outfit is nothing but mud!" she exclaimed before she could stop herself.

"The better to match your face, Lady Alina," Luka said, grabbing on to his right arm, which was hanging uselessly at his side. "What the devil did you think you were going to do out there?"

Alina accepted the handkerchief Tatiana handed her and began wiping at her face even as the coach moved forward once more, clearly sacrificing passenger comfort in favor of speed. "I tried to avenge your death—not that you're dead, but you know what I mean—and this is the thanks I get?" she asked as they were all bracing themselves so not to be tossed around the interior of the coach. "Questions, and that face of yours, Luka? Oh, don't try to hide it now. I saw your smile. Or did you think I would be content to simply *cower* here and have a fit of the vapors or something while highwaymen attacked us?"

"Highwaymen," the major said quietly, sobering. "Yes. It would appear that England is not quite so civilized as the English would like us to believe."

"Clearly not! Do you suppose they have followed us from Portsmouth? That they saw my trunks being unloaded, and my cloak? Oh, I should have been ruthless with anyone who dared to attempt to steal my cloak, let me tell you that!" She accepted another pristine linen square Tatiana had unearthed from the large bag at her feet and promptly ruined it by wiping it over her face and hands. The farther removed from the heat of battle she got, the more she regretted her impulsive action. But someone had shot Luka. And that had made her *so* angry!

The facts that, now that they were safe and on the move again, her hands had begun to shake and her stomach felt exceptionally queasy, and she believed she could begin to weep rather copiously if anyone so much as looked at her slightly askance, were all suddenly being brought very much home to her. She'd been reckless, and she could have been dead.

Why did she not stop to consider the consequences before she acted? Why did the illogical and impossible always seem rational and infinitely plausible when her wild Romany blood was up, as Tatiana had always told her?

Alina was proud of her Romany blood, but even as she looked for some excuse to explain away her more rash and ridiculous actions, she did not think it fair to blame that blood. She knew where the blame truly lay, and it was with her.

Just another failing she would have to apply herself to correcting before she became a bride. And just another reason to resent the absent Justin Wilde. If he had done his duty, he would have been riding in the coach with her—the coach that would be on its way to London—and nowhere near those hideous highwaymen. He would have taken up the brace of pistols and defended her. Why, if she looked at the thing long enough and hard enough, it was all his fault that she was sitting here, her beautiful new outfit ruined, muddy water dripping off the tip of her nose.

All of which she would tell him when he came to fetch her from this Ashurst Hall they were heading for. If he came to fetch her.

Beside her, as he attempted to insert a much-folded cloth inside his unbuttoned jacket, Luka groaned, and Alina brought her straying mind back to attention.

"Oh, I'm so sorry, Luka, I'm neglecting you. Are you all right?" she asked him. "Tatiana, why didn't you help Luka out of his jacket, so that we can see to his wound? Oh, never mind, you were probably too busy watching me make an utter cake of myself. Here, let's do it now."

"I was told we were only little more than a mile from Ashurst Hall just before we were attacked, my lady," he told her. "I can wait until we arrive. You shouldn't have to see the wound. It isn't seemly."

"Neither is bleeding yourself dry," Alina pointed out, but the coach had now turned, and the wheels were suddenly covering much smoother ground, the ruts and jaw-jarring potholes of the other road no longer in evidence.

"My lady…your clothing?"

Tatiana's warning brought Alina back to her own personal dilemma. That was probably vain of her, but she couldn't help herself. She was about to meet Justin's friends—an English duke and duchess, no less—and she was going to see them for the first time while looking as if she'd just finished rolling about in a pigsty. Oh, how Aunt Mimi would have laughed to see her like this, and then pointed out that it was no less than she would have expected from her mongrel niece.

"I'm going to blame him for *that,* too," Alina declared as Tatiana, being a down-to-earth sort in times like these—at least once the shooting and the shouting were over—asked her ladyship to please spit on the corner of yet another linen square, so that the servant could wipe some of the dirt off her ladyship's cheeks.

But then I might allow him to kiss me again...

CHAPTER FIVE

JUSTIN WILDE ARRIVED at Carleton House just after midnight, clad in his usual impeccable evening clothes and looking fresher—and smelling better—than most of the other guests of His Royal Majesty, the Prince Regent.

His appearance in the midst of the *haut ton* was a surprise, and presented a dilemma to everyone else present. Did they pretend not to see him? Did they nod as he passed—after all, he would not have gained entry without an invitation from the Prince Regent. Did they dare to approach him, clap him on the back, behave as if they were delighted to see him again, after dealing him the cut direct only a few months earlier, when he'd first returned to London? So much of society was in knowing whom to speak to and whom to avoid.

But he did look dashing, his well-remembered handsome, impeccable self. All that fashionably styled dark hair above those oddly unreadable green eyes. The way his black evening clothes fit his exemplary body. His snowy-white neckcloth always above reproach, tied in an intricate style of his own design, one that had never been successfully copied. That insouciant walk, as if he saw nothing in the world he feared. Pockets so deep his wealth seemed to have no measure at all. He was a true *rara avis* in all respects, the compleat, set-up gentleman. And hadn't he always had a smile for everyone, a joke for the men, a compliment for the ladies?

Yes, Baron Wilde was a bit of all right, really. Perfect in so many ways. Shame about him in that duel over his slut of a wife, firing early like that and shooting poor what-was-his-name in the back. Bloody coward…

No one could possibly imagine that the subject of their mingled awe, envy and repulsion had just spent the better part of two days in the saddle, or that he was harboring thoughts of committing dire physical mayhem on the body attached to the pudgy, beringed fingers he was now bowing over with such grace.

But, then, that had always been Justin's way. His smile belonged to everyone; his thoughts were his own.

During his first years in town, he had been sought after, admired, hugely popular with not only the ladies but their mamas, and welcomed by other gentlemen to be one of any party or sporting event. Because he was pretty and mannerly. Because he was entertaining. Because he genuinely enjoyed life.

Before.

Before, in his shallow and trivial youth, he'd married Sheila Broughton after being dazzled by her pretty face, and the way, frankly, they seemed to turn all heads whenever they entered a room together. She had fit him well, rather like his perfectly tailored waistcoats.

Better he should have married his tailor....

He'd never loved her. After the first few months of their marriage, he hadn't liked her, either, any more than she had liked him. He'd married her fine good looks, and she'd pledged herself to his title and deep pockets.

Still, they could have stumbled along, together yet not together, for several dozen years. Many did.

It was Sheila's lack of discretion that had brought both of them down, and taken Justin to that dew-covered lawn where his damned unerring aim had put a period to both Robbie Farber's existence and his own frivolous life as he had known it.

Eight years. Eight long years spent exiled from his country, his estates. Eight interminable years of doing whatever was asked of him, in the hope of gaining a pardon that would reunite him with his homeland and keep his neck out of a noose.

He'd returned to Mayfair only a few months ago, to learn that memories in the *ton* were longer than he would have imagined. There had been no welcome from anyone save Tanner Blake, Duke of Malvern, and Rafe Daughtry, Duke of Ashurst. But even those friendships hadn't softened society's condemnation of him. The three days he'd spent at his town house had been enough to convince him that he had rushed his reentry into Society, and he had taken himself off again, prepared to await the following spring season before trying again.

Now he was back, only two months passing between a nearly universal cut direct from those who had eight years earlier called themselves his friends and tonight's very visible acceptance by the Prince Regent—all part of the bargain they had struck.

Justin could hear the whispers, even as he could not make out the words. When he bowed his way back from the prince, it would be to see those same people who had judged him, had shunned him, now taking their cue from the prince and rushing up as if they were delighted to see him again.

And he could, in return, be delighted to see them, allow himself to be brought back into favor. Even as he cursed them all for sycophants and fools, while also cursing himself for ever believing this life was the one he wanted, the life he'd sacrificed so much to regain.

"A word in your ear, sir?" Justin suggested quietly. "You may frown as you lead me off, as if preparing to give me one last stern scold before welcoming me back into the fold of sheep standing all about us now, breathlessly anticipating your reaction and ready to take their cue from you."

"Damn you, what are you up to, Wilde? Where's the gel?" the Prince Regent asked sotto voce as he allowed two footmen to help him to his feet. He pointed toward a door off in a corner, and Justin fell into step directly beside him, in just the way George Brummell had dared to do, as if declaring them not only friends, but equals. Oh, this would add to his consequence; being so publicly taken off for a private coze with the heir to the throne. How Prinny must hate that. "What are you doing here, Wilde? It was to be tomorrow night, at Covent Garden."

"What? And miss this delightful gathering?" Justin responded lightly, insinuating his arm through the prince's crooked elbow, knowing the man had no choice but to allow the intimacy. "Imagine my delight, sir, when I returned to London and espied the invitation waiting for me on my desk."

He refrained from mentioning that the invitation had served to remove the problem of how to break into Carleton House at four in the morning and somehow make it past the guards.

"One of my fool secretaries must have already added you back to my invitation list. You shouldn't be on that list yet, not until you're bracketed with the gel. It was a mistake."

"I wondered as much. But then I thought, my,

how can I resist? After all, the wish of our Royal Highness can be nothing less than my command. I fair flew through my toilette, I tell you—taking only a miserly three hours to make myself presentable—and then hastened straight here. Please forgive my tardy and doubtless disheveled appearance. Although my man, Wigglesworth, persists in telling me that this waistcoat flatters me no end."

"Humph," the Prince Regent responded, which was as good as a compliment on Justin's attire, combined with a curse that His Royal Highness would never see a waistcoat so fine himself…or be able to see past it to his toes, either, come to that.

They'd entered the anteroom now, and Justin carefully first shut, then locked the door, deftly pocketing the key.

"The gel?" the prince said without preamble. "Where the devil is the gel? Did you forget her on the docks? Can't you get the straight of anything, Wilde? She's supposed to be with you."

Justin's smile never wavered. It was the sort of smile that could make a guilty man feel the sudden need to find a quick exit. "You mean, sir, where is the daughter of one Lady Anne Louise Farber, sister to Robbie Farber, once Earl of Birling, and the man I shot down eight years ago for having maligned my then estranged wife's nonexistent reputation?"

The prince shot a quick look toward the door. "You, um…you found that out quickly."

Justin raised one well-defined eyebrow, feigning surprise even as his every suspicion was confirmed. "Oh? So you're already aware of the connection? My, my, and here I was, prepared to give you the benefit of the doubt, call the whole thing coincidence and be done with it. After all, how can a mere loyal subject even begin to conceive that his presumptive sire might be so devious, so cold-bloodedly calculating?"

"It wasn't like that, Wilde. Not at the beginning, at least."

"At least? Tell me, is it still considered regicide if you're no more than a sorry excuse for a regent, and not the king? Or, knowing the mood of the populace, would I be looked upon more as a hero if I were to wring your damn neck for you in the next minute?"

The prince's normally pink cheeks disappeared in the full, florid flush that now possessed him from cravat to hairline. "You cannot speak to me this way! I'll summon the guards."

"Do that," Justin continued almost affably. "I've locked the door you keep eyeing—the only door to this quaint little closet set aside for your assignations with any of the plump, aged ladies you seem to enjoy having play mother to you. By the time the guards manage to break it down, you'll be on the floor, your face blue and your tongue swollen half out of your mouth. Not a pretty picture, I promise you. They won't even be able to shove your tongue back in your head for the state funeral. They'll have to snip it off."

The man who lived only for the day he would become His Majesty, George the Fourth, winced, and nearly gagged.

"Ah, so you do remember who I am and what I do, don't you, sir? Who you and others like you made me? One minute, no more—that's all it would take. But it would be the longest, and the last, minute of your life."

The prince's eyes shifted to the door, and then back to the key Justin was dangling in front of his face. "I didn't set out to have it happen this way," he said, nearly pleaded. "When Francis came to my ministers for our help with his problem and his possible solution, he mentioned the name Farber. I remembered the name. That's when I realized I had just the man for what he wanted done."

"Me."

"Yes. You. You're just the right man. I read the dispatches, you know. You have no conscience, no scruples. Everyone agreed you were perfect."

Justin refused to react to the prince's opinion of his character, or the lack thereof. "Counted on that, did you? And that's why you summoned me from Vienna. That's why you offered me the pardon I'd begun to believe would never become fact. That very expensive pardon with all those intricate strings tied to it. How wonderful for you that you could benefit your own pocketbook, even as you assisted your new ally."

"Well, yes," the Prince Regent admitted, relaxing slightly. "That did work out rather conveniently for me, I will admit to that. My creditors have become increasingly strident. Why should the benefits all run in Francis's direction?"

"Stupid, yet clever. The two, combined, make you a very dangerous man, Your Royal Highness. There are times I not only wonder if a monarchy is necessary, but if any of you should be allowed to breed. Eight years. Eight years I've thought of nothing but returning to England. To my homeland and my home. Now I find myself wondering what all the fuss was about, why I even cared."

"If that's true, Wilde, I am deeply sorry. But I immediately saw that you were the obvious choice. Who better than the Crown's own assassin to protect the lady from an assassin?"

Justin's eyes went cold. "Please, allow us both now to put an end to that particular comedy. You could have found someone else to do what Francis needs done—and what your new bosom chum the king of Austria needs done has nothing to do with safeguarding the lady, but very much to do with ridding Francis of a nuisance. I am simply an added amusement you've thrown into the mix. How jolly for you, to know that you've bracketed Birling's niece to the man who killed him. Why, I imagine you think it all but borders on the poetic."

The prince said nothing. Which spoke volumes.

Disgusted but not surprised, Justin pushed harder, needing to hear what this pathetic man had to say. "Admit it. I want to hear you say it. If I were to fail to eliminate Francis's enemy and the Lady Alina were to die because of that failure, her death would mean nothing to you."

"Who?" The Prince Regent, known for many things, was not often included on any list numbering the sharpest knives in his chef's kitchen.

"Never mind," Justin said, suddenly unpardonably weary of this conversation. "I know what you want me to do."

"You've always known that. I want you to marry the gel."

"So you say. From where I stand, it seems you wish me to assassinate a very powerful and visible public figure for you and your royal friends, while you both keep your hands and your countries clean of the dead. And the devil with what happens to *the gel*."

Prinny had the wit to at last look somewhat sheepish. "All right, yes, I will admit to not considering the possible problem with the woman. But you are now her protector, and she could have none better. Marry her, and keep her safe from this man the king is convinced wishes her dead. Yes, making the man dead in the process. They're one and the same, really, as long as he dies. And what do you care about this man? You've killed so many. Then you'll be free of any further obligation. You have my word on that, damn it."

"You'll forgive me if I remain less than confident."

"As for this young woman who so concerns you? You will bring her here, present her to me. Why, it would be my honor to give the bride away at Saint Paul's. That should make up for something, showing you are totally accepted by me, by the Crown. And then remain here in town for the small season?"

Justin didn't answer, but only bowed. "You really are a fool, aren't you? And now, as I'm fairly certain I've outstayed my welcome, I think it is time I rejoined my affianced bride."

He turned toward the door, the key once more in his hand.

"Wait! I have to know. Would you have done it?" the Prince Regent asked, his voice trembling slightly. "Would you have...murdered me? Because you wouldn't have outlived me for more than a few heartbeats, once my guards arrived. Had you thought of that?"

"Why do you think you're still alive, Your Highness? Much as I know you hadn't planned it this way, you've actually unwittingly given me something to hope for, to live for. Or, I should say, *someone*."

Justin held open the door to allow the Prince Regent to exit ahead of him, but the man stopped just at the threshold, his gaze on the assembled guests in the larger room, his complexion paling this time rather than flushing. "Wait. You didn't answer me. I admit I didn't consider the young lady in all of this, the possible danger to her. But you will protect, you've said as much. Now will you be bringing the gel here to London? That was the arrangement. To bring her here, present her to me, use the special license I managed for you. I didn't mean what I said. And then all will be forgiven, yes?"

Justin wondered how and when the prince would get back to the subject that most concerned him— after the worry over where his not-always-loyal subjects might put his sliced-off tongue before they buried him.

"I thank you, sir, but in point of fact I prefer to handle arranging my own nuptials. There will be ample time to visit London in the spring, during the season. For now, I should think my soon-to-be wife and I will adjourn to my estate and get to know each other. Oh, dear, wait a moment. Now you're frowning again, aren't you? That rascal Wilde, you're thinking, he's making a muddle of everything. I'm supposed to have my fiancée make her curtsy to you tomorrow night at Covent Garden, when that fierce-looking gentleman in the uniform of the Austrian high command isn't present, as he is tonight. Shame, shame on me."

"You already saw him? But you came into the room and headed straight to me. Like Doomsday, you know, no matter how you smiled."

"Men who labored as I did don't survive long if they fail to enlarge their powers of observation. Yes, I saw him. *Inhaber* Jarmil Novak, and your guest. Allow me, please, to hazard a guess—he is Francis's new Minister of Trade, and simply delighted to be on our shores, although probably not because of any fervor to encourage England's importation of fine Austrian cheeses. He has to know without having been told that he's been sent here to eliminate the last of the Valentin's, never thinking that it is he who is to die. I was wondering how you'd bring us all together."

"So damned smug, figuring it all out. Aren't you clever? You're not amusing, Wilde. Not at all."

"Unforgivable of me, I'm sure. And yet I will persevere. He arrived with quite a surprisingly large retinue, didn't he? Big, strapping fellows, part of his own private regiment? You have all the makings of a splendid entertainment, and all of it to take place here in London, where you can watch it unfold. You really should thank King Francis. He has no idea how solving his problem for him has become your personal delight. Too bad that the lady and I won't be obliging you."

"Wilde, wait! Don't you dare to turn your back on me. We have an agreement. I can still destroy you. I can snap you in two the way I snapped George when he dared to ridicule me, so that you'll never be able to show your face in London society again. Worse, I still could order you tried for murdering poor Robbie Farber, and have you hanged."

The guests closest to them heard most of what had been said, and were doing their best to pretend that they hadn't, even as they, collectively, all leaned in closer, as if they were on a ship that had begun listing to starboard.

As long as he would be the subject of gossip all over Mayfair by tomorrow, as long as he was so determinedly burning his bridges, Justin thought he might as well give them all something more to natter about over their morning chocolate.

"Why, Your Royal Highness," he said, shock in his every word, "are you saying that your signature is not your bond, your word not your oath? Can it be that your personally signed pardon, bestowed upon me only after I had gratefully and without question poured fifty thousand pounds into your private coffers, means nothing if you say it means nothing?"

"With those words, you have just nullified your pardon and forfeited your life," the Prince Regent whispered fiercely.

"Possibly, sir. Probably. But not the lady's. You might wish to warn *Inhaber* Novak of that fact, if not alert him to the target on his own back. Even on yours, if the lady is harmed. You and your new friend Francis played your game poorly, Highness, as I've already seen your cards. You will see mine only as I lay them out. But trust me on this. Mine are better. Oh, one thing more about the way I play the game. You were a lucky man tonight, as I very rarely bluff. I won't do it again."

Justin turned on his heels and strode out of the large reception room, feeling every eye on his back, with two particular sets of those eyes boring straight into it.

Riding clothes and his mount were both waiting for him at his town house, and he was changed and in the saddle within a quarter hour. He probably would not see London again in his lifetime, and for some reason this fact did not bother him. After so many years of longing for this city, this country, he could find no love in his heart for either.

He would not have believed this possible, only two short days ago. But that was before he saw a pair of frightened golden eyes looking to him for answers and reassurance. He'd been handed a gift, a way to do penance for so many crimes, so many mistakes.

Justin Wilde may have failed himself over the years, damned his own soul any number of times… but he would not fail her.

CHAPTER SIX

THE GIGGLES DREW HIM. Young, unaffected. The joy of life being enjoyed. He'd laughed like that, he was sure. Long ago. A lifetime ago.

He'd spent another day and a half in the saddle, riding across country, backtracking, until he was convinced he wasn't being followed, that his destination was known to him and only to him. Because the last damned thing he'd ever do would be to bring the hell following him down on his friends.

Justin Wilde had done a lot of stupid things in the course of his two and thirty years. If he were to apply to his friends for a list, the length of it might surprise even him. But threatening the life of the heir to the throne of England had been the topper. That step, once taken, was impossible to correct, even if he'd wanted to, and he didn't.

Because he'd never felt more free, even with the full might of England out to find him, jail him, execute him.

He was tired, filthy dirty thanks to the road dust, and more than slightly damp due to the early-afternoon rain, when he slid off his horse in the stable yard of his good friend Rafe Daughtry. Too dirty to present himself at the front door of Ashurst Hall, he'd planned to enter through the kitchens and sneak up to his assigned room, where Wigglesworth could render one of his miracles and make him human again.

But that was before he'd heard the giggles.

Alina. The woman he'd thought of night and day since the moment he'd first seen her on the docks in Portsmouth. The woman he'd dreamed of last night as he slept beneath the hedgerows. The woman who could never really be his.

Damn. He'd never before recognized this streak of melodrama he seemed to possess. He'd have to stop thinking like some lovesick swain and remember who he was. And the danger that followed him.

One of Justin's own outriders had been lounging on a bale of hay, using a single stick of that hay to pick at his teeth. He didn't bother to rise until he belatedly realized that the ragtag rider was his always immaculately groomed employer. He hastened to assist him with his mount, noticing that Justin's gaze was on the open door to the stables.

"Lady Alina, my lord," he offered without being asked. "Sounds like music, don't it? But I'm keepin' one eye on her, yes, I am. We all are, my lord. She just don't like stickin' in one place too long, she says."

"And what is she doing?"

"Don't know, my lord. I was told to watch, not to look."

"Very good. I'll see for myself."

Brushing at the front of his jacket with his gloved hands, Justin left the sunshine of the stable yard for the cool stable, pausing just inside it until his eyes became accustomed to the darker interior. Rafe kept a fine stable, stalls lining it in both directions, the whole of it built into the side of a hill, so that hay and other supplies could be moved by cart, directly into the upper floor of the vast structure.

As Justin stood there, a few bits of hay came drifting down from the wooden plank ceiling above him.

And he heard another giggle.

A man could get very disturbing ideas, hearing a woman's giggle coming from a hayloft.

He turned to the man, who was kicking at the dirt just outside the doorway, as if there was some invisible line he dared not cross.

"She's alone?"

"Oh, yes, my lord. Came back from her ride and went on in there, and didn't come back out."

"Thank you. What's your name?"

"Willis, sir. Did I do somethin' wrong?"

"No, Willis, you did not. Protecting the Lady Alina is paramount, but I will take it from here now. You may return to your post."

Justin headed for the ladder that wasn't much more than a series of foot-wide slats hammered onto one of the beams, marveling that a woman in a riding skirt would attempt let alone manage the vertical climb. Lady Alina, it would appear, was a young woman who went where she wished to go, when she wished to go there, no matter the difficulty.

He supposed, if he thought about it, he could come to at least two other conclusions. The young woman in question was fairly fearless. And the young woman was probably more than slightly reckless. A prudent man would store all three conclusions away for future reference.

He removed his hat and flung it on the hard-packed dirt floor, as nothing much could be done to the hat than hadn't already been accomplished by the rain and the fact that he'd used it for a pillow as he slept beneath the hedgerows last night, before pulling himself up to the floor of the loft.

Following the giggles, he soon located Lady Alina in a small walled-off area of the large loft. She was lying on her back in the soft, fragrant straw.

And she was covered in kittens.

At the moment, she was holding up one of the furry black-and-white balls of fur and then bringing it down to her face, nuzzling the lucky thing nose to nose, as its littermates—Justin counted at least six of them—variously snuggled against her side or climbing over her as if she were some mighty Gulliver and they were the inquisitive Lilliputians.

The mother cat, that had obviously accepted the intruder, wasn't quite as certain of Justin's appearance, and strutted over to him, her tail high, her back slightly arched. "Put a scratch in these boots, Mother, and there will be no saving you from Wigglesworth's wrath," he warned, and Lady Alina immediately sat up, looking at him with those wide, golden eyes.

He'd surprised her, surely. But she didn't look shocked. On the contrary, she appeared to be pleased.

Or he was weary enough to allow wishful thinking to cloud his heretofore clear judgment.

Her pins had fallen out of her hair. Ebony curls tumbled all around her head and shoulders. Sunlight streaming in through a barred window shone on her emerald-green riding habit and touched on her slightly reddened cheeks as she quickly put down the kitten and began buttoning up her jacket, for several of the buttons had slipped their moorings as she played with the frisky litter.

Justin caught a glimpse of snow-white skin and the soft curve of a breast above a silk chemise.

He swallowed like a schoolboy.

"You're here," she said unnecessarily as she began pulling bits of hay from her curls.

"Your powers of observation are astounding, Alina, if a trifle belated. Still, I couldn't be more delighted with my welcome," he told her, striving to get himself back under control, appear nonchalant while all he wished to do was take her in his arms and hold on tight to the best thing to have happened to him. Instead, he bent to pick up the kitten Alina had been playing with and brought it to his face. "Lucky little man, aren't you?" he said before carefully putting it back down in front of its worried mother.

"Do you always sneak up on people unannounced?" Alina asked as he held out a hand to assist her. She ignored it, and got to her feet unaided. She began working at her hair, tugging loose more bits of hay.

"Your pardon, I'm sure. Clearly I should have had Willis announce me. He could beat on a drum, or perhaps crash some cymbals? Here, don't do that, you're only making more tangles. Let me play at lady's maid."

She looked at him for a long moment, and then lowered her arms and nodded. "At least you look worse than I do," she said as if that made everything all right. "Wigglesworth told me you are always impeccable. Clearly I should not believe all that Wigglesworth tells me."

"I wouldn't believe the half of it," Justin told her as he fought the impulse to thread his fingers through her hair. Her soft, silky, wonderfully warm hair. "I vastly overpay the fellow."

If he just slipped his hands into the soft curls at either side of that sweet little face, and then gently drew her toward him, then he might kiss that full pink mouth, taste her sweetness once more, lose his wickedness in her innocence…

"What are you looking at? Do I have dirt on my nose?"

Justin pulled his mind from foolish fantasies and stepped away from her. "No," he said shortly. "Are you ready to return to the house? I've a great need for a bath and a change of clothes before I find our hosts and thank them for their kindness in taking care of you while I was gone."

She gave a rather imperious toss of her head, marred only by the sort of snorting *hrummph* that accompanied the gesture. "You make it sound as if I'm some infant and need taking care of. Which I don't, thank you. I'm quite out of charity with you at the moment. And if Brutus hadn't gotten in the way, I would have shot that man."

As she attempted to rush past him, Justin grabbed at her elbow and spun her around to face him. "Would you mind repeating that last little bit, kitten?"

Alina pulled her arm free of his grasp. "Don't call me that, even though I'm certain you think it's charming. You think *you're* charming. Wigglesworth insists that you're charming. Is it charming, my lord, to go riding off, leaving me in a strange land, surrounded by strangers, and having Luka shot into the bargain?"

Justin's blood froze in his veins. "Luka has been shot?"

"Yes, and my best traveling ensemble has been destroyed. Not that anything so trivial is so important as Luka being shot. But if you'd not had us riding all over this silly island while you did some flit as if you couldn't stand being with me—with us all a moment longer, instead of taking us to London, as you were supposed to do, then we wouldn't have been accosted by highwaymen intent on stealing my cloak. I shouldn't have flaunted it on the dock, granted, because that was horribly stupid of me now that I've had time to reflect on the thing. But still, it's mostly all your fault."

Justin's head was spinning, a circumstance that he felt no need to apologize for, as the woman could have been speaking a language he didn't understand for all the sense he could make of her words. He decided the cloak and the silly island could be disregarded as superfluous to the point for the moment, and instead concentrated on the words *Luka shot* and *highwaymen*.

"You were accosted by highwaymen on the way here, and Luka was shot?"

She looked at him in wide-eyed exasperation. "Didn't I already *say* that? Yes, we were accosted by highwaymen, and Luka was shot. And then I ended up in the mud and Brutus scooped me up and all but threw me back into the coach. For a man who doesn't speak, he can certainly make his point extremely clear."

Justin relaxed, but only slightly. She was clearly safe, and the major's wound couldn't have proved fatal, or else she wouldn't have been out here, giggling with kittens. "I find myself powerless to resist asking, kitten. How did you end up in the mud?"

"That isn't important to the point," she told him, shifting her gaze away from him. "Luka wants to see you as soon as you've returned. He is very put out with you."

"It would appear he's not the only one. Alina, I had to leave. But I could only leave if I believed that you would be safe until my return, which you most obviously were. But you think I was running away from you and our…arrangement. Don't you?"

"No, of course not. Don't flatter yourself. I don't even know you. I could not care a drop why you left."

She lied badly, and Justin's heart lifted with delight.

He put a bent finger beneath her chin to hold her in place, so that she had no choice but to meet his gaze. "Ah, but I care what you think of me. We have an adventure ahead of us, Alina. I need you to feel able to trust me. Without question, without hesitation."

"I don't understand. Are you speaking of our marriage?"

"There will be no marriage, kitten. I wouldn't so abuse you as to saddle you with a fugitive for a husband."

She blinked, but then looked at him rather intensely. "A fugitive from what? No, now you're lying to me. You're an English nobleman. You are your king's choice for my husband. Of course we're going to marry, it's all arranged. You're making no sense."

Why couldn't he have left this for later? Why couldn't he simply continue to enjoy this moment, this unexpected interlude?

He knew the answer. The more he was with her, the more he would miss her when he had to go.

There was no good place to start, no easy way to say so much that had to be said. And no time to say it all, damn it. He may have avoided the king's men on his way to Ashurst Hall, but the *Inhaber*'s men, those Alina had believed to be highwaymen, had to have followed them from Portsmouth. Someone was watching, and that someone had seen him ride into the stable yard, and word was undoubtedly already on its way to London and *Inhaber* Novak.

"We have to leave," Justin said, taking her hand and leading her toward the ladder. "Tomorrow morning at dawn, no later. There will be time for explanations once I have you somewhere safe."

He descended the ladder first, and then helped guide her down until she was standing in front of him once more. "I feel safe where I am, thank you. Charlotte has been everything that is kind, and Rafe apologized most profusely about the highwaymen, who he says have been a problem these past few months. I feel eminently safe here, thank you, except perhaps not quite so much now that you're here, too. You really are a very strange man, you know. Are you really a fugitive?"

Justin picked up his hat and offered Alina his arm. "So, from your question, I take it that trusting me implicitly is not under consideration?"

"Without question or hesitation I believe I can say yes, that's correct," Alina told him as they walked toward the house. "And I will add that this supposed marriage of convenience we both agreed to has been very much less than convenient since the moment I first saw you preening on the dock."

"I wasn't preening," Justin objected, laughing. "I was standing there awestruck, as I was supposed to do, my considerable consequence totally eclipsed by my affianced wife, whom I'd supposed to be fat and with a hairy chin, when I thought of her at all."

"Oh," she said in a small voice. "So I don't repulse you?"

Justin stopped on the brick path and turned her around to face him. She meant it, she really didn't understand just how beautiful she was. "Repulse me? You thought that? Your country has no mirrors?"

She put the back of her hand to her mouth for a moment, as if sorry she'd let the words escape her, but quickly rallied. "What was I supposed to think? You all but ran out of my…my bedchamber at the inn, and then you rode off the next morning without so much as another word to me. I know I'm only a woman, but women can think, too, you know. And I think you behaved like a man who very much wished to be anywhere this woman wasn't."

Justin threw back his head and laughed; a laugh so free and open he actually amazed himself, for he had guarded his emotions for too many long years. "God, you're adorable. No wonder your aunt wanted you gone."

Alina rolled her eyes at this. "She considers me painfully young and gauche."

"She considers you competition would be more to the point. But back to what we were discussing."

"We weren't discussing anything," Alina said testily. "You have been making pronouncements, for the most part, and very little sense for the rest of it. Fugitive or not, I don't think I want to marry you, and not because you say we won't. Our children would all be idiots."

"Blithering, drooling idiots, yes, I agree, if that makes you happy. But you do realize that we would then be flouting the wishes of two separate royal edicts."

"Oh. And that's why you're a fugitive? You went to London and told your Prince Regent that you refuse to marry me. Will they hang you now?"

"If they catch me, that's the least they'll do, but not for the reason you think. So you really don't wish to marry me?"

She hesitated, as if searching for just the correct words to answer him. "You already don't wish to marry me, so what I might want or not want doesn't matter, does it? If you want, you can take me to my mother's family, and I'd promise not to ever be any bother to you."

"Kitten, it's too late for that, as you bother me very much. The devil and the delight of it is that you don't seem to have any real understanding of just how and why you do."

She threw up her hands in exasperation. "There you go again, making absolutely no sense. I bedevil you, I delight you. You run from the sight of me, you come back again saying we must leave here and go somewhere safe, but you don't want to marry me. You say you're a fugitive and then you— Oh! I don't know *what* you're saying or doing."

She had a temper. Good. Fearless, possibly reckless, and with a temper. If the gods had ordered up a woman for him, they could not have done better. Except that the gods also had a sense of humor, and they had conjured her up for him knowing he would not be able to keep her. He put his hands on her slim shoulders. "All right, kitten—"

"I am not a kitten!"

"You're certainly not purring, I'll grant you that. I know you don't understand what I'm saying. I've barely begun to understand most of it myself, as even my mind isn't accustomed to running in such devious circles. But understand this, Alina. What I am *doing* is saving you from the man who is trying to kill you."

"Kill me?" Her eyes went so wide it was almost laughable. "Who is it that's supposed to be killing me?"

He'd rather have gotten her full attention by kissing her. But then, Justin Wilde had long ago learned that one does not always get what one wishes for.

He walked her toward a nearby bench, sat her down, and proceeded to tell her everything he'd learned in London.

ALINA'S HEAD WAS STILL positively spinning as she stepped out of her tub and into the large white towel Tatiana held out for her to wrap herself in before moving to the fire so that one of the Ashurst maids could brush her hair dry.

"Thank you, but no," she told the maid as she put out her hands for the brushes. "You may go now."

"Sit, my lady," Tatiana said, already going down

on her knees. "I'll do that for you, and you can tell me why you sent the maid away."

Alina subsided onto the hearth carpet, sighing as Tatiana began working the brushes through her wet hair. "Danica isn't going to come walking in here, her ears flapping as they do when she tries to pretend she isn't listening, is she?"

"Not since I locked the door to the dressing room and hid the key in my pocket, my lady, no. Although when she's done packing up most of your belongings and discovers she's locked in there it might get a little noisy. I could see when you came upstairs that something was troubling you. Is it that his lordship has come back, or that he says we must leave this lovely place tomorrow morning?"

"It is lovely here, isn't it?" Alina said, knowing she was only delaying the inevitable. "If everyone in England is as friendly and kind as the duke and duchess, I will find it easier to be happy in a strange land. I wonder if the baron's estate is even half so pretty."

"Is that where we're going, my lady? I thought we were bound for London."

Alina tipped her head so that all her long, thick hair fell to one side. Tatiana lifted its bulk, fanning it out over her arm to catch the heat from the fire. "I don't know," she said quietly. "There are so many things I don't know...."

Tatiana's hands stilled on the brushes. When she

spoke again, it wasn't the voice of the sweet, paid companion, but that of a woman who cared, and cared deeply. "He told you? The Englisher told you? The major said he might, once he'd come back. He should not have done that. He puts his nose where it does not belong. We would have kept you safe."

Alina closed her eyes, took a deep, shuddering breath. Now, at last, she believed, really believed: someone wanted her dead, needed her dead. "Does everyone know but me? Does Danica know?"

Tatiana made a rude sound. "That one? What good is she? She knows nothing but laces and crimping irons and how to be annoying. What did his lordship tell you?"

Slowly, to be certain she had the right of it, Alina repeated all that Justin had told her.

She was, save her aunt, the last Valentin. Not that Aunt Mimi mattered, for she had already refused to help the Romany lay claim to the land disputed between them and *Inhaber* Novak. If anything happened to her niece, she would sign whatever documents the *Inhaber* put in front of her (for a fee, surely), revoking all possible claim to the land that her silly, romantic niece would just as surely have signed over to the Romany. But as her father's daughter, Alina stood first, and her aunt second. Eliminate the first, the second becomes first. It was that simple, Justin had told her as he held her hand, as he'd dabbed her damp cheeks with his handkerchief.

He'd been so sweet, so caring—how could he still insist he could not marry her?

Alina did not believe her aunt wished her dead or knew about the plot, but she also did not think the woman would go into mourning for her niece unless she could find a becoming wardrobe in black. She'd probably just ask for the return of the Valentin jewels, and then bury her niece with the garnets. Alina had said as much to Justin, and that had made him laugh.

But there was very little else to make either of them smile.

Everything about this business of the land was complex. Francis did not want to be forced to make the decision between the Romany claim and Novak's claim. But she understood that; the man had many problems.

After that, complex rapidly became murky. The king wanted the *Inhaber* dead, out of his way, for reasons that most probably went beyond the matter of some disputed land. So the English Prince Regent had agreed to welcome Novak to England, and then have him assassinated by Justin Wilde, the husband who was, after all, only protecting his wife and himself, since a wife's possessions automatically became the possessions of the husband.

"And this killing of the *Inhaber* would have taken place in far-off England, with no hint of blame or conspiracy falling on King Francis?" she'd asked

Justin, thinking perhaps she at last understood the impossible to understand. "And that's the reason why you will be a fugitive? Your Prince Regent has agreed to make you into a murderer, hasn't he?"

He'd agreed that she was correct.

And she'd known he had just lied to her. She felt certain—no, the look on Justin's face had told her—that there was more, but that the entire truth would have to wait for another day. She had already begun a mental list of questions for the moment that day arrived. Beginning with *why you, Justin? Why did the Prince Regent, of all the men in England, choose you?*

"Those weren't highwaymen that attacked our coaches, Tatiana," she said now, willing herself to relax as the companion went back to brushing her hair for her. "They were sent by *Inhaber* Novak. And you knew that, Luka knew that. Everyone knew that except me. That's why we have to leave here, because his lordship doesn't want his friends put in any danger, to which I certainly agree. But I don't know where we're going, because he won't tell me."

"Does *he* know?"

Alina turned about so quickly, one of the brushes caught in her hair. "Do you think he doesn't? That he'd planned to leave me here with Luka, all unknowing, until I told him about the attack on the road? Do you think he is just taking us away now, without a destination in his mind? But that would be…"

"Yes?" the companion prompted.

"That would be something he might do," Alina admitted, thinking of the man she had only just barely begun to know, if at all. "I don't think he planned to go to London and confront his Prince Regent, but he did it once he'd figured out that he was to play the role of dupe, as he termed it, in all of this. He probably was very angry, and said terrible things to the Prince Regent. Mostly, I think he was showing off. He's a very strange man, Tatiana. And now he's a fugitive, an outlaw."

"The major trusts him."

"Luka is in bed with a wounded shoulder and is all but useless. He has little choice but to trust someone else. He told me as much when I went to see him earlier and demanded that he tell me the entire truth." She took Tatiana's hands in hers. "How did this happen? How did I go from silly girl to silly woman to a woman marked for death, all without noticing?"

"You were busy ordering bride clothes, my lady."

"Please, don't remind me of just how shallow and silly I have been. Do you know what I should do? I should return home and fight for the land. I may not have much Romany blood, but it would be my honor to give the land to them and confound the *Inhaber*.

And the king as well, I suppose. Is it very much land, do you know?"

Tatiana shrugged. "I don't know, but it is not important, my lady. It isn't the land the Romany want, it's the having it. If the *Inhaber* dies and you were to live, then yours is the only claim. The king would be forced to honor it. And the *Inhaber* deserves to die, for so many reasons. That is why the major has allowed any of this. His lordship sticking his nose where it has no place to be is making things difficult for all of us."

"I won't tell him that," Alina said, sighing. "It would only make him happy, I'm sure. And still I'm left asking—where will he take me?"

"That I do not know, my lady. I do know *how* he will take you. We who care for you did not arrive on these shores unprepared to protect you. We simply could not know that your bothersome betrothed would not take you straight to London. But that's all been fixed, and we are ready now."

Alina looked at her companion blankly, only smiling after the woman had begun her explanation.

CHAPTER SEVEN

CHARLOTTE DAUGHTRY HAD been so kind and so very welcoming these past days. She hadn't so much as blinked when Alina arrived covered in mud, as if visitors came to her door every day in that same sorry condition.

What Alina saw in the duchess was not simply a beautiful woman, but a very practical one, the sort who managed everyone around her without making anyone *feel* managed. Her husband, the duke, obviously adored her, as did all of the servants.

And if there was one thing Alina knew, it was that you could not fool the servants. They were the ones who saw you most, and at your most vulnerable. Anyone could manage to be polite and friendly in company. It was behind closed doors that the real person was revealed.

She'd also observed Charlotte with her son, one of the sweetest infants she'd ever seen, and one of the most fortunate. Little Rafael Fitzpatrick Daughtry had his mother's soft eyes and his father's determined chin, and he seemed to smile all the time.

Alina had caught herself wondering how the product of a mix of her and Justin Wilde would look, and then quickly had banished the thought because first, well, first they'd have to…do that.

Except that this afternoon, when Justin had sat so close to her, and he'd looked at her in that strange way, and even as he told her things she found difficult to believe, she'd found herself half hoping he'd kiss her. And those parts of her that had slumbered for so long had stirred yet again. It was all very… interesting. She'd found herself watching his hands tonight at dinner, how they held a glass, how he used them when speaking. She watched his mouth, the slight upturn of his lips when he was genuinely amused. Her breath had caught in her throat when a lock of that dark hair had dared to fall forward onto his smooth forehead, and he'd casually brushed it back with his spread fingers…wondering what he would do if she copied his gesture when they were alone.

"You seem distracted, my dear," Charlotte whispered as she pretended to be admiring the embroidery on the sleeve of Alina's gown as they returned to the drawing room after a relaxed and delicious dinner. "Are you nervous now that Justin has returned? He's harmless, or so says Rafe's sister Lydia, who knows him much better than I. Although, from everything I've heard about him, I'm frankly surprised that he'd agree to an arranged marriage, no matter if the king himself had asked it of him. That doesn't seem anything like him, especially after his first marriage, which Rafe tells me was disastrous."

Alina shot a quick, involuntary look toward the two men standing in front of the mantelpiece, sharing drinks and conversation. "His first marriage, you said?"

Charlotte took her new friend's hand and led her to a lovely flowered couch, urging her to sit down. Which Alina did, although she was faintly surprised that her suddenly stiff legs remained capable of bending at the knees. "Oh, Alina, I'm so sorry. I should have realized you might not know. But it was all very long ago, almost ten years, I believe. You stay here, and I'll go fetch you a glass of wine. You're terribly pale."

Alina nodded, her gaze still on Justin. She told herself she didn't care, that a marriage that was no longer a marriage was no concern of hers. Just as she'd told herself that it didn't matter that Baron Wilde was such an arresting figure, so very handsome. And clean, and young, and as prospective husbands went, probably a most wonderful catch. If she'd been looking for a husband, which she hadn't been. But since being presented with him, she'd fairly well accepted him as such…right up until the moment he'd announced that there would be no marriage.

Could he really decide that on his own, when

the announcement of their upcoming nuptials had already been made in Francis's court? The banns had been read in church for the third time only two days before she had begun her journey to England.

She probably ought to tell him that. Tell him that, at least in her country, they were already as good as married. Or would that make her seem a pathetic creature?

What he'd done was to put her in some sort of Limbo; that's what he'd done when he'd announced they would not marry. And told the Prince Regent as much, if he could be believed. She'd left her home an affianced bride, and landed in England only to be rejected by her affianced husband.

It was all so humiliating.

For some reason, one she didn't care to delve into too deeply, or else she would look more foolish than she already believed herself to be, this unforeseen development upset her more than the thought that *Inhuber* Novak wanted her dead.

And now to learn that Justin had been married before? What would be next? Did he have an entire gaggle of children hidden away somewhere she wasn't going to know about, either?

"Here you are, dear," Charlotte said, handing her a glass as she sat down beside her. "I was cudgeling my brain as I was pouring your glass, and I'm afraid I cannot remember much of what Rafe told me about Justin's marriage. She had an accident of some sort while Justin was on the Continent. Really, it's nothing to concern you. I shouldn't have mentioned it at all. He'll tell you everything in his own time. After all, you've barely met, haven't you? Truth to tell, I find it disturbingly medieval that you two should be all but ordered to wed each other in the first place. And if Rafe heard me say any of what I've just said, he'd remind me that none of this is any of my business."

Alina smiled. "No, I think you're correct. It's very strange. I had thought only royal princes and princesses were married off to strangers for the sake of some government alliance. But I was given a choice—my aunt was very specific about that. It's my decision to be here." She looked over at Justin again, still deep in conversation with the duke. "I don't know why his lordship agreed."

"And I don't know why I'm continuing to tell tales, but I am. According to Tanner, Lydia's husband, the Prince Regent has some sort of control over Justin. What sort of control I don't know, but it would seem that in order to remain in England, Justin has to do whatever the Prince Regent requires of him. He's only recently returned, you know—or perhaps you don't—after living abroad even since before his wife died, even throughout the war with France. I really should pay more attention, but as I always profess to abhor gossip, I try not to listen *too* well when people tell me things, or at least to forget them as soon as I'm told. Ah, and here's the tea tray. Thank you, Grayson."

As Charlotte went about the business of pouring tea, Alina sat very still, digesting all of this. So that was why he'd gone to London. To inform His Royal Majesty that he would no longer obey him. And that was why he'd called himself a fugitive. It had nothing to do with her, or whether or not it would be so horrible for him to marry her. Here she'd been, thinking herself repulsive to him in some way. Too young, too silly, too foreign—something. And all the time, as she'd variously worried, fretted and considered wreaking mayhem on the man, it hadn't been her at all. It had been Justin's private problems with the Prince Regent that had sent him haring off to London.

There were a few things she knew—very few. There were a few more things she'd guessed, rightly or wrongly. It had never occurred to her that she was no more than a convenient reason for Justin to go to the man and, in the words she'd overheard one day from one of the grooms, tell His Royal Highness to *bugger off*.

He was either very brave, or the most foolish, dangerous man in creation.

Alina put her hand to her mouth and pretended a huge yawn. "Oh, I'm so sorry, Charlotte. I can't seem to keep my eyes open. Would you mind terribly if I excused myself and went upstairs? I've already been warned that we're making a very early start in the morning."

Charlotte rose at once, announcing that Alina would be leaving them, and the two men immediately joined them to say their good-nights.

"It has been our pleasure to have you here, my dear. I won't see you in the morning before you go, I'm afraid," the duke told her, and then surprised her by kissing her on the cheek. "I know this man. He'll let no harm come to you," he whispered softly before stepping back.

Alina smiled her thanks and had already turned toward the foyer when Justin took her hand and threaded her arm through his. "You look rather pale. Wrestling with kittens has fatigued you?"

"Wrestling with many things has fatigued me," she countered as they stopped in the foyer and she reluctantly withdrew her arm. "But I am confident that I shall find answers to all that troubles me very soon. In fact, I'm convinced of it. Until we meet again, my lord, good night."

She ascended the first few steps sedately, but once she was sure Justin had returned to the drawing room, she hiked up her skirts and raced to her bedchamber, for once praying that Danica was waiting to help her into her nightclothes. After all, the sooner she was thought to be safely tucked up in bed, the sooner she would see Danica's disapproving back following her pimple-dotted front toward the door.

"Is that the best I've got, out of all these trunks of clothes?" she asked almost plaintively a few minutes later as she stood in the middle of the room, stripped to her chemise, and looked at the same night rail she'd worn that first evening in Portsmouth.

"I can only lay out what is there to lay out, my lady. It is you who chose to think only of how you could impress everyone with your fine gowns."

Alina made a face as the chemise fell away and she immediately became half-buried in yards of aged white muslin dropped over her head by the dresser. She had to fight her way free, shoving her arms into the sleeves that covered her past her wrists, and then stepped back as Danica went to close the dozen or more front buttons that would cover her almost halfway up her neck.

"Thank you, that will be all," she said, covering yet another feigned yawn. "I'll wear the rose tomorrow to travel, Danica."

"You'll wear the blue. Everything else is packed."

"But…but the blue was ruined in the mud."

"A few stains, here and there, but good enough to ride in a coach, bad enough to not suffer too much if you see a puddle you might wish to jump up and down in…my lady."

"Danica, you're impertinent, do you know that?" Alina wanted the woman gone, not just from her bedchamber at this moment, but from her life, her employ. "And clearly you are unhappy here. Perhaps you should return home. I am certain his lordship can arrange suitable transport."

The dresser didn't burst into tears, nor did she throw herself at Alina's feet and beg for her position, but her stern face did take on a faintly wounded expression. "This is how I'm thanked for leaving my homeland in order to serve the daughter of the good and kind General Leopold Valentin, so beloved of his countrymen, so mourned upon his death at the hands of the outlaw Bonaparte, so—"

"Oh, Danica," Alina exclaimed in a horror of remorse, clasping the unbending woman to her. "I'm sorry. I'm so, so sorry."

Danica took hold of Alina's shoulders and sternly put her at arm's length, her hatchet face once more implacable. "*Gut.* Good. Then that is settled, you have apologized as you should, and we will speak no more of this. You will wear the blue."

"Uh…yes?" Alina said, caught between surprise and an insane urge to laugh. "I will wear the blue. Most definitely. I can't imagine why I thought otherwise. I'll braid my hair myself—you just go to bed now. Good night, Danica."

Once the woman was gone, Alina stripped off the offending night rail and climbed back into her chemise, which at least didn't button to her chin, and then wrapped herself in the ermine-tipped cloak already laid out for the morning chill.

Before she could reflect too much over what she was about to do, she then opened the door to the hallway, stuck her head out far enough to be certain she would not be observed, and then raced on bare tiptoes down the length of the corridor before entering Justin's chamber, closing the door and flattening her back against it to catch her breath. She'd made it!

And then she very nearly leapt out of her skin when Justin spoke to her.

"You were somehow detained? I'd expected you a full ten minutes ago, and was just now feeling I'd misjudged you. How gratifying to see that I haven't. You're as foolish as you are brave."

The silky voice had come from somewhere in the dimness lightened by only a few candles. "And looking quite fetching, I might add," Justin said as he stepped forward, making himself visible in the candlelight.

"You knew I'd come? You've been waiting for me?" Alina shook her head at her own foolishness. "Yes, of course you did, of course you are. Now I feel foolish and…predictable."

Justin took her arm and led her toward the fire and the pair of facing leather wingback chairs that were much like the pair in her own chamber. As she'd already decided these chairs were less than comfortable, she sank to her haunches on the hearth rug, the cloak forming a velvet puddle around her.

Justin looked toward one of the chairs, and then shrugged his shoulders as if to say why should he be any different than his guest, at which point he also lowered himself to the floor, still holding a snifter of brandy delicately in one hand. He looked... magnificent. Without his evening jacket, with his shirtsleeves hanging loosely, the neat ruffling of his cuffs tickling at the backs of his hands, with his neckcloth gone and his waistcoat undone, he managed to look both wonderfully groomed and approachable. Human.

She should remember that he was probably neither.

"How did you know I'd come to see you?"

"I couldn't be certain," he told her, swirling the brandy in the snifter. She felt her eyes drawn to it, losing herself in its honeyed highlights. "If you hadn't, I would have found my way to your chamber. Charlotte, you see, apologized to me after you'd gone. She believes she may have been indiscreet."

With some effort, Alina tore her gaze from the brandy snifter. "About your dead wife, yes. But you would have told me in your own good time."

"If I didn't disappear again, as I did from Portsmouth."

"I hadn't thought of that, but yes, I suppose so. But mostly, if you were to go through with the marriage, that is, which you aren't, so I really have no reason to be curious about your...personal past."

"Ah, but you'd give that fine cloak to know, wouldn't you?"

"I most certainly would not," she protested, finally unable to resist looking him in the eye. He had such arresting green eyes, different from any color she'd ever seen. "But I do have a perfectly lovely reticule with seed pearls stitched all over it in the design of a peacock, if you think you'd fancy it."

"Now I've upset you."

"You can't upset me, my lord, if I don't wish to be upset. I am only curious about the man I am not going to marry. Anyone would be, you know. You're exceedingly strange. May I have a sip? I've never tasted brandy, but I like the smell of it. You warm it with your hands, don't you?"

He offered her the snifter, and she took it with both hands, holding it beneath her nose and breathing in its heady fragrance before touching the glass to her lips. The moment the warmed liquid hit her tongue she had to force herself not to gasp, and determinedly took a long swallow before handing the thing back to him.

"Here," he said, holding out a handkerchief he'd produced from somewhere on his person. "Your eyes are tearing. You are supposed to sip, kitten, and then hold the brandy in your mouth for a few moments, allow it to caress your tongue, and only then swallow. When something is good it is to be savored. Not gulped."

And then, without taking his eyes off her, he raised the snifter to his own mouth and demonstrated what he meant.

Those slumbering parts of her had clearly only been napping since she'd first seen him again this afternoon. Now they yawned, stretched and slowly began to wake up once more. "Why do you make me feel this way when you look at me?" she asked him before she could stop herself. "I don't like it."

"No, kitten, you don't understand it. There's a difference."

His gaze was steady, unwavering and mind-shatteringly unnerving. She tried to get up to leave this man and his unsettling way of saying what she didn't think he knew. But when he held out his hand she subsided, sighing.

He took her hand in his, stroked his thumb against her palm.

The entire world seemed to have suddenly narrowed to include only the two of them, wrapped inside the soft glow from the fire. He was so intensely male. She, for the first time in her life, believed she might know what it meant to be a female.

"You want to kiss me again, don't you?" she asked him quietly.

"No, kitten. That is precisely the last thing I want to do."

She looked down at her hand, lost in his, believing his touch put the lie to his words. "Forgive me.

There was a time, my lord, when I thought I was a fairly intelligent person. Do you think it's that the air here in England is different? Is that why I've been so very stupid ever since I left the ship? Or... or perhaps it was the brandy, because, you know, I've never really drunk strong..."

His finger beneath her chin signaled that he wanted her to raise her head, look at him. Her heart beating madly, her breath somehow gone, she couldn't seem to refuse.

"Have you ever wondered about the difference between what we know we shouldn't do and what, against all good sense, we find we have to do?" he asked her, his face close to hers, the smell of brandy on his breath somehow intoxicating her more than the drink itself. "And, much as I shouldn't want to do this, kitten, I find that I have to.... I really, really must...."

Alina's eyelids fluttered closed as, only his light touch beneath her chin holding her in place as if she had lost the power to move, he put his lips to hers. And this time he didn't move away again.

She didn't know what to do, how to react. She tried pursing her lips, but that didn't seem right. She tried simply tightening them against her teeth, and half felt, half heard his soft chuckle, so she knew that had to be wrong, as well. She probably looked like Danica in one of her disapproving attitudes.

So when Justin put the pads of his thumbs to

either side of her mouth and began to lightly massage her skin, she simply relaxed, deciding that he knew much better than she what a kiss between a man and a woman was all about.

"Better," he breathed, moving back slightly, just enough to look into her eyes. He tipped his head slightly to one side, his eyes alight with mischief. "Now let's try that again, shall we?"

"I…but I…"

He didn't allow her to finish, which was probably a good thing, as she had no idea what she might have said, but just captured her mouth even as she was speaking.

He kissed her, and then he kissed her again, and yet again. Each time she felt she learned more, until she actually became frustrated each time he withdrew, and found herself lifting her face to him, seeking out his next kiss.

He nipped lightly at her upper lip, which rather tickled. He actually drew her full bottom lip between his teeth, and ran his tongue along the soft underside of it, sending a trumpet blast to her sleeping parts and rousing them to full attention.

And when she sighed, and he insinuated his tongue into her mouth, probing, touching, stroking… why, she thought she might simply go mad.

She raised her arms to slide them around his neck, her cloak falling away without notice or care. It was only important that she hang on, keep him close, urge him closer. Because there was more than awareness in her now. There was hunger, a hunger she didn't understand but felt certain only he knew how to feed.

His hands went to her head, and she could feel the slight tug as he pulled the pins from her hair, slid his fingers into the tumbling curls even as he sighed against her mouth. He liked that? That was good, because she liked it, as well. Very much.

Now his hands were on her shoulders, and he was kissing her ear, his breath hot against her, sending shivers down her arms. He was pressing kisses along the length of her neck, and she was falling...no, he had her. He had her safe, and if they were falling, they were falling together, until she was lying on the soft velvet cloak.

And he was still kissing her, his fingers lightly tugging at the squared neckline of her chemise, his lips following the descent of the lace-edged silk, setting her skin on fire, making it impossible for her to breathe, but only possible to gasp in surprise as her breasts were suddenly free of the silk and he was touching her...touching her everywhere, kissing her everywhere, whispering that she was beautiful, she was everything, she was heaven and hell and the world in between....

His mouth closed over one taut, straining nipple, and Alina pressed her head back, raising her chin, raising her upper body toward him, offering she knew not what, as long as he didn't stop, never stopped.

She wanted to be touched, needed to be touched. Would simply die if this feeling went away.

His fingers closed over her other nipple, squeezing, rubbing, and she cried out at the intensified pleasure that shot through her, caused an ache to begin between her thighs. She dragged her nails down his back, feeling the ripple of his muscles beneath the fine lawn of his shirt, the faint shuddering of those same muscles as she cupped her breast, lifting it for him as he stroked the very tip with his wonderfully rough fingers.

She was his instrument, and he was composing a symphony upon her body. She soared, she swept, she sighed. She urged, she purred, she demanded. Because there was more, there had to be more. No symphony, no matter how wonderful, doesn't build, and build, the way she felt her senses building, without a heart-pounding crescendo somewhere, a thrilling climax, a sound so perfect and wonderful that it stops your heart, your breathing, only to take you up, up, into the stars before at last returning you to earth.

She was his instrument, and as Justin strummed her, his tongue flicking at her in time with his stroking thumb, his thigh somehow insinuated between her thighs, pressing hard against her, urging her to return that pressure.

Without thought, without shame, she responded, rubbing herself against him. With growing awe, she knew there was a crescendo coming to her, an ending to the symphony, yes, but one that she had to know.

And yet, when it happened, when the glorious became nearly intolerable, when her body at last found its own music, as her eyes flew open wide and she could only hold on to Justin as every cymbal crashed, and her heart became a tympani, she was still aware somewhere inside of her that it wasn't enough.

Not for her. Not for him.

Justin covered her breasts and rolled onto his back, taking her with him, pressing her cheek against his chest as his arm came around her and held her close.

They lay there for some time, feeling the heat from the fire, barely stirring when a log burned through and crashed in the grate. Alina's breathing at last returned to something less frantic, and her heartbeat was no longer audible in her ears.

And still she said nothing. Justin said nothing.

The mantel clock chimed out the hour, and at last Justin moved. He kissed the top of her head, and then helped her sit up, lifted her cloak up and around her shoulders.

She looked at him in open curiosity. "Why…why was that all?"

He retrieved his snifter of brandy and downed the remainder of its contents.

"You're supposed to sip, remember?"

He put down the snifter and, at last, he smiled at her. "I should be shot," he said affably enough. "That...uh...that wasn't intended. It was to start and end with a kiss."

Alina drew the edges of the cloak close together over her breasts. "I know. Tatiana explained it all to me. Gentlemen can be overcome by lust at the drop of a hat. They can't help themselves. It wasn't your fault."

"Tatiana? She said that? And who, pray, is this font of wisdom?"

"My companion. She was once my maid, but now she's my companion, and Danica is my dresser."

"I see. And which is which, may I ask, so that I can thank your companion for having explained it *all* to you?"

"Now you're being facetious. I know I really don't know anything. In point of fact, until just now I thought the whole thing..." She stopped herself.

Justin helped her to her feet. "Yes? You thought the whole thing what?"

Alina bent her head and muttered the word beneath her breath.

He leaned closer, pushing her tangled curls away from her face. "Your pardon, kitten. I didn't quite catch that."

"Repulsive," she said quietly, and then looked up into his face. "I thought the entire thing repulsive. There, I've said it."

"Ah, I see. Now I wonder if Tatiana's explanations left much to be desired, or if I should thank her again, as she made it much easier for the reality to exceed your woefully low expectations. Although I will tell you, I believe that I am not completely without talent, and that you are delightfully teachable. That is who I was supposed to be tonight, wasn't it, my curious little kitten? Your teacher? Your small experiment in what it means to be a woman? It may be a little late for warnings, but you should know that it is dangerous to play with me."

She wasn't certain which most upset her, his words or his tone. She only knew that the next thing she was aware of was the stinging of her palm after it had connected with his smiling face.

"Good," Justin said as she turned and began to run toward the door, her face aflame with shame. "We'll deal much better these next days if you hate me. Or at least I will."

She whirled about to face him, her cloak swirling around her feet—which would have been marvelously dramatic, she supposed, except that she nearly tripped over the thing as she walked back to him.

"I don't understand you. I don't understand any of this very much, but I don't understand you most of all. Why are you here? You've already told your

Prince Regent that you won't do as he wants you to do. You won't marry me. So what does it matter to you if *Inhaber* Novak wants to kill me? I am none of your concern. You've made your own bed with your Prince Regent, for whatever reasons, so why don't you just go lie in it, and leave me to myself? Luka is more than capable of protecting me. He was a soldier, and loyal to my father. You were nothing but a, a— Oh, and that's another thing! I have no idea what you were, what you are. So thank you very much, my lord, but we won't be requiring your services anymore. Luka will shoot the *Inhaber* dead and then take me to my mother's family. You, my lord, can...can simply go to straight to hell."

"Wait," Justin said quietly, just as she was about to make a second attempt at a dramatic exit, this time first carefully raising her cloak hem above her bare ankles. "There is no good time to tell you this. There is no family here in England for you to go to, Alina."

"There's not?" Alina felt the first stirrings of what could turn out to be real panic. "But—"

"Your mother had a single surviving relative, a sibling, a brother, Robert, Earl of Birling. He died without issue a little over eight years ago, in a duel. Everything was entailed, and there were no more living male relatives to inherit. The titles, the lands, everything reverted to the Crown at that time. Your mother didn't know, Alina, because when she married your father the Farber family cut her off and had nothing to do with her ever since. She never told you that?"

Alina stumbled to a chair and sat down with a thump. "No…no, she never said anything." She looked up at Justin, her eyes awash in tears. "Disowned her? Why?"

"Your mother was several years older than her brother, who was a contemporary of mine. I don't know the entire story, but there was something about the disgrace of having the only daughter married to…to a bloody foreigner. I'm sorry, that's all I know."

Alina rubbed her hands together in her lap. "So I am totally alone. Aren't I, Justin? Except for Aunt Mimi, of course, but I could not go back to her. I really couldn't. And…and you won't marry me."

He took hold of the desk chair and put it down in front of her, backward, and straddled it. His face was so serious, she felt frightened.

"No, kitten, I can't marry you. I told you, I'm a fugitive. Once you're safe, I'll be leaving England, never to return, or at least not until the Prince Regent is dead and unable to refute his signed pardon I have safely tucked away. Even a week ago I would have given everything I own to remain here, but now leaving is not only necessary, but I'm actually glad to be going. There's nothing here I want anymore save for a few friends. My estate is in the hands of my longtime manager, and will wait for me. It's not entailed in any event. What fortune that has remained here is my own and is already on its way to join with the bulk of my funds in Brussels."

"It all sounds so neat and tidy, the way you say it. And bloodless. You really don't care, do you? It's not a sham. You'd be safe in Brussels?" She didn't know why she asked that last question, why it was suddenly so important to her that he be safe.

He shook his head. "Once I make it to Brussels, I'll set sail for America. I've had my fill of kings, a surfeit of kings. The Americans got rid of us, and I think they had the right of it."

"America," she repeated. "That's a world away."

"A lifetime away. But you'll be fine here, Alina. While I was in London I made arrangements with my banker. My town house in London is now yours, as is a small estate located very near my friend Tanner Blake and his wife. I've already alerted them that you will soon be taking up residence, and I know Tanner will agree to manage your finances for you until such time as they present you next season in London and you capture the eye of half the gentlemen there. You are, no matter what, the granddaughter of an English earl, the daughter of a war hero. Prinny won't say a word against you. He can't, not after half of London is already sending around the word that I paid him fifty thousand pounds for the pardon he gave me."

Alina's head was spinning. She would be safe. She would be her own person, here in England. He was giving her the world. This man who barely knew her, this man who owed her nothing, was giving her everything. "I, um, I…thank you. You didn't have to…that is, there was no reason for you to…thank you."

He reached out and took her hand. "There was every reason, Alina. That's what you don't know but the Prince Regent did. Your uncle's duel was with me, and I fled England to escape the hangman for putting a period to Robbie Farber's existence. The Prince Regent summoned me back, pardoned me, so he could use me to rid Francis of this *Inhaber* Novak. And also to have himself a giggle or two at my expense, I'm sure, knowing I could not turn away from this chance to make up for my crime. I doubt he's considered the possibility of your death any more real than he would a play at Covent Garden. The man already half believes he fought with Wellington at Waterloo. Insanity seems to be his father's gift to him."

Alina pulled her hand free. "You? You shot my uncle? My mother's brother? *You?* Why?"

"That's not important. I have no excuses to offer you. Only my apology, and my thanks for allowing me this chance to make some small amends in the only way I can. The Prince Regent knew that, as well. He knows I can rid you and Francis of the

Inhaber because that's what I do, what I've done these past long eight years. I'm not a nice man, Alina. In fact, I am the utter antithesis of the sort of man you deserve."

She would not listen to such foolishness. He was being forced to assassinate the *Inhaber*—for her! He was doing it all for her, as he was giving her his possessions, cutting himself off from his own country, making himself into a fugitive. As some sort of penance for something that had happened so many years ago? Dear God! He was many thin things, perhaps, as he insisted, but he was not an evil man. How could she convince him? She felt so powerless, and so very sad.

"Alina, don't let your mind wander. Listen to me. Once the *Inhaber* is dead, both Francis and my Prince Regent will know they've gone as far as they can go. That will…be made clear to them. They'll both accept their losses and move on to the next intrigue. With monarchies, there is never a lack of intrigue. The Regent will find it easier to forget I ever existed. Your Romany will get their pitiful piece of land, and Francis will find a way to take it away again, one that doesn't involve you. Please, kitten, take what I'm offering you. It's all I have to give."

"My life. You're offering me my life."

"On the contrary, Alina. I prefer to see the thing as you saving mine. As for the rest—for tonight—

that was my mistake, not yours. It's best if we simply forget it ever happened."

She nodded, unable to say anything else, knowing he would not listen to her anyway, and got to her feet. She walked toward the door slowly, stopping once to look back at him, and then left, softly closing the door behind her.

CHAPTER EIGHT

JUSTIN MELTED INTO THAT peculiar darkness that comes just before dawn. The ground was unfamiliar, but the rules remained the same. See. Do not be seen. Act, don't think. Don't look in the face, not if you can help it. No one's nightmares were ever haunted by the remembrance of a turned back, a soft sigh as a soul surrendered to the afterworld.

Never hesitate.

Don't think of the child. Never, never think of the child.…

He'd left the first body behind the buttery. The man had been easy, half asleep at his post. Another reason to strike just before dawn: guards were at their most vulnerable as the night ended, as they congratulated themselves for a job well done and dreamed of a hot breakfast.

The second had proved more difficult, one of those rare soldiers that actually possessed some skills other than marching in a straight line and never thinking independently. But, in the end, he'd been no match for Brutus, and his neck had snapped like a dry twig.

Justin tapped Brutus on the shoulder and pointed toward the stand of trees set back about fifty yards from the gravel drive that led to Ashurst Hall. He then pointed to himself, and then to a similar grouping of trees on the other side of the drive. Brutus could move with the grace of a much lighter man, but he could not hope to conceal his bulk out in the open, crossing the drive.

No words were necessary. The man nodded once, showing his understanding, and the two parted ways.

Bent nearly in half, his knife concealed up his sleeve so that the blade didn't glint in the fading moonlight, Justin moved soundlessly over the gravel and slipped into the shadows.

There had been four men. Now there were two. Rafe's estate manager had seen the strangers indiscreetly and fatally advertising their presence in a local tavern, and they'd been under observation ever since. For two days and nights, as they'd watched Ashurst Hall, Ashurst Hall had been watching them. Now it was time they were gone.

Justin circled through the trees, his breathing slow and measured, his eyes on the ground, avoiding any errant twigs or loose stones, yet always flicking up, watching the shadows, separating tree from bush, at last locating the shadow that didn't fit either category.

Waiting, his ears alert for Brutus's signal that he'd gotten his man, Justin slid the blade forward, his hand closing familiarly on the hilt of the knife he'd had specially made for him at considerable expense in Spain after nearly losing his life to an inferior weapon. A workman is only as good as his tools, he'd known, and when your work is kill or be killed, there is no room for mediocre tools.

The short, shrill whistle broke the early-morning silence, and Justin was running and on his man before the fellow could fully rise from his crouch at the unexpected sound.

One arm encircling the man's chest, the tip of the Spanish knife lightly pressing against his throat, seemed to steal all thought of resistance, and the fellow began pleading in German, "Don't kill me, don't kill me."

"But it would be so easy, and relatively painless," Justin replied in flawless German. "Are you quite sure? Why should I spare you?"

"I do only what I'm told. A man has to live."

"Not necessarily. But you're a very fortunate man. Your companions are dead, all four of them."

"Four? But there were only three others. Please, sir, don't kill me."

At times, it was almost too simple to present a challenge. Having had Rafe's reconnaissance so easily proved correct, Justin slipped one leg between the man's thighs and, with a flick of his bent leg, had the man sprawled on the ground on his back. His captive lay there, showing no inclination to run, panting beneath his ridiculous mustachios and sideburns that had helped identify him and his compatriots in the village. After all, who outruns a knife in the back?

The knife was replaced by the pistol Justin carried in his waistband.

"We will now have a friendly chat about *Inhaber* Novak, my fuzzy friend."

"The *Inhaber?* But how did you—"

"*Shh,*" Justin warned affably. "You have but one job now, my friend, other than to remain alive, and that is to answer my questions. Now, are you listening carefully? You really don't want to get any of the answers wrong, do you?"

The man shook his head furiously, his eyes never leaving the barrel of the pistol.

"Good. You know the *Inhaber's* location, hmm?"

"Lon-London, sir. There is a hotel…the Pulteney. The Russian Tsar headquartered there during the Allies Peace Celebrations, so the *Inhaber* wished to set himself up there, as well. It…it is very fine."

"How personally gratifying for the *Inhaber* and his consequence, I'm sure. The Pulteney is quite a lovely establishment. Now, if it wouldn't be too much trouble, you will tell me where he is." To be certain the man understood the seriousness of his question, Justin cocked the pistol.

The man swallowed, shook his head. "But I told you."

Justin sensed Brutus's presence behind him. "Brutus, do I look stupid? More importantly, do I look harmless? And even more, do I seem to you a man who suffers fools gladly?"

Brutus growled low in his throat.

"He...he's on his way here," the hireling said quickly, his terrified gaze on Brutus. "We were to watch here, and wait for him, and the others. And... and have two of us follow you if you tried to take the girl away."

"Thank you. Brutus's imposing presence to one side, I had begun to worry I'd somehow lost my touch." Justin eased his pressure on the hammer of the pistol and returned the weapon to his waistband before pulling a folded letter from his pocket. "Not to insult your powers of retention, my good man, but I have composed a missive to your employer, one which you will deliver personally. You are hereby commissioned to present my compliments to the *Inhaber,* as well as the information that the lady has departed Ashurst Hall as of this morning. Observe."

As if to give credence to his words, the sounds of harness and coach horses could be heard from the drive. Brutus hauled up the man by his collar and turned him to watch as two coaches appeared out of the early morning mist and then disappeared into the distance. Brutus's whistle had not only alerted Justin. Wigglesworth had been stationed just outside the front door to Ashurst Hall and had flown into action the moment he'd heard the signal, quickly herding Alina and her small entourage into the pair of traveling coaches.

Once he had seen what he was meant to see, the *Inhaber*'s minion was roughly redeposited on the ground. He drew himself up into a fetal position, covering his head with his arms. "Please don't let him hurt me."

Justin rubbed at his forehead and sighed. "More and more, the world is populated by idiots, Brutus," he complained wearily. "He won't hurt you," he then assured the whimpering man. "This letter saves your life. Here, sit up, take it. There's a good fellow. Now, why don't you just run off and play postman. Go on, *run.*"

The man didn't need a second invitation. He snatched the letter and took to his heels, heading, Justin knew, for the place where he and his compatriots had tied up their four horses, knowing that what he would find there would be those same four horses, only now, thanks to some of Rafe's men, three of them were roped together into a line and had bodies strapped across their saddles.

When it came to making statements, Justin knew nothing made more of an impression than a show of power. In this case, his.

It also made it easier for him and Brutus to mount their own horses and follow.

"Lovely morning for a ride," he remarked to his friend as the now-rising sun made it less than child's play to follow the tracks of the four horses. "And much too lovely a morning to die, Brutus, so we will approach with caution. The *Inhaber* may not believe I am a gentleman of my word and am in fact breaking it by following that fool up ahead of us."

Brutus made a noise that could be interpreted as amusement.

With luck, and he knew he'd need it, the *Inhaber* also would still be abed, wherever he was, and his guard would not be too numerous, and as hapless as the four he'd put to guarding Ashurst Hall. Money could buy many things, even men. It could not insure competence or inspire loyalty.

Justin wanted this over, the *Inhaber* dead, Alina safe. He and Rafe had agreed that this would be the easiest, the quickest way to guarantee both. That success this morning would also hasten Justin's departure from England, never to see Alina again, could not be a factor. Giving her his possessions to make up for having killed her uncle, no matter how justified, was not his penance, as he'd thought it would be. Never seeing her again, never holding her, never smiling at her frank speech and her attempts at being worldly and sophisticated? Never really *knowing* her?

That was to be his true penance, and it would last a lifetime.

Luka had his orders. Employing a circuitous route, he was to remove Alina to the home of Rafe's sister Nicole and her husband, Lucas Paine, Marquess of Basingstoke, and once she was safe, from there to Malvern, and the home of Rafe's other sister, Lydia, and her husband, Tanner, Justin's closest friend.

Once the *Inhaber* was dead, Justin would get word to his friends before himself heading to Dover, the port of choice, it seemed, for those finding it necessary to escape England. Byron had made his a dramatic exit, Brummell had slipped the web of creditors to make for Calais, and soon Justin Wilde would escape the hangman via the same route, his destination Ostend, then Brussels and, finally, a ship bound for America.

A world away, as Alina had said last night—had there been a hint of sadness in her voice?

Brutus put out his arm and grunted, bringing Justin back to his surroundings. Damn. He'd nearly ridden straight down the hill leading into the small village, his mind elsewhere. His friend looked at him quizzically, or at least Justin decided the look was quizzical; with Brutus, it was difficult to tell.

"My apologies," he said as he saw the four horses

tied up in front of a ramshackle inn, the only building of more than two stories the backwater village could boast of, and only then because there was precious little of note elsewhere on the single street that bisected the rutted dirt road that clearly was meant to lead somewhere else.

He doubted the place even had a name. Which made it perfect, in so many ways, both for the *Inhaber* and for Justin.

They turned their mounts into the trees bordering the road. Battling low branches, they walked the horses a good twenty yards before dismounting and leading them farther into the trees, where they tied their reins to branches. "We don't know how many there are. Are you ready?"

In answer, Brutus pushed back his coat, revealing an amazing total of five heavy, workmanlike pistols stuck into his stout waistband. He then pulled knives from both his boot tops, and two more from elsewhere on his person.

"Only four?" Justin asked facetiously.

Brutus reached up behind his back and extracted a fifth knife from its sheath hidden beneath his coat, this blade even uglier than the others.

"My faith has been restored, but with only a modicum of luck, you won't need any of them. Unless the *Inhaber* is a complete fool, he'll be heading out shortly, to regroup somewhere else."

Brutus carefully replaced the knives, looking only

slightly crestfallen. The man did enjoy the exercise of a good fight now and then.

Rafe had insisted that he go with Justin, as well as some of his own men from the estate, but Justin had refused. He'd worked alone for too many years, and with Brutus for the last five. He had his own way of doing things, ways the large man understood, and too many people presented opportunities for too many mistakes. Not that he didn't trust Rafe Daughtry, but he would not chance having that man's blood on his hands in order to solve his own problems.

Brutus slung Justin's custom-designed rifle over his shoulder and followed him. When Justin hunkered down at the crest of the small hill that looked down on the few buildings, Brutus hunkered down behind him. When Justin pulled out a collapsible spyglass and lifted it to his eye, Brutus squinted. When Justin inhaled, he smelled the sausages Brutus had ingested for breakfast two hours earlier.

Justin stood up once more and looked about, noting the substantial cover of the trees, the fine elevation that had him looking down at the inn roof and the cleared ground around the building. He could not have asked for better; barely a test of his particular skills, actually.

"Now we wait. This terrain reminds one of Remiremont, does it not? The same sort of fine vantage point. May we have the same success here today."

No more than ten minutes later, they watched the

team that pulled the black traveling coach being led from the stables, to be maneuvered into the traces with more haste than expertise.

"He's already on the move. Our friend the *Inhaber* must be an early riser," Justin said to Brutus unnecessarily, thinking of their mounts, which had never been pressed to a gallop on their more than ten mile ride here, but which were nonetheless not precisely fresh. He held out his hand for the rifle. "We'll make the first shot count, Brutus, as we won't get a second chance."

As Justin dropped to his knees and removed his hat and gloves, tossing them aside, Brutus went down on all fours in front of him, offering his back as a human platform Justin could use to steady his arms and the rifle.

Justin raised the rifle and sighted down it to a spot approximately six feet beyond the door leading to the dirt yard and the coach, his heart rate slow, his breathing slower.

He could do this. He had to do this.

How many times had he been in this position? Too many. The French major who'd ordered the execution of British soldiers after they'd surrendered. The titled English general who'd been passing secrets to the French, supposedly brought down by an enemy sniper and transported home to be buried with honors so that no shame could be associated with the family name. The Swedish diplomat who had resisted the break from Bonaparte and had fought against the institution of a secret treaty between his country and Britain and Russia against France. The pompous Austrian financier—for reasons Justin hadn't even bothered to learn, because by then he had been past caring. Did any soldier marched onto a battlefield stop to ask the name and occupation of the enemy he had been ordered to kill?

For Justin, the only difference was that he had often dined with his unknowing target only a few hours earlier, and more than once had even bedded the man's wife.

The hustle and bustle in the yard below him increased, until at last the coach seemed to contain its limit of trunks and other luggage, and the outriders were all mounted and ready to leave.

Justin relaxed his shoulders as the door to the inn opened one last time, taking in a long breath, ready to let it ease back out as he squeezed the trigger and put an end to Alina's danger, and quite possibly to his own future.

He heard the cries before he saw the man he'd first seen at Carleton House. *Inhaber* Novak emerged from the inn carrying two poorly dressed children, girls of no more than ten. He held one clamped tight in each arm; both struggled to be free of his viselike grip. Human shields.

For a moment, Justin thought he might vomit. He dropped the rifle as the *Inhaber* covered the few feet between the inn and the coach, ducked his head and disappeared inside. Moments later both children exited the equipage, roughly tumbling to the ground and then quickly regaining their feet and running toward the frantic woman who had just exited the inn.

The coach sprang forward, the half-dozen outriders flanking it as it headed for the roadway and quickly disappeared, leaving behind only clouds of choking road dust, three horses and their dead riders, and the baron, the fugitive Justin Wilde, who could only look down impotently at his badly trembling hands.

"He knew," he said at last. "That's where he got the idea. Damn him, how did he know?"

The big man picked up the rifle and then held out one hamlike hand to assist Justin to his feet before patting him on the back and making sympathetic sounds.

"Yes, you're right, my friend," Justin said, determined to shake off what had just very nearly happened, what had happened before. "No sense rehashing my failure. He can't know for certain I was even here. And he has the letter. It's not as if we're totally out of the game."

Brutus, clearly trying to cheer his friend, pressed his hands together and put them to his cheek, tipping his head almost girlishly as he smiled a wide, gap-toothed smile.

Justin nodded. "Yes, and we'll see the pretty lady again. And the scowling major, who warned me I was doomed to fail, so that he made plans of his own, thank God, and will no doubt enjoy hearing of my lack of success," he added as Brutus made a show of twirling the ends of an enormous, nonexistent mustache. "Come along. We're off to Basingstoke."

ALINA WATCHED AS WIGGLESWORTH carefully picked his way toward her along the narrow, rutted track that was somewhat the worse for wear after a morning of rain, the expression on his face a mix of horror and determination.

He was dressed as always in shimmering silver satin and ridiculous amounts of dripping lace, the style of his suit one that hadn't been seen in England or anywhere else in many a year, but one that matched his, as Tatiana termed it, hoity-toity ways.

Lifting his befeathered tricorn hat from his powdered wig, the valet swept Alina an elegant bow and then gave in to his obvious distress. "Surely, my lady, this is a jest. We cannot possibly be abandoning the comfort and consequence presented by my lord's fine coaches in favor of—" he pointed toward the gaily painted caravans in abject horror "—*those*."

"Oh, Wigglesworth, but we are. And we do it, I understand, with the full blessing of his lordship. The coaches will return to the main road as soon as we transfer the most basic of our needs to these two fine equipages that have been waiting here for us, the bulk of our baggage still visibly strapped to the coaches and ready to lead anyone who might somehow stumble over them and then follow them off on a merry chase while we safely proceed to our next destination."

Wigglesworth looked about in panic as a few—a very few—bits of baggage were lowered to men waiting to transfer them to the caravans. "I see none of his lordship's baggage, my lady. His ensembles? His linens? His tins of food? But…but how is he to perform his toilette? How am I to present him in his best light? How…how will he *survive?*"

Alina's smile faded. "His lordship most probably won't be here at all, Wigglesworth. The coaches go to a seaport by the name of Rye, the major tells me, and he will be reunited with his belongings when they are shipped off to their final destination in Brussels. Mine," she added without much interest, "remain for the most part at Ashurst Hall, and the trunks you see are in fact empty."

The valet looked to the coaches and then back to the pair of gaily painted caravans. "But…but where am *I* to be? Nobody told me."

"Why, I don't think I know, Wigglesworth. I'm sorry. I supposed you'd continue on to Rye with the coaches, and I imagine the baron did as well, although the major insists that no bad penny ever disappears forever, and he is confident the baron will show up here eventually, which will mean he has failed to…to eliminate our problem as simply as he'd hoped."

Had she ever prayed harder for failure, even as she stormed heaven with entreaties to keep Justin safe? And did that make her the most terrible person in the world?

Wigglesworth turned his hat round and round in his hands, clearly caught on the horns of a dilemma.

If he opted for Rye and a reunion with his employer in Brussels, he could continue on in comfort, as he'd been doing for the past three or more hours, ever since leaving Ashurst Hall. Unless, of course, the *Inhaber*'s men accosted the coaches and became perturbed when they did not discover Lady Alina inside one of them. Why, they might even take out their anger and frustration on his fragile body, mightn't they?

With Brutus nowhere to be found, he would be defenseless. After all, he might pretend that it was his sartorially enhanced figure and his consequence as the baron's man that opened inn kitchens and such to him and his demands, but he knew it was Brutus standing at his back as he made those demands, smiling his gap-toothed smile as he drew up his hands into huge fists, who made the difference between success and being stuffed upside down in the midden.

On the other hand, if his lordship was not successful in his mission—heaven strike him down for thinking such a calumny!—who would take care of him if his own personal manservant had been too particular to travel in a rackety contraption that looked very much like a small red house on wheels, accompanied only by Lady Alina and a gaggle of variously toothless and garishly clad creatures who all seemed to be even now gaping at him as if he were the most amusing creature on earth? Who would shave his lordship if he were not available? Who would see to it that his linen was spotless? Who would cut the fat off his meat? Why, the man couldn't exist without him!

When the coachies climbed back up on the boxes, Wigglesworth turned and ran toward them, waving his arms wildly and calling out, "Wait! Wait!"

"Comin' with us, pretty man?" one of the coachies called down to him.

"I…don't be ridiculous! Someone has to remain to protect the lady, what with all you huge, strapping men deserting her here, in the middle of God only knows where," Wigglesworth declared even as he climbed halfway into the coach and pulled out his most important case, the one containing all his most prized possessions (including a half-dozen bars of scented soap; he was already convinced there could be no soap in either of the caravans).

He stepped back onto the roadway and pointed imperiously at a large black trunk strapped to the boot of the first coach. "And that one."

"Nope," the coachie said, shaking his head. "Stays with the coach."

Wigglesworth was not by nature a brave man. One might say he was not by nature even a timid man. But he did have his priorities, and his limits. Traveling without his lordship's own fresh linens exceeded those limits.

A rather dashing yet dainty ivory-handled pocket pistol of a type most often seen in the reticules of the more daring ladies in society appeared in Wigglesworth's hand. "It might well not prove a fatal shot, but I won't miss, either," he told the coachie. "The black trunk, if you please. Now."

One of the outriders, who had been amusing himself by dancing about behind Wigglesworth, imitating him for the delight of his fellows, had nearly reached the valet when Alina pressed the barrel of the pistol she'd earlier taken for herself from the coach into the small of his back.

"Let him alone, please," she said quietly. "Clearly he is under considerable duress. We will take this one trunk. In point of fact, you, personally, will off-load it for him and place it in one of the caravans. Are we agreed on that?"

"Yes, milady," the outrider said meekly, and Alina quickly put the pistol behind her back and smiled at Wigglesworth as he turned to her in triumph at having rescued the precious trunk.

"So, you're going to travel with us," she said, happily letting go of the pistol as Tatiana casually strolled past behind her and took it from her. "Does that mean that you think his lordship will be joining us?"

"I pray he won't, as he is certainly unused to such...simplicity," the valet answered, sighing and looking rather longingly at the coaches as they moved off, heading once more to the main road. "But as I do him no good at all in Rye or on a ship bound to wherever it will be bound, I see my place as here. His lordship will have me fetched in any case," he added more brightly. "He can't survive without me, you understand."

"We're ready to go, my lady," Tatiana said, joining them. "He is to come with us?"

Wigglesworth drew himself up straight. "He is."

Tatiana nodded, eyeing him up and down as if measuring him. "When we get to the camp, I'll see if someone can find him some clothes. Perhaps one of the children has extra."

The valet's eyes grew so wide they seemed in danger of popping straight out of his head. "I beg your pardon," he said haughtily.

"Not mine you should be begging," the companion said, winking at Alina. "It's everyone who has to look at you who you should be apologizing to. My lady—that is, *Magdaléna*—there is clothing for you in the first caravan. Danica is grumbling mightily, but she is seeing to sorting it all out and will help you change. Then we must be going."

Alina thanked Tatiana and then looked kindly at the woe-begotten face of the valet. "We have to do this, Wigglesworth. The major arranged it all even before the ship docked here in this country, and the Romany will protect us as we travel on. We will keep to the back roads the Romany know so well, and we will be safe. But not if we don't appear to be Romany ourselves, or otherwise all this fine subterfuge will have gone for naught. You do understand, don't you? It will be an adventure, Wigglesworth, a grand adventure."

"Playing the page and watching as that rascal Napoleon greeted his lordship at the Grand Trianon at Versailles, all unknowing we were there to steal his plans for the proposed march on Russia, my lady. *That* was a grand adventure. *This,* begging your ladyship's pardon, is a mockery of all that is civilized. If I am needed, I will be in my...domicile."

And with that, Wigglesworth was off, heading for the caravan holding his case and the coveted black trunk. He was no longer tiptoeing through the mud, but rather ignoring it, strutting with his nonexistent stomach pushed out, his shoulders flung back, his arms straight as they sawed back and forth through the air, front to back.

"It's called a *vardo,* not a domicile," Alina was left to say quietly, knowing she had just been firmly put in her place.

CHAPTER NINE

As THEY HAD BEEN HEADING in nearly diametrically opposite directions, and because Justin could only estimate where, generally, the Romany camp might be, it was not until he smelled the smoke from the cooking fires that he was able to track it to its source...and to Alina.

He knew that their progress for the past mile or more had been noted, could actually feel the eyes watching him and Brutus from the trees, and that comforted him, although he wouldn't be truly at ease until he saw Alina.

He'd been alone for a long time, and had convinced himself that he would continue alone, without feeling the loss. And then Alina had stood at the head of the gangplank in that ridiculous cloak and his carefully crafted world had tipped on its axis. Before he'd known who she was, why they'd been brought together the way they had, he'd already known she was someone who could shake him to his core—wake him up, because he'd been asleep for too many years, even as he'd traveled the Continent doing the Crown's bidding, even as he'd believed his one true happiness would be attained only if he could return to England, no matter what the means, or the cost.

Now the prospect of departing England, never to return, seemed a simple thing. Watching Alina leave him last night had been the most difficult thing he'd ever done, but he had been right to send her away. He didn't know if he could survive leaving her another time.

But he'd find out....

They rode into the camp at a sedate walk, and he counted the caravans. Eight in total, and in varying stages of repair and disrepair. He'd never known this many caravans to travel together here in England. That could be problematic, most especially when he informed the major that at least two of them would have to go.

The last thing he wanted was to attract attention as "those damned thievin' Gypsies" often did in the less enlightened areas of the country. If there was one sin Justin rarely committed, it was overestimating the intelligence of his fellow man and thereby underestimating the chances of something or someone totally unrelated to the point causing trouble for him.

As he led the way through the camp, caravans on either side of the clearing, mongrel dogs barked and ran around the horses as the men, from boy to man to aged grandfather, fingered the weapons stuck into their wide waistbands. Women raised themselves from their vigils over the campfires, pressed hands to aching backs as they pushed their ample bosoms forward and eyed him with a frank appraisal that had him smiling and tipping his hat to them all.

"Brutus," he said, his lips barely moving, "as I lack eyes in the back of my head and am loathe to turn around as we travel this gauntlet, I do hope you're smiling as you demonstrate how harmless you are. And perhaps a cheery wave to those kiddies over there wouldn't come amiss. We'll dismount at the last caravan once we're past it and wait for someone to alert the major that we're here. Unless Wigglesworth does it for us. What the devil is he doing here?" he ended as his valet cried out his name in a voice that could probably be heard for miles.

"My lord!" Wigglesworth yelled once more. "Thank the lofty heavens you have come to rescue me! I vow, I cannot exist like this for another moment!"

Justin turned the bay about and looked back from whence he'd come, taking in the small clearing and the caravans and the Romany who still watched him, but now with wide smiles on their faces.

"Wigglesworth?" he said in some astonishment a moment later. "What in the name of all that's wonderful are you supposed to be? My God, man, have you no pride?"

"Not any longer, my lord, no," the valet said, sighing deeply as he waited for Justin to dismount. "It was either this or show my head to the world, which I most firmly and reasonably refused to do."

Justin attempted to take in the apparition standing before him clad in a voluminous homespun blouse, its rather indiscreet neckline embroidered in red and green thread, a wide green sash about his waist above a black skirt, also embroidered, the fabric shiny in places from wear, all but threadbare in others. Atop his head was one of his wigs, still showing signs of the powder he used on them all, but combed out so that it hung in straggled disarray to his—dear God—bony bare shoulders.

From somewhere behind him, Justin could hear Brutus gasping for breath.

Justin was a gentleman, raised to never betray shock or surprise unless either was expected of him. It took all of his long years of hiding his true feelings to help him maintain a bland countenance at the moment, however.

"Please pardon my curiosity, but what would be wrong with your head, Wigglesworth, that you'd consent to…this."

The valet walked closer and crooked his index finger, so that Justin lowered his head to listen to the man's confidence.

"I have no hair, my lord."

"Really." Justin bit the insides of his cheeks. "All

these years together, Wigglesworth, and I had no idea. None at all?"

"I shave it off every morning, my lord. My wigs fit much better that way. Many in the last century did the same."

"Yes, I seem to remember something about that. So, beneath that fairly ruined wig there is…"

"Nothing save my bald pate, my lord. I attempted to tie one of those colorful handkerchiefs about my head, as some of these people seem to do, but it… it kept sliding off, my lord." Wigglesworth lifted his chin in something nearing defiance. "I cannot allow anyone to see my naked head, my lord. It isn't proper, and might frighten the ladies."

"At the moment, Wigglesworth, you're doing a fair job of frightening me, if you're at all concerned with my sensibilities. But I'll bow to your ingenuity if you're content with the costume."

"Disguise, my lord, not a costume," the valet corrected. "I am incognito."

"Not to mention incomprehensible, and rendering me nearly incoherent," Justin muttered under his breath as his attention turned to the far side of the camp, because he believed he had heard his name being called. "As long as you're happy, Wigglesworth."

"Happy? I am submerged in the depths of despair and still sinking, my lord, but to serve you, I will not complain. Oh, and my name is now Papin, my lord, for the duration of my incognito, um, incognito-ness. It means gray-haired lady."

"How very wonderful for you. But if we are to be players in this, *Papin,* I am no longer *my lord,* or even *sir.* For the nonce, you must address me as Justin."

Wigglesworth staggered where he stood. "But I couldn't!"

"You'd rather find a new employer once I am caught out and hanged? You'll not find another as lenient as me so easily."

Wigglesworth stood there, silent, before saying, "Just—Justin would not be good, my lord. Someone might still suspect. Better you take a Gypsy, er, Romany name. I will go ask the old lady who gave me my name, and—"

"Justin!"

All thoughts of his name, or Wigglesworth and his skirts—not to mention his chicken breast—fled as Justin turned to watch Alina running toward him across the field.

She was clad in a costume much like Wigglesworth's: a blouse, a scarf tied about her waist, a full skirt to her ankles. But that was where all similarity ended.

Her unbound hair trailed out behind her as she ran, her bright red skirt held up and showing glimpses of several lace-edged white petticoats. Her breasts strained against the ruffled neckline of her blouse, and the bright green scarf turned her waist into an incredibly small span, one he could easily encircle with his hands.

He took two steps toward her, ready to open his arms and catch her as she flung herself against him. He would lift her high off the ground, twirl her about and then draw her slowly down his body until he could kiss her smiling mouth.

Except that, still a good ten yards away, she suddenly stopped running, even as his imagination continued traveling down a path he knew he should not tread. He could see her composing herself before she began to walk toward him again.

Had she remembered that she should be angry with him? Even as he had brought himself back to the knowledge that he had no right to her affection?

"You're safe," she said at last. "Not…not that I was worried."

"Good. The last thing I would care to do, Alina, would be to cause you worry. You look…well. There was no trouble making the exchange? Are the accommodations suitable?"

"The accommodations are marvelous," she told him, finally smiling again. "I have always wanted to ride in a *vardo,* but I wasn't allowed, of course. To think I had to travel all the way to England to finally get my wish. Luka will want to know that you're here. He's asleep in the last *vardo,* back that way. It's probably too soon for him to be attempting to take command. He's feverish again. Tatiana and I were putting cool wet cloths on his head when someone told me you had arrived."

"Then perhaps it's as well that I'm here, although you have to have realized that I am here because I failed. Your nemesis is still breathing."

"Yes, but so are you," Alina pointed out, as if that balanced the scales. "Does this mean we will not be traveling to your friends at Basingstoke?"

He chose his words carefully. "No, nothing has changed there. I want to keep heading north, until you're safe at Malvern. I made more than one plan, and the second may work where the first failed. Alina—"

"Magdaléna," she corrected, pulling out her skirt and slowly turning in a full circle in front of him, pausing with her back to him to look over her shoulder at him in a way that pierced his heart. "I am Magdaléna, a simple Romany girl and no longer *my lady*. We've been practicing all afternoon, Tatiana and Danica and I, so that we are never caught in a mistake."

"Yes, Wigglesworth—that is, Papin—told me. He tells me the name means gray-haired lady. But by the look on that fellow's face over there, the one eavesdropping on us even now, I'm not convinced that's correct."

Alina lowered her head, her cheeks flushing. "Poor Wigglesworth. No, Papin does not mean gray-haired lady. I was told it means *goose*." She looked up at Justin again. "But Luka would not allow any of the other names they wanted to give the poor fellow. I think some of the suggestions were rather... naughty."

"I'll remember that when Wigglesworth comes to me with my name for the duration."

"You can simply ask Luka. He speaks Romani." She then looked past him and waved to Brutus, apologizing for not greeting him at once.

Justin knew he could dredge his mind for days and not come up with the name of another woman who had even taken the time to say hello to Brutus. Or worry herself about Wigglesworth, for that matter. Add to that the fact that, rather than hiding in her caravan, terrified, she seemed to be enjoying herself mightily.

"This is an adventure for you, isn't it, kitten?" he asked her as they walked between the rows of caravans on their way to see Luka.

"My father often told me that all of life should be an adventure. Yes, I am enjoying myself, except for the times I remember that *Inhaber* Novak wants to see me dead in order to steal lands from these wonderful people. You never saw him today?"

"I saw him," Justin answered shortly. "I will see him again. You're not to worry about the man."

"I worried more that I wouldn't see you again. I know what you said. That I should forget what happened ever happened. That you think I was only…curious. But how can that be, Justin? Something did happen. How can something have changed nothing?"

Justin stopped walking and turned her to him, his hands on her upper arms. "Nothing has changed, kitten. My plans have only been delayed."

Her eyes searched his as if looking for answers to questions she wasn't sure she dared ask, but could not resist asking. "You left this morning without a word of goodbye. Was…was that easy for you? Because it wasn't easy for me."

"Christ…" Justin took her hand in his, and they continued walking toward the last caravan. She held on tight, trusting him. Him! Nobody should ever trust him, let alone an innocent young woman like Alina. "I knew last night was a mistake. I knew it, and yet I allowed myself to…" He squeezed her hand. "You're young, vulnerable. And I'm a very bad man."

"The Bad Baron. Yes, Charlotte told me some call you that."

"I've been called worse by those who know me best. Listen closely, Alina. You don't care about me. You don't know me. What happened…what very nearly happened last night would have been the same with any man who knew only the half of what I know. You were curious, any fool could have seen that, and I was available. I didn't rouse your heart, kitten. I awakened your body. That's all it was. That's all it could ever be for us, for reasons I've already explained. Someday, someday soon, you'll travel to London with Tanner and Lydia, and you'll meet a man worthy of you. In a year, you won't even remember me."

"Don't say that!" she commanded, cutting him off. "How dare you presume to tell me what I think, what I feel? How *dare* you!" And then she turned on her heel and ran from him, her glorious black hair lifting in the breeze the way it had a lifetime ago, when his heart had swelled as she'd run toward him.

ALINA REMAINED IN HER caravan for several hours, until dinner was over and the children had all been gathered up and tucked into their beds. Only then did she venture out into the center of the camp, on the hunt for Stefan, the young Romany who had driven their caravan that afternoon.

Stefan was very pretty. Even Danica, who never unbent enough to indulge in casual conversation, had remarked that Stefan could snap his fingers at any silly female and have her come running to him.

Stefan didn't walk. He swaggered. His coal-dark hair was long, and he tossed it often, rather like a girl. His eyes were as blue as a summer sky, and ringed with long, curling lashes that rightfully belonged on a girl. His teeth were so white, they gleamed. He wore his full, blousy shirt open to the waist and tucked into tight-fitting leather breeches that ended just below his knees. Below his knees, his strong calves positively bulged with muscle.

He wore his face shaved smooth, but had a considerable amount of dark, curling hair on his remarkably muscled chest.

He sang like an angel, and had done so most of the afternoon, often turning about to peer inside the caravan to be sure his three female passengers were listening appreciatively.

Alina thought he was probably the most beautiful man she'd ever seen. And the most immensely silly.

But he'd do.

Carefully avoiding Luka's caravan, as she'd waited until Justin had entered it again a quarter hour earlier, she flung her black wool shawl up and over her head so that it settled low across her shoulders, and then began strolling along the clearing, past the eight campfires that illuminated the area.

She smiled to the women sitting on the steps of their caravans, knitting, mending, some turning cards over on small tables and nodding at what they saw. A young mother nursed her infant, a corner of her shawl covering her breast.

The men, those who had not disappeared into the trees to set up a perimeter guard, smoked long pipes as they rested their feet on the stones around the campfires, talking and laughing amongst themselves, one of them daring to whistle as Wigglesworth pranced by on his way back from the nearby stream carrying a shallow copper basin and some toweling, his expression a study of injured dignity.

Brutus appeared from between two of the caravans just as Alina approached, and the whistling and laughing abruptly stopped. The large man had that effect on people.

"They mean no harm to him, Brutus," Alina told him, and the man nodded his agreement, and then shrugged.

"And you'll see to it that they do no harm," she said, smiling. "It must be very gratifying to be able to command so much respect merely by being you. That's called consequence, Brutus. You were blessed with consequence. Why, I believe there have been princes and kings who have not commanded a room the way you do, simply by entering it."

Brutus seemed to chew on this thought for a few moments, and then nodded his thanks. Or she supposed so, anyway.

"Was there anyone else at the stream when you were there, Brutus?" she asked, having walked the entire camp and seen no sign of Stefan.

The big man nodded, and then pointed toward Alina's assigned caravan before seeming to mime a person holding reins, driving a team of oxen.

"Ah, Stefan. Stefan is at the stream. Thank you, Brutus, that's just who I was looking for."

Brutus smiled, clearly happy to have pleased her, tugged at his forelock and lumbered on, following after the bewigged and beskirted goose.

Alina waited until anyone who had been watching the exchange between her and Brutus went back to what they had been doing, and then she slipped silently into the gap between two of the caravans and headed for the stream she had visited earlier, having volunteered to help bring water for the cooking pots.

She found Stefan easily, and watched him as he stood on the bank, his long legs spread as if he'd just laid claim to the ground around him, one hand on his hip, the other just then very precisely and almost ceremoniously bringing a thin black cheroot to his lips. He inhaled deeply, and then blew out a stream of smoke that seemed blue-white in the fading light as it wreathed his head before blowing away in the breeze. Everything he did, every move he made, seemed to Alina to be planned, practiced, deliberate, even when he thought himself alone.

Except for the cheroot, and the hair on his chest, he reminded her very much of her Aunt Mimi.

"Stefan," she said before she could change her mind. "What are you doing here?"

He swiveled about slowly, moving first his head, so that she had no choice but to look into his eyes, his slow smile, before he turned to fully face her, holding out his hand to her, palm up. "Come, Magdaléna, see the moon as it rises in all its glory. The smoke from the fires obscure, but here, at the water's edge, there is nothing to hamper our view of the wise man who smiles down on all of us."

"Some of us more than others, do you think?" she asked as she joined him, noticing that once again his shirt was opened to his waist, baring his chest to the moonlight even as he raised his face to it, as well.

"Moon baths are salubrious to the complexion. I wait here until it is fully risen, and then I shall bathe in it."

Alina covered an involuntary giggle with a cough. "Really? I...I'd never heard of that, Stefan. You... you do have a lovely complexion."

He nodded, accepting her compliment as his due as he fingered the single gold hoop earring in his right ear. "The sun? The sun is not good for the complexion. Look at those who seek it and see the leather they call skin. But the moon? The moon washes all clean."

"I had thought that the job of soap and water. That's...fascinating. Really."

He denied the moon the pleasure of his face as he lowered his chin and turned to her, his smile confident. "You should bare your complexion to the moonlight, Magdaléna. I have with me a blanket. We could bathe...together."

Only the elders knew that Alina was their key to the land they coveted, as Luka believed that the fewer who knew, the fewer who could make a mistake and give her away. Stefan had not been told who she was, that she was anything more than what she appeared to be, as she'd changed her clothing in the caravan before they'd joined with the other wagons. To him, she must be simply another Romany girl to seduce with his vaunted beauty and ridiculous prattle about moon bathing.

"I don't think so, no," she told him, careful to maintain her smile. "But perhaps a kiss? A single kiss in the moonlight? It…it would seem a shame to waste it."

He looked crestfallen for a moment, but then shrugged his wide shoulders before tossing his cheroot into the stream. "A kiss tonight, a hope for tomorrow," he said, taking her hand and pressing her palm against his bare chest. "You will dream of me, and I of you, and tomorrow night, beside another stream, we will visit the moon again…and perhaps the stars, as well."

"But for now," she reminded him, "only a kiss. You have to promise, Stefan."

"Agreed, it is a promise. But you will ask for more."

Alina closed her eyes as he lowered his head toward her. She knew now not to purse her lips, nor to tighten them against him. Instead, she opened her mouth slightly and prepared herself for the first small explosions inside her to begin, the first stirrings of what she knew now as desire.

And there was nothing. Nothing happened... except that her palm began to tickle against the hair on his chest.

She ground her mouth against his, and he responded by clasping her close against him, insinuating his tongue between her lips.

And nothing happened.

He wasn't clumsy. He didn't attempt to overpower her. He was very gentle as he cupped her left breast, actually, and probably very practiced. He rubbed lightly at her nipple through the thin material, moaned low in his throat as if pleased by the feel of her.

But nothing happened.

"I...I'm sorry," she said as he dropped his hands from her and stepped back, looked down into her face. "That was...very nice."

"For me, Magdaléna, a moment in heaven. But not for you. Stefan knows this. There is another. But for another, you would be mine. The fault lies with him, not me."

She did not wish to discuss Justin. "The *fault?* Stefan, this... What happened just now is nothing to do with *you*. And there is no one else."

He brightened. "No? Then the fault is with you. This happens with females. But I can fix that. I will merely redouble my efforts, and you will soon swoon and sigh. *Oh, Stefan, Stefan,* you will cry. *Yes, Stefan, yes.*"

He reached for her, but Alina only laughed and deftly danced out of his reach…and straight into Justin's arms.

"Dear me, I feel decidedly *de trop,*" he said, steadying her. "Shall I go away, and leave you two your privacy?"

"No!" Alina exclaimed, and then quickly lowered her voice. "That is, Stefan and I were just talking. Weren't we, Stefan?"

Stefan pointed at Justin with his chin and sneered. "Who is this? Your father?"

Alina looked up at Justin, wide-eyed. He looked so…so at a loss for words. She couldn't help herself. She began to laugh. She laughed so hard, in fact, that she found herself clinging to him as he continued to stare at Stefan until it seemed that his mistake had finally penetrated the young Romany's brain, and he took to his heels, returning to the camp.

"Stop it," Justin said quietly once the young man was gone.

But she couldn't. She'd attempted her small experiment, she had proved Justin wrong…and now Stefan had mistaken her almost lover for her *father?*

"But…but it's so *funny!*"

"I fail to see the humor."

"Oh, pooh, Justin, of course you do," Alina said,

using her sleeve to wipe at her streaming eyes. "Stefan is such a *child*. Not a man at all, even if he is older than me. He sees you as ancient. Do you feel ancient, Justin?"

"I *feel* like turning you over my knee. What the devil maggot did you take in your head? Bathing in moonlight? Allowing a lummox like that to kiss you? *Paw* you? What did you think you were doing? Were you trying to make me jealous?"

Alina sobered as suddenly as she had burst into laughter. "And now you think this is about *you*. Do all men think they are the most important creatures in nature?"

Finally, Justin smiled. "Yes, kitten, we do. It's an illusion women have allowed us from the beginning. Our mistake is in ofttimes believing what you all tell us."

"Oh," she said quietly. "Well, then, I suppose that's all right. And I wasn't in any danger, you know. I told Stefan one kiss, and he agreed."

The smile disappeared. "He sounded as if he'd agreed. Did he act as if he'd agreed?"

"Well…no. But if you hadn't stood in front of me like some great wall for me to run into, I would have been safely back in the camp, and we wouldn't be having this conversation, would we?"

"Ah, so now it's not Stefan's fault, or your fault… but once again my fault. A thousand apologies, I'm sure."

"I accept your apologies, all thousand of them. And one more, for saying that it didn't matter who kissed me last night because I was simply being… awakened. Even you would have to agree that Stefan is exceedingly handsome—"

"Even if he is thick as a plank," Justin inserted neatly.

"Well, yes, there is that. But it was not his mind that I was kissing, was it? Are you hairy?"

"I beg your pardon?" Justin said in a faintly strangled voice.

"Stefan is very hairy. On his chest. I don't think I like that. Not that I considered the thing until now, but there is such a thing as too much of anything, don't you agree?"

Justin rubbed at his forehead. "I can't believe we're having this insane conversation. Alina, no more experiments, please. I shouldn't have said what I did. You're infatuated with me, and I thank you for that—it's quite flattering. But the fact remains that in a few months you will be making your debut in London and I will be in America, a fugitive from English justice."

"But if you weren't? In America, I mean. If you were in London with me…?"

"Geography changes nothing. I'm also too old for you, Alina," he said, probably believing he was being logical.

She could also be logical. "My father was fifteen

full years older than my mother. Besides, we are already betrothed. That's next door to being married. Tatiana told me. So what we did…almost did…was not wrong. I don't understand why you are so set against it. You did kiss me, and if we don't always like kissing other people but we like kissing some of them, then we must feel *something* for that other person. Please, Justin, I don't want you to be a fugitive. If you marry me, then you will have obeyed your Prince Regent. He will forgive you, and you can remain in England. It's…it's as if you aren't running only from England, but from me, as well."

Justin rubbed at her upper arms, and she shivered even though she wasn't cold.

"You're forgetting the *Inhaber,* Alina. He must die or else he'll kill you, so he is already a dead man as far as I'm concerned."

Alina had forgotten. With her head so full of Justin, of finding some way to keep him here in England with her, she had forgotten the *Inhaber,* the disputed lands—all of it. But now she remembered. "Why would everyone find it so easy to see you as a murderer? Because of what you did to my uncle all those years ago?"

A shadow seemed to cross Justin's face, even though the full moon continued to shine down brightly.

"There are those who say it was an unfair fight, that I fired early."

She tipped her head to one side and looked up at him with some intensity. "And did you? Fire early, that is."

"I fired on two," he told her, his voice dull. "Some say his back was turned. Some say he'd turned to fire early, into my back, and that I was warned just in time to save myself."

Alina swallowed down hard. "And what do you say?"

"I say it was a long time ago, and we should let the dead rest. All the dead men. All the shadows I can't let touch you in your innocence. You came into my life years too late, Alina. I'm already lost."

And she knew she was losing him, losing the arguments she could not believe she had brought to him in the first place. She had been all but begging him to marry her! Why did she feel frustration, but no shame? Was this what it was like to be a woman? Or was she a headstrong girl who simply could not hear the word *no* without trying to turn it to a *yes?*

"You can't be right," she told him fiercely. "We are two people, Justin, that's all. We're not simply the tools of our countries. That ceased to be the truth when you kissed me. All we have to do is start from here, from today. Yesterday doesn't matter."

"And tomorrow may never come?" he asked her, his smile sad and knowing. "That was my argument to myself last night, but the clear light of morning showed me the error in my thinking. I've killed men, Alina. For good reasons, for bad reasons, for no reason at all that I bothered to ask about before going off to put an end to their existence. I've done things no fine words or thoughts could reconcile with the actions of an honorable man, a soldier. For eight years, I was the Crown's assassin, as I attempted to procure a pardon for killing my man in a duel. Not for king and country, Alina, for myself, for my own selfish gain."

Alina blinked at the tears stinging her eyes. Yes, she was losing him. Without ever having him, she was losing him. This time, forever. "But that's the past. The past is over."

He shook his head slowly. "It's too late. Killing those men killed a part of me. I can't run from the truth of who and what I am, but I'll be damned if I'll make you a part of it."

She wiped at her wet cheeks and threw back her head defiantly. "You can say those words to me ten thousand times, Justin, but I will never believe them. Until, someday, you don't believe them, either. You don't have to be the one to kill the *Inhaber*. If Francis wants him dead, he'll be dead. You're killing him to save me, when it is so obvious to me that you never want to kill again. You didn't have to shower me with your money and your property the way you have done. You never had to tell me about my uncle, who I am convinced was a coward and a fool. You never...you never had to stop last night when you knew I was there for the taking. Justin Wilde is a good man. You're the only one who doesn't believe in him. But I do. And I'm not giving up on him until he learns that."

She didn't run from him this time. She simply turned and left him there in the moonlight. Perhaps, she thought, the wise old man in the moon might shine down some wisdom on him....

CHAPTER TEN

MORNING CAME EARLY AFTER a nearly sleepless night, and Justin left a hand-wringing Wigglesworth behind in the caravan to tend to Luka while he visited the stream to wash himself in the cold water before donning the clothes he'd been given.

He didn't shave (or allow Wigglesworth to shave him, which had something to do with the hand-wringing). He didn't brush his hair into its usual style after washing it in the stream, but only shook his head hard and then raked his fingers through the damp locks and let them settle where they would. He donned the black leather trousers and pulled on the soft, low-heeled black suede boots that ended just below his knees, and then tucked the full-sleeved white shirt into his waistband, buttoning all but three buttons, so that his shirt collar lay open. He wound the long red cloth around his waist twice, and then knotted it so that the fringed ends hung to his knees.

Lastly, he added an inferior but highly decorated

blade to his sash and slid his Spanish-made knife into his right boot.

When he reentered the camp, it was as Markos, and nobody looked at him a second time as he accepted a tin cup filled with hot coffee from one of the women before returning to the caravan. As he went, he saw that the oxen were being hitched to the caravans, and, indeed, two of the caravans had already left the camp, as he had asked. They were still too many, he thought, but he was also loath to give up more of the men who had sworn to protect Alina.

Luka was sitting up in his narrow bed, filling his face and his mustachios with chopped eggs, his trembling hands giving the lie to his insistence last evening that he was fine, and ready to take charge once more.

"The fever?" Justin asked Wigglesworth, just then adjusting his straggly wig over his "naked pate."

"Still with us, I'm afraid, my—Markos. He says there is no time for it until we reach Basingstoke at the least, but the ball has to come out, and he needs medicine. One of the elders was here while you were gone, and he says he knows a surgeon in a town only a few miles from here. We're heading there as soon as the ladies have breakfasted."

"It's not necessary," Luka protested, nearly spilling the contents of his bowl as he sank back against the cushions behind him. "After Leipzig, I fought on for a full week, chasing the Little Corporal back to France to harass him in his retreat, and all with a ball in my thigh."

"How commendable," Justin said, relieving the man of the bowl. "And if you were to succumb to this fever due to some overweening sense of honor or bravado, you'll die with the comfort of knowing there will be a fine statue of you erected in some quaint village square somewhere, for the pigeons to decorate with their usual flair."

"Go to blazes, Wilde," Luka said, and then winced as he tried and failed to sit up once more.

"Markos. I am Markos, remember? And you, my friend, are in no fit state to insult me. Now, tell me what the Romany do when they encounter a village? We'll take only this caravan into the town, I assume, and leave the others in some makeshift camp until we return?"

"No. This is a village they visit each time they come this way. They usually camp for the night and the villagers come to buy goods, to be entertained. It would be odd if they didn't stop, and cause more comment about my wound. Yet another reason to leave the ball where it is until we reach Basingstoke. It will only be two more days."

"Yes, oxen don't move with the speed of horses, do they? My plan had been to alert you that the *Inhaber* still draws breath, and then leave you to carry on while I went on the hunt once more. Now I will

be delayed until you've reached not only Basingstoke, but Malvern. Lucas Paine is a good man, but
he'll ask too many questions I don't care to answer.
Tanner will simply ask what I want him to do, and
then do it."

"I still don't understand what happened yesterday.
You said you tracked the *Inhaber* to some small inn.
Why did you let him go?"

Justin saw a quick flash of the *Inhaber* as he ran
from the inn, the two little girls clasped to him like
living armor. "My vantage point wasn't one that
pleased me. If I'd shot and missed, I would have
destroyed any chance that he'd consider my offer."

"Yes, the letter you gave to his henchman. You
never said what it contains."

"No, I didn't, did I? And now it's time we were on
the road. Wigglesworth, your wig has slipped down
over your ear. Have you, I wondered, considered a
judicious application of glue?"

Leaving the major to stew, and Wigglesworth to
ponder, Justin stepped outside the caravan to see
Brutus standing with his legs wide and braced, his
massive arms folded across his chest, staring at
Stefan, who had been about to climb onto the box of
the caravan taken over by Alina and her women.

"And a cheery good morning to you, Brutus. Is
there a problem?"

"He won't let me pass," Stefan said, pouting.

"Magdaléna wishes for me to drive her, as I did yesterday. I sing for her."

"Like the proverbial angel, I'm sure," Justin said, all smiles and affability. "However, unless you'd like to be able to join a real angels' chorus in the next two minutes, I suggest you find something to occupy you elsewhere. No, no, don't look at him," he went on as the youth shifted his gaze to Brutus. "This is between you and me. I'd much rather we cried friends and moved on, but if you've a mind to be difficult, your difficulty rests with me."

"It would not be a fair fight. You carry a knife," Stefan accused.

"No, I carry two. Fighting fair, as you term it, is for those with no expectation of dying peacefully in their own beds after a long and fulfilling life. But, please, it's such a beautiful morning, and I am your guest. You agree to keep your distance from the girl, and I will allow you to keep the hand that dared to touch her."

"You want her?" Stefan declared with amazing bravado. "I give her to you. Her and the oxen both. May you be in good voice."

As the young Romany stomped off, Justin turned to Brutus. "And may I be in good voice? Is that some obscure Romany curse, do you think? That was stupid of me, baiting the boy like that. Unforgivable. It's never wise to make enemies, Brutus, remember that. This is where women will get you, if you allow it. Puffing up and strutting, squawking discordantly, like a peacock out to intimidate his fellows in order to keep the peahen for himself."

Brutus grunted and nodded before stepping aside so that Justin, noting that everyone else seemed ready to quit the camp, could mount the box behind the team of oxen.

Loiza, introduced to him last evening as the leader of this clan of Romany, stood in the clearing and waved his arms to the drivers, motioning for them to alternately, one by one, move out into a line.

Justin unwound the thick leather straps that served as reins from the large foot brake and looked out over the pair of broad backs. Releasing the brake, he flicked the reins as he would for a team of horses.

The oxen remained placidly standing there.

He couldn't be certain, but he thought they might be snoring.

Now here was a dilemma. He'd ridden any horse that could be ridden, driven any horse that could be driven. But he'd never sat up behind a pair of hulking great oxen who ignored him with such admirable panache.

Loiza shouted something to him in Romani, but Justin didn't understand. He saw the stout whip standing in its holder and picked it up, flicked it expertly just above the team's heads, a move that had no effect on them.

"I suppose I should tell you. Stefan sings to them,"

Alina said from behind him, and Justin turned to
see that she'd opened the top half of a narrow door
just behind his seat and was poking her head and
shoulders through the opening. "He sang to them
most all of the afternoon yesterday."

May you be in good voice.

"So it *was* a curse." Justin figuratively tipped his
hat to Stefan, who was standing in the clearing, his
smile so broad it nearly split his face in two. "Excuse
me," he said, setting the brake—probably an unnecessary precaution. "I believe I have some groveling
to do."

Several hours later, Justin sat on his horse and
watched as the caravans formed a broken circle in
the middle of a grassy field just far enough away
from the market town of Farnham that the castle
keep was only partially visible above the trees.

As soon as the last caravan was in place, the
makeshift camp turned into a beehive of activity,
everyone seeming to know what he or she was to
do, including Alina, who apparently believed she
would be accompanying Luka and Loiza into Farnham itself, to see the surgeon.

"No, you're staying here," Justin told her, dismounting in front of the caravan just as she was about
to climb its steps and go inside. "The major will be
fine with Loiza. He told me he's been coming here
twice a year for the past decade and more. Nobody

will think anything of seeing him. But you...stand out."

Luka, who had managed to get to his feet, appeared in the doorway of the caravan to add his voice to Justin's, at which point all thought of conversation abruptly stopped. The man was clad in Romany garb, his right arm in a sling. Neither of these things was surprising. What was rather shocking was Luka's clean-shaven face.

"Luka! I would not have known you," Alina exclaimed as he slowly made his way down the few built-in steps to the ground, Wigglesworth descending behind him and looking quite pleased with himself for having a hand in the major's transformation.

"Resigning from your king's army a little sooner than you'd thought, my friend?" Justin said, surprised to see how much younger the other man looked now that all those whiskers were gone.

Luka raised his hand and stroked at his cheeks and chin. "I would say I did it so as to further disguise myself, but in truth, I could not overcome a strong urge to prove to you that I do possess an upper lip," he answered, suppressing a grin. "Lady Alina, the baron is correct. You must remain here, as we have no idea where...a certain person might be. But you're safe enough here. Perhaps you can help the women when the townspeople come to buy their wares."

Alina looked ready to launch a protest, but then

merely shrugged her shoulders—wonderfully visible thanks to the fetching cut of her blouse. "At least I can watch over the children while the women work."

Justin assisted the major to the waiting horse and helped him mount; the man had sworn he could ride without tumbling to the ground in a dead faint. "She pretends this is all a game, but she knows how serious the situation is, and she'll behave. She's had a considerable lot to deal with in these past few days, one way or another." *No thanks to me,* he added silently.

Luka nodded his head. "She is her father's daughter. Perhaps even more determined. And fearless. All her concern yesterday was for you, with none reserved for herself. But you don't care, do you? We are not your friends, and the *Inhaber* is not your enemy. Your Prince Regent is the one you would destroy if you could, for his betrayal of you. Wigglesworth told me all about your supposed arrangement, believing he could gain my sympathy, and he did, to a point. You've been used badly, Justin Wilde, but you are not without blame. Now Lady Alina pays the price. And her every tear damns you to hell."

Justin watched as Loiza led the way out of the camp, Luka behind him and with Stefan belatedly bringing up the rear, a rifle slung across his back.

Justin's hands balled into fists at his sides. He hadn't attempted to refute anything the major had said because the man was right, straight down the line.

Except for one thing. He did care.

He cared very much.

ALINA SAT ON A LOW STOOL placed on the thick grass, surrounded by Romany children as well as other young ones who had come to the camp with their mothers.

All around them were the sounds of voices, some raised in song, some sharp with haggling, and much laughter in between. The whirr of the whetstone as one of the men worked the pedals as he sharpened knives brought to him from Farnham kitchens competed with the sound of a small hammer attacking the dents in a cooking pot.

She put the last few touches on her drawing of a sweet little cherub whose huge blue eyes had stared at her intently the entire time she'd been sketching him. "Here you are, sweetheart," she said, tearing off the page and handing it to the child, who immediately squealed in delight and then ran to show his mother his new treasure. "Now, who's next?"

Justin leaned against one of the caravans, watching as a young boy missing several of his top teeth shot both hands into the air as he yelled, "Me, me! But with teeth, please? Mama promised I'd get more."

Alina's clear laugh floated to Justin, washed over him, and he smiled.

She was so many different people, all wrapped up together to make her irresistible to him. The haughty Lady Alina, surveying her domain on the Portsmouth docks. The practical daughter who thought it perfectly understandable that she learn to shoot in order to protect her home from French invaders. The Romany Magdaléna, turning a plan to hide her from the *Inhaber* into a grand adventure. The insistent debater, throwing out arguments in order to get her own way.

The frightened, inquisitive girl, determined to become a woman.

Two more days, and he'd know if *Inhaber* Novak had taken the bait. Two more days, and he'd have his answer. He wasn't going to accompany Alina all the way to Malvern and the home of his friend Tanner Blake. That had been a lie, convenient to tell, necessary that everyone believe.

He would leave them all at Basingstoke and ride to Sandhurst, there to meet with one of the few other men he trusted with his life, and had done more than once during his years on the Continent.

Captain Richard Matterly was now an instructor at the Royal Military College at Sandhurst, the relatively new invention that would turn the next generation of rosy-cheeked English sons into hardened soldiers.

Justin had penned two letters before leaving Ashurst Hall. One to the *Inhaber,* putting forth his offer and directing him to reply via a missive delivered to Captain Matterly, and another to Richard, warning him that he would be watched and that Justin would contact him to relieve him of the *Inhaber*'s reply.

Two more days. One more night. And then the rest of his life. Alone.

"May I stand with you, my lord?" Wigglesworth whispered, coming up to him so quietly that Justin realized he was making a very poor guard at the moment.

"You don't add to my consequence in that rig out, but I will allow it, yes. Is there a problem?"

"Yes. There is a man, and he keeps looking at me. I…I think he wishes to purchase…my favors."

"Oh, I hardly think—" Justin's amusement at this bit of ridiculousness evaporated as his every muscle tensed. "Where is he? Show me this admirer of yours. Discreetly, Wigglesworth, if you please. Don't look his way or point him out. Just talk to me."

"Yes, my lord. There are many people here, but if you look past the lady with the rather formidable girth, the one with the berries on her hat, then it is that man in the poorly cut blue frock coat, standing just outside the major's domicile. He was attempting to speak with my lady's dresser, when I went to the stream to launder your smallclothes, but she was having none of him. Then he saw me, and all thoughts of dallying with her fled his mind. He has been watching me ever since, even if he tries not to look as if he is. I think it is the new way I've tried with the wig, my lord. I should have thought earlier to add these bows."

"And now you've led him to me," Justin said quietly. "Very good, Wigglesworth."

"Papin, my lord."

"Oh, I fear that with the introduction of your gentleman admirer we've passed beyond that, Wigglesworth. Go search out Brutus, discreetly please, if you will be so kind. Tell him Lady Alina is not to leave his sight until I return, nor should anyone be allowed to approach her."

"Immediately, my lord. But where are you going?"

"Hunting," Justin said shortly, as the nondescript man in the bad frock coat seemed to have noticed that he was no longer unnoticed and had begun sidling toward the gap between two of the caravans. Anxious to escape…or anxious to have Justin follow him? "Now, go."

Justin was on the other side of the grassy clearing and did not cut straight across it in some hurried pursuit sure to capture Alina's attention. Instead, he faded into the growing shadows between two caravans and then beyond them, into the trees.

Swiftly working his way parallel to the caravans, he circled around until he was deep in the
trees behind Luka's caravan, just in time to intercept the man in the frock coat. The man had been
walking backward, stepping carefully, a pistol in his
hand, certain pursuit, if it came, would come from
the camp. Which may have accounted for his sharp
intake of breath when he felt the tip of Justin's knife
pressing just beside his spine.

"Leaving so soon?" Justin asked conversation-
ally—in German. "But everyone is so happy. I understand there will be food later, and dancing. Oh,
yes, and you will oblige me by dropping that evil-
looking pistol. Now."

The man raised his arms, pistol still in hand, as
if to show that he was harmless, but still keeping his
back to Justin. "I don't know what you're saying, you
crazy Gypsy! Just go on and rob me. Nice fat purse
for you in my waistcoat. Go on, take it!"

Justin was surprised. He'd been expecting one
of the *Inhaber's* men. "You're English? Oh, and as
you didn't understand me, you will now greatly relieve my mind by dropping that evil-looking pistol.
There's a good fellow. Now turn around so I can get
a good look at you."

The man did as he was told. Justin always appre-
ciated cooperation, it made things so much easier.

The man's dark eyes widened with relief and no
small shock. "Lord Wilde? Is that you? Oh, thank

God. I only saw you the once, on the dock at Portsmouth. But it is you, isn't it? Please, I can explain."

Justin lightly turned the knife in his hand, so that they were both aware of its continued presence. "Really?" he drawled. "And I cannot tell you how much I am looking forward to that explanation. But first, you seem to have the advantage of me. Who are you?"

"Your pardon, my lord. My name is Phineas Battle," the man supplied helpfully, lowering his arms to his sides. "Late of His Majesty's army and for the moment employed by a person or persons who wish to remain—"

"Don't bother to finish with that drivel," Justin said, holding up his hand. "I think I'd rather guess in any case. You're not really sure who hired you, but you do have a fairly good suspicion it was someone important."

"I really couldn't say, sir. I have considered that possibility, but felt it prudent to keep my questions to myself. I was told that you are a very clever man. Yes, yes, exceedingly clever. And in disguise, no less. That was a man back there, wasn't it, all dressed up that way? I confess, I couldn't stop staring. But I am quite harmless, my lord, with orders to watch over the lady and yourself, without being detected, of course. You haven't made my mission at all easy for me. I'm not accustomed to such deviousness."

"Clearly. A thousand pardons, I'm sure," Justin

said, still trying to sort things out in his head. Battle had to be the Prince Regent's man. "You were sent to watch over us, you say? To what end?"

Battle, a man with the look of an underpaid clerk, frowned. "I beg your pardon, my lord?"

"To what purpose, Phineas," Justin repeated, as the question had seemed to take the man off guard, as might happen to someone forced to deviate from a prepared script. But that didn't make sense, not if the man was sent to observe without being detected. Did Justin have Wigglesworth's unusual attire to thank for discovering yet another twist in what was already a complicated plot? Or was he being led into some sort of trap?

"I was to report to…my employer. Your location and destination, my lord. That is all."

That did smack of something the Prince Regent would have ordered. Would Justin really dare to defy him, not come to London as ordered? Yes, Justin could understand Prinny's desire to know that information.

Or had he been supposed to discover Battle, so that the man could feed *him* information, perhaps deliver a threat? Also possible.

But wait.

Why this man? Why this sad excuse, this little clerk who was so obviously incompetent in the role of spy? And why wasn't he sweating, swallowing over and over again to ease his dry mouth? Justin was holding a knife on the little clerk, and the little clerk wasn't sweating.…

"Something niggles at the edges of my brain, Phineas. Why you? Why were you chosen for this mission? Exactly what did you *do* in His Majesty's army?"

"*Do,* sir?"

Justin maintained a casually interested expression. "It isn't a difficult question. Unless, of course, the answer proves troublesome."

"Not troublesome at all, my lord. I was merely a soldier. And perhaps not a very good one." Battle raised his arms slightly, and shrugged.

Justin cursed himself for a gullible idiot even as he dropped to the ground, rolling to his left and coming up with both Battle's pistol and the Spanish knife. He didn't bother aiming the pistol, as he was fairly certain it wasn't loaded, or else Battle would never have been so eager to put it in Justin's possession. Still, just to be safe, he flung the pistol into the trees.

His movements had been swift, fluid and took only two heartbeats before he was on his feet once more, but already Phineas Battle held a short, wicked-looking two-sided knife in each palm, probably lowered by some mechanism beneath the ill-fitting frock coat, activated when he shrugged his shoulders.

Battle was also in a crouch, moving his arms side

to side, the blades gleaming. "What was it, my lord, if I may ask? I was being so very helpful, letting you discover me, telling you just what you wanted to hear. What do I do wrong?"

As they began to circle each other, Justin kept his eyes on Battle's waist, the center of the man's body. No matter which way a man moved, the first indication was always at the waist; nobody moves feet or arms first, nothing is done without that telltale giveaway.

"You were too meek, Phineas, too eager to give up, give everything away. You volunteered too much, and overplayed your hand. It's always the little things. Now, as you're about to kill me anyway, don't you first want to regale me with how clever you really are?"

"Not particularly, no, as I've already ordered my dinner at the inn for seven o'clock, and I wouldn't wish to be late. My instructions were to follow you until you'd exterminated a certain foreign minister by the name of Novak."

"One wonders why you simply weren't hired for the job."

Battle smiled, even as the two men continued to circle each other, feel each other out. Neither had yet to attempt a single move with the knives, a mutual show of respect for the other's abilities. "I don't think the lady would have fancied me as her affianced husband, do you?"

"You know more than I would have suspected. How?"

"My employer's minion likes his gin and his ladies. Provide both, and a determined man can learn much that is necessary to keep himself alive. But we digress and, as you told me, I've already talked too much. Still, as you are a fellow assassin, I will make allowances. Indeed, I've often wished we could have met during the war, broken open a few bottles and talked. I thought there were perhaps some things I could learn from you, as I was told you were the master of our craft."

"You're about to learn if you were told correctly," Justin pointed out to him, adjusting his stance slightly, as Battle was a good five inches shorter than he. Whether his own height would prove an advantage or a disadvantage, he had still to find out.

"Ah, very droll, sir," Phineas said as Justin feinted with the knife and then quickly drew back once more. "In honor of your reputation, I will tell you this, because I know you want to hear it. I was here today only to keep you on point, as it were, remind you that you have a job of work still to do. My real assignment is, of course, to silence you after you'd dispatched your man to his greater reward."

"Of course. I should have seen that for myself." Justin began altering the configuration of their invisible circle, counting his sideways steps and his distance from a network of large, barely concealed tree roots hiding amid the long grass and fallen leaves. Carefully, he moved back a few inches after every dozen steps, so that Battle stepped slightly forward to keep their distance unchanged; each new maneuver bringing the track of the circle into closer proximity with the tree roots.

"Yes, yes, so now you understand. But we've finished talking, my lord. I thought you could teach me, but it seems that your skills have suffered since the war. Still, as we appear to be at an impasse and it is getting on toward dinnertime, and much as it will undoubtedly pain my employer, you really do have to die now."

"It would appear that one of us does," Justin said, having decided that although Battle had been carrying the pistol in his right hand, he was in reality, left-handed. Clever, clever boy, although if he routinely employed those little toys he was brandishing now, he was probably proficient with both hands. A fair fight could prove injurious, if not deadly. With Alina to protect, much as he no longer valued his own life, he could not die now.

Careful to only keep up the count in his head, and not betray himself by looking at the ground, Justin suddenly lunged forward clumsily with the knife, demonstrating a sad lack of expertise. The now overconfident Battle's instinctive reaction was to laugh and dance backward. His left foot landed awkwardly amid the web of tree roots. He lost his balance, and fell.

He looked up at Justin in real surprise, and perhaps even a little professional admiration, and then down at his chest, and the hilt of Justin's blade that protruded from it. And then he died.

Phineas Battle was laid to rest deep in the trees once it was fully dark, rolled into the grave dug by Brutus and then covered with dirt and leaves, until there was no indication that the ground had been disturbed.

"Poor Phineas," Justin told Brutus. "Some lessons can only be learned once, but by then it's too late."

CHAPTER ELEVEN

ALINA REMAINED WITH THE children and the women until the townspeople had drifted back to Farnham and the last cooking pot washed, the last Romany child tucked up in bed.

She had looked in on Luka earlier, but he was still asleep after his visit to the surgeon, and Wigglesworth was tending to him in any case. She'd asked where Justin could be, as she hadn't seen him in several hours. She'd been told that he and Brutus had taken the job of guarding the camp while the men played the instruments as their women danced for the townspeople, who expected this sort of entertainment.

She'd enjoyed her day, most especially her time spent with the children, and then the mothers. All of the Romany were by legend at least loosely related by blood, the sister of one of those Alina spoke to was married to the brother of her sister's husband, and three generations of this particular family traveled together in England as they did each year, before retiring to Wales for the winter. They had none of them been to the Continent in more than a generation, but they each held dear their memories of summers wandering France, winters camping on land surprisingly no more than twenty miles from Alina's childhood home.

Some of these exotic nomadic people had seen Rome, others had walked the streets of Toulouse... and many of their family had died in the wars against Bonaparte.

"Brutus, there you are," she called to the man as she took one last circuit around the camp on what was proving a fruitless search. "Have you perhaps seen my sketchbook? I thought I left it on one of the tables, but now I— *Oh, no!*"

She hiked up her skirts and took off in a panicked run as she saw Justin carrying her sketchbook toward her caravan, idly leafing through the pages as he walked along. She'd told herself she wouldn't speak to him until he came to her, but now she had no choice.

"Justin, wait! Stop! That's mine, don't look at it."

He turned to her, smiling, and held up the page he'd been looking at. "A *fish,* Alina? You shoved a fish in my mouth? Ah, and it's dated, as well, how wonderful. The day we met, isn't it? Clearly your first impression of me wasn't overwhelming positive."

"What a dreadful, wretched man you are!" She

reached for the sketchbook but he held it up over his head, and she wasn't about to be so undignified as to jump up and attempt to snag it from his fingers. Besides, it was far easier to ball up her fingers into a fist, and punch him in the stomach.

Laughing, pretending to be mortally wounded, he handed over her property. All except for one page, she noticed, one he had previously ripped from the sketchbook.

"What did you take? Justin? What did you take? I did not give you permission to take anything."

"Then, kitten, we're even, aren't we? I did not give you permission to sketch me."

Not only dreadful and wretched, but also much too pleased with himself. She turned over page after page, until she'd figured out what sketch he'd taken. She looked at him quizzically. "But…but that was a sketch of me, dressed in these clothes. It was only so that I'll always remember. What could you possibly want with that?"

He put his crooked finger beneath her chin and looked down into her face in the near darkness broken only by the nearby campfires and the full moon. "The same thing as you, albeit for different reasons. So that I'll always remember," he told her quietly. "It's getting late, and it has been a full day for everyone, one way or another. Let me walk you back to your caravan."

That was the last thing she wanted.

"I…I'm not in the least sleepy. Can't we take a walk? I barely saw you today, and you'll be gone in another few days. Besides, I wanted to tell you something important one of the women told me earlier. About *Inhaber* Novak."

"Ah, that dreary man again. The woman knows him?"

Alina began walking in the direction of the stream, as the Romany knew all of the streams and ponds, always camping near a supply of clean water. Justin had no choice but to follow if he wanted to hear what she had to tell him.

They had to proceed single file along the narrow path cut through the underbrush, so it was only after she'd dropped to her knees on the soft grass that he could either sit with her or stand there like some great looby, pretending he didn't want to sit beside her, which he would not like at all.

"This had better be good, kitten, because otherwise I'd have to think you have lured me out here for some nefarious purpose." But he smiled as he said the words, and she was of a mood to forgive him most any of his silliness, if she could only be alone with him.

"It's very tragic, Justin, and explains much of why the Romany don't want the *Inhaber* to have this land that is disputed, and even why they are so willing to help us."

"Luka paid them. It was all arranged."

"And the Romany never refuse an open hand holding gold or silver," Alina told him, arranging her skirts about her. She really did love this skirt, and wished her own clothing could be as adaptable to running, to twirling about as she'd done during the dancing (even though she wasn't very adept at it), and to sitting on a stream bank with a man she hoped with all her heart would soon be kissing her. "They are only romantic to us, Justin. In truth, they are an exceedingly practical people. You have to be, I suppose, when you are continuously outlawed and looked upon as little more than animals."

"Your own Romany blood is boiling?"

"I suppose so, yes. If the land that belonged to my father's family through his mother is really mine to give where I will, then I will give it to these people."

"Don't, kitten," Justin warned her, taking her hand. "From what I've managed to learn from Luka, the land covers only a few square miles, and most of it is uninhabitable in any case. You don't want your new friends dying over it. Because, *Inhaber* or no, you alive or dead, Francis is not going to allow the Romany even an inch-wide foothold in what he sees as his country, his kingdom. He'll find some excuse to brand anyone who tries to live there as thieves and traitors, and the land will be forfeit."

"I know you've told me that," she said, prepared to argue. "But what else can I do?"

"Kings don't like to lose, kitten, and they never do so gracefully, so it will be up to you to be graceful for him. Once the *Inhaber* has been dispatched, you will write a letter to Francis, gifting him with the land you were told is yours, in thanks for having shown you such kindness in the past. Or some such drivel. That's the only way I can know you're safe here in England."

"But these people! I would be betraying them."

Justin reached out and stroked her cheek. "You aren't listening. If any of them try to go back there, they'll die. I just made the same argument with Luka and Loiza, and they agree. In fact, Loiza had already come to that conclusion on his own. They want Novak dead for quite another reason. That's why they're helping us."

"Oh," Alina was crestfallen, on more than one count. She was not going to be able to see herself as some bountiful mistress, bestowing great gifts on her subjects. And the most important thing she was going to tell Justin was something he already knew. "Then I suppose I have nothing else to tell you."

"If you were going to tell me that the *Inhaber* raised himself a small army of Romany in order to look loyal to the king, and then sent them off to fight in France—women and children naturally following after their men—and then left them there alone and without provisions, to be slaughtered by the French?

Then no, you have nothing new to tell me. But I do have something to tell you."

"You're not leaving? You found a way to stay? No, don't say anything. I see your answer in your eyes." She turned her head away and folded her hands in her lap. "Tell me what you want to tell me."

"I know why Francis wants *Inhaber* Novak dead."

She turned her head quickly, to look at him. "It's not because of the land?"

"No. That was convenient. Loiza is a very intelligent man. He knew when he first heard the story of the disputed land that it was something that was not new to anyone. Francis could take the land at anytime. Your king wants Novak dead because he is powerful, and because he knows things about the king that would not endear him to his allies. Allies such as my own government."

Alina listened as Justin explained what had gone on at the Congress of Vienna, which he had attended in part himself. The allies had carved up what remained of the Holy Roman Empire, dubbed the new collection the German Confederation, and Francis, who most coveted his title of Holy Roman Emperor was now, to his chagrin, no more than Francis of Austria.

"Quite a comedown from Emperor, you'll agree," Justin said as Alina listened intently. "So, kings being kings, your Francis smiled and agreed and feted the tsar and Prussia's Frederick and all the others, all the while negotiating a secret treaty with King Louis of France. There could be another war, kitten, or at least a coup that topples Francis, if anyone were to know about this."

"But…but what does the *Inhaber* have to do with anything?"

"Novak was Francis's secret emissary to King Louis. That was when Francis trusted him. He trusts him no longer, obviously, and envisions a world without the man in it. But not by his hand, and not inside his country. Let England grovel and apologize for the actions of the rogue Baron Wilde, that terrible murderer, while Francis declares a month of national mourning for the great *Inhaber* Novak. I would give most anything to be able to stand face-to-face with Prinny and explain all of this to him, spell it out so that even that imbecile could understand, but that isn't going to happen."

"But when you kill the *Inhaber,* you'll have made terrible trouble for England, yes?"

"I'm not going to kill the man. I've killed enough men. Let Francis deal with Francis's problems, and let the Prince Regent have to explain away why he failed and yet should still be allowed to retain any gold your king undoubtedly paid him."

"But—but if you don't kill him, he will kill me."

"Not once he knows what I know. He'll forget about you and the disputed land entirely."

Alina made a face. "Well, that's very nice, but you're saying I'm not important. Not at all?"

"Rather lowering, isn't it? To be nothing but a tool in the hands of someone else, someone who sees a way to use you to his own ends. But you're not safe yet, Alina. Not until I can meet with Novak and get him to listen to reason. None of which is a foregone conclusion."

"You will be careful, won't you?"

"I always try to be, yes."

"Your Prince Regent is going to have even more reason to hate you if you spare the *Inhaber,* isn't he?"

"He should never have attempted political intrigue, or any other kind, for that matter. He isn't very good at it. The buffoon can't even manage his own wife. But he may assuage his injured sensibilities by remembering the fifty thousand pounds he coerced from me."

Alina put her hand on his forearm. "And allow you to stay in England?"

"At the rate I've been burning bridges these past days? No, that isn't possible."

"Let me go with you, Justin. There is less for me here in England than there is even for you. Why can't I go with you? You kiss me as if you are not repulsed by me, and you know that I…care."

"It's because *I* care…" His voice trailed off, and he turned to look out across the stream and the path of moonlight that led to the other shore. "While you were sketching the children this afternoon, Alina, I killed a man."

She couldn't hold back the gasp of surprise and shock. But how? How could he still look the same as he'd done earlier? How did you kill a man, and then continue on as if nothing had happened? "That's not true. You're lying to me, trying to frighten me."

His voice sounded dull, without emotion, as he answered her. "I dispatched him as if he were an annoying fly, or a cockroach under my foot. He was alive, now he's dead. Do I feel remorse? No, I don't. Nor do I feel joy or shame, or justified in any way. I lost some essential part of what we need inside us to be truly human, and I lost it a long time ago. There's no bringing it back, and I won't subject you to what's left of me. You have your whole life ahead of you, Alina. Mine is behind me, as what happened today proved to me yet again."

Alina had so many questions, but none of them were important. If Justin had killed a man, he'd had a good reason. If this was blind faith in a man she barely knew, then so be it. She could only do what her heart told her was right, as her mother had done before her, giving up her family, her home, her country, for the man she loved. Surely she could sacrifice a little pride.

She blinked back tears and felt a new determination overtaking her. She went up on her knees and moved slightly behind Justin to wrap her arms around him, rest her cheek against his shoulder. He said he felt nothing, but she didn't believe him. No matter why he'd killed, he had to be feeling something. He was vulnerable tonight, or else he wouldn't have told her anything at all.

He needed her. She was sure of it.

"If not a lifetime, then just this one night? Please. Tonight we don't have to be who we are, or even who we think we are…or aren't. I can simply be your Magdaléna, and you my Markos. Two simple people, living a simple life, one with no complications. Can't we pretend, just for tonight?"

He put up his hands, touching hers. "Alina, don't do this.…"

She would say it, all of it, now. While he was still here.

"Don't do what, Justin? Don't wonder what it would be like to lie in your arms? Don't yearn to have you touch me again? Don't long to kiss you, and hold you, and find out if you can fill this aching void inside of me I didn't know existed until you came into my life? Maybe you don't feel what I feel, or maybe you're lying to me, and to yourself. Maybe you're afraid that if you touch me, really touch me, you won't be able to leave me.

"Are we both to spend the rest of our lives not

knowing if those lives could have been different, better? You say you have no life, Justin. Or is it that you're afraid of life? Is it the chance of feeling again that's so frightening to you? If I'm not afraid, then how can you—"

Smothering a curse, he pulled her forward onto his lap and crushed his mouth to hers, a move meant to silence her, she supposed. She believed she could taste the desperation in his kiss as his hands moved over her roughly, pushing the blouse from her shoulder, digging his fingertips into her soft flesh.

She clung to him as he ravaged her mouth, kissing her half in demand, half in supplication. She grabbed at his jaw, holding him still, and returned his passion with some of her own, biting his lower lip until she could taste blood and then plunging her tongue inside his mouth to join with his, duel with his.

His hand found her bare breast beneath the thin lawn of her blouse, and she cried out when he pinched her taut nipple, sending sharp spikes of desire down her body and to the heated ache between her legs.

She couldn't be still, couldn't have enough of him. In desperation she grabbed at her skirts and struggled to hike up the fullness of heavy fabric and the cotton slips beneath, taking his hand and pressing it to her bare thigh.

She whimpered against his mouth as he reached up and roughly tore her last undergarment from her.

She grabbed onto his shirtfront and raised her hips instinctively, the tightening between her thighs so pleasurable, simply in the anticipation of his touch. She knew what he wanted, because she wanted it, as well.

She couldn't know all that he knew; the unknown was still ahead of her, but she wasn't frightened. She welcomed it, all but begged for it. She spread her legs as wide as she could, her heels digging into the soft grass as she raised herself to him again. *Touch, touch, touch. Take what's there for you, take it all, give back what you can. I'm here for you. Touch me. Love me....*

Still with his mouth on hers, Justin ground his hand against her in an intimacy she encouraged, gasping with unexpected pleasure as he then stroked her, learning her even as she learned from him. She felt herself rising to some precipice, the same one she had fallen off the other night, only to be left wanting.

More. The word repeated itself inside her head. *There has to be more.*

She put her hand flat against his chest and pushed with all of her might, freeing herself from his grasp and quickly rising to her feet.

"Alina. Dear God, I've hurt you. I must be out of my mind."

She couldn't speak, had no words to say what she needed to say. Her hands went to the long scarf tied about her waist, her fingers fumbling to undo the clever knot. The scarf had barely fallen to the ground before she was pulling the loose blouse up and over her head, tossing it aside as she reached for the buttons at her waistband.

There was no shame, no thought of maidenly reserve as the skirt and petticoats puddled at her feet and she was entirely naked, standing there in the moonlight, offering herself to this man.

Still unable to speak, she took his hands and pulled him to his knees along with her. Her breath coming fast and hard, she tugged his shirt free from his waistband, pushing back the material so that the buttons strained in their moorings. She felt a frustration so great she nearly screamed with it.

"Please," she managed at last, her mouth close to his. "I want this for you, too. I'm not afraid, Justin. And I want no half measures. If we're to be together only this once, then let it be completely. Don't you need me? I need you, Justin. I need you in ways I still don't even understand. Help me. Let me help you…"

His clothing melted away somehow and she was now free to touch him, learn him as he was learning her. The ripple of his muscles told her when she was pleasing him, and that pleasure came back to her twofold.

"Two people," he whispered as he took hold of her

shoulders, easing her back onto her petticoats and following her down. "We're just two people…"

His kisses were deep, and drugging. His hands touched her in ways not possible before, with an intimacy that bordered on worship. He was becoming lost in her, and that's what she wanted for him.

He took her hand and guided it down between her legs as he whispered into her ear. "Feel what I feel, Alina…touch what I touch. That's your heat, that's your agony, there lies your white-hot center. All the pleasure, all the longing. And just when you think you can't bear the pleasure anymore, that's when your body longs for mine. Inside you. Deep inside you. There. Right there. That's it, sweetheart. Touch yourself. Feel the silk of you."

"Justin…"

"I'm going to hurt you, kitten. I don't want to, but I am. But what you want lies beyond the now, what you're feeling now. What lies beyond is why we were created. God's joke is that you should feel pain this first time, and that I'd rather die ten deaths than hurt you."

Alina's breath caught on a sob. She tugged her hand free of his and attempted to pull him up and over her body. "I'm not frightened. Don't be frightened for me. Please."

He kissed her, held that perfect kiss as he moved between her legs. When the pain came she barely felt it, and it was swiftly gone, to be replaced by a new fullness that, of all things, had her smiling against his mouth.

And then he began to move, his rhythm slow, careful, even as his short hard breaths matched her own, so that she bit at his shoulder in a new and different frustration, urging him on, her fingernails digging into his back. What she didn't know, her body did, and her body knew there was even more. Without conscious thought, she raised her legs and clamped them around his back, taking him deeper, wanting him even deeper inside her. "We're not two people anymore, Justin, we're one. Don't hurt for me...I'm not afraid..."

He kissed her again and then pushed himself up on his palms, looking down into her face, searching for some lie in her words, so that she reached up and cupped his cheeks in her hands.

He began to move more purposefully, his thrusts deeper, growing faster, with more of his strength behind them. His gaze locked with hers, he ground against her, until her eyes widened and her breath caught and what he had called her "white-hot center" pulsed in a glorious ecstasy that only increased as she felt his own body do the same. On and on and on, until he collapsed against her and there was nothing but the night and the moon and their mingled breathing.

And the tears that mingled on their cheeks.

Because it had been so right. Because it had been so good.

Because they might neither of them ever feel this way again.

JUSTIN STAYED THE NIGHT in Sandhurst after he'd retrieved the *Inhaber*'s answering letter from his friend at their arranged meeting place, for no good reason other than he knew he should stay away from the Romany camp...and Alina.

Briefly, he debated with himself the wisdom of traveling on to London, finding some way to confront the Prince Regent, but he knew that for what it was: a dangerous as well as fruitless enterprise. Even if he could convince the royal buffoon of what he knew, there would be no forgiveness. He'd threatened the man's life, and then publicly announced that he'd pocketed fifty thousand pounds in return for a worthless pardon. By now everyone in Mayfair knew about it, and those in the countryside, at their estates, were reading letters from their friends, recounting Prinny's latest scandal.

No. There was no possible way he could remain in England. As he'd told Alina as he'd left her outside her caravan, after they'd shared one last kiss, he had burned too many bridges.

And now he had committed the worst crime of all. He'd stolen Alina's virginity. He could spend hours over the bottles he'd taken with him to his small room at the run-down inn where he'd met with Richard, telling himself that he'd been temporarily out of his head. That the events of the day and the encounter with Phineas Battle had affected him more than he would ever allow anyone to know. That he'd needed a pair of warm arms around him, had desperately needed to be reminded that a part of him at least was still alive, was still capable of feeling. That he wasn't a cold-blooded murderer, but only a man doing what he had to do, and that maybe, just maybe, he deserved some happiness.

But in the morning, when the sun rose and his head throbbed and his mouth tasted as if something foul had died there, when the nightmare that woke him to feel his heart pounding so fast he thought he might die banished the memory of Erich's face, he saw the truth. He deserved nothing but the hell he had made of his life.

He washed and dressed with some care, knowing Wigglesworth would not approve of even his best efforts, but at least he was once again clean-shaven and in his own clothes. He paid his bill and ventured out into the streets, a London gentleman on the stroll, swinging his cane idly as he sought out his breakfast and took in his surroundings, pausing to admire the facade of one of the many churches, lingering over a glass of wine at a quaint outdoor café. And all the time watching, assuring himself he wasn't being followed.

He was back to playing the game he'd played for eight long years. And he hated it. Had he ever walked a street without having a care for his back? Had he ever smiled without first calculating the effect of that smile? Had he ever in the last long eight years been free to simply *be?*

Two people, just two people...

Enough! He'd detected nobody following him, and if someone did, well, he'd take care of that annoyance somewhere along the road. He returned to the inn and ordered his bay saddled for the ride to Basingstoke. There he would meet Alina and Luka, Wigglesworth and Brutus. There he would answer Lucas Paine's questions with careful lies and flatter the Lady Nicole into sharing something of her wardrobe with Alina before sending her on to Malvern Hall, another two full days' travel away.

He'd promise to join her there, once his business with the *Inhaber* was completed.

That would be another lie, the last he would tell her. Or was it to be the last he would tell himself? Because from the first moment she'd looked into his eyes, she'd found a part of him he'd thought long ago gone, and now she'd given him not only her body, but her trust, her belief that he was somehow better than he knew himself to be.

Was it his past that kept him away from all she offered to him? Or was it his fear that he could never be what she believed him to be?

How many shadows did it take to submerge a soul into eternal darkness, with no hope of redemption?

CHAPTER TWELVE

"Nicole, darling, precisely what is it you think you're doing?"

Alina bit back a giggle as she watched Lucas Paine, Marquess of Basingstoke, attempt to extricate his wife from the caravan sitting in the circular drive in front of a most spectacularly enormous estate home. "Delicious as the view is from where I'm standing, I don't think backing out is the proper way to exit one of these things."

"I was only taking one last look," his wife explained reasonably once he'd taken hold of her at the waist and lifted her to the ground. "It's amazing, Lucas. There's an entire *world* inside there, and it all fits together in a space half the size of my dressing room. Alina, explain to me how three of you slept in there."

"I'm afraid the answer is, not very comfortably. My dresser snores with a dedication that could probably mow down an entire forest. But the drivers have to leave now, Nicole, to return to their camp. Stefan?"

The young Romany, who'd been pretending not to look at the marchioness even as he devoured her with his eyes, stepped forward and bowed to Alina.

"Oh, for goodness' sake," she said, feeling annoyed rather than flattered. "We've been on the road for days. It's ridiculous for you to begin bowing now."

"Yes, my lady," Stefan responded, bowing yet again. "And we visited the moonlight. I will forever treasure that moment."

"You'd be better forgetting it," Alina said, feeling hot color run into her cheeks.

"But how can I, my lady? We were there, you and I, and—"

"I will count to three, Stefan, and you will be up on the box, singing to your oxen. Understood?"

Stefan shot one more look at the marchioness, touched his fingers to the gold hoop in his ear and then did as Alina said.

"You and that near-god, in the moonlight?" Nicole slipped her arm through Alina's. "You do realize that I won't rest until I hear the remainder of that story."

"It wasn't what you think," Alina said quickly. "It was…it was more in the nature of an experiment."

Nicole's eyes positively twinkled in her beautiful face. "Wait, don't say anything else until we're inside and I've fetched Lydia from wherever she is. Then you can tell us both about this…experiment. And be prepared for questions, as I will insist on hearing all of the details."

The caravan moved off, Stefan singing to his oxen in a clear baritone. His lordship, clearly having intercepted and understood a look from his wife, said something about a pressing meeting with his estate manager and took himself off as Nicole dragged Alina back inside the house.

Nicole told her to wait in the main salon, instructed one of the footmen to have tea and cakes served in the next ten minutes, and then took off up the stairs more in the way of a carefree young girl than a lofty marchioness.

This left Alina free to wander into the lovely blue-and-white room and sit herself down rather primly on one of the soft couches arranged in a grouping in front of one of the three massive fireplaces.

Ever since their arrival at Basingstoke the previous evening, Alina had felt as if she'd been dropped headfirst into a whirlwind. Her aunt Mimi had told her that the English were a cold and haughty people, and that she must be on her best behavior at all times or else she would reflect badly on everyone from King Francis himself down to the lowliest scullery maid in his palace.

And yet, within an hour of her arrival, Alina had found herself luxuriating in a hot bath attended to by not only the marchioness but also her sister, the Duchess of Malvern. A duchess! Alina had never been naked in front of anyone save Tatiana…and Justin, of course…and suddenly she was submerged to her shoulders in lovely scented bubbles while Lady Nicole twirled about the room wearing her Romany clothes and the duchess reclined on a chaise, daintily eating grapes.

Alina learned that the women were not only sisters, but twins, and that they were both newly married. Yet, if she hadn't been told, she would never have believed the two were even distantly related.

Nicole was the most gloriously different and exciting creature, both alive and lively. Her hair was black, as was Alina's, but her eyes were not the drab golden-brown of Alina's, but nearly violet in color, and fringed with long dark lashes that made the violet all the more startlingly beautiful. Her skin was softly kissed by the sun, and she possessed the most delightful dusting of freckles across her nose and cheeks. She looked like mischief, and the Romany clothing suited her perfectly.

By contrast, the duchess was a blonde, with huge, innocent-looking blue eyes and a smile that was warm, welcoming, yet slightly reserved. She moved with the sort of easy grace that cannot be learned; you had to be born with it, Alina was sure. And when she looked at her husband, the duke, she became probably the most stunningly lovely woman Alina had ever seen.

Ah, yes, the duke. Tanner Blake, Duke of Malvern,

and the man to whom Justin was entrusting her: her life, her newly acquired estate and fortune, even her town house in London. Justin had seemed to have it all perfectly worked out, except that the duke was not at Malvern. He was here, at Basingstoke.

Justin would probably be unhappy about that, when he learned of it.

It might be perverse of her, but as she'd been having her life controlled by the man from the moment she'd first set foot in England, she believed she'd rather enjoy his reaction once he deigned to arrive from wherever it was he'd disappeared to this time.

Once Tatiana had wrapped her in a wondrously thick white robe and she had been settled in front of the fire, Alina had dismissed her maid-cum-companion with the information that she would manage brushing her own hair and that the woman should retire for some much-needed rest in a real bed.

She'd taken the silver-backed brushes from the woman only to have them snatched away by Nicole, who'd gone down on her knees behind her and begun drawing the brushes through her damp hair, exclaiming at the hints of red and gold picked out in the firelight.

"Tell us more about your adventure," Nicole had suggested as Alina closed her eyes, luxuriating in the warmth of the fire and the gentle strokes of the brush, so unlike the rough tugging that was all Tatiana seemed able to manage. "Lucas only told me Justin's letter to him said we're to watch over you until you can leave for Malvern, which of course you can't, not with Lydia and Tanner here. And Charlotte's letter, which arrived by post this morning, only told me that I was to treat you kindly because you will have had a difficult journey. Dearest Charlotte—she was once in charge of us, you know. It's so difficult for her to remember that I'm a grown woman now. She keeps expecting me to do something outrageous, heaven only knows why."

Lydia had nearly choked on a grape, but then recovered quickly.

"We'll ignore her as well, won't we? I really don't know Justin Wilde, except for what my sister has told me, and all she has told me is that he dresses well and can be very witty when he thinks anyone might see more in him than he would like, whatever that means. Is he really such a rogue?"

For the next hour, Alina had answered the twins' questions, knowing she was being gently interrogated, but not really minding, as she was talking about Justin. If he couldn't be here with her, talking about him seemed the next best thing and kept her from worrying about him overmuch. After all, he said he'd meet her here, and Wigglesworth had assured her that the baron always kept his promises.

Besides, he wouldn't leave her now. He simply couldn't. So she'd regaled them with her adventures,

making Nicole laugh as she recounted her ignomini-
ous encounter with a mud puddle, and delighting in
Lydia's sympathetic noises and smothered giggles as
she described Wigglesworth in all of his womanly
garb.

An adventure. That's how she described all that
had happened to her. A grand adventure. She did
not mention Justin other than to inform them that
he was her betrothed, and that he was off doing
something somewhere, but would surely explain everything when he arrived. She most certainly didn't
tell them about the night beside the stream, or his
revelation that he had been killing people.

Except that Lucas and Tanner seemed somehow to
know that, and at breakfast this morning, whenever
the ladies' conversation drifted toward the absent
baron, the two men had gently steered it back to
safer territory.

So they knew. Perhaps not what was occurring
at that moment, but they knew Justin. They knew a
man whose history was still much of a mystery to
her, and they seemed to sense that whatever Justin
was about now, it wasn't the stuff of friendly meal-
time conversation.

*I killed a man this afternoon. He was alive, and
now he's dead.*

"Lydia, don't dawdle, you know you want to hear
this as much as I."

Alina shook herself back to the present, watching

as the sisters entered the main salon, Nicole's violet eyes alive with mischief, Lydia looking more sedate, almost indulgent of her twin's enthusiasm. Alina felt a momentary pang that she had been denied siblings, most especially a sister. How wonderful it must be to have someone always there to confide in when the need arose, someone who understood you better than anyone else and who had only love for you, as you did for her.

"You didn't see him, Lydia," Nicole was saying, "so I'll describe him for you. He was tall, enormously tall, or perhaps he just seemed that way because of how he held himself so erect. Oh, I don't know how to describe it."

"Stefan poses like a man looking in a mirror, and liking very much what he sees," Alina supplied helpfully.

"Yes! That's it exactly. You know, now that I think about it, he's probably fairly insufferable. Was he insufferable, Alina?"

"I think I prefer the word *oblivious*—to anyone and anything other than himself. But I used him badly, I'm afraid."

By the time she was done recounting what had happened at the stream, and even admitting why she had approached Stefan in the first place, Nicole was wiping her streaming eyes and Lydia was rubbing her palms together as if they itched.

But then Lydia said quietly, "You're in love with

him, aren't you? The baron. Does he know?" And even Nicole's smile faded.

The room became very quiet.

Alina had been alone for so long. And even when her mother had been alive, she had been sickly and often kept to herself, as if to shield her daughter from any unpleasantness. With her father off to war, they had remained in the country, fairly isolated. Alina had learned to amuse herself, in daydreams mostly, probably remaining young longer than other girls her age, many of whom had been married at sixteen and seventeen and had gone on to have babies of their own while Alina had been left to those daydreams... and been taught to shoot and to throw a knife so that the hilt didn't hit the target first, because her father didn't know anything else to teach her. But if, as she'd felt herself changing, the world around her looking different to her, if she'd had any questions for her mother they still hadn't been the sort of questions she would have had for her now.

She hadn't anyone to consult when Justin barged into her daydream and made the world so very real so very suddenly. But that wasn't his fault.

She'd bungled everything with him, she knew that. She'd been young and gauche and most likely much too honest. Instead of helping him, she'd probably only compounded his problems.

She needed to stop lying to everyone—and to herself. Alina looked down at her hands, unsurprised to see that she'd entwined her fingers together and that her knuckles had turned quite white. "It doesn't matter. He's leaving England in a few days, for America. Because, you understand, he has burned too many bridges and his life is over and there's no place for me in what's left of it."

And then she cried…and told these two warm and wonderful women who could have been her sisters everything that was in her heart.

THERE WAS NOTHING IN the world to compare with the English countryside. Justin had traveled through Europe, its towns, its cities. He'd seen grape vine-yards and snow-topped mountains and lush plains planted with wheat and fed by wide blue rivers. He'd sipped tsipouro at a small café in Athens while look-ing out over the Aegean Sea, walked the same streets once trod by Julius Caesar and his legions, ridden in a dogsled toward the colorful spires of St. Basil's in Moscow, and visited the royal mounds of Gamla Uppsala in Sweden.

But nothing he had seen or experienced could take the place of the sight of his most neat and or-derly England. The carefully manicured fields, the hedgerows and stone walls that divided them and yet at the same time bound them all together. The church spires always visible in the distance. The ruins, the manor houses, the quaint villages, the thatch-roofed farmhouses, the fat cows in the meadows, the rosy-cheeked children laughing on the village green. Even the rain; the rain was different in England.

It was time he was truthful, if only to himself.

This was his country. His home. It wasn't always right, its leaders not always wise, its fights not always fair or justified. There was poverty, there was greed. But there was also good. So very much *good*. England. Always to endure.

Justin reined in his mount at the crest of a hill overlooking Basingstoke, where Alina waited for him. He wondered what she'd thought when she'd caught her first glimpse of this, one of the premier estates in Hampshire, larger even than Ashurst Hall. She'd probably been impressed; God knows he'd been when he'd caught his first sight of it through the trees.

His own Hampshire estate was only half the size, but Justin believed its setting was equally fine, and that if anyone thought they required more than twenty bedrooms, then that person lived a life much different from his own.

Alina would never see his Hampshire estate, the one he'd carried a picture of in his heart for the past eight years. He couldn't allow himself to see her there, or even to imagine her there, especially if the Prince Regent found some way to confiscate the property that had been in the Wilde family since the fifteen hundreds. But she'd be fine with his town house, and with the much smaller estate near Malvern, in Worcestershire.

He'd never see her reaction to either of those places, either. He'd never watch, his pride in her absolute, as she charmed the *ton* with her wit and beauty, her wonderfully wise innocence. He'd never waltz with her in the candlelight, playfully hand her the reins as they drove through Hyde Park. Because he'd be a world away from her.

And it was all his fault.

Why, for only the second time in his life, had he acted without a single thought to the consequences?

His first thoughtless action had been to respond in anger when the surgeon in attendance had shouted out *he turns early* the day Robbie Farber's insane action had robbed him of his life and Justin of his country.

Why, having had eight long years to reflect on the danger of choosing his battles poorly, had he done what he'd done? What maggot had got into his brain so that he'd confronted the Prince Regent —for the love of God, threatened to strangle the miserable excuse for royalty where he stood?

But he already knew the answer. Alina. He'd acted in some misguided idea he was safeguarding her, and with no thought to himself.

No, that wasn't completely true. He'd also been angry—incensed!—that the Prince Regent had inadvertently shown him a future, and then taken it away by pairing him with the niece of the man he'd killed.

He could only hope that he'd put enough fear into the Prince Regent that he now regretted his insane plot that could include Alina's death at the hands of *Inhaber* Novak. Justin had seen the confusion in the man's eyes when he'd pushed at him; clearly he hadn't thought all the way through the thing, past the part where he would no longer be bothered with one Baron Justin Wilde. It was always those who had never killed, never seen a battlefield, never felt their own life in danger, who plotted most with the lives of others, blithely believing in that most terrible of axioms: the end justifies the means.

And yet. And yet.

And yet there was no way to erase what had been done. No way to change the past. No way to deal with this damn *Inhaber*. No way to assuage the Prince Regent. No way to remain in England.

No way to ever see Alina smiling up at him as he gently laid her down on the ancestral bed of the Wildes and, together, they set the course for their future. Love. Children. A lifetime together...

"Are you planning on spending the day here? I admit this aspect is one of my favorites, but I believe there's someone down there, waiting for you. God only knows why—you look like hell. Tanner, I barely remember Justin from our salad days in London, so you be the judge. He looks like hell, yes?"

Justin turned about in his saddle to see Lucas Paine walking his mount toward him, followed closely by— "Tanner? What in bloody blazes are you doing here?"

"Hear that, Lucas? I told you that's what he'd say," the Duke of Malvern said as the three men shook hands. "Not so much as a single hello, just what in hell am I doing here. You're becoming damned predictable, Justin. Although threatening the life of our future king? I wouldn't have won any wagers betting against that one as being too mad even for you."

Justin looked at his smiling friend in complete amazement. "How...?"

"How could I have known?" Tanner Blake removed his curly brimmed beaver to run a gloved hand through his dark blond hair. "How could I not? It's all over Mayfair. That, and the fact that Prinny coerced fifty thousand pounds from you to secure that pardon you wanted so badly and labored so diligently to deserve—I seem to have been indiscreet there, telling all who would listen how well you'd served the Crown. Difficult as it is to fathom, as you're no longer the easiest fellow to get along with, it would seem that the sympathies of the *ton* are firmly with you, and our Prince Regent has taken to his bed, to be bled by his leeches and fretted over by his latest aged *cherie amour.*"

Justin's hands tightened so on the reins that the bay began to dance sideways in protest. Because, even though it was his life they were talking about, all he really wanted to know was how Alina was, was she all right, happy. Had she asked about him, cursed him; was she waiting for him. "That…that doesn't seem possible."

"It's London, Justin," Lucas Paine said as the three headed their horses toward the estate house. "Anything is possible, and the more absurd that anything is, the more possible it becomes. Hell, man, the populace tosses eggs at Prinny's coach when he dares to go abroad. You were only a little more… direct in your protest. But he's not yet forgiven, isn't that right, Tanner?"

"Far from it. Not since the Austrian government has lodged a formal protest with our government over the unprovoked murder of three of its citizens at the hands of one Baron Wilde. Oh, and there is supposedly a witness, although he keeps babbling about a giant more than he does about you. Would you happen to know anything about that, Justin?"

"They were sent to kill Alina," Justin protested, and then shook his head. "But you're right. I didn't have to dispatch them. I could just as easily have disabled them. I was…making a statement." *Mine.*

Do what you want to me, but this is what happens when you touch what is mine.

"You were making a mess more of mess," Lucas Paine said with the certainty that his most recent guest wouldn't kill him on his own property, with his brother-in-law as witness. "Although I don't blame you. They'd already made one failed attempt on her life while you were busier in London than Puss in Boots, frightening the piss out of Prinny. Somebody had to pay for that."

"I suppose so, Lucas," Tanner agreed as they rode three abreast along the wide gravel drive toward the front doors. "Then again, diplomacy has never been Justin's strong point. And we'd have to consider his cloak-and-dagger years for the Crown. War changes a man, God knows I know that. Perhaps he saw the elimination of those men as nothing more than expediency, reducing the number of the enemy, and nothing out of the ordinary for him. It's understandable."

"All right, we'll give him the three men. But what about the colonel-in-chief, this Novak fellow who seems involved somehow?"

Justin sat forward in the saddle and looked across at the two men. He really needed to begin paying attention. "Yes, what does he do about the *Inhaber* Novak? Pray do continue your discussion, and don't consider me in the slightest. Why, I might not even be here."

Tanner grinned at him. "Yes, I'd already noticed that your mind seems elsewhere. But good God, Justin, you should have heard us before you got here. I felt like an old biddy full of gossip and in a fever to tell somebody what I knew as I raced here from London, thanks to a letter from Charlotte telling me you'd been to Ashurst Hall, and another from Lucas here, telling me where you were heading. It's a good thing Lydia was already in residence, visiting her sister, or she would have missed all the fun, and we all know she's fond of you, Lord only knows why. By the way, the ladies are, however, all out of charity with you at the moment. As your friend, I thought I should warn you."

They dismounted as three footmen hastened to take the reins of their horses. "The ladies? If I were to count noses on these ladies," Justin inquired carefully, thinking of Alina, "how many noses would I be counting?" *Other than Alina's.* God, what a mess he'd made!

"Three. Oh, wait. Four?" Tanner laughed. "Do we include your man Wigglesworth in that? It seems that some jokester in the Romany camp decided it would be great good fun to hide his usual clothing, so that he arrived here in his incognito-ness, as he kept indignantly informing anyone who was listening rather than simply being doubled over in laughter. The skirts, and most especially the bows in his wig, didn't help his case, let me tell you."

Justin wanted to be where he wasn't, and he wasn't inside Basingstoke, hunting down Alina. But the game must be played. "He has to be devastated, and a devastated Wigglesworth, gentlemen, can be worse than a toothache. I'm tempted to call back my horse and ride on. Where is he, Lucas?"

"One of the Gyp—pardon me. One of the Romany brought the clothing early this morning, all brushed and pressed and ghastly. It seems your man Brutus paid a small visit to the camp last night. I believe his powers of persuasion saved the day. At any rate, I imagine he's in your assigned rooms, once more properly overdressed and breathlessly awaiting your arrival. Shall we get back to counting noses?"

Justin's head was spinning. He was in no shape to confront Alina. He looked as if he'd been dragged through one of the hedgerows backward. More importantly, he wasn't in control of himself. For the first time in too many years, he was worried that he had something to lose...and even more worried that he might already have lost it.

And Tanner knew it. Not Lucas, who couldn't know that he was on the very edge of tossing aside whatever sangfroid he'd always prided himself on possessing. But Tanner knew. He had to get away from them, regroup. Only then could he see Alina again.

It also wasn't lost on him that this singular woman he hadn't known existed until a few short days ago had the power to reduce him to a quivering mass of nerves and apprehension....

He looked at the open doors to the house and very deliberately shrugged his shoulders. "I imagine I'll be able to work that out for myself when we meet for dinner. For now, I've barely slept in days. Would it be cowardly of me to postpone meeting the ladies until I've slept, had a bath and perhaps some food that doesn't move around on the plate of its own accord?"

"What do you say, Tanner?" the marquess asked in mock seriousness. "Shall I agree to harbor this dastardly fugitive?"

"He did make a cake out of Prinny. There's that in his favor," Tanner pointed out. "Although I'd still like to hear more about this Novak fellow and why Justin's been racing about the countryside, gleefully dispatching his attendants. We can't seem to figure that one out, can we?"

"Oh, the devil with the both of you merry imbeciles," Justin declared, climbing the front steps two at a time and striding into the entrance hall. "I think I'd rather face your wives. But not until I've had some damned sleep. Wigglesworth! Show yourself, man, I'm in need of a bed!"

Justin Wilde had relied on himself for so many years. He'd operated in the shadows of life, shunning his friends, protecting them from the man he'd become. He'd turned to Rafe and Tanner and Lucas only because he had no choice; he'd needed a safe place for Alina. Not for himself, for her.

But somehow Alina had opened that door he'd so firmly shut the day he'd fled England and the hangman. Now the door seemed easier to open to others. Because of her. Because she took him on faith, took him on trust, and believed she saw something still good inside him long after he'd thought he'd traveled beyond caring what anyone thought of him.

The laughter of his old friend and his new friend followed Justin up the curving staircase and, strangely, his step felt lighter than it had done in days. Was there hope? Was there really a way out of this damnable mess he'd help create?

And where the devil was Alina?

LET HIM COME TO YOU. That's what they'd told her. *You were very brave,* Lydia had said as she'd handed Alina a handkerchief when tears threatened yet again. *You went to him. You bared your heart to him. He has his demons, yes. We all have demons of some sort. I know this won't be easy for you, as you're more like Nicole than could possibly be comfortable for you, but it's up to Justin now to realize that your love is greater than his fears for you. He's a much better man than he believes himself to be. I know, because he was enormously helpful to Tanner and me during a...a difficult time.*

Nicole's advice had been equally as heartfelt, but

more direct. *No, no, we don't let him come to you.
We make him come to you. And I'm less kind than my
sister. Demons or no, he has behaved abominably.
Of course he'll marry you. He compromised you.
Even the Bad Baron is aware that there are rules a
gentleman can break, and those he cannot.*

And that, Alina had decided during a mostly
sleepless night, was now the problem. She and Justin
had been formally betrothed, albeit by proxy, an
agreement between her king and his Prince Regent.
The banns had been read in her home church. A
substantial dowry had been agreed upon and sent
off to London (and probably had gone straight to
the Prince Regent, but that didn't make it any less
official, did it?). That was all troublesome, but there
had to be ways and ways to wriggle out of the betrothal, as Justin had so clearly stated he wished to
do.

The easiest, of course, was for him to take himself and his demons off to America. Nicole had said
something very interesting about that, as well. *If he
didn't care for you, he'd marry you. It's because he
cares that he's being so ridiculous, you know. Men
and their honor can be extremely annoying at times,
and when their hearts are involved, annoying can
turn even the best of them into blockheads.* Even
Lydia had nodded her agreement.

But then, Alina knew, there was still the worst
of it: she'd seduced him. She hadn't known there

was a term for what she'd done that night at the stream, but Nicole did, and the word was *seduced*. How that compared to being compromised, Alina wasn't too clear about, but it seemed to her that she was as guilty, or even more guilty, than Justin. All that business about gentlemen succumbing to uncontrollable lust at the drop of a hat. If truth be told, and she might as well be truthful, if only to herself, she'd rather counted on that....

Poor Justin. He'd been under constant duress ever since she'd first stepped onto the dock at Portsmouth, and all because of her. Well, mostly because of her.

He shouldn't *have* to marry her just because she was in love with him.

The kindest thing she could do would be to relieve him of any sense of obligation to her. Then, if Nicole and Lydia could be believed, there might still exist a way for him to remain in England, which he could not do if he did something terrible to the *Inhaber* because of her. Clearly she was a complication he didn't need.

Alina looked around the conservatory, where she had been sitting for half the afternoon on the twins' orders, waiting for Justin to come to her. She would soon grow whiskers, waiting for him to come to her. But both Nicole and Lydia had agreed on that one single point: the next move had to come from him.

Perhaps someone would be kind enough to gather

her dry and withered remains after she'd expired here among all the pretty flowers, waiting for him—

"Alina?"

She nearly cried out as Justin walked toward her, looking as wonderfully exquisite as he had that day on the docks. He'd made a handsome, roguish Romany, but when rigged out in his marvelous London finery, there could be no other man on earth who looked so fine. He stopped on his way, plucked an orchid from its curving stem and carried it with him, depositing it in her outstretched palm before sitting down beside her.

"Beautiful, but not perfect. They have no scent, you know," he said just as if the last words he'd said to her before these hadn't been *I can never forgive myself for what I've done to you....*

She lifted the bloom to her face and inhaled deeply. It was a pretty flower, a lovely gesture, but she'd rather he'd kissed her. "I can imagine that this one does. Nothing is ever perfect, except in our imaginations. The rest of the time, we simply have to learn to muddle through, taking the good with the bad."

"And what are we muddling through today?" he asked, lifting her hand and pressing his lips against her suddenly heated skin.

He wasn't going to be serious, which meant that, inside, he was very serious indeed. She longed to slap him.

Why didn't he kiss her somewhere other than her hand?

"I'm not sure. I would imagine you'd know that better than I. Are the duke and duchess about to take me off to Malvern so that you can go kill somebody else?"

"Would you go with them if I asked it of you?"

Still they hadn't looked at each other. Not really. Physical intimacy beneath the moonlight, it would seem, resulted in nervous avoidance in the mundane, everyday world. *Did we really do that? It had all seemed so natural, so wonderful, at the time. So why are we so loath to be reminded of it now?*

"I don't think so, no. I believe I am done being shunted off somewhere else each time you decide what you think is best for me. I've already lost my beautiful new wardrobe to Ashurst and my caravan to Basingstoke. I imagine the only thing I have left to lose to Malvern would be…you."

He avoided a direct answer, a fact she didn't miss. She was learning him, she really was. He should be careful about that, not that she was going to warn him.

If she looked at him, would he kiss her?

"You enjoyed the caravan?"

"I enjoyed the…adventure. The Romany have a freedom we can never have, even as they are at times persecuted and even shunned for who they are. But at least they have each other, and the streams, and the moonlight. People who don't understand such things say they have no home, but Loiza told me their hearts and homes travel with them, and that it's only the heart that needs a home."

"And what of the land? The *Inhaber* seems to want it very much, and I say that with my tongue so firmly in my cheek I'm surprised you can understand what I'm asking."

Alina sighed. No, he wasn't going to kiss her. He was going to *talk*. Did he have any idea how fatigued she was with *talking?* "You were right. Loiza says it would bring them only sorrow. But, Justin," she said, turning to look at him for the first time since he sat down beside her, "the land is not mine to give, not really. It's not his to take, either. It's disputed. Correct?"

"You've been thinking, haven't you?" He smiled, stroked the back of one finger down her cheek, so that she was caught between sighing and leaning against him and wanting to shake him for not really listening to her.

Very nice, the way he touched her. Almost as if he could not sit so close to her and not touch her.

But she'd rather he kissed her.

She slapped his hand away (thinking this a good compromise between the two) and got to her feet. If he wanted to talk, then he should be prepared to listen, as well!

"I refuse to discuss this with you anymore, Justin.

All you can think of doing is going around killing everyone. Shooting the *Inhaber* because he tried to have me shot, which he did, and it was horrible of him and he probably deserves to die for any number of good reasons, but that doesn't make it right that you be the one to kill him. Just when your friends think they can find a way to rescue you from all your follies—yes, I heard about the Prince Regent, yet again—you will ruin everything by thinking there is no solution except to hunt down the *Inhaber* and... and execute him. That's what you were doing while you were gone, wasn't it. Finding some way to kill the man? Or is he already dead?"

He stood up as well and took hold of her by the shoulders, obviously knowing what she knew—that she was ready to run from the conservatory.

Don't touch me. Don't touch me unless you mean it. Don't talk to me. Hold me. Don't you want to hold me?

"I was attempting to *contact* the man, Alina. There's a difference. Contrary to what you think, an impression I imagine you gained from me, I do not *go around killing* everyone." And then he smiled. "Sometimes I only threaten to kill them."

Alina rolled her eyes in frustration. "Now you're making a joke, which only tells me that you're thinking again what a bad man you are, and all of that drivel you keep mouthing every time I try to tell you that I—"

She clamped her mouth tightly shut on the words *love you*. She wasn't going to say those words. They'd only make him feel more obligated to her.

"Every time you try to tell me what, Alina?" he asked her, stepping closer, so that her heart began to pound almost hurtfully in her chest.

"Nothing," she said, looking down at her shoe tops, her borrowed shoe tops, and felt herself slowly begin to shatter into very small pieces. She couldn't help herself. She was only one woman, and only very newly a woman at that, and she had been bartered by her king like so much produce, betrothed to a man she didn't know, dropped into a foreign country only to learn her only living relative really was her odious aunt Mimi and there would be no cousins or uncles and aunts to welcome her. She'd been submerged in a mud puddle, nearly shot, been hidden away with the Romany, had kissed a fool, had been introduced to parts of her body and feelings, both physical and emotional, she hadn't until that moment known existed, and…and… "You keep trying to make things better for me, and you only keep making them worse for both of us!"

He stepped back, shock evident in his expression. "Well, so much for Justin Wilde, the better man. I wondered how long it might take you to realize the gravity of my sin against you. No matter the provocation, the circumstances, I should be shot for touching you."

"Shot! Do you hear yourself? Everything is life and death to you," she accused, waving her arms (in what she would later think the way of a demented windmill). "The *Inhaber* wants me dead, so he must die. Your Prince Regent connives with my king, so you puff yourself up and run off to threaten his life. I don't know why the man you killed while we were with the Romany had to die, because you didn't tell me, but I'm certain he did something worthy of dying for."

"I suppose," Justin said tightly, "that your conclusion would depend on where you were standing when the man produced a pair of wicked-looking knives and announced that he was going to kill me."

Some of the wind went out of her sails. "Oh. Well, then I guess that was all right." *And don't you laugh at me now. Don't you dare laugh at me!*

Justin took her hands and pulled her back down on the bench. "Contrary to what you may think, kitten, I do not rise from my bed every morning and think to myself, ah, and who might I kill today? I thought I was done with that when the war ended. I prayed I was done with it long before the war ended. I bought my way back to England, intent only on living out my life in my homeland. I didn't ask for anything I had to do in these past few days. But I won't apologize for it. I did what I was trained to do. I'm talking about something entirely different here, and you know that as well as I. Knowing I couldn't marry you, knowing I couldn't ask you to give up everything and follow me as I escape to America, knowing that of all the men in the world I am the one man least worthy of you, I took your virginity."

"That...that doesn't matter," she said, her head down, watching as he took her hands in his, lightly squeezed her fingers. "I mean, that last part. I made you do it."

He'd probably forgotten that part. *You can't steal what is freely given.*

"Oh, kitten," he said, chuckling softly, "you mustn't believe everything your companion told you. I knew exactly what I was doing, including what a bastard I was for not putting a stop to it. I simply couldn't find it in myself to give a damn. At the time. Now, however, we have to deal with the consequences, which means we must marry. Then they can hang me."

"Hang you? But you said you didn't kill the *Inhaber.*"

"No, but it does seem that three of his men, all military attachés and completely innocent of any wrongdoing, I'm told, although they looked very much like hired thugs to me, seem to have been killed, and I have been named as their murderer."

Her heart sank to the toes of her borrowed slippers. If the man had to be so excessively good at something, couldn't it have been something less *lethal?*

"The *Inhaber* is telling everyone this because he wants you arrested so he is free to come after me," Alina said, marveling at the words as they came out of her mouth. She was beginning to think like a devious person. And Justin had been forced to think this way for all those long years he refused to talk about with her other than to say that those years had killed something important inside him. She was beginning to understand how that could happen. "But he could not chance killing Lady Wilde, could he, especially if she were to make herself very visible in London? That would be too suspicious, and make for strain between our two countries."

"Very good, kitten. Your mother was English, the daughter of an earl. Your country is England. Your death would cause a strain between two new and still tenuous allies who seem to have less in common now that their common enemy is gone. You'd be safe."

"Then I refuse to marry you," she said firmly.

"Alina, for the love of God—"

"No, Justin. Either you find a way to assuage the *Inhaber* and your Prince Regent and make both of us safe here, or I refuse to be safe and you dead. I won't have it."

"You won't *have it?*"

For a handsome man, he could look very silly, what with his eyes all wide like that and his neck turning a deep red above his pristine white neckcloth.

Suddenly she felt very brave.

"No, Justin, I won't. You're so intent on how terrible you are, and on being some sort of martyr or atoning for past sins, or whatever you think it is you're doing, and I am thoroughly out of patience with you. So, no, I won't do it. If you're going to save my honor or whatever such ridiculousness you've been spouting, then you'll simply have to find another way. Because I will not marry a dead man!"

Then, because brave wasn't the same as fearless, she stood, turned on her heels and ran out of the conservatory, on the hunt for Nicole and Lydia, who would surely hide her until Justin no longer looked as if he'd explode at any moment.

She certainly hoped those two wonderful women would be able to come up with some sort of miraculous ideas as to what they could all do next, because, after having knocked Justin back on his heels, Alina had completely run out of ideas.

And he still hadn't kissed her.

CHAPTER THIRTEEN

THE FOLLOWING EVENING, after a dinner attended only by the three gentlemen, Justin stood at the opened window of his bedchamber as fading sunlight turned the evening to a misty portrait of muted colors and soft outlines, and looked down into the garden three stories below.

Alina was walking there with the marchioness and the duchess, and the three of them had their heads together like true conspirators. It had been the sound of their conversation wafting up to him that had drawn him, and now he was too fascinated to turn away. They reminded him of three beautiful, perfect flowers, dressed in their gowns of yellow, pale green and softest rose, rivaling any blooms in the gardens.

They'd been constant companions, taking their meals together, shunning male company, and all with the excuse that Alina was not quite well…although, oh no, not ill enough to have the doctor sent for. *She'll be fine,* they said. *We're simply bearing her company.*

And Tanner and Lucas seemed to have swallowed this story whole. Either that, or they were better at subterfuge than he'd formerly have given either of them credit for possessing, and were both in whatever plot was going forward up to their starched cravats, and knew more than they were saying.

Had she told the women why she and he were at odds? Had she told them *everything?*

Of course she had. Who else did she have to talk to, if not Lydia and Nicole? Surely not her companion, she of the "uncontrolled lust at the drop of a hat." Look where *that* particular conversation had led them!

No wonder he was in so much trouble. He was only a man, for all his supposed sophistication and talents. What man had ever outcomplicated a woman?

And no wonder she had refused to come down to dinner last night, and turned away the notes he'd sent to her bedchamber. Headache be damned—she simply was refusing to see him while she and the ladies made their plans.

Plans that had to include his downfall, that was certain. He could only guess at how much he was intended to suffer before that downfall.

He'd told Alina he couldn't marry her—for very reasonable reasons—and she'd fought him. He'd told her they had to marry—again, for exceedingly reasonable reasons—and she'd thrown his offer back in his face.

Now, most probably on the advice of two women he would have otherwise thought of as perfectly intelligent human beings, she wouldn't speak with him at all.

He had become so frustrated with his inability to find a way to circumvent the ladies and see Alina that he'd actually appealed to Tanner and Lucas for their help.

The next time he considered going to his friends for their advice, he'd have to grab up several bottles of wine, lock himself in a cabinet and drink until he'd overcome the impulse.

"The great Justin Wilde, flummoxed by a slip of a girl?" Tanner had looked at him in feigned astonishment. "The same man who could so coldly and calmly threaten the life of the Prince Regent can't so much as say *boo* to that sweet girl who my wife tells me is so young and innocent it's nearly painful? It's lowering, Justin, I have to tell you. I've lost all faith in you. But I bow to my wife's wisdom on this. Sorry."

Lucas Paine had been even less help. "Lydia sees young and innocent, but my wife sees independent and determined. As Nicole is more than generously gifted with both attributes herself, I believe I'll take her at her word. My advice? Well, actually, I don't have any. I rather enjoy Nicole the way she is."

Justin took a sip of his wine and looked down into the garden again. Now they were laughing. *Laughing!* The *Inhaber* was still out there; Alina knew the man wanted her dead. Justin still couldn't be certain he wouldn't be locked up in chains for having threatened the Prince Regent, or if his pardon had been revoked, three charges of murder were soon to be placed at the feet of this same man who was to become her husband, except that she'd refused him—and she was *laughing?*

He hated war. But, damn it all to blazes, war between men was reasonably straightforward, even in his job of spy and assassin; both sides had them. War between a man and a woman had no rules, or at least none the men were informed about by the women, who also seemed to possess all the weapons.

Without consciously searching out the memory, he was suddenly reminded of one of his least-favorite schoolboy lessons, his assigned reading of Aristophanes' *Lysistrata*. But surely the women weren't plotting to withhold their…favors from the men until this small "war" was settled. Were they?

If so, he could probably expect a visit from Tanner and Lucas in his very near and unpleasant future. At least then perhaps they wouldn't be so damned jolly!

Ah, they were moving on, the ladies on the stroll. At least Alina had moved on, rather aimlessly walking ahead of the other two down the path toward the large hedge maze Lucas had told him was more than two hundred years old.

Wait a moment. Did Nicole just take a quick peek up at his open window? Had she seen him standing there, gawking like a fool?

He leaned closer to the sill.

Now she was whispering in Lydia's ear and pulling rather inelegantly on her sister's arm when her sister began to turn her head, probably to also look up at the window.

He could imagine the whispered conversation:

He's up there, poor lovesick fool, watching us. Shh, don't let Alina hear us.

He's up where, Nicole? Let me—

No! Don't look, don't turn around!

"From this evidence, my lord Wilde," Justin intoned in mock gravity of purpose, "it may be reasonably deduced that you do not remain unobserved." A niggling thought knocked on the back of his mind, one that was calling out helpfully: *You've completely lost control of what's left of your wits. You do know that, don't you?*

What followed below him was a pantomime wherein Nicole crossed her arms and seemed to shiver in the cool, early evening air, Lydia nodded her head in agreement before taking a few steps toward Alina's departing back and saying a few words, Alina resuming her walk toward the maze, Lydia and Nicole turning to head for the steps to the terrace—obviously to fetch shawls—and Nicole hanging back as her sister mounted the steps, looking up at Justin's window, putting her fists rather belligerently on her hips, tilting her head, and then finally throwing her arms wide as if to say, "Well, what are you waiting for?" before disappearing out of sight.

Justin scribbled a mental note to himself to be extremely nice to Lucas Paine; the man must really have his hands full. Although he'd said he rather liked Nicole the way she was. And Tanner seemed to be more than content with Lydia, which made perfect sense to Justin, as he'd been half in love with the lady herself before it became clear that she had eyes only for his friend.

Now he knew why he had been drawn to Lydia. It was because he would have been half in love with Nicole as well, if he'd met her before now.

Alina was a delicious mix of the two wives of his friends, and possibly with a touch of the gracious and intelligent Charlotte Daughtry thrown in for good measure, for Alina certainly seemed to like *managing* people, a thought that pleased him even as that small voice knocking on the back of his brain told him that he had only one option open to him now that he fully understood what lay in front of him. Surrender. Complete and total surrender.

His.

"Wigglesworth?" He called out, turning from the window. "Fetch me a blanket."

The valet hurried into the bedchamber from wherever he'd been lurking, awaiting his master's next request, looking splendidly outlandish in his satins and refreshed wig. "A blanket, my lord? Goodness, who opened that window? Have you taken a chill? I have something in my case for that, a mixture one of the Romany ladies was kind enough to press on me for the paltry sum of threepence when I—"

"Never mind, Wigglesworth." Justin cut him off impatiently, striding to the large bed and stripping off the heavy tapestry-like coverlet. He wound it around and around as he walked to the open window. Then he tossed the probably priceless bit of silk down onto the flagstones below.

"My lord! That…that was Flemish, sir, and now most probably ruined.… I think I feel faint."

"Not yet, Wigglesworth," Justin warned him as he dealt with his evening jacket, removing it with some effort as it had been tailored to fit him within an inch, before tossing it in the valet's general direction. "You will oblige me by withholding your apoplexy until after you have found Brutus and told him to station himself at the entrance to the maze, barring the way to anyone who might dare to enter, including the master of this house. Understood?"

"The…the maze, my lord?"

"I believe that's what I directed, yes," Justin said

as he stripped off his neckcloth and opened the top button of his shirt.

"If his lordship is perhaps *warm...*"

"I'm not stripping to the buff, Wigglesworth. I'm merely..." He stopped himself before he said *stripping for battle*. "Now go, man, do what I've asked. No! Wait! The servant stairs, Wigglesworth. They lead down to the kitchens and the rear of the house, yes? Show me where they're located in this hulking pile of a place, because I'll be damned if I'm using the main staircase and giving them all a show as they watch from the main salon, which I'm sure they're all already doing."

"My lord," Wigglesworth lamented, wringing his hands and clearly on the verge of tears. "I am aware, we are all aware, that you have been placed under a considerable strain these past—"

"You have three seconds to do as I'm asking, man, or that wig gets stuffed in the chamber pot. I haven't yet decided if you'll still be wearing it when that happens."

Not quite a full minute later, Justin stepped out of the back door he'd been led to by a clearly terrified kitchen maid. It was short work to locate the coverlet—it was damned large and twice as heavy; he might have chosen better—fold it as best he could and then toss it over his shoulder as he took off for the path leading to the maze.

There would be a moon soon, but for now the

night was still caught between dusk and dark, and it was easy for him to navigate the twisting brick path. He hefted the coverlet when it began slipping from his shoulder. It was only moderately cool now, but he was prepared for an evening chill. It wasn't her emerald and ermine-tipped cloak in front of the fireplace at the inn, or the bright skirts and petticoats of her Romany clothes on the bank of the stream, but a priceless Flemish silk coverlet would serve the purpose.

Someday he really ought to try taking Alina to his bed. If, when the mess was finally over, he still possessed one.

He hastened his step.

As he did not encounter Alina along the way, it was obvious to him that he'd been correct in his assumption—the twins had directed her to enter the maze without them, as they went back to the house for shawls, or lanterns, or both.

Brutus wasn't at the entrance to the hedge maze when Justin reached it, but he knew he could rely on the man to do what he was told. The precisely trimmed ten-foot-high hedge would do the rest.

Justin plunged into the maze with more haste than knowledge of the twists and turns of the thing, and a frustrating five minutes later he knew himself to be hopelessly lost. Thanks to the height of the hedges, he couldn't even see the estate house in order to regain his bearings.

"From Paris to Warsaw in the dead of winter, without a map, and while being pursued by a full French company, and you found your way," he grumbled to himself. "And now, when it's even more important, you let a damn fool hedge defeat you?"

"Justin?"

He turned about in a full circle, but he was still alone on the path. "Alina?"

"Justin. It is you. What are you doing out here?"

He turned to his left, sure the voice had come from the other side of the hedge. "Getting myself lost, apparently. Where are you?"

"Lost," she said, her voice sounding small. "I studied the map earlier, and thought I knew the key, but I must have taken a wrong turn somewhere. I wanted to surprise Lydia and Nicole by making my way to the gazebo in the center of this dratted thing before they returned. Now, again, what are you doing here? I'm not speaking to you, you know."

"On orders from *les jumeaux terribles,* I imagine. The terrible twins. Although I am, for the moment, in charity with them both. Unless we never find our way out of here, that is, and have to be rescued, which would force me to reconsider my current sympathetic feelings for the women who have told you to avoid me."

"They…they sent you after me? Have you come to apologize?"

"Certainly," he said, trying to peer through the dense hedge, but to no avail. He'd give his best curricle for a sharp sword at the moment. "For trying not to embroil you in my sad and sorry life via matrimony, for pointing out the logic of temporarily aligning you matrimonially with that same complicated—and, as it happens, probably temporary—life, I most humbly apologize. For shunting you from pillar to post these past days, for depriving you of your wardrobe and your caravan, I beg your pardon. Whatever you might wish me to apologize for, consider me figuratively at your feet, begging forgiveness. I will not, however, make the same mistake as I did yesterday. I will not apologize for taking your virginity. I do try not to make the same blunder twice."

He waited, but she didn't answer him.

"Alina? Alina!"

"I…I remembered where I made the incorrect turn," she said from behind him, and he turned about sharply to see her standing only a short ten paces behind him. "You were saying something? I followed the sound of your voice, but I'm afraid I couldn't make out your words."

God. How beautiful she was.

"It doesn't matter," he told her quietly, careful not to move, because he couldn't know if she'd turn and run off again, like some woodland sprite, leaving him lost again, not in the maze—the devil take the maze—just simply *lost*. "I was, in my own insufferable and fairly self-serving way, trying to tell you I'm sorry. And I am, Alina. I'm so, so sorry I've hurt you. That was never my intention."

She took two small steps toward him. "What on earth is that great lump hanging over your shoulder?"

He looked to the coverlet as if he'd forgotten it was there. "This? I think this is called, in the vernacular, a good idea at the time I first had it. Now I feel like an idiot. A presuming idiot at that. In reality, it's…it's, um, the coverlet from my bed. I rolled it up and threw it out the window."

A slow smile began on Alina's face and put an unholy twinkle in her eyes. "You really are the Bad Baron, aren't you? Well, I suppose it is your turn."

"My turn for what?" he asked as she took his hand and led him back the way she'd come. Her hand was so small in his. Amazing how it was large enough to hold all of his heart.

"Your turn to seduce me. You did come out here planning to seduce me, Justin, didn't you?"

"I could lie and say no, but the coverlet rather gives me away, doesn't it? I can remember a time I believed I was successfully subtle in advancing my interests."

She grinned up at him. "I don't believe I knew you then. That must have been a long time ago."

"Touché, kitten. Every time I attempt to tell myself

I'm too aged for you, you turn me into the rawest of green youths. May I ask where we're going?"

"To the gazebo, now that I remember the way. Can I assume we won't be disturbed?"

They turned yet another corner, which was when, in the increasing dark, he finally saw the small square metal marker at the side of the path. The one with an engraved *M* on top and an arrow pointing forward on its side. He pulled on her hand, halting her as he then looked to his right, toward a second small square metal marker, this one with an *H* on top and an arrow pointing in the opposite direction on its side.

He remembered the sight below his window. The three women, lingering there, when there were at least several dozen other places they could have stopped to have their conversation. The laughter, sure to rise up to his open window, the only open window out of the half dozen in the chamber, the one Wigglesworth (a man incapable of intrigue; witness his recent incognito-ness) hadn't opened because he was surprised to see that it wasn't shut. The easy way Alina had gone off on her own rather than returning to the house with the other two...connivers.

Damn. He was being led about like a monkey on a chain.

"Brutus is guarding the entrance by now," he said after a moment during which he mentally kicked himself halfway across the maze. "There is only the one, isn't there?" He gave his head a quick shake. "I'm most probably going to pay dearly for asking this question, kitten, but I'm afraid curiosity has won out. Was Nicole the only one who knew I was standing at my window, watching the three of you?"

"Does it matter?" she asked him, pulling him around one more turn and into a clearing holding an ironwork fantasy of a gazebo at its center.

"Does it matter? It should, at least I think so. But I'm finding it difficult to come up with a good argument, considering I'm where I've been trying to be since you ran off on me yesterday and locked yourself away."

"I allowed myself to be convinced," she told him quietly as they mounted the three shallow steps and entered the gazebo. He dropped the coverlet onto the floor, and drew her down instead on the wide chaise longue that occupied most of the small space. "But by this afternoon, I began to feel silly. You kept sending me notes I wasn't brave enough to read or else I'd surely lose my resolve, and I was becoming quite sick of my bedchamber, pretty though it is. But Lydia and Nicole insisted that you had to come to me, not I to you. So…so Nicole and I put our heads together and…"

"Not Lydia?" Justin asked, for he knew how proper the lady Lydia could be, bless her.

"She thought truthfulness would be the better route, but when we discussed the thing, and found that the truth was rather convoluted, and would probably only lead to another argument, she added her agreement. I was the only one not sure it would work, that you'd follow me. But I thought you might not be able to help yourself."

While she explained, he'd been pulling the pins from her hair. Now the long dark tresses fell down past her shoulders like some warm, living veil.

"It's that uncontrollable lust business again, isn't it? You still half believe in it."

She busied herself unbuttoning his waistcoat and shirt, even as she avoided his gaze. The timid temptress. She made him want her more than he already did, which had seemed impossible only moments earlier.

"I don't...I don't think the failing is strictly a problem for you gentlemen, you know. I did worry, a little, but Nicole and Lydia assured me that ladies can also...harbor yearnings of that sort. Which... which is a good thing, Justin, because I have been... yearning nearly from the moment you returned me to my caravan." She sighed almost theatrically. "Are you ever going to kiss me?"

He shook his head slightly, even as he reached for the thankfully few buttons at the back of her gown and undid them, one by one. "Not yet, kitten, no. I think I want to hear more about this yearning of yours."

He slid the gown from her shoulders, baring her

breasts. Her nipples were taut, revealing her arousal, as did the increasingly rapid rise and fall of her chest as her breaths quickened, shortened. He'd barely touched her, and she was already responding. The pleasurable coil in his gut tightened.

"Justin, please…" She pressed her hands against his thighs. "But you're going to insist, aren't you?"

"Oh, yes. I really must insist. Tell me, kitten. Tell me all that you feel…all that you yearn for."

"This is my punishment for avoiding you. Very well. But I don't know how to describe what it's like for me. I…I yearned for this feeling I'm feeling now. There's…there's this almost pleasant thickness that begins just at the base of my throat, and it seems somehow connected to…other parts of my body."

He nuzzled the side of her neck, his blood running hot. "Yes…go on.…"

"There's this… A strange sort of anticipation of your touch, as if I'm somehow already feeling your mouth against me, your tongue stroking me, your fingers pinching me lightly as you rub at me, again and again, making me grit my teeth and beg you for more, beg you to feed this hunger that robs me of my breath and— *Yes. Yes, like that. Oh, Justin…*"

He lowered her all the way back onto the soft cushions, suckling at her budding nipple, playing her with his hands and tongue, glorying in her unashamed moans of pleasure as she cupped her own breasts for him, raised them to his mouth as if offering him the gift of her, a gift he greedily took.

He kissed her heated flesh, easing her gown down, pressing a kiss against her flat stomach as she lifted her hips, helping him free her of her garments.

He'd dreamed of this, lain awake thinking about this, nearly lost his mind envisioning this moment. She'd been a virgin, she wouldn't have understood such undiluted intimacy. She might not understand now, but she was fearless, he knew that. And she trusted him.

He probed her navel with his tongue, stroked her flat lower belly with his thumbs, was driven on by the way, once again, she instinctively raised her hips to him, her body telling him that it was ready for what he would do next…even if her mind still wondered.

He eased her suddenly taut thighs apart and sought her out with both hands, to find her wet and slick and swollen with desire. He knew what to do, how to stroke her, how to reach her, and when her thighs fell open bonelessly, he knew he'd moved her past the point of any lingering modesty. When he finally brought his mouth to her, she reacted with a low moan of pleasure, not shock or dismay.

Like spreading the petals of a delicate, exotic flower, he fully explored her, finding the white-hot center of her and then sealing his lips against her, stroking that center of her pleasure with his tongue before sucking it into his mouth, feeling her small explosions as they rippled through her body and his.

She was still for long moments, pressing against him, blatantly prolonging her enjoyment, before she seemed to come alive with a fury that surprised him. She reached down for him, pulling at him, her fingers curling into his back as she urged him upward.

He was powerless to resist.

Now he was the boneless one, somehow turned onto his back as she knelt beside him, tearing at his buttons, whimpering softly as she divested him of his clothing, and then pulling him back across her body as she collapsed once more onto the cushions.

There was a fierce desperation in the kisses she pressed on his face, his throat, his chest, in the way her fingernails dug into the bare flesh of his back, the way she moved her body beneath his. She needed him. She'd been pleasured, but not fulfilled. She needed him for that. She needed to feel whole, and she couldn't do that until their two halves were joined.

She didn't say the words, but her actions told him all he needed to know, all he'd never hoped to experience. His woman. Wanting him, only him. Needing him…as he needed her, only her.

Her sigh when he sank into her nearly unmanned him, and he felt tears stinging at the backs of his eyes. She took him into her, held him tightly, brought her legs up and over his back in order to take more of him, all of him. She gave herself even as she invited him to take what he needed.

And all he needed, all he'd ever needed, all he would ever need, was her.

CHAPTER FOURTEEN

ALINA LAY WITH HER HEAD on Justin's gently rising and falling bare chest, listening to his steady heartbeat. Beneath the coverlet he'd pulled across them earlier, her hand rested at his waist, her left leg drawn across his as she melded against him, into him, imprinting him with her body, branding him as hers.

She loved when he touched her, reveled in the sensations he so easily aroused in her, exulted in his loss of control as he plunged deep inside her, briefly taking them both out of the world and into a fleeting realm of delight surely no two other humans had ever known.

But this was somehow even better. Lying here with him as he slept. The thickness at the very bottom of her throat, the fullness in her chest, were not the stirrings of passion, of need. This was an ache of love, filling her up with an emotion that encompassed every feeling she'd ever had, and then doubled it.

She would protect him, comfort him, hold him

when he was ill or in pain. Her arms would cradle his children, the milk from her breasts would give them sustenance. He was hers, always hers, and she would die for him, live for him, be nothing without him.

There was passion for his body, and she'd gloried in it. But this was a passion for him, for Justin, the man. The way he smiled at her with his eyes as well as his mouth, a smile that seemed reserved only for her. The way he teased her, even how their wills clashed. His affection for Brutus, and his amused tolerance of Wigglesworth's antics. The loyalty he inspired in his true friends. The way he walked, as if the world belonged to him, the way he took her hand in his as if that was the most natural thing in the world to do.

The way he *cared,* when he did everything to show that he did not.

Alina drew in a breath, let it out in a shuddering sigh. What *was* she going to do with him?

"Kitten?"

She smiled against his chest. "You know, Justin, it's a good thing they weren't puppies in that barn. I've learned to tolerate *kitten,* but *pup* would have been quite unacceptable."

His low chuckle pleased her. As did the way he put his arm around her and pulled her close against him. "I thought you were the most beautiful woman I'd ever seen. You don't know what it took for me not to join you in that hay and cover you with kisses. But then I remembered what I had to tell you."

"Do we have to talk about any of that now? Life was still so uncomplicated that day, before you told me about my uncle, the *Inhaber* and your ridiculous notions."

He pushed himself up against the cushions, drawing her along with him. "I beg your pardon? I never have ridiculous notions."

She rolled her eyes; clearly even the best of intentions couldn't last, for she longed to box his ears. "Yes, you do. And since most of them come from some ridiculous notion of protecting me from you, I believe I have the right to say whether or not they are ridiculous."

He wrapped a coil of her hair around his finger before letting it drop onto his chest. "I believed I was protecting you from my unworthy self. The past had just come rushing up into my face, along with all its attendant demons, and I thought the past was all that was left of me. Not enough to build a future on, and not fair of me to impose on you, either. You looked at me with such innocence and trust, as if I were some fairy-tale knight in his polished armor. I wasn't, kitten. I'm not. Your *Inhaber* knew it."

Alina pulled the coverlet along with her as she sat up, facing him in the moonlight. She couldn't really see his face clearly, but she knew he was wearing that maddening mask of indifference he tried on with everyone, fooling most of them she was sure, but not her. Never her.

"What does the *Inhaber* have to do with your demons, as you call them? Are you telling me you know him? You've met him? What does he know?"

"No, we've never met. But what happened couldn't have been coincidence. He's heard of me, somehow, about my time in Bohemia."

She was rapidly running out of patience with him now. "Justin, if the *Inhaber* knows something about you that upset you so much that you refused to honor our betrothal because of it, I have the right to know what that something is, and if you continue to be so *cryptic,* I will probably hit you."

He was silent for long moments, during which Alina wondered if he was going to continue to be so stubborn and how she'd ever find a way to get through the walls he'd kept about him, obviously for years.

"Let me begin at the beginning, when I was not much older than you are now, kitten," he said at last, and she nearly cried out in relief. Nothing he might tell her could possibly be worse than not knowing. "Please don't think of anything I'm going to say as putting forth excuses. There are no excuses."

"Will you hold my hand while you tell me?" she asked quietly, putting out her hand to him. She was already crying silent tears when he took that hand in his and squeezed it softly.

And then he told her.

He'd been wild in his youth, wonderfully well-named. Blessed with an ancient title, nearly bottomless wealth, a pleasing countenance and several varied talents that meant that most anything he attempted came easily to him—perhaps too easily. You don't value what you don't earn.

He'd excelled at school, kept up an easy friendship with most everyone he met, and when he came to London he came to conquer it. And did. He could outfence, outshoot, outfight and outride anyone, including his teachers. He didn't seem capable of losing at cards, or with women. His was a charmed life, a gift from the gods, and he enjoyed it to the top of his bent...and then beyond. Until the pleasures began to pall, the achievements coming too easily.

So he married, as this seemed the next logical thing to do. He chose a young woman who was nearly equally popular within the *ton,* a beautiful woman who would look good on his arm. Together, they would continue to effortlessly swim through life, hosting balls and perhaps the occasional musical or literary evening, but otherwise go their own way.

But she'd been indiscreet. Not once, but several times, leading to that misty morning and the reflexive shot that ended Robbie Farber's life and changed Justin's forever.

Within days he was in Brussels, then Vienna, and from there into oblivion. Until, months later, sunk in drink and despair at his lost life, he was approached by a man bearing a letter from his widowed mother. There was a way, she'd written, a path not easily traveled, but he wasn't without talents that could be valuable to the Crown during this terrible time. If he did as he was told, made himself valuable to the war effort, there would be a pardon at the end of his service.

He'd resisted, argued that he'd rather fight in the army as the lowliest field soldier, but in the end he'd agreed. With every other door closed to him, he had no choice but to go through the only one left open.

The French welcomed him, the banished and disgraced Englishman with the ready wit, the deep pockets, the pleasing countenance. Oh, yes, when they conquered the English he would be delighted to take them on a tour of London. He taught the ladies bawdy songs, played and drank deep with the gentlemen. Money, his own, ran through his hands and into theirs, and they liked him all the better.

And then, in the cold gray of dawn, he would lay in wait on a hilltop and put a rifle shot squarely between the eyes of a French field marshal as he stepped outside his tent to relieve his bladder.

Better a single shot than dozens of volleys in a

battle that would no longer be necessary. It wasn't honorable, and the Crown would have denied responsibility. But it was effective.

For the first three years, he kept count of his kills. He added Brutus and somehow acquired Wigglesworth, or perhaps it was Wigglesworth who'd acquired him. He was always on the move, always playing a part, a role.

And the war dragged on.

And his mother died.

And he became more reckless, less caring. Until he realized he no longer felt much of anything about anyone, most especially himself. He no longer kept count of his kills.

Until Trebon.

Alina knew Trebon, had even once, as a child, visited the small Bohemian city with her father.

Justin's hand tightened on hers, so that her fingers hurt with the pressure, but she ignored the pain, unwilling to stop him now when, obviously, he was so close to telling her the worst of what he saw as his eternal damnation.

He'd been sent there to eliminate a traitor, a merchant who had been forwarding dangerous information to the French. More than that, Justin hadn't asked. This was, after all, only another job of work, as he'd begun to think of his activities, another stepping-stone that would lead back to England.

He'd spent a few days in the ancient city, acting

the tourist while, as usual, tossing his money and his smiles and his wit about willy-nilly, introducing himself through forged letters of recommendation. He'd met with the widowed merchant, dined with the man, even been introduced as *that amusing Britisher* to the man's youngest child, the fourteen-year-old Erich, spending one pleasant afternoon teaching the boy how to shoot.

Erich had been polite, if not proficient, and in the end he'd shyly produced some poetry he'd written and read it to Justin, telling him that his papa disapproved, and that he was a sad disappointment to the man, unlike his brothers, who were already off fighting the evil Bonaparte.

Knowing he'd tarried too long, become too involved, but seeing something in young Erich's eyes that he knew he'd not seen in his own for too many years, Justin returned to the manor house that same night, intent on completing his latest job of work. Theodor Janosi had to die. His traitorous actions were costing too many lives; he had even put his own soldier sons in danger by diverting supplies from his factory to the French. He had to be stopped, and it was Justin's job to stop him.

Justin fell silent for so long that Alina believed he would refuse to tell her the rest. And it would be terrible, what he would say, she knew that in her heart.

"Erich, Justin?" she asked him softly. "What happened to him?"

"He…he died. That bastard must have sensed my presence and pulled Erich from the shadows, where I hadn't seen him standing, placing him in front of him as a shield just as the knife left my hand. His own son."

Alina bit her bottom lip until she tasted blood.

"I killed Janosi with my bare hands, Alina," Justin told her quietly. "I was nothing more than a wild animal. I beat him until every bone in both my hands seemed broken. I continued to beat him long after he was dead, until I simply couldn't hit him anymore. Brutus helped me bury Erich beneath the tree where he'd read me his poetry that afternoon. I…I, um, told them that I was finished, done, and six months later they finally took me at my word. I was sent to Vienna to help with the negotiations when Bonaparte at last admitted defeat, and remained there until long after his escape and recapture. Until I was finally offered the pardon that had cost young Erich his life. You know the rest."

Alina used the coverlet to wipe at her streaming eyes. "It wasn't your fault, Justin."

"No," he said with that maddening flippancy she'd learned he used to protect himself. "It was Janosi's fault. No, wait. It was my mother's fault. No, Bonaparte's. How about your uncle the earl? If he hadn't turned early, I would have never met Erich, would I, and the boy would still be alive and writing his poetry. *It's my fault, Alina.* Put the blame where it belongs, and it belongs with me. I thought I could forget, put the past in the past, tell myself I'd done enough penance, that I deserved the life I'd once had and so stupidly thrown away. When the pardon arrived, even with all the strings Prinny attached to it, I took a chance and came home."

"Only to have one of those strings show up in the form of the niece of the man you'd killed in the duel that had started it all. Oh, Justin, how cruel that was for you."

Now she understood why he'd been so incensed with the Prince Regent, and why he'd gifted her with his belongings while telling her he would not marry her. He had been performing some sort of penance.

Until she'd seduced him, in her selfishness, her curiosity, her determination that she could change his mind about their marriage. But he'd still refused to *burden* her with his supposedly terrible self, until after the *Inhaber* had— "Justin? You still didn't tell me about the *Inhaber*. You said he knew. Do you mean he knew about…Erich?"

He brought her hand to his lips, kissed it. "The morning I sent you off from Ashurst Hall, it was so that I could follow the *Inhaber*'s man and dispose of our…problem in the way I know best."

She listened as he told her how that terrible man

had exited the inn carrying the two little girls, using them as shields so that he could safely reach his coach. Justin had been waiting, his finger caressing the trigger of his rifle, only to see that stomach-clenching sight, only to relive the moment Theodor Janosi had pulled young Erich into the path of the knife.

"He's an evil man," she said, wrapping her arms around Justin's neck. "A coward. But I'm glad you didn't kill him. I spoke with Tanner earlier today, and he swears to me there is a way out for us, Justin, if you'll only agree. We can appease your Prince Regent. We can find a way around your...zeal with the men who attacked my coach. But only if you let the *Inhaber* live. There has to be a way to let him live, so that...so that we can live."

"There is," he told her, dropping a kiss on her nose and then actually smiling. Perhaps he was pretending again, or perhaps he felt lighter somewhere in his soul now that he'd told her about Erich. "I never told you what I wrote to him in that letter I sent to him via his henchman."

She sat back on her heels, trying to make out his features in the darkness. "No, you didn't. What did you write in that letter?"

"That, at a time and place of his choice, and for the mere pittance of ten thousand pounds, I'd hand you over to him."

Alina tried to speak. She opened and closed her mouth several times, but no words would come.

"He replied via a friend of mine in Sandhurst, agreeing to the terms, if I produced Luka, as well. Do you happen to know why he's interested in your *secretary?*"

"You...you weren't really going to hand me over to the man. I know you wouldn't do that, that it's all a trick. But it would be encouraging to me if you were to say the words."

"Come here," he told her, reaching for her.

She allowed him to pull her against his chest, but then she carefully took a pinch of his chest hair and gave it a sharp tug, so that he cried out in mock pain. "You have a most terrible, devious mind, Justin Wilde. The *Inhaber* believes he will have all three of us served up to him on a platter, doesn't he? While you have, in turn, learned where he will be, and even when. But now you won't kill him, because then there is no hope of you marrying me now that I am so thoroughly and happily compromised, and then not being hanged the next day. And I very much wish to marry you, so that you can compromise me every night for the rest of our very long and uneventful lives."

"That is what tonight is about, isn't it? I've surrendered. Completely, utterly and quite happily." He kissed her hair, her brow. "You're forgetting only one thing, kitten. The bastard still needs you dead in order for him to have the only claim to that damned land."

"But we settled that, didn't we? The Romany don't want the land, so I don't have to worry about depriving them of it, and if I write a letter to the king, giving up all claim to the land, then it is over. Oh."

"Yes, kitten, *oh*. You can't give up land that isn't indisputably yours to give. I believe you're the one who pointed that out to me."

"Yes, somebody pointed that out to me, I think. Perhaps the *Inhaber* has some idea how we could arrange matters?"

"Other than eliminating you and tossing the disputed claim into the lap of your aunt?"

"Who would renounce any claim immediately, for a price. Why can she do what I can't? I'm certain Luka told us that's what she'd do. He also told me that I couldn't give up the land, remember? He said that, didn't he? We really do need to speak with Luka, now that the horrible *Inhaber* is going to be allowed to grow fat and old."

"Yes, I think we do, kitten. I've never quite understood this business about the land. I'll admit that."

"You were too busy killing people and ruining me," Alina told him, trying not to smile. "It's understandable. Yes, tomorrow we need to speak with Luka." She slid her hand lower on his belly. "Tomorrow."

"The land. I should have concentrated more on the

land, Alina. All I really heard was that your life was in danger. Your king needs the *Inhaber* dead. I was chosen to marry you because the *Inhaber* wants you dead, and I was the most likely man to successfully assassinate him while protecting my betrothed wife, keeping your king's hands clean. Then I realized that Robbie Farber had been dug up and thrown into the mix, and went charging hotfoot after that idiot Prinny, burning bridges everywhere I went. I should have thought more about the land...."

He remained distracted, but she was determined.

She slid her hand lower, finding and capturing him. He was silk against her skin, his own skin so smooth and pliant as she closed her hand and began gently pulling on him, then pressing down, the silk now sheathing a growing hardness.

She tugged lightly again, moving his soft skin up, down. Again. He seemed to grow beneath her fingers.

Did that feel good to him? He wasn't talking to himself anymore, so she thought she was safe in assuming that it did.

He reached for her, but she evaded him, going to her knees and pushing the coverlet down so that she could better concentrate on her discovery of this new power she apparently possessed.

She dared to touch the very tip of him with one inquisitive finger, and found him to be moist with a droplet she then spread over the entire tip. Silk on silk.

She had done this to him? Her touch had done this? What he had done to her, she could do to him?

Fascinating.

Amazing what could be dared in the nighttime, when there was no room for thoughts other than the next pleasure.

She moved her hand faster, thoughts of how he'd moved inside her causing her to feel a clenching between her thighs each time she stroked the length of him. She lowered herself onto her haunches, her knees spread, and continued to stroke him, moving her hips as she closed her eyes and lowered her head, imagining him inside her. Big. Strong. Silk and hard, throbbing heat.

When he slid his hand between her legs she moaned in pleasure and anticipation. His thumb grazed her, again and again, spreading her, finding that small, hot center that took pleasure and turned it into need. Deep, teeth-grinding, jaw-clenching greed to feel more, more.

Then he slipped his fingers inside her, deep inside her, and she thought she might come apart, not possibly survive such intense bliss. She matched her deep strokes with his, her eyes still closed, her heart pounding so fast and hard she could hear it in her ears.

What he had done to her, she could do to him?

She wanted him to forget. She longed for him to be healed. There were no miracles that could erase the past, but there could still be a future. What he'd thought dead inside him was only in hiding, waiting to be reawakened, to fill him once again. He was beautiful, so very beautiful. In his mind and in his heart. She would not give up on him, even if he'd given up on himself.

The passion she'd felt, the carnal pleasure that so inflamed her, began to merge with the true love she felt for this man, this good man. They couldn't be separated and, combined, she knew she had the power to show him how much she loved him, trusted him, believed in him.

What he had done for her, she could do for him.

She lowered her head even more…and found out that she was right.

CHAPTER FIFTEEN

"WELL, IT'S YOU, JUSTIN," Nicole said in seeming surprise as he entered the morning room. "I would have thought you'd still be abed, as you hadn't come in from wherever you'd gone off to before Lucas and I finally gave up on playing the good hosts and went upstairs."

"Nicole," Lucas said quietly from his seat at the head of the table. "You promised you'd be good."

Justin laughed, then rounded the table and placed his hand on the back of Nicole's chair. "Lucas, I'm going to kiss your wife."

The marquess languidly waved a slice of toast above his plate. "I have no opposition. Nicole?"

Her answer was to push back from the table and stand up, wrapping her arms around Justin as he bussed her firmly on the cheek. "I knew all you needed was a nudge. Lydia, come here," she said as Tanner and her sister entered the morning room. "You probably get one, too."

"No, she gets two, because I know she allowed

herself to be convinced." He kissed Lydia on both cheeks as he wrapped her in a hug. "Thank you."

Lydia blushed prettily and kissed him back. "We were terrible, weren't we? I don't know what we would have done if it had rained," she said seriously, sending a faintly harassed look toward her twin. "No, that's not true. I do know, and may I say, Justin, you can thank your lucky stars that the night was dry."

Nicole giggled and bent her head to concentrate on her breakfast.

The three men all shook hands, Justin accepting their congratulations before realizing that he had never formally asked for Alina's hand in marriage. He'd been foisted on her, he'd rejected her, he'd reneged on his rejection, she'd rejected his renege—but he'd never actually proposed to her, and she'd never actually said yes.

"Excuse me," he said putting down the plate he'd been about to fill at the buffet—he had the most ravenous appetite this morning. "There's something I need to fetch from my chamber."

He headed for the now-familiar servant stairs, forgoing the main staircase, not wanting to pass Alina on the way, and entered his bedchamber in time to see Wigglesworth standing in front of the cheval glass in the dressing room, caught in the act of replacing his wig.

"Ye-gods, man, you were right—the women

needed to be spared that particular sight. You're bald as a doorknob."

"My lord!" Wigglesworth exclaimed, clapping the wig to his head, sideways, as it turned out, covering himself as if his modesty had been violated. "You are supposed to be breakfasting. If I cannot count on you to be where you say you are going to be—well, then there's no hope, is there?"

Justin bit back a grin at the reprimand. "A thousand apologies, Wigglesworth. I can only say that I will strive to be more dependable in future."

"Just so, yes, my lord," the valet said, nodding his head, causing the wig to turn a bit more, so that the beribboned queue slid forward over his nose. "I have just inspected the Flemish silk, and am delighted to report that it has suffered no more damage than a few broken threads, which I have repaired. But you won't be tossing it out the window again, will you, my lord? I do not know if it could sustain a second insult."

"I believe I will be able to restrain myself. Wigglesworth, where's my jewelry case?"

"Ah, my lord, so you noticed." The valet gave a final adjustment to his periwig, pulling it down snugly over his ears, and toddled over to the tall dressing chest, going up on the toes of his heeled shoes and opening the top drawer. "I didn't wish to say, my lord, but I did think the onyx studs would have been more the thing with that waistcoat. The brushed gold is acceptable, but much better suited to the—"

Justin reached inside the case and extracted what he wanted. "Yes, thank you, Wigglesworth. I'll be returning to the morning room now. Please feel free to dance a jig or whatever else it is you do when I'm not here."

He chose the servant stairs yet again, and this time the kitchen staff didn't even bother to look up from their chores, probably having decided that the gentry were simply queer, and to basically ignore them when they popped up where they had no business being.

When he reentered the morning room it was to see Alina standing at the heavily laden sideboard, a plate in her hand as she seemed to be having some difficulty choosing from the considerable choices before her.

She looked wonderful, most especially when he considered that they had not stolen back into the house until nearly dawn, startling the boy who was building up the fire in the kitchen hearth. He'd dropped a log on his foot and begun to yelp, causing Alina to attempt to go to him to be certain he was all right before Justin held her back and, instead, tossed the boy a gold crown, which immediately put a halt to his injured cries.

They'd whispered and giggled like children themselves as they stole up the servant stairs, him dragging the Flemish silk with him, and he'd kissed her thoroughly at her door before finally returning to his own bedchamber, where he'd collapsed into a short but dreamless sleep until his rumbling stomach woke him.

Ah, how good it was to be alive again...or perhaps alive, truly alive, for the very first time in his life. There were still problems to be solved, waters to be smoothed and one huge dilemma in the form of the *Inhaber* to be dealt with, but he wasn't going to think about them today. Today was for Alina. Tomorrow he would have to let the world back in.

But not today.

"Alina," he said when she turned to look at him, her smile unabashedly gleeful, unashamedly lover-like. She positively glowed. For him. He wasn't a humble man, had never been, but he felt humble now. Humbled and grateful. "There's something I forgot to do."

Her smile faded. "Where are you going this time? I thought we'd have just this one day...."

Before she could get the bit between her teeth—wives did that, didn't they, when they thought their husbands had gone beyond the pale—he went to her, took her free hand in his and dropped to one knee.

"Justin!"

There was a general scraping of chairs as the other four occupants of the room, along with two footmen who had been charged with lifting the lids on the silver servers, all turned to see why Alina had sounded so shocked.

"*Shh,* kitten, I'm about to make a public cake of myself," he said, reaching into his pocket and extracting the ring he had taken from his jewelry case.

Not the one Sheila had worn, and not the ring he had purchased for his unknown bride, but the betrothal ring that had been in his family for over three hundred years, the one his mother had worn until the day she died and it was sent to him, finally catching up to him somewhere in Spain and giving him a reason he hadn't needed to drink himself into a stupor for three days.

The gold had been refilled where it had been worn thin on so many Wilde bride hands. Its size had been changed and changed again, to fit several dozen fingers. A few lost stones had been replaced around the center diamond. If the ancient portrait in the Long Gallery could be believed, the original center stone hadn't been an emerald-shaped diamond at all, but a round ruby. But for all the changes, all the years, it was still the Wilde betrothal ring; that's what tradition was all about.

And now it would grace the finger of another Wilde bride.

"But, Justin, we're already—"

"Not correctly," he told her as, behind him somewhere, Lydia could be heard sniffling. "This is not anyone else's decision. This is you, kitten, you and me." He paused, smiled, looked around at the other occupants of the room. "Well, almost you and me. But we'll endeavor to ignore them."

"Oh, Justin…"

"Here, I think we can dispense with this," he said, taking the empty plate from her hand and replacing it on the sideboard, then taking her hand in both of his. "Lady Magdaléna Evinka Nadeja Valentin…"

"You remember that entire mouthful?"

"Alina, be good. Now, what was I doing?"

"You were being imperious."

He playfully squeezed her fingers. She'd never feared him, had completely failed to be overly impressed with him, had always seen through him as if he were a pane of glass to her. She'd seen all the way to his soul, the one he'd believed he had lost long ago.

"Alina, I'm still accused of murdering the men sent to attack your coach. I threatened the life of the Prince Regent and could be clapped in chains at any moment. My pardon for killing your uncle in a duel and thus robbing you of any living relatives save your odious aunt Mimi may be revoked. I still don't know what will happen with that damnable *Inhaber*. For all of those reasons, I may have to flee England yet again, this time to never return."

"For God's sake, Lucas, stop him," Nicole implored sotto voce. "He'll talk her out of it yet."

Tanner gave a bark of laughter, quickly stifled, probably thanks to a speaking look from his wife.

"You're to be witnesses, not participants," Justin said, never taking his gaze away from Alina's somewhat pinched, white face. "Alina, I love you. I'd die for you, but I'd much rather live for you, and for our children, and for the happiness I know we can bring each other, hopefully—please, God—here in England, surrounded by our very good and wonderfully meddlesome friends, building a life together. Please, before this becomes any more farcical...will you do me the not unmixed honor of becoming my wife?"

"Tell him you need a few moments to consider," Tanner advised. "He could do with a little more time on his knees. I know I'm certainly enjoying the sight of a humble Justin Wilde."

"Well, *I* am not!" Alina said feelingly. She took the ring from Justin's hand and slipped it onto her finger, then took his hands as if to pull him to his feet. "There. It's done, finally. Will you kiss me now, Justin? Am I destined to always having to ask you to kiss me?"

He slipped his arms about her waist. "You haven't yet said yes, kitten."

She rolled her eyes. He loved when she did that, how she never held back her feelings, good, bad or indifferent. No, never indifferent, and never indecisive. Alina always knew just what she thought, and just what he should be thinking.

Going up on tiptoe, she clasped his face between her hands and brought her mouth to his, kissing him deeply, thoroughly. As their delighted audience applauded approvingly, Lucas instructed one of the footmen to tell the butler to bring up several of his best bottles of wine from the cellars so that they could toast the happy couple. Through it all, she kissed him, and he kissed her back, until one of them—he'd never remember if it had been her or him—began to smile. And then to laugh.

"You're such a wonderful idiot. I've said yes a dozen times," Alina told him as they broke the kiss and once more stood there, lightly holding on to each other's hands, devouring each other with their eyes.

"I think you have your answer, my friend," Tanner said, clapping him on the back as the ladies drew Alina aside to hug her and admire the Wilde ancestral betrothal ring. "And for all the trouble you're in, damn me if you're not still the luckiest devil I know."

TODAY WOULD BE THEIR day, one devoted only to each other, with no shadows from the past, no worries about what was still an uncertain future.

Wearing a ruby-red riding habit borrowed from Nicole and matched with a Basingstoke mare only a little too gentle for her taste, Alina had enjoyed a ride with Justin that had taken them to the village and an establishment called the Crown and Bell.

Over Justin's protests, they sat in the public taproom rather than a private dining room, and Alina entertained herself by smiling at the farmers and laborers who sat at the many scarred wooden tables pretending they hadn't noticed the finely dressed young miss sitting in the corner with that handsome, well dressed, yet evilly scowling gentleman.

Also over his protests, she drank a mug of the inn's own beer, warm and fairly bitter, and, as she told him, not even a patch on the beer brewed near her childhood home. Justin had seemed amazed that she'd been allowed beer, but she'd never told him that she actually had, and simply allowed him to assume she spoke from experience.

The fib, the omission, had been to test him, although he couldn't know that. To test him, and her "fibbing ability," which Nicole had assured her all females possessed, if they only worked at it. Not that anyone should go about telling lies—fibs—willynilly. But sometimes they were for the greater good, and that made them all right. Especially when they were meant to protect men, who were notoriously unable to protect themselves when they thought their honor was involved.

Alina knew someday she really had to hear the history of Nicole and Lucas's courtship. Especially if the head-shakings and sighs of Lydia when the subject was even casually touched upon meant anything.

"Justin," Alina said quietly, drawing her finger around the wet circle left by the mug, "would you ever lie to me?"

He hesitated only the merest heartbeat before saying he would never lie to her for her to believe him.

"Good. Then I will never lie to you in the same way that you will never lie to me."

He put his elbow on the tabletop and propped his chin in his hand. "Other than to hint very broadly that you've been imbibing beer since your childhood, you mean?"

She sat back, alarmed. "You knew I was fibbing?"

"Kitten, you have the most expressive face in creation. You could no more hide an untruth than fly to the moon."

This was unsettling. "What does my expressive face do that gives me away?"

He reached across the table and gave a small flick to the side of her nose. "Oh no, kitten. If I tell you, you'll be careful not to do what you do, and then where would we be?"

"Is it my eyes?" she persisted. "Do I squint? Or perhaps I frown? I might do that, as I really don't like being untruthful—it seems such a waste of energy. Please, Justin, tell me. I won't rest until you tell me."

"Absolutely not. I'm in love—I haven't turned imbecilic. Now, drink up the remainder of that beer, and we'll head back to Basingstoke. I still need to speak with Luka."

She eyed the beer as if a snake had just poked its head above the surface of it. "I really don't like it," she admitted, "although you probably know that, too. No, don't say anything, because I already know the answer. You certainly can be insufferable, Justin. You should have told me I wouldn't like it. And why must you speak with Luka? You said that tomorrow could wait for tomorrow, remember?"

He took her arm in his and walked them out of the taproom, pretending not to notice as she gave a quick wave of goodbye to the young man in the homespun smock and leather gaiters who had been looking at her shyly for the past hour—although she did see him smile while pretending to be stern.

As he helped her up onto the sidesaddle, he said, "Tomorrow I meet with the *Inhaber,* remember? Much as I'd like to forget, much as I wish he'd simply go away. I have a few questions for Luka."

"About the land. I remember." She turned the mare, and they walked the horses toward the end of the village. "The Romany don't want it, I don't want it. I still don't see why we can't simply give it to him. According to Loiza, it isn't even very good land. It's really no more than a symbol. Do people actually die for symbols?"

"All the time, kitten, yes. People hate, fight and die for the damndest things. That's probably why I never questioned what Luka told us about the land. And the *Inhaber* did send his men to kill you. That's something not easily forgotten. Or forgiven. Shaking the man's hand tomorrow will not be the easiest thing I've ever done. Luckily, I've had considerable practice in being duplicitous."

She wished he wouldn't talk like that about himself. He'd been a soldier. Granted, not the usual sort, but a soldier for it all. Besides, that was the past. It was now, and tomorrow, and the rest of their lives that were important.

There was a break in the neat hedgerows, and Alina turned the mare into the field beyond, leaving Justin little choice but to follow her. She rode between the harvested rows until she reached the end of the field and a small, nearly circular stand of trees where the land was too rocky to be cultivated. There she dismounted without his help and tied the reins to a low-hanging branch.

He dismounted as well, shaking his head. "There are at least three dozen beds at Basingstoke, kitten. We really should try at least one of them."

"Oh, so you are assuming I'm about to seduce you, Lord Wilde. Is it my turn? Why, I believe it is. Perhaps later. Right now, I really think we should talk about the *Inhaber*." She walked over to a fallen tree trunk and sat down, then waited for him to join her. "Are you really going to include Luka? Because if it comes to a fight, he's still injured."

"Worried about your secretary, Alina?"

"No, I'm worried about you. See? I'm not fibbing, because you can tell, so I may as well be honest, even if that makes me a bad person. You'd be so busy rescuing him that you might forget to rescue yourself. I think he should be made to remain here, at Basingstoke. You're not taking me, correct?"

He lifted her gloved hand to his lips, turning it so that he could kiss the bared flesh at the inside of her wrist. "Because if it comes to a fight, I'd be too busy rescuing you to remember to rescue myself? Yes, that's correct. Brutus and I will do very nicely on our own. We always have."

"You didn't answer me. Are you taking Luka?"

"No, I'm not I never planned to include him."

She sighed, that one worry assuaged at least. "But you still have no idea what you're going to say to the man? He'll see soon enough that Luka and I aren't with you. He'll be very angry."

Justin leaned in, began nuzzling the side of her throat. "I suppose I could prevail upon Wigglesworth to don his incognito-ness yet again, and hope the *Inhaber* is shortsighted. Must we really discuss this now? I'd really much rather you seduced me." He took her hand, laid it in his lap, proving to her that he wasn't completely joking. "Here, let me help you, if you don't know how to make the first move."

"Justin," she said quietly, tugging to free her hand from his grip.

"Darling. Try that, kitten. Try calling me *darling*."

"*Justin*. The children."

He licked her earlobe. "Exactly. The first one won't mind being conceived in a— Damn." He straightened quickly, thankfully also releasing her hand so that she could move it away from its most compromising location.

She put a smile on her face and waved to the half-dozen children who were crossing the field not twenty yards from them. "Wave to them, Justin. I think they might believe you were hurting me."

"You're not the one in pain," he grumbled as he got to his feet, not only tipping his hat to the children, but removing it to hold in front of him. "We really have to begin considering making love indoors."

Alina waved again as the children waved and then began to run across the field once more. "Tatiana naps in her room in the attic each afternoon, but Danica never seems to leave my dressing room. I think she knows. She looks at me all disapproving, so I'm more than fairly certain she knows."

"Wigglesworth dances the jig in my dressing

room," Justin told her as they retraced their steps to the horses.

"Oh, he does not. You really shouldn't tease him so. He worships you. Justin?"

Something in her voice as she said his name must have alerted him, as he turned to her immediately, taking her hands in his. "Kitten, I really don't want to discuss tomorrow with you. I want us to enjoy today."

"Because you think it may be all we'll ever have?"

"No." He looked at her so seriously, she had to believe him. "I think I can…redirect the man, point him toward a more pressing problem he doesn't seem to know he has. My problem is in getting close enough to him to have that conversation without having to dispose of any more of his men. I'm also going to pray that he's so grateful to me for passing along the information I have for him that he'll withdraw his accusations about his deceased guards. My worry, since you won't rest until I tell you, is how in God's name I'll ever be able to mend fences as it were, with His Royal Highness. If I fail there, it doesn't matter where else I might succeed."

Alina's heart skipped a beat. He was genuinely worried about the Prince Regent. Her new friends had been correct; he already had more than enough on his plate, so it was clearly up to them to rescue him from the worst of his folly.

And it wasn't as if she'd actually be *lying* to him, which she now knew wouldn't work, thanks to her so depressingly expressive face. She simply had to keep him occupied, his mind on other things until it was tomorrow and time for him to ride off to meet with the *Inhaber*.

She looked out over the field, and the children were gone. Good.

"You know, *darling*," she said, taking his hand and leading him back toward the trees once more, "this tiny forest is fairly dense, and there is all of this late-afternoon shadow, isn't there? Why, I imagine if we were to go no more than a few feet off the path, we'd all but disappear."

Really. It was so easy to distract men. She might even call it child's play....

CHAPTER SIXTEEN

THEY'D RETURNED TO Basingstoke to find that, for reasons only women knew—and definitely reasons only women understood—Alina was not left alone again with Justin until tea was served at ten o'clock and all three ladies announced they were retiring for the night, leaving the men to amuse themselves as best they could without feminine company.

Which meant that all three men made for the terrace and lit up cheroots Lucas passed around. Fragrant blue smoke began to rise in the cool evening air. Nice, actually quite good tobacco, but Justin would rather be with Alina.

"What the devil was that about?" he asked his friends as Tanner handed him a glass of port, not his favorite drink, but he'd manage it. "Why have your wives suddenly turned into duennas?"

Lucas blew out a thin stream of smoke, and then smiled. "If I might quote my wife?"

"As she seems to be the one in charge, yes, do that."

"Nicole believes you have been indiscreet enough.

From now until the wedding—you do have one in mind fairly soon, correct?—you are to behave yourself. Again, not my words. Oh, and Lydia agrees. Actually, I understand she more than agrees. It would seem our dearest lovers have turned into wives. It would be depressing, except that they're enjoying themselves so much."

"There's a special license waiting at my town house in London, courtesy of Prinny. If I can dare show my face there, that is. Clearly, as if I didn't have enough as it is, I now have new incentive to get back in the man's good graces."

"Prinny has no graces," Tanner said, leaning his elbows on the balustrade. "I was one of those unfortunate enough to see him harnessed and then winched up in the air so that he could be lowered onto his horse for some ceremony in Hyde Park. Richard led his men into battle in the Crusades. Henry fought side by side with his army at Agincourt. The Louis we propped up on a throne in Paris is so fat he can't lift his foot high enough not to trip over his own red carpet, and our own poor king George is mad as a hatter and has been fitted for his own straitjacket. Prinny can't even mount a horse without aid, and the only place he's led his countrymen is into debt. Truly, our only hope is that Princess Charlotte will grow up to be another such as Elizabeth, and bring some honor back to the monarchy."

"Elizabeth, as I recall," Justin pointed out, "had

somewhat of a penchant for chopping off heads. A man in my current position might be grateful that Prinny can be so easily distracted by simply placing a new, expensive toy in his greedy hands."

Tanner and Lucas exchanged looks Justin did not miss, but could not interpret.

He tossed his barely smoked cheroot out onto the grass. "Pleasant as this company is, if I'm not to be allowed to see Alina any more tonight, I may as well go visit the major and discuss something that's been troubling me. I'll be gone by first light and hopefully returned in one piece by noon, free of at least half my problems. Wish me luck?"

"Will you need it?" Tanner asked him.

"I don't know. I may have used up the last of my store of luck when the Fates gave me Alina. But even the Fates can't be that cruel."

"We've both offered several times to accompany you," Lucas said, walking with him to the French doors leading back into the main salon. "That offer still stands."

Justin clapped the man on the shoulder. "If your lovers have become wives, then their lovers have become husbands. And husbands don't go skulking about old church ruins, pistols drawn, exposing themselves to danger not their own. But thank you. Thank you both, most especially for keeping Alina safe here."

This time he only caught out Lucas shifting his

gaze toward Tanner, who'd remained still, his expression impassive.

"She will be safe here, correct?" he asked Lucas.

"She'll be as safe as she can be, definitely," Lucas answered.

Justin nodded. He was becoming an old woman, fretting when there was no need to fret. He smiled, shook both men's hands and headed upstairs to see the major, his mind already on the following morning and his meeting with the *Inhaber,* most especially the logistics that would be involved in getting past the man's guards.

Strange that he'd always planned how he would eliminate somebody. He'd never before had to plan for a way to keep his intended target alive.

Alina hadn't actually said the words, but he thought she knew: killing was easier.

At the head of the staircase, he nearly turned for his bedchamber rather than have another dreary conversation about the *Inhaber* Novak, but then headed for the major's bedchamber. He supposed he'd owed the man an explanation as to why he would not be accompanying him tomorrow morning.

He rapped on the major's door, and then was forced to wait a full minute before the man bid him enter, only to find him fully dressed and reclining atop the coverlet, his arm tucked in its sling. Strange again. Alina had told him that the major had been up and about yesterday, and that he'd thrown off the sling, protesting that he was no longer so ill as to be kept confined to his bed.

"You've looked better," he said smoothly as Luka slid to the edge of the bed and stood up, rather dramatically holding on to the bedpost for support.

It might be prudent to tear his mind away from Alina, away from the *Inhaber,* away from the Prince Regent, and concentrate a bit more on the earnest, clean-shaven major. A friend is not a friend merely because he says he is your friend. *You've been asleep, Wilde. Lost in love and misery. Time to wake up!*

"The fever came back today. Knocked me flat, I'm afraid."

"Ah, damned plaguey things, fevers. I hesitate to further distress you, but I find that before I go hunting up your *Inhaber* tomorrow morning for our hopefully productive tête-à-tête, I have a few questions about this disputed land that's caused us all so much bother."

"Tulk. Then it's true—you're actually going to *talk* to him at this meeting you've arranged. Lady Alina told me you hope to settle everything...amicably. But I didn't really believe her. As if such a thing is possible with a monster like the *Inhaber* Novak. You were bent on killing him. You went off to kill him that morning, remember? We'd discussed it, you understood. You agreed. It was the plan then, and it should be the plan now."

Well, now the fellow was looking a little more robust, and his color was better, as well.

"Ah, yes, the *plan*. It came to me late, this revelation I've had, Major, but I've realized that I followed other plans, created by others, only implemented by me, for too many years. Always with the assumption that the cause was right and just, or at least right and just to somebody's mind. Now I find myself chafing at the notion of possibly being forced back in the role of tool, a weapon without choices of my own."

"But that is who you are." The major's lips curved in a smile; he'd have been well served to keep the mustachios, as at least this particular smile was neither pleasant nor flattering, but revealing. "I suppose we take off the gloves now, as you English say? In truth, I've been wondering when you'd come to me about the land. It was my mistake that got you to finally wondering in the first place, wasn't it?"

Justin hid his surprise at the man's unexpected candor—and that hint of disdain that was rather troubling. Had he been so intent on Alina, on his feelings of guilt concerning her uncle and the threat to her from the *Inhaber,* that he'd overlooked what was directly beneath his nose? He quickly cudgeled his brains for what had to be the correct response to the major's question; there was no room for error now. Not when he'd stumbled onto something he didn't yet understand.

"Yes, certainly. Time for candor. And it was

dashed clumsy of you, I agree," he improvised smoothly, walking over to the decanter and glasses that stood on a table near the windows. "But clumsy of me as well for taking so long to realize what had been staring me in the face. Wine?"

"Thank you, no," the major said, his tone once more light, conversational. "So, what exactly gave me away?"

Justin grabbed onto the seeming discrepancy he and Alina had discussed only that afternoon. "Must we?" he asked, turning about, one of the wineglasses in his hand. "Oh, very well. It made no sense, you see, that Alina could not sign away the land to the *Inhaber,* yet her detestable aunt Mimi could. A piddling thing, especially stacked up against all that has transpired these past days. The man's attack on Alina's coach, his minions armed to the teeth and skulking about Ashurst Hall? Both events lent considerable credence to the notion that her life is in danger, and the *Inhaber*'s permanent removal the only real solution. Yet it continues to niggle, that small discrepancy."

The major nodded. "Yes. Just as I thought. Loiza had several strong words for me on that subject after he'd spoken with Lady Alina."

"She is the one who first picked up on the thing, truth be told," Justin said, nodding, and at the same time surreptitiously measuring the major, wondering what he'd missed, how he'd so badly misjudged him. Weighing the notion that the sling would make a convenient hiding place for a knife or small pistol. "Tell me more about your king, and exactly why he wants the *Inhaber* dead."

The major didn't strike him as a man who believed confession good for the soul. He did, however, strike him as a man who would play for time until he learned whether or not more decisive measures were necessary. As Justin was doing himself.

And him standing here in his evening clothes, and without his knife or any weapon close to hand. Still, a bit of well-placed pressure on the man's wound should be enough to incapacitate him. If not, snapping off the head of the wineglass on the table behind him would turn the stem of the glass into a tolerable weapon.

Standing here, holding forth on what is at least outwardly a civilized conversation, while contemplating grinding his fingers into a gunshot wound, putting a wineglass stem through a man's throat. God, had he ever thought like a normal man? What all had he lost on the day thoughts like these became normal to him?

"The king? You still think this is about the king? That I would risk so much for *him?*"

At last Justin believed he understood. "You're Romany, aren't you? That business about the *Inhaber* hiring Romany as part of the army he raised, and then abandoning them to be slaughtered by the French—men, women, children. That's true?"

"Unfortunately for my family, yes. From that day onward, the *Inhaber* has been marked for death. But he stubbornly refuses to die. Instead, he continues to prosper."

Justin wanted to keep him talking, perhaps lower his guard. "How inconsiderate of the fellow. It all begins to come clearer, although far from completely transparent. No wonder you had found it so simple to arrange the caravans, the Romany protection for Alina."

"Loiza is my uncle, and it was always planned to remove Lady Alina to the caravans, where I—we would be safer. In any event, she was never to be harmed or exposed to any real danger. The rest?" The major made a crude hand gesture that had Justin raising one eyebrow in near admiration. "Yes, the rest is lies. There is no disputed land, there never has been, other than in convenient legend. The land had only been a plausible story, although the lie difficult to maintain."

"Oh, I wouldn't be so sure of that, Major. I swallowed the whole thing like some idiot schoolboy for longer than it pleases me to realize, among other things I may have overlooked. Discovering a fellow assassin so close to Alina did nothing to change my mind. Your hireling, I suppose? He seemed almost eager to guide my suspicions to my Prince Regent, and I remember myself being damnably eager to point him in that same direction. Information you spoon-fed him, I'm sure."

Luka shrugged, both his injured and uninjured shoulders. So expressive, the Romany. Sometimes to their detriment.

"It was imperative that you didn't think too much, but only believed what was in front of your eyes. That was Loiza's idea, once he decided I had bungled things. We'd considered others before choosing you, and that particular man had been brought to our attention. It was easy enough to hire him to lurk about the encampment in order to reinforce in you the belief that Lady Alina was in grave danger. He assured us he could speak with you and convince you of everything we needed you to believe. But something clearly went wrong."

"For him, certainly. Although I congratulate your uncle on this much, as I certainly was distracted. Led by the nose might be more accurate, if personally damning. But now you're attempting to tell me that Alina has never been in danger. You disappoint me. I thought there were to be no more lies."

"I'm telling you the truth. At least the truth as we'd hoped it would be."

"Ah, I'm relieved. I was beginning to wonder if there could be any truth left anywhere in this," he said quietly, remembering that the *Inhaber* had specifically asked that the major accompany them to their meeting. "You're a bit of a bastard, aren't you, Major? I actually pitied you, believing you were in love with her. But that day the coach was attacked? That bullet had never been meant for Alina. It had been meant for the target it found."

"The *Inhaber* had to know I would come hunting him when he learned I was to come here with Lady Alina. In Prague there had been…other attempts, but the man is always well protected. My name was somehow connected to those attempts, which is why I was asked to see the king in the first place. He made it clear to me what he wanted, and that he would help me. Yet even here in England, I would never again be allowed close to the *Inhaber*."

Justin's mind was whirling. "But someone at the English court, someone who had just been wed to one of his countrywomen, someone he would never question—that someone would be allowed close. Someone who believed he had good reason to want the *Inhaber* dead. Most importantly, preferably someone who wouldn't muck up the job the way you had, someone already known—modesty aside—as being very good at what he did. Befriend the man, dine with him, and then…eliminate him, probably with what some might term extreme malice. Instead, Alina very nearly died."

"I didn't choose the time and place of the confrontation—he did. I *was* protecting her, you know. I would have suggested the caravan to you when I told you about the *Inhaber,* after that first night at the inn in Portsmouth, as my uncle was already waiting for us on the road to London. That was always the plan, for she and I to disappear while you executed the *Inhaber* for us."

"How terribly inconsiderate of me, I'm sure. Hearing all of this, I'm amazed you can contain your contempt for me."

The flushed cheeks were back. "You made a confusion of everything. It was you who put all of us in danger with your mad decision to send her to Ashurst Hall. She could have been injured in the cross fire during the attack, which made it my duty to protect her. I owed her father that much. And may I remind you that, by doing so, I presented my unprotected back to the enemy."

"And now I imagine you believe I should be searching about for a medal to pin on your front? Forgive me if I leave it to others to do you that honor. Your king, I would imagine. I wonder, Major, how much of what you're doing can be laid at the door of revenging your fellow Romany, and how much at the door of your own personal ambition. Does Loiza wonder, as well?"

"My uncle may have considered this, yes. I am not in favor at the moment." The major shifted uncomfortably in his seat, wincing as the movement caused his shoulder to remind him of his wound—or he meant to remind Justin of his wound, assuming a gentleman wouldn't strike an injured man. And how wrong he was. Justin hadn't been a gentleman for a long time.

He allowed the silence to grow, until the major apparently felt it necessary to fill it.

"I may have been promised…something, once the *Inhaber* was no longer a problem for the king. But that's of no matter. He needs to die."

"Somebody should, yes, I agree. I could begin a list."

"It was never meant to be so complicated. Your damn Prince Regent—"

"Please, leave the damning of our future king to those who will be His Royal Highness's subjects, if you don't mind. I should have known he didn't come up with such an intricate plot on his own. He did try to appear brilliant and conniving, I'll give him that, but he hasn't the brain for intrigue."

"True enough. He was most concerned in deciding how much he might be able to profit if he assisted our king in a matter that had nothing to do with his own interests."

Justin laughed. It wasn't a pleasant sound, even to his own ears.

"Finally, something that makes sense in all of this. Prinny the plotter made no sense. Prinny the greedy buffoon and even dupe? Yes, that I can understand and even somewhat forgive. He can't help who he is. It was *you* who dangled the idea in front of his face of having me buy my way back to England. No wonder he's taken to his bed. He had no idea what I was talking about when I accused him of plotting Alina's murder."

"To be fair, King Francis didn't know, either. But I tell you again, Lady Alina was never in any danger."

"She was very nearly shot! *I killed people,* damn you to hell. For what?" Justin took a calming breath. He wondered if the major knew that he was seeing him through a red veil of anger. Then the rest of what the major had said penetrated his brain. "What do you mean, your king didn't know?"

Luka sighed rather dramatically. "Kings know what they want to know. And then, like all royalty, they walk away. Minions do the rest. This doesn't surprise you, does it, Justin?"

"Lord Wilde, thank you. Only my friends address me as Justin, *Major.*"

"Yes, the inestimable Baron Wilde," the major said, and now his tone took on somewhat of an edge. "We heard about the boy in Trebon. And what you did to the father. A killer without mercy, without conscience. You were perfect for our needs. Did you really think that fat flawn in London came up with your name on his own?"

Justin ignored the question. "Why not just come to me, hire me to assassinate the man for you?"

"Would you have done it? What could we have offered you?"

Justin didn't answer.

"We had our choice of many men, but Trebon made it clear that you were the one we wanted, especially after our failed attempts, because now the *Inhaber* was never alone or unprotected. We know everything about you. Tell me—the man who insulted your wife. We heard you shot him in the back at the count of two," the major said almost gleefully. "Is that true?"

"Yes, of course, as I kill children and unarmed men, just as you said, without mercy or conscience. I'm a very bad man," Justin said, not giving a damn what Luka thought of him. It was enough that the major had not stumbled on the fact that Robbie Farber had been Alina's uncle. God only knew what the major would have done with that information. Perhaps there was such a thing as Fate.

Luka nodded his head, as if a suspicion had been proved true. "I thought we had chosen the wrong man that day on the dock. You play the game well, my lord, but the savage lies not far beneath the so-civilized surface. It is not only what the king will do for me that is important. What is left of my family needs to see the *Inhaber* dead. We, all of us, need to know he suffered, as did the merchant in Trebon. I was glad you failed the day you went riding after him. A quick death is not what we wished for him.

Now I suppose we will have to satisfy ourselves if you merely tell me where we can find him. I need you to do that now, my lord."

"I'm afraid you and your hoped-for fortune are doomed to disappointment, Major. I'll be damned if I'll give you his location so that you and your family can murder him and place the blame on me. He can cool his heels where he is, and then return to London. I don't—"

Justin remembered the letter. The one where he'd offered up Alina in exchange for ten thousand pounds. The letter he'd signed with his usual flourish. Even if the *Inhaber* had destroyed the letter, there was still the matter of the man's presence in London. There was no choice now; he had to meet with him. Explain. Grovel yet again, and this time to a real bastard of a man, not simply a well-born buffoon.

"Something has changed your mind, my lord, I can see it in your eyes. You will meet with the *Inhaber* tomorrow, won't you? Tell me, tell me the place of this meeting."

"Major, you're still alive for only two reasons. The first is that I would not have Alina if not for your insane and, frankly, self-serving plotting. The second is that Loiza and the others I met in the camp have my sympathy for what *Inhaber* Novak did to their families. But if you want him dead, you'll have to find a way to do that without me. I'm done, do you understand that?"

"A man like you? The madman of Trebon? A man like you does not find it so easy to be *done*."

"Don't push me, Major, or I might prove you right. I'll proffer your thanks to the marquess and give your farewells to Alina. Brutus will meet you at the stables in one hour, to escort you back to your uncle's camp. It seems you are to be a disappointment to him once again."

He turned away, but then, as if he'd just thought of something else, he turned back once more. It was a maneuver that had served him well before, had even saved his life. "That morning at the inn," he said, "when you were so adamant I not leave Alina with you while you traveled to Ashurst Hall. It seems a lifetime ago. I truly believed you were concerned for her. For the sake of her affection for you, I'd like to continue to believe that."

The major drew himself up straight. "I would of course have been upset had any real harm come to her. She is the daughter of my commander. Still, she is only a woman. They have their place in life. They were born to be useful to us, and sacrifices must sometimes be made. That is simply the way of the world."

"Ten minutes," Justin bit out between clenched teeth. "Brutus won't be happy if he's kept waiting.

No, that's not fair. You're injured. I'll give you the full hour, and then Brutus can carry you out."

"Carry—?"

Justin knocked the major to the floor with a fist flush to the jaw, then swiftly stepped down hard on his injured shoulder until the man's eyes rolled up in his head. Then, to satisfy his curiosity, he rummaged inside the man's sling, to be rewarded when his hand closed around the small pistol hidden there.

He pocketed the weapon that probably would have been shoved into his back before he'd made it safely out of the room.

"You should have paid more attention to your own argument, Major," he calmly told the unconscious man. "You were right—it's not that easy for someone like me to be done."

But ten hours later, he very nearly was.

The *Inhaber* might not have been as grateful for the information Justin gave him as one would suppose, as he'd already decided that his king was very much looking forward to attending his funeral. But once the farce of the disputed land was cleared up—the man had thought Lord Wilde mad when he'd read his letter—he'd agreed to reconsider the charges of the murder of his guards, accusing instead one Major Luka Prochazka.

This seemed reasonable to the newly civilized Baron Wilde, and he instructed Brutus to please put the *Inhaber* down, as the man's already red face was beginning to turn somewhat blue. He'd then tossed the *Inhaber* the keys to the cellars of the ruined church where the meeting had taken place, so that he could release his henchmen, who had surrendered with even more alacrity than Justin could have hoped.

A well-armed and growling Brutus did have that effect on some people, the last-moment addition of a crossbow an almost inspired touch.

With the letter that could have damned him (for the third or fourth time, he'd rather lost count of his recent indiscretions) now destroyed, all that was left was to ride back to Basingstoke, soundly kiss Alina, assure her he was fine and then gather up the inestimable Wigglesworth and hotfoot it to Carleton House, where he would grovel for, hopefully, the last time.

Except, when he rode up to the front doors of Basingstoke at noon, it was to be told that the master and mistress were not at home. Indeed, they had all, master, mistress, duke, duchess and the dear Lady Alina, departed for London within minutes of sunrise that very morning, a journey of nearly fifty miles that would require several changes of horses and the constitutions only the young possessed.

As Justin went tearing up the stairs, already ripping at his neckcloth and shouting for Wigglesworth, the butler called after him, "The Duke and Duchess of Ashurst will be meeting them there, my lord. I overheard Lady Nicole say as much to her sister the duchess. I imagine it will be quite the merry party. You are to join them at Carleton House this evening at eleven, if you wish, although you will be cutting it rather fine, won't you, my lord?"

The butler quickly clapped his hands over the ears of the youngest footman standing in the entrance hall as Justin offered his sentiments concerning what he *wished....*

"NICOLE, SIT STILL," Charlotte Daughtry begged, not for the first time since the twins had joined Alina and the duchess in the luxurious town carriage and headed off for Carleton House.

Alina had been taken to the duke's residence because her baggage had come to London with Charlotte and Rafe, leaving the twins to complete their toilettes in Tanner's Mayfair residence, so they had still to see Alina's gown for the evening. Charlotte thought that delicious, proving that though she might have been a practical sort, she could very much enjoy surprising the two young brides who had once been her charges.

"But it's so annoying. With all these coaches clogging the streets, it will take us forever to arrive. Justin can't get there ahead of us, or it won't matter when we get there, for he'll have already ruined everything."

Alina's stomach performed a small flip as she

sat on the facing seat, and it wasn't because she was riding backward, especially not at the snail's pace they were traveling. "She's right, Charlotte. That could be disastrous. He'd strut into the Prince Regent's presence, perfect as Wigglesworth can make him, imperiously demanding to see me and be assured I'm fine."

"Just before he tears a strip off your hide for having come to London without him," Lydia pointed out reasonably. "Tanner and Rafe have wagered fifty pounds on how long it will take him to turn from terrified fiancé to infuriated lover."

Nicole laughed. "Well, now that we're all such a *jolly* party, I must say I'm pleased that Lucas was clever enough to confine our party to just two coaches. What do you think they're discussing back there behind us? How to subdue Justin if he becomes violent?"

"Justin doesn't become violent," Alina told her rather proudly. "He becomes efficient. And if he were to think that any harm might come to me, I believe he could become prodigiously efficient."

"Oh, Lord, she's right," Lydia breathed, shaking her head. "Sometimes I wonder not only why my mind manufactures ideas such as this, but why I ever think to voice them in front of my sister."

"But it is a brilliant idea," Charlotte said soothingly. "It's just as your aunt Emmaline has always said—sometimes men simply have to be saved from themselves."

Alina giggled and sank back into the cushions. She had yet to meet the twins' aunt, but she already liked her. Emmaline, she'd been told, was also married to a duke: the Duke of Warrington. She giggled again, knowing her nerves were badly rattled, unable to stop herself. But her aunt Mimi had always impressed upon her something she called the *privileges of rank*. Tonight Alina was absolutely knee-deep in dukes, and adding in the marquess made everything all the better. Bless Justin, he might think he was alone in his life, but he had very good, loyal and well-placed friends.

Perhaps enough of them to keep him from some dank cell, if Lydia's idea failed, if she, Alina, could not do her part as she was so determined to do.

The coach moved ahead yet again, and Nicole leaned forward to peer out the window. "We're finally here. I can actually see a small mob of people waiting to mount the steps to the front doors. I'd always thought London was very thin of company at this time of year."

"He's still the Prince Regent, still the heir to the throne," Charlotte reminded them. "If His Royal Highness wishes to commemorate the anniversary of the Great Fire with tonight's reception, then who are we to question his judgment?"

Nicole laughed. "Especially when it so neatly

dovetails with our own plan. How fortunate Rafe received that invitation. Ah, at last." She reached for the handle, ready to open the door herself before Charlotte restrained her. "Impatience. The greatest of my sins."

"Really? I don't remember being offered a vote in that," Lydia said, and her sister looked at her in amused surprise, so that she shrugged delicately and added, "Tanner tells me I should speak my mind more often, rather than to keep my thoughts inside as I have always done. He said it would be very... freeing. I think he's right."

"And I think I'm extremely grateful the two of you are married now, and no longer Rafe's and my responsibility. Shall we go? Alina? Are you all right, dear?"

She nodded, not quite sure she could trust her voice, and within minutes they were all slowly making their way up the outer steps and then up the curving marble staircase that led to the first floor of the Prince Regent's London residence.

She could feel eyes on her, both from the men and the ladies. She could hear the whispers. She took herself back to the Portsmouth docks and the first time she had set foot on English soil, the homeland of her mother.

And then, in her mind's eye, she replaced this multitude of well-dressed gentlemen and their perfumed and bejeweled ladies with the sailors, dockworkers, even the prostitutes on those docks. After all, people were people, weren't they?

Besides, it made the whole thing easier. Especially if she continued to believe that Justin would soon be here. She did not doubt that he would have been successful in his dealings with the *Inhaber*. It was as Wigglesworth had assured her—the baron always prevailed. Perhaps not at first, but in the end the result was always the same. Success.

To divert her mind, she held on to the curved railing and took in her surroundings. There certainly was a multitude of gold gilt everywhere, along with crystal and stucco and a flotilla of candles that could easily have lit up a village. And yet the entire structure seemed somehow fragile to her, as if it might be only the stucco and gilt that held it all together and they were all fortunate to not have the vaulted roof tumble down on them at any moment.

She raised her eyes to the enormous chandelier at the very top of the staircase. Was that a crystal dove at the center of it? With its eyes picked out in rubies? How ludicrous!

"I'm not afraid anymore," she whispered to Lydia as they passed beneath the chandelier. "Anyone who must try with such dedication to impress his guests cannot be anything other than terrified that he will not measure up to whatever is expected of him. Poor man."

Lydia leaned close to whisper. "That *poor man* is

one day to be George the Fourth, King of England. And you *pity* him?"

"Yes. He is probably much like my aunt Mimi. So very concerned with all that is outside of her, so that no one will notice that there is very little inside of her."

"No wonder Justin loves you. And you will balance his cynicism for his fellow man with your compassionate heart."

"No, it is all of you who are so compassionate, so extraordinarily kind. The Prince Regent could very easily take you all in disfavor for what you're doing tonight."

"We've already discussed this, haven't we? We'd be very poor friends if we did not support Justin now. We're prepared for the prince's punishment, and even more certain there will be one. We'll survive it, knowing we've done the right thing." She squeezed Alina's gloved hand. "Now, are you ready? We're next to be announced. Thank goodness they limit the introduction to only the most senior titles, or we'd have another five minutes ahead of us to get through."

Alina took a deep breath, then nodded. She only flinched the first time one of the pair of liveried footman—were they twins? did it matter?—rapped the bottom of his staff sharply against the marble floor and announced in a near bellow, "Your Royal Highnesses! The Duke and Duchess of Ashurst!"

The second footman followed with, "Your Royal Highnesses! The Duke and Duchess of Malvern."

"Your Royal Highnesses! The Marquess and Marchioness of Basingstoke!"

And then, as her new friends stood with the ladies to the left, their husbands to the right, as though an honor guard of lesser mortals sent ahead of her, "Your Royal Highnesses! Lady Magdaléna Evinka Nadeja Valentin!"

Alina took five steps forward into the vast ballroom and raised her gloved hands to the hood of the cloak fashioned from a thin ivory whisper of silk and antique Austrian lace that had made her such a curious and intriguing sight to the others on the stairs.

The Duke of Ashurst himself stepped forward as she lowered the hood and untied the silken strings at her throat, lifting it all away from her shoulders to reveal what had been so well hidden.

Several gasps were heard, and a ripple of low whispers began spreading out across the ballroom. *"Who is she?"* Alina heard. And *"My God—magnificent!"*

Ah, if only Justin could be here beside her. He would be so proud. She also thought he would appreciate such a moment. He was so delightfully vain.

Alina's gown had been her greatest achievement in her purchases, other than the velvet, ermine-tipped cloak that she had once sworn she loved with all her heart.

She knew the material of her gown to be extraordinary, appearing as liquid gold, its simple bodice devoid of ruffle or sleeves. The bodice stopped at the high waist, accented by an intricate, braided knot of material, and the nominally full front piece of the skirt was seemingly made up of hundreds of pleats that ran vertically down to within a whisper of the floor. There were forty-two pleats, actually; Danica had told her that several times, having been the one who had to make them perfect with the pressing iron in an obscenely brief amount of time.

Emeralds and diamonds were everywhere. In Alina's dark hair, which was piled at least six inches high, with ringlets caressing her neck. In her ears, on her wrists, over top her long gloves…and in the heavy necklace that possessed the famed Valentin emerald at its center. How Aunt Mimi had coveted that necklace that was never truly hers.

In the midst of all the quiet, Alina heard what she thought might be something that sounded very much like *coo* from somewhere behind her. She had no idea what it might mean, but she decided she would choose to be flattered.

Her chin high, she surveyed the dockworkers and sailors and prostitutes in her mind's eye and then took the arm the Duke of Malvern offered her and proceeded directly down the center of the enormous chamber, toward the pair of thrones sitting on a cleverly tiered dais. The royal princess Charlotte occupied the smaller throne, her father the monstrously large and overly carved creation beside it.

An Ashurst footman followed them, the velvet-and-ermine cloak cradled in his outstretched arms.

Her heart pounding, her expression one of the confidence she tried with all her might to believe she possessed, Alina dropped into a deep curtsy that spread the deceptive fullness of her gown into a graceful golden puddle. "Your Royal Highness," she said, holding out her right hand as she kept her chin high, refusing to lower her gaze as she knew she should. "My affianced husband, Lord Wilde, sends his most abject apologies for his tardiness. He assures me he will be arriving shortly to apologize personally. And to thank you, as I do now, for being the wisest of men, who has in his infinite wisdom and charity bound our two hearts together. We are both of us now and forever your most grateful and loyal subjects."

The world stopped, held its collective breath.

Alina remained deep in her curtsy, at last lowering her head, baring the nape of her neck, as if in supplication. Her outstretched hand remained steady.

Just as she thought she had surely failed, she heard the creak of bone stays. She believed she could sense the Prince Regent rising from his red-velvet-and-gold-gilt throne. A fleshy hand took hold of hers, and she was drawn to her feet.

He bent over her fingertips, not actually kissing them, but still quite graciously, as if acknowledging her extraordinary and faintly exotic presence.

And the world breathed again.

"The shimmer of your gown is as nothing when matched with the worth of the true gold I see in your eyes, madam. The emeralds, however, are astounding. You've brought a present for me? From your king?" the Prince Regent asked in a curiously high-pitched voice.

Alina carefully recited the words Lucas had also penned for her, working on the two short speeches, refining them again and again during their hurried journey.

"For Her Royal Highness Princess Charlotte, sir, a gift from Lord Wilde and myself, if it pleases you. There is not another like it anywhere, as is proper, for only the daughter of the most beloved Florizel can do it justice. May she wear it in good health for the next fifty years."

Rafe nodded to the footman, and he stepped forward so that the duke could lift the cloak and flourish it, the ermine tails showing to their best advantage.

From her throne, the princess inclined her head and smiled.

"My compliments, madam. You may inform your

affianced husband that he has gained himself a most delightful and formidable advocate," the Prince Regent said quietly.

There was the sound of some commotion at the doorway to the ballroom, and Alina hid a smile.

"I believe it may be possible that you might tell him yourself, Your Highness."

She didn't turn to watch, even as another round of gasps danced about the ballroom, even as she heard and recognized the confident footfalls of her beloved approaching.

Only when she felt his presence beside her did she dare to look at him. Oh, he was such a handsome fellow in his finery. Even if his neckcloth was slightly askew, and his hair somewhat the worse for the hat that must have sat on it for several long hours. She bit back a smile. The man actually smelled a bit of horse. Poor Justin. How his consequence must be suffering, that he was not his usual pristine and perfect self.

And how important she must be to him.

"Justin," she said quietly.

"Alina," he drawled almost languidly, without so much as nodding his head in her direction. "Imagine seeing you here. Was Basingstoke that much of a bore in my absence?"

Oh, dear. If he grew any more polite, she felt sure the pressure building up inside of him would soon have the top of his head exploding into pieces. He must be very worried about her.

"Your Royal Highness," Justin said then, as he moved closer to the dais and bowed deeply to the Prince Regent, his voice so low, so intimate, that even Alina had difficulty hearing him. "My betrothed means well, but she is not a part of this. I am here to tell you that I was wrong and present myself for punishment. What transpired between us the last time I was in this building was unforgivable, the worst of it being that I misjudged you, and that I likewise misjudged my deep love and devotion for this country. I offer no excuses. No apology, no matter how abject or sincere, can adequately correct the insult I have dealt you. I can only say that I will do anything you ask, Your Highness. I am yours to command."

"How delightful, if difficult to believe. Yet rather easy to prove," the Prince Regent said just as quietly, "Would you give her up if I were to ask it of you—for love of Crown and country?"

At last Justin turned his head to look at Alina. His eyes widened slightly, which served to warm her heart quite a lot. He took her hand in his, which brought tears to her eyes.

Please, Lord, let him behave. Please make him be diplomatic. Please don't let him say anything witty and damning....

Justin turned back to the Prince Regent. "No," he said flatly.

The future king at last showed that he wasn't as shallow and perhaps even stupid as many of his subjects would believe. He nodded, smiled—he was really rather handsome when he smiled, Alina thought charitably—and said, "Take her home, Wilde, now. Leave this very minute. Your lady, and your impertinent friends. We look forward to the pleasure of your company again in the spring. But not until then, not any of you. Do we understand each other?"

They were prepared for this. They knew this could be their very public punishment so that the Prince Regent might have his small victory. *Say yes, Justin,* Alina prayed silently. *They're your friends, our friends. Take what they've offered. You're not alone. You'll never again be alone....*

"Yes, Your Highness," Justin said.

EPILOGUE

ALINA RAN ALONG THE PATII that wound through trees just budding with bright, spring-green leaves, her muslin skirts hiked almost above her knees as she laughed, occasionally daring a glance back to search out her pursuer.

Just as she burst from the shade of the trees, into the grassy clearing that bordered one of the streams flowing through the country estate, she found herself caught up and swung high off the ground.

"Justin! How do you always do this?" she exclaimed, resting her hands on his broad shoulders. "We always begin together, yet even when I manage to elude you, I can never arrive here first. You must know a secret path."

He lowered her slowly, their bodies touching in that now-familiar and yet still so thrilling way, until their lips met in a brief kiss before he set her back on her feet. "Perhaps I am a *mullo,* and flew here in the form of a bat," he said teasingly as they walked hand in hand to the edge of the stream.

"No," she protested, her good humor fled. "Loiza has told me stories of these supposed vampires. To the Romany a *mullo* is a terrible dead person who returns only to do malicious things. You do good things. You gave Loiza some of your land."

"*Our* land, kitten, and he refused the deed, only accepting the offer to set up camp there whenever he wished. And in return he gave me your caravan," Justin pointed out. "I think that you're taking my selfishness for more than it is."

She glanced back at the gaily painted caravan that had been her refuge for several days during that terrible and yet glorious time and now sat permanently here, a wedding gift from her husband. She hadn't told him, but she valued this gift more than any of the others, including the sable-trimmed cloak he had been so proud of. Cloaks, furs, jewels: they were all simply *things*. The caravan was and would always be their most private refuge, something much more special, something totally theirs.

"You also arranged for Loiza to be able to return Luka's body to Prague, for burial."

"And to watch as the *Inhaber* Novak was publicly executed for having murdered the major right on the streets of London. I enjoyed listening to Loiza's recounting of that particular event. Darling, I'm trying my best to be good, but don't paint me as more than I am."

"If you promise not to paint yourself as less than you are," she bargained, taking his hand and leading him toward the caravan. "I must insist you be your wonderful, witty, imperious self when we all travel to London next week. Lydia wrote to me, you know. She says that it is definite, and the princess Charlotte will be presenting the Prince Regent with his first grandchild before the year is out. You must remember to congratulate him when we appear at Carleton House."

"Why?" Justin teased as he took a key from his pocket and unlocked the door to the caravan. "He had nothing to do with it."

"I see I should have made myself more clear. You will please be witty and imperious *except* when speaking to the Prince Regent. Honestly, Justin, do you *like* being banished to the country for months at a time?"

"As long as you're here with me, I believe I might even prefer it. Now, kitten, I assume you invited me to join you here for some reason?"

Accepting the support of his hand, Alina mounted the three steps to the caravan and ducked inside, quickly stepping to her right so that he would have an unimpeded view of the interior.

"Well, hello," he said as he joined her, his smile, as always, melting her heart. "Would that be a splendid new and infinitely larger bed I'm seeing, or an invitation? Or, if I'm a very lucky man, and I thank the Fates that it appears that I am—both?"

She smiled, her heart full, and reached up to undo his neckcloth. "And I am a very fortunate woman."

* * * * *

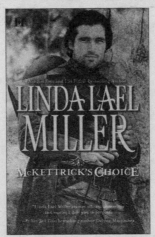

"Jim Butcher is a brilliant world-builder."
—*Midwest Book Review*

Praise for
CURSOR'S FURY

"Butcher deftly mixes military fantasy and political intrigue in the rollicking third Codex Alera book . . . Readers will cheer Tavi every step of the way." —*Publishers Weekly*

"The author of the Dresden Files modern fantasy series is equally familiar with old-style 'classic' fantasy, demonstrating his skill in complex plotting and vivid world-crafting to masterly effect."
—*Library Journal*

"Plenty of military action and some interesting revelations about Tavi's past make this one of the best volumes yet in this entertaining series."
—*Locus*

"Butcher keeps the action plausible . . . The action scenes are tense and well played out." —*The Green Man Review*

...'t miss

...AIN'S FURY
...**C**UR OF THE CODEX ALERA
BO...

Available now

D0092530

continued

Ace Books by Jim Butcher

FURIES OF CALDERON
ACADEM'S FURY
CURSOR'S FURY
CAPTAIN'S FURY

CURSOR'S
FURY

BOOK THREE OF THE CODEX ALERA

JIM BUTCHER

ACE BOOKS, NEW YORK

THE BERKLEY PUBLISHING GROUP
Published by the Penguin Group
Penguin Group (USA) Inc.
375 Hudson Street, New York, New York 10014, USA
Penguin Group (Canada), 90 Eglinton Avenue East, Suite 700, Toronto, Ontario M4P 2Y3, Canada
(a division of Pearson Penguin Canada Inc.)
Penguin Books Ltd., 80 Strand, London WC2R 0RL, England
Penguin Group Ireland, 25 St. Stephen's Green, Dublin 2, Ireland (a division of Penguin Books Ltd.)
Penguin Group (Australia), 250 Camberwell Road, Camberwell, Victoria 3124, Australia
(a division of Pearson Australia Group Pty. Ltd.)
Penguin Books India Pvt. Ltd., 11 Community Centre, Panchsheel Park, New Delhi—110 017, India
Penguin Group (NZ), 67 Apollo Drive, Rosedale, North Shore 0632, New Zealand
(a division of Pearson New Zealand Ltd.)
Penguin Books (South Africa) (Pty.) Ltd., 24 Sturdee Avenue, Rosebank, Johannesburg 2196,
South Africa

Penguin Books Ltd., Registered Offices: 80 Strand, London WC2R 0RL, England

This is a work of fiction. Names, characters, places, and incidents either are the product of the author's imagination or are used fictitiously, and any resemblance to actual persons, living or dead, business establishments, events, or locales is entirely coincidental. The publisher does not have any control over and does not assume any responsibility for author or third-party websites or their content.

CURSOR'S FURY

An Ace Book / published by arrangement with the author

PRINTING HISTORY
Ace hardcover edition / December 2006
Ace mass-market edition / December 2007

Copyright © 2006 by Jim Butcher.
Excerpt from *Captain's Fury* copyright © 2007 by Jim Butcher.
Cover art by Steve Stone.
Cover design by Rita Frangie.
Interior text design by Kristin del Rosario.

ISBN: 978-0-441-01547-4

ACE
Ace Books are published by The Berkley Publishing Group,
a division of Penguin Group (USA) Inc.,
375 Hudson Street, New York, New York 10014.
ACE and the "A" design are trademarks belonging to Penguin Group (USA) Inc.

PRINTED IN THE UNITED STATES OF AMERICA

10 9 8 7 6 5 4 3 2 1

CURSOR'S FURY

Men plan.
Fate laughs.

FROM THE WRITINGS OF GAIUS QUARTUS,
FIRST LORD OF ALERA

Tavi made a steeple of his fingers and stared down at the *ludus* board. Squares of black and white lay in eleven rows of eleven, and painted lead figurines, also of black and white, stood in serried ranks upon them. A second board, five squares by five, rested on a little metal rod, its center over the lower board's center, occupied by only a few pieces. Casualties of war sat on the table beside the board.

Midgame was well under way, and the pieces were approaching the point where exchanges and sacrifices would have to be made, leading into the endgame. It was the nature of *ludus*. Tavi's dark Legions had taken heavier losses than his opponent's, but he held a stronger position. So long as he kept the game running in his favor—and provided his opponent wasn't laying some kind of fiendish trap Tavi had overlooked—he stood an excellent chance of victory.

He picked up one of his Lords and swept the piece up onto the raised skyboard, representing the skies above the field of battle, bringing added pressure onto the beleaguered positions of the hosts of the white foe.

His opponent let out a low, relaxed sound that was like nothing so much as the growl of some large and sleepy predator. Tavi knew that the sound indicated the same emotion a mildly amused chuckle might have in a human being—but never for a second did he forget that his opponent was not human.

The Cane was an enormous creature, and stood better than nine feet tall when upright. His fur was dark and thick, a heavy, stiff coat over the whole of his body, save for upon his paw-hands, and in patches where heavy scar tissue could be seen on the skin beneath his fur. His head was that of an enormous wolf, though a bit stockier than the beast's, his muzzle tipped with a wide, black nose, his jaws filled with sharp white teeth. Triangular ears stood erect and forward, focused on the *ludus* board. His broad tail flicked back and forth in restless thought, and he narrowed scarlet-and-golden eyes. The Cane smelled like nothing else Tavi had ever encountered, musky, musty, dark, and something like metal and rust, though the Cane's armor and weaponry had been locked away for two years.

Varg hunched down on his haunches across the board from Tavi, disdaining a chair. Even so, the Cane's eyes were a foot above the young man's. They sat together in a plainly appointed chamber in the Grey Tower, the impregnable, inescapable prison of Alera Imperia.

Tavi permitted himself a small smile. *Almost impregnable. Not quite inescapable.*

As always, the thoughts of the events of Wintersend two years past filled Tavi with a familiar surge of pride, humiliation, and sadness. Even after all that time, his dreams were sometimes visited with howling monsters and streams of blood.

He forced his thoughts away from painful regrets. "What's so funny?" he asked the Cane.

"You," Varg said, without looking up from the *ludus* board. His voice was a slow, low thing, the words chewed and mangled oddly by the Cane's mouth and fangs. "Aggressive."

"That's how to win," Tavi said.

Varg reached out a heavy paw-hand and pushed a white High Lord figure forward with a long, sharp claw. The move countered Tavi's most recent move to the skyboard. "There is more to victory than ferocity."

Tavi pushed a *legionare* figure forward, and judged that he could shortly open his assault. "How so?"

"It must be tempered with discipline. Ferocity is useless unless employed in the proper place . . ." Varg reached up and swept a Steadholder figure from the skyboard, taking the *legionare*. Then he settled back from the board and folded his paw-hands. ". . . and the proper time."

Tavi frowned down at the board. He had considered the Cane's move in his planning, but had deemed it too unorthodox and impractical to worry much about it. But the subtle maneuvers of the game had altered the balance of power at that single point on the *ludus* board.

Tavi regarded his responses, and dismissed the first two counters as futile. Then, to his dismay, he found his next dozen options unpalatable. Within twenty moves, they would lead to a series of exchanges that would leave the Cane and his numerically superior forces in command of the *ludus* board and allow them to hunt down and capture Tavi's First Lord at leisure.

"Crows," the boy muttered quietly.

Varg's black lips peeled away from his white teeth, an imitation of an Aleran smile. Granted, no Aleran would ever look quite so . . . unabashedly carnivorous.

Tavi shook his head, still running down possibilities on the game board. "I've been playing *ludus* with you for almost two years, sir. I thought I had your tactics down fairly well."

"Some," Varg agreed. "You learn quickly."

"I'm not so sure," Tavi said in a dry tone. "What is it I'm supposed to be learning?"

"My mind," Varg said.

"Why?"

"Know your enemy. Know yourself. Only then may you seize victory."

Tavi tilted his head at Varg and arched an eyebrow without speaking.

The Cane showed more teeth. "Is it not obvious? We are at war, Aleran," he said, without any particular rancor beyond his own unsettling inflections. He rolled a paw-hand at the *ludus* board. "For now the war is polite. But it is not simply a game. We match ourselves against one another. Study one another."

Tavi glanced up and frowned at the Cane. "So that we'll know how to kill one another come the day," he said.

Varg let his silence speak of his agreement.

Tavi liked Varg, in his own way. The former Ambassador had been consistently honest, at least when dealing with Tavi, and the Cane held to an obscure but rigid sense of honor. Since their first meeting, Varg had treated Tavi with an amused respect. In his matches with Varg, Tavi had assumed that getting to know one another would eventually lead to some kind of friendship.

Varg disagreed.

For Tavi, it was a sobering thought for perhaps five seconds. Then it became bloody frightening. The Cane was what he was. A killer. If it served his honor and his purposes to rip Tavi's throat out, he wouldn't hesitate for an instant—but he was content to show polite tolerance until the time came for the open war to resume.

"I've seen skilled players do worse in their first few years in the game," Varg rumbled. "You may one day be competent."

Assuming, of course Varg and the Canim did not rip him to pieces. Tavi felt a sudden, uncomfortable urge to deflect the conversation. "How long have you been playing?"

Varg rose and paced across the room in the restless strides of any caged predator. "Six hundred years, as your breed reckons it. One hundred years as we count them."

Tavi's mouth fell open before he could shut it. "I didn't know . . . that."

Varg let out another chuckling growl.

Tavi pushed his mouth closed with one hand and fumbled for something relevant to say. His eyes went back to the *ludus* board, and he touched the square where Varg's gambit had slipped by him. "Um. How did you manage to set that up?"

"Discipline," Varg said. "You left your pieces in irregular groups. Spread them out. It degrades their ability to support one another, compared to adjacent positioning on the board."

"I'm not sure I understand."

Varg started positioning pieces again, as they were at the confrontation, and Tavi could see what the Cane meant. His forces stood in neat rows, side by side. It looked awkward and crowded to Tavi, but the overlapping combat capabilities more than made up for the difficulty of arranging it, while his own pieces stood scattered everywhere, each move the result of seeking some single, specific advantage in order to dominate the board.

Varg restored the table to its game positioning, flicking his tail in emphasis with his words. "It is the same principle as when your Legions face our raiding parties. Their discipline mitigates their physical weakness. No amount of rage can match discipline. Unwisely employed aggression is more dangerous to oneself than any enemy, cub."

Tavi frowned at the board and grunted.

"Concede?" Varg asked.

"Game isn't over yet," Tavi said. He couldn't see how to defeat Varg's positioning, but if he pressed on, he might find an opportunity, or Varg might make some kind of mistake Tavi could capitalize upon. He pushed a Knight to Varg's Steadholder, taking the piece and beginning the vicious exchange.

After a dozen moves, Tavi did not find a way to beat the Cane. His defeat looked inevitable, and he grimaced and lifted a hand to knock his First Lord onto its side in capitulation.

Someone pounded on the door to the cell—really, Tavi thought, it was more like a Spartan apartment than a prison, a large suite that included a bed large enough to suit even the Cane as well as a sitting area and a reading area—and a guard opened the wooden door outside the prison suite. "Excuse me young man. A courier from the Citadel is here upon the Crown's business. He wishes to speak to you."

"Hah," Tavi said, and flashed Varg a smile as he lowered his hand. "Duty calls. I suppose we'll have to call this one a draw."

Varg let out another amused growl and rose as Tavi stood to face him. The Cane tilted his head slightly to one side. Tavi mimicked the gesture, though a little more deeply. "Until next week, then. Please excuse me, sir."

"Duty neither makes nor needs excuses, cub," Varg said. He flashed his fangs in another smile at the guard. The man didn't precisely flinch, but it seemed to Tavi that he had to fight not to do so.

Tavi withdrew to the barred door that faced the cell, never turning his back on Varg. He slipped through the door after the guard unlocked it, then followed him down two flights of stairs to a small, private office. It was a very plain affair, its walls lined with shelves of books, an unadorned table and chairs of gorgeously polished dark wood, a ledger desk, and a writing desk. A plain white porcelain pitcher sat on the table, beaded with droplets of water.

A small, stout, and somewhat myopic man sat in one of the chairs. He wore the red-and-blue-trimmed tunic of a senior functionary in the Citadel. The guard nodded to the man and withdrew into the hallway, shutting the door behind him.

Tavi frowned, studying the messenger. There was something familiar about him. Tavi did not recognize his face, but that meant little in the teeming mass of Alera Imperia's Citadel.

The messenger's head tilted slightly, and he remained silent.

Then Tavi grinned and swept into a formal bow. "Your Majesty."

The messenger let out a bark of a laugh, a pleased sound. As he did, his form wavered and shifted, sliding into a larger, leaner frame, until Gaius Sextus, First Lord of Alera and the mightiest of its furycrafters, sat before Tavi. His hair was thick, well trimmed, and silver-white, though it and the lines at the corners of his eyes were the only features about the man that made him look older than a well-preserved forty years or so. There was an aloof, wolfish quality to the way he held himself, confident in his power, his intelligence and experience. Tavi idly noted that the First Lord had evidently altered his clothing when he changed, as it still fitted him despite Gaius having added six inches of height.

"How did you know?" Gaius murmured.

Tavi frowned. "The eyes, sire," he said, finally.

"I changed them," Gaius countered.

"Not their shape or color," Tavi explained. "Just . . . your eyes. They were yours. I'm not sure how I knew."

"Instincts, I suppose," Gaius mused. "Though I wish it weren't. If you had some kind of innate talent we could define, perhaps we could teach your technique to the rest of the Cursors. It could prove extremely valuable."

"I'll work on it, sire," Tavi said.

"Very well," Gaius said. "I wanted to speak to you. I read your analysis of the reports you've been tracking."

Tavi blinked. "Sire? I thought those were for Captain Miles. I'm surprised they reached you."

"In general, they wouldn't. If I tried to read every paper in the Citadel, I'd be smothered within a day," Gaius said. "But Miles thought enough of your argument that he passed it on to me."

Tavi took a deep breath. "Oh."

"You make a convincing case that now is the time for action against the more ambitious High Lords."

"Sire," Tavi protested. "That wasn't necessarily my position. Miles wanted me to write in opposition to his preferred strategies. I was just advocating it to help him find weaknesses in his own planning."

"I'm aware," Gaius said. "But that makes your conclusions no less credible." He frowned, eyes on one of the plain bookcases. "I think you're right. It's time to make the High Lords dance to *my* tune for a change."

Tavi frowned again. "But . . . sire, it could escalate into a real disaster."

Gaius shook his head. "The escalation is coming regardless of what we do. Sooner or later, Kalare or Aquitaine will move on me in force. Best to move now, on my own schedule, rather than waiting for them to prepare."

"Optionally, sire," Tavi pointed out. "It could fall flat, too."

Gaius shook his head, smiling. "It won't."

"How do you know?"

The First Lord bobbed an eyebrow. "Instinct."

Tavi chuckled despite himself. "Aye, sire." He straightened. "What are my orders?"

"We still need to see to your military training," the First Lord mused, "but none of the Legions I prefer are due to begin a training cycle until next year." Gaius drew a leather letter case from within his tunic and tossed it to Tavi. "You'll need something to fill your time. So you're going on a trip."

Tavi frowned down at the case. "Where?"

"The Vale," Gaius replied. "To the ruins of Appia, to be precise, to study with Maestro Magnus."

Tavi blinked and stared. "What?"

"You've finished your second term as an academ, and great furies only know what you might find to amuse yourself if left to your own devices here. I read your paper on the Romanic Arts. So did Magnus. He needs a research assistant," Gaius said. "I suggested you, and he jumped at the chance to have you for six months."

Tavi gaped. "But . . . sire, my duties . . ."

Gaius shook his head and said, "Believe me, I'm not handing you a gift, Tavi. I may need you in position there, depending on how matters fall out. Unless, of course, you do not wish to go."

Tavi felt his mouth curve into a slow, disbelieving smile. "No, sire! I mean, uh, yes, sire! I'd be honored."

"Excellent," Gaius said. "Then pack to leave before dawn. And ask Gaele to deliver those letters for you."

Tavi drew in a sharp breath. Gaele, a student and classmate of Tavi's, had never really been Gaele. The true student had been murdered, doubled, and coldly replaced before Tavi had the chance to get to know the real Gaele. The spy who had done it, a Kalaran Bloodcrow called Rook, had been Tavi's friend for two years before he'd discovered her murderous true identity.

Instead of turning her in, though, Gaius had decided to allow her to remain in her role, in order to use her to feed disinformation to her master. "You think she'll pass this to Kalare?"

"This? Absolutely," Gaius said.

"May I ask . . . ?" Tavi said.

Gaius smiled. "The envelope contains routine mail and one letter to Aquitaine, informing him of my intention to adopt him legally and appoint him my heir."

Tavi's eyebrows shot up. "If Kalare gets wind of that, and believes it, you think it will push him to act before Aquitaine solidifies his claim to the throne."

"He'll react," Gaius agreed. "But I'm not certain as to the manner of his reaction. He's slightly mad, and it makes him difficult to predict. Which is why I want as many eyes and ears as I can spare in the south. Make sure you keep my coin with you at all times."

"I understand, sire," Tavi said, touching the old silver bull hung on the chain around his neck. He paused as a bitter taste of memory poisoned his mouth. "And Gaele?"

"Should this succeed, she will have outlived her usefulness to the Crown," Gaius said in a voice as quiet and hard as stone.

"Yes, sire," Tavi said, bowing. "What about Fade, sire?"

Gaius's expression darkened an almost-imperceptible shade. "What about him?"

"He's been with me since . . . since I can remember. I assumed that . . ."

"No," Gaius said in a tone that brooked no dissent. "I have work for Fade to do as well."

Tavi met Gaius's uncompromising eyes for a long and silent moment. Then he nodded slightly in acquiescence. "Yes, sire."

"Then let's waste no more time." Gaius rose. "Oh," he said in a tone of afterthought. "Are you by any chance sleeping with the Marat Ambassador, Tavi?"

Tavi felt his mouth drop open again. His cheeks heated up so much that he thought they might actually, literally, burst into flame. "Um, sire . . ."

"You understand the consequences, I assume. Neither of you has furycraft that would prevent conception. And believe me when I say that paternity complicates one's life immensely."

Tavi wished desperately that the earth would open up, swallow him whole, and smash him into a parchment-thick blob. "We, uh. We aren't doing *that*," Tavi said. "There are, uh, well, other. Things. That aren't . . ."

Gaius's eyes sparkled. "Intercourse?"

Tavi put a hand over his face, mortified. "Oh, bloody crows. Yes, sire."

Gaius let out a rolling laugh. "I dimly remember the concept," he said. "And since young people always have done and always will do a poor job of restraining themselves, at best, I suppose I must be satisfied with your, ah, alternate activities." The smile faded. "But bear in mind, Tavi. She's not human. She's Marat. Enjoy yourself if you must—but I would advise you not to become too deeply attached to her. Your duties will only become more demanding."

Tavi chewed on his lip and looked down. In his excitement, he had overlooked the fact that if he was sent away, he would not see Kitai for half of a year. He didn't like that notion. Not at all. They found time to spend together on most days. And most nights.

Tavi felt his blush rising again, just thinking of it. But he felt faintly surprised at how much he disliked the idea of being parted from Kitai—and not just because it would mean a severe curtailing of his, ah, alternate activities. Kitai was a beautiful and fascinating young woman—clever of wit, quick of tongue, honest, loyal, fierce, and with a sense of innate empathy that Tavi had only seen previously in watercrafters like his aunt, Isana.

She was his friend. More than that, though, he was attached to Kitai by an unseen bond, some kind of link between them that each Marat shared with a totem creature. Every Marat Tavi had ever seen had been in the company of their totems, what Kitai called a *chala*. Her father, Doroga, the head of the Gargant Clan, was never to be seen outside the company of the enormous black gargant named Walker. He could count the number of times he'd seen Hashat, head of the Horse Clan, walking on her own feet with one hand.

Tavi nursed a secret concern that if he was separated from Kitai, it might put some kind of strain upon her, or harm her in some way. And after this visit to the south, he would be entering into his required three-year term with the Legions, which could take him to the far-flung reaches of the Realm—and which would certainly not be near Alera Imperia and Kitai, her people's ambassador to the Crown.

Three years. And after *that*, there would be another assignment. And another. Cursors in service to the Crown rarely spent much time in one place.

He already missed her. Worse, he hadn't told Gaius about the bond and what he feared it might do to Kitai. He had never explained his suspicions about the bond to the First Lord. Beyond a formless anxiety about the notion, he had no sharply defined reason why—but his instincts told him that he should be very wary about revealing anything Gaius might see as an ability to influence or manipulate one of his Cursors. Tavi had grown up on the frontiers of the Realm, dangerous lands where he'd spent most of his life learning to listen to his instincts.

Gaius watched the expressions play over his face and nodded, perhaps mistaking Tavi's concerns for romantic regrets. "You begin to understand."

Tavi nodded once, without lifting his eyes, and carefully kept his emotions in check.

Gaius blew out a breath, resumed his disguised form, then headed for the door. "You'll do as you wish, Tavi, but I trust your judgment. Start packing, Cursor. And good luck."

Unseasonably rough weather slowed the pace of the Knights Aeris bearing Rook to her master in the south, and it took her nearly five days to make the trip. That time had been pure torture for her. She had no talent for windcraft herself, which meant that she could only sit in the enclosed windcraft-borne litter and stare at the package of folded documents sitting on the seat opposite her.

Nausea unrelated to the litter's lurching through rough winds wound through her. She closed her eyes so that she wouldn't have to look at the bundle of missives she'd secretly copied from official documents in the capital. She'd bought copies of some from unscrupulous, greedy palace staff. She'd stolen into empty offices and locked chambers to acquire others. All contained information of some value, crumbs and fragments that meant little alone, but that would be assembled into a more coherent whole with the help of similar reports from her fellow bloodcrows.

Ultimately, though, none of them mattered. Not anymore. The topmost document on the stack would render it all obsolete. When her master learned what she had found, he would be forced to move. He would begin the civil war every Aleran with half a mind had known was coming. It would mean the death of tens of thousands of Alerans, at the very least. That was bad enough, but it wasn't what made her feel the most sick.

She had betrayed a friend to attain this secret. She was not the naïve youngster she pretended to be, but she was not much older than the boy from Calderon, and in the time she'd known him she'd grown to like and respect him and those around him. It had been a torment of its own, knowing that her friendship and laughter was nothing but a facade, and that if her friends knew her true purpose in the capital, every single one of them would not have hesitated to assault and imprison her.

Or even kill her outright.

It made it harder to play her role. The camaraderie and easy contact was seductive. She had entertained idle thoughts of defection, despite her determination to focus on other things. If she hadn't been a skilled watercrafter, she would have left tears on her pillow each night—but even that much would have jeopardized her cover, so she willed them away.

Just as she was doing now, as the litter finally descended into the sizzling, steaming heat of late summer in Kalare. She had to look calm and professional for her master, and her fear at the mere thought of failing him made a rush of terrified, acidic vertigo whirl through her. She clenched her hands into fists, closed her eyes, and reminded herself in a steady rhythm that she was his most valuable tool and too successful to discard.

It didn't help much, but at least it gave her something to do during the last few moments of the flight, until the rich, vaguely rotten vegetable stench of Kalare made its way into her nose and throat. She didn't need to look out the window and see the city, as busy at dusk as at dawn. Nine-tenths of the place was worn, muddy squalor. The enclosed litter descended upon the other tenth, the splendor of the High Lord's Tower, landing upon the battlements as such litters did many times each day.

She took a deep breath, calmed herself, took up her papers, raised her hood to hide her identity from any observer, and hurried down the stairs to cross a courtyard into the Tower proper, the High Lord's residence. The stewards on duty recognized her voice and did not ask her to lower her hood. Kalarus had impressed upon them his will regarding Rook's visits, and not even his guards would dare his anger. She was hurried directly to the High Lord's study.

Kalarus sat at his desk within, reading. He was not a large man, nor heavily built, though perhaps a bit taller than average. He wore a shirt of light, almost gauzy grey silk, and trousers of the same material in dark green. Every single finger bore a ring set with a variety of green stones, and he wore a steel circlet across his brow. He was dark of hair and eye, like most southerners, and modestly handsome—though he wore a goatee to hide his weak chin.

Rook knew her role. She stood beside the door in total silence until Kalarus glanced up at her a few moments later.

"So," he murmured. "What brings you all the way back home, Rook?"

She drew back her hood, bowed her head, and stepped forward to lay the missives upon her master's desk. "Most of these are routine. But I think you'll want to read the topmost document without delay."

He grunted and idly reached out, toying with the paper without unfolding it. "This had better be earthshaking news, Rook. Every moment you are gone from your duties to Gaius risks your cover. I should be unhappy to lose such a valuable tool over a foolish decision."

She fumed with anger, but kept it inside and bowed her head again. "My lord, in my best judgment, that information is an order of magnitude more valuable than any spy, however well placed. In fact, I'd bet my life on it."

Kalare's eyebrows lifted a fraction. "You just did," he said quietly. Then he opened the paper and began to read.

Any man with Kalare's power and experience concealed his emotions and reactions as a matter of course, just as Rook hid her own from the High Lord. Anyone with sufficient skill at watercrafting could learn a very great deal about a person from those reactions, both physical and emotional. As a matter of course, the most powerful lords of Alera trained themselves to restrain their emotions in order to foil another's crafting.

But Rook did not need to make an effort to read the man with crafting. She had a knack for reading others, honed over the years of her dangerous service, and it had nothing to do with furycraft. She could not have picked out any single change in his features but was perfectly certain that Kalare had been startled and badly shaken by the news.

"Where did you get this?" he demanded.

"From a palace page. He overslept and had to sprint for the windport. As we are friends, he asked me to deliver his messages for him."

Kalare shook his head. "You believe it genuine?"

"Yes, my lord."

The fingers of his right hand began a flickering, twitching, trembling motion, drumming quietly on the desk. "I would never have thought Gaius would make peace with Aquitaine. He hates the man."

Rook murmured, "Gaius needs him. For now. Necessity can trump even hatred."

Her heart fluttered as that last phrase left her mouth tinged with a featherlight portion of bitter irony. Kalare did not notice. His fingers twitched even faster. "Another year to prepare, and I could have crushed him in a single season."

"He may well be aware of the fact, my lord. He seeks to goad you into premature action."

Kalare frowned down at his fingers, and they slowly stilled. Then he folded the message, over and over again, eyes narrowed. Then his lips parted, baring his teeth in a predatory smile. "Indeed. I am the bear he baits. Gaius is arrogant and always has been. He is certain that he knows everything."

Rook nodded, adding nothing.

"He is about to learn that *this* bear is a great deal larger and more dangerous than he believed." He stood up, jerked on a summoning bell's cord, then beckoned and caused his furies to open a nearby chest and to toss a dozen rolled maps onto its surface. "Pass the word to my captains that the time has come. We mobilize and march within the week. Tell your people to put pressure upon the Cursors again."

Rook bowed. "Aye, my lord."

"And you . . ." Kalare smiled. "I have a special assignment for you. I had thought to attend to it personally, but it would seem that I must take my vengeance by proxy."

"The Steadholder?" Rook asked quietly.

"The bitch from Calderon," Kalare corrected her, a dangerous edge in his voice.

"Yes, my lord. It will be done." She bit her lips. "My lord . . . if I may?"

Kalare gestured at a door on the other side of the study, a solar for reading and entertaining intimate guests. Rook crossed the room and opened the door upon a spacious chamber with thick carpeting, richly furnished.

A small girl with glossy black hair sat on the floor with a young maid, playing with dollies. When the door opened, the child's caretaker glanced up, rose, bowed to Rook, and retreated without another word.

"Mama!" shrieked the child in glee. She rose and rushed over to Rook, who caught her daughter up into a tight hug. "I missed you, Mama."

Rook squeezed tighter, and awful, bitter tears escaped despite her determination not to weep. "I missed you, too, Masha."

"Is it time, Mama?" her daughter asked. "Do we get to go to the country and have ponies now?"

"Not yet. But soon now, little one," she whispered. "Soon, I promise."

The little girl looked up at her with enormous eyes. "But I miss you."

She hugged the child close to escape the pain in her eyes. "I miss you, too. I miss you so much." Rook sensed Kalare's presence behind her, in the doorway to the solar. She turned and faced him without looking at his eyes. "I'm sorry, little one. I can't this time. I have to go now."

"B-but you just got here!" Masha wailed. "What if I need you and I can't find you?"

"Don't worry," Kalare told Rook in a smooth, gentle voice incongruous to the hard glitter in his eyes. "I'll make sure my faithful retainer's daughter is safe. You have my promise on that. I value your loyalty very highly."

Rook turned away, putting her body between Masha and Kalare. She hugged the weeping little girl as a trickle of bitter, furious, terrified tears washed over her face.

She heard Kalare turn away and walk back into his study, chuckling under his breath. "More than he bargained for. Far more indeed."

Ehren sat at the rickety desk in the open-walled bungalow, sweat dripping off his nose and onto the accounting ledger before him and beading into droplets upon a leather slave's collar that would streak infrequently down his thin shirt. The Sunset Isles could grow hideously warm in the summer, though thank the great furies that it was finally beginning to wind down. Bugs swarmed around Ehren's head, and tiny swallows darted through the wide-open wall windows, snatching at them. His hand cramped every few moments, forcing him to set aside the quill pen he used. He had just laid it down when a cadaverously thin man strode through the door.

"Ehren," he snapped, the name viciously snarled. "By the bloody crows I didn't buy you to sit around staring out a window."

Ehren's frayed temper made the thought of breaking the fool's neck rather tempting—but a Cursor did not allow such personal matters to interfere in his duties. His job was to remain invisible in the Sunset Isles, watching and listening and sending reports back to the mainland. He picked up the pen again, ducked his head, and said in a meek voice, "Yes, Master Ullus. Sorry. Just resting my fingers."

"You'll rest them in a gibbet if I see you lazing about again," the man said, and stalked over to a low cabinet stocked with dirty glasses and bottles of cheap rum. Ullus immediately set about the task of making the glasses dirtier and the rum more worthless, as he did most days, while Ehren continued to labor on the impossibly incomplete accounts ledger.

Sometime later, a man came into the room. He was not large, but had the lean, seedy look Ehren had come to associate with the pirates who would terrorize merchant shipping before slipping back into the myriad hiding places in the Sunset Isles. His clothing showed much wear and exposure to salt and wind and sun, and he wore mismatched bits of finery, the decorative trophies of a successful pirate.

And yet . . . Ehren frowned and kept his eyes on the ledger. The man didn't carry himself like a pirate at all. Most of them tended to be as ragged, undisciplined, and unkempt in mannerism as in appearance. This man looked cautious and sober. He moved like the best professional fighters, all relaxed awareness and restraint. Ehren judged that he was no pirate at all, but a cutter—an assassin who would trade death for gold if the price was right.

Ullus rose to his feet and rocked unsteadily back and forth on his heels. "Sir . . ." he began. "Welcome to Westmiston. My name is Ullus, and I am the senior trade manag—"

"You are a fence," the man said in a quiet voice.

Ullus dropped his mouth open in a facade that would not have convinced an intelligent child. "Good sir!" he exclaimed. "I do not know where you have heard this slander, but—"

The man tilted his head slightly and focused his eyes on Ullus. Ehren's master was a drunken fool, but neither too drunk nor too foolish to recognize the danger glinting in the man's eyes. He stopped talking, shut his mouth, and swallowed nervously.

"You are a fence," the stranger continued in the same quiet tone. "I am Captain Demos. I have goods to liquidate."

"Certainly," Ullus said, slurring the word. "Why, just bring them here, and I should be glad to give you fair value for them."

"I don't care to be cheated," the man said. He drew a piece of paper from his pocket and tossed it at Ullus's feet. "This is a listing. You will sell them at my price or buy them yourself before I return in three weeks. I will pay you a tithe as commission. Cheat me a single copper ram, and I'll cut your throat."

Ullus swallowed. "I see."

"I thought you would," the man said.

Ullus picked up the list and read it. He winced. "Captain," he said, his tone cautious, "you'll get a better price for these farther east."

"I do not sail east," the man said.

Ehren sighed and dipped his quill, focusing on looking bored, miserable, and surly in order to disguise his sudden excitement and interest. Westmiston was the westernmost human settlement in the Sunset Isles. The only civilization west of here all belonged to the Canim. Their main trade port was ten days sailing from Westmiston, and at this time of year, about eleven days back.

Three weeks.

Captain Demos was carrying something to the Canim.

"Come," Captain Demos said. "Bring your slave and a cart. I sail within the hour."

Tavi pulled on the rope until he thought his spine would snap from the strain. "Hurry!" he said through gritted teeth.

"You can't rush true learning, my boy," said the old man from where he knelt at the mechanism's release pin. Magnus fussed and grunted over the device for a moment, then crudely forged metal scraped on metal. "Research is the essence of academia."

Sweat broke out over Tavi's whole body. "If you don't get that pin in soon, the arm is going to slip and throw you halfway across the Vale," Tavi growled.

"Nonsense, my boy. I'm well out of the way. It will shatter like the last one." He grunted. "There, it's in. Easy does it."

Tavi slowly relaxed his hold on the rope, though his hands and arms screamed for relief. The long wooden arm of the device quivered, but remained bent back, locked into place and ready to be released. The haul rope, hooked up to several of the spinning wheels Magnus had manufactured, sagged to the ground.

"There, you see?" he said proudly. "You managed it all by yourself."

Tavi shook his head, panting. "I still don't understand how the wheels work."

"By condensing your strength into a smaller area," Magnus said. "You hauled forty feet of rope to move the arm back only five feet."

"I can do the math," Tavi said. "I'm just . . . it's almost unreal. My uncle would have trouble bending that thing back, and he's a strong earthcrafter."

"Our forefathers knew their arts," Magnus cackled. "If

only Larus could see this. He'd start frothing at the mouth. Here, lad. Help me with the ammunition."

Together, Tavi and Magnus grunted and lifted a stone weighing better than fifty pounds into place in the cup at the end of the engine's arm, then they both stood back from it. "Maybe we should have used some professionally manufactured parts."

"Never, never," Magnus muttered. "If we'd used crafted parts, we'd just have to do the whole thing again without them, or else Larus and his kind would discredit us based on that fact alone. No, my boy, it had to be done just as the Romans did it, just like Appia itself."

Tavi grunted. The ruins of the city of his forefathers stood all around them. They had been built upon the crown of an ancient mountain worn down to the size of an imposing hill, and everything had been made of stone. The walls of dozens and dozens of buildings, now reduced to jagged stone by time and the elements, surrounded them. Grass and trees grew among the ruined houses and old city walls. Wind sighed among the stones, a constant, gentle, and sad song of regret. Deer paced silently on streets so faded they could only be seen to be man-made if viewed from a distance, and sheltered among the walls during infrequent storms. Birds nested upon the remains of statues ground to featurelessness by time.

The stones used in ruined Appia's construction did not have the smooth arcs and precise corners of furycrafted rock, but were built piecemeal, from smaller stones that yet bore traces of tool marks, a practice some of the ancient, stone-carved texts Magnus had uncovered in the catacombs beneath the ruins called "quarrying." Other carvings, apparently of the Romans in action, had survived the years of weathering in the stillness of the caves, and it was from one of those carvings that Magnus and Tavi had seen the war engine engaging in a battle against a foe that seemed to be some kind of monstrous, horned giant.

In fact, everything Tavi had seen and learned there made it quite clear that the ancestors of the Alerans had, like himself, possessed no furycraft whatsoever. It was a fact so self-evident that Tavi wanted to scream with frustration every time he thought of how "scholars" like Maestro Larus at the Academy casually dismissed the claim without bothering to examine the evidence.

Which was why Magnus insisted upon using only crude and inefficient manual labor for every step of the creation process of the war engine. He wanted there to be no way to dismiss the fact that it was at least possible to manage such things without the use of furycraft.

"I understand why we have to do it like this, sir. But the Romans had a lot more practice than we do. Are you sure this one will work?"

"Oh," Magnus said. "As sure as I can be. The fittings are stronger, the beams thicker. It's quite a bit more stable than the last one."

The last engine had simply shattered into a mound of kindling when they tested it. The current model, the fifth of its line, was considerably more sturdy. "Which means if it explodes again, it's going to throw a lot more pieces around. And harder."

They looked at one another. Then Magnus grunted and tied the end of a long cord to the pin that held the arm back. The pair of them backed away a good twenty paces. "Here," Magnus said, offering Tavi the cord. "I did the last one."

Tavi accepted it warily and found himself smiling. "Kitai would have loved to see this. Ready?"

Magnus grinned like a madman. "Ready!"

Tavi jerked the cord. The pin snapped free. The mechanism bucked in place as its arm snapped forward, and threw the stone into a sharp arc that sent the missile soaring into the air. It clipped a few stones from the top of a ruined wall, arched over a low hilltop, and dropped out of sight on the other side.

Magnus let out a whoop and capered about in a spontaneous dance, waving his arms. "Hah! It works! Hah! A madman, am I?"

Tavi let out an excited laugh of his own and began to ask Magnus how far he thought the engine had thrown the stone, but then he heard something and snapped his head around to focus on the sound.

Somewhere on the other side of the hill, a man howled a string of sulfurous curses that rose into the midmorning spring sky.

"Maestro," Tavi began. Before he could say more, the same stone that they had just thrown arched up into the air and plummeted toward them.

"Maestro!" Tavi shouted. He seized the back of the old man's homespun tunic and hauled him away from the engine.

The stone missed them both by inches and smashed into the engine. Wood shattered and splintered. Metal groaned. Chips broke off the stone and Tavi felt a flash of pain as a chunk the size of his fist struck his arm hard enough to make it go numb briefly. He kept his body between the wiry old Maestro and the flying debris and snapped, "Get down!"

Before Magnus had hit the ground, Tavi had his sling off his belt and a smooth, heavy ball of lead in it, as a mounted man rounded the side of the hill, sword in hand, his string of profanity growing louder as he charged. Tavi whirled the sling, but the instant before he would have loosed, he caught the sling's pouch in his free hand. "Antillar Maximus!" he shouted. "Max! It's me!"

The charging rider hauled on the reins of his horse so hard that the poor beast must have bruised its chin on its chest. The horse slid to a stop in the loose earth and stone of the dig site, throwing up a large cloud of fine dust.

"Tavi!" the young man atop the horse bellowed. Equal measures of joy and anger fought for dominance of his tone. "What the crows do you think you're doing? Did *you* throw that stone?"

"You could say that," Tavi said.

"Hah! Did you finally figure out how to do a simple earth-crafting?"

"Better," Tavi said. "We have a Romanic war engine." He turned and glanced at the wreckage, wincing. "Had," he corrected himself.

Max's mouth opened, then shut again. He was a young man come into the full of his adult strength, tall and strong. He had a solid jaw, a nose that had been broken on several occasions, wolfish grey eyes, and while he would never be thought beautiful, Max's features were rugged and strong and had an appeal of their own.

He sheathed his weapon and dismounted. "Romanics? Those guys who you think didn't have any furycraft, like you?"

"The people were called Romans," Tavi corrected him. "You call something Romanic when it was built by Romans. And yes. Though I'm surprised you remember that from the Academy."

"Don't blame me. I did everything I could to prevent it, but it looks like some of the lectures stuck," Max said, and eyed Tavi. "You nearly took my head off with that rock, you know. I fell off my horse. I haven't done that since—"

"The last time you were drunk," Tavi interjected, grinning, and offered Max his hand.

The big young man snorted and traded a hard grip with Tavi. "Furies, Calderon. You kept growing. You're as tall as me. You're too old to grow that much."

"Must be making up for lost time," Tavi said. "Max, have you met Maestro Magnus?"

The old man picked himself up off the ground, brushing away dirt and scowling like a thunderstorm. "This? *This* mental deficient is Antillus Raucus's son?"

Max turned to face the old man, and to Tavi's surprise his face flushed red beneath his tanned skin. "Sir," Max said, giving an awkward duck of his head. "You're one of the people my father bid me give his regards should I see you."

Magnus arched a silvery eyebrow.

Max glanced at the wreckage of the engine. "Uh. And I'm sorry about your, uh . . . your Romanic thing."

"It's a war engine," Magnus said in a crisp tone. "A Romanic war engine. The carvings we've found refer to it as a mule. Though admittedly, there seems to be some kind of confusion, since some of the earlier texts use the same word to describe the soldiers of their Legions . . ." Magnus shook his head. "I'm wandering again, excuse me." The old man glanced at the ruined war device and sighed. "When is the last time you spoke to your father, Maximus?"

"About a week before I ran off and joined the Legions, sir," Max said. "Call it eight years or so."

Magnus's grunt conveyed a wealth of disapproval. "You know why he doesn't speak to you, I take it?"

"Aye," Max said, his tone quiet. Tavi heard an underpinning of sadness in his friend's voice, and he winced in sympathy. "Sir, I'd be glad to fix it for you."

"Would you now?" Magnus said, eyes glinting. "That's quite generous."

"Certainly," Max said, nodding. "Won't take me a minute."

"Indeed not," Magnus said. "I should think it a project of weeks." He lifted his eyebrows and asked Max, "You were aware, of course, that my research compels us to use strictly Romanic methods. No furycrafting."

Max, in the midst of turning to the war engine, paused. "Um. What?"

"Sweat and muscle only," Magnus said cheerfully. "Everything from harvesting timber to metal fittings. We'll rebuild it. Only the next one needs to be about twice as large, so I'm glad you're volunteering your—"

Tavi got nothing more than a flicker of motion in the corner of his eye to warn him, but suddenly every instinct in his body screamed of danger. "Max!" Tavi shouted, even as he dived at the Maestro again.

Max spun, his sword flashing from its sheath with the speed only a windcrafter could manage. His arm blurred into two sharp movements, and Tavi heard two snapping sounds as Max cut a pair of heavy arrows from the air with the precision only a master metalcrafter could bring to the sword, then darted to one side.

Tavi put a low, ruined wall between the attackers and the Maestro and crouched there. He looked over his shoulder to see Max standing with his back to a ten-foot-thick stone column that had broken off seven or eight feet above the ground.

"How many?" Tavi called.

"Two there," Max replied. He crouched and put his hand to the ground for a moment, closing his eyes, then reported, "One flanking us to the west."

Tavi's eyes snapped that way, but he saw no one among the trees and brush and fallen walls. "Woodcrafting!" he called. "Can't see him!"

Max stepped out to one side of the column and barely darted back before an arrow hissed by at the level of his throat. "Bloody crowbegotten woodcrafting slives," he muttered. "Can you spot the archers?"

"Sure. Let me just stick my head out and have a look around, Max," Tavi said. But he fumbled at his belt pouch and withdrew the small mirror he used for shaving. He lifted it above the ruined wall in his left hand and twisted it back and forth, hunting for the reflection of the archers. He found the attackers within a second or two—though they had been under a woodcrafting when they attacked, they must have dropped it to focus their efforts on precision archery. Half a second after Tavi spotted them, another arrow shattered the mirror and laid open his fingertip halfway to the bone.

Tavi jerked his hand back, clutching at the bleeding finger. It only tingled, but there was enough blood that Tavi knew it would be quite painful momentarily. "Thirty yards, north of you, in the ruin with the triangle-shaped hole in the wall."

"Watch that flanker!" Max shouted, and flicked his hand around the column. Fire streaked from his fingertips, blossoming into an enormous cloud that reached toward the archers. Tavi heard Max's horse scream in panic and bolt. Max sprinted around the far side of the column in the flame's wake.

Tavi heard a crunch of stone on stone to the west and rose to a tense crouch, sling in hand and ready. "Hear that?" he whispered.

"Yes," Magnus grunted. "If I reveal him, can you take him?"

"I think so."

"You think so?" Magnus asked. "Because once I draw him out, he's going to send an arrow at my eye. Can you take him or not?"

"Yes," Tavi said. Somewhat to his own surprise, his voice sounded completely confident. To even more surprise, he found that he believed it. "If you show him to me, I can handle him."

Magnus took a deep breath, nodded once, then rose, flipping his hand in the general direction of their attacker.

The earth rumbled and buzzed, not with the deep, growling power of an earthquake, but in a tiny if violent trembling, like a dog shaking water from its fur. Fine dust rose from the ground in a cloud fifty yards across. Not twenty paces away, the dust cloud suddenly clung to a man crouched beside a row of ferns, outlining him in grime.

The man rose at once and lifted his bow, aiming for the old Maestro.

Tavi stood, whipped the sling around once, and sent the heavy lead sphere whistling through the air.

The attacker's bow twanged.

Tavi's sling bullet hit with a dull smack of impact.

An arrow shattered against a tumbledown rock wall two feet behind Maestro Magnus.

The dust-covered woodcrafter took a little stagger step to one side, and his hand rose toward the quiver on his shoulder. But before he could shoot again, the man's knees seemed to fold of their own accord, and he sank to the ground in a loose heap, eyes staring sightlessly.

From several yards to the north came a ring of steel on steel, then a crackling explosion of thunder. A man let out a brief scream cut violently short.

"Max?" Tavi called.

"They're down!" Max called back. "Flanker?"

Tavi let out a slow sigh of relief at the sound of his friend's voice. "Down," he replied.

Maestro Magnus lifted his hands and stared at them. They trembled violently. He sat down very slowly, as though his legs were no more sturdy than his fingers, and let out a slow breath, pressing a hand to his chest. "I have learned something today, my boy," he said in a weak voice.

"Sir?"

"I have learned that I am too old for this sort of thing."

Max rounded a corner of the nearest ruined building and paced over to the still form of the third man. Blood shone scarlet on Tavi's friend's sword. Max knelt over the third man for a moment, then wiped his sword on the man's tunic and sheathed it on his way back to Tavi and Magnus.

"Dead," he reported.

"The others?" Magnus asked.

Max gave the Maestro a tight, grim smile. "Them, too."

"Crows." Tavi sighed. "We should have kept one alive. Corpses can't tell us who those men are."

"Bandits?" Magnus suggested.

"With that much crafting?" Max asked, and shook his head. "I don't know about that third one, but the first two were as good as any Knight Flora I've ever seen. I was lucky they were dividing their attention to conceal themselves on those first two shots. Men that good don't take up work as bandits when they can get paid so much more to serve in someone's Legion." He squinted back at the dusty corpse. "Hell, what did you hit him with, Calderon?"

Tavi twitched the hand still holding his sling.

"You're kidding."

"Grew up with it," Tavi said. "Killed a big male slive after one of my uncle's lambs when I was six. Two direwolves, a mountain cat. Scared off a thanadent once. Haven't used it since I was thirteen or so, but I got back into practice to hunt game birds for the Maestro and me."

Max grunted. "You never talked about it."

"Citizens don't use slings. I had enough problems at the Academy without everyone finding out about my expertise in a freeholding bumpkin's weapon."

"Killed him pretty good," Max noted. "For a bumpkin weapon."

"Indeed," Magnus said, his breathing back under control. "An excellent shot, I might add."

Tavi nodded wearily. "Thanks." He glanced down at his bleeding finger, which had begun to swell and pulse with a throbbing burn.

"Crows, Calderon," Max said. "How many times have I told you that you need to stop biting your nails?"

Tavi grimaced at Max and produced a handkerchief. "Give me a hand, here."

"Why? You obviously aren't taking very good care of the ones you've got."

Tavi arched an eyebrow.

Max chuckled and bound the cloth around Tavi's finger. "Just to keep the dirt out and stop the bleeding. Once that's done, get me a bucket of water and I can close it up."

"Not yet." Tavi pushed himself to his feet and turned in the direction of the pair of archers. "Come on. Maybe they were carrying something that can give us a clue about them."

"Don't bother," Max said, squinting at a point in the distance. His voice became very quiet. "It'll take a week to find all the pieces."

Tavi swallowed and nodded at his friend. Then he went and stared down at the man he'd killed.

His bullet had hit the man almost exactly between the eyes, with so much force that it had broken something in his head. The whites of his sightless eyes were filled with blood. A thin trickle of it ran from one of the man's nostrils.

He looked younger than Tavi had expected, somehow. He couldn't have been much older than Tavi himself.

Tavi had killed him.

Killed a man.

He tasted bile in his mouth and had to look away, fighting away a sudden attack of nausea that threatened to empty his stomach right onto his boots. The struggle was a vain one, and he had to stagger several paces away to throw up. He calmed himself afterward, spitting the taste out of his mouth. Then he shut his sense of revulsion and guilt away into a quiet closet in his mind, turned back to the corpse, and systematically went through the man's belongings. He focused on the task to the exclusion of everything else.

He didn't dare start thinking about what he had just done. There was nothing left in his belly to come up.

He finished and went back to the Maestro and Max, fighting not to break into a run. "Nothing," he said quietly.

Max exhaled, a trace of frustration in it. "Crows. I wish we at least knew who they were after. Me, I guess. If they'd been here before me, they'd have killed you already."

"Not necessarily," Magnus said quietly. "Perhaps someone sent them to track you back to one of us."

Max grimaced at Magnus, then glanced away and sighed. "Crows."

"Either way," Tavi said, "we may still be in danger. We shouldn't remain here."

Max nodded. "Kinda works out then," he said. "The Crown sent me to bring your orders, Tavi."

"What are they?"

"We're taking a trip to the Blackhills at the southern tip of Placida's lands. There's a new Legion forming there, and Gaius wants you in it."

"When?"

"Yesterday."

Tavi grunted. "That won't please my aunt and uncle."

"Hah," Max snorted. "It won't please Kitai, you mean."

"Her, too. She—"

Magnus sighed. "Crows, Antillar. Don't start him talking about his girl again. He won't shut his mouth about her."

Tavi scowled at Magnus. "I was just going to say that she was supposed to come with my family to our get-together in Ceres next month. I'm going to miss it."

"And missing it is a bad thing?" Max frowned, then said, "Oh, right, I forgot. Your family *likes* having you around."

"It's mutual. I haven't seen them in more than two years, Max." He shook his head. "Don't get me wrong. I know this is important but . . . two years. And it isn't as though I'll make a good *legionare*."

"No problem," Max said. "You're going in as an officer."

"But I haven't even served my compulsory term. No one makes officer their first tour."

"You do," Max said. "You aren't going as yourself. Gaius wants eyes and ears in the command structure. You're it. Disguise, false identity, that kind of thing."

Tavi blinked. "Why?"

"New concept Legion," Max said. "Aquitaine managed to push the idea through the Senate. You're to be serving with the First Aleran. Ranks and officers both consist of equal numbers of volunteers from every city. The idea is—"

Tavi nodded, understanding it. "I get it. If there's someone from every city in the Legion, that Legion could never pose a military threat to any single city. There would be officers and *legionares* in the ranks who wouldn't stand for it."

"Right," Max said. "So the Aleran Legion would be free to wander anywhere there was trouble and pitch in without ruffling anyone's feathers."

Tavi shook his head. "Why would Aquitaine support such a thing?"

"Think about it," Max said. "A whole Legion of folks from all over Alera training near Kalare's sphere of influence. People always coming and going, messengers and letters from all over the Realm. Do the math."

"Espionage hotbed," Tavi said, nodding. "Aquitaine will be able to buy and sell secrets like sweetbread at Wintersend—and since they'll all be near Kalare and far from Aquitaine, he stands to gain a lot more intelligence on Kalare than he gives away about himself."

"And Gaius wants to know all about it."

"Anything more specific?" Tavi asked.

"Nope. The old man has flaws, but suppressing initiative in his subordinates isn't one of them. This is a spanking new Legion, too. No experience, no battle standard, no combat history, no tradition to uphold. You'll blend right in with the other green officers."

Tavi nodded. "What kind of officer am I supposed to be?"

"Third subtribune to the Tribune Logistica."

Magnus winced.

Tavi arched a brow at the Maestro, and asked Max, "Is that bad?"

Max grinned, and Tavi found the expression ominous. "It's . . . well. Let's just say that you won't ever run out of things to do."

"Oh," Tavi said. "Good."

"I'm going, too," Max said. "As myself. Centurion, weapons trainer." He nodded at Magnus. "So are you, Maestro."

Magnus arched a brow. "Indeed?"

"Senior valet," Max said, nodding.

Magnus sighed. "It could be worse, I suppose. You wouldn't believe how many times I've had to play scullion somewhere."

Tavi turned and blinked at Magnus in pure shock. "Maestro . . . I knew you were in the First Lord's counsel, but . . . you're a *Cursor*?"

Magnus nodded, smiling. "Did you think I made it a point to have wine and ale on hand for passing merchants because I was lonely for company the past twelve years, my boy? Drunken merchants and their guards let out quite a bit more information than anyone realizes."

"And you never *told* me?" Tavi asked.

"Didn't I?" Magnus said, eyes sparkling. "I'm sure I did, at some point."

"No," Tavi said.

"No?" Magnus shrugged, still smiling. "Are you sure?"

"Yes."

Magnus let out a theatrical sigh. "I thought I had. Ah, well. They say memory is the first thing to go." He glanced around him. "Though I'll miss this place. At first my work here was just a cover story, but crows take me if it hasn't grown on me."

Tavi shook his head. "Shouldn't I know *something* about soldiering if I'm planning to be an officer there? What if someone puts me in charge of something?"

"You're only technically an officer," Max assured him. "Everyone is going to walk on you, so don't worry about being in command. But yeah, you need the basics. I'm to give them to you on the way there. Enough that you should be able to fake it until you pick it up for real."

Magnus heaved himself to his feet. "Well then, lads. We're wasting daylight, and we'd best not wait for more assassins to arrive. Maximus, go catch your horse and see if our visitors left any nearby, if you would. I'll put together enough food to last us a while. Tavi, pack our things."

They set about preparing to leave. Tavi focused on the task at hand the whole while—packing saddlebags, satchels, bundling

clothes and equipment, inspecting weaponry. The assassins'
three horses became pack animals once Max rounded them up,
and shortly after high noon the three of them rode out, the
string of spare mounts in tow. Max set a brisk pace.

Tavi tried to keep his mind on his work, but the steady
throb from his wounded finger made it difficult to concentrate.
Before they crested the rise that would put ruined Appia behind them, he glanced back over his shoulder.

Tavi could still see the dusty dead man sprawled in the ruins.

◻◻◻◻◻ CHAPTER 2

Amara hadn't seen the Count of Calderon for months. When
she and her escort of Knights Aeris swept down into the
Calderon Valley, and to Bernard's fortress-town of Garrison,
she felt a flutter of excitement low in her belly.

To her surprise, Garrison had grown visibly, even in the
weeks since she had last visited. What had begun as a tent
town on the Aleran side of the fortress walls had become a
collection of semipermanent wooden homes, and she could
see that Bernard had found the money to hire enough
earthcrafters to begin erecting buildings of stone, which
would provide shelter from the deadly furies of this frontier
of the Realm.

The really surprising development was what was happening on the *outside* of the protective walls of the fortress. Tents
were spread out over the ground into an open market, and she
could see a few hundred people moving about them, doing
business as they might on any market day. That wasn't so terribly unusual. The shocking thing was that most of the people
moving around the improvised market were Marat.

The pale barbarians and their beasts had been little but an

infrequent and vicious menace from the perspective of Aleran history, and only twenty years or so earlier, an invading horde had massacred the Crown Legion, which was still recovering from heavy losses in a previous campaign. Thousands of *legionares* and camp followers and holders of the valley had died in a single day, including Princeps Gaius Septimus and all but one of his personal armsmen—Sir Miles, now Captain of the newly re-created Crown Legion.

It had been one of Alera's bitterest defeats, and though the First Lord and his Legion had scoured the valley of Marat, nothing could bring his son and heir back from the grave. Alerans died. The next First Lord died. There was no shortage of hard feelings between Alerans and their barbarian neighbors.

And yet, there were the peddlers and merchants, doing business with the Marat as they might in any town in the Realm. Many horses grazed lazily over the plain leading deeper into Marat territory, and Amara could see two dozen massive gargants doing the same. A group of perhaps a dozen wolves loitered in the morning sunshine on a mound of weather-worn boulders half a mile away. The Horse and Gargant tribes were, more than any other Marat, allies of the Alerans—or more precisely, allies of Bernard, Count of Calderon, and so their presence was understandable. But the Wolf tribe had struck her as the cruelest and most bloodthirsty of the Marat, and had invariably been a foe of the Realm.

Times, it would seem, were changing, perhaps for the better, and she felt a fierce surge of pride that Bernard had been one of the people responsible for that change.

Amara tried to remain relaxed and calm, but despite her efforts, she found herself hundreds of yards ahead of her escort. The sentry over the gate called up a relaxed challenge and waved her in before she'd finished giving her name. After years of visiting the Count of Calderon, most of the *legionares* regularly stationed there knew her face by now, especially the remaining veterans of Giraldi's century. Those men, cut down to a bare sixty serving *legionares*, were the only century in the history of the Realm to have twice received the scarlet stripe of the Order of the Lion for valor, and they enjoyed sporting the red blazon on both legs of their uniform trousers with the same casually false disregard other *legionares* did their weaponry and armor.

Amara swept down into the courtyard, willing her wind fury, Cirrus, to bring her to earth still moving, and stepped with unconscious grace into a smooth trot that carried her across the courtyard and up the stairs that led to the Count's office and chambers. She went up the stairs two at a time, though she knew it made her look like an overeager girl bound for the arms of her lover—but she couldn't manage any more than that.

Before she reached the top of the stairs, the door above her opened and Bernard appeared in the doorway. He was a large man, broad-shouldered and strong, his dark hair and beard, both clipped short in Legion fashion, salted with threads of premature silver. His strong, weather-darkened face broke into a wide smile, and he caught Amara up in his arms as though she weighed no more than a newborn lamb. She twined her arms around his neck and buried her face into the space between his throat and his shoulder, holding tight and breathing in the scent of him—leather and fresh-cut hay and woodsmoke.

He promptly carried her inside, into his spare, utilitarian office, and she nudged the door shut with her foot in passing.

As soon as they were alone, she caught his face between her hands and kissed his mouth, slowly, luxuriously, thoroughly. He returned the kiss with slowly building heat for several moments before breaking it off to murmur, "Are you sure this is the best way to conceal our marriage?"

Amara looked up at him, smiling, then nuzzled close and closed her teeth on the skin of his throat, a quick, delicate little bite. "What married couple," she murmured, her fingers already undoing the buttons of his tunic, "behaves like this?"

His voice deepened into a rough growl, and she felt him shift her weight to hold on to one arm, while the other slid along her thigh. "But no one's watching us now."

"I like to be thorough," she replied, lips moving against his skin, her breath coming more swiftly. "It's the safest thing."

Her husband's growl deepened into a rumble, and he abruptly turned with her and sat her on the edge of his oaken desk. There was the sound of steel rasping on steel as he drew the dagger from his belt and set it beside her on the desk. She protested, "Bernard, not ag—"

His mouth covered hers in a sudden, scorching kiss that briefly silenced Amara. He opened the heavy jacket of her flying leathers, and one hand tightened on the small of her back, all but forcing her to arch her body to meet his mouth as he nuzzled her through the thin muslin of her blouse. His teeth scored lightly over the tips of her breasts, a sharp and sweet little agony, and the sudden inferno that the touch ignited erupted through her body, utterly robbing her of the ability to speak anything but a low and desperate moan of need.

She found herself squirming, hips grinding against his, as he took up the knife and with quick, certain flicks, cut the leather cords binding the seams on the outside of one leg of her leather breeches. Far from objecting, she urged him to hurry with her hands and body and mouth, and began tearing at his own clothing as she felt the air touch more and more naked skin.

Her eyes met his, and as she always did, Amara felt stunned at the depth of desire in them, that this man, her secret husband, actually *wanted* her so very badly. At first she had hardly believed what she had seen in his face, and even now it was a feeling that remained fresh and new. More, it sparked an answering desire far beyond anything she had ever dared hope to feel. For Amara, it was exhilarating that a man should want her so genuinely, so desperately. This man. Her husband, her lover.

He made Amara feel beautiful.

He kissed her, hands and mouth roaming over her until she thought she would lose her mind. She let out a low cry, gave her desires free rein, and he took her there on the desk, his presence, his strength, his scent, his touch all blending into torturous pleasure she could hardly endure. Her desire to touch and to feel drove all thoughts from her mind. Nothing mattered but what she could taste, hear, feel, smell, and she embraced it with abandon.

Hours later, she lay with him in his wide bed, her long, slender limbs twined with his. She could not remember precisely when he had carried her into his chambers, but the angle of the sunlight striking one wall through a high, narrow window told her that afternoon was rapidly fading toward twilight. She was naked, but for the single silver chain she wore around her neck, and Bernard's heavy Legion ring set with a green stone that hung upon the necklace. One of his arms was around her, and his body was a heavy, relaxed presence.

Amara lay there, sleepy and content, idly stroking one of her own slender, honey brown hands over the cords of muscle in one of his arms. She had seen Bernard casually lift loads that even a gargant would not consider a light burden, through the power given him by his earthcrafting, and she found it eternally amazing that so strong a man could be so very, very gentle, too.

"I missed you, my lady," he murmured, his voice pitched low, a lazy, satisfied growl in his tone.

"And I you, my lord."

"I've been looking forward to this trip."

Amara let out a wicked little laugh. "If you had your way, we'd stay right here."

"Nonsense," he said, but smiled as he did. "I miss my nephew."

"And that's what you've been looking forward to," she murmured. She moved her hand. "Not this."

Her husband's eyelids fluttered shut and he let out a low hiss. "Don't get me wrong. Mmmm. I have no objections to that. None at all."

He felt the soft, dark hairs of his chest brush against her cheek as she smiled. "I suppose it works out then."

Bernard laughed, a relaxed and warm sound. He tightened his arm around her slightly and kissed her hair. "I love you."

"And I you."

He fell quiet for a moment, and she felt herself tense up a little. She could sense that he wanted to ask her, and that he was uncertain about whether or not to speak. His hand slid over her belly, strong and gentle.

She knew that he could not feel the scars that the Blight

had left over her womb, but she flinched for an instant regardless. She forced herself to remain quiet and relaxed, and covered his hand with both of hers. "Not yet," she said. She swallowed, and said, "Bernard . . ."

"Hush, love," he said, voice strong and sleepy and confident. "We'll keep trying."

"But . . ." She sighed. "Two years, Bernard."

"Two years of a night here, a night there," he said. "We'll finally have some time together in Ceres." His hand drifted over her skin, and Amara shivered. "Weeks."

"But love. If I can't give you a child . . . your duties as a Count call for you to pass the strength of your crafting down to children. You owe it to the Realm."

"I've done my part for the Realm," Bernard said, and his tone became unyielding. "And more. And I will give the Crown its talented children. Through you, Amara. Or not at all."

"But . . ." Amara began.

He turned to face her, and murmured, "Do you wish to leave me, my lady?"

She swallowed and shook her head, not trusting herself to speak.

"Then let's have no more talk of it," he said, and kissed her rather thoroughly. Amara felt her protests and worries beginning to dissolve into fresh heat.

Bernard let out another low growl. "Think we've thrown off sufficient suspicion for this visit, my lady?"

She laughed, a throaty sound. "I'm not sure."

He let out another low sound and turned his body to her. His hand moved, and it was Amara's turn to shiver in pleasure at a touch. "We'd best play it safe, then," he murmured. "And attend to duty."

"Oh," she whispered. "Definitely."

In the coldest, darkest hours of the night, Amara felt Bernard tense and sit bolt upright in bed, his spine rigid with tension. Sleep dragged hard at her, but she denied it, slipping from the depths of formless dreams.

"What is it?" she whispered.

"Listen," he murmured.

Amara frowned and did. Gusts of winds rushed against the stone walls of Bernard's chambers in irregular surges. From far away, she thought she could hear a faint sound on the wind, inhuman shrieks and moans. "A furystorm?"

Bernard grunted and swung his legs off the side of the bed and rose. "Maybe worse. Light." A furylamp on the table beside the bed responded to his voice, and a golden glow arose from it, allowing Amara to see Bernard dress in short, hurried motions.

She sat up in bed, pressing the sheets to her front. "Bernard?"

"I just have to make sure it's being taken care of," Bernard said. "It won't take a moment. Don't get up." He gave her a brief smile, then paced out across his chambers and opened the door. Amara heard the wind slam against it, and the distant sound of the storm rose to a deafening howl until he shut the door behind him.

Amara frowned and rose. She reached for her flying leathers, then regarded the sliced ties with a sigh. Instead, she dressed in one of the Count of Calderon's shirts and draped one of Bernard's capes around her. It was large enough to wrap around her several times and fell past her knees. She closed her eyes for a moment and breathed in the lingering scent of her husband on the fabric, then opened the door to follow him.

The wind hit her like a physical blow, a cold, wet wind heavy with a fine mist. She grimaced and willed her wind fury, Cirrus, into the air around her in order to shield her from the worst of wind and rain.

She stood at the top of the stairs for a moment, peering around the fortress. Furylamps blazed against the storm, but the wind and gusts of cold rain blunted their radiance, reducing it to little more than spheres an arm's length across. Amara could see men hurrying through the storm-cast shadows and standing their watches atop Garrison's walls in armor and spray-soaked cloaks. The barracks that housed the contingent of Knights attached to the forces under Bernard's command opened, men spilling out of them and hurrying for the walls.

Amara frowned and called to Cirrus again. The fury lifted her in a smooth rush of wind from the steps and deposited her on the heavy stone roof of the building, which allowed her to see over the fortress walls and out over the plains beyond.

The furystorm lurked there like an enormous beast, out over the broad, rolling plains that marked the beginning of Marat territory. It was an enormous, boiling cauldron of lightning and scowling storm cloud. Its own inner fires lit the lands about in a display brighter than the light of a strong moon. Pale, luminous forms swept in and around bolts of lightning and rolling mist—windmanes, the savage and deadly furies that accompanied the great storms.

Lightning flashed abruptly, so brightly that it hurt Amara's eyes, and she saw fire reach down from the storm in a solid curtain that raked at the ground and sent earth and stone spraying up from the impact in clouds and pieces she could see from miles away. Even as she watched, whirling, twitching columns of firelit cloud descended from the storm and touched upon the earth, darkening into half a dozen howling funnels that scattered earth and stone into a second, earthbound storm cloud.

She had never seen a storm of such raw, primal power, and it frightened her to her bones—though not nearly as much as when the tornados, each howling like a thing in torment, turned and flashed across the lightning-pocked earth toward the walls of Garrison. More wails, though infinitely smaller, rose in ragged dissonance as the windmanes came soaring down from the clouds overhead, outriders and escorts for the deadly vortices.

Heavy iron alarm bells sounded. The gates of the fortress opened, and perhaps two dozen Aleran traders and half as many Marat came running through them, seeking shelter from the storm. Behind her, she could hear other bells ringing as the folk of the shantytown were admitted to enter the safety of the stone shelters within the fortress.

Cirrus whispered a warning into her ear, and Amara turned

to find the nearest of the windmanes diving upon the men on the walls over the gate. A flash of lightning showed her Bernard, his great war bow in hand, bent to meet the wild fury's attack. It glittered off the tip of his arrow—and then the heavy bow thrummed and the arrow vanished, so swiftly did the war bow send it flying.

Amara found her heart in her throat—steel was of absolutely no use against windmanes, and no arrow in the Realm could slay one of the creatures. But the windmane screamed in agony and veered off, a ragged hole torn in the luminous substance of its body.

More windmanes dived down, but Bernard stayed on the wall, calmly shooting those glitter-tipped arrows at each, while the Knights under his command focused their attention upon the coming storm.

The Knights Aeris of Garrison, windcrafters at least as strong as Amara, each and every one, as well as those who had escorted her here, lined the walls, shouting to one another over the maddened, furious howls of wind and storm. With a concentrated effort, each of them focused upon the nearest of the whirling tornados, then together they let out a sudden shout. Amara felt a shift in air pressure as the Knight's furies leapt forth at their command, and the nearest tornado abruptly wobbled, wavered, and subsided into a murky, confused cloud that slowed and all but vanished.

More windmanes shrieked their anger and dived at the Knights Aeris, but Bernard prevented them from drawing near, sending unerring shots through each of the glowing, wild furies as they charged. Together, the Knights focused on the next tornado, and the next, each one being dispersed. In only moments, the last of the tornados bore down upon the walls, but it withered and died before it could quite reach them.

The storm rolled overhead, rumbling, lightning flashing from cloud to cloud, but it had a weary quality to it, now. Rain began to fall, and the thunder shrank from great, roaring cracks of sound to low, discontented rumbles.

Amara turned her attention to the walls, where the local Knights Aeris were returning to their quarters. She noted, in passing, that the men hadn't even bothered to don their armor. One of them, in fact, was still quite naked from bed, but for the *legionare's* cloak he held wrapped around his waist. Her own escort looked a bit wild around the eyes, but wry remarks and lazy laughs from the Knights of Garrison seemed to be steadying the men.

Amara shook her head and descended back to the stairs, retreating into Bernard's chambers. She slipped some more wood onto the fire and stirred it and its attendant furies to greater heat and light. Bernard returned a few moments later, bow in hand. He unstrung it, dried it with a cloth, and set it in a corner.

"I told you," he said, amusement in his tone. "Nothing worth getting out of bed for."

"Such things are common here?" she asked.

"Lately," he said, frowning faintly. He had gotten soaked in the rain and spray, and he peeled wet clothing on his way to stand beside the fire. "Though they've been rolling in from the east lately. That's unusual. Most of the furystorms here start up over old Garados. And I can't ever remember having this many this early in the year."

Amara frowned, glancing in the direction of the surly old mountain. "Are your holders in danger?"

"I wouldn't be standing here if they were," he replied. "There are going to be windmanes out until the storm blows itself out, but that's common enough."

"I see," she said. "What arrows did you use on those windmanes?"

"Target points, covered in a salt crystal."

Salt was the bane of the furies of the wind and caused them immense discomfort. "Clever," Amara said. "And effective."

"Tavi's idea," Bernard said. "He came up with it years ago. Though I never had the cause to try it until this year." He broke into a sudden grin. "The boy's head will swell when he hears about it."

"You miss him," Amara said.

He nodded. "He's got a good heart. And he's the closest thing I've had to a son. So far."

She doubted it, but there was little use in saying so. "So far," she said, her tone neutral.

"Looking forward to Ceres," Bernard said. "I haven't spoken to Isana in weeks. That's strange for me. But I suppose we'll have time on the trip."

Amara said nothing, and the crackling of the fire emphasized the sudden tension that built up between them.

Bernard frowned at her. "Love?"

She drew in a breath and faced him, her eyes steady on his. "She declined the First Lord's invitation to be transported by his Knights Aeris. Politely, of course." Amara sighed. "Aquitaine's people are already bringing her to the conclave of the Dianic League."

Bernard frowned down at her, but his eyes wavered away, moving to the warmth of the fire. "I see."

"I don't think she would have cared to keep much company with me anyway," Amara said quietly. "She and I . . . well."

"I know," Bernard said, and to Amara, her husband suddenly looked years older. "I know."

Amara shook her head. "I still don't understand why she hates Gaius so much. It's as though it's personal for her."

"Oh," Bernard said. "It is."

She touched his chest with the fingers of one hand. "Why?"

He shook his head. "I'm as ignorant as you are. Ever since Alia died . . ."

"Alia?"

"Younger sister," Bernard said. "She and Isana were real close. I was off on my first tour with the Rivan Legions. We were way up by the Shieldwall, working with Phrygia's troops against the icemen. Our parents had died a few years before, and when Isana went into service in the Legion camps, Alia went with her."

"Where?" Amara asked.

Bernard gestured to the western wall of the room, indicating the whole of the Calderon Valley. "Here. They were here during the First Battle of Calderon."

Amara drew in a sharp breath. "What happened?"

Bernard shook his head, and his eyes looked a bit more sunken. "Alia and Isana barely escaped the camp before the horde destroyed it. From what Isana said, the Crown Legion was taken off guard. Sold its own lives to give the civilians a chance to run. There were no healers. No shelter. No time. Alia went into childbirth, and Isana had to choose between Alia and the baby."

"Tavi," Amara said.

"Tavi." Bernard stepped forward and wrapped his arms around Amara. She leaned against his strength and warmth. "I think Isana blames Alia's death on the First Lord. It isn't rational, I suppose."

"But understandable," Amara murmured. "Especially if she feels guilty about her sister's death."

Bernard grunted, lifting his eyebrows. "Hadn't ever thought of it that way. Sounds about right. Isana has always been the type who blames herself for things she couldn't have done anything about. That isn't rational, either." He tightened his arms on Amara, and she leaned into it. The fire was warm, and her weariness slowly spread over her, making her feel heavy.

Bernard gave her a last little squeeze and picked her up. "We both need more sleep."

She sighed and laid her head against his chest. Her husband carried her to the bed, undressed her of the clothing she'd thrown on before rushing into the rain, and slipped into the sheets with her. He held her very gently, his presence steady and soothing, and she slipped an arm around him before falling into a doze that quickly sank toward deeper sleep.

She considered the furystorm in the drifting stillness that comes just before dreams. Her instincts told her that it had not been natural. She feared that, like the severe storms of two years ago, it might be a deliberate effort on behalf of one of the Realm's enemies to weaken Alera. Especially now, given the events stirring across the Realm.

She choked down a whimper and pressed herself closer to her husband. A quiet little voice in her thoughts told her that she should take every moment of peace and safety she could find— because she suspected they were about to become memories.

Tavi didn't get his sword up in time, and Max's downward stroke struck his wrist at an appallingly perpendicular angle. Tavi heard a snapping sound and had time to think *Those are my wrist bones* before the world went suddenly scarlet with pain and sent him to one knee. He keeled over onto his side.

Max's *rudius*, a wooden practice blade, hit his shoulder and head quite firmly before Tavi managed to wheeze, "Hold it!"

At his side, Maestro Magnus flicked his own *rudius* at Max in a quick salute, then unstrapped his wide Legion shield from his left arm. He dropped the *rudius* and knelt beside Tavi. "Here, lad. Let me see."

"Crows!" Max snarled, spitting. "You dropped your shield. You dropped your bloody shield again, Calderon."

"You broke my crowbegotten arm!" Tavi snarled. The pain kept burning.

Max tossed his own shield and *rudius* down in disgust. "It was your own fault. You aren't taking this seriously. You need more practice."

"Go to the crows, Max," Tavi growled. "If you weren't insisting on this stupid fighting technique, this wouldn't have happened."

Magnus paused and exchanged a look with Max. Then he sighed and removed his hands from Tavi's injured arm, taking up shield and *rudius* again.

"Ready your shield and get up," Max said, his voice calm as he recovered his own *rudius*.

Tavi snorted. "You've broken my bloody arm. How do you expect me to—"

Max let out a roar and swept the practice weapon at Tavi's head.

Tavi barely threw himself back in time to avoid the stroke and he struggled to regain his feet, balance wavering because of the pain and the heavy shield on his left arm. "Max!" he shouted.

His friend roared again, weapon sweeping down.

Magnus's *rudius* swept through the air and deflected the blow, then the old Maestro shouldered into Tavi's shield side, bracing him long enough to get his balance underneath him.

"Stay in tight," Magnus growled, as Max circled to attack again. "Your shield overlaps mine."

Tavi could hardly make sense of the words for the pain in his arm, but he did it. Together, he and Magnus presented Max with nothing but the broad faces of their shields as a target, while Max circled toward their weak side—Tavi.

"He's faster and has more reach than me. Protect me or neither of us will hold a sword." Magnus's elbow thumped swiftly into Tavi's ribs, and Tavi pivoted slightly, opening a slender gap in the shields through which Magnus delivered the quick, ugly chop Tavi had been less than enthused about learning.

Max caught the blow on his shield, though barely, and when his reply stroke came whipping back, Tavi stretched his shield toward Magnus, deflecting the blow while the Maestro recovered his defensive balance.

"Good!" Magnus barked. "Keep the shield up!"

"My arm—" Tavi gasped.

"Keep the shield up!" Max roared, and sent a series of strokes at Tavi's head.

The boy circled away, staying tight against Magnus's side, and the old Maestro's return strokes threatened Max just enough to keep him from an all-out assault that would batter through Tavi's swiftly weakening defenses. But Tavi's heel struck a stone, he misstepped, and moved a little too far from Magnus's side. Max's *rudius* clipped the top of Tavi's skull, hard enough to send a burst of stars through his head despite the heavy leather helmet he wore for their practice bouts.

He fell weakly to one knee, but some groggy part of his brain told him to keep his shield close to Magnus, and he foiled a similar strike Max directed at the Maestro on his return stroke. Magnus's *rudius* flashed out and tapped Max hard at the inner bend of his elbow, and the large young man grunted, flicked his *rudius* up in a salute of concession, and stepped away from the pair of them.

Tavi collapsed, so tired that he felt he could barely keep breathing. His wounded wrist pounded in agony. He lay there on his side for a moment, then opened his eyes to stare at his friend and Magnus. "Through having fun?"

"Excuse me?" Max asked. His voice sounded tired as well, though he was barely panting.

Tavi knew that he probably should keep his mouth shut, but the pain and the anger it begat paid no attention to his reason. "I've been bullied before, Max. Just never figured you'd do it."

"Is that what you think this is?" Max asked.

"Isn't it?" Tavi demanded.

"You aren't paying attention," Magnus said in a calm voice, as he stripped himself of the practice gear and fetched a flask of water. "If you got hurt, it was a result of your own failure."

"No," Tavi snarled. "It is a result of my friend breaking my arm. And making me continue this idiocy."

Max hunkered down in front of Tavi and stared at him for a silent minute. His friend's expression was serious, even . . . sober. Tavi had never seen that expression on Max's face.

"Tavi," he said quietly. "You've seen the Canim fight. Do you think one of them would politely allow you to get up and leave the fight because you sustained a minor injury? Do you think one of the Marat would ignore weaknesses in your defense out of courtesy for your pride? Do you think an enemy *legionare* will listen while you explain to him that this isn't your best technique and that he should go easy on you?"

Tavi stared at Max for a moment.

Max accepted the flask from Magnus after he finished, and drank. Then he tapped the *rudius* on the ground beside him. "You cover your shieldmate no matter what happens. If your other wrist is broken, if it leaves you exposed, if you're bleeding to death. It doesn't matter. Your shield stays up. You protect him."

"Even if it leaves me open?" Tavi demanded.

"Even if it leaves you open. You have to trust the man beside you to protect you if it comes to that. Just as you protect him. It's discipline, Tavi. It is literally life and death—not just for you, but for every man fighting with you. If you fail, it might not only be you who dies. You'll kill the men relying on you."

Tavi stared at his friend, and his anger ebbed away. It left only the pain and a world full of weariness.

"I'll ready a basin," Magnus said quietly, and paced away.

"There's no room for error," Max continued. He unstrapped Tavi's left hand from the shield and passed him the water.

Tavi suddenly felt ragingly thirsty and began guzzling it down. He dropped the flask and laid his head on the ground. "You hurt me, Max."

Max nodded. "Sometimes pain is the only way to make a stupid recruit pay attention."

"But these strokes," Tavi said, frustrated but no longer belligerent. "I know how to use a sword, Max. You know that. Most of these moves are the clumsiest-looking things I've ever seen."

"Yes," Max said. "Because they fit between the shields without elbowing someone behind you in the eye or unbalancing the man on your right or making your feet slip in mud or snow. You get an opening for maybe half a second, and you've got to hit whatever you're swinging at with every ounce of force you can muster. Those are the strokes that get the job done."

"But I've already been trained."

"You've been trained in self-defense," Max corrected him. "You've been trained to duel, or to fight in a loose, fast group of individual warriors. The front line of a Legion battlefield is a different world."

Tavi frowned. "How so?"

"*Legionares* aren't warriors, Tavi. They're professional soldiers."

"What's the difference?"

Max pursed his lips in thought. "Warriors *fight*. *Legionares* fight *together*. It isn't about being the best swordsman. It's about forming a whole that is stronger than the sum of the individuals in it."

Tavi frowned, mulling the thought over through a haze of discomfort from his throbbing wrist.

"Even the most hopeless fighter can learn Legion technique," Max continued. "It's simple. It's dirty. It works. It works when the battlefield is cramped and brutal and terrible. It works because the man beside you trusts you to cover him, and because you trust him to cover you. When it comes to battle, I'd rather fight beside competent *legionares* than any duelist—even if it was the shade of Araris Valerian himself. There's no comparison to be made."

Tavi looked down for a moment, then said, "I didn't understand."

"You were at a disadvantage. You're already a fair hand with a blade." Max grinned suddenly. "If it makes you feel any better, I was the same way. Only my first centurion broke my wrist six times and my kneecap twice before I worked it out."

Tavi winced at his own wrist, now swelling up into a large, plump sausage of throbbing torment. "Naturally, it only stands to reason that I would learn more quickly than you, Max."

"Hah. Keep that talk up, and I'll let you fix that wrist on your own." Despite his words, though, Max looked concerned about him. "You going to be all right?"

Tavi nodded. "I'm sorry I snapped at you, Max. It's just . . ." A little pang of loneliness hit Tavi. It had become a familiar sensation over the last six months. "I'm missing the reunion. I miss Kitai."

"Can't a day pass without you whining to me about her? She was your first girl, Calderon. You'll get over it."

The little lonely pang went though him again. "I don't want to get over it."

"Way of the world, Calderon." Max reached down to slide Tavi's good arm over one of his broad shoulders and lifted him from the ground. Max helped him over to their camp's fire, where Magnus was pouring steaming water into a mostly full washbasin.

Twilight lingered for a long time in the Amaranth Vale, at least compared to Tavi's mountainous home. Every night, the trio had stopped traveling an hour before sundown, in order to give Tavi lessons in the use of Legion battle tactics and techniques. The lessons had been arduous, mostly practice exercises with a weighted *rudius*, and they'd left Tavi's arm too sore to move after the first couple of evenings. Max hadn't judged Tavi's arm ready to train until two weeks of exercises had hardened the muscles in it into sharp, heavy angles beneath the skin. Another week had served to frustrate Tavi thoroughly with the seemingly clumsy techniques he was being forced to learn—but he had to admit that he'd never been in better fighting condition.

Until Max had broken his wrist, at least.

Max eased Tavi down beside the basin, and Magnus guided the broken wrist down into the warm water. "You ever awake through a watercrafted healing, boy?"

"Lots of times," Tavi said. "My aunt had to see to me more than once."

"Good, good," Magnus approved. He paused for a moment, then closed his eyes and rested the palm of his hand lightly on the surface of the water. Tavi felt the liquid stir in a swift ripple, as though an unseen eel had darted through the water around his hand, then the warm numbness of the healing enveloped his hand.

The pain faded, and Tavi let out a groan of relief. He sagged forward, trying not to move his arm. He wasn't sure it was possible to fall asleep sitting up, and with both eyes slightly open, but he seemed to do so, because the next time he glanced up, night had fallen, and the aroma of stew filled the air.

"Right, then," Magnus said wearily, and withdrew his hand from the washbasin. "Try that."

Tavi drew his arm out of the tepid water of the washbasin and flexed his fingers. Soreness made the movement painful, but the swelling had all but vanished, and the throbbing pain had faded to a shadow of what it had been before.

"It's good," Tavi said quietly. "I didn't know you were a healer."

"Just an assistant healer during my stint in the Legions. But this kind of thing was fairly routine. It'll be tender. Eat as much as you can at dinner and keep it elevated tonight if you want to keep it from aching."

"I know," Tavi assured him. He rose and offered the healer his restored hand. Magnus smiled a bit whimsically and took it. Tavi helped him up, and they both went to the stewpot over the fire. Tavi was ravenous, as always after a healing. He wolfed down the first two bowls of stew without pausing, then scraped a third from the bottom of the pot and slowed down, soaking tough trailbread in the stew to soften it into edibility.

"Can I ask you something?" he said to Max.

"Sure," the big Antillan said.

"Why bother to teach me the technique?" Tavi asked. "I'll be serving as an officer, not fighting in the ranks."

"Never can tell," Max drawled. "But even if you never fight there, you need to know what it's about. How a *legionare* thinks, and why he acts as he does."

Tavi grunted.

"Plus, to play your part, you've got to be able to see when some fish is screwing it up."

"Fish?" Tavi asked.

"New recruit," Max clarified. "First couple of weeks they're always flailing around like landed fish instead of *legionares*. It's customary for experienced men to point out every mistake a fish makes in as humiliating a fashion as possible. And in the loudest voice manageable."

"That's why you've been doing it to me?" Tavi asked.

Both Max and the old Maestro grinned. "The First Lord didn't want you to miss out on too much of the experience," Magnus said.

"Oh," Tavi said. "I'll be sure to thank him."

"Right, then," Magnus said. "Let's see if you remember what I've been teaching you while we ride."

Tavi grunted and finished off the last of his food. The practice, the pain, and the crafting had left him exhausted. If it had been up to him, he would have simply lain down right where he was and slept—which had doubtless been intentional on behalf of Max and Magnus. "I'm ready when you are." He sighed.

"Very well," Magnus said. "To begin, why don't you tell me all the regulations regarding latrines and sanitation, and enumerate the discipline for failure to meet the regulations' requirements."

Tavi immediately started repeating the relevant regulations, though so many of them had been crowded into his brain over the past three weeks that it was a challenge to bring them up, tired as he was. From sanitation procedure, Magnus moved on to logistics, procedures for making and breaking camp, watch schedules, patrol patterns, and another hundred facets of Legion life Tavi had to remember.

He forced his brain to provide facts until weariness was interrupting every sentence with a yawn before Magnus finally said, "Enough, lad, enough. Get some sleep."

Max had collapsed into lusty snoring an hour before. Tavi sought his bedroll and dropped onto it. He propped his arm up on the leather training helmet as an afterthought. "Think I'm ready?"

Magnus tilted his head thoughtfully and sipped at his cup of tea. "You're a quick study. You've worked hard to learn the part. But that hardly matters, does it." He glanced aside at Tavi. "Do you think you're ready?"

Tavi closed his eyes. "I'll manage. At least until something beyond my control goes horribly wrong and kills us all."

"Good lad," Magnus said, with a chuckle. "Spoken like a *legionare*. But bear something in mind, Tavi."

"Hmmm?"

"Right now, you're pretending to be a soldier," the old man said. "But this assignment is going to last a while. By the time it's over, it won't be an act."

Tavi blinked his eyes open to stare up at the sea of stars now emerging overhead. "Did you ever have a bad feeling about something? Like you knew something bad was about to happen?"

"Sometimes. Usually set off by a bad dream, or for no reason at all."

Tavi shook his head. "No. This isn't like those times." He frowned up at the stars. "I know. I know it like I know that water's wet. That two and two is four. There's no malice or fear attached to it. It just *is*." He squinted at the Maestro. "Did you ever feel like that?"

Magnus was silent for a long moment, regarding the fire with calculating eyes, his metal cup hiding most of his expression. "No," he said finally. "But I know a man who has a time or two."

When he said nothing more, Tavi asked, "What if there's fighting, Maestro?"

"What if there is?" Magnus asked.

"I'm not sure I'm ready."

"No one is," the Maestro said. "Not really. Old salts strut and brag about being bored in most battles, but every time it's just as frightening as your first. You'll fit right in, lad."

"That's not something I've had much practice in," Tavi said.

"I suppose not," Magnus said. He shook his head and took his eyes from the fire. "Best I rest these old bones. Best you do the same, lad. Tomorrow you join the Legions."

⊶⊶⊶ CHAPTER 4

They rode into the First Aleran Legion's training camp in the middle of the afternoon. Tavi idly picked a few loose black curls from his collar, rubbed his hand over the stiff brush of short hairs left on his head, and glared at Max. "I just can't believe you did that while I was asleep."

"Regulations are regulations," Max said, his tone pious. "Besides. If you'd been awake, you'd have complained too much."

"I thought it was every soldier's sacred right," Tavi said.

"Every soldier, yes, sir. But you're an officer, sir."

"Who should lead by example," Magnus murmured. "In grooming as well as uniform."

Tavi glowered at Magnus and tugged at the loose leather jacket he wore, the leather stiff and heavy enough to turn a glancing blow of a blade, dyed a dark blue in contrast to the lighter tunic he wore beneath. He wore a Legion-issue belt and blade at his side, and though his favored training had been in a slightly longer weapon, the standard sidearm of the Legions felt comfortable in his grasp as well, particularly after the practices with Max and the Maestro.

The Legion camp was fully the size of his uncle's stronghold at Garrison, and Tavi knew that they were of similar size for a reason: all Legion camps were laid out in precisely the same fashion in order to make sure that all commanders, messengers, and various functionaries of the armed forces always knew their way around any given camp, as well as making it possible for militia newly recalled to duty to fit in with the highly disciplined, organized troops of a Legion. Garrison, Tavi realized, was quite simply a standard Legion camp built from stone instead of canvas and wood, barracks replacing tents, stone walls and battlements replacing portable wooden palisades. It housed less than the full complement of men it could, and while Lord Riva claimed that this was because of his confidence in Count Bernard's alliance with the largest clans of Marat in the lands beyond Garrison, Tavi suspected it had far more to do with funds being skimmed from Riva's military budget and into other accounts.

The land around the camp had been trampled thoroughly by thousands of marching feet in the past several weeks. The thick, green grass common to the Vale was mashed flat, only in places rebounding from repeated trampling. Tavi could see several hundred troops at training even now, at least half a dozen cohorts of recruits drilling in the brown-gold tunics they would wear until they'd earned their steel armor. They bore large wooden replicas of actual shields, weighted and heavier than the actual items, as well as wooden poles the length of the common Legion fighting spear. Each recruit, of course, bore his own weighted *rudius*, and the marching men had the slack-faced, bored look of miserable youth. Tavi caught not a few resentful glares as they rode by the marching recruits, swift and fresh and lazy by comparison.

They rode into what would have been the eastern gates of Garrison, and were halted by a pair of men dressed in the arms and armor of veteran *legionares*. They were older than the recruits outside, and more slovenly. Both men needed a shave and, as Tavi approached near enough to get a whiff of them, a bath.

"Halt," drawled the first, a man a few years Tavi's senior, tall and broad and sagging in the middle. He dragged most of a yawn into the word. "Name and business, please, or be on your way."

Tavi drew rein on his horse a few feet away from the sentry and nodded to him politely. "Rufus Scipio, of Riva. I'm to serve as subtribune to the Tribune Logistica."

"Scipio, is it," the *legionare* drawled. He pulled a wadded-up sheet of paper from a pocket, brushed what looked like bread crumbs from it, and read, "Third subtribune." He shook his head. "To a post that barely needs a Tribune, much less three subbies. You're in for a world of hurt, little Scipio."

Tavi narrowed his eyes at the veteran. "Has Captain Cyril given nonstandard orders with regard to the protocols of rank, *legionare*?"

The second *legionare* on duty stepped forward. This one was short, stocky, and like his partner, had a belly that also spoke of little exercise and much beer. "What's this? Some young Citizen's puppy thinks he's better than us enlisted men 'cause he's taken one turn around the rose garden with a Legion that never marched out of sight of his city?"

"That's always the way," drawled the first man. He sneered at Tavi. "I'm sorry, *sir*. Did you ask me something? Because if you did, something more important bumped it clean out of my head."

Without a word, Max hopped down off of his horse, seized a short, heavy rod from his saddlebag, and laid it across the bridge of the first sentry's nose with a blow that knocked the large man from his feet and slammed his back onto the dirt.

The second sentry fumbled at his spear, the tip of the weapon dipping toward the unarmored Max. The young man seized it in one hand, locking it in place as immovably as if within stone, and swung the smaller sentry into the wooden palisade with such force that the entire section rocked and wobbled. The sentry bounced off and hit the ground, and before he could rise, Max thrust the end of his wooden baton beneath the man's chin and pushed. The smaller sentry let out a choking sound and froze in place on his back.

"Sir," Max drawled lazily to Tavi. "You'll have to forgive Nonus," a thrust of the stick made the smaller man let out a croaking squeak, "and Bortus, here." Max's boot nudged the first sentry's ribs. The man didn't even twitch. "They managed to buy their way out of being cashiered out of Third Antillan a few years back, and I guess they just weren't smart enough to remember that a lack of proper respect for officers was what got them into trouble in the first place."

"Antillar," choked the smaller man.

"I'm not speaking to you yet, Nonus," Max said, poking his centurion's baton into the underside of the *legionare's* chin. "But I'm glad you recognize me. Makes it convenient to tell you that I'm serving as centurion here, and I'll be in charge of weapons training. You and Bortus just volunteered to be the target dummies for my first batch of fish." His voice hardened. "Who is your centurion?"

"Valiar Marcus," the man gasped.

"Marcus! Could have sworn he retired. I'll have a word with him about it." He leaned down, and said, "Assuming that's all right with Subtribune Scipio. He's within his rights to go straight to lashes if he'd like it."

"But I didn't . . ." Nonus sputtered. "*Bortus* was the one who—"

Max leaned on the baton a little harder, and Nonus stopped talking with a little, squealing hiccup of sound. The big Antillan looked over his shoulder at Tavi and winked. "What's your pleasure, sir?"

Tavi shook his head, and it was an effort to keep the smile from his face. "No point in lashes yet, centurion. We won't have anything to build up to, later." He leaned over and peered at the larger, unconscious *legionare*. The man was breathing, but his nose was swelling and obviously broken. Both of his eyes had already been ringed with magnificent, dark purple bruises. He turned to the man Max had left conscious. "*Legionare* Nonus, is it? When your relief arrives, take your friend to the physician. When he wakes up, remind him what happened, hmmm? And suggest to him that at least while on sentry duty, greeting arriving officers with proper decorum should perhaps be considered of somewhat more importance than taunting puppies raised in rose gardens. All right?"

Max jabbed the baton into Nonus again. The *legionare* nodded frantically.

"Good man," Tavi said, then clucked to his horse, riding on without so much as looking over his shoulder.

He only got to hear Magnus descend from his own mount, fuss for a moment over the state of his saddlebags, then present his papers to the prostrate sentry. He cleared his throat, and sniffed. "Magnus. Senior valet to the captain and his staff. I can't abide the state of your uniform. My bloody crows, this fabric is simply ridiculous. Does it always smell so bad? Or is that just you? And these stains. How on earth did you manage to . . . no, no, don't tell me. I simply don't want to know."

Max burst out into his familiar roar of laughter, and a moment later he and Magnus caught up to Tavi. The pair of them rode through row after row of white canvas tents. Some of them looked Legion-perfect. Others sagged and drooped, doubtless the quarters of fresh recruits still finding their way.

Tavi was surprised at how loud the place was. Men's voices shouted to be heard over the din. A grimy, blind beggar woman sat beside the camp's main lane, playing a reed flute for tiny coins from passersby. Work teams dug ditches and hauled wood, singing as they did. Tavi could hear a blacksmith's hammers ringing steadily nearby. A grizzled old veteran drilled a full cohort—four centuries of eighty recruits each—at the basic sword strokes Tavi had learned so recently, facing one another in a pair of long lines and going through drilled movements by numbers barked by the veteran, shouting in response as they swung. The strokes were slow and hesitant, incorrect movements aborted in midmotion to follow the instructor. Even as he watched, Tavi saw a *rudius* slip from the hands of a recruit and slam into the kneecap of the man beside him. The stricken recruit howled, hopping on one leg, and blundered into the man on his other side, knocking half a dozen recruits to the ground.

"Ah," Tavi said. "Fish."

"Fish," Max agreed. "It should be safe to talk here," he added. "There's enough noise to make listening in difficult."

"I could have handled those two, Max," Tavi said quietly.

"But an officer wouldn't," Max said. "Centurions are the ones who break heads when *legionares* get out of line. Especially troublemakers like Nonus and Bortus."

"You know them," Tavi said.

"Mmmm. Served with them, the slives. Lazy, loud, greedy, drunken, brawling apes, the both of them."

"They didn't seem happy to see you."

"We once had a discussion about the proper way to treat a lady in camp."

"How did that turn out?" Tavi asked.

"Like today, but with more teeth on the ground," Max said.

Tavi shook his head. "And men like that are given status as veterans. They draw higher pay."

"Outside a battle line they aren't worth the cloth it would stain to clean their blood off a knife." Max shook his head and glanced back at them. "But they're fighters. They know their work, and they've been in the middle of some bad business without folding. That's why they got out under voluntary departure rather than forced discharge for conduct unbecoming a *legionare.*"

"And it also explains why they're here," Magnus added. "According to the records, they're honorable veterans willing to start with a fresh Legion—and that kind of experience is priceless for training recruits and steadying their lines in battle. They know they'll have seniority, that they won't have to do the worst of the work, and that they'll get better pay."

Max snorted. "And don't forget, this Legion is working up in the bloody Amaranth Vale. Plenty of freemen would kill to live down here." Max gestured around them. "No snow, or not to speak of. No rough weather. No wild, rogue furies. Lots of food, and they probably think this is a token Legion that will never see real action."

Tavi shook his head. "Aren't men like that going to be bad for the Legion as a whole?"

Magnus smiled a little and shook his head. "Not under Captain Cyril. He lets his centurions maintain discipline in whatever way they see fit."

Max twirled his baton with a sunny smile.

Tavi pursed his lips thoughtfully. "Will all the veterans be like them?"

Max shrugged. "I suspect that most of the High Lords will do everything in their power to keep their most experienced men close to home. No Legion has too many veterans, but they all have too many slives like Nonus and Bortus."

"So you're saying the only men in this Legion will be incompetent fish—"

"Of which you are one," Max said. "Technically speaking, sir."

"Of which I am one," Tavi allowed. "And malcontents."

"And spies," the Maestro added. "Anyone competent and friendly is likely a spy."

Max grunted. "They can't all be rotten. And if Valiar Marcus is here, I suspect we'll find some other solid centurions where he came from. We'll slap the scum around enough to keep them in line, and work the fish until they shape up. Every Legion has this kind of problem when it forms."

The Maestro shook his head. "Not to such a dramatic degree."

Max shrugged a shoulder without disagreeing. "It'll come together. Just takes time."

Tavi nodded ahead of them, to a tent three or four times the size of any others, though it was made of the same plain canvas as all the rest. Two sides of the tent were rolled up, leaving the interior open to anyone passing by. Several men were inside. "That's the captain's tent?"

Max frowned. "It's in the right place. But they're usually bigger. Fancier."

Magnus let out a chuckle. "That's Cyril's style."

Tavi drew his mount to a halt and glanced around him. A slim gentleman of middle age appeared, dressed in a plain grey tunic. The eagle sigil of the Crown had been stitched into the tunic over his heart, divided down the middle into blue and red halves. "Let me take those for you, gentlemen." He glanced at each of them and then abruptly smiled at the Maestro. "Magnus, I take it?"

"My fame precedes me," the Maestro said. He pushed the heels of his hands against the small of his back and winced, stretching. "You have the advantage of me."

The man saluted, fist to heart, Legion fashion. "Lorico, sir. Valet. I'll be working for you." He waved, and a young page came over to take the horses.

Magnus nodded and traded grips with the man, forearm to forearm. "Pleased to meet you. This is Subtribune Rufus Scipio. Centurion Antillar Maximus."

Lorico saluted them as well. "The captain is having his first general staff meeting, sirs, if you'd care to go inside."

Max nodded to them. "Lorico, could you direct me to my billet?"

"Begging your pardon, centurion, but the captain asked that you attend as well."

Max lifted his eyebrows and gestured to Tavi. "Sir."

Tavi nodded and entered the tent, glancing around the place. A plain *legionare's* bedroll sat neatly atop a battered old standard-issue travel chest. They were the only evidence of anyone residing in the tent. Several writing tables stood against the walls of the tent, though their three-legged camp stools had been drawn to the tent's middle, and were occupied by one woman and half a dozen men. There were another score or so of armored men crowded into the space the tent provided, all of them arranged in a loose half circle around an unremarkable-looking bald man in armor worn over a grey tunic. Captain Cyril.

Legion armor always made a man's shoulders look wide, but Cyril's looked almost deformed beneath the pauldrons. His forearms were bare, scarred, the skin stretched tight over cords of muscle. His armor bore the same red-and-blue eagle insignia Tavi had seen on Lorico's tunic, somehow embedded into the steel.

Tavi stepped aside to let Magnus and Max enter, and the three of them came to attention while Lorico announced them. "Subtribune Scipio, Astoris Magnus, and Antillar Maximus, sir."

Cyril looked up from the paper he held in his hand and nodded to them. "Good timing, gentlemen. Welcome." He gestured for them to join the circle around him. "Please."

"My name is Ritius Cyril," he continued, after they had joined the circle. "Many of you know me. For those who don't, I was born in Placida, but my home is here, in the Legions. I have served terms as a *legionare* in Phrygia, Riva, and Antillus, and as a marine in Parcia. I served as a Knight Ferrous in Antillus, as a Tribune Auxiliarus, Tribune Tactica, and Knight Tribune, as well as Legion Subtribune. I have seen action against the Icemen, the Canim, and the Marat. This is my first Legion command." He paused to look around the room steadily, then said, "Gentlemen, we find ourselves in the unenviable position of pioneers. No Legion like this one has ever existed. Some of you may be expecting to serve in a token fighting force—a political symbol, where the work will be light and the business of war will seldom cross paths with us.

"If so, you are mistaken," he said, and his voice turned slightly crisp. "Make no mistake. I intend to train this Legion to be the equal of any in the Realm. There is a great deal of work ahead of us, but I will ask nothing more from any of you than I do of myself.

"Further, I am as aware as any of you of the various agendas of the lords and Senators who supported the founding of this Legion. Lest there be any misunderstandings, you should all know now that I have no patience for politics and little tolerance for fools. This is a Legion. Our business is war, the defense of the Realm. I will not allow anyone's games to interfere with business. If you are here with your own agenda, or if you have no stomach for hard work, I expect you to resign, here and now, and be gone after breakfast tomorrow." His gaze swept the room again. "Are there any takers?"

Tavi arched a brow at the man, impressed. Few would dare to speak so plainly to the Citizenry, of which most of the officers of every Legion were members. Tavi glanced around the gathering of listeners. None of them moved or spoke, though Tavi saw uncomfortable expressions on several faces. Evidently, they were no more used to being spoken to in no uncertain terms than Tavi was to hearing them so addressed.

Cyril waited for a moment more, then said, "No? Then I will expect you all to do everything in your power to fulfill your duties. Just as I will do all in my power to aid and support you. That said, introductions are in order."

Cyril went around the room and delivered terse introductions of each person there. Tavi took particular note of a beefy-looking man named Gracchus, Tribune Logistica and Tavi's immediate commander. Another man, a weathered-looking veteran whose face had never been pretty even before all the scars, was identified as Valiar Marcus, the First Spear, the most senior centurion of the Legion. When Cyril reached the end of the introductions, he said, "And we have been the beneficiaries of some unanticipated good fortune. Gentlemen, some of you know her already, but may I present to you Antillus Dorotea, the High Lady Antillus."

A woman rose from where she sat on the stool in a grey dress that bore the First Aleran's red-and-blue eagle over the heart. She was slim, of medium height, and her long, fine, straight dark hair clung to her head and shone as if wet. Her features were narrow and vaguely familiar to Tavi.

Beside him, Max sucked in a startled breath.

Captain Cyril bowed politely to Lady Antillus, and she gave him a grave inclination of her head in response. "Her

Grace has offered her services as a watercrafter and healer for the duration of our first deployment," Cyril continued. "You all know that this is not her first term of service with the Legions as a Tribune Medica."

Tavi arched an eyebrow. A High Lady, here in the camp? That was anything but ordinary for a Legion, despite anything the captain might have said to the contrary. The high blood of Alera wielded an enormous amount of power by virtue of their incredible talent of furycrafting. A single High Lord, Tavi had been told, had the strength of an entire century of Knights, and Antillus, one of the two cities that defended the great northern Shieldwall, was renowned for its skill and tenacity in battle.

"I know it isn't traditional, but I'll be meeting with each of you separately to take your oaths. I'll send for each of you over the next day or two. Meanwhile, Lorico has your duty assignments and will show you to your billets. I would be pleased if you all would join me at my table for evening meals. Dismissed."

Those seated on stools rose, and the men parted politely to let Lady Antillus leave first. There were a few murmurs as they left, each taking a leather message tube from Lorico.

"Go on, lads," Magnus murmured to them without even opening his leather tube. "I'll get started here. Good luck to you both." He smiled and stepped back into the captain's tent.

Tavi walked away with Max and read his orders. Simple enough. He was to report to Tribune Gracchus and assist with the management of the Legion's stores and inventory. "He was different than I expected," Tavi said.

"Hmmm?" Max asked.

"The captain," Tavi said. "I thought he'd be more like Count Gram. Or perhaps Sir Miles."

Max grunted, and Tavi frowned at his friend. The big Antillan's face was pale, and his brow was beaded with sweat. That was hardly new to Tavi, who had nursed Max out of hangovers more than once. But now he saw something different in his friend's face, behind the distraction in his expression. Fear.

Max was afraid.

"Max?" Tavi asked, keeping his voice low. "What's wrong?"

"Nothing," Max said, the word quiet and clipped.

"Lady Antillus?" Tavi asked. "Is she your . . ."

"Stepmother," Max said.

"Is that why she's here? Because of you?"

Max's eyes shifted left and right. "Partially. But if she's come all this way, it's because my brother is here. It's the only reason she'd come."

Tavi frowned. "You're scared."

"Don't be stupid," Max said, though there was no heat in the tone. "No . . ."

"But—"

Something vicious came into Max's voice. "Leave off, Calderon, or I'll break your neck."

Tavi stopped in his tracks and blinked at his friend.

Max froze a few steps later. He turned his head a bit to one side, and Tavi could see his friend's broken-nosed profile. "Sorry. Scipio, sir."

Tavi nodded once. "Can I help?"

Max shook his head. "I'm going to go find a drink. A lot of drinks."

"Is that wise?" Tavi asked him.

"Heh," Max said. "Who wants to live forever?"

"If I can—"

"You can't help," Max said. "Nobody can." Then he stalked away without looking back.

Tavi frowned after his friend, frustrated and worried for him. But he could not force Max to tell him anything if his friend didn't want to do so. He could do nothing but wait for Max to talk about it.

He wished Kitai was here to talk to.

But for now, he had a job to do. Tavi read his orders again, recalled the camp layout Max and the Maestro had made him memorize, and went to work.

Isana awoke to a sensation of emptiness in the rough, straw mattress beside her. Her back felt cold. Her senses were a confused blur of shouts and odd lights, and it took her a moment to push away the sleepy disorientation enough to recognize the sounds around her.

Boots raced on hard earth, the steps of many men. Grizzled centurions bellowed orders. Metal scraped on metal, armored legionares walking together, brushing one another in small collisions of pauldrons, greaves, swords, shields, steel armor bands. Children were crying. Somewhere, not far away, a war-trained horse let out a frantic, ferocious scream of panic and eagerness. She could hear its handler trying to speak to it in low, even tones.

A breath later, the tension pressed in on her watercrafter's senses, a tidal flood of emotion more powerful than anything she had sensed in the dozen or so years since she and Rill, her water-fury, had found one another. Foremost in that vicious surge was fear. The men around her were terrified for their lives—the Crown Legion, the most experienced, well-trained force in Alera, was drowning in fear. Other emotions rushed with it. Primarily excitement, then determination and anger. Beneath them ran darker currents of what she could only describe as lust—and of another emotion, one so quiet that she might not have noticed it at all but for its steady and growing presence: resignation.

Though she did not know what was happening, she knew the men of the Legion around her were preparing to die.

She stumbled up off the mattress, dressed in nothing but

her skin, and managed to find her blouse, dress, and tunic. She twisted her hair into a knot, though it made her shoulders and back ache abominably to do it. She took up her plain woolen cloak and bit her lip, wondering what she should do next.

"Guard?" she called, her voice tentative.

A man entered the large tent immediately, dressed in armor identical to that worn by the rest of the legionares, save perhaps for sporting an inordinate number of dents and scratches. His presence was a steady mix of perfect confidence, steely calm, and controlled, rational fear. He stripped his helmet off with one hand, and Isana recognized Araris Valerian, personal armsman to the Princeps.

"My lady," he said, with a bow of his head.

Isana felt her cheeks flush and her hand drifted to the silver chain around her throat, touching the ring that hung upon it beneath her clothing. Then she moved it down, to rest on the round, swollen tightness of her belly. "I'm hardly your lady," she told him. "You owe me no fealty."

For a moment, Araris's eyes sparkled. "My lady," he repeated, with gentle emphasis. "My lord's duties press him. He bid me find you in his stead."

Isana's back twinged again, and if that wasn't enough, the baby stirred with his usual restless energy, as though he heard the sounds in the night and recognized them. "Araris, my sister . . ."

"Already here," he said, his tone reassuring. The unremarkable-looking young man turned to beckon with one hand, and Isana's little sister hurried into the tent, covered in Araris's own large grey traveling cloak.

Alia flew to Isana at once, and she hugged her little sister tightly. She was a tiny thing who had taken after their mother, all sweetness and feminine curves, and her hair was the color of fresh honey. At sixteen, she was an aching temptation to many of the legionares and men among the camp followers, but Isana had protected her as fiercely as she knew how. "Isana," Alia panted, breathless. "What's happening?"

Isana was nearly ten years her sister's senior. Alia's furycrafting talents, like Isana's, ran to water, and she knew that the girl would hardly be able to remember her own name under the pressure of the emotions rising around them.

"Hush, and remember to slow your breathing," she whispered to Alia, and looked up at Araris. "Rari?"

"The Marat are attacking the valley," he replied, his voice calm and precise. "They've already breached the outpost at the far end and are marching this way. Horses are being brought for you. You and the other freemen of the camp are to retreat toward Riva at all speed."

Isana drew in a breath. "Retreat? Are the Marat really so many? But why? How?"

"Don't worry, my lady," Araris said. "We've handled worse."

But Isana could see it in the man's eyes, hear it quavering in his voice. He was lying.

Araris expected to die.

"Where?" she asked him. "Where is he?"

Araris grimaced, and said, "The horses are ready, my lady. If you would come this w—"

Isana lifted her chin and strode out past the armsman, looking left and right. The camp was in chaos—or at least, the followers in the Legion's camp were. The legionares *themselves were moving with haste, with anxiety, but also with precision and discipline, and Isana could see the ranks forming along the palisade around the camp. "Do I need to go find him myself, Rari?"*

His tone remained even and polite, but Isana could sense the fond annoyance behind his reply. "As you wish, my lady." He turned to the two grooms holding the reins of nervous horses nearby, flicked a hand, and said, "You two, with me." He started striding toward the eastern side of the camp. "Ladies, if you will come this way. We must make haste. I do not know when the horde will arrive, and every moment may be precious."

And it was then that Isana saw war for the first time.

Arrows flew from the darkness. One of the grooms screamed, though he was drowned out by the cries of the horse whose reins he held. Isana turned, her heartbeat suddenly thunder in her ears, everything moving slowly. She saw the groom stagger and fall, a white-feathered Marat arrow protruding from his belly. The horse screamed and thrashed its head, trying to dislodge the arrow sunk into a long line of muscle in its neck.

Cries came from the darkness. Marat warriors, pale-haired, pale-skinned, erupted from the beds of supply wagons brought into the camp earlier in the afternoon, brandishing weapons of what looked like blackened glass and stone.

Araris turned and moved like lightning. Isana could only stare in shock as three more arrows flickered toward her. Araris's sword shattered them to splinters, and a casual flick of one of his steel-encased hands prevented even those from striking her face. He met the group of howling Marat and walked through them like a man in a crowded market, shoulders and hips twisting, bobbing up onto his toes to slide between passersby, turning a neat pirouette to avoid stumbling over something on the ground.

When he stopped, every one of the Marat lay on the ground, food for the crows.

He flicked his sword to one side, cleaning it of blood, sheathed it, and extended his hand as though nothing of note had happened. "This way, my lady."

"This way, my lady," murmured a low, richly masculine voice, "we needn't worry about being too long parted. I'm sure you can see the advantages."

Isana jerked her head up from where she had dozed off in the comfortable seating within the litter the Aquitaines had sent to fly her down from Isanaholt. The vivid dream, full of the details of memory, lingered for longer than it usually did. Dreams of that last night had repeated themselves endlessly for the last two years. The fear, the confusion, the crushing weight of guilt replayed themselves to her mind as though she had never felt them before. As though she was innocent again.

She was sick of it.

And yet the dreams also restored to her those brief moments of joy, the heady excitement of those springtime days of youth. For those few seconds, she did not know what she did now. She had a sister again.

She had a husband. Love.

"I just bought you a brand-new girl, Attis," teased a woman's voice from outside the litter, the tone clear and confident. "You'll be amused until I return."

"She's lovely," said the man. "But she's not you." His tone turned wry. "Unlike the last one."

The door to the air coach opened, and Isana had to call upon Rill to halt tears from filling her eyes. Isana's fingers touched the shape of the ring beneath her blouse, still on the chain around her neck. Unlike her, it had remained bright and untarnished by the passage of years.

She shook away the remnants of the dream as best she could and forced her thoughts back to the moment.

High Lord Aquitainus Attis, who five years ago had perpetrated a plot resulting in the deaths of hundreds of her neighbors in the Calderon Valley, opened the coach door and nodded pleasantly to Isana. He was a lion of a man, combining grace of motion in balance with physical power. His mane of dark golden hair fell to his shoulders, and nearly black eyes glittered with intelligence. He moved with perfect confidence, and his furycrafting was unmatched by anyone in the Realm, save perhaps the First Lord himself.

"Steadholder," he said politely, nodding to Isana.

She nodded back to him, though she felt her neck stiffening as she did. She did not trust herself to sound civil when speaking to him, and so remained silent.

"I quite enjoy my holidays abroad," murmured the woman, her voice now near at hand. "And I am perfectly capable of looking after myself. Besides. You have your own work to do."

The woman entered the coach and settled down on the opposite bench. High Lady Aquitaine Invidia looked every inch the model of the elite Citizenry, pale, dark-haired, tall, and regal. Though Isana knew that Lady Aquitaine was in her forties, like her husband and Isana herself, she looked barely twenty. Like all blessed with sufficient power at watercrafting, she enjoyed the ongoing appearance of youth. "Good evening, Isana."

"My lady," Isana murmured. Though she had no more love for the woman than she did for Lord Aquitaine, she could at least manage to speak politely to her, if not warmly.

Invidia turned to her husband and leaned forward to kiss him. "Don't go staying up to all hours. You need your rest."

He arched a golden brow. "I am a High Lord of Alera, not some foolish academ."

"And vegetables," she said, as if he hadn't spoken. "Don't gorge yourself on meats and sweets and ignore your vegetables."

Aquitaine frowned. "I suppose you'll act like this the entire time if I insist upon joining you?"

She smiled sweetly at him.

He rolled his eyes, gave her a quick kiss, and said, "Impossible woman. Very well, have it your way."

"Naturally," she said. "Farewell, my lord."

He inclined his head to her, nodded at Isana, shut the door, and withdrew. He thumped the side of the litter twice, and said, "Captain, take care of them."

"My lord," replied a male voice from outside the door, and the Knights Aeris lifted the litter. The winds rose to the low, steady roar that had become familiar to Isana in the last two years, and unseen force pressed her against her seat as the litter leapt into the skies.

Several moments passed in silence, during which Isana leaned her head against her cushion and closed her eyes, in the hopes that the pretense of sleep would prevent the need for conversation with Lady Aquitaine. Her hopes were in vain.

"I apologize for the length of the trip," Lady Aquitaine said after a few moments. "But the high winds are always tricky at this season, and this year they are particularly dangerous. We must therefore fly much lower than we usually would."

Isana did not voice the thought that it was still a great deal higher than a walk along the ground. "Does it make a difference?" she asked, without opening her eyes.

"It is more difficult to stay aloft closer to the earth, and more difficult to fly quickly," Lady Aquitaine replied. "My Knights Aeris must count the journey in miles instead of leagues, and given the number of stops we must make to visit my supporters, it will take us a great deal longer to reach our destination."

Isana sighed. "How much longer?"

"Most of three weeks, I am told. And that is an optimistic estimate that assumes fresh teams of Knights Aeris await us at way stations."

Three weeks. Rather too long a time to pretend to be asleep without openly insulting her patron. Though Isana knew her value to the Aquitaines, and knew that she could afford to avoid the usual fawning and scraping such powerful patrons required, there were limits she would be ill-advised to press. Consequently, she opened her eyes.

Lady Aquitaine curled her rich mouth into a smile. "I thought you would appreciate the information. You'd look rather silly sitting there with your eyes closed the whole way."

"Of course not, my lady," Isana said. "Why would I do such a thing?"

Invidia's eyes hardened for a moment. Then she said, "I am given to understand that you plan a small reunion with your family in Ceres."

"After the meeting with the League, of course," Isana said. "I have been assured of alternate travel arrangements back to Calderon if my plans should inconvenience you."

Invidia's cool features blossomed into a small, even genuine, smile. "Hardly anyone fences with me anymore, Isana. I've actually looked forward to this trip."

"As have I, my lady. I have missed my family."

Invidia laughed again. "I shall ask little of you beyond our visits with my supporters and the League meeting," she said. Then she tilted her head to one side and leaned forward slightly. "Though you have not been apprised of the meeting's agenda."

Isana tilted her head.

"Gracchus Albus and his staff have been invited to attend."

"The Senator Primus," she murmured. Then her eyes widened. "The emancipation proposal to the Senate?"

Lady Aquitaine sighed. "If only the rest of the League perceived the significance as well as you."

"They should spend time running a steadholt," Isana said, her tone wry. "It makes one acutely aware of the extended consequences of small but significant actions."

The High Lady moved one shoulder in a shrug. "Perhaps you are correct."

"Will Gracchus support the proposal?"

"He has never been a foe of the abolitionist movement. His wife, daughter, and mistresses assure me that he will," Lady Aquitaine said.

Isana frowned. She disapproved of such manipulations, though it was the Dianic League's first and favorite tool. "And the Senate?"

"Impossible to say for certain," Lady Aquitaine said. "There is no knowing what debts may be called in on such an important issue. But enough to make a real fight of it. For the first time in Aleran history, Isana, we may abolish the institution of slavery. Forever."

Isana frowned in thought. It was indeed a worthy goal, and one that would rally the support of folk of conscience everywhere. Slaves in most of the Realm faced a grim lot in life—hard labor and little chance of ever working their way free, even though the law required owners to sell a slave's freedom should he ever earn his (or her) buying price. Female slaves had no recourse to the uses their bodies were put to, though neither did males, when it came to it. Children were all born free, legally at least, though most owners employed various forms of taxation or indenture for them, which amounted to outright enslavement from birth.

The laws of the Realm were supposed to protect slaves, to limit the institution to those who had been willing to enter bondage and who could, in time, repay their indenture and walk free again. But corruption and political influence allowed each High Lord virtually to ignore the laws and to treat slaves in whatever fashion each saw fit. In the time since she had become Lady Aquitaine's ally in the Dianic League, Isana had learned more than she had ever dreamed about the abuses slaves suffered in much of the Realm. She had thought her own encounter with the slaver Kord was nightmarish enough to last a lifetime. She had been sickened to learn that in much of the rest of the Realm, his conduct was but marginally worse than average.

The Dianic League, an organization consisting solely of female Citizens of the Realm—those with status, influence, but little actual, legal power—had struggled for years to engender support for the abolishment of slavery. For the first time, they were in a position to cause it to be, for while the High Lords and the First Lord controlled the military assets of the Realm, the criminal codes of Alera, and the enforcement of civil law, it was left to the elected Senate to create and administer those laws.

Slavery had been a civil institution since its inception, and the Senate had the power to pass new laws regarding slavery—or to abolish it altogether. The Dianic League considered it the first step toward gaining legal parity for the women of the Realm.

Isana frowned. Though Lady Invidia had always been true to her word and her obligations as patron, Isana harbored no illusions that she had any personal interest in emancipation. Even so, it was difficult for Isana to resist the inherent lure in the accomplishment of such a dream, the destruction of such an injustice.

But then, she was hardly in any condition to think with the cool, detached logic required by politics. Not with a reunion with her loved ones so near at hand. Isana wanted nothing so much as to see Tavi again, whole and well—though the uncomfortable silences resulting from slips in conversation, when one of them mentioned something loosely related to politics or loyalty, made it a somewhat bittersweet proposition. She wanted to speak with her brother again. Between running the steadholt and the infrequent but regular voyages from her home on behalf of Invidia Aquitaine, there had been fewer and fewer opportunities to get together with her little brother. She missed him.

The irony in traveling halfway across the Realm to break bread with them again—and taken there by the Aquitaines, no less—was not lost on Isana. Neither was the sobering reality that she had brought it all upon herself, by allying herself with her current patron, one with ruthless, ambitious designs upon the Crown.

Even so, Isana forced herself to push her family from her thoughts and regard the situation with detached intellect. What did the Aquitaines have to gain by outlawing slavery?

"This isn't about freedom," she murmured aloud. "Not for you. It's about crippling Kalare's economy. Without slave labor, he'll never profit from his farmlands. He'll be too busy fighting to remain solvent to rival your husband for the Crown."

Lady Aquitaine stared at Isana for a moment, her expression unreadable.

Isana did not let her eyes waver from her patron's. "Perhaps it's just as well that many in the League do not perceive as much as I do."

Lady Aquitaine's expression remained detached. "Do I have your support—and confidence—in the matter or not?"

"Yes. As I promised," Isana said. She leaned back in her seat and closed her eyes again. "Nothing I do can stop you from scheming. If some good can be accomplished along the way, I see no reason not to attempt it."

"Excellent," Lady Aquitaine said. "And practical of you." She paused for a thoughtful moment, and Isana could feel the sudden weight of the High Lady's full attention. "Hardly a freeman in the Realm would be able to recognize the situation for what it is, Isana. It makes me wonder where you acquired the necessary perspective for these kinds of politics. Someone must have taught you."

"I read," she said, not needing to falsify the weariness in her voice. "Nothing more." Isana used years of practice and experience to keep any expression from her face, but in the wake of the dream, it was almost painfully difficult to prevent her hand from rising to touch the outline of the ring hanging over her heart.

There was another long silence, and Lady Aquitaine said, "I suppose I must applaud your scholarship, then."

The weight of her attention passed, and Isana almost sagged with relief. It was dangerous, lying to the High Lady, whose talent for watercraft and thus for sensing lies and deceptions was greater than even Isana's own. The woman was capable of torture, of murder, even if she preferred to use less draconian tactics. Isana had no illusions that those preferences were the result of practical logic and self-interest, rather than ethical belief. If necessary to her plans, Lady Aquitaine could kill Isana without batting a long-lashed eyelid.

Should it ever come to that, Isana would die before speaking.

Because some secrets had to be kept.

At any price.

◦◦◦◦◦ Chapter 6

The life of a *legionare*, even that of officers, had, in Tavi's opinion, been vastly overrated. By the time a week had passed in the camp of the First Aleran, he had come to the conclusion that the vaunted glory and prestige of the officers corps was nothing more than a fiendish ploy on behalf of the Citizenry, designed to drive the ambitious to foaming insanity.

And that went double for the high reputation of the Cursors, which had gotten him ordered into this crowbegotten Legion to begin with.

Tavi had considered himself a stalwart, stoic, strong-minded agent of the Crown, especially after the trials he had faced at the Academy, where his time and focus had been in constant demand. There, he'd often been unable to find enough hours in the day to sleep, and constant runs up a monstrously sadistic stairwell had tested his physical and mental limits. There were some days where he had broken down into screaming fits of frustration, just to blow off steam.

The Legion life was worse.

Tavi tried not to give such cynical thoughts too much of his attention, but standing in the light, wooden storage building through the second chorus of yet another furious rant from Tribune Gracchus, to which he was not expected or allowed to respond, it was hard to keep from feeling somewhat bitter about the entire situation.

"Do you have any idea of the chaos you've caused?" Gracchus demanded. The beefy man slapped a pair of fingers against his opposite palm every few syllables, then jabbed them accusatorily at Tavi at the end of each sentence. "The measure of flour for each *legionare* is a precise calculation, Subtribune, and it is not subject to arbitrary adjustments by striplings on their first tour."

There was a pause as Gracchus drew breath, and Tavi promptly interjected, "Yes, sir." He had learned Gracchus's rant-rhythm before the end of the second day.

"That's why we *use* standardized, regulation measuring cups in the first place."

"Yes, sir," Tavi said.

"By introducing your shoddy replacements, you have thrown off my estimates, which will disrupt stores calculations for more than a month, Subtribune. I have every right to have you flogged for such a thing. In fact, I could have you up on charges for it and disenfranchised to repay the provisions budget."

"Yes, sir," Tavi repeated.

Gracchus's eyes were already beady. He narrowed them even farther. "Do I detect insubordination in your tone, Subtribune?"

"Sir, no sir," Tavi replied. "Only disagreement."

The Tribune's scowl darkened. "Do tell."

Freed to speak, Tavi kept his tone mild. "More than a score of veterans had complained to their centurions that they were receiving smaller measures of bread at meals. When enough of them had done so, the centurions requested that the First

Spear look into the matter. He did. Per standard procedure, the First Spear approached a Subtribune Logistica. I happened to be the first one he found."

Gracchus shook his head. "Do you have a point, Subtribune?"

"Yes, sir. I investigated the matter, and it seemed likely that some of the flour was going missing between the storehouse and the mess." Tavi paused for a moment, then said, "I started by verifying the accuracy of the measuring cups. Sir."

Gracchus's face went florid and angry.

"Though the cups appear to be standard-issue, sir, they are in fact forgeries that hold nine-tenths of what the actual cups will contain. I asked one of the smiths to beat out a few cups of the proper size, sir, until they could be replaced with standard-issue gear."

"I see," Gracchus said. His upper lip had beaded with sweat.

"Sir, I figure that someone must have replaced the cups with forgeries, then skimmed the excess flour off to a market for it—or perhaps they were utterly unscrupulous thieves with the gall to sell the excess grain back to the Legion at a profit." Tavi shrugged his shoulders. "If you wish me to face charges, sir, I understand your decision. But I estimate that the amount of money gained from this business wouldn't buy much more than a silver ring and a new pair of boots. I think we caught it before any real harm could be done."

"That's enough, Subtribune," Gracchus said in a quivering voice.

"Of course," Tavi went on, "if you wish to put me up on charges or take disciplinary measures against me, the captain would be obligated to open an investigation. I'm sure he'll be able to sort out exactly who was stealing what from whom, sir. That might be for the best."

Gracchus's face turned purple. He closed his eyes, and the silver ring on his left hand rapped nervously upon his breastplate. His new boots rasped against the floor as he shifted uncomfortably in place. "Subtribune Scipio, you are sorely trying my patience."

"Beg pardon, sir," Tavi said. "That was not my intention."

"Oh yes it was," Gracchus snarled. "You're lucky I don't drop you into a pit where you stand and close it after you."

From the entry to the building, someone coughed politely and rapped knuckles against wood. "Good afternoon, sirs," said Maestro Magnus, stepping forward to smile politely at them. "I hope this is not a bad time."

Gracchus's stare was almost poisonous, and Tavi was sure that if looks could kill, he would already be a dead man. "Not at all, centurion," he murmured, before Gracchus could answer. "How may I assist you?"

"Captain Cyril's compliments, Tribune, and will Subtribune Scipio join him at the practice field?"

Tavi frowned at Magnus, but the old Maestro's expression told him nothing. "With your permission, sir?"

"Why not," Gracchus said, his voice smooth. "I can use the time to consider how best to employ your energies. Something in the way of sanitation, perhaps."

Tavi managed not to scowl at the Tribune, but felt his cheek twitch in a nervous tic. He saluted, then departed with Magnus.

"Was that about the measuring cups?" Magnus murmured, after they had walked away.

Tavi arched a brow. "You knew about it?"

"Tribunes Logistica skimming from their Legion is not precisely unheard of," Magnus said. "Though in general they cover their tracks a little more carefully. Gracchus lacks the guile to do it well."

They strode past one neat row of tents after another. In the week since they'd arrived, the fish had at least learned the proper procedure for pitching a tent. Tavi frowned at Magnus. "Did the captain know?"

"Naturally."

"Then why didn't he do something about it?" Tavi asked.

"Because while Gracchus might be an incompetent embezzler, he's a capable logistics officer. We need him. Had the captain ordered an official investigation, it would have stained Gracchus's honor, ruined his career, and discharged him from the Legion over a few bits of jewelry and new boots."

Tavi grimaced. "So the captain is letting it slide."

"He's not a legate, Tavi. He's a soldier. His job is to build and maintain the Legion as a strong, capable military force. If that means ignoring an indiscretion or three within his senior staff, he's willing to pay that price."

"Even if it means short rations for the Legion?"

Magnus smiled. "But they aren't getting short rations, Subtribune. The cups have been replaced, the problem eliminated."

"The First Spear." Tavi sighed. "The captain sent him to me."

"He did no such thing," Magnus replied, smile widening. "Though I might have misunderstood some comments he made, and shared my misunderstanding with Valiar Marcus."

Tavi grunted and thought about it for a moment. "It was a test," he said. "He wanted to see how I'd react to it."

"Many men would have blackmailed their way into a share of the profits," Magnus said. "Now the captain knows you're honest. Gracchus's greedy impulses have been checked. The *legionares* are getting their full measure of food, and the Legion still has its Tribune Logistica. Everyone's a winner."

"Except me." Tavi sighed. "After today, Gracchus is going to have me knee-deep in the latrines for a month."

"Welcome to the Legions," Magnus agreed. "I suggest you regard it as a learning experience."

Tavi scowled.

They walked out the west gate and received overly precise salutes from the two fish standing sentry in their brown tunics and training weapons. A few hundred yards from the gate, there was a wide field, furycrafted into a perfectly flat plane. A broad oval of stone road ringed the field—a practice course of roadway, built with the same properties as the roads throughout the Realm.

Four full cohorts of recruits were on the track, attempting to speed-march in formation. Properly utilized, the furies built into the Realm's roads would enable a traveler to maintain a running pace for hours at a time with little more effort than walking. The recruits, for the most part, were not utilizing the road properly, and instead of moving in neat ranks their formation resembled a comet—a solid leading element led the way, followed by stragglers who grew progressively slower, more distant, and more exhausted.

In the center of the field, centurions drilled some recruits in weapon play, while others practiced with the true steel shields of a full *legionare*, learning a basic metalcrafting discipline that would enable them to make their shields stronger and more able to resist impacts—and that would, incidentally, carry over into similarly reinforcing their weapons and armor. Still other recruits sat in loose groups around their instructors, being shown the correct way to wear and maintain armor, how properly to care for weaponry, and dozens of other facets of Legion business.

Tavi and Magnus waited for a comet-shaped cohort of fish to pound past on the training road, then walked across it toward a wooden observation platform at roughly the field's center. The grounds around the tower served as a watering station for the thirsty recruits and also featured an infirmary for the recruits who had succumbed to fatigue or who had, like Tavi, earned a pointed lesson from the weapon instructors.

Captain Cyril stood atop the observation platform, and the sun shone off his armor and bald pate. He leaned against a guardrail, speaking quietly with Tribune Cadius Hadrian, a small, slender man who stood beside him in the light armor and woodland colors of a scout. Hadrian pointed at the running trainees on the back stretch of the track and murmured something to the captain. Then he pointed toward a group of fish strapping into bulky suits of training armor. Cyril nodded, then glanced down to see Tavi and Magnus at the base of the platform.

Cadius Hadrian followed the captain's look, then saluted and slid down the platform's ladder to the earth. The leader of the Legion's scouts nodded silently to Tavi and Magnus as they saluted him, and paced away.

"I've brought him for you, sir," Magnus called. "And I told you so."

Captain Cyril had a blocky, largely immobile face, tanned to leather by his time in the field, and even a small smile sent creases across his features. "Send him up."

Tavi turned to the ladder, and Magnus touched his arm. "Lad," he murmured, almost too low to be heard. "Remember your duty. But don't play him false."

Tavi frowned, then nodded to Magnus and scaled the ladder to join the captain on the platform. He reached the top, came to attention, and saluted.

"At ease," Cyril said easily, beckoning with one hand as he turned back to the field. Tavi stepped up to stand beside him. Neither said anything for several moments, and Tavi waited for the captain to break the silence.

"Not many novice subtribunes would stand up to their commanding officer like that," Cyril finally murmured. "That takes a certain amount of courage."

"Not really, sir," Tavi said. "He couldn't come against me without revealing what he'd done."

Cyril grunted. "There are ways he can get around it. Not to hurt your career, perhaps, but he can make your duties unpleasant."

"Yes," Tavi said, simply.

Cyril smiled again. "A Stoic, I see."

"I'm not afraid of work, sir. It will pass."

"True enough." The captain turned speculative eyes on Tavi. "I looked into your records," he said. "You aren't much of a furycrafter."

A flash of irritation mixed with pain rolled through Tavi's chest. "I've just got my Legion basics," Tavi said—which was true, as far as the false records provided by the Cursors were concerned. "A little metal. I can handle a sword. Not like the greats, but I can hold my own."

The captain nodded. "Sometimes men go out of their way to conceal their talents, for whatever reason. Some don't want the responsibility. Some don't want to stand out. Others will embarrass an illegitimate parent should they do too much. Like your friend, Maximus."

Tavi smiled tightly. "That's not me, Captain."

Cyril studied Tavi for a moment, then nodded slowly. "I don't have those kinds of gifts, either. Pity," he said, and turned back to the field. "I was hoping I might round up a few more Knights."

Tavi arched an eyebrow. "Knights? Don't we have a full complement, sir?"

Cyril's armor rasped as he shrugged a shoulder. "We have Knights, but you know what a valuable commodity that kind of talent can be. Every High Lord in the Realm wants all the Knights he can beg, buy, borrow, or steal. Especially given the tensions lately. Our Knights are largely, ah . . . how to phrase this."

"Fish, sir?" Tavi suggested. "Knights Pisces?"

The captain snorted. "Close enough. Though I would have said young and clumsy. We've only got one Knight Ignus, and he's currently being treated for burn wounds." Cyril shook his head. "A batch of a dozen or so Terra and Flora aren't bad, but they've got a lot of work to do, and there aren't nearly enough of them. We've got no Knights Ferrous at all. And all the rest, sixty of them, are Knights Aeris."

Tavi lifted his eyebrows. "Most Legions would kill to have that many Knights Aeris, sir."

"Yes." Cyril sighed. "If they could fly."

"They can't?" Tavi asked. "I thought that was what you had to be able to do to *be* one of those, sir."

"Oh, they can get into the air, for the most part. Getting *down* again in one piece has proven something of a problem. If Tribune Fantus and young Antillus hadn't been there to lessen the impacts, and Lady Antillus hadn't come down with her son, we'd have had fatalities already."

Tavi frowned, then said, "Perhaps Maximus could help them out? Instructing them, I mean."

The captain broke out into a single bark of laughter. "It would be inappropriate. And I need him where he is. But even if I didn't, I wouldn't let him anywhere near the Knights Pisces. Have you seen him *fly*?"

Tavi frowned for a moment and thought about it. "No, sir."

"He doesn't fly so much as make these great, bounding hops. He can land on his feet sometimes. Other times, he hits something. We pulled him out of a peat bog once. I can't tell you how many times he's broken his legs."

Tavi frowned. "That . . . hardly sounds like Max, sir."

"I would imagine he doesn't talk about it much. He never got it down, but I didn't think he'd ever give up trying. Then I saw him ride in here. Damn shame. But it happens like that sometimes."

"Yes, sir," Tavi said, unsure what to say.

"Scipio," the captain went on. "I haven't asked you for your oath to the Legion yet."

"No, sir. I figured that's what this was about."

"It is," Cyril said. He narrowed his eyes. "I'm no fool, lad. A lot of men are here for their own reasons. And some are here for someone else's reasons."

Tavi looked out over the practice field and remained silent, unsure what to say.

"I'll only ask you this one question. Can you swear your loyalty to this Legion, to these men, and mean it beyond any doubt, any question?"

"Sir . . ." Tavi began.

"It's important," the captain said. "We all need to know that we can rely upon one another. That we will serve the Crown and the Realm regardless of the hazard or difficulty. That we will not leave a brother behind, nor hesitate to give our lives for one another. Otherwise, this is no Legion. Just a mob of men with weapons." He faced Tavi, and said, "Can you look me in the eyes and swear that, young man?"

Tavi looked up and met Cyril's eyes. "I am here to serve the Crown, sir. Yes."

"Then I have your oath?"

"You do."

The captain stared at Tavi for a moment, then nodded once, sharply, and offered his hand. Tavi blinked for a second and traded grips with Cyril. "I work my people hard, Subtribune. But I suspect we'll get along. Dismissed."

Tavi saluted, and the captain returned it. Tavi turned to the ladder, but paused when a wave of shouts rose up from below. He looked up to see a small mob of recruits in their brown tunics rushing for the infirmary, bearing an injured man. Blood stained them, and the grass behind them as they passed.

"Help!" one of them shouted, voice high with panic. "Healer!"

They grew closer, and Tavi could see more blood, pale flesh, and a sopping, bloody cloth pressed against the throat of a limp man whose skin was a shade of grey. A healer appeared from one of the large tents, and Tavi saw the man's expression flash with alarm. He started barking orders at once.

The recruits shifted their grip on him to let the healer get close, and the injured man's head lolled limply toward Tavi, eyes glassy and sightless.

Tavi's heart stopped in his chest.

It was Max.

oooo CHAPTER 7

Amara frowned down from her seat in the gallery of one of the large lecture halls of the Collegia Tactica, one of the great prides of the city of Ceres and the largest military academy in Alera. She was one of only a handful of women present in the hall, among perhaps five hundred men, most of them wearing Legion tunics and armor. The gallery above the floor seats had been filled to overflowing with curious young nobles and other students of the Collegia, and she sat between a pair of young men who seemed uncertain of how to address a young woman who bore a faint dueling scar on one cheek and a sword upon her hip.

The hall's presentation platform was the size of a small theater stage, and was also crowded with people. A half circle of chairs lined the back of the platform. Several older men sat in the chairs, most of them experienced military commanders, retired and now serving as Maestros for the Collegia. In the next to last chair sat Centurion Giraldi, arguably the most heavily decorated noncommissioned officer in Alera, now that he bore not simply one but double scarlet stripes of the Order of the Lion down the outside seams of his uniform trousers. The grizzled, stocky old soldier had walked with a limp ever since sustaining injuries in battle with the monstrous creatures called the "Vord." Giraldi's grey hair was cut in a *legionare's* short brush, his armor bore the nicks and dents of a lifetime of battle, and he looked intensely uncomfortable sitting before such a large audience.

Beside Giraldi sat Senator Guntus Arnos, Consul General of the Collegia. He was a short man, barely more than five feet tall, dressed in the formal, deep blue robes of the Senate. His grey hair was oiled and drawn back into a tail, his hands were steepled in front of his face, and he wore an expression of sober, somber judgment. He probably practiced it in front of a mirror, Amara thought.

Bernard wore his colors of green and brown, his sturdy and sensible tunic a marked contrast to Senator Arnos's rich robes. He stood at the podium at the platform's center, facing those present in the hall with a demeanor of calm, competent composure.

"In short," he said, "I believe that these Vord are far and away the deadliest threat this Realm has ever known." His voice carried clearly through the hall thanks to the windcraftings built into the place to make sure speakers could be clearly heard. The windcrafted acoustics were necessary. The hall was filled with a continual low buzz of whispers and quiet speech.

"That single Vord queen entered my holdings," Bernard continued. "Within a month, the Vord had become a force that destroyed two-thirds of my command, including a half century of Knights, and the entire population of a frontier steadholt. Their use of tactical judgment, as Centurion Giraldi and I have enumerated it to you today, proves that these creatures are more than mere beasts. They are an intelligent, coordinated threat to all of mankind. If we do not exercise the highest levels of caution, immediately stamping out an infestation, that threat may well grow too swiftly to be stopped." Bernard exhaled, and Amara could see a bit of relief on her husband's face, though few others would have. Bernard was glad to be finished. "At this time, I will open the floor to questions."

Several dozen hands went up at once, but then faltered and lowered again as Senator Arnos calmly raised his own hand.

Bernard frowned at the hall for a moment, until Giraldi nudged Bernard's leg with his cane. Bernard glanced at him, then to Arnos.

"Of course, Senator," he said. "Please."

Arnos rose and faced the hall. "Count Bernard," he said. "I have heard several tales of what happened out in Calderon, and each seemed less plausible than the last. I confess that, upon the surface, your own tale sounds more fantastical than the others."

A low, rumbling round of chuckles rolled through the hall.

Bernard's eyes narrowed a bit, and Amara recognized the first sign of his irritation. "Be that as it may, honored Senator," he replied, "I fear that I have nothing to offer you except the truth."

"The truth," Arnos said, nodding. "Of course. But I think we all know how . . . amorphous, shall we say, the truth can be."

"Forgive me," Bernard said. "I did not mean to confuse you, Senator. I must amend my statement. I have nothing to offer you except fact."

"Fact," Arnos said, nodding again. "Excellent. I have questions about some of the facts you have presented today."

Amara got a sickly little feeling in her belly.

"By all means," Bernard said.

"Do I understand you correctly that you learned of these creatures' presence from a barbarian Marat?"

"From Doroga of the Sabot-Ha," Bernard said. "The most powerful and influential of their chieftains."

"But . . ." Arnos shrugged a shoulder. "A Marat."

"Yes," Bernard said.

"That is how you know that they are called the Vord?"

"Yes."

"In fact," Arnos continued, "no Aleran had ever heard of this creature before the barbarian told you of it."

"Given the kind of danger the Vord represent, I suspect that by the time one learns of them, it may already be too late to fight them. Without Doroga's warning, we might already have lost half the Realm."

"And you believe that?" Arnos asked.

"Yes," Bernard said.

"And yet, according to the barbarian, his own unlettered, tribal, pauper-folk, without a civilization, without furycrafting, somehow managed to defeat them in the past."

Bernard paused for a moment before speaking. Amara recognized the gesture: it was the same one he got on his face before rebuking a particularly foolish subordinate. "They did not defeat the Vord, Senator," Bernard said. "The refugees of their civilization managed to flee and survive."

"Ah," Arnos said, skepticism flavoring the sound. "Come now, Count. What surety can you give that the entire situation was not some kind of ploy on behalf of the Marat? There are many dangerous creatures in the world. It seems to me that we had nothing to fear from these Vord before the Marat spoke to you about them."

Bernard's jawline twitched. "Doroga very nearly gave his life in defense of me and mine, when we fought the Vord together. He lost nearly two thousand of his own people fighting them before they came to Calderon."

Arnos waved a vague hand. "Come now, Your Excellency. The Collegia contains a thousand years of military history, hundreds of battles faithfully recorded, large and small. The morale of a military force in the field breaks well before it sustains fifty percent casualties. Are we really to take the barbarian's word that his people fought on after losing *ninety* percent of their force?"

"If Doroga says so. I believe him."

The Senator permitted himself a small, sly smile. "I see. It would appear, then, that your struggle together against these creatures the barbarian knew all about has engendered within you a sense of trust." He paused, then added lightly, "Or credulity."

Bernard stared levelly at Arnos for a long moment. Then he drew in a breath, and said in a patient tone, "Senator, disregarding any evidence I did not see with my own eyes, the Vord are still clearly an intelligent, resourceful, ruthless foe who will not discriminate between armed forces and noncombatants. They clearly possess the wherewithal to inflict tremendous damage upon anyone unfortunate enough to be near them."

Arnos shrugged a shoulder, still wearing the faint smile. "Perhaps. But their most vaunted, feared trait seems to be their ability to reproduce at such a fantastic rate. That if even one of them remains, they could repopulate themselves at tremendous speed." He tilted his head, and said, "Yet, it has been three years since you fought them, Count, and they have not been seen again. I cannot help but wonder whether or not it might have been a lie, told to you by the Marat in order to heighten your sense of danger, and therefore the amount of trust you would place in them after successfully overcoming it."

"Do you mean to say that Doroga lied to me?"

"He *is* a barbarian, after all, Count."

Bernard gave the Senator a tight smile. "The Marat's tribal tongues had no word for 'lie' until they met us, Senator. The very idea of speaking falsehood was introduced to them only a few generations ago, and it never picked up much of a following. For one Marat to call another a liar is a challenge to a fight to the death, and one that is never refused. Doroga is no liar."

"I see no way to be sure of that."

"I do, Senator," Bernard said. "I believe him. I am a Count, a Citizen of the Realm, a veteran of the Legions who has shed and spilled blood in defense of Alera. I will vouch for his word with my own."

"I'm sure you would," Arnos said, his tone that of the kindly grandfather speaking to a foolish youth. "I have never questioned your sincerity. But I suspect that the Marat has manipulated you."

Bernard stared at the Senator and rolled his shoulder in a

gesture Amara had seen him use when preparing to shoot his war bow. Bernard's voice suddenly rang out sharp and clear, though still perfectly polite in tone. "Senator. If you call my friend a liar one more time, I will take it badly."

"Excuse me?" Arnos said, his eyebrows rising up.

"I suggest you find an alternate shortsighted, egomaniacally ridiculous reason to blatantly, recklessly ignore an obvious threat to the Realm simply because you don't wish it to exist. If you cannot restrain yourself from base slander, I will be pleased to meet you in *juris macto* and personally rip your forked tongue from your head."

The muttering in the room stopped, and a bottomless silence fell.

Amara felt a rush of fierce, pleased pride flash through her, and she found herself smiling down at Bernard.

Arnos's face flushed dark red, almost purple. Without another word, he turned and strode from the hall, steps sounding angrily on the hall's floor. A little more than a third of the room, including several of the men also on the raised platform, rose and followed the Senator out.

When they had gone, Bernard shook his head and cast an almost imperceptible wink in her direction. "All right," he said. "Next question."

A small forest of hands went up. Those men who remained, all of them wearing Legion uniform tunics or armor, or with their hair cropped Legion fashion, settled down to listen.

Amara descended to the hall floor after Bernard's talk was over. He was shaking hands with the few members of the Collegia's staff who had remained when Senator Arnos left. Giraldi hovered in the background, leaning on his cane, and traded gibes with several other old soldiers apparently of his acquaintance.

Amara smiled as Bernard broke away from the men and came to her. "You will rip his forked tongue from his head?"

He gave her a fleeting smile. "Too much, you think?"

Amara imitated Arnos's clipped Rhodesian accent. "You *are* a barbarian, after all, Count."

Bernard let out a rumble of a laugh but shook his head. "He didn't believe me."

"He's one fool," Amara replied. "We knew when we set out to come here that there would be plenty of them around."

"Yes. I just didn't think that one of them would be the Senator holding the purse strings for all the Crown funds for the Legions." Bernard shook his head. "And he has a following. Maybe I should have let him strut a bit."

"If you had, you wouldn't be you," Amara replied. "Besides, you struck a solid note with the active duty soldiers here. They're the ones whose opinions will matter most."

"They're also the ones who will suffer the most from budget cuts," Bernard said. "It's hard to fight anyone when your equipment is wearing out and falling apart around you. Much less something like the Vord."

"And would kissing up to the Senator make him more likely to increase the gold allowed to the Legions in order to increase their scouts and other auxiliary troops?"

"Perhaps not," Bernard admitted.

"Then don't gnaw at it. You've done what you can. And I should imagine that the cadets who were here will be talking about the way you dropped that challenge to the Senator for years. A source of long-term amusement."

"At least I accomplished something positive. Why didn't you say so?"

She laughed and took his arm as they left the lecture hall and strolled across the campus.

He smiled and tilted his head at her. "You look . . . I don't know. Happy, today. You haven't stopped smiling."

"I don't look happy," she said.

"No?"

"No, Your Excellency." She took a deep breath, then said, "I look late."

He stared at her blankly for a moment. "You look . . ." Then his eyes widened. "Oh. *Oh!*"

She looked up at her husband and smiled. For a moment, she thought her heart might simply fly from her chest and take to the sky. She couldn't resist a little skip and a burst of wind from Cirrus, which carried her seven or eight feet off the ground, spun her about in a dancer's twirl, and dropped her back down to Bernard's side.

His smile stretched ear to ear. "Are you . . . I mean. Are you sure?"

"As much as anyone can be, this soon," she replied. "Perhaps you were right all along. This is the first time we've been together for more than a few days at a stretch."

Bernard let out a laugh, picked her up, and all but crushed her against him in a bearish embrace, drawing stares from cadets passing between classes all around them. Amara reveled in it. It was when she felt his strength, that casual, enormous power, that she felt the most soft, the most yielding—the most feminine, she supposed. He made her feel beautiful. Granted she wore a sword at her hip, and could use it to deadly effect if necessary—but it made it no less pleasant to feel otherwise for a time.

"I do need to breathe," she murmured a moment later.

He laughed and put her down again, and they kept walking together, now very close, his side pressed to hers, his arm around her shoulders. "How long have we been here?"

"Six weeks," Amara murmured. "As you well know."

"Has it been that long?" Bernard asked.

She gave him a look from beneath lowered lashes. "It can be difficult to judge the passing of time when one so seldom leaves his bedchamber, my lord."

He let out a low, pleased sound, something between a chuckle and a contented growl. "That's hardly my fault. The outside world holds little to interest me compared to the company I keep there."

"My lord," she said, miming a shocked face. "Whatever could you mean?"

His fingers tightened on the curve of her waist, above one hip, stroking lightly. She shivered. "Let me show you."

"What about Giraldi?" she asked.

"He isn't invited."

She dug her elbow lightly into Bernard's ribs. "We're not leaving him alone tonight, are we?"

"No, no. He'll meet us for dinner when we pick up Isana. He's teaching some basic combat classes, meanwhile, as something of a celebrity instructor."

"Good," Amara said. "He'll get into trouble without something to keep him occupied."

"I thought you were married to me," Bernard said.

"I pick my battles," Amara said. "You're going to find trouble regardless of what I do. Perhaps it's a family trait. It would explain you and your nephew both."

"That isn't fair," Bernard said. "Tavi gets in much more trouble than I do."

"He's younger," Amara said with a sly, sideward glance, nudging him with her hip.

"I'll show you young," Bernard growled—but he glanced over his shoulder in the middle of the statement, and the smile faded from his face as he did.

"What is it?" Amara asked, leaning her head against him as if nothing had happened.

"There are two men following us," Bernard said. "But I'm not sure that they are our escort."

"What escort?" Amara asked.

He arched an eyebrow and glanced at her.

"All right." She sighed. "The Cursors have teams watching over a number of possible loyalist targets. I didn't want you to feel insulted."

She paused to straighten the hem of her skirts and called to Cirrus, spinning the fury into a new kind of crafting, one that would bend the light entirely back upon itself, blinding her to what lay before her, but letting her see what was behind. It was a difficult crafting to form and a strain to hold on to, but a quick look was all she needed.

"Those men aren't our escort," she said quietly. "I don't know them."

Bernard's eyes narrowed. "Something does not smell right, then."

"Yes," Amara said. "I don't like the way this smells at all."

CHAPTER 8

"Bloody crows," Cyril snarled. "Get moving, Subtribune."

Tavi grasped the outside of the ladder with his hands and slid down it, feet pressing the sides of the ladder rather than using the rungs. He hit the ground, flexed his legs to absorb the shock, and sprinted for the infirmary tents. He heard Captain Cyril land behind him, then keep pace with Tavi despite the weight of his armor.

"Make a hole!" Tavi shouted at the recruits gathered outside the tent, doing his best to imitate Max's tone, volume, and inflection when he issued orders. "Captain coming through!"

Fish hastened to stand aside, most of them throwing hasty, suddenly remembered salutes as Cyril came through. Tavi swept the tent flap aside and held it for the captain, then followed him in.

The healer within was a veteran named Foss. He was most of seven feet tall, built like a Phrygian mountain bear, and his armor was of the style of standard Legion-issue from nearly forty years ago and looked slightly different than the current design. It bore an impressive number of dents and dings, but was impeccably maintained, and the man moved in it like it was his own skin. Foss had a short, thick brush of grey hair cropped close to his head, and deep-set, narrow eyes.

"In the tub," he snarled to the fish carrying Max, gesturing them to a long wooden watercrafter's trough filled with water. "Careful, careful. Crows take it, man, do you want to tear the wound open even farther?"

They got Max into the tub, still in his armor. The water covered him up to his chin, with his head resting on a supporting incline. Muttering darkly to himself, Foss reached in and adjusted the incline, lowering it until the water covered all of Max but his lips, nose, and eyes. Then he knelt behind Max and thrust his hands into the water, closing his eyes.

"Give him room to work, recruits," Captain Cyril said in a quiet voice. He pointed at the opposite corner of the tent, and the bloodstained young men hastened to obey him.

Tavi bit his lip, staring at his friend. Max's skin looked strange—waxy and colorless. He couldn't see if Max still drew breath.

"Healer," Cyril murmured a moment later.

"Give me some quiet here," growled Foss, his rumbling basso threatening. After a good half a minute, he added, "Sir." He went on muttering to himself under his breath, mostly colorful vulgarities from what Tavi could hear. Then Foss drew in a breath and held it.

"He's been hurt before," Tavi said to the captain. "Do you think he'll be all right?"

Cyril never took his eyes from Max. "It's bad," he said shortly.

"I saw him run through. That should have killed him. But he was up and walking inside four hours."

Cyril's gaze moved to Tavi, his expression remote, hard, though his voice remained very quiet. "Your babbling might distract Foss. If you want to help your friend, put your bloody teeth together and keep them that way. Or get out."

Tavi's cheeks flushed with warmth, and he nodded, closing his jaws with an audible click. It was a physical effort to stop talking. Max was his friend, and Tavi felt terrified. He did not want to lose him. His instincts screamed at him to shout, to order the healer to work faster, to do *something*. But he knew that he couldn't.

Tavi hated the helpless feeling that knowledge sent through him. He'd had a lifetime to get familiar with it, when his lack of furycrafting continually put him at a disadvantage in virtually every facet of his life. He would have given anything to have a healer's skill at watercrafting, to be able to help his friend.

The captain was right. The best thing he could do for Max was to shut his mouth and wait.

There wasn't a sound for nearly two minutes, and every second of it felt like a week.

Then Foss exhaled a low, agonized groan, bearish body sagging forward over Max.

Max suddenly jerked and drew in a ragged, choking breath.

Foss grunted, still sagging, and his rumbling voice sounded unsteady. "Got him, Cap," he said after a moment. "It was real close."

Tavi heard Cyril exhale slowly himself, though he kept his face from any expression. "I thought Lady Antillus was here today," he said. "How is it that she was not here to care for Maximus?"

Foss shook his head and slowly sat up again, drawing his arms from the bloodied water to sit down immediately on the canvas floor. "Lunch with her son, she said."

"Ah, yes. Family lunch," Cyril said. "How is he?"

"Bad, Cap. He's tougher'n a gargant leather boot, but he bled out more than I've ever seen a man survive."

"Will he recover?"

Foss shook his head again. "Wound is closed. He's breathin'. But losing that much blood can do bad things to a man's head. Maybe he wakes up. Maybe he doesn't. Maybe he wakes up, and he ain't himself no more. Or can't walk. Or he wakes up simple."

"Is there anything we might do to help him?"

Foss shrugged and from his sitting position fell wearily onto his back, rubbing at his forehead with one blunt-fingered hand. "Don't know that he needs anything but time. But I'm just an old Legion healer. Maybe the High Lady knows better than me, or can see more than I can about him."

"Crows," the captain muttered. He turned and frowned at the recruits, still in their corner—eight of them, Tavi noted, a spear of men who would march in file together and share the standard Legion tent. "File leader," Cyril commanded.

One of the young men, a tall and gawky youth, came to attention and saluted. "Captain, sir."

"What's your name, son?"

"Schultz, sir."

"Report," Cyril said. "What happened, recruit Schultz?"

"It was an accident, sir."

Cyril was silent for a second, staring at the recruit, who swallowed and blanched and grew even more rigid.

"The captain knows it was an accident, recruit," Tavi said. "Tell him the particulars of it."

The boy's face reddened. "Oh. Sir, sorry, sir, yes, sir. Um. We were our cohort's strongest spear at our sword lessons. First ones to get issued live swords, sir. Centurion Antillar had us running our drills with live blades for the first time, all in a row, sir. He was going to show us to our whole cohort, sir, before they got their blades. He went up and down the line, watching us, calling our mistakes, sir."

"Go on," Cyril said. "How was he injured?"

The boy shook his head. "Sir, it was an accident. He had just corrected me and he was walking away from me, where he could watch the whole line of us. And I went through a number eight thrust." The recruit shifted his feet into a fighting stance and swept his right arm straight up from down low by his leg. Such a stroke from a sword could disembowel a man, and though difficult to use, in the close press of combat it could be devastating. "And the sword . . . just slipped out of my hand, sir."

"It slipped," Cyril said quietly, his gaze level.

The recruit snapped back to attention. "Yes, sir. I haven't ever had that happen before. It slipped and it flew out spinning and it struck Centurion Antillar in the side of the neck, sir." He looked down at himself, and for the first time seemed to see the blood all over him. "I didn't mean it to happen, sir. Not at all. I'm sorry, sir."

The captain folded his arms. "He had just finished correcting you. He had his back to you. Your sword inexplicably flew from your grasp and struck his throat. You say it was an accident."

"Yes, sir."

"And you expect me to believe that?"

The recruit blinked at him. "Sir?"

"Men have lost their tempers with their centurions in the

past. Sometimes they were angry enough to kill them. Perhaps you couldn't stand Antillar's criticism of your technique. It's a hot day. You've not eaten. Maybe you lost your temper and killed him."

The recruit's mouth dropped open. *"Sir . . ."* He shook his head. "I'd never, no sir, Centurion Antillar, no sir."

"We'll see," Cyril said quietly. "I will be looking into this more thoroughly. Get back to your cohort, recruits. Schultz. Don't attempt to leave the camp. The men who I'd send to hunt you down would have orders to execute you on sight."

The young man swallowed and saluted again.

"Dismissed."

Schultz led his fellow recruits out of the tent, and only a second later the flap flew open again and an armored Knight entered, accompanied by the beautiful Lady Antillus. The Knight jerked to a stop upon seeing Max in the tub, his mouth dropping open. Lady Antillus drew in a breath, placing the fingers of one hand over the bodice of her blue-on-blue silk gown, her eyes wide.

For some reason he could never have put a name to, Tavi did not believe Lady Antillus's gesture was a genuine one. It was too smooth, perhaps, too flowing to be true shock and distress.

"Great furies preserve," she said. "What has happened to my stepson?"

"According to the recruit whose weapon struck him, it was a training accident, my lady," Cyril said.

Lady Antillus's expression grew distressed. "He looks horrible. I take it that Foss has seen to him?"

Foss grunted from the floor. "Aye, m'lady. But he lost a lot of blood."

"What is his prognosis?" she asked the healer.

"Um. What?" Foss asked.

"He's not in immediate danger," Tavi interjected. "But the extent of the damage that may have been inflicted by blood loss is not yet clear."

Lady Antillus's attention turned to Tavi, and he could feel the full, throbbing force of her personality behind that gaze. She was not a tall woman, in particular, and she had dark hair that fell in a straight, shimmering curtain to her hips. Her face was pale, with a touch of the perpetually ruddy cheeks that come to those living in the northern climates, and her eyes were the color of deep amber. She had stark cheekbones and thin lips, and taken together it made her look too harsh to be conventionally beautiful—but the grace of her carriage and the steady, burning fires of intelligence in her amber eyes combined into an impressive, attractive whole.

Once again, Tavi was struck with the notion that she looked familiar to him, but for the life of him he could not track down the proper memory.

"I don't believe we've spoken, young man," she said.

Tavi bowed to her at the waist. "Subtribune Rufus Scipio, m'lady. I, of course, know who you are."

The Knight stepped forward, staring at the silent Max. It wasn't until he did that Tavi realized that he was several years younger than Tavi himself. He was a little under average height and slender. His hair was long and auburn, his eyes ivy green, and his armor was of masterful quality—and completely unmarred.

"Mother," the young Knight said quietly, "he looks like death. Shouldn't we . . . do something? Take care of him?"

"Of course, we—"

"No," Captain Cyril said, overriding her with his own voice.

Lady Antillus stared at Cyril in shock. "Excuse me?"

The captain bowed slightly toward her. "Beg pardon, lady. I ought to have said, 'not yet.' The centurion has endured a great shock, but his injuries have been ably closed. I judge that he needs rest, first. Any further crafting could tax whatever strength remains in him and do more harm than good."

"Right," the young Knight said, nodding. "He's got a point, Mother—"

"Crassus," Lady Antillus snapped, her voice cool and edged.

The young Knight dropped his eyes and shut his mouth at once.

Lady Antillus turned back to Cyril. "In good conscience I

must ask: Are you actually arrogant enough to think you know better than a trained watercrafter? Are you a Tribune Medica, Captain?"

"I am the Tribune Medica's commanding officer, *Tribune*," Cyril said in a perfectly calm voice. "I am the man who can tell the Tribune Medica either to follow her orders or depart the service of this Legion."

Lady Antillus's eyes widened. "Do you dare speak to me so, Captain?"

"Leave this tent. That is my order, Tribune."

"Or what follows?" she asked in a quiet voice.

"Or I will discharge you in dishonor and have you escorted from this camp."

Lady Antillus's eyes flashed with anger, and the air of the tent suddenly became stiflingly warm. "Beware, Cyril. This is foolishness."

The captain's mild tone never changed. "This is foolishness, *what*, Tribune?"

Heat rolled off the High Lady as if from a large kitchen oven, and she spat, "Sir."

"Thank you, Tribune. We'll discuss this again when Maximus has had the chance to rest." Then his own eyes and expression hardened for the first time, and the captain's face looked harder than the steel of armor or sword. His voice dropped to barely a murmur. "Dismissed."

Lady Antillus spun on her heel and stalked from the tent. The heat of her anger lingered, and Tavi felt his face beading with sweat.

"And you, Sir Crassus," Cyril said, his voice assuming its more usual, brisk tones. "We'll take care of him."

Crassus nodded once without lifting his eyes, then hurried out.

Silence fell over the tent. Cyril let out a long breath. Tavi mopped at the sweat now running into his eyes. The only sound was that of droplets of water falling from the crafting tub as Max breathed, the slight motion overflowing the tub's edge, here and there.

"Someone's never getting promoted ever again," observed Foss from his place on the floor.

Cyril showed the exhausted healer a fleeting smile before shrugging his shoulders and straightening his spine, reassuming his usual air of detached command. "There's not much trouble she can cause for me by accusing me of issuing orders to a lawful subordinate."

"Not official trouble," Tavi said quietly.

"What are you saying, Subtribune?"

Tavi glanced at his friend, silent in the tub. "Accidents happen."

Cyril met Tavi's eyes and said, "Aye. They do."

Tavi tilted his head. "You knew. That's why you welcomed Max to the staff meeting. To warn him that she was here."

"I simply wanted to make an old friend welcome," Cyril said.

"You don't think that recruit hurt Max. You knew that she was outside. That was for her benefit, to make her think that you didn't realize what was happening."

The captain's frown deepened. "Excuse me?"

"Captain," Tavi began. "Do you think that Lady—"

"No," Cyril said, sharply, raising warning a hand. "I don't think that. And neither do you, Scipio."

Tavi grimaced. "But it's why you didn't want her close to Max."

"I simply gave her an order and made sure she followed it," Cyril said. "But be careful with your words, Scipio. Should you say the wrong thing and be overheard, you'll find yourself in *juris macto* with the High Lady. She'd burn you to cinders. So unless you get something solid, so solid that it will stand up in a court of law, you keep your mouth shut and your opinions to yourself. Do you understand me?"

"Yes, sir," Tavi replied.

Cyril grunted. "Foss."

"I never hear or remember or repeat anything, sir."

"Good man," Cyril said. "When Maximus wakes up, we need to have a familiar face here. He's going to be confused, disoriented. As strong as he is, he could do some damage if he panicked." Cyril drummed his fingers idly against the hilt of his sword. "I've got an hour or so. Scipio, go tell Gracchus that I'm giving you special duty for a day or two. Get a big meal. Bring some food with you. I'll spell you, or send the First Spear in my place."

Tavi swallowed. "Do you really think he's in danger, sir?"

"I've said everything I intend to. The important thing now is to prevent any further accidents. Now move."

"Yes, sir," Tavi said, and saluted.

But then he paused at the door to the tent. Max was helpless. It was a horrible, cynical thought, but what if the captain's confrontation with the High Lady had been staged for Tavi's benefit? What if by walking away from Max, Tavi was in fact condemning his friend to death?

Tavi looked over his shoulder at the captain.

Cyril stood over the tub. He looked up at Tavi and arched an eyebrow. Then the captain frowned, and Tavi had the uncomfortable impression that Cyril had seen the direction of Tavi's thoughts.

Cyril met Tavi's gaze, his eyes steady. Tavi could see the strength in the man—not the raging strength of storms that underlay Gaius's rage, or the smoldering fire of Lady Antillus's anger. This strength was something older, humbler, as steady and sure as the rolling hillsides of the Vale, as set in place as the ancient, worn old mountains around it, as unchanging in the face of turmoil as waters of a deep well. Tavi couldn't have said how he knew it, but he did: Cyril respected the power of those like Lady Antillus, but he did not fear them. He would neither bow his knee nor stain his honor for her or her like.

"Maximus is Legion," the captain said, chin lifted proudly. "If harm comes to him, it will be because I am dead."

Tavi nodded once. He touched his fist to his heart and nodded to the captain. Then he turned and hurried from the tent to follow Cyril's orders.

Tavi spent the day and most of the night in the tent by his friend's side. Valiar Marcus had spelled him for time enough to bathe and eat a cold meal. Captain Cyril himself had come in the hours before dawn, and Tavi had simply thrown himself down on the floor and slept, armor and all. He awoke stiff and sore in midmorning, and stretched the kinks out, doing his best to ignore the complaints of his body. The captain had waited until Tavi was fully awake before departing, leaving him to resume his watch over his friend.

Foss came in now and again, checking up on Max.

"Shouldn't we get him into a bed?" Tavi asked.

Foss grunted. "Take his armor off. Water is better, so long as he doesn't get cold."

"Why?"

"M' fury's still in it," Foss said. "Doin' what she can to help 'im."

Tavi smiled. "She?"

"Bernice. And don't give me no mouth, kid. I know you Citizens make fun of us pagunus types for giving them names. Back in my home, they'd look at you just as funny for sayin' they didn't need them."

Tavi shook his head. "No, I'm not criticizing you, healer. Honestly. It's the results that matter."

"Happen to be of the same mind m'self," Foss said, grinning.

"How'd you wind up here?" Tavi asked.

"Volunteered," Foss said. He added hot water from a steaming kettle to the tub, careful not to let it burn the man within.

"We all volunteered," Tavi said.

Foss grunted. "I'm career Legion. Shieldwall. Antillus to Phrygia and back, fighting off the Icemen. One hitch for one city, then one in the other. Did that for thirty years."

"Got tired of the cold?" Tavi asked.

"Manner of speakin'," Foss confirmed, and winked at Tavi. "Wife in Phrygia found out about the wife in Antillus. Thought I might like to see what the south was like for a spell."

Tavi chuckled.

Max said, his voice very weak, "Don't play cards with him, Calderon. He cheats."

Tavi shot up off the camp stool and went to his friend. "Hey," he said. "You decide to wake up, finally?"

"Got a hangover," Max said, his voice slurred. "Or something. What happened to me, Calderon?"

"Hey, Max," Tavi said, gentle urgency in his voice, "don't try to talk yet. Wake up a little more. Let the healer see to you."

Foss knelt by the tub and peered at Max's eyes, telling the young man to follow his finger when he waved it around. "Calderon?" he asked. "Thought you were Rivan."

"Yes," Tavi said smoothly. "My first hitch was in Riva. I was in one of the green cohorts they sent to Garrison."

Foss grunted. "You was at Second Calderon?"

"Yes," Tavi said.

"Heard it was pretty bad."

"Yes," Tavi said.

Foss peered up at Tavi from under shaggy black brows, his eyes thoughtful. Then he grunted, and said, "Maximus, get out of that tub before I drown you. I never cheated at cards in my life."

"Don't make me hit you," Max said, his voice only a shadow of itself. He started to stir up out of the tub but groaned after a second and sagged back.

"Bucket," Foss said to Tavi. Tavi grabbed a nearby bucket and tossed it to Foss. The healer deposited it on the floor just as Max turned on his side and threw up. The healer supported the wounded *legionare* with one broad arm. "There now, man. No shame in it. You had a close call."

Max sagged back a minute later, then blinked his eyes several times and focused them on Tavi. "Scipio," he said, gentle emphasis on the word. Max had recovered his wits, Tavi surmised. "What happened?"

Tavi glanced up at Foss. "Healer? You mind if we have a minute?"

Foss grunted, got up, and left the tent without speaking.

"You had a training accident," Tavi said quietly, once Foss had left.

Max stared at Tavi for a long minute, and Tavi saw something like despair in his friend's eyes. "I see. When?"

"About this time yesterday. One of your recruits lost his grip on his *gladius* and threw it through your neck."

"Which one?" Max asked in a monotone.

"Schultz."

"The crows he did," Max muttered. "Kid's got some real metalcraft, and he never even knew it until he joined up. He gets some experience, he could be a Knight. He didn't slip."

"Everyone says he slipped," Tavi said. "The captain agrees that in the absence of other evidence, it was an accident."

"Yeah. Captains always do," Max said, his tone flat and bitter.

"What?" Tavi asked.

Max shook his head and sat upright in a slow, painful-looking motion. Water sluiced down over the heavy muscles of his shoulders and back, smooth rivulets broken by the heavy, finger-thick ridges of scar tissue that crisscrossed his upper back. He rubbed a hand over the back of his neck, and gingerly touched the stripe of furycrafted pink skin where the sword had struck him. "Toss me that towel."

Tavi did. "This isn't the first time something like this has happened to you, is it?"

"Fifth," Max said.

"Crows," Tavi muttered. "And it's her?"

Max nodded.

"What do we do about it?" Tavi asked.

Max dried off, the motions slow, halfhearted. "Do?"

"We've got do something."

Max looked around until he spotted his uniform pants and tunic on a nearby chair, folded and laundered. He dropped the towel on the floor and shambled over to his clothes. "There's nothing to do."

Tavi peered at his friend. "Max? We have to do something."

"No. Leave it."

"Max—"

Max froze, his shirt in his hands, his shoulders and voice tight. "Shut up. Now."

"No, Max. We've got to—"

Max spun, and snarled, "What?" As he spoke, the ground lashed up at Tavi and bounced him into the air and to one side. He landed in a sprawl.

"Do *what*?" Max snarled, sweeping his tunic like a sword at one of the tent's support posts in a gesture of futile rage. "There's nothing I can do. Nothing anyone can do." He shook his head. "She's too smart. Too strong. She can get away with whatever the crows she wants to." He ground his teeth, and the tunic burst into sudden flame, white-hot tongues of it licking up around Max without harming his skin. Tavi felt the heat, though, intense, just short of painful. "Too . . ."

Max dropped his arms in a limp, weak gesture, flakes of black ash that had been his tunic drifting down. He sat down and leaned his back against the support post and shook his head. Tavi gathered himself to his feet and watched as Max's head fell forward. He was silent for a time. Then he whispered, "She killed my mother. I was five."

Tavi went to his friend's side and crouched beside him.

"People like her get to do what they please," Max said quietly. "I can't just kill her. She's too smart to be caught. And even if she was, she has family, friends, contacts, people she controls and blackmails. She'll never face justice. And one of these times, she'll get me. I've known that since I was fourteen."

And suddenly Tavi understood his friend a little better. Max had lived his life in fear and anger. He'd run away to join the Legions to escape his stepmother's reach, but he knew, or rather, was convinced that he'd only managed a stay of execution. Max believed that she would kill him, believed it on a level so deep that it had become a part of who and what he was. That was why his friend had caroused so enthusiastically in the capital, why he had blown off most of his classes at the Academy, why he had made merry with wine, women, and song at every opportunity.

He believed he would never live to die of old age.

Tavi put his hand on Max's shoulder. "No one's invincible. No one's perfect. She can be beaten."

Max shook his head. "Forget it," he said. "Stay clear. I don't want you to get caught up in it when it happens."

Tavi hissed out a breath of frustration and rose. "Bloody crows, man. What is the matter with you?"

Max never looked up. "Just go away."

Footsteps approached the tent, then Maestro Magnus thrust his head inside, looking around quickly. "Ah," he said. "He's awake?"

Foss nudged in past Magnus and scowled at Tavi. "That's it. Everyone out."

"What?" Tavi asked.

"Everyone out. Patient needs to clean up, dress, get some water in him, and let me check him before he'll be able to move around. You people staring at him won't help. So get out."

"Actually, a fair idea," Magnus said, giving Tavi a direct look.

Tavi nodded at him, and said, "All right. I'll be outside, Max."

"Yeah," Max said, waving a vague hand. "Out in a bit."

Tavi slipped out of the tent, walking close to Magnus. "Where have you been?" Tavi asked him.

"Keeping an eye on our Tribune Medica," Magnus replied. He led Tavi on a brief walk, away from the tents and past several groups of drilling recruits, variously shouting and being shouted at by instructors, creating plenty of noise in which to hide any conversation. "Has anyone come?"

"The captain and the First Spear," Tavi said quietly. "This morning that Knight, Crassus, was standing not far off, but he didn't come over."

"Were you able to find out about that messenger that keeps

going back and forth between Tribune Bracht and the village?" Magnus asked.

"I've been with Max," Tavi said. "Maestro, that's more important than—"

"Our duties?" Magnus asked archly. "No, Tavi. The security of the Realm is more important than any one of us. Remember why we are all here."

Tavi ground his teeth together but nodded once, sharply. "I should be able to find out in the next day or so."

"Good. While you're at it, I want you to find out whatever you can about the master farrier and his staff. And that veteran squad from the fifth cohort."

"I already did that last," Tavi said. "They're aphrodin addicts. They've been buying it at the bordello in the camp."

Magnus hissed through his teeth. "Addicts can still be spies. Find out who deals with them there. Whom they talk to."

Tavi coughed. "That's really more in Max's traditional waters than mine."

"Great furies, man. I'm not letting Maximus anywhere near an aphrodin den at a time like this. He'll get himself killed."

"Sir, Max likes to chase the ladies and drink, and furies know how well I know it. Sometimes he'll drink laced wine. But he isn't . . . that doesn't control him."

"It's got nothing to do with whether or not he's able to control himself," Magnus said. "But it will be far too easy for someone to arrange an accident for him if he's lying drugged and besotted in a pleasure den when he should be watching for a knife in the back."

"From his stepmother?"

"Careful," Magnus said, looking around. "Has Max ever spoken to you of his family?"

"No," Tavi said. "But I always thought the scars on his back said plenty about them."

Magnus shook his head. "Maximus is the illegitimate, publicly acknowledged son of High Lord Antillus. The High Lord married three years after Maximus was born, a political arrangement."

"Lady Antillus," Tavi said.

"And Crassus was the product of their union," Magnus said.

Tavi frowned. "She thinks Max is a threat to Crassus?"

"Maximus is popular in the northern Legions and with at least one other High Lord. He's a powerfully gifted furycrafter, he may one day be one of the finest swordsmen in Aleran history, and he made a great many friends at the Academy."

"Uh," Tavi said. "He was friendly. I don't know if most of those who spent time with him would count as 'friends,' per se."

"You'd be surprised how many times alliances have been forged between former casual lovers," Magnus replied. "More to the point, he is known to be friendly with the First Lord's page, among others, and has a widely known defiant streak when it comes to authority."

"Max doesn't want to be a High Lord," Tavi said. "He'd run screaming within half an hour. He knows it."

"And yet," Magnus said, "he has made allies. He has a power base of influence among several Legions, and with several Lords—including those in the personal retinue of Gaius himself. Forget your personal knowledge of him and think of it in terms of an exercise, lad. What if he decided that he *did* want it?"

Tavi wanted to protest, but he ran through the angles in his mind, playing things out in numerous possibilities directed by logic, instinct, and the examples of history, as he had been taught by the Cursors.

"He could do it," Tavi said quietly. "If something happened to Crassus, Max would be the only reasonable choice. Even if it didn't, if Antillus's Legions favored Max over his little brother, if he had support from other High Lords and the First Lord, that would be the end of the matter, practically speaking. It wouldn't even be particularly difficult for him."

"Precisely."

"But he doesn't want that, Maestro. I know him."

"You do," Magnus said. "But his stepmother doesn't. And this isn't young Antillar's first accident." As he finished the sentence, they completed their brief circuit of the interior of the practice field, returning to the infirmary. They were in time to see Lady Antillus and Crassus cross the practice track and walk toward the infirmary tent.

"Max is afraid of her," Tavi murmured.

"She's had a lifetime to teach him fear," Magnus said, nodding. "And she's deadly clever, lad. Powerful, wicked, devious. Several disturbing fates have befallen her foes, and not a shred of evidence has been found, not a drop of blood stained her hands. There are few in the Realm as dangerous as she."

"She looks familiar," Tavi said quietly. "Like someone I should know."

Magnus nodded and said, "There are many who say her nephew Brencis is almost a mirror image of her."

Tavi clenched his teeth. "Kalarus."

"Mmmm," Magnus said, nodding. "Lord Kalare's youngest sister—and only surviving sibling."

Tavi shook his head. "And Max's father married her?"

"As I said. A political marriage." Magnus watched them approaching. "I doubt Lord Antillus likes her any better than Max does. And now, young Scipio, I'm off to attend to the captain and do a great many other things. I think you should entertain the Lady and her son until Maximus gains his feet and can face her in the open, in front of witnesses."

Tavi grimaced. "I'm not good at smiles and charm."

"Now, now. You're a loyal servant of the Realm, Scipio. I'm sure you'll manage." Magnus smiled at him, but whispered, "Be careful." Then he saluted Tavi and vanished into the normal, bustling industry of the Legion camp.

Tavi watched him go for a second and turned his gaze to Lady Antillus and her son. She wore the sky blue on deep blue of the city of Antillus. Max had once remarked that the city colors had been chosen based on what shade the skin of one's . . . well, *parts*, assumed when exposed to the weather in winter and autumn, respectively. From a purely aesthetic perspective, the dress flattered her face, her hair, her figure in every measurable sense. Tavi thought that the blue made her skin look too pale, somehow, as though it was a covering for a mannequin rather than for a human being.

She was speaking quietly, emphatically, to Crassus. Her son was dressed in the brown training tunic of the Legion, though he wore his armor over it—a mark of respect for someone new to the Legions. Only the most solid and promising recruits wore steel before the recruits were issued it generally. Or the most well connected ones, Tavi supposed. Though he could hardly cast stones on *that* account, all things considered. Crassus was scowling, an expression that made his face look more petulant than formidable.

"I don't understand why we can't just get it over with," he was saying.

"Darling child, you have the judgment of a goat," Lady Antillus snapped back. "I have some experience in these matters. One cannot rush them." She put her hand on her son's arm, a motion that silenced him, as Tavi approached.

"Good afternoon, Your Grace," Tavi said, bowing to Lady Antillus, combining it smoothly with a salute. He nodded to Crassus. "Sir Knight."

Crassus saluted Tavi, fist thumping against his breastplate. "Subtribune."

Lady Antillus bowed her head very slightly to Tavi, giving him a flinty look.

"I've been meaning to ask you, Your Grace," Tavi said. "I am told that the training regimen of our novice Knights has been, ah, taxing on those involved. I thought that we might find a way to add more milk or cheese to the younger Knights' rations if they've been breaking bones a bit too often."

"It probably isn't a terrible idea," Lady Antillus allowed, though the words seemed to come out reluctantly.

"We'd be grateful for the gesture, sir," Crassus said, his tone respectful, carefully neutral.

"You'll be glad to know that Maximus is recovering well," Tavi said, smiling politely. "In fact, he was rising to dress a few moments ago."

Lady Antillus looked past Tavi to the tent, frowning. "Was he? Did he seem himself?"

"As far as I could tell, Your Grace," Tavi said. "I believe that the captain intended to check on him as well."

Her tone turned flat, and she dropped even the pretense of being polite. "Did he."

"He takes the well-being of his men very seriously," Tavi said, trying to sound cheerfully oblivious to her reaction.

"Like a mother cares for her son, I suppose?" she muttered. She glanced at Crassus. "Perhaps we should go in immediate—"

"I also wished to ask you," Tavi said, walking over her words. "Maximus's injury is really rather unusual given that we haven't seen any actual combat. The healers in my last Legion favored strong wine and rare meat to restore an injury with so much blood loss, but I've read others who favor an herbal tea and increased vegetables."

"Read whom?" Lady Antillus demanded.

"Lord Placidus's treatise on common military injuries and complications, Your Grace."

Lady Antillus rolled her eyes. "Placidus should stick to tending his cows and leave the healing of nonedibles to those who know better," she said.

Tavi frowned at her, tilting his head. "How so, lady?"

"To begin with, Placidus rarely has to deal with injuries sustained upon a strenuous campaign," she said. "His forces are generally deployed on a short-term basis, and their provender reflects that fact. His herbals are fine for men who are eating fresh meat every day or two, but for men marching on jerky and hardtack, the dietary requirements for . . ." She frowned at him for a moment, her eyes narrowed. Then she waved one hand in a dismissive gesture. "Though I suppose Maximus is hardly the victim of a winter's privation, is he? Give him whatever is the most cost-effective."

"Yes, Your Grace," Tavi said, bowing his head. "Is there anything I should know about the preparation?"

"Why, Subtribune," Lady Antillus said. "If I didn't know better, I would think you were trying to interfere with my visit to my stepson."

Tavi lifted both eyebrows. "Your Grace? I'm sure I don't know what you mean."

She gave him a prim little smile. "I'm sure you don't know

what you're playing with, Scipio." She glanced at the tent, then back at Tavi. "How long have you known my Maximus?"

Tavi fixed her with the same cheerful smile he had always used when his aunt Isana had asked him loaded questions, relying upon her empathic senses to gather information from the answers. He had learned to baffle her before he turned thirteen years old. He certainly wasn't going to allow *this* creature to do what his aunt could not. "A season or so. We traveled here together from the capital."

She frowned faintly, narrowing her eyes. "You seem quite close to him for such a brief acquaintance."

Tavi threw in a bit of truth in order to confuse the issue. "We were attacked by armed bandits on the way here. We fought them together."

"Ah," Lady Antillus said. "A bonding experience. Are you sure you didn't meet him before that?"

"Your Grace?" Tavi said. "No, I'm certain that I'd have remembered it. Max is the sort to stand out in one's memory."

Crassus snorted quietly.

Lady Antillus glared at her son, then turned back to Tavi. "I was told he was quite close to a page in service to the Crown."

"Could be, Your Grace," Tavi agreed. "But you'd have to ask him about it."

"Would I?" she pressed. "Are you sure you are not the young man from Calderon, Subtribune?"

"I was only stationed there for a week or so before the battle, Your Grace. After that, I was based at a town named Marsford, about twenty miles south of Riva."

"You are not Tavi of Calderon?" she asked.

Tavi shrugged his shoulders at her and smiled. "Sorry."

She answered his smile with her own, wide enough to show her sharply pointed canines. "Well. That's cleared up. Now be a dear for me, Subtribune, and light this campfire?"

Tavi felt his smile falter for a second. "Beg pardon?"

"The campfire," Lady Antillus said, as though speaking to the village idiot. "I think an herbal tea would be nice for all of us to enjoy if Maximus is up and about. You've had your basic furycrafting. I've seen your record. So, Subtribune Scipio. Light the campfire."

"Mother, I'll get it for—" Crassus began.

She flicked her hand in a slicing gesture, and her smile grew wider. "No, darling. After all, we are Legion, are we not? I have given dear Scipio a lawful order. Now, he must follow it. Just like all the rest of us."

"Light the fire?" Tavi asked.

"Just a little firecrafting," she said, nodding. "Go ahead, Subtribune."

Tavi squinted at her, then up at the sun and chewed on his lip. "I'll be honest with you, Your Grace. Fire isn't my best subject. I haven't practiced it since my tests."

"Oh, don't sell yourself so short, Scipio," Lady Antillus said. "It isn't as though you're some kind of freak with no crafting at all."

Tavi made himself smile as naturally as he knew how. "Of course not. But it might take me a moment."

"Oh," she said, gathering her skirts and stepping away from the campfire, laid but not lit, before the infirmary tent. "I'll give you a bit of room, then."

"Thank you," Tavi said. He went over to the fire, squatted, and drew his knife. He took one of the more slender sticks lying in an upright tent-shaped stack, and struck a small mound of shavings from it in rapid order.

Tavi glanced up to find Lady Antillus watching from ten feet away. "Don't let me distract you," she said.

Tavi smiled at her. Then he rubbed his hands on his thighs and stretched them out over the tinder, narrowing his eyes.

Behind him, Max emerged from the tent and walked toward them, his steps growing louder. "Oh," he drawled, his voice still a bit weak. "Hullo, stepmother. What are you doing?"

"Watching your friend Scipio demonstrate his firecrafting skills, Maximus," she said, smiling. "Don't spoil it by helping. He'll miss the chance to prove himself."

Max's steps faltered for a second, but he kept walking. "You can't take his basic fieldcraft on faith?"

Lady Antillus sounded like she was almost laughing. "I'm

sorry, darling. Sometimes I just need to have my trust in others vindicated."

"Scipio . . ." Max said, lowering his voice.

"Leave off, Max," Tavi growled. "Can't you see I'm concentrating, here?"

There was a brief silence in which Tavi's imagination provided him with an image of Max staring openmouthed at his back. Then he set his shoulders, let out a quiet grunt of effort, and a wisp of smoke curled up from the tinder.

Tavi leaned over and blew gently on the spark, feeding it more shavings, then small pieces, then larger ones, until the fire was going strong and set to the prepared sticks of the campfire. They took in short order, and Tavi brushed off his pants, rising.

Lady Antillus stared at him, with her smug smile frozen stiffly upon her lips.

Tavi smiled at her again and bowed. "I'll fetch water for the tea, Your Grace."

"No," she said, her voice a little too clear and sharp and polite. "That's all right. I've just remembered another obligation. And Crassus must return to his cohort."

"But—" Crassus began.

"Now," Lady Antillus said. She dismissed Max with a glance and shot Tavi a spiteful glare.

Tavi dropped the false smile he'd been wearing. Suddenly, he found the memory of Max's pale face, the water pink with his blood, growing in his mind. In the space of a breath, it became painfully sharp and clear. A breath later, Tavi recalled with sickening clarity the cruel, vivid scars that crisscrossed his friend's back—the marks of a many-tongued lash barbed with bits of metal or glass. To leave such vicious scars, the injuries had to have been inflicted on him before Max had come into the power of his furies, when he was twelve years old. Or younger.

And Lady Antillus—and her son—had been responsible for it.

Tavi found himself planning quite calmly. The High Lady had enormous power of furycrafting, and so would have to be the first target. If she did not die all but instantly, she might be able to prevent an injury from killing her, or to strike out with power enough to slay Tavi as she died. Where she stood, the lunge would be a little long, but so long as she did not absolutely expect a physical attack, he should be able to drive his slender poniard up through the hollow of her throat and into her brain. A twist, a ragged extraction to tear the wound wider, and he would be left with only Crassus.

The young Knight had little experience, and it was the only thing that would have let him react in time to save his life. A sharp blow to the throat, a gouge to the eyes, and the young lord would be in too much pain to defend himself effectively. Tavi could take a length of wood from the newly lit fire, a rather symbolic statement, he thought, and finish Crassus off with a sharp blow to his unarmored temple.

And suddenly Tavi froze.

The rage he felt fled, and instead he felt sickened, as if the cold dinner he'd eaten last might come flying back out of his mouth. He realized that he was standing in the bright afternoon sun, staring at two people he hardly knew, planning to murder them as coolly and calmly as a grass lion would stalk a doe and her fawn.

Tavi frowned down at his hands. They had started shaking a little, and he wrestled with the bloodthirsty thoughts that had risen up in him, pushing them away. He had actually done violence to other people, classmates at the Academy who had been bullying him at the worst possible time. Tavi had hurt them, and badly, because he'd had little choice in the matter. He had felt sick afterward. Though he had seen the ugly aftermath of that kind of violence, he was nonetheless capable of planning such a brutal attack. It was frightening.

More frightening still, he was all but certain he could actually do it.

But whether or not Max's injuries were their doing, regardless how burning hot the rage Tavi felt in his belly, murdering Lady Antillus and her son would not wipe Max's wounds away—to say nothing of the consequences that would fall on Tavi, and upon the First Lord, by reflection.

She was not the kind of foe one could simply assault and do away with. She would have to be overcome by other means—and if what Magnus said was true, Lady Antillus was a dangerous opponent.

Tavi smiled faintly to himself. He could be dangerous as well. There were more weapons in the world than furies and blades, and no foe was invincible. After all, he had just turned her trap back upon her rather neatly. And if he had outwitted her once, he could do it again.

Lady Antillus watched his face as the thoughts flowed through his head, and seemed hardly to know how to react to Tavi's changing expression. A flash of unease went through her eyes. Perhaps, in his anger, he had let too much of his emotions slip free of his control. It was possible she had sensed his desire to do her harm.

She took her son's arm and turned without a further word, walking away with regal poise. She didn't look over her shoulder.

Max rubbed a hand through his short hair, then said, "All right. What the crows was that all about?"

Tavi frowned at the retreating High Lady, then at Max. "Oh. She thought I was someone you knew at the Academy."

Max grunted. Then he flicked his hand, and Tavi felt a tightness against his ears. "There," Max rumbled. "She can't possibly overhear us."

Tavi nodded.

"You lied to her," Max said. "Right to her face. How the hell did you manage that?"

"Practice," Tavi said. "My aunt Isana is a strong water-crafter, so I was motivated to figure it out as a child."

"There aren't many who can do something like that, Calderon." Max gestured at the fire. "How the crows did you do that? You been holding out on me?"

Tavi smiled. Then he reached down to his trousers and drew out a rounded lens of glass from his pants pocket and turned his palm enough to show it to Max. "Nice, sunny day. Old Romanic trick."

Max looked down at the glass and made a small choking sound. Then he shook his head. "Crows." Max's face turned pink, and his shoulders shook with restrained mirth. "She was listening for your fury. And she never heard it. But you got the fire anyway. She'll never think of . . ." This time he did burst out into the rolling laughter Tavi was familiar with.

"Come on, Scipio," Max said. "Let's find something to eat before I fall down."

Tavi put the glass away and grunted. "Last meal for me. Gracchus is going to have me knee-deep in latrines as soon as he finds out I'm not sitting up with you anymore."

"That's the glamorous officer life for you," Max said. He turned to swagger toward the mess, but his balance swayed.

Tavi was beside his friend in an instant, providing support without actually reaching out for him. "Whoah. Easy there, Max. You had a close call."

"I'll be all right." Max panted. Then he shook his head, regained his balance, and resumed walking. "I'll be fine."

"You will be," Tavi said, nodding. After a moment, he added more quietly, "She isn't smarter than everyone, Max. She can be beaten."

Max glanced aside at Tavi, head tilted, studying him.

"Well, crows," he said at last. "If *you* can do it, how hard can it be?"

"I've got to stop encouraging you." Tavi sighed. "But I'll watch your back. We'll figure something out."

They walked a few more paces before Max said, quietly, "Or maybe she'll just kill both of us."

Tavi snorted. "I'll handle her by myself if you aren't up to it."

Max's eyebrows shot up. Then he shook his head, and his fists slammed gently down on the pauldrons of Tavi's armor, making the steel ring out a gentle tone. "You'd never let me live that down," he said.

"Bloody right I wouldn't," Tavi said. "Come on. Let's eat." He walked steadily beside his friend, ready if Max's balance should waver again.

Tavi shivered, and in the corner of his eye caught Lady An-

tillus watching them cross the camp, never quite openly staring at them. It was the steady, calm, cautious stare of a hungry
cat—but he could feel that this time, rather than tracking
Maximus, her dark, calculating eyes were all for him.

✕✕✕✕ CHAPTER 10

"And it is with great pleasure and pride," Lady Aquitaine addressed the assembled Dianic League, "that I introduce to some
of you, and reintroduce to many of you, the first female Steadholder in Aleran history. Please welcome Isana of Calderon."

The public amphitheater of Ceres was filled to its capacity
of four thousand, though perhaps only half of them were actual members of the Dianic League, the organization consisting of the leading ladies of the Citizenry. Few of the women in
attendance bore a title lower than Countess. Perhaps two hundred had been freemen who won their Citizenship through the
formal duel of the *juris macto*, or who had served in the Legions, mostly in service as Knights, though half a dozen had
served as rank-and-file *legionares*, disguising their sex until
after they had proven themselves in battle.

Of them all, only Isana had attained her rank through
rightful, legal appointment, free of any sort of violence or
military service. In all of Aleran history, she was the only
woman to do so.

The rest of those present were mostly men, and by and
large members of the abolitionist movement. They included a
dozen Senators among their number, their supporters and contacts in the Citizenry, and members of the Libertus Vigilantes,
a quasi-secret organization of militant abolitionists within the
city of Ceres. The Vigilantes had spent years persecuting slave

traders and slave owners within the city. It was not unusual to find an insufficiently paranoid slaver hung from the top of a slave pen by his own manacles, strangled by one of his own chains. The elderly High Lord Cereus Ventis, though the legal master of the city, did not command the respect of the Vigilantes or their supporters, nor possess the resolve to come down on them with all the power at his disposal, and had consequently failed to quell the violence.

Any remaining folk there were either spies who would report back to the Slavers Consortium or simply curious onlookers. The amphitheater was a public forum, open to any Citizen of the Realm.

The crowd applauded, and their emotions flowed over Isana like the first incoming wave of an ocean tide. Isana closed her eyes against it for a moment, fortifying herself against its impact, then rose from her seat, smiled, and stepped to the front of the stage, to the podium beside Lady Aquitaine.

"Thank you," she said. Her voice rang clearly throughout the amphitheater. "Ladies, gentlemen. A man I once knew told me that giving a speech is like amputating a limb. It's best to finish it as quickly and painlessly as possible." There was polite laughter. She waited for it to fade, then said, "The institution of slavery is a blight upon our entire society. Its abuses have become intolerable, its legal safety mechanisms nonfunctional. Everyone here knows that to be true."

She took a deep breath. "But not everyone here has been taken captive by a slaver, illegally and against her will. I have." She glanced aside at Lady Aquitaine for a moment. "It's a terrible thing to feel so helpless. To see . . ." She swallowed. "To see what happens to women in such a situation. I hardly believed the rumors of such things—until they happened to me. Until I saw them with my own eyes."

She turned back to the audience. "The stories may sound like nightmares. But they are true. Through the course of this summit, you have heard testimony from freed slaves, men and women alike, of atrocities that have no place in any society living under the rule of law."

"We find ourselves in a unique position to destroy this cancer, to cleanse this festering wound, to make a change in our Realm for the better. We have a responsibility to our fellow Alerans, to ourselves, and to our progeny to do so. Senators, Citizens, I ask that you all support the Lady Aquitaine's emancipation proposal. Together, we can make our lands and people whole once more."

She took a step back from the podium and nodded. The crowd rose to their feet in enthusiastic applause. Their approval flooded over her in another wave of emotion, and she could hardly keep her feet beneath it. She had no illusions about the skill of her oratory. Of course the abolitionists would support Lady Aquitaine's emancipation legislation. The speech and the crowd's public approval, at the conclusion of the weeks-long summit, was little more than a formality.

She took her seat again while Senator Parmos rose to the podium, to expound upon the abolitionist movement's enthusiastic support. Parmos, a talented speaker, a master of the subtle firecrafting of the inspiration and manipulation of emotion, would in all likelihood hold the crowd spellbound for an hour or more with the power of his words.

"Very good," Lady Aquitaine murmured as Isana sat down beside her. "You have a natural talent."

Isana shook her head. "I could have cawed like a crow, and they would have reacted the same way."

"You underestimate yourself," Lady Aquitaine replied. "You possess a quality of . . . integrity, I think describes it best. It sounds sincere. It gives your words additional weight."

"It doesn't sound sincere. It is sincere," Isana replied. "And I have no integrity anymore. I sold it three years ago."

Lady Aquitaine gave her a wintry little smile. "Such sincerity."

Isana inclined her head in a slight nod and did not look at the woman beside her. "Does this appearance conclude my obligation for today?"

Lady Aquitaine arched an eyebrow. "Why do you ask?"

"I'm meeting my brother for dinner at Vorello's."

"A very nice dining house," Lady Aquitaine said. "You'll

like it. We're almost done with this trip. I'll have one or two more meetings before I can return to Aquitaine. If I require your presence, I shall send for you."

"Very well, my lady," Isana said, then pretended to listen to Senator Parmos speak. Eventually, his voice rose to a thundering crescendo of a conclusion that brought the entire amphitheater enthusiastically to its feet. The tide of their emotion, fanned to fiery heat by the Senator's speech and firecraft, disoriented Isana, and left her with a giddy, whirling miasma of a sensation that managed to be exhilarating and uncomfortable at the same time.

Isana had to leave the amphitheater. When Lady Aquitaine rose and began to thank and dismiss the gathering, Isana slipped off the stage and out a side exit of the sunken bowl of the amphitheater. The dizzying pressure of the crowd's emotions waned as she walked away from the theater. She paused beside a small public garden, trees and flowers centered around an elegant fountain of black marble. The spring sun was hot, but the mist rising from the fountain, together with the trees' shade, kept the whole of the little garden cool and comfortable. She sat down on a carved-stone bench and pressed her fingertips against her temples for a moment, forcing herself to relax and slow her breathing.

"I know just how you feel," said a rather dry, feminine voice from nearby. Isana looked up to see a tall, willowy woman with rich red hair and a deep green gown seated upon the bench beside hers. "It's Parmos," the woman continued. "He's not happy until the audience is a few seconds short of becoming a riot. And I don't like his speechmaking voice. It's too syrupy."

Isana smiled and inclined her head. "High Lady Placida. Good afternoon."

"Steadholder," Lady Placida, said with exaggerated formality. "An' it please thee, I would fain speak with thee a while."

Isana blinked at her. "Your Grace?"

She held up a hand. "I'm teasing, Steadholder. This certainly is anything but a formal setting. How would it suit you if I called you Isana and you called me Aria?"

"I'd like that."

Lady Placida nodded sharply. "Good. Many Citizens assign far too much importance to the privileges of rank without placing complementary weight upon their duties. I'm glad to see that you aren't one of them, Isana."

Uncertain of how to respond politely, Isana nodded.

"It grieved me to hear about the attack upon you at Sir Nedus's manor on the night we met."

Isana felt a twinge of pain, low on her abdomen, near her hip. The arrow wound had healed cleanly, but there was a very faint scar, hardly more than a discoloration upon her skin. "Nedus was a good man. And Serai was more of a friend than I had at first believed." She shook her head. "I wish things had happened differently."

Lady Placida smiled, though there was sadness at the edges of it. "That's the way of things. It's easy to see what choices one should have made after it is too late to go back. I shall miss Serai. We were not close, but I respected her. And I enjoyed her talent for puncturing pompous windbags."

Isana smiled. "Yes. I wish I had known her longer."

Silence fell for a moment before Lady Placida said, "I met your nephew, back during that Wintersend excitement."

"Did you?" Isana asked.

"Yes. A most promising youth, I thought."

Isana lifted an eyebrow and studied Lady Placida for a moment, and asked, cautiously, "Why would you say that?"

Lady Placida spread her hand in a languid, seed-scattering gesture. "He impressed me with his intelligence. Cleverness. Determination. He is a most well spoken young man. I share a similar respect for several of the young people who are his friends. You can tell a great deal about a person by looking at the people who share his life."

Isana did not miss the implication of Lady Placida's statement, and she nodded in thanks of the compliment. "Tavi's always been very bright," Isana said, smiling despite herself. "Too much so for his own good, I think. He's never let anything hold him back."

"His . . . condition," Lady Placida said with deliberately delicate phrasing. "I have never heard of anything quite like it."

"It's always been a mystery," Isana agreed.

"Then I assume his situation has not changed?"

Isana shook her head. "Though goodness knows, there are plenty of people with many crafting skills who never do anything constructive with them."

"Very true," Lady Placida agreed. "Will you be in Ceres for long?"

Isana shook her head. "A few more days at most. I've been away from my steadholt too long as it is."

Lady Placida nodded. "I'll have a mountain of work waiting for me as well. And I miss my lord husband." She shook her head and smiled. "Which is somewhat girlish and silly of me. But there it is."

"Not silly," Isana said. "There's nothing wrong with missing loved ones. I hadn't seen my brother in nearly a year. It was nice to visit him here."

Lady Placida smiled. "That must have been a relief from what Invidia has you doing."

Isana felt her back stiffen a little. "I'm not sure what you mean."

Lady Placida gave her an arch look. "Isana, please. It's clear she's managed to attach some strings, and equally clear that you don't care for the situation."

Strictly speaking, Isana should have denied it. Part of her agreement with Lady Aquitaine had been to support her publicly. But this was hardly a public forum, was it? So instead, she remained silent.

Lady Placida smiled and nodded. "Isana, I know how difficult this kind of situation can be. Should you need to talk to anyone about it, or if it progresses to something you are not willing to tolerate, I would like to offer you my support. I don't know the particulars, so I cannot know how I might be of help to you—but if nothing else, I could at least listen to what you chose to share and offer advice."

Isana nodded, and said, carefully, "That's . . . very kind."

"Or a most manipulative way to suborn information from you, hmm?"

Isana blinked, then felt herself smile a little. "Well. Not to put too fine a point on it, but, yes."

"I sometimes grow bored with tactful evasions," Lady Placida explained.

Isana nodded, then said, "Assuming that you are sincere: Why would you offer such help to me?"

Lady Placida tilted her head to one side and blinked. Then she took Isana's hand, met her eyes, and spoke. "Because you may need it, Isana. Because you seem to me to be a decent person in unenviable circumstances. Because I can judge from the child you raised that you are a person worthy of my respect." She shrugged a shoulder. "Not terribly aloof and aristocratic of me, I know, but there. The truth."

Isana watched Lady Placida steadily and in growing surprise. Through the touch of her hand, Isana could sense the clear, chiming tone of absolute truth in her voice. Lady Placida met her eyes and nodded before withdrawing her hand.

"I . . . Thank you," Isana said. "Thank you, Aria."

"Sometimes, just knowing that the help is there, if you need it, is help enough in itself," she murmured. Then Aria closed her eyes, inclined her head in a little bow, and departed the little garden, gliding away into the streets of Ceres.

Isana sat for a moment more, enjoying the murmur of the fountain, the cool shadows beneath the trees. She had grown weary of fulfilling her obligations to Lady Aquitaine over the past three years. There had been many distasteful things about it, but the most distressing facet of the matter was the helplessness of it. There were few people in all Alera as powerful and influential as Lady Aquitaine.

The First Lord, of course, would never be a source of support or comfort. His actions had made that quite clear. Other than Gaius, there were fewer than a score of people whose power approached that of the Aquitaines, many of them already allies. There was no more than a handful of folk who had both the power and the inclination to defy Aquitaine Invidia.

The High Lady Placidus was one of them.

Aria's presence, and her offer, had provided a sense of

comfort and confidence that felt like a cold drink in the middle of a hot, endless day. Isana felt surprised at her reaction. Aria had done nothing more than speak idle words during a casual meeting, and nothing about them would bind her to them. Yet Isana had felt the truth in the woman's voice and manner. She sensed Aria's genuine compassion and respect.

Isana had once shared a similar contact with Lady Aquitaine. Isana had indeed felt the truth in her voice, but the sense of the woman had also been utterly different. Both women were the sort to keep their word—but what was primarily integrity in Aria was, in Lady Aquitaine, simple calculation, a kind of enlightened self-interest. Lady Aquitaine was an expert at negotiations, and to negotiate one needed a reputation of keeping one's end of the bargain, for good or ill. She had a steely resolve to make sure that she paid what she owed—and more to the point, to be paid what was owed her. Her honesty had more to do with calculating debt and value than it did with right and wrong.

It was one of the things that made Lady Aquitaine particularly dangerous, and Isana suddenly realized that she feared her patron—and not merely for what Lady Aquitaine might do that would touch upon Isana's loved ones. Isana feared her, personally, sickeningly.

She'd never realized that. Or perhaps it would be more accurate to say that she'd never allowed herself to realize it before now. Aria's simple offer of support had created another possibility for the future. Perhaps it was the relief Isana had needed to allow herself to face the fear she had kept hidden away. Isana had found hope again.

She shivered and put her face in her hands. Silent tears came, and she did not try to stop them. She sat in the peace of the little garden and let some of her bitter fear wash out with her tears, and in time, when the tears had passed, she felt better. Not buoyant, not ecstatic—but better. The future was not set in stone, no longer unremittingly dark.

Isana murmured to Rill to cleanse the tears from her eyes and restore the reddened skin of her face to its natural color, and left the garden to face the world.

Max regarded Tavi, grinning. "They say if you breathe through your mouth instead of your nose, it will help you keep your breakfast down."

Tavi sighed. He looked down at himself. His trousers were soaked to above midthigh and stained with the most vile effluvia imaginable. More of it had splattered onto his tunic, arms, neck, and he felt sure there was some in his hair and on his face. "And slog around in that with my mouth open? Smelling it is bad enough. I don't want to taste it, too."

Max lounged on a camp stool next to the practice grounds, watching Schultz and his spearmates drilling with live steel and their shining new armor. Schultz was running the drill, while Max watched over the recruits. "Schultz!" Max called. "Relax a little. You hold your shoulders that tight, it's going to slow down your thrust."

Tavi grunted. "He still thinks you're going to kill him?"

"It was fun at first," Max said. "Useful, too. But it's been almost a month. I think he's getting it figured out now."

Tavi grunted and grabbed a ladle in a nearby bucket of water.

"Hey," Max protested. "Downwind."

Tavi idly flicked the ladle of water at Max, then drank one of his own, being careful to swallow in small, controlled motions. He had learned to his own dismay that gulping down liquid on a stench-soured stomach could produce unpleasant results.

"What's he got you doing now?" Max asked.

"Inspections." Tavi sighed. "I have to take measurements of each latrine, make sure it's got the right dimensions. Then estimate volume and compare the rate that they're all filling up. Then I have to supervise the digging of new ones and filling in the old ones."

"That stomach bug clear up?" Max asked.

Tavi grimaced. "Finally. Took four days. And the captain's asked Foss to brew me up some kind of tea to help me fight off other sicknesses."

"How's that working out?"

"I'd almost rather get the diseases. You should smell that stuff Foss makes."

Max grinned. "And if *you* think it smells bad . . ."

"Thank you. I needed a little more humiliation," Tavi said.

"In that case, you should know what the *legionares* are calling you."

Tavi sighed. "What?"

"Scipio Latrinus. Is that enough humiliation for you?"

Tavi suppressed a flash of irritation. "Yes. That's perfect, thank you."

Max glanced casually around, and Tavi could feel the air around him tightening as Max ensured privacy. "At least it's given you a good excuse to go to the Pavilion every night. And I've noted that you aren't whining about Kitai anymore."

"I'm not?" Tavi asked. He frowned and thought about it. That hollow, unpleasant sensation in his stomach, the empty pang, had been absent for some time, and his frown deepened. "I'm not," he mused.

"Told you you'd get over her," Max said. "I should have bought you a girl for the evening weeks ago. Glad you did it on your own."

Tavi felt his face heat up. "But I didn't."

Max's eyebrows lifted straight up. "Ah," he said. He squinted at his recruits and said, "You didn't buy a boy, did you."

Tavi snorted. "No," he said. "Max, I'm not there to enjoy myself. I go there for the job."

"The job," Max said.

"The job."

"You go to the Pavilion because it's a duty."

"Yes," Tavi said, half-exasperated.

"Even though there's all those dancers and such?"

"Yes."

"Crows, Calderon. Why?" Max shook his head. "Life is too short to pass some things by."

"Because it's my job," Tavi said.

"Easy to argue that you have to maintain your cover," Max pointed out. "A little wine. A girl or two. Or three, if you can afford it. What's the harm?"

Tavi frowned and thought about it. Max was quite correct when he said that the girls at the Pavilion could be quite enticing, and Tavi had avoided watching them dance. It was a given that any dancer with earthcrafting would use it to hone the appetites of the men watching. Often, several danced at once, and such an environment was geared to fleece the pockets of the legionares who succumbed to their urges. Since the legionares by and large went there with exactly that purpose in mind, it tended to work out.

Tavi had been propositioned by several of the doxies there, but had declined to purchase anyone's charms for a night or to sample the wine and other intoxicants available. He had no intention of clouding his judgment—his wits were what had kept him alive.

"You should enjoy yourself," Max said. "No one would begrudge you that."

"I would," Tavi said. "I need to keep my wits about me."

Max grunted. "True, I suppose. As long as you aren't constantly mooning over Kitai, I guess it's all right if you don't tumble a doxy now and then."

Tavi snorted. "Glad you approve."

Three cohorts of recruits, nearly a thousand legionares, pounded by on the practice road, now moving in a solid block and in full armor. Their footsteps thundered in uniform rhythm, even through the muting effect of Max's screen. After they passed, and the racket faded away, Max asked, "Turn up anything?"

Tavi nodded. "Found two more legionares reporting to that contact from the Trade Consortium."

"Do we know who he's reporting to yet?"

"He thinks he's reporting to a Parcian merchant's factor."

"Heh," Max said. "Who is the factor working for?"

Tavi shrugged a shoulder. "I crossed a few palms. I might get something tonight." He gave Max an oblique look. "I heard about an unlicensed slaver operating nearby. Apparently grabbed a couple of camp followers. But someone beat him unconscious, tied him to a tree, sneaked past his guards, and released his slaves."

Max lowered his windcrafted screen long enough to stand up and shout, "Crows take it, Karder, get that shield up or I'll give you a few lumps on top of your fool head to remind you! If Valiar Marcus's spear humiliates my best, you'll all be running circles for a week!"

Recruits gave Max sidelong, dark looks until Schultz bellowed them back into formation.

"Yeah?" Max said to Tavi, sitting down again. "I heard the same thing. Good for whoever did that. Never liked slavers."

Tavi frowned. "It wasn't you?"

Max frowned back. "It wasn't you?"

"No," Tavi said.

Max pursed his lips, then shrugged. "Wasn't me. There are a lot of Phrygians hereabouts. They hate slavers. Crows, plenty of folk do. I hear that Ceres has a whole big gang of men in masks who roam around at night and hang any slaver they can get their hands on. They have to employ a whole army of personal guards to stay safe. Gotta love a town like Ceres."

Tavi frowned and glanced eastward.

"Oh, right," Max muttered. "Sorry. Your family reunion."

Tavi shrugged a shoulder. "We were only planning on being there for a month or so. They've probably left already."

Max watched the recruits at their drill, but his expression turned a bit bleak. "What's it like?"

"What is what like?"

"Having a family."

Tavi drank another ladle of water. "Sometimes it felt like they were strangling me. I knew it was because they cared, but it still drove me mad. They were worried about me because of my crafting problem. I liked knowing that they were there. I always knew that if I had a problem, they'd help me. Sometimes at night, I would have a bad dream or lie awake feeling sorry for myself. I'd go and look in their rooms and see they were there. Then I could go back to sleep."

Max's expression never changed.

Tavi asked, "What was your family like?"

Max was quiet for a second, then said, "I don't think I'm drunk enough to answer that question."

But Max had been the one to bring up the subject. Maybe he wanted to talk and just needed some encouragement. "Try," Tavi said.

There was a longer silence.

"Notable for their absence," Max said, finally. "My mother died when I was five years old. She was a slave from Rhodes, you know."

"I knew."

Max nodded. "I don't remember much about her. My lord father all but lives at the Shieldwall. He only comes back to Antillus during the summer, then he's got a whole year's worth of work to make up for. He'd sleep maybe three or four hours a night, and he hated being interrupted. I'd maybe have dinner with him once, and a furycrafting lesson or two. Sometimes I'd ride with him to review the new recruits. But neither of us talked much." His voice grew very quiet. "I spent most of my time with Crassus and my stepmother."

Tavi nodded. "Wasn't fun."

"Crassus wasn't so bad. I was older and bigger than him, so there wasn't much he could do. He followed me around a lot, and if he saw something of mine that he liked, he'd take it. She'd give it to him. If I said anything, she'd have me whipped." He bared his teeth in a rictus of a smile. "Course, if I did *anything*, she'd have me whipped."

Tavi thought of his friend's scars and clenched his jaw.

"At least, until I came into my furies." His eyes narrowed. "When I figured out how strong I was, I blew the door to her private chambers to cinders, walked in, and told her that if she tried to have me whipped again, I'd kill her."

"That's when the accidents started," Tavi guessed.

"Yeah."

"What happened?"

"First one was at flying lessons," Max said. "I was hovering a couple of feet outside the city walls, maybe thirty feet up. A jar of rock salt fell out of a window of a tower, hit the wall, and pieces flew through my windcrafting. Disrupted it. I fell."

Tavi winced.

"The next time was in the winter. Someone had spilled water at the top of a long staircase, and it froze. I slipped on it and fell." He took a deep breath. "That's when I ran off and joined the Legions in Placida."

"Max," Tavi began.

Max abruptly rose to his feet, and said, "Feeling kind of nauseous. Must be your stench."

Tavi wanted to say something to his friend. To help him. But he knew Max, and he was too proud to accept Tavi's sympathy. Max had ripped open old wounds in speaking of his family and didn't want anyone to see the pain. Tavi cared about his friend, but Max wasn't ready to let anyone help him. It was enough for one day.

"Must be my stench," Tavi agreed quietly.

"Work to do," Max said. "My fish have a practice bout with Valiar Marcus's veteran spear in the morning."

"Think they'll win?"

"Not unless Marcus and all his men have heart attacks and drop dead during the bout." Max glanced over his shoulder and met Tavi's eyes for a moment. "The fish can't win. But that isn't the point. They just need to put up a decent fight."

Max meant more than the words were saying. Tavi nodded at his friend. "Don't count the fish out yet, Max," he said quietly. "You never know how things are going to turn out."

"Maybe," Max said. "Maybe." He gave Tavi a token salute as he lowered the screen, nodded, and walked back out onto the practice field. "Crows, Scipio!" he said when he was thirty paces away. "I can still smell you all the way from *here*. You may need a bath, sir!"

Tavi debated finding Max's tent and rolling around in his cot for a while. He rejected the idea as unprofessional, however tempting. Tavi glanced at the lowering sun and simply headed from the practice field over to the domestics' camp.

Camp followers were as much a part of a Legion as armor and helmets. Six thousand or so professional soldiers required a considerable amount of support, and the domestics and camp followers provided it.

Domestics were by and large childless, unmarried young women serving a legally required term of service with a Legion. They saw to the daily needs of the *legionares*, typically consisting mostly of food preparation and laundry. Other domestics helped repair damaged uniforms, maintained spare weaponry and armor, handled the delivery of packages and letters, and otherwise assisted in the duties required by the camp.

While the law required nothing more than labor, placing that many young women in close proximity to that many young men inevitably resulted in the growth of relationships and the conception of children—which was the point of the law, Tavi suspected. The world was a dangerous place filled with deadly enemies, and the people of Alera had need of all the hands they could get. Tavi's mother and his aunt Isana had been serving a three-year term of service with the Legions when he had been born, the illegitimate son of a soldier and a Legion domestic.

Other followers of the Legion included domestics who had decided to remain in a more permanent capacity—often as the wife to a *legionare* in every sense but the legal one. While *legionares* were not permitted to marry legally, many career soldiers had a common-law wife in the camp following or a nearby town or village.

The last group was those folk who sensed an opportunity near the Legion. Merchants and peddlers, entertainers, craftsmen, doxies, and dozens of others followed the Legion selling their goods and services to the regularly paid and relatively wealthy *legionares*. Still others simply lurked nearby, intending to follow the Legion and wait until the conclusion of a battle, hoping to loot whatever could be had in the fighting's aftermath.

The camp followers formed in a loose ring around the wooden fortifications of the Legion, their tents ranging from surplus Legion gear to garishly colored contraptions to simple lean-tos and shelters made of a sheet of canvas and rough-cut wooden poles. Lawless folk abounded, and there were parts of the camp where it would be very foolish for a young *legionare* to wander after dark—or a young officer, for that matter.

Tavi knew the safest routes through the camp, where *legionares'* families tended to gather for mutual protection and support. His destination was not far past the invisible boundary of the "decent" side of the camp.

Tavi walked up to Mistress Cymnea's Pavilion, a ring of large, garishly colored tents, pitched together to form a large circle around a central area like a courtyard, leaving only a narrow walkway between tents to allow entry. He could hear the sound of music, mostly pipes and drums, inside, as well as the sound of laughter and raucous voices. He slipped into the open ring of well-trampled grass around a central fire.

A man the size of a small bull rose from his seat as Tavi entered. He had weather-reddened skin and no hair, not even eyebrows or eyelashes, and his neck was as thick as Tavi's waist. He wore only tooled-leather breeches and boots, and his hairless upper body was heavy with muscle and old scars. A weighty chain around his neck marked him as a slave, but there was nothing like mildness or submission in his expression. He sniffed, made a face, and gave Tavi a steady glower.

"Bors," Tavi said politely. "Is Mistress Cymnea available?"

"Money," Bors rumbled.

Tavi already had his money pouch off his belt. He dumped several copper rams and a few silver bulls into his palm and showed them to the huge man.

Bors peered at the coins, then nodded politely at Tavi. "Wait." He lumbered off toward the smallest tent in the circle.

Tavi waited quietly. In the shade beside one of the tents sat Gerta, a vagabond Mistress Cymnea had taken in and something of a fixture outside her tents. The woman wore a dress that looked more like a shapeless sack than clothing, and smelled none too clean. Her hair was a dark, brittle bush that clung together in mats and stuck out at improbable angles, showing only a part of her face. She wore a binding across her eyes and nose, and beneath the grime on her skin, Tavi could see the angry red pockmarks of a recent survivor of the Blight or one of the other dangerous fevers that could strike down the folk of Alera. Tavi had never heard the simple woman speak, but she sat in place playing a small reed flute in a slow, sad, and haunting melody. A beggar's bowl sat on the ground before her, and as he always did, Tavi dropped a small coin into it. Gerta did not react to his presence.

Bors reappeared and grunted at Tavi, tilting his head toward the tent behind him. "You know the one."

"Thank you, Bors." Tavi put his money away and headed for the smallest of the tents—though even so, it was larger than even the captain's tent within the fortifications.

The interior of the tent was carpeted with rich rugs, the walls hung with fabrics and tapestries to make it look almost like a real, solid chamber. A young girl, perhaps twelve years old, sat in a chair near the door reading from a book. Her nose wrinkled, and without looking up from the book she called, "Mama! Subtribune Scipio is here for his bath!"

A moment later, the curtains behind the child parted, and a tall woman entered the front chamber. Mistress Cymnea was a dark-eyed brunette taller than most men, and looked like she could pick an armored *legionare* off the floor and throw him out of her tent, if there was a need. She was dressed in a long gown of wine red silk, worn with an intricately embroidered corset of black and gold. The gown left her broad shoulders and arms bare, and emphasized the curves of her figure.

She swept into a graceful curtsey, and smiled at Tavi. "Rufus, good evening. I would say that this is a pleasant surprise, but I could time my baking on your arrival if I had a mind."

Tavi bowed his head in reply and smiled back at her. "Mistress. Always nice to see you."

Cymnea's smile widened. "Such a charmer. And I can, ah, see that you are still in disfavor with Tribune Gracchus. What can the Pavilion provide for you this evening?"

"Just a bath."

She made a mock-severe expression at him. "So serious for a man so young. Zara, darling, run and prepare the good Scipio's bath."

"Yes, Mama," the girl said. She got up and scampered out, taking her book with her.

Tavi waited a moment, then said, "I hate to be too forward but . . ."

"Not at all," Cymnea said. She wrinkled her nose. "Given your fragrant circumstances, the less time spent in close quarters, the better."

Tavi bowed his head, half-apologetically. "Were you able to learn anything?"

"Of course," she said. "But there is a matter of price to consider."

Tavi winced, but said, "I can go somewhat higher than yesterday's amount, but for more than that . . ."

Cymnea waved a hand. "No. This isn't about money. The information has the potential to be dangerous."

Tavi frowned. "How so?"

"Powerful men might not appreciate potential enemies learning more about them. If I share the information, I might pay a price for having done so."

Tavi nodded. "I understand why you might be concerned. I can only assure you that I will keep the source of the information confidential."

"Yes? And what guarantee do I have of that?"

"You have my word."

Cymnea burst out into a merry peal of laughter. "Really? Oh, young man, that is just so . . . so very charming of you." She tilted her head at Tavi. "But you mean it, don't you."

"I do, Mistress," Tavi said, meeting her eyes.

She stared at him for a moment. Then she shook her head, and said, "No, Scipio. I haven't done as well as I have by taking foolish chances. I'm willing to trade for the information, but only in kind. Something that might protect me in return."

"Such as?" Tavi asked.

"Well. Such as who *you* are working for. That way, if you talked about me, I'd be in a position to talk about you."

"Sounds fair," Tavi said. "But I can't."

"Ah," she said quietly. "Well. There we are, then. I'll return your silver."

Tavi held out his hand. "Don't. Consider it a retainer. If you come across anything juicy that offers you less risk, perhaps you'd pass it along."

Cymnea tilted her head and nodded once. "Why would you trust me to do that?"

Tavi shrugged a shoulder. "Call it instinct. You run an honest business, in its way." He smiled. "Besides. It isn't my money."

Mistress Cymnea laughed again. "Well. I haven't done as well as I have by turning away silver, either. Zara should have your bath ready by now. I believe you know the way?"

"Yes, thank you."

She sighed. "Honestly. It isn't as though I mind your business, but Gracchus seems to be taking your chastisement a bit far."

"I'll manage," he said. "As long as I can get a bath at the end of the day."

"Then I'll not keep you from it," she said, and smiled.

Tavi bowed his head to her and left the tent. He crossed the little green courtyard, where the blind woman played her reed pipe. The tent where wine and girls were served erupted into a louder round of roars and shouts than were normal this early in the evening, drowning out the reed pipe for a time. Bors turned his head toward the sound, the motion reminding Tavi of a dog taking note of activity in its territory.

Tavi walked to another tent, this one bright blue and green. Inside, several alcoves had been partitioned with heavy drapes, each one containing a large, round wooden tub big enough to fit two or three people comfortably. Loud splashing and a woman's giggles came from one of the curtained chambers. In another, a man slurred out a quiet song in a drunken voice. Zara appeared from behind another curtain and nodded to Tavi. Then she emerged, holding a gunnysack, and wrinkled her nose at the smell as he entered.

Tavi slipped into the alcove and drew the curtain shut. He removed his filthy clothing and passed it out through the curtain to the waiting girl. She took it from him with brisk motions, tucked it into the gunnysack, and carried it out at arm's length, to have it laundered, swiftly dried, and brought back to him.

A large bucket of lukewarm water sat beside the tub, a washcloth upon it. Tavi used it to wipe the worst of the grime from his body before testing the steaming water. He added a bit more hot water from a large container on a swinging arm next to the tub, then sank into it with a sigh. Warmth enfolded him, and he luxuriated in it for a time. The work Gracchus had assigned him was as strenuous and tiring as it was distasteful, and he looked forward to soaking tired muscles in hot water at the end of each day.

He thought about his family for a moment and felt bad to have missed their reunion in Ceres. He had to admit, though, that it would have been awkward speaking to his aunt now that she had thrown her support to Lord and Lady Aquitaine. So long as the conversation didn't come anywhere near politics, things might have been all right—but Tavi's training as a Cursor meant that he was involved with politics nearly every waking moment, in one fashion or another.

He'd missed his uncle, too. Bernard had always shown Tavi the consideration and respect that he'd never realized were all too uncommon. Tavi felt proud that his uncle had proven himself a hero of the Realm, and on more than one occasion, and he had been looking forward to Bernard's reaction upon seeing Tavi after his years of education and training. Bernard had worked hard to make sure Tavi had the raw materials to build an honorable life for himself. Tavi wanted Bernard to see with his own eyes what his nephew had made with them.

And Kitai . . .

Tavi frowned. And Kitai. She would have been there. If Tavi had not felt the little lonely pangs that had plagued him since leaving her in Alera Imperia, it was not because he no longer desired her company. She was often in his thoughts, especially her laughter and her pointed wit, and if he closed his eyes he could picture her face—exotic and arrogantly lovely with her canted Marat eyes, white silken hair, her long, strong limbs, tight with shapely muscle, skin softer than . . .

In the other alcove, the woman's giggles segued into quite different high-pitched sounds, and Tavi's body reacted to the thoughts of Kitai and the sounds of the nearby doxy with an almost-violent enthusiasm. He ground his teeth, suddenly sorely tempted to follow Max's advice. But no. He needed all of his focus and attention to be on his duty, to be alert for even the smallest scrap of intelligence he could report back to the First Lord. The last thing he wanted to do with his time was to undermine his own effectiveness with foolish—if undeniably alluring—distractions.

Besides. He didn't want one of Cymnea's girls there with him. He wanted it to be Kitai.

His body made its agreement with the sentiment uncomfortably clear.

Tavi groaned and sank under the water for as long as he could hold his breath. When he surfaced, he seized the nearby bowl of soap and a clean washcloth and scrubbed his skin until he thought it might slough off, struggling to turn his thoughts to something less involving. Clearly, he missed Kitai. Clearly, he wanted to be near her as much as he ever had. But if so, then why had the odd, uncomfortable sensations of loneliness that had spurred him to speak about her ceased?

He had always felt the pangs when he thought about . . . her presence, he supposed. Her voice, her touch, her features all felt like something perfectly natural to his world, as much a part of it as sunshine and air. When he had been touching her, even only so much as holding hands, there had been a kind of peaceful resonance in the touch, something warm, reassuring, and deeply satisfying. It was the memories of their loss that had brought on the unpleasant sensation of loneliness. Even now, the memories should, by all rights, have brought on more of the same.

But they didn't. Why?

He had just finished rinsing himself of the soap when it hit him, all at once.

Tavi snarled a muted curse, heaved himself out of the tub. He seized a towel, quickly swiped it over his body, and snatched up a plain robe folded on a nearby chair, shoving his still-damp arms into it. He stalked out of the bathing tent into the central yard.

The wine tent was in an uproar of one kind or another, and Tavi emerged in time to see Bors lumber up to its entrance and go inside. He spotted the blind woman beside one of the tents, still playing her reed pipe, and stalked toward her.

"What are you *doing*?" he hissed at the woman.

The blind woman set her pipe down and her mouth quirked into a smile. "Counting the days until you realized who I was," she replied. "Though I was about to start counting the weeks."

"Are you insane?" Tavi demanded in a harsh whisper. "If someone realizes that you are Marat—"

"—they will be considerably more observant than you, Aleran." Kitai sniffed.

"You were supposed to be in Ceres at the family reunion."

"As were you," she said.

Tavi grimaced. Now that he knew who "Gerta" truly was, the disguised elements of Kitai's appearance seemed painfully obvious. She had dyed her fine, silvery white hair to crude black and let it grow matted and tangled deliberately. The pockmarks on her face were doubtless some kind of cosmetics, and the blind woman's bandage covered her exotic, canted eyes.

"I can't believe the First Lord just let you ride away."

She smiled, and it showed very white teeth. "No one has ever told me where I may or may not go. Not my father. Not him. Not you."

"All the same. We need to get you out of here."

"No," Kitai said. "You need to learn to whom the Parcian merchant's factor reports his information."

Tavi blinked at her. "How did you . . ."

"If you recall," she said, smiling, "I have very good ears, Aleran. And as I sit here, I learn much. Few guard their words near a madwoman."

"You've just been sitting *here*?"

"At night, I can move more freely and learn more."

"Why?" Tavi asked.

She arched her brows. "I do what I have done for years now, Aleran. I watch you and your kind. I learn of them."

Tavi let out a short, exasperated breath, but touched her shoulder. "It is good to see you."

She reached up and squeezed his hand with hers, her fingers fever-warm, and she made a small, pleased sound. "I did not enjoy your absence, *chala.*"

There was a shriek from the far side of the Pavilion, then a mussed, besotted *legionare* flew out of the wine tent. Bors came out after him a second later and applied sweeping kicks from his great booted feet to wherever he could reach upon the drunk, until the man had been driven from the Pavilion.

Kitai withdrew her hand from Tavi's, and the spot felt peculiarly cool in the absence of her heated skin. "Now, Rufus Scipio. It will be strange for you to be seen conversing with a simpleton. Go away. You'll scare off the game."

"We must speak again," Tavi said. "Soon."

Kitai's lips curled up into a sensual little smirk. "There are many things we must do, soon, Aleran. Why ruin them with talk?"

Tavi flushed, though the sunset was particularly red tonight, which might have hidden it. Kitai lifted her reed flute to her lips again, hunching down once more into her role. Bors returned from evicting the rowdy drunk and settled down into his spot by the fire. Tavi shook his head and returned to the bath tent to await his laundered clothing.

He closed his eyes and sat listening to Kitai's flute as he did, and found himself smiling.

◦◦◦◦ CHAPTER 12

Vorello's Pool was one of the most beautiful places Isana had ever visited. Centered around a crystalline pool in the base of a rocky grotto, the whole of the dining house had seemingly been built from the trees and vines planted within the grotto and growing as living partitions, bridges, and stairways. Ta-

bles were arranged upon rocky shelves around the pool at
varying heights. Several tables were set upon flat stones rising
from the pool itself, and employees of the hotel would ferry
customers out to the tables with graceful boats propelled by
furies within the pool's waters.

Furylamps cast luminous color over each table, and the
colors constantly, slowly shifted and changed from hue to
hue. From a distance, it looked like a cloud of fireflies hovering over the surface of the water. More lights within the
pool itself shone up, also changing colors over time, casting
shadows up the walls of the grotto and half-shadowing each
table.

Singers, mostly young women, stood upon a number of
raised rocks or sat upon the low-hanging branches of one of
the trees. They sang songs of beauty and sadness in quiet,
hauntingly lovely voices. Instrumental music supported the
voices, drifting through the restaurant with no evident source.

One of the staff showed Isana to a table, set upon a rocky
outcropping over the pool, framed by the embrace of the long,
strong roots of a tree above. She had hardly settled into her
seat before Bernard and Amara arrived, with Giraldi trailing
in their wake.

Isana rose to meet her little brother's bearish, affectionate
embrace, and knew at once that something had happened. Her
entire sense of him was filled with a brimming excitement and
mirth that she hadn't felt in him since . . . Isana drew in a
sharp breath. Since he'd been married. She stared at his face
for a moment, his own happiness drawing a smile onto her
face, then glanced aside at Amara.

The Countess looked as she always did—distant, golden,
and difficult to read. She had the warm, honey brown skin
characteristic of the folk of sunny Parcia in the south, and her
straight, fine hair was almost the precise same shade, giving
her, in stillness, the appearance of a statue, some work dedi-
cated to a huntress figure, lean and intense and dangerous.
Isana had come to know that it was only part of the Countess's
personality. Her beauty could best be seen in motion, as she
walked or flew.

Isana glanced aside at Amara, and the Countess avoided her eyes. Amara's cheeks flushed with color, and her usual reserved expression changed, becoming something young and girlish and delighted. She fidgeted in place, and she and Bernard's hands found one another without either of them seeming to be aware of it before she became still again.

"Well," Isana said to her brother. "Shall I order a bottle of something special?"

"Why would you ask that?" Bernard said, his tone smug.

"Because she's not stupid," growled Giraldi. The old centurion, grizzled and stalwart despite his limp, stepped around Bernard to bow politely to Isana. She laughed and gave him a fond embrace. Giraldi smiled, evidently pleased, and said, "But don't buy any special drink on my account. Just something that will make me think the food tastes good if I drink enough of it."

"Then you'll need almost nothing," Amara said. "The food here is wonderful—though the gourmands from my own home city disdain it. They hate it when any cook makes them eat too much by daring to exceed their expectations, I think."

Giraldi grunted and looked around. "I don't know. Awful lot of upper crust in this place." He nodded at a table above their own. "High Lady Parcia, there, having dinner with High Lady Attica's daughter. Couple of Senators, over there. And that's Lord Mandus, from Rhodes. He's the Fleet Tribune in their navy. They aren't the sort of folk that eat decent food."

Amara laughed. "If the meal isn't to your liking, centurion, I'll pay someone to fetch you a steak and a pitcher of ale."

Giraldi grinned and subsided. "Well, then."

Isana paused to regard Amara. There was a warmth in her voice and manner she had never sensed there before. Isana already respected Amara, but to see her and Bernard together and so clearly happy, made it very difficult for her not to share some portion of her brother's affection for the young woman. She was wearing a dress, too, which was unusual in Isana's experience. Isana did not miss the fact that the Cursor wore a gown in the rich green and brown Bernard had chosen for his colors, and not the somber, muted tones of red and blue generally favored for formal wear by the Cursors and other servants of the Crown.

Isana had always maintained a certain distance from the Cursor, the young woman who owed her personal loyalty to Gaius Sextus. Isana's harsh feelings toward the First Lord had spilled over onto Amara. She knew, on some level, that it was unfair of her to hold the sins of the liege against the Cursor who served him, and yet she had never been able to bring herself to give Amara a chance to prove herself in her own right.

Perhaps it was time for that to change. Bernard clearly adored the young Countess, and she had obviously brought Isana's little brother a great deal of happiness. If what Isana suspected was true, Amara might be around for a very long while. That was reason enough to force Isana to face the fact that she owed it to her brother to attempt at least to make peace with the Cursor.

Isana bowed her head to the Countess, and said, "You look lovely tonight, Amara."

The Cursor's cheeks flushed again, and she met Isana's eyes for a moment before smiling. "Thank you."

Isana smiled and turned to sit down as Giraldi drew out her seat for her. "Why thank you, centurion."

"Ma'am," the old soldier said. He waited for Amara to be seated, then lowered himself into his own chair, leaning on his cane and briefly grimacing in discomfort.

"The leg never healed any better?" Isana asked.

"Not that I noticed."

Isana frowned. "Would you like me to take a look at it?"

"Count brought in some big healer from Riva. It's been poked enough. Problem isn't the wound. The leg is getting old," Giraldi said, a small smile on his lips. "It had a good run, Isana. And I can still march. I'll finish this hitch. So don't you worry about it."

Isana felt the little spike of disappointment and regret in Giraldi's voice, but it was a small thing beside his resolve and his pride—or perhaps more accurately, his self-satisfaction, a form of inner peace. Giraldi had been badly wounded in battle against the Vord at the Battle of Aricholt, but he had never faltered in his duty, never failed to fight in defense of the Realm. He had spent a lifetime in the Legions and in service to the Realm, and made a difference by doing so. That knowledge formed a bedrock for the old soldier, Isana reasoned.

"How have your presentations gone?" she asked, looking at Giraldi, then Bernard.

Bernard grunted. "Well enough."

"Well enough with soldiers," Giraldi corrected. "The Senators are all certain that we poor countryfolk have been bamboozled by the Marat, and that the Vord aren't really anything to worry about."

Isana frowned. "That hardly sounds encouraging."

Bernard shook his head. "The Senators won't be doing the fighting. The Legions do that."

To Isana, he sounded like a man trying to convince himself of something. "But doesn't the Senate administer the Crown's military budget?"

"Well," Bernard said, frowning. "Yes."

"We've done all we can," Amara said, and put her hand over Bernard's. "There's no reason to blame yourself for the Senate's reaction."

"Right," Giraldi said. "His mind was made up even before you threatened to rip his tongue out for him."

Isana blinked at Giraldi, then at Bernard. Her brother cleared his throat and blushed.

"Oh, dear," Isana said.

A server arrived just then with a light wine, fruit, and bread, and told them that the evening meal would be served shortly.

"What about you, Steadholder?" Amara asked, once the server had withdrawn. "What were the results of the League's summit with the abolitionists?"

"Complete success," Isana replied. "Senator Parmos addressed the entire assembly this afternoon. He's going to sponsor Lady Aquitaine's proposal."

Amara's eyebrows lifted. "Is he?"

Isana frowned. "Is that such a surprise?"

"Yes, actually," Amara said, frowning. "From my understanding of the situation in the Senate, any emancipation legislation would have been blocked by the southern Senators. Between Rhodes and Kalare, they have votes enough to kill any such motion."

Isana arched an eyebrow. Amara's information was doubtless obtained from the Crown's intelligence network. If Amara had been unaware of the shift in the balance of power, then it was entirely possible that the First Lord was, too. "The Rhodesian Senators have cast their support to the abolitionists."

Amara stiffened in her seat. "*All* of them?"

"Yes," Isana said. "I thought you'd know already."

Amara shook her head, her lips pressed together. Isana could feel the Cursor's anxiety rising. "When did this happen?"

"I'm not sure," Isana said. "I overheard two members of the League discussing it during Lady Aquitaine's tour. Perhaps three weeks ago?"

Amara suddenly rose, her voice tight. "Bernard, I need to contact the First Lord. Immediately."

Bernard frowned at her in concern. "Why? Amara, what's wrong?"

"It's too much," Amara said, her eyes focused elsewhere, her voice running in quick bursts that mirrored her furious thought. "Kalare's being forced into a corner. He won't take covert measures. He can't. Between emancipation laws and the letter . . . we're not ready. Oh, crows, not ready."

Isana felt the Cursor's anxiety begin to change into rising fear. "What do you mean?"

Amara shook her head rapidly. "I'm sorry, I don't dare say more. Not here." She looked around quickly. "Bernard, I need to get to the river, immediately. Isana, I'm sorry to disrupt the dinner—"

"No," Isana said quietly. "It's all right."

"Bernard," Amara said.

Isana looked across the table at her brother, who was frowning deeply, eyes focused on the sky above the open grotto.

"Why," he asked quietly, "are the stars turning red?"

Isana frowned and stared up at the sky. She could not see the full glory of the stars in the furylit beauty of the city of Ceres, but the brightest stars were still visible. The entire western half of the sky was filled with crimson pinpoints of light. As she watched, the white stars overhead burned sullen, and the scarlet light spread like some kind of plague to the east, marching slowly and steadily forward. "Is it some kind of furycrafting?" she murmured.

In the grotto around them, the singers fell quiet one by one, and the music trailed off to silence. Everyone started staring up and pointing. A confused tide of emotion pushed against Isana's senses.

Amara looked around them. "I don't think so. I've never seen anything like that. Bernard?"

Isana's brother shook his head. "Never saw anything like it." He glanced at Giraldi, who shook his head as well.

The confusion around Isana became something thicker, almost tangible, and tinged with more than a little fear. Over the next several seconds, the tide of emotion continued to grow, getting rapidly more distracting. Seconds after that, the sensations pressed so loudly against Isana's thoughts that she began to lose track of which were her own emotions and which came from without. It was excruciating, in its own way, and she suddenly found herself in a battle to hold on to her ability to reason. She put her hands to the sides of her head.

"Isana?" said Bernard's voice. It sounded like it was coming from very far away. "Are you all right?"

"T-too many people," Isana gasped. "Afraid. They're afraid. Confused. Afraid. I can't push it out."

"We need to get her out of here," Bernard said. He stepped around the table and picked Isana up. She wanted to protest, but the pressure against her thoughts was too much to struggle against. "Giraldi," he said. "Get the coach."

"Right," Giraldi said.

"Amara, watch for those two that were shadowing us. Be ready to knock someone down if you have to."

Isana heard Amara's voice grow suddenly tense. "You think this is an attack of some kind."

"I think we're unarmed and vulnerable," Bernard said. "Move."

Isana felt her brother walking and opened her eyes in time to see the grotto's pool passing beneath them as he walked over an archway. Desperate, she reached out to Rill, calling up the fury to let the emotions washing over her pass through her, into the water. If she could not stand against the tide of emotion, perhaps she could divert it.

The pressure eased, though it was strenuous to maintain the redirection. It was enough to let her remember her name and to have the presence of mind to look up and see what was happening.

Sudden excitement, exaltation and battle lust, washed over her, near enough to make her feel as though she stood too close to a forge. She looked up and saw confusion, patrons and staff rising and moving toward the exits, and among them she saw a number of men in the clean white tunics of restaurant staff moving with professional, calculated haste, expressions sharp with eagerness and purpose.

Even as she watched, one of the men closed in behind Mandus, the Rhodesian Fleet Tribune, seized his hair, bent his head back, and cut his throat with swift efficiency.

More excitement made Isana look up. Three more men stood on the ledge above them, crouched and ready to leap. Each wore a white tunic, each bore a short, curved, cruel-looking sword, and steel collars shone upon their throats.

Her own sudden terror destabilized her crafting and plunged her into an ocean of confusion and fear.

"Bernard!" she cried.

The three assassins leapt down upon them.

CHAPTER 13

Without Isana's warning, Amara would surely have died.

Her eyes were scanning what lay before them, looking for the two men who had shadowed her and Bernard after the presentation at the amphitheater. A shrill scream of horror drew Amara's eyes to the far side of the grotto, where she saw Fleet Tribune Mandus, his throat opened, the cut hopelessly deep and precise, fall to his knees and slump to his side to die on the floor.

When Isana cried out her warning, Amara had her back to the assassins. She spun and managed to dart aside from the nearest man's first, sweeping cut. Two of the men were falling upon Bernard and Isana, and burdened as he was with his sister, Bernard would never be able to defend himself.

Amara called to Cirrus, and her fury came rushing down into the grotto at her call. She hurled a raw gale at the two men, catching them in midair. She flung one of them over the side of the walkway and he fell toward the pool. The other managed to get his hand on an outthrusting branch of one of the trees and flipped himself neatly down to the ground beside Bernard. The assassin turned to Amara's husband, sword in hand, but Amara had delayed him for the few critical seconds that would have made the attack a success.

"Giraldi!" Bernard bellowed. He turned and all but threw Isana into the grizzled soldier's arms. Then the Count of Calderon seized one of the heavy hardwood chairs, and with a surge of fury-born strength, swung the sixty-pound chair into the assassin, driving the man hard into a rocky wall of the grotto.

Amara turned to throw her hand out and force her own attacker back with a blast of wind, but the man hurled a small cloud of salt from a pouch at his belt, and Amara felt Cirrus buck in agony upon contact with the substance, the fury's concentrated power dispersed, temporarily, by the salt.

The average hired cutter did not venture forth with a pouch of salt at hand and ready to throw—which meant that the man had come for Amara, specifically.

The assassin advanced with the speed of a professional fighter and sent two quick cuts at her. Amara dodged the first cleanly, but the second blow slid over her hip and left a long, shallow cut that burned like fire.

"Down!" Bernard thundered. Amara threw herself to the ground just as Bernard flung the heavy hardwood chair. It struck the assassin with a dull, crunching sound of bones breaking upon impact and drove the man hard against the trunk of a tree.

The assassin bounced off the tree trunk, seized the chair, and flung it out over the grotto and into the pool. Though his rib cage was horribly deformed by the power of the blow Bernard had dealt him, the man's expression never changed— an odd little smile beneath wide, staring eyes.

Amara stared at the assassin in shock as he lifted his sword and came at her again, hardly slowed by the blow that should have killed him. She started to back away, but felt empty air beneath her heels and instead spun and leapt, arms reaching out to seize an overhanging tree branch. The assassin's sword whipped at the air behind her, missing, and with a snarl of fury the man lost his footing and plunged into the pool below them.

Behind Bernard, the first assassin rose from the blow her husband had dealt him, and though his left arm dangled uselessly, broken in many places, he came forward with his sword, wearing the same staring, mad smile as the other man.

Bernard put the dining table between himself and the assassin, then drew back a booted foot and kicked it at him. It struck the assassin and knocked him off-balance, and in the second it took him to recover it, Bernard raised a hand and clenched it into a fist, snarling, "Brutus!"

Bernard's earth fury, Brutus, came to his call. The stone arch heaved and rippled, and suddenly the rock stretched itself into the shape of an enormous, stone hound. Green gemstones glittered where a dog's eyes would be, and Brutus's mouth opened to show rows of obsidian black fangs. The fury rushed forward toward the assassin, ignored several blows from the assassin's sword, and clamped its jaws down on the man's calf, locking him in place.

Without an instant's hesitation, the assassin swept his blade down and severed his *own* leg just below the knee to free it from Brutus's grasp. Then he rushed Bernard again, awkward and ungainly, blood rushing from the wound. He let out an eerie cry of ecstasy as he did. Bernard stared at him in shock for half a second, then the man was on him. Brutus tossed its great head and threw the severed leg aside, but it would take the fury endless seconds to turn around. Amara gritted her teeth but was effectively trapped, hanging there from the branch. She could climb up, then to the ground again, but by then it would be over—and Cirrus would not recover in time to let her fly to Bernard's aid.

Everything slowed down. Somewhere on one of the levels far above their own, there was a flash of light and a thunderous explosion. Steel rang on steel somewhere else. More screams echoed around the grotto.

Bernard was not slow, especially for a man his size, but he did not have the speed he would need to have a fair chance of combating the assassin unarmed. He lunged to one side as the man swung, putting his body between Isana's and the man's steel blade. The blade struck, and Amara's husband cried out in pain and fell.

The assassin seized Bernard by the hair—but instead of cutting his throat, he simply threw the wounded man aside and raised his sword to strike down at Isana.

Desperate, Amara called to Cirrus—not to push her toward the assassin, but away. She clung to the branch as the weakened wind fury pushed her back. She pushed with all of her strength, then abruptly released the crafting. The branch, bent by the force of the wind, suddenly snapped back. Amara

swung on the branch as it did and used its backsweep to pro-
pel her, feetfirst back toward the assassin.

She drove her heels into the assassin's chest, all her body
rigid to support the vicious blow. She struck cleanly and hard,
and the force of the blow snapped the man's head forward and
back. She heard bones break, and the assassin fell into a limp
mass of bloodied flesh with Amara atop him.

She rolled away from him and seized his sword, crouched
on all fours, blood staining her green gown. She stared in shock
at the man. The assassin still clung to life, madness burning in
his eyes as he let out a final, short, violent cry. "Brothers!"

Amara looked up. Several of the attackers in the grotto had
finished their bloody work, and at the dying man's call, the
faces of another dozen men with metal collars and lunatic
eyes turned toward her. Their path to the exit, a walkway
through the trees and a second stone arch, was already filled
with more of the men. They were cut off.

"Bernard," she said. "Can you hear me?"

Bernard pushed himself to his feet, his face pale and tight
with pain. He glanced back and forth and saw the men approaching and reached for another heavy chair. He let out a
choke of pain as he picked it up, and Amara could see a stab
wound in the slablike muscles of his back.

"Can you fly?" he asked, his voice quiet. He closed his
eyes for a moment, and the chair in his hands abruptly twisted
and writhed, suddenly as lithe as a willow branch. The various
pieces of the chair elongated and wound and braided themselves together into a thick fighting cudgel as if of their own
volition, a massively heavy club that would prove deadly
when driven by an earthcrafter's physical strength. "Can you
fly?" he asked again.

"I'm not leaving you."

He shot a quick glance at her. "Can you carry my sister out?"

Amara grimaced and shook her head. "I don't think so.
Cirrus was hurt. I don't think I could lift myself out yet, much
less her."

"I've got her, Bernard," Giraldi said, grimacing. "But you
should take her. I'll rear-guard you while both of you get out."

Bernard shook his head. "We stay together. Either of you ever seen men fight like these?"

"No," Amara said.

"No, sir."

"There are a lot of them," Bernard commented. Indeed, the nearest band of half a dozen had made their way down the pathway above them and were nearly close enough to rush them. At least a dozen more blocked their escape and slowly closed so that they would attack in time with the first group. Fires burned on some of the upper levels. A pall of smoke tainted the air and concealed the bloody stars.

"Yes," Amara agreed quietly. She hated that her voice shook with her fear, but she could not stop it. "Whoever they are."

Bernard put his back to Amara's, facing the men coming from farther down the slope. "I'll set Brutus on them," he said quietly. "Try to knock them down. We'll try to run through them."

The plan was hopeless. Brutus, though terribly powerful, was anything but swift, and would be of only limited use in close-quarters combat. Not only that, but employing the fury on its own would rob Bernard of the lion's share of the strength the fury could provide him. These men, whoever they were, were capable and madly determined. They would never reach the door.

But what else could they do? Their only other option was to fight back-to-back until they were slain. Bernard's plan offered at least a wisp of hope, strictly speaking, but Amara knew that it was only a matter of choosing between final deeds before the end.

"Ready?" he asked quietly.

Amara ground her teeth. "I love you."

He let out the low, satisfied growl he often uttered after kissing her, and she could hear the fighting grin that stretched his lips. "And I you."

She heard him take a deep breath, just as the men above them prepared to leap down, and he let out a roar. "Brutus!"

Once again, the great stone hound bounded up out of the earth. It lurched toward the group coming up the rocky shelf, and bayed, its mountainous voice the basso rumble of stones grating together under enormous strain. The first assassin raised his weapon, but the stone hound simply hurtled into him, ducking its head and slamming its shoulder into the man's chest. Blood burst from the assassin's mouth in a sudden froth. Brutus swung its great head and threw the assassin back into a pair of his companions.

One of them screamed and fell from the ledge to land upon his back on a stone standing a few inches out of the surface of the water. He let out a short gasp and slipped limply beneath the pool's surface. The other stumbled, and Brutus plunged over the man, paws landing like sledgehammers, crushing the assassin into a shapeless mass.

Bernard charged in behind Brutus, and Amara darted along in his wake. Behind her, the men on the upper level had paused for a second at Bernard's yell, then leapt forward in what seemed a superhuman grace and disdain for pain or death.

Bernard's cudgel struck down another attacker on the first swing, but she heard the snarl of pain the movement drew from him. Brutus continued its charge, but by then, the assassins farther back in the line had spotted the stone hound. One of the men bounded over Brutus entirely, invisible to the earth fury while airborne, and engaged Bernard. Behind him, other assassins rapidly backed up to the wooden bridge, getting their feet up off the stone of the grotto.

Amara heard a breath behind her and barely had time to turn and parry a heavy slash from the nearest of the attackers behind them. The force of the blow knocked her back into Bernard, whose forward momentum had died as the assassin in front of him menaced him with his blade. Amara parried another blow, her back to her husband's, calling upon Cirrus to provide whatever quickness he could to her limbs. Her riposte was a silver-and-scarlet blur of bloodied steel that struck the man on the neck, just above the steel collar.

Her cut had been too shallow to open the artery in the man's neck, but he let out a shout that sounded more like a

sound of pleasure than agony and pressed his attack more furiously than ever.

Bernard let out a shout of effort, followed by a heavy thud-
ding sound behind her. Steel whistled in the air, and Bernard
cried out again.

"No!" Amara screamed, terror making her voice shrill.

And then, behind the attackers coming down the walkway
at her, Amara saw a man in the somewhat grimy white tunic of
a cook or scullion, in contrast to the clean white smocks that
the assassins wore. He was of medium height and build, and
his hair was long, shaggy, and greying. He landed on the walkway in catlike silence, a worn old *gladius* in his right hand,
and with a single simple, ruthlessly efficient motion drove the
blade through the base of the nearest assassin's skull.

The man dropped as if he'd simply fallen asleep. His killer
glided forward to the next assassin on the walkway, dark eyes
gleaming behind the curtain of ragged hair. The next man in line
fell to the same stroke, but dropped his blade to the stone with a
clatter of metal, and the next assassin in the line whirled around.

"Fade?" Amara shouted, parrying again.

The slave never slowed. A quick bob to one side stirred
some of the hair from around his face, revealing the hideous
scarring on one entire cheek, the Legions' brand burned into
cowards who had fled the field of battle. Fade's blade moved
in graceful, deceptively lazy-looking circles, shattering the
assassin's weapon with contemptuous ease, then sheared off
the top quarter of the man's skull on the next stroke. Fade
kicked the dying man into the one in front of him and simply
strode down the rock walkway. His sword arm moved in
small, simple, unspectacular-looking movements, shattering
blades and bodies with equal, dispassionate ease.

Assassins fell, every single injury a blow to the neck or
head, and when Fade's sword struck them they did not move.
Ever again.

The last one, Amara's opponent, shot a swift glance over his
shoulder. Amara howled her defiance and swung her captured,
curved blade with both hands. She struck true, and buried the

weapon to the width of its blade in the assassin's skull. The man stiffened and twitched, sword falling from his fingers.

Fade gripped the sword's hilt and ripped it from the assassin's skull, simultaneously sending him falling from the ledge, then murmured, "Excuse me, Countess."

Amara gaped for a second, stunned, then slipped aside to let Fade through. The slave nudged Bernard to one side, into the grotto wall, caught a blow intended for the Steadholder on his blade. Fade moved forward to the wooden walkway like a dancer, swords spinning, blocking, killing. The assassins pressed forward to attack.

They died. They never came close to touching him.

In the space of four or five seconds, Fade slew nine or ten men, left a legless casualty on the stone behind him for Brutus to crush, and kicked another off the walkway and into the pool below. On the far side of the walkway, he dropped into a crouch, swords ready, eyes scanning all around him.

"F-fade?" Bernard rumbled.

"Bring Isana," the slave snapped to them. "Countess, take the lead." He dropped the curved sword and glided back over the bridge to get a shoulder beneath Bernard's arm and assist the dazed Count to his feet.

"Fade?" Bernard said again, his voice weak and confused. "You have a sword?"

The man did not answer Bernard. "We have to get them out of here, now," he told Amara. "Move and stay together."

Amara nodded and managed to gather up the Steadholder and stagger along behind the swordsman.

"What are you doing here?" Bernard asked. "I thought you were in the capital, Fade."

"Be quiet, Count," Fade said. "You're losing blood. Save your strength."

Bernard shook his head, then suddenly jerked, tensing. "I-Isana!"

"I've got her," Giraldi grunted.

Bernard blinked once, then nodded and bowed his head, hobbling along only with Fade's help.

Corpses and blood littered the restaurant. The collared assassins had spared none they could reach. Elderly men and women, even children lay where they had fallen, wounded, dead, or dying. Fade led them to the street outside the restaurant, where the nightmarish results of the attack seemed intensified. Many had managed to flee the restaurant, though their wounds had been mortal. Wounds that sometimes looked minor could prove fatal within a moment or two, and many who thought that they had escaped the slaughter had only survived long enough to die on the street.

People screamed and shouted, rushing back and forth. The signaling horns and drums of Ceres' civic legion were already converging on the spot. Other folk lay on the ground, curled up into a tight ball, sobbing in incapacitating hysteria, just as Isana was. Amara realized, with a sickening little burst of illumination, that whatever had incapacitated Isana had done it to those folk as well.

They were all watercrafters, the only folk who might possibly save the lives of many of the wounded. They had all been struck down, and though others struggled to close wounds and stop bleeding, they had little more than cloth and water to work with.

Blood had spread into a scarlet pool, half an inch deep and thirty or forty feet across.

And then the great chimes in Ceres's citadel began to ring in deep, panicked strokes, sounding the alert to the city's legions. Horns began to blow the Legion call to arms.

The city was under attack.

"Bloody crows," Amara whispered, stunned.

"Move!" Fade snarled. "We can't let her—"

Then the slave suddenly glanced up. He dropped Bernard and threw himself at Giraldi and Isana, hand outstretched.

An arrow, a black shaft with green-and-grey feathering flickered through the air and slammed completely through Fade's left hand. A broad, barbed arrowhead erupted from his flesh.

Without blinking, he pointed with his sword to a nearby rooftop, where a shadowed figure quickly vanished from view. "Countess! Stop him!"

Amara seized Fade's blade from his hand, called to Cirrus, and flung herself into the sky. She streaked toward the rooftop and saw the dark figure, bow still in hand, crouching to climb down.

Rage and fear made it impossible for Amara to think. It was on pure reflex that she cast Cirrus out in front of her, the sudden rush of wind throwing the cloaked figure from the rooftop to fall twenty feet to the ground. The archer landed with a sickening, crunching sound and let out a high-pitched scream of pain.

Amara darted down into the alley, alighting on the stone almost atop the fallen woman, and struck downward as the woman raised the bow. The sword shattered the wood, and the woman fell back with another cry.

Gripping the sword tight, Amara drove it down at the archer's throat and set the point against her skin so that it was drawing a bead of blood. She could see by the light of a nearby furylamp, and so she ripped the hood from the woman's head.

It was Gaele—or rather, it was the mask Kalare's head spy, Rook, wore when she was serving the Cursors in the capital, a spy within the midst of Kalare's enemies.

The woman met Amara's eyes, her features pleasant but plain, and her face was pale. Her leg was twisted beneath her at an unnatural angle.

And she was weeping.

"Please," she whispered to Amara. "Countess. Please kill me."

ᴏᴏᴏᴏᴏ CHAPTER 14

Events proceeded at a pace which Amara remembered as a blur of desperate communications, shouted commands, and scrambling dashes from one building to the next while the panicked city of Ceres girded itself for battle.

By the deepest hours of the night, it all culminated in a meeting within the private garden of the High Lord Cereus, within the walls of the High Lord's Tower, the final redoubt and bastion of the city's defenses, and the most secure location in the city.

Amara arrived first, with Bernard and Giraldi. Bernard had, maddeningly, staggered up from a healer's watercrafting tub and refused to leave her unprotected for the space of a minute since the attack at the restaurant. Giraldi claimed that he had to remain nearby as well, in order to protect his Count, but Amara was not fooled. The men had decided that she needed protecting, and as far as they were concerned, that was that.

A wizened old majordomo showed them to the garden, a simple affair of flowers and trees that might be found at any steadholt in the Realm, and that the High Lord Cereus tended to with his own hands. The garden was arranged around a perfectly circular pool. Its mirrored surface reflected the colors of the low furylamps throughout the garden, as well as the sullen red light of the stars.

Servants produced food, and Amara's belly remembered that they'd been attacked before she'd had the chance to eat. Giraldi made both her and her husband sit, while he brought them food and stood over them as he might over his grandchildren, making sure that they ate before sitting down with a small round of cheese, a loaf, and a pitcher of ale for himself.

A few moments later, Lord Cereus arrived. Among the Citizenry of the Realm, Cereus Macius was something of a rarity—a silver-haired, elderly man. Either he had lacked the talent for preserving his outward youth, or he had simply never bothered to maintain it. There were rumors that Cereus's furycrafting abilities were somewhat stunted when it came to watercrafting, though Amara had no way to know if the rumors were based on fact, or if the fact of his appearance had given birth to the rumors.

Cereus was of medium height and slender build, with a long, morose-looking face and blunt, strong fingers. He entered, two hard-faced men flanking him, hands on their swords. Upon seeing Bernard and Giraldi, the two men paused and narrowed their eyes. Bernard and Giraldi returned their scrutiny with matching impassivity.

"I wonder, Countess Amara," Cereus murmured, his tone whimsical. "Are we to let them sniff one another's rumps and become friends, or should we tie their leashes to separate walls to avoid trouble?"

"Your Grace." Amara smiled and rose, bowing deeply. "They mean well."

Cereus took her hands in both of his, smiling, and nodded back to her. "You may be right. Gentlemen, if there's fighting to be done tonight, I'd prefer that it not be in my garden. Very well?"

The two bodyguards nodded and withdrew by half a step and no more. Giraldi grinned and went back to his food. Bernard smiled and bowed to Cereus. "Of course, Your Grace."

"Count Calderon," Cereus said. "Welcome. Though I fear you have come to my city at a most unfortunate time."

"I am here, Your Grace," Bernard said firmly. "And I offer you whatever aid I can provide."

"Thank you," Cereus said, no trace of irony in his words. "Countess, are the others coming?"

"Yes, Your Grace," she said. "But it may take more time. Most of the survivors were badly traumatized by the city's panic."

Cereus grunted and lowered himself stiffly onto a richly, beautifully carved wooden bench. "Understandable." He squinted at Bernard. "Your sister, the . . ." He blinked as if mildly disbelieving, ". . . Steadholder. The woman Steadholder. She's a talented watercrafter, yes?"

"Yes," Bernard said.

"How is she?"

"Exhausted. Sleeping," Bernard replied. "She'd had a difficult day even before the stars changed."

"The panic was extremely painful to those of sensitivity to such things. If there is anything I can do to help her, please send word to me," Cereus said.

Bernard bowed his head. "Thank you, Your Grace. Your offer of secure quarters was more than generous enough. She's resting comfortably."

Cereus squinted at Giraldi. "Is that ale? Real, honest ale?"

Giraldi belched.

"Crows and thunder," Cereus said. "Do you have another mug, soldier?" Giraldi did. Cereus sipped, let out a long sigh, and settled back down on his bench. "My daughter, you see," he explained. "She'll not let an old man have a well-earned draught. Says it isn't good for my heart."

"Got to die of something," Giraldi observed. "Might as well put back a few pints while you wait to see what it is."

"Exactly," Cereus said. "The girl's got a heart of gold, but she doesn't see that." He glanced over his shoulder, at the battlements rising above the garden, and the old lord's face settled into deeper lines, marks of worry and grief etched in the shadows on his face. Amara watched as he settled down to sip carefully at the ale and wait for the others to arrive. It didn't take long. Within half an hour, High Lord Cereus's little garden was crowded with visitors. "Well," he said, looking around with a somewhat lost expression on his face. "I suppose we should begin."

Cereus rose. He stepped up onto his bench with an apologetic expression and rapped a ring against his now-empty mug. "My lords, ladies. Welcome. Would that it were a happier occasion." He smiled faintly and gestured. "I have asked you here on behalf of the First Lord and his Cursor, Countess Amara. Countess."

Lord Cereus stepped down from the bench with a visible expression of relief.

Amara bowed her head to Cereus, took a small coin from her pocket, and dropped it into the pool, murmuring, "Amaranth waters, hasten word to thy master."

The water's surface rippled around the vanished coin, then began to stir. Then an extrusion of water rippled forth and resolved itself into the form of a tall, slender man in his late prime, colors slowly seeping into the shape of his tunic and breeches, forming into the blue and scarlet of the House of

Gaius. Similarly, his hair became a seemingly premature grey-white, though he had seen nearly fourscore years.

Amara bowed her head. "My lord, we are ready."

The First Lord's image turned to face Amara and nodded. "Go ahead. Lords Atticus and Placidus"—he made a gesture as two more watery forms began to take shape on either side of his own—"will be joining us as well."

Amara nodded and turned to face the others in the garden. "My lords and ladies, I know that the past few hours have been confusing and frightening. The First Lord has instructed to me to share what information we have about recent events.

"We do not yet know the background and particulars of the attackers who struck last evening," Amara said. "But we do know that they attacked almost every member of the Dianic League, as well as the faculty and staff of the Collegia Tactica, the captain and Tribunes of the First Ceresian, and a number of visiting military officers who were attending a symposium at the Collegia.

"The assassins proved deadly and efficient. High Lady Rhodes was slain, as was High Lady Phrygius, Senator Parmos, and seventy-six other Citizens who had been targeted by the assassins. Several more citizens, including Lady Placidus, are missing." She reached into a pouch at her side and drew out the hinged metallic ring of a discipline collar, a slaver's device used to control troublesome slaves. "What we know is that each of the attackers wore a discipline collar, like this one. Each of them bears an engraving that reads: *Immortalis*. Each of the men involved in the attack appeared to be twenty years of age or younger. Each of them displayed an almost superhuman ability to withstand pain, and they were apparently acting without fear or regard for their own lives.

"We are fairly certain that these Immortals, for lack of a better term, are slaves trained, conditioned, and collar-disciplined from childhood to be soldiers. Simply put, they are highly proficient madmen with no conscience, no doubt, no aversion to pain, and a perfect willingness to sacrifice their own lives to accomplish their mission. Fewer than one target in four survived the attacks."

Quiet comments went around the little garden. A large, heavily built man with dark hair and an iron grey beard, wearing Legion armor, rumbled, "We all have some idea what they can do. But do you know who sent them?"

Amara took a deep breath and said, "Full, legal corroboration should be complete in a few days, but the given the timing of events, I am confident of what we will find. Last night, apparently simultaneously with the attacks here, Lord Kalarus mobilized his Legions."

Several people drew in sharp breaths. Low mutters ran through the garden again, voices quicker, nervous.

"One of Kalarus's Legions assaulted the western foothills of Parcia and diverted the Gaul through the floodplain. The Third Parcian Legion was forced to abandon the stronghold at Whiteharrow, and Kalarus's Legions now control the passes down out of the Blackhills.

"At the same time," Amara continued, "two more Legions assaulted the camp of Second Ceres, taking them completely by surprise. The attackers offered no quarter. There were fewer than a hundred survivors."

Lord Cereus's face became even more pale, and he bowed his head.

"Those Legions," Amara said, "are already marching on the city. Their Knights Aeris and other advance elements are already in the area, and we anticipate that the main body of troops will arrive within half a day."

"Pah," scoffed a voice from the edge of the garden. "That's ridiculous."

Amara turned to the speaker, Senator Arnos, dressed in the formal scholar's robes of the Collegia Tactica and wearing a haughty expression. "Sir?" she inquired politely.

"Kalarus is ambitious, but he is no fool. You would have us believe that he would make open war upon the whole of the Realm and leave his own city unprotected?"

"Unprotected, sir?" Amara asked mildly.

"Three Legions," Lord Arnos said. "Each High Lord has three Legions at his command. That is the law."

Amara blinked slowly at Arnos, then said, "Law-abiding High Lords do not make war upon the whole of the Realm and send fanatic madmen to assassinate their fellow Citizens. Generally speaking." She turned back to the others present, and said, "In addition to the forces already mentioned, two more of Kalare's Legions have already seized the bridges over the Gaul at Hector and Vondus. Intelligence suggests that another Legion will join the two on their way here, and that he holds at least one Legion in mobile reserve." She glanced back at the Senator. "If it makes you feel any better, sir, Kalarus also has a Legion stationed at Kalare to secure his city."

"Seven," muttered the grey-bearded soldier. "Seven bloody Legions. Where the crows did he hide four entire *Legions*, Countess?"

"For the time being, that is of secondary importance," Amara said. "What matters is that he has them, and he's using them." She took a deep breath and looked around the room. "If Kalarus's forces take Ceres, there will be nothing to stand between them and the capital."

This time there were no mutterings—only silence.

The First Lord's rich, smooth voice murmured, "Thank you, Countess. Lord Cereus, what is the status of your defenses?"

Cereus grimaced and shook his head. "We aren't ready for something like this, sire," he said, his tone frank. "With Second Legion destroyed, I have only First Legion and the civic legion to man the walls—and we're going to be spread thin. Against three entire Legions and their Knights, we'll not hold for long. If Kalarus himself is with them . . ."

"I remember a young soldier," Gaius said, "who once told me that the more desperate and hopeless the battle, the more he wanted to face it and take the field. That he lived for such challenge."

"That soldier grew up, Gaius," Cereus said in a tired voice, without looking up. "He wed. Had children. Grandchildren. He got old."

Gaius regarded Cereus for a time, then simply nodded. "First Imperian must hold the northern pass from the Blackhills while Second Imperian secures the capital. I'm dispatching Third Imperian to your aid, but they cannot reach you before Kalare's forces. The Crown Legion, however, was on maneuvers south of the capital, and I ordered them to your aid within an hour of the first attack. They've been force-marching through the night, and Sir Miles should be arriving with his men within hours."

Cereus exhaled, evidently relieved. "Good, good. Thank you, old friend."

Gaius nodded, his stern features softening for a moment. Then he said, "There's no denying that you're still outnumbered, but all you need do is stand fast. I have already asked High Lords Placidus and Atticus to send relief forces to link up with Third Imperian. Aquitaine, Rhodes, and Parcia will be joining forces to retake the bridges over the Gaul."

Cereus nodded. "Once they do, you'll have Kalarus's Legions cut off from retreat or reinforcement."

Gaius's image nodded. "You have only to hold out, Macius. Don't risk your people on anything heroic."

"EXCELLENT ADVICE," boomed a voice that seemed to resonate up from the water of the pool. It rang off the walls around the little garden, unpleasant and sharp.

The pool stirred once more, and at its far side another shape rose—forming into a man Amara recognized as Kalarus Brencis, High Lord of Kalare. In person, he was not a particularly imposing figure of a man—tall, but thin, and his eyes always seemed sunken in shadows, giving his face a gaunt, stark look, his hair straight, fine, and limp. The figure formed from the waters of the fountain, though, was taller by half than the other forms there, and built with more apparent muscle than the actual Kalarus carried. "Gentlemen. Ladies. I trust, by now, that the shape of things to come is obvious to . . . well, not to *everyone* so much as to everyone who has *survived*." The image's teeth showed in a vulpine smile. "Thus far, at any rate."

Amara shot a glance at the image of Gaius. The First Lord looked from her to Cereus. The old High Lord sat very still and very quiet, not moving.

"Brencis," the First Lord said, his tone calm, "am I to understand that you are confessing before those here that you are to blame for these murders? And that you have unlawfully set your forces against those of your fellow High Lords?"

Kalarus's image turned to the First Lord's, and said, "I've looked forward to this since I was a boy, Gaius." He closed his eyes and exhaled in pleasure. "Shut your crowbegotten mouth, old man."

Kalarus's image clutched his hand into an abrupt fist, and the water-image of Gaius suddenly exploded into individual droplets that splashed back down into the pool.

Amara, and everyone else in the garden, drew in a sudden, sharp breath at Kalarus's display of power. He had simply cut the First Lord's contact through the pool, a show of furycrafting strength whose implications were terrifying. If Kalarus truly held as much or more power than the First Lord . . .

"Out with the old," Kalarus said, his image turning to address those in the garden. "And in with the new. Think carefully, fellow Alerans, which you would choose to be. We all know that the House of Gaius has failed. He has no heir and plays games with all the Realm at stake rather than accept his fall from power—and would drag each of you down to the grave with him. You can be a part of the next great age of Aleran civilization—or you can be paved under it."

Senator Arnos rose and faced Kalarus's image. "Your Grace," he said. "While your power and temerity are very much in evidence, surely you must see that your military position is untenable. Your opening moves have been audacious, but you cannot hope to prevail against the joined might of the other cities of the Realm and their Legions."

Kalarus let out a booming laugh. "Joined might?" he asked. "Ceres will fall within the day, and I will press on to Alera Imperia herself. There is not enough free might to prevent it." The image turned to Lord Placidus, and said, "Sandos, I had no idea that Aria had a birthmark on her left thigh." His gaze swiveled to the image of Lord Atticus. "Elios, may I compliment your daughter on a particularly lovely head of hair—a small section of which will be delivered to you by messenger, so that you may know that she is in my protective custody."

"Protective custody?" Amara asked sharply.

Kalarus nodded. "Quite. My lords Atticus and Placidus, my quarrels have never been with you or your cities, and I desire none now. I am holding those two as guarantors against your neutrality. I do not ask you to forsake any vow or to turn against the First Lord—only stand from my way. I give you my word that if you do so, when matters settle down, they will be returned to you, otherwise unharmed."

Cereus rose slowly to his feet and walked down to the edge of the pool. "This is why you have come here, Kalarus?" he asked quietly, not looking at the image. "To make promises to your neighbors that you will not attack them, even while you assault another before their very eyes?"

"I am delivering my terms to *them*," Kalarus said. "My terms for *you* are somewhat different."

"I am listening," Cereus said quietly.

"Yield your city to me now," Kalarus said. "And I will spare your life and that of your family. You will be free to depart and make what life you would elsewhere in the Realm."

Cereus's eyes narrowed. "You would seek to cast me from my family's home? To force me to abandon my people?"

"You should be grateful I'm giving you a choice," Kalarus replied. "Defy me, and it will go hard for you, and for your line. I promise to be thorough. I know all of their names, old man. Your three daughters. Your son. Your eleven grandchildren."

"You would threaten babes in arms, Kalarus? You're a madman."

Kalarus barked out a laugh. "A madman? Or a visionary. Only history will decide—and we all know who writes the histories." Kalarus's teeth showed again. "I'd prefer you to fight so that I might destroy you. But we both know that you aren't a fighter anymore, Macius. Walk away while you still can."

High Lord Cereus faced Kalarus's image for a silent minute before he lifted a hand, clenched it into a fist, and snarled, "Get out of my garden."

The waters of the pool rippled, and Kalarus's image, like

Gaius's had, fell back into droplets of water that splashed into the pool.

"Threaten my granddaughter. I'll wring your skinny throat, you cowardly slive." Cereus growled at the pool. Then he turned to face the assembly. "Ladies and gentlemen, I have a city to defend. I welcome any help you might give. But if you don't intend to fight, you should depart the city as quickly as possible." He turned a hard look at the pool where Kalarus had stood. "If you can't help, then stay the crows out of my way."

Then the old man, his anger wrapped around him like a cloak, spun on his heel and strode from the garden barking orders to his startled-looking men, his voice ringing from the walls.

The others in the garden just stared after Cereus, startled at the change in the man. Then they began to speak quietly, most moving to leave. Amara turned to the images of Lords Placidus and Atticus. "My lords, please. Before you go, a word on behalf of the First Lord?"

The water-forms nodded, and Amara waited until the garden had emptied again. "My lords, may I ask your intentions?"

Lord Placidus, a plain, stocky man of unremarkable height and crystal blue eyes shook his head. "I'm not sure, Countess. But if he has Aria then . . ." The High Lord shook his head. "There are a number of dangerously volatile furies who are restrained from doing harm by my wife's will. If she dies without taking the proper measures to keep them neutralized, several thousand of my holders would perish. I have no qualms about sending my Legions into harm's way—but I am not willing to sacrifice the populations of entire steadholts. Women. Children. Families."

"You would let the Realm fall instead?" Amara asked.

"The Realm will stand, Countess," Placidus said, his voice hardening. "Only the face beneath the crown will change. I have never made it a secret that I wish nothing to do with the politics of the Crown. In point of fact, if Gaius's page hadn't publicly manipulated us into supporting him, my *wife* might now be with me, safe and unharmed."

Amara ground her teeth, but nodded once. "Very well, Your Grace." She turned to High Lord Atticus. "And you, sir?"

"I gave one daughter to Gaius already," Atticus said, his voice bitter. "My Caria, taken to wife and held hostage in the capital. Now Kalarus has taken the other daughter. I see little difference between the two. But Gaius asks me to sacrifice men and blood, while Kalare wishes me merely to stand aside." He bared his teeth, biting off the words. "So far as I am concerned, you can all cut each other to shreds and let the crows pick clean your bones."

He turned, and the water-image flowed back down into the pool.

Lord Placidus grimaced at the departed lord of Attica. "I have no love for Kalarus or what he stands for," he told Amara. "I have no qualms about facing him on the field of battle. But if I must choose between the First Lord's life and those of my wife and thousands of my holders, I do not choose Gaius."

"I understand," Amara said quietly.

Placidus nodded once. "Tell Gaius I'll not contest him should the Legions need passage through any of my lands. It is all I can offer."

"Why?" Amara asked him, her voice very quiet.

Placidus was silent for a moment. Then he said, "Most High Lords marry for advantage. For political alliance." The image of Placidus shook its head as it slipped back down into the pool, receding. "I loved her, Countess. Still do."

Amara stared at the rippling pool for a moment, then sighed and settled down onto a nearby bench. She shook her head, struggling to work her way through a dozen trains of thought. She looked up a moment later, to find Bernard standing over her, offering her a mug of Giraldi's ale. She drank it off in a single, long pull.

Kalarus was far stronger than anyone had anticipated and had found some way to secretly train and transport entire Legions of men. He was ruthless, clever, and determined—and worst of all, to Amara's way of thinking, was that Lord Cereus's accusation seemed distressingly accurate. Kalarus might well be as mad as Cereus claimed. Though the forces of the Realm had the strength to beat him back, if only just, Kalarus had chosen a particularly vicious moment in which to attack and had struck at the most vulnerable point. If he moved swiftly enough, his coup might well succeed.

In fact, she could not think of anything the First Lord might do to stop him.

She could understand what Placidus had done, on one level, but on another she burned with fury at the man's decision to turn aside from the First Lord. He was a High Lord of Alera. He was honor-bound to come to the aid of the First Lord in the face of insurrection. Amara wished no harm to come to Lady Placida or to any innocent holders, of course, but she simply could not reconcile Lord Placidus's choice with his obligations as a Citizen and Lord of the Realm.

Bernard's ring, on its chain around her neck, felt heavy. She could hardly be the first to cast that particular stone. After all, hadn't she put her own desires ahead of her duties?

Bernard settled down next to her and exhaled slowly. "You look exhausted," he said quietly. "You need to sleep."

"Soon," she answered. Her hand found his.

"What do you think?" he asked her. "About all this."

"It's bad," she said quietly. "It's very bad."

Gaius's voice rolled through the little garden, rich and amused. "Or perhaps it only seems so on the surface, Countess."

ꚉꚉ CHAPTER 15

Amara blinked, rising abruptly, and turned to find Gaius standing behind them in the flesh, emerging from a wind-crafted veil so fine and delicate that she had never had an inkling that it had been present. "Sire?" she said. "You were *here* all along? But Kalarus . . ."

The First Lord arched an eyebrow. "Kalarus Brencis's ego is enormous—and an enormous weakness. The larger it grows, the more of his view it will obstruct, and I have no objections to feeding it." Then he smiled. "And my old friend Cereus needed someone to remind him of what he is capable. It was generous of Kalarus to volunteer."

Amara shook her head. She should have known better. Gaius Sextus had not retained his rule in the face of dangerous, ruthless men like Kalarus by being weak or predictable. "My lord, you heard what Lords Atticus and Placidus said."

"I did indeed," Gaius said.

Amara nodded. "Without their forces to help hold Ceres, Kalarus's gambit may well succeed."

"I give him five chances in six," Gaius agreed.

"Sire," Amara said, "this is . . . this . . ." Her outrage strangled her voice for a moment, and she pressed her lips firmly together before she said something that, in the eyes of the law, could not be retracted.

"It's all right, Cursor," Gaius said. "Speak your mind freely. I will not hold anything you say as a formal accusation."

"It's *treason*, sir," Amara spat. "They have an obligation to come to the defense of the Realm. They owe you their loyalty, and they are turning their backs on you."

"Do I not owe them loyalty in return?" Gaius asked. "Protection against threats too powerful for them to face? And yet harm has come to them and theirs."

"Through no fault of your own!" Amara said.

"Untrue," Gaius said. "I miscalculated Kalarus's response, his resources, and we both know it."

Amara folded her arms over her stomach and looked away from Gaius. "All I know," she said, "is that they have abandoned their duty. Their loyalty to the Realm."

"Treason, you say," Gaius murmured. "Loyalty. Strong words. In today's uncertain clime, those terms are somewhat mutable." He raised his voice slightly and glanced at the far corner of the little garden. "Wouldn't you agree, Invidia?"

A second veil, every bit as delicate and undetectable as Gaius's had been, vanished, replaced by the tall, regal figure of Lady Aquitaine. Though her eyes looked a bit sunken, she showed no other signs of the trauma the city's sudden surge of panic had inflicted upon its more powerful watercrafters. Her expression was cool, her pale face lovely and flawless, her dark hair held back into a wave that fell over one white shoulder to spill over her gown of crimson silk. A circlet of finely wrought silver in the design of laurel leaves, the badge of a recipient of the Imperian Laurel for Valor, stood out starkly against her tresses, the ornament emphasized by its contrast against her hair.

"I think," she said, her tone steady, "that regardless of our ongoing differences, we can both recognize a greater threat to our plans when it appears."

Amara drew in a sharp breath, and her eyes flicked from Lady Aquitaine to Gaius and back. "Sire? I'm not sure I understand. What is she doing here?"

"I invited her, naturally," Gaius said. "We have a common interest in this matter."

"Of course," Amara said. "Neither of you wishes to see Lord Kalarus"—she emphasized the name ever so slightly—"on the throne."

"Exactly," said Lady Aquitaine with a cool smile.

"Kalarus's timing was quite nearly perfect," Gaius said. "But if the Legions of Attica and Placida are freed to act, we should be able to stop him. That's where you and Lady Aquitaine come in, Countess."

Amara frowned. "What is your command, sire?"

"Simply put, rescue the hostages and remove Kalarus's hold on Lords Placidus and Atticus with all possible haste." Gaius nodded toward Lady Aquitaine. "Invidia has agreed to assist you. Work with her."

Amara felt her spine stiffen, and she narrowed her eyes. "With . . . her? Even though she is responsible for—"

"For saving my life when the Canim attacked the palace?" the First Lord said gently. "For taking command of a situation which could have dissolved into an utter disaster? For her tireless efforts to rally support for emancipation?"

"I am aware of her public image," Amara said, her voice sharp. "I am equally aware of her true designs."

Gaius narrowed his eyes. "Which is the very reason I offered her this opportunity to work together," he said. "Even if you do not believe that she believes in acting for the good of the Realm, I am sure that you trust her ambition. So long as she and her husband wish to take the throne from me, I am confident that she would do nothing that would give it to Kalarus."

"You cannot trust her, sire," Amara said quietly. "If she gets the chance to move against you, she will."

"Perhaps so," Gaius said. "But until that time, I am confident of her assistance against a common foe."

"With reason," Lady Aquitaine murmured. "Countess, I assure you that I see the value of cooperation in this matter." The tall woman's eyes suddenly burned hot. "And politics aside, Kalarus's murderous attempt upon my life, on the lives of my clients, upon so many Citizens and members of the League cannot be ignored. Any animal as vicious and dangerous as Kalarus must be put down. It will be my pleasure to assist the Crown in doing so."

"And when that is done?" Amara asked, her tone a challenge.

"When that is done," Lady Aquitaine said, "we will see."

Amara stared at her for a moment before turning to Gaius. "My lord . . ."

Gaius lifted a hand. "Invidia," he said. "I know that you are still weary from tonight's trauma."

She smiled, the expression elegant and not at all weary. "Of course, sire. Countess, High Lord Cereus has offered the safety and security of his guest wing to all those attacked by Kalarus's Immortals. Please call on me at your convenience."

"Very well, Your Grace," Amara said quietly.

Lady Aquitaine curtseyed to Gaius. "Sire."

Gaius inclined his head, and Lady Aquitaine departed the garden.

"I do not like this, my lord," Amara said.

"A moment," the First Lord said. He closed his eyes and muttered something, making a pair of swift gestures with his hands, and Amara sensed furycraft at work, doubtless to ensure a few moments of privacy.

Amara arched an eyebrow at him. "Then you do not trust Lady Aquitaine."

"I trust her to bury a knife in my back at her earliest opportunity," Gaius replied. "But I suspect her contempt for Kalarus is genuine, as is her desire to recover the abducted members of the League—and her aid could be priceless. She is quite capable, Amara."

The Cursor shook her head. "And the busier she is with me, the less time she has to plot against you."

"Essentially," Gaius said, a smile toying at the corners of his mouth, "yes. Make whatever use of her you can and recover those hostages."

Amara shook her head. "He can't possibly be holding them nearby. Not someone as powerful as Placidus Aria. He'd need to have her within his own lands—probably at his citadel."

"I agree," Gaius said. "There has been much movement in the upper air over the past day, but I am sure that at least some travelers have departed for Kalare. You need to decide upon your course of action and leave before the sun is fairly risen tomorrow."

Amara frowned. "Why, sire?"

"You may note," Gaius said, "how the recent discussion avoided one particular subject most scrupulously."

"Yes. The stars," Amara said quietly. "What happened to them."

Gaius shrugged. "I've nothing but suspicions, at this point."

"I don't even have that much," Amara said.

"I believe," Gaius said, "that it is some working of the Canim. The change came from the west and spread over toward the east. I suspect that it is some kind of very high, very fine cloud, that colors the light of the stars as they shine down."

"A cloud?" Amara murmured. "Can you not simply examine it?"

Gaius frowned faintly. "In fact, no. I've sent dozens of furies up to investigate. They did not return."

Amara blinked. "Something . . . damaged them?"

"So it would seem," Gaius said.

"But . . . I did not think the Canim could do such an enormous thing. I know their rituals give them some kind of rude parallel to Aleran furycraft, but I never thought that they could manage something on this scale."

"They never have," Gaius replied. "But the remarkable thing about this working of theirs is that it has had some far-reaching effects I have never encountered before. I have been unable to observe activities and events passing in the Realm beyond perhaps a hundred miles of Alera Imperia. I suspect that the other High Lords have been similarly blinded."

Amara frowned. "How could the Canim have done such a thing?"

Gaius shook his head. "I've no way of knowing. But whatever they have done, the upper air groans with it. Travel has become quite dangerous in only a few hours. I suspect that it will only become worse as time passes. Which is why I must take my leave at once. I have a great many things to do, and if air travel becomes as difficult as I suspect it might, then I must set out at once—and so must you."

Amara felt her eyes widen. "Do you mean to say . . . sire, is Kalarus conspiring with the Canim?"

"It would seem a rather large coincidence that he would be in position to attack in so many places, with such precision, and just at the moment when the most powerful furycrafters in his path would have been disabled—just precisely at the same time the Canim released this working."

"A signal," Amara said. "The stars were a signal for him to begin."

"Probably," Gaius replied.

"But . . . sire, *no one* has ever found common ground with the Canim. No Aleran would ever . . ." She broke off and bit her lip. "Mmm. But the facts suggest that one has. I sound like Senator Arnos."

"Far less tiresome," Gaius said. He put a hand on Amara's shoulder. "Countess, I have two things to tell you. First, if Kalarus manages to prevent Placida and Attica from sending reinforcements, he will in all probability seize the capital and its furies. Aquitaine and the other High Lords will contest him. Our Realm will dissolve into utter chaos. Tens of thousands will die, and if Kalarus truly has thrown in his hand with the Canim, we may be facing the end of the Realm entirely." He lowered his voice, emphasizing the words. "You *must* succeed. At *any* cost."

Amara swallowed and nodded her head.

"Second," he said, more quietly, "there is no one else in the Realm to whom I would sooner entrust this task than you, Amara. In the last few years, you have rendered more courageous service than most Cursors do in a lifetime. You do them great honor—and I am proud to have the loyalty of so worthy an individual."

Amara felt her back straighten as she looked up at the First Lord. Her throat felt tight, and she swallowed and murmured, "Thank you, sire."

He nodded once, and withdrew his hand. "Then I leave you to it," he said quietly. "Good luck, Cursor."

"Thank you, sire."

Gaius flicked his hands a few times, and the privacy furycrafting dissipated, vanishing from Amara's senses. At the same time, a gentle wind that hardly stirred the plants of the garden lifted Gaius from the ground, even as he wove another delicate veil around himself, vanishing as he took almost silently to the skies.

Amara stood staring up after the departed First Lord for a moment. Then she felt Bernard's presence at her side. He slipped an arm around her waist, and she leaned against him for a moment.

"I don't like this," he said.

"Nor I," Amara replied. "But that doesn't matter. You and Giraldi should go and inform the Steadholder of what happened here."

"Giraldi can take care of it," Bernard said. "I'm going with you."

"Don't be ridiculous," Amara said. "Bernard, you're—"

"Your husband. A veteran. An expert hunter and woodsman," he said. His jaw set into a line. "I'm going with you."

"I'm not—"

"Going to stop me from going with you. No one is."

Amara's chest suddenly felt very tight. She turned to her husband and kissed him once, on the mouth, and very lightly. Then she said, "Very well. If you're going to be a mule about it."

Giraldi limped up to them and grunted. "Now you be careful, sir. I don't want to be the only centurion in the Legions to get two of his commanders cut down."

Bernard traded grips with him. "Keep an eye on 'Sana. When she wakes up, tell her . . ." He shook his head. "Doesn't matter. She knows better than I what I'd say."

"Course," Giraldi agreed. Then he caught Amara in a rough hug, hard enough to make her ribs creak. "And you. Don't let him distract you none."

Amara hugged back, and said, "Thank you."

The old centurion nodded, saluted them, fist to heart, and limped from the garden.

"Very well, my lady," Bernard murmured. "Where do we begin?"

Amara frowned, and narrowed her eyes. "With someone who has seen Kalarus's operation from the inside, and who might know his plans." She turned to Bernard and said, "We're going to the dungeons."

◁◁◁◁ CHAPTER 16

"You told the assembly that all of Kalarus's assassins had died rather than be captured," Lady Aquitaine murmured as they descended the last steps to the cells beneath Lord Cereus's citadel.

"Yes," Amara said. "I did. But this one we took alive. It is she who attempted to take the life of Steadholder Isana."

"She?" Lady Aquitaine asked, her tone interested. "The others were all men."

"Yes," Amara replied. "She was one of Kalarus's blood-crows. It is possible that she might know something of his plans. She was high in his councils."

"And therefore loyal to him," Lady Aquitaine mused. "Or at least very much under his control. Do you actually believe she will divulge such information to you?"

"She will," Amara said. "One way or another."

She could feel the pressure of Lady Aquitaine's gaze on the back of her head. "I see," the High Lady murmured. "This shall be interesting."

Amara put a hand on Bernard's shoulder to signal him, and stopped on the cold stone stairway before her. She turned to face Lady Aquitaine. "Your Grace, I ask you to remember that you are here to assist me," she said quietly. "I will do the talking."

The High Lady narrowed her eyes, for a moment. Then she nodded, and Amara resumed her pace.

The "dungeon" of the citadel of Ceres was seldom in use. In fact, it appeared that the chilly place was primarily used for storing foodstuffs. Several crates of cabbages, apples, and tubers had been stacked neatly in the hall outside the only closed and guarded doorway. A *legionare* wearing a tunic in the brown and grey of the House of Cereus stood outside the door, a naked sword in his hand. "Halt, sir," he said, as Bernard entered the hall. "This area is off-limits."

Amara slipped around Bernard. "*Legionare* Karus, isn't it?" she asked.

The man came to attention and saluted. "Countess Amara? His Grace said you're to have access to the prisoner."

Amara gestured at Bernard and Lady Aquitaine. "They're with me."

"Yes, Your Excellency." The guard withdrew to the door, drawing the key from his belt. He hesitated for a moment. "Countess. I don't know who that woman is. But . . . she's hurt pretty bad. She needs a healer."

"I'll take care of that," Amara told him. "Has she tried to speak to you?"

"No, ma'am."

"Good. Leave the keys. I want you to take station at the

bottom of the stairs. We're not to be disturbed for any but Lord Cereus or Gaius Sextus himself."

The *legionare* blinked, then saluted. "Yes, ma'am." He took up his shield by its carrying strap and marched to the bottom of the stairs.

Amara turned the key smoothly in the well-kept lock, and opened the door. It swung on soundless hinges, and Amara frowned.

"Problem?" Bernard whispered.

"I suppose I expected it to clank. And squeak."

"First dungeon?"

"Except for where they locked me up with you."

Bernard's mouth quirked into a small smile, and he pushed the door the rest of the way open and entered the room first. He stopped there for a moment, and Amara saw him stiffen and heard him draw in a sharp breath. He stood stock-still for a moment, until Amara touched his back, and Bernard moved aside.

Rook had not been treated kindly.

Amara stood beside her husband for a moment. The blood-crow had been chained to the ceiling, the cuffs cutting into her wrists, held so that her feet barely touched the floor. Her broken leg was wholly unable to support her weight. A six-inch-wide circle grooved into the floor had been filled with oil, and dozens of floating wicks surrounded the prisoner with fire, preventing the use of any water furies—which she obviously possessed, if able to change her appearance to double for the student murdered several years before. Her tenuous connection with the earth, as well as a lack of proper leverage, would make the use of earth furies a useless gesture. No living or once-living plants adorned the room, ruling out much use of wood-crafting, and the close quarters would make the use of any firecrafting essentially suicidal. Metalcrafting might be able to weaken the cuffs, but it was something that would take a great deal of time and effort, and Rook would have neither. This deep beneath the surface, wind furies would be of very limited use—a fact not lost on Amara, who never felt comfortable when Cirrus was not readily available.

That left only simple ingenuity as a possible threat to her captors—and no one who had worked long in Kalarus's service would be in short supply. Or at least, would not be under normal circumstances. Rook hung limply in the chains, her good leg trembling in a kind of constant state of collapse, barely able to keep enough weight off her suspended shoulders to keep them from being dislocated. Another day or so and it would happen in any case. Her head hung down, hair fallen around her face. Her breathing came in short, harsh jerks, edged with sounds of basic pain and fear, and what little of her voice Amara heard was dry, ragged.

The woman was no threat to anyone. She was doomed, and she knew it. Part of Amara cried out at the woman's plight, but she pushed compassion from her thoughts. Rook was a murderer and worse. A bloody-handed traitor to the Realm.

All the same. Looking at the woman made Amara feel sick.

Amara stepped over the ring of floating candles, walked over to stand before her and said, "Rook. Look at me."

Rook's head twitched. Amara caught the dull shine of the low candlelight on one of the woman's eyes.

"I don't want to make this more unpleasant than it has to be," Amara said in a quiet tone. "I want information. Give it to me, and I'll have your leg seen to. Supply you a cot."

Rook stared and said nothing.

"It won't change what will happen. But there's no reason you have to be uncomfortable until your trial. No reason you should die in fever and agony while you wait."

The captive woman shuddered. Her voice came out in a rasp. "Kill me. Or get out."

Amara folded her arms. "Several thousand *legionares* are already dead thanks to your master. Thousands more will die in the coming battles. Women, children, the elderly and infirm will also suffer and die. In wars, they always do."

Rook said nothing.

"You attempted to murder Isana of Calderon. A woman whose personal courage, kindness, and integrity I have seen demonstrated more than once. A woman I count my friend.

Count Calderon here is her brother. And, of course, I believe you are acquainted with her nephew. With what they have all given in service to the Realm."

Rook breathed in short, strangled rasps, but did not speak.

"You face death for what you have done," Amara said. "I have never been one to believe in spirits bound to earth for their crimes in life. Neither would I wish to have such deeds as yours on my conscience."

No response. Amara frowned. "Rook, if you cooperate with us, it's possible that we can end this war before it destroys us all. It would save thousands of lives. Surely you can see that."

When the spy did not reply, Amara leaned in closer, making eye contact. "If you cooperate, if your help makes the difference, the First Lord may suspend your execution. Your life may not be a pleasant one—but you will live."

Rook drew in a shuddering breath and lifted her head enough to stare at Amara. Tears, absent until then, began to streak down her cheeks. "I can't help you, Countess."

"You can," Amara said. "You must."

Rook ground her teeth in agony. "Don't you see? I *can't.*"

"You will," Amara said.

Rook shook her head, a slight motion of weary despair and closed her eyes.

"I've never tortured anyone," Amara said quietly. "I know the theory. I'd rather resolve this peaceably. But it's up to you. I can go away and come back with a healer. Or I can come back with a knife."

The prisoner said nothing for a long moment. Then she inhaled, licked her lips, and said, "If you heat the knife, it's easier to avoid mistakes. The wound sears shut. You can cause a great deal more pain with far less damage, provided I do not faint."

Amara only stared at Rook for a long, silent moment.

"Go get your knife, Countess," Rook whispered. "The sooner we begin, the sooner it will be over with."

Amara bit her lip and looked at Bernard. He stared at Rook, his face troubled, and shook his head.

"Countess," murmured Lady Aquitaine. "May I speak to you?"

Rook looked up at the sound of her voice, body tensing.

Amara frowned but nodded to Lady Aquitaine, who stood silhouetted in the doorway, and turned to step close to her.

"Thank you," Lady Aquitaine said quietly. "Countess, you are an agent of the Crown. It is your profession, and so you are familiar with many of the same things as the prisoner. You are not, however, personally familiar with Kalarus Brencis, how he operates his holdings and uses his clients and those in his employ."

"If there is something you think I should know, it might be more productive if you told it to me."

Lady Aquitaine's eyes managed to be cold and perfectly restrained at the same time. "She asked you to kill her when you saw her?"

Amara frowned. "Yes. How did you know?"

"I did not," Lady Aquitaine replied. "But it is a position one can understand, given a few key facts."

Amara nodded. "I'm listening."

"First," Lady Aquitaine said, "assume that Kalarus does not trust her any farther than he can kick her, if it comes to that."

Amara frowned. "He has to."

"Why?"

"Because she's operating independently of him most of the time," Amara said. "Her role in the capital had her away from Kalarus for months at a time. She could have betrayed him, and he would never have known about it until long after."

"Precisely," Lady Aquitaine said. "And what might possibly compel her to perfect loyalty despite such opportunity, hmm?"

"I—" Amara began.

"What might compel her to deny potential clemency? To urge you to finish her as quickly as possible? To ask you to kill her outright from the very beginning?"

Amara shook her head. "I don't know. I take it you do."

Lady Aquitaine gave Amara a chill little smile. "One more

hint. Assume that she believes that she is being watched, by one measure or another. That if she turns against him, Kalarus will learn of it, and that regardless of how far away she is, he will be able to retaliate."

Amara felt her belly twist with nauseated horror as it dawned on her what Lady Aquitaine was speaking about. "He holds a hostage against her loyalty. Someone close to her. If she turns against him, he'll kill the hostage."

Lady Aquitaine inclined her head. "Behold our spy. A young woman. Unwed, I am certain, and without a family able to support or protect her. The hostage must be someone she is willing to die for—willing to face torture and agony for. My guess . . ."

"He has her child," Amara stated, her voice flat and cold.

Lady Aquitaine arched a brow. "You seem offended."

"Should I not be?" Amara asked. "Should not you?"

"Your own master is little different, Amara," Lady Aquitaine said. "Ask High Lord Atticus. Ask Isana her opinion on his decision to relocate her nephew to the Academy. And did you think he hasn't noticed your relationship with the good Count Bernard? Should your hand turn against him, Amara, do not think for a moment he would not use whatever he could to control you. He's simply more elegant and tasteful than to throw it in your face."

Amara stared steadily back at Lady Aquitaine. Then she said, in a quiet voice, "You are very wrong."

The High Lady's mouth curled into another cool little smile. "You are very young." She shook her head. "It is almost as though we live in two different Realms."

"I appreciate your insight into Kalarus's character—or rather the lack thereof. But what advantage does it give us?"

"The lever Kalarus uses," Lady Aquitaine said, "will serve you just as ably."

Amara's stomach turned in disgust. "No," she said.

Lady Aquitaine turned more fully to Amara. "Countess. Your sensibilities are useless to the rule of a realm. If that woman does not speak to you, your lord will fail to muster the support he needs to defend his capital, and whether or not he lives, his rule will be over. Thousands will die in battle. Food shipments will be delayed, destroyed. Famine. Disease. Tens of thousands will fall to them without ever being touched by a weapon."

"I know that," Amara spat.

"Then if you truly would prevent it, would protect this Realm you claim to serve, you must set your squeamishness aside and *make the difficult choice*." Her eyes almost glowed. "That is the *price* of power, Cursor."

Amara looked away from Lady Aquitaine and stared at the prisoner.

"I'll talk," she said finally, very quietly. "I'll cue you to show yourself to her."

Lady Aquitaine tilted her head to one side and nodded comprehension. "Very well."

Amara turned and went back over to the prisoner. "Rook," she said quietly. "Or should I call you Gaelle?"

"As you would. Both names are stolen."

"Rook will do, then," Amara said.

"Did you forget your knife?" the prisoner said. There was no life to the taunt.

"No knife," Amara said quietly. "Kalarus has abducted two women. You know who they are."

Rook said nothing, but something in the quality of her silence made Amara think that she did.

"I want to know where they have been taken," Amara said. "I want to know what security precautions are around them. I want to know how to free them and escape with them again."

A short breath, the bare specter of a laugh, escaped Rook's lips.

"Are you willing to tell me?" Amara asked.

Rook stared at her in silent scorn.

"I see," Amara said. She beckoned with one hand. "In that case, I'm going to leave."

Lady Aquitaine—and not Lady Aquitaine—stepped into the light of the circle of fire. Her form had changed, growing shorter, stockier, so that the dress she wore fit her badly. Her features had changed, skin and face and hair, to the perfect mirror of Rook's own face and body alike.

Rook's head snapped up. Her tortured face twisted into an expression of horror.

"I'll go for a walk outside," Amara continued in a quiet, remorseless voice. "Out in public. With her. Where everyone in the city might see. Where anyone Kalarus has watching will see us together."

Rook's face writhed between terror and agony, and she stared at Lady Aquitaine as if physically unable to remove her gaze. "No. Oh furies, *no*. Kill me. Just *end* it."

"Why?" Amara asked. "Why should I?"

"If I am dead, she will be nothing to him. He might only cast her out." Her voice dissolved into a ragged sob as she began to weep again. "She's only five. Please, she's only a little girl."

Amara took a deep breath. "What is her name, Rook?"

The woman suddenly sagged in the chains, wracked with broken, harsh sobs. "Masha," she grated. "Masha."

She pressed closer, seizing Rook by the hair and forcing her to lift her face, though the woman's eyes were now swollen, mostly closed. "Where is the child?"

"Kalare," sobbed the spy. "He keeps her next to his chambers. To remind me what he can do."

Amara steeled herself not to falter, and her voice rang on the stone walls. "Is that where they've taken the prisoners?"

Rook shook her head, but the gesture was a feeble one, an obvious lie. "No," she whispered. "No, no, no."

Amara held the spy's eyes and willed resolve into her own. "Do you know where they are? Do you know how I can get to them?"

Silence fell, but for Rook's broken sounds of grief and pain. "Yes," she said, finally. "I know. But I can't tell you. If you rescue them, he'll kill her." She shuddered. "Countess, please, it's her only chance. Kill me here. I can't fail her."

Amara released Rook's hair and stepped back from the prisoner. She felt sick. "Bernard," she said quietly, nodding at a bucket in the corner. "Give her some water."

The Count did, his expression remote and deeply troubled.

Rook made no sign that she noticed him, until he had actually lifted her head and used a ladle to pour some water between her lips. Then she drank with the mindless, miserable need of a caged beast.

Amara wiped the hand she'd touched the spy with upon her skirts, rubbing hard. Then she stepped outside and got the keys to the woman's shackles from the *legionare* on guard. As she stepped back into the cell, Lady Aquitaine touched her arm, her features returned to normal, her expression one of displeasure. "What do you think you are doing?"

Amara stopped in her tracks and met the High Lady's cold gaze in a sudden flash of confidence and steel-hard certainty.

Lady Aquitaine's eyebrows rose, startled. "What are you *doing*, girl?"

"I'm showing you the difference, Your Grace," she said. "Between my Realm. And yours."

Then she went to Rook and removed the shackles. Bernard caught the spy before she could collapse to the floor. Amara turned and summoned the *legionare*, then sent him to fetch a healer's tub and water to fill it.

Rook sat leaning weakly against Bernard's support. The spy stared up at Amara, expression mystified. "I don't understand," she said. "Why?"

"Because you're coming with us," Amara said quietly, and her voice sounded like a stranger's to her ear, certain and powerful. "We're going to Kalare. We're going to find them. We're going to find Lady Placidus and Atticus's daughter and your Masha. And we're going to take all of them away from that murderous slive."

Bernard shot a glance up at her, hazel eyes suddenly bright and somehow wolfish, glowing with a fierce and silent pride.

Rook only stared at her, as though she was a madwoman. "N-no . . . why would you . . . is this a trick?"

Amara knelt and took Rook's hand between hers, meeting her eyes. "I swear to you, Rook, by my honor that if you help us, I will do everything in my power to take your daughter safe away from him. I swear to you that I will lay down my own life before I let hers be lost."

Rook stared at her in silent shock.

Without ever looking away from the prisoner's eyes, Amara pressed her dagger into the spy's grasp, and lifted it so that Rook held the blade against Amara's throat. Then she dropped her hands slowly away from the weapon.

Bernard let out a short, sharp hiss, and she felt him tense. Then abruptly he relaxed again. She saw him nod at her out of the corner of her eye. Trusting her.

"I have given you my word," she said quietly to Rook. "If you do not believe me, take my life. If you wish to continue your service to your lord, take my life. Or come with me and help me take your daughter back."

"Why?" Rook demanded in a whisper. "Why would you do this?"

"Because it is right."

There was an endless, silent moment.

Amara faced Rook, calm and steady.

Then Amara's knife clattered to the stones. Rook let out a sob and collapsed against Amara, who caught her and supported her weight.

"Yes," Rook whispered. "I'll tell you anything. Do anything. Save her."

Amara nodded, lifting her eyes to Bernard. He laid his hand on Amara's hair for a moment, fingers warm and gentle. He smiled, and she felt her own smile rise to answer his.

"Your Grace," Amara said after a moment, looking up, "we need to depart at once. The guard should be bringing a healing tub. Could you please see to Rook's injury?"

Lady Aquitaine stared down at the three on the floor, her head tilted to one side, frowning as if faced with a mystifying silent theater performed by lunatics. "Of course, Countess," she said after a moment, her voice distant. "I am always glad to serve the Realm."

Tavi slept in a tent he shared with several other junior officers. In the middle of the night, unusual noises disturbed his rest, and a moment later Max shook him roughly awake. "Come on," Max ordered him in a low, growling whisper. "Move it."

Tavi rose, pulled on his tunic, grabbed up his boots, and followed Max out into the night. "Where are we going?" Tavi mumbled.

"To the captain's tent. Magnus sent me to get you," Max said. "Something's up." He nodded down another row of tents as they passed, and Tavi looked up to see other figures moving quietly through the night. Tavi recognized the shadowy profile of one of the Tribunes Tactica, and a few moments later, the ugly, rough features of Valiar Marcus, the First Spear, appeared from the night and fell in beside them.

"Marcus," Max muttered.

"Antillar," the First Spear said. "Subtribune Scipio."

Tavi abruptly stopped in his tracks, and looked up. The sky was overcast, making the night very dark, though the clouds were low and swift-moving. Thunder rumbled far in the distance. Through gaps in the cloud cover, the stars glowered down in sullen shades of crimson. "The stars," he said.

Max looked up and blinked. "Bloody crows."

The First Spear grunted without slowing his pace.

"What's happening?" Tavi asked him, catching up.

The First Spear let out a snort but said nothing, until they arrived together at the captain's tent. The senior officers were there, much as they had been on the day Tavi arrived. Magnus and Lorico were both there, and passing out mugs of strong tea to the officers as they arrived. Tavi took one, found a quiet spot against the wall of the tent, and drank the hot, slightly bitter tea while struggling to blink the sleep from his eyes. Gracchus was there, and looking hungover. Lady Antillus was at hand as well, seated with her hands folded in her lap, her expression distant and unreadable.

Tavi had begun to feel almost as though he could string several thoughts together into something resembling intelligence when Captain Cyril entered, immaculately groomed, fully armored, the picture of self-possessed command. The quiet murmurs of the sleepy officers came to a sudden halt.

"Gentlemen, Your Grace," Cyril murmured. "Thank you for coming so promptly." He turned to Gracchus. "Tribune Logistica. What is the status of the stores of standard-issue armor and weaponry?"

"Sir?" Gracchus said, blinking.

"The armor, Tribune," Cyril said in a rock-hard voice. "The swords."

"Sir," Gracchus said. He rubbed at his head. "Another thousand sets to go, perhaps. Inspections should be finished in another week."

"I see. Tribune, do you not have three junior officers to assist in inspections?"

Max let out a quiet, nasty little laugh from beside Tavi.

"What?" Tavi whispered.

"Legion justice is slow but sure. This is why the captain wanted you here," Max said. "Listen."

"Yes, sir," Gracchus mumbled.

"And in a month's time, you and your three assistants have been unable to complete this fundamental task. Why is that?"

Gracchus stared at him. "Sir, I was aware of no particular need. I had my officers working on several different—"

"Latrines?" Cyril asked in an arch tone. "Armor and sidearm inspections are to be completed by dawn, Tribune."

"B-but why?"

"Perhaps this isn't as important as your nightly binges at the Pavilion, Tribune," Cyril said in an acidic tone, "but captains appoint a Tribune Logistica because they like to make sure our *legionares* have armor and swords when they march to battle."

Electric silence gripped the room. Tavi felt his spine straighten in surprise.

"Finish the inspections, Tribune. You'll do them walking on the road if you must, but you *will* complete them. Dismissed." Cyril turned his attention from Gracchus to the rest of the room. "Word reached me moments ago. We are at war."

A low murmur of responses went through the officers in the tent.

"I have my orders. We are to proceed west to the town at the Elinarch. The bridge there is the only one over the entire western leg of the Tiber River. The First Aleran is to secure that bridge."

The officers murmured again, low and surprised.

The Tribune Auxiliarus, Cadius Hadrian, stepped forward. His voice was deep and very quiet. "Sir. What about the stars?"

"What about them?" Cyril asked.

"Do we know why they've changed color?"

"Tribune," Cyril said calmly, "stars do not concern the First Aleran. Our only concern is that bridge."

Which Tavi took to mean that Cyril had no idea, either.

Valiar Marcus took a step forward from his place against the tent's wall, and said, "Captain. With all due respect, sir, most of the fish aren't ready."

"I have my orders, First Spear," Cyril said. He looked around at the officers, and said, "And now you all have yours. You know your duties." He lifted his chin, and said, "We march at dawn."

◦◦◦◦◦ CHAPTER 18

When the stars burned red, the inhabitants of Westmiston did not panic so much as freeze in place, like a hare who senses a predator nearby.

Ullus had shaken Ehren from his sleep without a word, and

they had gone out of the bungalow to stare up in total silence. The other folk of Westmiston did the same. No one carried a light, as though afraid to be noticed by something looking down on them.

No one spoke.

Waves broke on the shore.

Wind stirred fitfully, restlessly.

The sullen light of the stars illuminated nothing. The shadows grew, their edges indistinct, and within the light all movement was veiled, blurred, making it difficult to tell the difference between stationary objects, living things, and the shadows themselves.

The sun rose the next morning, pure and golden for a few moments—but then it took on a sullen, sanguine hue. The colors of sunset looked bizarre with the light coming down from overhead, strong and bright. It was unsettling. Few folk moved about Westmiston. Those who did sought wine, rum, and ale. The captain of the only ship currently in the harbor was murdered in the street at noon, cut down by his own crew when he ordered them down to the harbor to set sail. The body lay untouched where it fell.

Sailors stared fearfully up at the sky, muttering darkly under their breaths and making superstitious gestures of warding and protection. Then they drank as much alcohol as possible, walking over their former captain's remains to enter the wine house.

Ullus stepped out of his bungalow to squint up at the sky, fists on his hips. "Bloody crows," he complained, his tone personally offended. "Everyone in the whole crowbegotten town is staying indoors. This could be bad for business."

Ehren set his pen down for a moment and rested his forehead on the edge of his desk. He bit back a dozen insulting replies and settled for a sigh before he went back to his writing, and said, "You may be right."

Someone began ringing the town's storm bell.

Ullus shook his head with disgust, stalked over to a cabinet, and jerked out a large bottle of cheap rum. "Go see what that fool of a watchman is on about now."

"Yes, sir," Ehren said, glad to be able to move. Like everyone else, except possibly Ullus, Ehren was worried about the portents in the sky, the haze of blood over sun and stars. Unlike everyone else, Ehren knew about the vast storms that the Canim had hurled at the western shores of Alera only a few years ago. Ehren knew that their ritualists were capable of great feats of power rivaling or surpassing the furycraft of the Realm.

And Ehren knew that an unscrupulous captain with no time to spare and a suspiciously large load of goods to sell had, three weeks and one day ago, sailed from Westmiston for the Canim homeland.

The bloody-hued sky was surely no natural event. If, as he suspected, it meant that the Canim were exerting their power again, and this time on a scale no one had dreamed they could manage, then business was going to be *very* bad in Westmiston—and anywhere else within sailing range of Canim raiders.

He finished the line he was working on—his notes, encoded in a cipher known only to the Cursors, rather than the books Ullus assumed he was balancing. He'd already prepared a summary of all that he had learned in the past months, and only the last several days' worth of observations needed to be added to the small, waterproof case at Ehren's belt.

He did so, then left the bungalow, jogging down toward the harbor at an easy pace. His footsteps sounded loud in the unusual silence of the islands. It did not take him long to see why the watchman had begun ringing the chimes—a ship had arrived in the harbor. It took him a moment to be sure, but when he saw Captain Demos on deck, he recognized the vessel as the *Slive*. She had come in under a strong wind and full sail, and her crewmen moved with the jerking haste of tired men with no time to spare.

A sudden gust of cold wind pushed at Ehren, and he peered out at the western horizon. There, far out over the sea, he could see a long line of darkness on the horizon. Storm clouds.

The *Slive* spent its incoming momentum on a sudden turn,

and her timbers shook and groaned. A bow wave pressed out ahead of the vessel, high enough to send a sheet of seawater over the quay, before the ship itself bellied up to the quay, already facing back to the west, toward the mouth of the harbor, ready to run for open water.

Ehren was suddenly very sure that he wanted off the island.

He headed on down to the harbor and went out along the rickety old quay to the *Slive*.

Two men loitering on deck with bows in hand took note of him as he did. Ehren slowed his steps cautiously as he approached the ship, and he stood well back from the gangplank as it was cast down.

Captain Demos was the first man onto the plank, and he gave Ehren a flat stare with nothing human in it but for an instant of recognition. He nodded, and said, "The fence's scribe."

"Yes, Captain," Ehren said with a bow of his head. "How may I serve you?"

"Take me to your master, and be quick." He whistled sharply without using his fingers, and half a dozen men dropped what they were doing and came down the gangplank after him. Each of the men, Ehren noted, was large, armed, and looked unfriendly. In point of fact, every single man aboard was armed, even as they readied the ship to depart again. There were even a few pieces of armor in evidence— mostly abbreviated chain shirts and sections of boiled leather.

That was hardly the normal state of affairs, even on a pirate vessel. Weaponry presented nothing but a hindrance to a sailor in the rigging. Wearing even light armor on a ship was all but a death sentence should one fall into the sea. No sailor, pirate or otherwise, would don such gear without a compelling reason.

Ehren found Captain Demos staring at him with an unnerving amount of intensity and no expression on his face. His hand rested negligently on the hilt of his sword. "Question, scribe?"

Ehren looked up at Demos, sensing that he was in immediate danger. He bowed his head carefully, and said, "No, sir. It is no business of mine."

Demos nodded, and lifted his hand from his sword to gesture for Ehren to precede them. "Remember it."

"Yes, Captain. This way, sir."

Ehren led Demos and his men up to Ullus's bungalow. The fence came out to meet them, wearing a rusted old *gladius* through his belt, his face set in a scowl made fearless by drink. "Good day, Captain."

"Fence," Demos said, his tone flat. "I am here for my money."

"Ah," Ullus said. He looked at Demos's armed escort and narrowed his eyes. "Well as I said, sir, three weeks was hardly time enough in which to liquidate your articles."

"And as I said. You will pay me in cash for anything not sold."

"I wish I had enough to afford it," Ullus said. "But I don't have access to such a great amount of coin in this season. If you come back to me in the autumn, I should have more available."

Demos was silent for a moment. Then he said, "I regret it when business deals do not work out—but I made my position clear, fence. And whatever kind of snake you may be, my word is good." He turned his head to his men, and said, "Cut his throat."

Ullus's sword came to his hand readily enough, out before any of Demos's armsmen drew. "That might not be as easy as you think," he said. "And it will profit you nothing. My coin is hidden. Kill me, and you will not see a copper ram of it."

Demos lifted a hand, and his men stopped in their tracks. He stared at Ullus for a second, then said, "Bloody crows, man. You really are that stupid. I thought it was an act."

"Stupid?" Ullus said. "Not so stupid that I'd let you run roughshod over me on my own island."

Ehren remained very still, over to one side, where he might duck behind the bungalow should weaponplay commence. He felt the wind change quite suddenly. The fitful, restless breeze that had danced idly around the island for all of that day vanished. Something like the breath of some single, enormous beast rushed across the island in a single, enormous moan. The wind rose so suddenly that the pennons on the banner poles on the harbor snapped, their tips cracking like whips as the wind, hot and damp, sent the banners streaming to the horizon.

Demos's attention flicked to the wind banners, and his eyes narrowed.

Some instinct cried out to him, and Ehren turned to Demos. "Captain," he said. "In the interest of saving time, I have an offer for you."

"Shut up, slave," growled Ullus.

Demos glanced aside at Ehren, his eyes flat.

"I know where his coin is hidden," Ehren said. "Grant me passage to the mainland, and I'll show you where it is."

Ullus whirled on Ehren in a fury. "Who do you think you are, you greasy little tosspot? Hold your tongue." He brandished the rusty sword. "Or I will."

"Captain?" Ehren pressed. "Have we a bargain?"

Ullus let out a cry of pure rage and rushed at Ehren, sword rising.

Ehren's small knife appeared from its hiding place in his tunic's roomy sleeve. He waited until the last moment for Ullus's strike, and then slipped aside from it by the width of a hair. His knife struck out, a single stroke that left a cut two inches long and almost as deep.

Ullus's throat sprayed blood. The ragged fence collapsed to the ground like a groggy drunk abruptly sure that it was time for a nap.

Ehren stared down at the man for a moment, regret sharp in him. Ullus was a fool, a liar, a criminal, and he'd doubtless done more than his share of despicable deeds in his time—but even so, Ehren had not wanted to kill him. But if Ehren's instincts were correct, he'd had little choice. It was imperative that he leave the island, and Demos was his only way out.

He turned to Demos and leaned down to wipe the blade of his little knife clean on the back of Ullus's tunic. "It would seem that your own arrangement with Ullus has been resolved in accordance with your terms. Have we a new bargain, Captain?"

Demos stared at Ehren, with neither more nor less expression on his face than before. He looked briefly at Ullus's body. "It would seem I have little choice if I am to collect my coin."

"That's true enough," Ehren agreed. "Captain, please. I have a sense that we do not wish to stand around talking about this all day."

Demos's teeth showed in an expression that was not a smile. "Your technique is sound, Cursor."

"I don't know what you mean, sir."

Demos grunted. "They never do. Passage is one thing. Involving myself in more politics is another."

"And more expensive?" Ehren asked.

"Commensurate with the risk. Dead men spend no coin."

Ehren nodded once, sharply. "And your own loyalties, sir?"

"Negotiable."

"Ullus's coin," Ehren said. "And a like amount upon return to Alera."

"Double the amount on return," Demos said. "Cash, no vouchers or letters of marque. You're buying passage, not command of my vessel. And I'll have your word not to go out of my sight until paid in full."

Ehren tilted his head. "My word? Would you trust it?"

"Break it," Demos said, "and the Cursors will hunt you down for sullying their business reputation."

"True enough," Ehren said, "if I worked for them. Done."

Demos jerked his head in a nod. "Done. What do I call you?"

"Scribe."

"Take me to the coin, scribe." He turned to one of his men. "We set sail at once. Get a slave detail and take any women or children you can see on the way back."

The men nodded and started back to the harbor. Demos turned to find Ehren frowning at him. "We'd best move."

Ehren jerked a nod at him and led him to the back of the bungalow, where Ullus thought he'd built a clever hiding place into the woodpile. Ehren recovered the entirety of Ullus's cash fortune in a leather sack and tossed it to Demos.

The captain opened the sack and dumped some of its contents onto his palm. They were a mix of coins of all sorts, mainly copper rams and silver bulls, but with the occasional gold crown mixed in. Demos nodded and headed back for the ship. Ehren followed, walking on the man's left, a stride away, where he would have time and room to dodge should the pirate draw his sword.

Demos seemed briefly amused. "If I wished to be rid of you, scribe, I wouldn't need to kill you. I'd leave you here."

"Call it a professional courtesy," Ehren said. "You aren't a smuggler or a pirate."

"I am today," Demos said.

Armed members of the *Slive*'s crew rushed past. Behind them, Ehren heard screams as the men began seizing women and children and shackling them.

"And a slaver, too," Ehren said, trying to keep his tone calm. "Why?"

"This most recent enterprise has ended in a less-than-satisfactory fashion. I'll sell them when we reach the mainland and defray some of my expenses," Demos said. He glanced out to the west, as they headed down the quay, his eyes on the rising blackness of the storm there.

After that, Demos fell silent until they boarded the *Slive*. Then he began to give orders immediately, and Ehren hastened to stand out of the way. The slave patrol brought in a score of chained prisoners, while several other men fought a brief, ugly brawl with inhabitants of Westmiston who objected. A pirate was slain, the townsfolk beaten back with half a dozen dead. The women and children passed within a step of Ehren when the slavers hurried them into the hold, and he felt nauseated at their distress, their sobs, their cries of protest.

Perhaps he could find some way to help them when they returned to Alera. He folded his arms, closed his eyes, and tried not to think on it, while Demos and his crew rigged the ship and headed for the harbor, tacking against the strong wind while men strained at the oars to give the ship all possible speed while the darkness of the storm grew and grew, until it looked like nothing so much as great mountains looming up on the horizon. It was unnerving, as every sailor aboard the *Slive* threw his strength into driving the ship directly at that glowering, ominous tide of shadow, until they could clear the harbor and round the island.

They had just broken into the open sea when Ehren saw what his instincts had warned him about.

Ships.

Hundreds of ships.

Hundreds of enormous ships, broad and low-beamed, sailing in formation, their vast, black sails stretched tight and full by the gale sweeping along behind them. The horizon, from one end to the other, was filled with black sails.

"The Canim," Ehren whispered.

The Canim were coming in numbers more enormous than any in Alera's history.

Ehren felt his legs turn weak, and he leaned against the *Slive*'s railing for support, staring out at the armada plunging toward them. Distantly, in Westmiston, he could hear the storm chimes ringing in panic. He turned to see the drunken, disorganized crew of the other ship rushing down to the docks—but at the speed the Canim fleet was moving, they would never escape the harbor before they were cut off by black sails.

The *Slive* rounded the northernmost point of the island of Westmiston, and her crew adjusted the rigging for running before the wind instead of into it. Within minutes, the Aleran vessel's grey canvas sails boomed and stretched tight before the dark storm's windy vanguard, and the *Slive* leapt into the open sea.

Ehren paced slowly aftward, until he stood staring off the *Slive*'s stern. Ships detached themselves from the Canim fleet and fell upon Westmiston, wolves to the fold.

Ehren looked up to find Demos standing beside him.

"The women and children," Ehren said quietly.

"As many as we could carry," Demos said.

Smoke began to rise from Westmiston.

"Why?" Ehren asked.

Demos regarded the Canim fleet with dispassionate calculation. "Why let them go to waste? They'll fetch a fair price."

The man's lack of expression, whether in word, movement, or deed, was appalling. Ehren folded his arms to hide a shiver. "Will they catch us?"

Demos shook his head. "Not my ship." He lifted a hand abruptly and pointed out to sea.

Ehren peered. There, between the *Slive* and the oncoming armada, a sudden wave rose directly up from the sea, against the flow of the others. Ehren could hardly believe what he was seeing, until water began to break around the massive shape that had risen from the sea. He could see few details, from this distance, but the black, enormous shape that stirred the surface would have stood taller than the *Slive*'s sails.

"Leviathan," he breathed. "That's a leviathan."

"Little bit shy of medium size," Demos agreed. "They're territorial. Those Canim ships have been stirring them up as they passed for the last ten days."

A deep, booming thrum ran through the water, so powerful that the surface of the churning sea vibrated with it, tossing up fine spray. The ship shook around them, and Ehren clearly heard a plank give way and snap somewhere below them.

"Damage party, starboard aft!" Demos bellowed.

"What was that?" Ehren breathed. The soles of his feet felt odd, aftershocks of the vibration still buzzing against them.

"Leviathan complaining," Demos said. He glanced at Ehren, and one corner of his mouth might have twitched for a second. "Relax, scribe. I've two witchmen below. They'll keep us from bothering the leviathans."

"And the Canim?"

"We've seen four ships smashed, but it hasn't slowed them down. There, look."

The vast shape in the water moved for a moment, toward the armada, but then descended, water crashing into its wake, swirling in a vortex for a time even after the leviathan dived. By the time the first Canim ship reached the spot, there was nothing but a restless remnant of the enormous beast's presence, a rough-stirred sea. The Canim ship broached it, spray flying, and held its course.

"Say this much. Those dogs don't have a yellow bone in

them," Demos murmured, eyes distant. "All but the biggest leviathans get out of the way of that storm coming behind the Canim. They'll take a few more losses on the way over, but they'll get through."

"You were carrying a message to them?" Ehren asked.

"That's no business of yours," Demos said.

"It is if you're complicit with them, Captain. Did they simply let you escape them?"

"Didn't *let* me," Demos said. "But then I didn't give them much choice in the matter. They weren't as sneaky as they thought they were. Crows'll go hungry before I let some mangy dog-priest stick a knife in my spine."

"Priest?" Ehren asked.

Demos grunted. "Robes, books, scrolls. Talks a lot of nonsense. Name was Sarl."

Sarl. Formerly the chamberlain to Ambassador Varg at the capital—and the creature who had plotted with the Vord to strike down the First Lord. Sarl, who had escaped from Alera, despite all the efforts of the Legions and lords to find and stop him. Sarl, who, Ehren was now sure, must have had help inside of Alera.

"Kalarus," Ehren murmured.

Demos sent Ehren's earlier words back at him, imitating the scribe's inflection. "I don't know what you mean, sir."

Ehren studied the man for a moment, sure that the overt denial held covert confirmation. If so, then Demos had been hired by Kalarus to take a message to the Canim—who had promptly attempted to kill him before he could escape. Obviously, Demos had no intentions of participating with the authorities by way of retribution—that kind of criminal seldom found others willing to do business with them down the line. But he must have been angered by the betrayal, enough to let Ehren obliquely learn who had hired him and what was happening.

"You know what this means," Ehren said, shaking his head. "A messenger. This armada. It's war, Captain. And you are not the only one who has been betrayed."

Demos stared aft and said nothing. The darkness that was

the storm driving the Canim armada swallowed the island of Westmiston entirely.

Ehren turned to face Demos. "I'll triple the amount of your pay if you get us back to Alera in time enough to warn the Legions. No questions asked."

The mercenary glanced at him, silent for a long moment. Then his teeth showed again, and he nodded, very slightly, to Ehren. "Bosun!"

"Aye, skipper?"

"Reinforce the mainmast, hang out all the laundry, and warn the witchmen! Let's make the old bitch fly!"

ᗢᗢᗢᗢ CHAPTER 19

Isana opened her eyes and thought she was going to faint. Septimus, with his usual delicate, precise touch, had slipped a ring onto her finger so lightly that she had not felt him doing it.

The band looked like silver, but was so delicately wrought that she could barely feel its weight. The setting was of a pair of eagles, facing one another, supporting the jewel upon their forward-swept wings. The stone itself was cut into a slender diamond shape, but the gem was like nothing Isana had ever seen, brilliant red and azure, divided precisely down the center without any detectable seam.

"Oh," she breathed quietly. She felt her eyes bulging, her cheeks growing pink. "Oh. Oh, my."

Septimus let out a quiet laugh, and she could sense his pleasure at her reaction, and Isana felt that same surge of joy well up inside her, just as it had the first time she had heard his laugh. Her mouth failed her, and she only sat, staring up at Septimus, drinking in his features. Dark hair, intense green eyes, tall, strong. He was so handsome, his expressive face able to convey volumes of meaning without speaking at all, and his voice was low, rich, strong.

They sat together on a spread blanket at the shore of the little lake near the Legion garrison in the Calderon Valley, under the harvest moon. They had taken their meal together there, as they had so many times since the spring, feeding one another and speaking quietly, laughing, kissing.

He had asked her to close her eyes, and Isana had complied, sure that he was about to show her some new jest.

Instead, he had slipped a ring bearing all the marks of the House of Gaius onto her left ring finger.

"Oh, Septimus," Isana breathed. "Don't say it."

He laughed again. "My love, how could I not?" He reached out and took both of her hands in his. "I cursed my father when he sent the Legion all the way out here," he said quietly. "But I never thought I would meet someone like you. Someone strong and intelligent and beautiful. Someone . . ." He smiled a little, and it made his face look boyish. "Someone I can trust. Someone I want to stand beside me, always. I can't take the chance that I might lose you if the Legion is ordered elsewhere, my love." He lifted her hand and kissed it. "Marry me, Isana. Please."

The world started spinning in wild circles, but Isana could not take her eyes away from the only stable thing in it— Septimus, his eyes bright and intense in the moonlight.

"Your f-father," Isana said. "I'm not even a Citizen. He would never allow it."

Septimus flicked an irritated glance in the general direction of the capital. "Don't worry about that. I'll deal with Father. Marry me."

"But he would never accept it!" Isana breathed.

Septimus shrugged and smiled. "The shock will be good for him, and he'll get over it. Marry me."

Isana blinked, shocked. "He's the First Lord!"

"And I am the Princeps," Septimus said. "But our titles don't really come into it. He may be the First Lord, but he is also my father, and great furies know that we've locked horns more than once. Marry me."

"But it could cause you such trouble," Isana pressed.

"Because Father seeks to preserve the old ways, my love." He leaned toward her, eyes bright and intent. "He does not see that the time is coming when those ways must change—when they must make Alera a better place for everyone—not just for Citizens. Not just for those who have power enough to take what they want. The Realm must change." His eyes blazed, conviction and passion suffusing his voice. "When I become First Lord, I'm going to be a part of that change. And I want you with me while I do it."

Then he moved, pressed Isana gently down to the blanket, and kissed her mouth. Isana's shock was transformed into a sudden hurricane of delight and need, and she felt her body melt and move, pressing sinuously against his as he kissed her, his mouth soft, strong, hungry, searing hot. She had no idea how long the kiss went on, but when their lips finally parted, Isana felt as if she was on fire, burning from the inside out. The need was so great that she could barely focus her eyes.

His mouth slid over her throat, then pressed a slow, tingling kiss against the skin covering her fluttering pulse. He lifted his head slowly, and met her eyes with his own. "Marry me, Isana," he said quietly.

She felt an answering need in Septimus, the feral call of the flesh, the rising tide of his passion, the warmth and the love he felt for her—and then she saw something else in his eyes. There, just for an instant, was a flutter of uncertainty and fear.

Septimus was afraid. Afraid that she would say no.

It nearly broke Isana's heart, just seeing the potential for his grief. She lifted a hand to touch his face. She would never hurt him, never bring him pain. Never.

And he loved her. He loved her. She could feel it in him, a bedrock of affection that had grown and grown and grown, answered by the same in Isana.

She felt her eyes blur with tears at the same time she let out a breathless burst of laughter. "Yes," she said. "Yes."

A surge of Septimus's joy flowed into her, and she flung herself onto him, rolling him onto his back so that she could *kiss him, face and throat and hands, to taste him, to drink in the warmth and beauty of him. Reason disintegrated under the joy, under the need, and Isana's hands moved as if of their own will, tearing open his tunic so that she could run her hands and nails and mouth over the tight muscle beneath it.*

Septimus let out an agonized moan, and she felt his hips surge up against hers, felt the hot hardness of him pressed against her so tightly that she thought they might simply burst into flame together.

He seized her face between his hands and forced her eyes to his. Isana saw everything she'd already felt in them, saw how much he wanted to simply let go, give in to the moment. "Are you sure?" he said, his voice a growling whisper. "You've never done this. Are you sure you want this now?"

She couldn't trust her lips to answer, her tongue to function. They were far too intent upon returning to his skin. So she sat up and stared down at him, panting, mouth open, and dug her fingernails into his chest while arching her back, pushing her hips back and down against him, a slow, torturous motion.

Septimus could feel her, just as she could him. Words were neither needed nor wanted. His eyes glazed over with hunger and need, and he lifted her and pressed her down again, savagely took another kiss from her open, willing lips. His hand slid up one of her legs, brushing skirts aside, and there was suddenly nothing in her entire world but passion, sensation, pleasure.

And Septimus.

They lay in one another's arms much later, the moon now settling down, though dawn was nowhere near. Isana could hardly believe what was happening to her. Her arms tightened on Septimus in languorous wonder, feeling the warmth of him, the strength of him, the beauty of him.

He opened his eyes slowly, smiling at her the way he smiled at nothing and no one else, and it made Isana feel deliciously smug, delighted.

She closed her eyes and nuzzled her face into his chest. "My lord, my love."

"*I love you, Isana,*" he said.

The truth of it rang in Isana's heart. She felt it between them, flowing like a river, running endlessly through both. "I love you," she whispered, and shivered in pure delight. "This is . . . this is like a dream. I'm terrified that if I open my eyes, all of this will be gone, and I'll find myself in my cot."

"*I couldn't bear it if this wasn't real,*" *Septimus murmured into her hair. "Best you stay asleep then."*

Isana opened her eyes and found herself in a strange bed-chamber.

Not in the moonlight.

Not young.

Not in love.

Not with him.

Septimus.

She'd had the dream before—memories, really, perfectly preserved, like a flower frozen in a block of ice. They made the dream so real that she could never remember, while it happened, that she was dreaming.

It hurt just as much to awake from the dream as it had all the times before. Slow, slow agony pierced her, taunted her with what might have been and never would be. It was pure torment—but to see him again, to touch him again, was worth the pain.

She didn't weep. She was long since past the tears. She knew the memories would fade before morning, washed away into pale ghosts of themselves. She just held on to those images as tightly as she could.

The door opened, and Isana looked up to find her brother leaning in the doorway. Bernard entered at once, strode to her bedside, and gave her a warm smile.

She tried to smile back. "Bernard," she said in a weary voice. "At some point, I would like a few weeks to go by in which I do not faint during a crisis."

Her brother leaned down and enfolded her in a vast hug. "Things will settle down again," he told her. "Lord Cereus says it's because your watercrafting is so strong, without being complemented by enough metalcraft to endure your own empathy."

"Lord Cereus," Isana said. "Is that where I am?"

"Yes," her brother answered. "In his guest quarters. Cereus has offered the hospitality of his citadel to the Citizen refugees trapped here."

Isana lifted both her eyebrows. "Trapped? Bernard, what is happening?"

"War," Bernard said shortly. "Lord Kalarus marches on Ceres with his forces. There will shortly be battle joined here."

"The fool." Isana shook her head. "I take it there is not time to leave?"

"Not safely," Bernard said. "You were particularly targeted by the assassins who attacked the restaurant, and there are agents of Kalare in the city and advance forces already in the area. You're safest here. Giraldi will stay here with you, as will Fade."

Isana sat bolt upright. "Fade. He's here, in Ceres."

Bernard hooked a thumb over his shoulder. "In the hall, in fact. And armed. And I've never seen *anyone* fight like he did." Bernard shook his head. "I always thought him just a disgraced *legionare*."

"Why is he here?" Isana demanded. "Why is he not with Tavi?"

Bernard blinked mildly at her. "Tavi? I know Gaius took Fade to the capital to serve as a slave in the Academy . . ." His frown deepened. "'Sana? You're upset . . ."

Isana forced herself to set aside the rising sense of panic, smoothing her expression back to calm. "I'm sorry . . . I'm just so . . . I'll be all right, Bernard."

"You're sure?" Bernard said. "'Sana, I . . . well, when you told me to buy Fade, I did it. Never asked you why. I was sure you had your reasons, but . . ." A heavy silence fell, and Bernard asked, "Is there anything you should tell me?"

Isana dared not meet her brother's eyes. "Not yet."

Bernard frowned at the answer.

Before he could ask another question, Isana nodded at

Bernard's working clothes, his woodland cloak. "Where are you going?"

He hesitated for a moment and gave her a lopsided smile. "Can't say," Bernard said. "Not yet. Mission."

"What mission?" Isana asked. She tilted her head to one side and then said, "Ah, I see. Amara's mission."

Bernard nodded, somewhat sheepishly. "Yes."

"She makes you happy, doesn't she."

Her younger brother's face spread into a little smile. "Yes."

As Isana had Septimus. A little pang went through her, but she covered it with a smile. "From the rumors I've heard," Isana added drily, "*very* happy."

"*Isana,*" Bernard rumbled, his face flushed.

Isana let her lips curl around a small silent chuckle. "Leaving soon, I take it?"

"Before it gets light. I was about to go," he said. "I was hoping you'd wake first."

"Will you . . ." She frowned. "Is it . . ."

He smiled at her and touched her shoulder again. "I'll be fine. I'll tell you all about it when we get back."

She could feel Bernard's confidence and honesty, through his touch on her shoulder, but she also felt uncertainty and fear. Though her brother was not in fear of his life, or ruled by his trepidations, he knew full well that he was going into danger and that nothing in the future was certain.

There was a knock at the door, and Giraldi opened it and stuck his head in. "Your Excellency," he said. "Your skinny Countess just blew past on her way to the tower. Said you should catch up."

Bernard nodded sharply, then turned and gave his sister another, tighter hug. Isana knew that her ribs weren't really about to collapse, as she had endured many such embraces from Bernard in the past, but she finally made a sound of complaint and pushed at him. It was, she sometimes thought, the only way he knew when to stop.

"Giraldi will be with you," he said. "Love you."

"And I you," Isana said. "Good luck."

Bernard bent down and kissed her forehead, then rose, leaving. "Take good care of her, centurion."

"Go teach yer grandmother to suck eggs," Giraldi muttered, winking at Isana.

"What?" Bernard called over his shoulder.

"Sir!" Giraldi answered. "Yes, sir."

"Terrible," Isana murmured. "The lack of discipline in today's Legions."

"Shocking," the veteran concurred. "Steadholder, you in need of anything? Victuals, drink?"

"Some privacy first," Isana said. "Then something simple?"

"I'll find it," Giraldi said.

"Centurion. If you would, please send Fade to speak to me."

Giraldi paused by the door and grunted. "That scarred slave? The one-man Legion?"

Isana stared at him for a moment, saying nothing.

"Seems kind of odd, old Fade would be out there at your steadholt all those years, and never saw him use so much as a knife. Figured all those scars on his arms were from working his smithy. Then tonight, he just went through those maniacs like they was made of cobwebs. Sort of makes a body wonder who he is."

Isana folded her arms, one finger tapping in slight impatience, and said nothing.

"Hngh," Giraldi grunted, limping out. "The plot thickens."

Fade entered a few moments later. He was still dressed in the simple, blood-sprinkled smock of a scullion, though he wore a Legion-issue sword belt and his old blade at his side. He had acquired a worn, old cloak of midnight blue, and wore the military boots of a *legionare*. A bloody rag was tied crudely around his left hand, but if the wound caused him pain, he showed no sign of it.

Fade shut the door behind him and turned to face Isana.

"Tavi?" she asked quietly.

Fade took a steadying breath. "On assignment. Gaius has him in the field."

Isana felt the first flutterings of panic. "Gaius knows?"

"I believe so," Fade said quietly.

"Tavi is alone?"

Fade shook his head, letting his long hair fall forward over his face, as usual, hiding much of his expression. "Antillar Maximus is with him."

"Maximus. The boy whose life Tavi had to save? *Twice?*"

Fade didn't lift his face, but his voice hardened. "The young man who twice proved his loyalty to his friend and the Realm. Maximus laid down his life to protect Tavi against the son of a High Lord. You cannot ask more than that of anyone."

"I don't deny his willingness to lay down his life," Isana retorted. "It is his *aptitude* for it that concerns me. Great furies, Araris, Antillar has *practice* at it."

"Lower your voice, my lady," Fade said, his tone warning and gentle at the same time.

She never understood how he could do that. Isana shook her head tiredly. "Fade," she corrected herself, "I'm not your lady."

"As milady wishes," Fade said.

She frowned at him, then dismissed the argument with an idle throwaway gesture of one hand. "Why didn't you stay with him?"

"My presence would have drawn attention to him," Fade said. "Gaius has inserted him into the newly formed Alcran Legion." He gestured at the horrible brand on his face, the coward's mark of a soldier who had fled combat. "I could not have remained nearby him. If I had to fight, it is probable that someone would recognize me, and it would raise a great many questions about why one of Princeps Septimus's *singulares*, supposedly dead for twenty years, was guarding the young man."

"Gaius didn't have to send him there," Isana insisted. "He wanted to isolate him. He wanted to make him vulnerable."

"He wanted," Fade disagreed, "to keep him out of the public eye and in a safe location."

"By putting him into a Legion," Isana said, her disbelief heavy in her tone. "At the eruption of a civil war."

Fade shook his head. "You aren't thinking it through, my lady," he said. "The First Alcran is the one Legion that will *not* see action in a civil war. Not with so many of its troops and officers owing loyalties to cities, lords, and family houses on both sides of the struggle. Further, it has been forming in the western reaches of the Amaranth Vale, far from any fighting, and it would not surprise me to learn that Gaius issued orders to send it even farther west, away from the theater of combat."

Isana frowned and folded her hands on her lap. "Are you sure he's safe?"

"Nowhere would be totally safe," Fade said in a quiet tone. "But now he is hidden among a mass of thousands of men dressed precisely like him, who will not enter combat against any of the High Lords' Legions, and who have been conditioned by training and tradition to protect their own. He's accompanied by young Maximus, who is more dangerous with a blade than any other man his age I've seen—save my lord himself—and a crafter of formidable power. Knowing Gaius, there are more agents nearby about whom I was told nothing."

Isana folded her arms in close to her body. "Why did you come here?"

"The Crown had received intelligence that you had been personally targeted by Kalare."

"The Crown," she said, "and everyone else who was at that Wintersend party, and the servants and anyone they might have spoken to, or who might have heard rumors."

"More specific," Fade said. "He asked me to watch over you. I agreed."

She tilted her head, frowning. "He asked?"

Fade shrugged. "My loyalty is not Gaius Sextus's to command, and he knows it."

She felt herself smile at him a little. "I can't trust him. I can't trust any of them. Not with Tavi."

Fade's expression never changed, but Isana felt a flash of something in the scarred slave she never had before—an instant of anger. "I know you only seek to protect him. But you do Tavi a grave disservice. He is more formidable and capable than you know."

Isana blinked her eyes. "Fade—"

"I've seen it," Fade continued. That same sense of anger in

him kept on rising. "Seen him act under pressure. He's more capable than most men, regardless of their skill with furies. And it's more than that . . ."

Isana wrenched her thoughts from her worries and really looked at the scarred man. His skin was too pale, blotchy with patches of red and glistening with a cold sweat. His eyes were dilated, and his pulse fluttered fast and hard in his throat and upon one temple.

"He makes those around him be more than they are," Fade snarled. "Makes them be better than they are. More than they thought they could be. Like his father. Bloody crows, like the father I left to *die* . . ."

Fade suddenly lifted his wounded hand and stared at it. He was trembling violently and there were flecks of white on his lips. He blinked in utter bafflement at his quivering hand, opened his mouth as though to speak, then jerked in a convulsive spasm that threw him onto the floor in a violent seizure. Seconds went by as he kicked and thrashed, then he let out a soft groan and simply went limp.

"Fade!" Isana breathed and pushed herself from the bed. The world pitched about, then left her on the floor. She did not have strength enough to stand, but she crawled on all fours to the fallen man's side, reaching out to touch his throat, to feel his pulse.

She could not find it.

⬦⬦⬦⬦⬦ CHAPTER 20

Isana thrust her hand down at Fade's chest, calling out to Rill to let her perceive the fallen man's body through a water-fury's senses. In the wake of her collapse, the effort was simply too much. Isana's head felt as if it would burst asunder in an explosion of pure agony, and her own heart labored in a sudden panic as she lost the strength to remain upright.

She let out a weak cry of purest frustration, then gritted her teeth and focused. Giving vent to her emotions would not help the stricken man beside her.

"Help!" she called. It sounded pathetically quiet, and she was sure the sound would not carry past the closed wooden door. She struggled to draw a deep breath and tried again. "I need help in here! Healer!"

At the second cry, the door slammed open, and Giraldi took one look around the room and spat a vile curse, limping badly as he rushed to Isana's side. "Steadholder!"

"Not me," she told him, weak and frustrated. "Fade collapsed. Not breathing. Healer."

The old centurion nodded sharply and rose to rush from the room at a pace that was surely dangerous to his crippled leg. He called out down the hall, and footsteps came running. Guards appeared, first, and within a minute they had escorted a young woman in a simple white gown into the room.

She was a pale creature, her skin so white that it almost seemed translucent, and her hair—quite short, for such a young woman—light and fine as cobwebs. Isana felt certain that her youth was genuine and not the result of watercrafting talent, though why she felt so Isana could not say. The healer's eyes seemed too large for her long, thin, somehow sad face, and were of a brown so dark that they looked black. The circles of weariness beneath her eyes stood out almost as vividly as violent bruises, and she carried herself with the brisk, sure manner of confidence Amara would only have expected in someone years older.

The young woman went to Fade at once and knelt to place her fingertips on his temples, her manner competent, professional, if somewhat weary. "Steadholder," she said, as she concentrated on her own furycraft, her eyes closed, "can you tell me what happened to him?"

"He collapsed," Isana said. Giraldi returned, and she was torn between a surge of gratitude and one of embarrassment as he simply hefted her back into her bed. "His conversation began to ramble. He was shaking. Then he fell down into a fit. He stopped breathing, and I couldn't find his pulse."

"How long ago?"

"Not two minutes."

The young woman nodded. "There's a chance, then." She raised her voice until it carried like a trumpet, ringing off the walls with a volume worthy of a centurion on a battlefield. "Where is my tub?!"

A trio of groaning young *legionares* came through the door bearing a heavy healing tub, sloshing water over its edges. They plunked it down even as the young healer divested Fade of his cloak, sword belt, and boots. At a nod from her, the guards in the room lifted his limp body into the tub.

The healer knelt behind the tub and placed her hands on Fade's head. "Step back," she said, in a tone that suggested she said it often. The guards hastily withdrew from the tub and out of the room. At a nod from Isana, Giraldi went with them.

The healer was silent for several seconds, her head bowed, and Isana had to restrain herself from shouting for the girl to hurry. Then the air in the room began to tighten, somehow, an odd sensation, like an unseen wind pressing against Isana's skin. The healer's fine hairs began to lift, one by one, away from her head, as if carried in a gentle updraft, though Isana could feel no air moving. She was still for a moment, then breathed out in a murmur, and what looked like tiny flickers of lightning played over the tub.

Fade reacted violently, body suddenly arching up, drawn as tightly as one of Bernard's hunting bows. He stayed that way for a moment, then subsided into the tub again and started coughing, a wet and fitful sound.

Isana's heart leapt up as the slave breathed again.

The healer frowned more intently, and Isana saw the water begin to stir in the tub, as it did when she worked her own healing furycraft, though only for a moment. Then the healer grimaced and lifted her hands from Fade's head. She moved around the tub and lifted his wounded hand. She unbound the kerchief wrapped around it and leaned down, sniffing. She drew her head away in a sharp little motion, turning her face away from the injury, then lowered his hand into the water.

"What is it?" Isana asked.

"Garic-oil poisoning," the young woman said.

"What's that?" Isana asked.

"Many weapon merchants in the southland preserve their weapons with an oil mixture that includes a tincture made from the oil in the hides of garim lizards."

"And it's poisonous?" Isana asked.

"Not always intentionally. But if the oil isn't mixed correctly, or if it's left out too long, the garic oil turns. Goes rotten. If it's on a weapon that inflicts a wound, the rot gets into the blood." She shook her head and rose. "I'm very sorry."

Isana blinked. "But . . . you healed him. He's breathing."

"For now," the healer said quietly. "Your friend is a metalcrafter, I take it?"

"Yes."

"Wounded during the attacks?"

"Defending me," Isana said quietly. "An arrow. It struck his hand."

The healer shook her head. "He must have been suppressing the discomfort. If he'd gotten to a healer within the hour, perhaps . . ."

Isana stared at her in disbelief. "What will happen?"

"Fever. Disorientation. Pain. Eventual loss of consciousness." The young healer grimaced. "It isn't quick. Days. But if he has family, you should send for them." She looked up at Isana, her dark eyes steady and sad. "I'm sorry," she said quietly.

Isana shook her head slowly. "Is there nothing to be done?"

"It has been healed, betimes. But it takes days, and most who try it die with the victim."

"You are not able to attempt it?" Isana asked.

The healer was still for a moment, then said, "I will not."

"Great furies," Isana breathed quietly. "Why not?"

"Legions march on my father's city, Steadholder. Battle will be joined. Men will be wounded and needed to return to the fight. If I'm attempting to heal him, it will mean the deaths of dozens or hundreds of my father's *legionares*." She shook her head. "My duty is clear."

"You're Cereus's daughter?" Isana asked.

The young healer smiled a little, though there was little joy or life in it, and dipped her head into a small bow. "Aye. Cereus Felia Veradis, Steadholder."

"Veradis," Isana said. She looked at the wounded man. "Thank you for helping him."

"Don't thank me," Veradis said.

"May I ask a favor of you?" Isana said.

The young woman nodded her head once.

"I would like a healing tub brought in here, please."

Veradis's eyebrows rose. "Steadholder, I am told your healing skills are impressive, but you are in no condition to attempt such a crafting."

"I believe I am a better judge of such things than you," Isana said quietly.

"My experience suggests that you aren't," Veradis said in a practical tone. "He is important to you. You aren't thinking clearly."

"That, too, is something only I can judge." She returned Veradis's gaze steadily. "Will you do me the favor, lady?"

Veradis studied her for a long moment. Then she said, "I will."

"Thank you," Isana said quietly.

"In the morning," Veradis said. "After you have slept. I will return and instruct you in the method. You will not worsen his chances with a few hours' delay."

Isana pressed her lips together in frustration, but then nodded. "Thank you."

Veradis nodded back and turned to leave. She paused by the door. "I'll send in a cot, and make sure there's an attendant near your door." She paused, just outside the room, and asked, "He is your protector?"

"Yes," Isana said quietly.

"Then I ask you to consider one thing before you begin. Should you die attempting to heal him, you will render his death meaningless. He will have sacrificed his life for his lady for nothing."

"I am not his lady," Isana said quietly.

"Yet you will risk your own life for him?"

"I will not stand by and watch him die."

Veradis smiled for just a second, and for an instant looked her age, young and lively. "I understand, Steadholder. Good luck."

ᗤᗤᗤᗤᗤ CHAPTER 21

Max looked blankly at Tavi for a second, then asked, "Are you insane?"

"This isn't complicated," Tavi told Max. "Take this hammer and break my crowbegotten leg."

It was hard to tell in the wan light of predawn, but Tavi thought he saw his friend turn a bit green. Around them were the sounds of the First Aleran preparing to march. Centurions bellowed. Fish apologized. Veterans complained. Outside the walls, the camp followers, too, were preparing to march.

"Tavi," Max protested. "Look, there's got to be some other way."

Tavi lowered his voice. "If there is, tell me. I can't use the furies in the road for myself or my horse, I can't ride in a wagon without looking awfully suspicious, and I sure as crows can't keep pace on my own for more than an hour or three. A broken leg takes days to heal up well enough to march on it."

Max sighed. "You're insane."

"Insane?" Tavi asked. "Have you got a better idea, Max? Because if you do, this would be a good time to share it with me."

Max let out an exasperated sound, muttering several choice curses under his breath. "Bribery," he said finally. "You grease the right palms, you can get out of almost anything. It's the Legion way."

"You can loan me some money, then?"

Max scowled. "Not right now. I lost it all to Marcus at a card game two nights ago."

"Well done."

Max's scowl deepened. "Where's *your* money?"

"I've been buying baths every night, remember? They aren't cheap."

"Oh."

Tavi slapped the handle of a small smithy's hammer into Max's hand. "Lower leg. We'll tell the medicos that a horse spooked and rolled a wagon wheel over it."

"Tavi," Max protested. "You're my *friend*. I don't hit *friends*."

"You hit me when we were training!" Tavi said, indignant. "You broke my *wrist*!"

"That's different," Max said, as if the distinction was perfectly obvious. "It was for your own good."

A column of mounted soldiers jogged by, tack and harness jingling. The riders were in a jovial mood, by their talk, and Tavi caught snippets of rude jokes, friendly insults, and easy laughter.

"The scouts have already left," Tavi said. He nodded at the mounted troop. "There goes the vanguard. We'll get the order to march in a minute, so stop acting like an old beldame and break my stupid leg. It's your *duty*."

"Crows take duty," Max said easily. "You are my *friend*, which is more important."

"Max, so help me, one day I'm going to beat some sense into your head with a rock," Tavi told him. "A big, heavy rock." He held out his hand for the hammer. "Give it."

Max passed the tool back to Tavi, his tone relieved. "Good. Look, I'll bet we could figure out some other way to—"

Tavi took the hammer in his grip, braced his right leg against the wheel of a nearby wagon, and before he could actually stop to think about it, he swung it hard into the side of his shin.

The bone broke with an audible crackling sound.

Pain flooded through Tavi's senses in a sudden fire, and it was all he could do not to scream. His whole body felt shockingly weak for a moment, as if the blow had transformed muscle and sinew to water, and he dropped to his rear, clutching at the wounded limb.

"Bloody crows and carrion!" Max swore, his eyes huge with surprise. "You're insane, man. *Insane!*"

"Shut up," Tavi said through clenched teeth. "And get me to a medico."

Max stared at him for another long second, then shook his head and said, bewildered, "Right. What are friends for?" He stooped down and moved as though to pick Tavi up and carry him as one would a child.

Tavi glared.

Max rolled his eyes and grabbed one of Tavi's arms instead, hauling it over his shoulder to support his weight.

A growling, rough voice said, "There you are, Antillar. Why the crows is your bloody century lined up beside Larus's . . ." Valiar Marcus drew up short as he spotted Max and Tavi, and the battle-scarred old veteran's ugly face twisted into a squint. "What the crows is this, Maximus?" He glanced at Tavi and threw him a casual salute. "Subtribune Scipio."

Tavi grimaced and nodded in response to the First Spear. "I was loading the wagon," he said, focusing on the words and trying to ignore the pain. "The horse spooked. Wheel went over my leg."

"The horse spooked," the First Spear said. He glanced at the horse hitched to the supply wagon.

The greying draft animal stood placidly in its traces with its head down, sound asleep.

"Um," Tavi said. He licked his lips and tried to think of something to tell the First Spear, but the pain of his leg made it difficult to come up with anything with his customary speed. Tavi glanced at Max.

Max shrugged at the First Spear. "I didn't see it happen. Just came along and there he was."

"There he was," the First Spear said. Valiar Marcus squinted at Tavi. Then he took two steps and bent down. He stood up again with the smithy's hammer. "Spooked horse. Wagon wheel." He squinted down at the hammer, then at the two young men.

Max coughed. "I didn't see anything."

"Thanks," Tavi muttered sourly.

"What are friends for," Max said.

Valiar Marcus snorted. "Antillar, get your century to its proper place and prepare to march." He glanced at Tavi. "Going to be a nice day to march, sir," he observed. "But I suppose not everyone has the same opinion."

"Um. Yes, centurion," Tavi replied.

The First Spear shook his head and tossed the hammer to Max. Max caught it neatly by the handle. "Best get the subtribune to a medico first," Marcus said. "Maybe drop that by the smithy wagons on the way, eh? Then get your fish to their place in the ranks. I'll tell the senior teamster to be more careful with this, ah, nervous horse, eh?"

The old horse let out a snore. Tavi hadn't known they could do that.

Max nodded, and threw the First Spear an awkward salute with the hand holding the hammer. It came dangerously close to braining Tavi in the temple, and he ducked aside from it, threatening Max's balance.

The First Spear muttered a chuckling oath beneath his breath and stalked off.

"Think he figured out your clever plan?" Max asked brightly.

"Shut up, Max." Tavi sighed, and the pair started limping for the medicos. "Is he going to talk? If someone starts asking questions, it isn't going to take them long to find out that I've got no crafting of my own. And I only know of one person in the whole bloody Realm like that. It will blow my cover."

Max grimaced. "Some spy you are. Maybe next time when I tell you the plan is crazy . . ."

"What? If you hadn't wasted time whining about it, we wouldn't be in this mess!"

"You wanna walk to the medico without me?" Max growled. "Is that it, Scipio?"

"If it will save me hearing more of your complaining, I might!" Tavi said.

Max snorted. "I ought to dump you in one of your latrines and leave you there." But despite his words, the big northerner bore Tavi toward the medical wagons, careful not to jostle his friend's leg.

"Just keep your mouth shut," Tavi said, when Max got him to the wagon. "Until we know what he's doing."

"Right," Max said. He left Tavi in the hands of the healers, then pulled his centurion's baton from his belt and jogged off to pull his soldiers into proper marching order.

Foss appeared from one of the other wagons. The bearish old healer hopped up into the bed of the wagon Tavi sat in and briefly examined his leg. "Hungh. Accident, huh?"

"Yes," Tavi said.

"Should have just bribed the First Spear to let you drive a wagon, kid. Don't have to be a real good bribe for something like that."

Tavi frowned. "How much? Once I get paid . . ."

"Cash only," Foss said, his voice firm.

"Oh. In that case, I told you," Tavi said. "It was an accident."

Foss snorted and poked at Tavi's leg.

It felt like a blade sinking into his skin, and he clamped his teeth together on a hiss of pain. "And I spent all my money at the Pavilion."

"Ah," Foss said, nodding. "Got to learn to balance your vices, sir. Lay off a little on the wenching, save something for avoiding work." He dragged a long, slender tub from the back of the wagon, and filled it from a couple of heavy water jugs. Then he helped Tavi remove his boot, an agonizing process that made Tavi promise himself that he would take off the boot before he broke his own leg, the next time.

Foss hadn't begun the healing yet when the Legion's drums rolled, putting the column on notice that it was almost time to move. A moment later, a clarion sounded from the head of the column, and the wagons and infantry began to move. At first, they moved quite slowly, until the men and horses reached the causeway, then they picked up speed. A double-quick march stepped up to a steady jog, and from there they increased the pace to a mile-eating lope that was not quite a full sprint. The horses, similarly, worked their way up to a canter, and the wagon jounced and jittered along behind them.

Tavi felt every bump in the road in his wounded leg. Each one sent a flash of pain through him that felt like some small and fiendishly determined creature taking a bite out of his leg. That went on for what felt like half a lifetime, until Foss finally seemed satisfied that the pace had steadied enough to allow him to work and slipped Tavi's wounded leg into the tub.

The watercrafting that healed the bone was quick, transforming the pain to a sudden, intense, somehow benevolent heat. When that faded a moment later, it took most of the pain with it, and Tavi collapsed wearily onto his back.

"Easy there, sir," Foss rumbled. "Here. Get some bread into you at least, before you sleep." He passed Tavi a rough, rounded loaf, and Tavi's suddenly empty belly growled. Tavi devoured the loaf, a small wedge of cheese, and guzzled down almost a full skin of weak wine before Foss nodded, and said, "That's good enough. Have you back on your feet in no time."

Tavi devoutly hoped not. He flopped back down, threw an arm across his eyes, and vanished into sleep.

He became dimly aware of alarmed shouts and blaring horns sounding a halt. The wagon slowed to a stop. Tavi opened his eyes to a sullen, overcast sky that flickered with flashes of reddish light and rumbled with threatening thunder. Tavi sat up, and asked Foss, "What's going on?"

The veteran healer stood up in the back of the wagon as it came to a halt, peering ahead. A drum rattled in a series of fast and slow beats, and Foss exhaled a curse. "Casualties."

"We're fighting already?" Tavi asked. He shook his head, hoping to slosh some of the sleep from it.

"Make a path!" called a woman's voice, louder than humanly possible, and Lady Antillus's large white horse thundered down the road, forcing *legionares* to scamper out of its path and other horses to dance nervously in place. She went by within a few feet of Tavi, her harness and coin purse jingling.

"Come on," Foss growled. "Nothing wrong with your arms, sir."

He motioned Tavi to help him, and the two of them wrangled a pair of full-body tubs from the wagon and to the ground. It hurt his leg abominably, sore muscles clenching into burning knots, but Tavi ground his teeth and did his best to ignore it. He and Foss dragged the tubs to the side of the causeway as Lady Antillus hauled her steed to a sliding halt and leapt down from the horse's back with an odd melding of poise and athleticism.

"Water," Foss grunted. Tavi pulled himself back into the wagon and began wrangling the heavy jugs to the end of the wagon. Wind rose to a thunderous roar, and Commander Fantus and Crassus shot down the road not ten feet above the ground, each man bearing an unmoving form over one shoulder. Lady Antillus, Foss, and four other healers met them, taking the wounded men from the Knights Aeris. They stripped the injured of armor with practiced efficiency and got both men into the tub.

Tavi observed from the bed of the wagon and kept his mouth shut. The men's injuries were . . . odd. Both were smeared with blood, and both thrashed wildly, letting out breathless cries of pain. Long strips of the skin on their legs were simply gone, in bands perhaps an inch wide, as though they'd been lashed with red-hot chains.

Once they were in the tubs, Lady Antillus stepped forward and seized one of the wounded Knights' heads. He struggled for a moment more, then eased slowly down into the tub, panting but not screaming, his eyes glazed. She did the same for the second man, then gestured to the healers and settled down to examine the men and confer.

More thundering hoofbeats approached, though this time they were well to the side of the road, away from the danger of spooking a nervous horse or trampling an unlucky *legionare*. Captain Cyril and the First Spear drew up to the healers. The captain dismounted, followed by Valiar Marcus, and looked around until he spotted Knight Tribune Fantus. "Tribune? Report."

Fantus grimaced at the two young men in the tub, then saluted Cyril. "We were attacked, sir."

"Attacked?" Cyril demanded. "By who?"

"By *what*," Fantus corrected. "Something up at the edge of that cloud cover. Whatever it was, I didn't get a good look at it." He gestured to Crassus. "He did."

Crassus just stared at the two wounded men, his face entirely bloodless, his expression nauseated. Tavi felt a spike of sympathy for the young man, despite his enmity for Maximus. Crassus had seen his first blood spilled, and he looked too young to be dealing with such a thing, even to Tavi.

"Sir Crassus," Cyril said, his voice purposefully pitched loudly enough to shock the young Knight from his motionless stare.

"Sir?" Crassus said. He saluted a beat late, as if just then remembering protocol.

Cyril glanced at the boy, grimaced, and said in a quieter voice, "What happened up there, son?"

Crassus licked his lips, eyes focused into the distance. "I was point man on the air patrol, sir. Bardis and Adrian, there, were my flankers. I wanted to take advantage of the cover, hide us in the edges where we could still watch the ground ahead. I led them up there."

He shuddered and closed his eyes.

"Go on," Cyril said, his voice quiet and unyielding.

Crassus blinked his eyes several times. "Something came out of the cloud. Scarlet things. Shapes."

"Windmanes?"

"No, sir. Definitely not. They were solid, but . . . amorphous, I think, is the word. They didn't have a fixed profile. And they had all these legs. Or maybe tentacles. They came out of nowhere and grabbed us with them."

Cyril frowned. "What happened?"

"They started choking us. Pulling at us. More of them kept coming." Crassus took a deep breath. "I burned off the one that had me, and tried to help them. I cut at them, and it seemed to hurt them—but it didn't slow them down. So I started chopping at those leg things until Bardis was free. I think Adrian had an arm free and struck, too. But neither of them could keep themselves up, so I had to catch them before they fell. Sir Fantus helped, or I would have lost one of them."

Cyril pursed his lips, brows furrowed in consternation. "Lady Antillus? How fare the men?"

The High Lady glanced up from her work. "They've been burned. Some sort of acid, I believe. It is potent—it is still dissolving flesh."

"Will they live?"

"Too soon to tell," she said, and turned back to the tubs.

Cyril grunted, rubbed at his jaw, and asked Fantus, "Did you get a feel for the crafting behind this overcast?"

"No," Fantus said. "It isn't furycrafted."

More thunder rumbled. Scarlet lightning danced behind veils of clouds. "It's natural?"

Fantus stared up. "Obviously not. But it isn't furycraft."

"What else could it be?" Cyril murmured. He glanced at the wounded Knights. "Acid burns. Never heard of a fury that could do that."

Fantus squinted up at the overcast sky, and asked, "What else could it be?"

Cyril's eyes followed the Knight Tribune's gaze. "Well. If life was simple and predictable, imagine how bored we'd all get."

"Bored is good," Fantus said. "I like bored."

"So do I. But it would appear that fate did not consult with either one of us." Cyril rubbed at his forehead with one thumb, his face distant, pensive. "We need to know more. Take your best fliers up and be on your guard. Get another look at them if you can. We need to know if they're going to stay up there in the cover or if they'll come down here for dinner."

"Yes, sir," Fantus said.

"Meanwhile, I want one tier of the air patrol to keep a relatively low ceiling. Say, halfway up. Then a second tier, above them, keeping an eye on the clouds. If there's trouble, the first tier can come up to help."

Fantus frowned. "That near the ground it's going to be tiring on the first tier, Captain. The men will have to take it in shifts. It will severely reduce the number of eyes we've got looking out for trouble."

"We aren't in hostile territory. Better that than to lose more of our Knights Aeris to these things. We're spread thin enough as it is. Do it."

Fantus nodded and saluted again. Then he went to Crassus and stood beside the young Knight, staring down at the men in the tubs.

Tavi glanced back at the tubs and nearly threw up.

One of the men was dead, horribly dead, his body shrunken and wrinkled like a rotten grape, gaping holes burned into the body. The other Knight was breathing in frenzied gasps, his eyes wide and bulging, while the healers worked frantically to save him.

"It would seem that someone is attempting to impede our progress," the captain said to the First Spear.

"Doesn't make much sense. The way we're marching, we're getting out of Kalarus's way. Totally out of the theater of this war. He should be happy to see us on the road."

"Yes," Cyril said. "But it would seem that someone wants us slow and blind."

The First Spear grunted. "Which means you want to move fast and find out what the crows is going on out here. Just to spite him."

Cyril's teeth flashed in a swift smile. "Take half a glass for the men and the animals to get some water. Then we're on the march again."

The First Spear saluted the captain and marched off, beckoning runners and delivering orders.

Cyril stared at the survivor of the attack. He was slowly easing down from his agonized thrashing. He stepped up to stand beside Crassus. The young Knight hadn't moved. His gaze remained on the sad, withered body of the dead man.

"Sir Crassus," Cyril said.

"Sir?"

The captain took the young man by his shoulders and gently forced his entire body to turn away from the corpse, and toward the captain. "Sir Crassus, you can do nothing for him. Your brother Knights need your eyes and thoughts to be upon your duty. They are who you should focus upon."

Crassus shook his head. "If I'd—"

"Sir Crassus," Cyril said, his tone quiet but hard. "Writhing in recrimination and self-doubt is a game your men cannot afford you to play. You are a Knight of the Realm, and you will comport yourself as such."

Crassus stiffened to attention, swallowed, and threw the captain a steady salute.

Cyril nodded. "Better. You've done all you can for them. Return to your duties, Sir Crassus."

"Sir," Max's half brother said. He began to look over his shoulder but arrested the movement with a visible effort, then donned his helmet and strode back toward the front of the column.

Cyril watched Crassus for a moment, then the healers began to back away from the second tub, with the air of men whose work had been completed. The young Knight in the tub, though pale as death, was breathing steadily while Lady Antillus continued to kneel beside the tub, her head bowed, her hands on the injured Knight's head.

Cyril nodded, and his gaze fell on Tavi. "Scipio?" he asked. "What happened to you?"

"Accident with a cart, sir," Tavi replied.

"Broke his leg," Foss provided with a grunt, as he returned to the wagon.

Cyril arched a brow and glanced at Foss. "How bad?"

"Lower leg, clean break. I mended it. Shouldn't be a problem."

Cyril stared at Tavi for a long moment, his eyes narrowed. Then he nodded.

Lady Antillus rose from the healing tub, smoothed her skirts, and walked sedately to the captain. She saluted him.

"Tribune," Cyril greeted her. "How is he?"

"I believe he is stable," Lady Antillus replied, her voice cool, calm. "Barring complications, he should survive. The acid ate away most of the muscle on his left thigh and his right forearm. He'll never serve again."

"There's more to serving a Legion than fighting," Cyril said quietly.

"Yes, sir," Lady Antillus said, her neutral tone speaking clearly as to her disagreement.

"Thank you, Your Grace," Cyril said. "For his life."

Lady Antillus's expression became remote and unreadable, and she inclined her head very slightly.

Cyril returned the nod, then turned to his horse, mounted, and headed back up the column.

Lady Antillus turned to Tavi after the captain left. "Scipio."

"Tribune," Tavi said, saluting her.

"Hop down from the wagon," she said firmly. "Let's see your leg."

"Excuse me?"

Lady Antillus arched a brow. "I am the Tribune Medica of this Legion. You are one of my charges. Now hop down, *Subtribune*."

Tavi nodded and eased himself down slowly, careful to put as little weight as he could on his wounded leg.

Lady Antillus knelt and touched the wounded leg for a moment, then rose and rolled her eyes. "It's nothing."

"Foss healed it," Tavi said.

"It is a minor injury," she said. "Surely, Scipio, someone with even your modest skills of metalcrafting could ignore any discomfort it might cause and march."

Tavi glanced back at Foss, but the healer was supervising the loading of the wounded Knight into the bed of the wagon and studiously kept his eyes away. "I'm afraid not, Your Grace," Tavi improvised, regarding her thoughtfully. "It's still fairly tender, and I don't want to slow the Legion."

Clearly, he hadn't fooled Lady Antillus by starting that fire. It was depressingly probable that she knew or at least strongly suspected his identity, and she was out to expose him. Given how badly he'd beaten her nephew, Kalarus Brencis Minoris, back at that fiasco during Wintersend, he wasn't surprised at her animosity. Even so, he couldn't allow her to prove to everyone in sight who he was.

Which meant that he had to act.

"I'm sorry, Your Grace," Tavi said. "But I can't put any weight on it yet."

"I see," Lady Antillus said. Then she reached out and firmly pushed on Tavi's shoulder, forcing his weight to the injured leg.

Tavi felt a flash of pain that shot from his right heel to his right collarbone. The leg buckled and he fell, pitching forward into Lady Antillus, almost knocking her down.

The High Lady let Tavi fall and recovered her balance. Then she shook her head, and said, "I've seen little girls in Antillus bear more than that." Her eyes fell on Foss. "I don't care to waste my time dealing with obvious shirkers. Watch the leg. Get him back on his feet the moment you deem him fit. Meanwhile, he can play nurse for the casualty."

Foss saluted. "Yes, Tribune."

Lady Antillus glared down at Tavi. Then she tossed her dark hair back over one shoulder, mounted her horse again, and kicked it into a run toward the front of the column.

After she was gone, Foss snickered. "You've got a nose for trouble, sir."

"Sometimes," Tavi agreed. "Foss. Assuming I can get some cash, how much are we talking, to ride in the wagon?"

Foss considered. "Two gold eagles at least."

Tavi returned his small knife to its sheath in his pocket, calmly loosened the neatly sliced strings of Lady Antillus's coin purse, and upended its contents into his hand. Three gold crowns, half a dozen gold eagles, and eleven silver bulls jingled together. Tavi selected a gold crown and flicked the coin to Foss.

The healer caught the coin on reflex and stared at Tavi, then at the silk purse. His eyes widened, and he made strangling sounds in his throat.

"That's five times your asking price," Tavi said. "And I'll help with your casualty the whole way. Good enough?"

Foss rubbed a hand back over his short-shorn hair. Then he let out a rough laugh and pocketed the coin. "Kid, you got more balls than brains. I like that. Get in."

⋙ CHAPTER 22

While dawn was half an hour away, Lady Aquitaine summoned four Windwolves, mercenary Knights long in service to the Aquitaines—and responsible for no few lost lives themselves. Allegedly responsible, Amara reminded herself firmly. There was no proof.

Amara, Bernard, Rook, and Lady Aquitaine met them atop the northernmost spire of Cereus's citadel. The Knights Aeris and the coach they bore swept up to the spire from within the city, keeping lower than the rooftops whenever possible.

They were dressed for travel—Amara in her close-fit flying leathers and her sword belt, Bernard in a woodsman's outfit of brown and green and grey, bearing his axe, bow, bedroll, and war quiver. Lady Aquitaine wore clothing similar to Amara's, though the leathers' layers sandwiched an impossibly fine mesh of steel, providing greater protection for the High Lady. She also wore a sword, something Amara had never pictured Invidia Aquitaine using—but she bore the long, slender blade as casually as Amara did her own.

Once the coach had landed, the door opened, and one of the most deadly swordsmen alive emerged from it. Aldrick ex Gladius stood half a head taller than even Bernard, and moved with a kind of placid grace, no motions wasted. He had a pair of swords belted to his left side, a Legion-issue *gladius* and a duelist's longblade. His wolfish grey eyes found Lady Aquitaine, and he gave her a curt nod. "Your Grace."

Behind him, a woman in a pale green gown peered at them from her seat in the coach, her beautiful, pale face a ghostly contrast with her dark hair and eyes. Amara recognized Odiana, another of Aquitaine's mercenary Knights. Her head tilted oddly to one side as she studied the others, and Amara saw the colors of her silk dress pulse and swirl, tendrils of dark red and vermilion slithering over the fabric covering her shoulders, a disquieting sight.

Aldrick stared at them for a moment, eyes never leaving Amara and Bernard. "This is too much load for the coach, milady. We'll never outrun their Knights Aeris."

Lady Aquitaine smiled. "It will just be the four of you," she told Aldrick. "The Countess and I will travel outside the coach. Assuming that is acceptable, Countess?"

Amara nodded. "I'd planned on it in any case."

Aldrick frowned for a moment, then said slowly, "This is not a wise decision, my lady."

"I'll survive having my hair blown about, thank you," she replied. "But I am willing to listen to an alternative suggestion, assuming you have one."

"Leave one of them here," he said immediately.

"No," Amara said. Her tone made the word into a command.

When Lady Aquitaine did not dissent, Aldrick's frown deepened.

"The sooner we leave," Lady Aquitaine said, "the farther away from the city we can get before daylight. Count Calderon, Madame Rook, please have a seat."

Bernard glanced at Amara, who nodded. Rook had been provided with a simple brown dress, and she had altered her features, though it had seemed considerably more of an effort for her than it had for Lady Aquitaine. She still limped slightly, and she looked exhausted—and there was a noticeable absence of weaponry on her person—but she entered the coach under her own power. Bernard and Aldrick faced one another for a second, before Aldrick bowed slightly, and said, "Your Excellency."

Bernard grunted, gave Amara a wry glance, and entered the coach. Aldrick followed him in, and the Knights Aeris at the carry poles hooked their flight harnesses to them and, with an unavoidable cyclone of wind, lifted the coach from the stones of the tower and launched into the air, slowly but steadily gaining altitude.

"Countess," Lady Aquitaine said, as they prepared to fly, "I assume you have seen aerial combat before."

"Yes."

"I haven't," she said in a matter-of-fact voice. "You're in command. I suggest that I attempt to veil us."

Amara arched an eyebrow at the proud High Lady, impressed. Invidia might be arrogant, ruthless, ambitious, a dangerous enemy—but she was no fool. Her suggestion was a good one. "That large a windstream will be difficult to hide."

"Impossible, in fact, if any Knights Aeris pass nearby," Lady Aquitaine said. "But I believe I will be able to reduce our chances of being seen at a distance."

Amara nodded. "Do it. Take position on the coach's left. I'll take the right."

Lady Aquitaine nodded, twisting her hair into a knot at the nape of her neck and tying it there. "Shall we?"

Amara nodded and called to Cirrus, and the two women stepped up onto the tower's battlements and leapt into the predawn sky. Twin torrents of wind rose and lifted them swiftly into the sky. They easily overtook the slowly rising wind coach, and Amara took up a position on the right side of the coach, between it and the general direction of Kalarus's approaching forces.

They had gained nearly four thousand feet of altitude before the sun rose, reducing the landscape beneath to a broad diorama, every feature on it seemingly rendered in miniature. If they continued ascending to risk the swift high winds of the upper air, the land would resemble a quilt more than anything else, but at sunrise Amara could still see details of the land beneath them—notably, travelers on the road from the south, fleeing toward the protection of the walls of Ceres.

And, beyond them, marching at speed down the road

toward Ceres, came Kalarus's Legions. Shadows yet blanketed much of the land below, but as the early golden light began to fall upon the column between gaps in the terrain, it glinted on their shields, helmets, and armor. Amara raised her hands, focusing part of Cirrus's efforts into bending the light, bringing the landscape beneath into crystalline, magnified focus. With the fury's aid, she could see individual *legionares*.

Both Legions below moved swiftly, their ranks solid and unwavering—the marks of an experienced body of troops. This was no ragged outlaw Legion, raised and trained in secret in the wild, its ranks consisting mostly of brigands and scoundrels. They must have been Kalare's regular Legions, those the city had maintained from time out of mind. Though they saw less action than the Legions of the north, they were still a well-trained, disciplined army. Mounted riders flanked the infantry in greater numbers than in most Legions, who typically maintained only two hundred and forty cavalry in a pair of auxiliary wings. There were perhaps three times that number in Kalarus's Legions, the horses all tall and strong, their riders wearing the green-and-grey livery of Kalare.

"Look!" called Lady Aquitaine. "To the north!"

Amara looked over her shoulder. Though very far away, Amara spotted another column of troops marching down toward Ceres from the foothills north of the city—the Crown Legion, coming to the city's defense. Amara noted with satisfaction that, as Gaius had promised, they were nearer Ceres than the southern Legions and would beat them to the city's walls.

Over the next few moments, the sun's golden light dimmed a shade and took on the same ruddy hue as the stars.

A disquieting sensation flickered through Amara's awareness.

She frowned and tried to focus upon it. As the sun's light changed, or perhaps as they rose higher into the air, there was a subtle shift in the patterns of wind around her. She could sense them through Cirrus as the fury became uneasy, the windstream it provided her wobbling in tiny fluctuations. The hairs on the back of her neck rose, and Amara suddenly had the distinct impression that she was being watched, that a malevolent presence was nearby and intent upon doing her harm.

She drew in closer to the coach's side, rising a bit to look over it at Lady Aquitaine. The High Lady had a frown on her face as she peered around her, one hand upon the hilt of her sword. She turned a troubled gaze on Amara. Roaring wind made conversation problematic, but Lady Aquitaine's shrug and a slight shake of her head adequately conveyed that she, too, had sensed something but did not know what it was.

Bernard leaned his head out the window of the coach, his expression concerned. Amara dropped closer, flying beside the coach closely enough to hear him. "What's wrong?"

"I'm not sure."

"That woman of Aldrick's is having some kind of seizure," Bernard called. "She's curled up in a ball on the floor of the coach."

Amara frowned, but just before she spoke she saw a shadow flicker across the wall of the coach. She put a hand on Bernard's face and shoved him hard, back into the coach, and used the impulse of it to roll to the right. World and sky spun end over end, and she felt an intruding windcrafting interfere with Cirrus's efforts to keep her aloft. Simultaneously, the form of an armored man in the green-and-grey colors of Kalare flew nearly straight down, sword gleaming red in the altered sunlight. The blade missed Bernard's head, and the Knight Aeris tried for a swift cut at Amara. She avoided it by darting straight up and watched the enemy Knight shoot far past them, fighting to pull out of his dive and pursue.

Amara checked around her again and saw three more armored figures half a mile above and ahead of the coach. Even as she watched, the three Knights banked, sweeping down to intercept the coach's course.

Amara called to Cirrus, and the furious winds around her let out a high-pitched whistle of alarm like the cry of a maddened hawk, to alert the others to the danger. She darted ahead of the coach, so that its bearers could see her, and flicked her hands through several quick gestures, giving orders. The bearers banked the coach to the left and put on all the speed they could muster. It leapt ahead through the eerie vermilion sky.

That done, Amara darted like a hummingbird to Lady Aquitaine's side of the coach, flying in close enough to speak.

"We're under attack!" she said, pointing ahead and above them.

Lady Aquitaine nodded sharply. "What do I do?"

"Keep the veil up and see if you can help the coach move any faster."

"I will not be able to aid you, Countess, if all my concentration is on the veil."

"Right now there are only four of them. If every picket Knight can see us from miles away, we'll have forty on us! Keep the veil up unless they get close. They'll have salt. They'll try to injure the bearers' furies with it and force the coach down. We have to stop them from getting that close. I want you to take position above the coach."

Lady Aquitaine nodded and flitted into position. "Where will you be?"

Amara drew her sword and regarded the diving Knights grimly. "Watch for any that get past me," she shouted. Then she called to Cirrus and shot up to meet the oncoming foe, swifter than an arrow from the bow.

The oncoming Knights Aeris hesitated for a moment as she rushed them, and she exploited their mistake by pouring on all the speed at her command. Amara was arguably the fastest flier in Alera, and the advancing Knights were unprepared for the sheer velocity of her charge. She was on the foremost Knight before the man had fairly drawn his sword and stabilized his windstream to support a blow. Amara swept past the man and struck, both hands on the hilt of her blade.

She had aimed for his neck, but he ducked at the last moment and her sword struck the side of his helmet. The sturdy blade shattered under the sheer force of the blow, metal shards tumbling in the scarlet light. Amara felt an instant of painful, tingling sensation in her hands, which then immediately went numb. Her windstream fluttered dangerously, sending her into a lateral tumble, but she gritted her teeth and recovered her balance in time to see the doomed enemy Knight plummeting toward the earth, knocked lethally senseless by the blow.

The other two Knights saw their comrade's plight and rolled into a dive, their furies driving them down faster than the unconscious Knight could fall—but it would be a near thing, both to catch him and pull out of the dive in time. The coach would have valuable minutes to flee, to place more distance between it and the observers, so that Lady Aquitaine's veil could hide it from sight once more.

Amara pressed her numb hands against her sides, keeping an eye on the diving Knights, and banked around to glide back to the coach. From here, she could see through the crafting Lady Aquitaine's furies held around the coach, though she could not make out many details. It was like staring at a distant object through the wavering lines of heat arising from one of Alera's causeways in high summer. If she'd been much farther away, she might not have seen the coach at all.

Amara shook her head. Though she could, if she had to, veil herself in a similar fashion, her own abilities would be pushed to their utmost to do so. Lady Aquitaine's veil was twenty times the volume, at least, and she did it while also muffling the gale that held them all aloft, as *well* as propelling herself. She might not have Amara's training or experience in aerial conflict, but it was a potent reminder of how capable— and dangerous—the woman truly was.

Something hit Amara from below, a sudden blow that drove the breath from her body and made her vision shrink to a tunnel of black with a vermilion sky at the far end. She'd been sinking in a shallow dive to rejoin the coach, and her own descent made the blow far more powerful than it might have been on its own.

For a second, she lost her reference to sky and earth completely, but her instincts warned her not to stop moving, and she called desperately to Cirrus for more speed, regardless of the direction in which she flew. She fought her way through the disorientation, past the pain in one thigh and the hollow-gut sensation of having her breath knocked from her, and realized that she was soaring almost straight up, bobbing and weaving drunkenly. Feathery, faint oceans of bloodred cloud surrounded them, a mere translucent haze.

Amara shot a glance over one shoulder and realized her mistake. Though she had been watching the descending pair of Knights, she had forgotten the first attacker, who had to have possessed speed to challenge Amara's own, to have ascended again so quickly.

Now he pressed hard behind her, a young man with muddy eyes and a determined jaw, now holding one of the short, heavy bows of horn and wood and steel favored by huntsmen in the rolling forests and swamps of the southern cities. He had a short, heavy arrow fitted to the string, the bow half-drawn.

She felt the air around her ripple, and knew that the knight had loosed the first shaft, and that she did not have time to evade it. Amara directed Cirrus to deflect the missile, the air between her shoulder blades suddenly as thick and hard as ice, but it struck with such force that Cirrus was unable to maintain the pace of her flight, and her speed dropped.

Which, she realized with a sudden surge of fear, had been the point of shooting at her in the first place.

The enemy Knight was upon her in an instant, the column of air that propelled him interfering with hers, and Cirrus faltered even more.

And to make things worse, that inexplicable sense of a hostile presence returned, stronger, nearer, more filled with anger and hate.

The enemy Knight shot ahead of her, above her, and his windstream abruptly vanished as he turned, an open leather sack in his hands, and hurled half a pound of rock salt directly into Amara's face.

Another whistling shriek split the air, this time agonized, as the salt tore into the fury in a cloud of flickering blue lights, briefly outlining the form her fury took most often, that of a large and graceful destrier whose legs, tail, and mane terminated in continuous billows of mist. The fury reared and bucked in torment, and its pain slammed against Amara's consciousness, and she suddenly felt as if a thousand glowing embers had crashed into her, the sensation at once insubstantial and hideously real.

With another scream, Cirrus dispersed like a cloud before high winds, fleeing the pain of contact with the salt.

And Amara was alone.

Her windstream vanished.

She fell.

She thrashed her arms and legs in panic, out of control, desperately calling upon her furycraft. She could not reach Cirrus, could not move the air, could not fly.

Above her, the enemy Knight recalled his fury and recovered his air stream, then dived down after her, fitting another arrow to his bow, and she suddenly knew that he did not mean to let her fall to her death.

He was a professional and would take no chances.

He would make sure that she was dead before she ever hit the ground.

Amara fumbled for her knife, a useless gesture, but twisting her hips to reach it sent her into an uncontrolled, tumbling spin, more severe and more terrifying than anything she had felt before.

She saw in flashes, in blurred images.

The ground waxed larger beneath her, all fields and rolling pastures in the ruddy sunlight.

The scarlet sun scowled down at her.

The enemy Knight raised his bow for the killing shot.

Then the misty scarlet haze they fell through *moved*.

Ground.

Sky.

Sun.

The scarlet haze condensed into dozens of smaller, opaque, scarlet clouds. Ruddy vinelike appendages emerged from the undersides of each smaller cloud, and writhed and whipped through the air with terrifying and purposeful motion.

An eerie shriek like nothing Amara had ever heard assaulted her ears.

A dozen bloody vines shot toward her pursuer.

The enemy Knight loosed his shot. The impact of the bizarre tendrils sent the shaft wide.

The Knight screamed, one long, continuous sound of agony and terror, a young man's voice that cracked in the middle.

Dark crimson cloudbeasts surrounded him, vines ripping, tearing.

His screams stopped.

Amara's vision blurred over, the disorientation too great, and she called desperately, uselessly to Cirrus, struggling to move as she would if the fury had been there to guide her. She managed to slow the spinning, but she could do nothing else. The land below rose up, enormous, prosperous—and ready to receive her body and blood.

Cirrus was beyond her call.

She was going to die.

There was nothing she could do about it.

Amara closed her eyes, and pressed her hands against her stomach.

She didn't have the breath to whisper his name. *Bernard.*

And then gale winds rose up to surround her, pressing hard against her, slowing her fall. She screamed in frustration and fear at her helplessness and felt herself angling to one side, pulling out of the fall as if it had been an intentional dive.

The land rushed up and Amara came to earth in the furrowed field of a steadholt. She managed to strike with her feet and tried to fold herself into a controlled roll to spread out her momentum. The rich, fresh earth was soft enough to slow her momentum, and after fifty feet of tumbling she fetched up to a halt at the feet of a steadholt scarecrow.

She lay on her side, dazed, confused, aching from dozens of impacts suffered during the landing, and covered with earth and mud and what might have been a bit of manure.

Lady Aquitaine alighted near her, landing neatly.

She was in time to be sprinkled with the blood of the Knight taken by the cloudbeasts. Amara had beat it to the ground.

Lady Aquitaine stared up in shock, bright beads of blood on one cheekbone and one eyelash. "Countess?" she breathed. "Are you all right?"

The coach descended as well, and Bernard all but kicked the door off its hinges in his hurry to exit and run to Amara. He knelt with her, his expression almost panicked, staring at her for a breath, then examining her for injuries.

"I managed to slow her fall," Lady Aquitaine said. "But she's been badly bruised and may have cracked some bones."

The words sounded pleasant to Amara, though she could not remember what they meant. She felt Bernard's hand on her forehead and smiled. "'M all right, my lord," she murmured.

"Here, Count," Lady Aquitaine said. "Let me help you."

They fussed over her, and it felt nice.

Fear. Pain. Terror. Too much of it for one day.

Amara just wanted to rest, to sleep. Surely things would be better after she rested.

"No broken bones," Lady Aquitaine said.

"What happened up there?" Bernard asked, his voice a low growl.

Lady Aquitaine lifted her eyes to the red skies above.

Droplets of blood still fell, tiny beads of red that had once been a human being.

She frowned and murmured, perplexed, "I have no idea."

⋈⋈⋈⋈ CHAPTER 23

The next morning, Isana woke when Lady Veradis opened the door. The pale young healer's dark-circled eyes were even more worn than the day before, but she wore the colors of her father's house in a simple gown. The young woman smiled at Isana and said, "Good morrow, Steadholder."

"Lady," Isana said, with a nod. She looked around the room. "Where is Fade?"

Lady Veradis entered the room, bearing a tray covered

with a cloth napkin. "Being bathed and fed. I'll have him brought in once you are ready."

"How is he?"

"Somewhat disoriented with fever. Weary. Otherwise lucid." She nodded at the food. "Eat and ready yourself. I will return presently."

Isana pushed worry from her mind, at least long enough to wash herself and partake of the sausages, fresh bread, and cheeses Veradis had brought. Once some of the food had touched her tongue, Isana found herself famished, and ate with abandon. The food would be necessary to keep her strength up during the healing, and she should take as much as she could.

A few minutes later, there was a knock at the door and Veradis asked, "Steadholder? May we enter?"

"Of course."

Veradis came in. Three guards bore a healer's tub readied with water. The tub wasn't as large as the one from the day before, and it bore spots of rust and wear that marked it as a well-worn member of its breed. It had probably been stored in a closet somewhere, forgotten until the sudden attack on the city demanded the use of every tub that could be found. The guards set it down on the floor, then one of them drew a low chair over to sit beside it.

A moment later, Giraldi came in, supporting Fade with one shoulder despite his limp and his cane. Fade wore only a long, white robe, his face was flushed with fever, his eyes glazed, and his wounded hand had swollen up into a grotesque mockery of itself.

Giraldi grimly helped the scarred man over to the tub and had to help Fade remove the robe. Fade's lean, wire-muscled body showed dozens of old scars Isana had never seen before, especially across his back, where the marks of the whipping that had accompanied his branding stood out from his skin, as thick as Isana's littlest finger.

Fade settled weakly into the tub, and when he laid his head back against the wooden rest, he seemed to fall asleep instantly.

"Are you prepared?" Veradis asked quietly.

Isana rose and nodded, without speaking.

Veradis gestured to the chair. "Sit, then. Take his hand."

Isana did so. The low chair put her head on a level with Fade's, and she watched the scarred slave's features as she reached down to take up his healthy hand and grip it between hers.

"It isn't a terribly complicated crafting," Veradis said. "The infection has a natural tendency to gather at the site of the wound. So concentrated, his body cannot drive it out. You must dilute the infection, spreading it more thinly throughout his body, where he will have a chance to fight it off."

Isana frowned and drew in a slow breath. "Spread the sickness throughout his whole body? If I stop, the infection could take root anywhere. One site is bad enough. I could not handle two at once."

Veradis nodded. "And it could take his body days to fight off the infection."

Isana bit her lip again. Days. She had never maintained a healing furycraft for more than a few hours.

"It isn't a very good way to help him," Veradis said quietly. "It is, however, the only way. Once you begin, you cannot stop until he has won through. If you do, the garic oil will corrupt his blood entirely. He'll die within an hour." She reached into a pocket and drew out a soft, supple cord, offering it to Isana. "Are you sure you wish to attempt this?"

Isana studied Fade's scarred face. "I can't tie that with one hand, lady."

The young healer nodded, then knelt and, very carefully, bound Isana's hand loosely together with Fade's. "A very great deal will depend upon him, Steadholder," she murmured as she worked. "Upon his will to live."

"He will live," Isana said in a quiet voice.

"If he so chooses, there is hope," Veradis said. "But if he does not, or if the infection is simply too great, you must end the crafting."

"Never."

Veradis continued as if Isana had not spoken. "Depending

on the progress of the infection, he may become delusional. Violent. Be prepared to restrain him. Should he lose consciousness altogether, or if he bleeds from the nose, mouth, or ears, there is little hope for his life. That's how you will know when it is time to break away."

Isana closed her eyes and shook her head, firmly, once. "I will not leave him."

"Then you will die with him," Veradis said, her tone matter-of-fact.

I should have, Isana thought bitterly. *I should have twenty years ago.*

"I strongly urge you not to throw away your life in vain," Veradis murmured. "In fact, I beg you. There are never enough skilled healers during war, and your talents could prove invaluable to the city's defense."

Isana looked up and met the young woman's eyes. "You must fight your battle," she said quietly. "And I must fight mine."

Veradis's tired gaze focused elsewhere for a moment, then she nodded. "Very well. I will look in on you if I can. There are guards in the hall. I have instructed them to serve as attendants, should you need food or any kind of assistance."

"Thank you, Lady Vera—"

Isana's words were suddenly drowned by a titanic booming sound, so loud that it shook the stones of the citadel and rattled the glass in the windows, cracking it in several places. There was a second boom. Then, much more faintly, a rumble of drums, a series of clarion calls of military trumpets, and a sound like wind rushing through thick forest.

Lady Veradis drew in a sharp breath, and said, "It's begun."

Giraldi stumped over to the window and peered out. "Here come Kalare's Legions. Forming up near the south gate."

"What was that sound?" Isana asked.

"Knights Ignus. Probably tried to blast the gate down, first thing." He squinted for a moment, then said, "Cereus's Legions are on the walls now. Must not have taken the gate down."

"I must go," Veradis said. "I am needed."

"Of course," Isana said. "Thank you."

Veradis gave her a fleeting smile, and murmured, "Good luck." She departed on silent feet.

"To all of us," Giraldi growled, frowning out the window. A series of smaller detonations came rippling through the predawn air, and Isana could actually see the light of the fires reflected against the glass.

"What's happening?" she asked.

"Kalare brought his firecrafters up. Looks like they're blasting the walls."

"Aren't they too thick to blast through?" Isana asked.

Giraldi grunted in the affirmative. "But it creates rough spots to help troops climb ropes and ladders. If they get lucky, they might crack the wall. Then they could bring in watercrafters and use them to widen the break or undermine the wall."

A brilliant glow suddenly poured through the windows, the light a cool, bluish color rather than the orange-gold of dawn.

Giraldi grunted. "Nice."

"Centurion?"

He glanced at her over his shoulder. "Cereus let the firecrafters go to town until he could tell where most of them were. Then he moved his Knights Flora to the walls and turned on every furylight and lamp in the city so they could see to shoot."

"Did it work?"

"Can't see from here," Giraldi said. "But the *legionares* on the walls are cheering them on."

"Perhaps they've killed Kalare's firecrafters, then."

"They didn't get all of them."

"How do you know?"

Giraldi shrugged. "You never get them all. But it looks like they've given Kalare's forces something to think about."

Isana frowned. "What happens now?"

Giraldi frowned. "Depends on how bloody they're willing to get. Cereus and his people are on their home ground, familiar with the local furies. It gives them an advantage over Kalare's Knights. They tried a lightning assault and failed. Now as long as Cereus keeps his Knights intact and uses them well, Kalare's forces will get massacred if they charge in against them."

"If they want to storm the city, they must destroy its Knights," Isana said. "Is that it?"

"Pretty much. They've got to know that time isn't on their side, too. They've got to take the city before reinforcements arrive. The only way to do it fast is to do it bloody." The old soldier shook his head. "This is going to be a bad one. Like Second Calderon."

Isana's memory flashed back to the battle. The corpses had been burned in bonfires that reached forty feet into the sky. It had taken most of a year to clean the blood and filth from the stones of Garrison. She could still hear screams, moans, cries of the wounded and dying. It had been a nightmare.

Only this time, it would not be a few hundred noncombatants in peril, but thousands, tens of thousands.

Isana shuddered.

Giraldi finally turned from the window, shaking his head. "You need anything from me?"

Isana drew in a deep breath and shook her head. "Not now."

"I'll leave you to it, then," Giraldi said. "I'll be right outside."

Isana nodded and bit her lip.

Giraldi paused at the door. "Steadholder. You thinking you can't do this?"

"I . . ." Isana swallowed. "I've never . . . I don't think I can do it."

"You're wrong," Giraldi growled. "Known you for years. Fact of the matter is, you can't *not* do it." He nodded to her and slipped outside. He shut the door behind him.

Isana bowed her head at Giraldi's words. Then she turned back to her patient.

She had treated infected wounds often, both in her capacity as a steadholt's healer and during her term of service in the Legion camps. Standard practice was to encourage increased blood flow through the site, then to painstakingly focus on the afflicted tissues, destroying the infection a tiny piece at a time. Once Rill had severely weakened the infection, the patient's body itself could eliminate whatever sickness was left in the wound.

She'd done it with training injuries in the camps, for young *legionares* too foolish to properly clean and care for a minor cut. She'd done it for holders and their children, even for livestock. Infections were a tricky business, requiring both delicacy, to finely control the actions of her fury, and strength, to assault the invading fevers. It had rarely taken her more than half an hour to render such a wound manageable once more.

Isana sent Rill gliding into the tub, surrounding Fade with the fury's presence. Isana's senses, extended through the water fury, usually felt the presence of an infection as a low, sullen, hateful kind of heat. Exposure to it was unpleasant but bearable, on a scale somewhat similar to being burned by a long day in the sun.

But Fade's injury was different. The instant her fury touched upon the battered man's wound, Isana felt it as a searing blaze, hotter than an oven, and she flinched back from it by pure reflex.

Fade groaned in his sleep and stirred before settling down again. He was in the grip of a fever dream. She felt his confusion as a series of flashes of one emotion, then another, none of them remaining long enough to be clearly understood. Isana set her jaw in determination. Then, focusing again on Rill, she pressed her senses back into the waters of the tub and reached for Fade's wounded hand.

As she touched upon the wound, she felt every muscle in her body grow suddenly tight, as the pulsing, malevolent fire of the garic-oil infection seared its way into her perceptions. She held herself against the pain, marshaling her thoughts and her focus, and pressed harder against the wound site.

She saw at once why Veradis regarded this crafting as a difficult and dangerous one. Infections had life of their own, and Isana had encountered several different breeds, attempting to spread through the body of the victim, like the freemen of a steadholt marching into a new wilderness to make it their own.

The garic fever, though, was no mere steadholt of settlers. It was a Legion, a horde, a *civilization* of tiny, destructive creatures. That was why the usual, uncomfortable heat was so much more intense and painful. The fever was already destroying Fade's hand, corroding the veins and vessels, working its way in threads and tendrils to the bones of his hand and wrist. If Isana attempted the usual course of action, attacking the fever directly, it would tear apart Fade's hand, allow the infection to spread to different areas of the body while maintaining its painful and dangerous density, send him into shock, and likely kill him. She could not simply attempt to crush it.

Instead, she would have to lay siege to the fever in the stronghold it had made of the wound. Attacking it by inches, she should be able to chip slowly away at the teeming mass of infection to wash it out through the blood in pieces small enough for Fade's body to combat them successfully. As she did so, she would simultaneously have to keep pressure against the infection, to keep it from fracturing into larger pieces as she undermined it, chipping it away.

But there was so *much* of the fever. It could take days for her to finish the job, and all the while, it would be attempting to grow, spread, and destroy. If she worked too swiftly, freeing masses of infection too large, Fade's body would not be able to combat them, and the infection would spread with lethal consequences. If she worked too slowly, breaking off pieces too small, the fever would breed faster than it could be destroyed. And all the while, she would be forced to endure the pain of proximity and keep her focus on the task.

It seemed almost impossible. But if she allowed herself to believe that, she would never be able to help him.

Giraldi was right. Isana would rather lose her own life than stand aside and watch as a friend died.

Isana tightened her fingers on Fade's hand and prepared to call out to Rill. She closed her eyes and tried to ignore the sounds of drums and trumpets and far-distant shouts of the wounded and dying.

Isana shivered. At least Tavi was safe and well away from this insanity.

The rest of the journey to Kalare was neither swift nor easy. Each day required severe effort on behalf of the Knights Aeris to keep the coach airborne and moving without rising more than a few hundred feet above the ground. It was grueling work. The fliers needed rest breaks every hour or so, and after three days both Amara and Lady Aquitaine began to take turns wearing flight harnesses yoked to the coach in order to give the men a chance to rest. Each night, after the meal, they devised the plan for rescuing the hostages.

The sky became covered with a low, growling overcast, perpetually rumbling with thunder and flickering with lightning, though no rain ever fell. The deadly scarlet haze now reached down to some point within the overcast. One afternoon, in an attempt to rise higher in the hopes of it making their travel quicker, Amara realized that they had accidentally ascended into the red haze, and she saw those deadly creatures begin to condense from the fine mist. Amara had led the coach in an emergency dive back out of the clouds, and no one was harmed, but they scarcely dared fly too much higher than the treetops lest the creatures renew the attack.

At Amara's command, they had ceased their journey two hours before sundown, the coach coming down into a region of heavy forest so thick that Lady Aquitaine had to land first and alone to employ her furies to will enough of the ancient tree branches to move so that the coach would have a place to come down.

Panting with effort and weariness, Amara unhooked the harness from the coach and sat down in place, leaning her back against the coach itself. By now, evening camp had become a routine, neatly organized without the need for her to issue any orders. She and the other three bearers settled down to rest, while the others brought out the canopies, prepared food, found water. To her embarrassment, she actually fell asleep, sitting against the coach, and she didn't wake until Bernard touched her shoulder and set a metal camp plate down onto her lap.

The heat of the plate on her thighs and the warmth of Bernard's hand on her shoulder stirred up a number of rather pleasant but inconvenient memories. She looked from his hand, warm and strong and quite . . . knowledgeable, up to her husband's face.

Bernard's eyes narrowed, and she saw an answering fire to her own in them. "There's a pretty look," he murmured. "I always enjoy seeing that one on your face."

Amara felt her mouth stretch into a languid smile.

"Mmm," Bernard rumbled. "Even better." He settled down beside her, a plate of his own in his hands, and the aroma of food suddenly washed through Amara's nose and mouth, and her stomach reacted with the same mindless, animal lust the rest of her felt by virtue of being near Bernard.

"Fresh meat," she said, after her third or fourth heavenly bite. "This is fresh. Not that horrible dried trail rope." She ate more, though the roasted meat was still nearly hot enough to sear the roof of her mouth.

"Venison," Bernard agreed. "I was fortunate today."

"Now, if only you could hunt down a bakery for fresh bread," she teased.

"I saw one," Bernard said, gravely. "But it got away."

She smiled and nudged his shoulder with hers. "If you can't get me bread in the middle of the wilderness, what good are you?"

"After dinner," he said, catching her eyes with his own, "we can go for a walk. I'll show you."

Amara's heart beat faster, and she ate the next bite of venison with an almost-wolfish hunger, never looking away. She wiped a little juice from the corner of her mouth with one fingertip, licked it clean, then said, "We'll see."

Bernard let out a low, quiet laugh. He studied the others at the fire for a moment, and said, "Do you think this plan will work?"

She considered while chewing. "Getting into the city, even the citadel, is fairly simple. Getting out again is the problem."

"Uh-huh," Bernard said. "A Cursor should be able to lie better than that."

Amara grimaced. "It's not Kalarus or his Knights or his Legions or his Immortals or his bloodcrows that I'm worried about."

"You're not?" Bernard asked. "I am."

She waved a hand. "We can plan for them, deal with them."

Bernard's eyes flicked over toward the fire and back to Amara, his look questioning.

"Yes," she said. "Getting in depends on Rook. I think she's sincere, but if she's setting us up for betrayal, we're finished. Getting out again depends on Lady Aquitaine."

Bernard scraped the last of his meal around his dish with his fork. "Both of them are our enemies." His upper lip twitched away from his teeth in a silent snarl. "Rook tried to kill Tavi and Isana. Lady Aquitaine is using my sister to promote her own agenda."

"When you put it that way," Amara said, trying to keep her voice light, "this plan sounds . . ."

"Insane?" Bernard suggested.

Amara shrugged a shoulder. "Perhaps. But we have few options."

Bernard grunted. "Not much to be done about it, is there."

"Not much," Amara said. "Compared to our allies, Kalarus's forces only seem mildly threatening."

Bernard blew out a breath. "And worrying about it won't help."

"No," Amara said. "It won't." She turned her attention back to her dish. When she finished it, her husband brought her a second plate, from where the others ate near the fire, and she set to it with as much hunger as the first.

"It's that much of a strain?" Bernard asked quietly, watching her. "The windcrafting?"

She nodded. She'd broken the hard trailbread into fragments and let them soak up juice from the roast to soften them, and she ate them between bites of meat. "It doesn't seem so bad, when you're doing it. But it catches up to you later." She nodded at the fire. "Lady Aquitaine's men are having thirds."

"Shouldn't you do that, too?" Bernard asked.

She shook her head. "I'm all right. I'm lighter than they are. Not as much to lift."

"You're stronger than them, you mean," Bernard murmured.

"Why would you say that?" Amara asked.

"Lady Aquitaine doesn't even take seconds."

Amara grimaced. It was one more thing to remind her of Invidia Aquitaine's abilities. "Yes. I'm stronger than they are. Cirrus and I can lift more weight with less effort than they can, relatively speaking. Lady Aquitaine's furies are such that her limits are more mental than physical."

"How so?" Bernard asked.

"Air furies are . . . inconstant, fickle. They don't focus well on any single thing for long, so you have to do it for them. It takes constant concentration to maintain flight. Lady Aquitaine does that easily. It takes even more concentration to create a veil, to hide something from sight."

"Can you do it?" Bernard asked.

"Yes," Amara said. "But I can't do anything else while I am—I can barely walk. It's more wearying and takes much more focus than flying. Lady Aquitaine can do both of them at the same time. It's something well beyond my own skills and strength alike."

"She's no more impressive than you are, in flight. She hardly seemed able to follow you when we dived out of that cloud the other day."

Amara smiled a little. "I've had more practice. I fly every day, and I only have the one fury. She's had to divide her practice time among dozens of disciplines. But she's been doing it longer than I have, and her general skills and concentration are far better than mine. With some time to focus on flying, to practice, she'd fly circles around me, even if her furies were only as strong as Cirrus—which they aren't. They're a great deal stronger."

Bernard shook his head, and mused, "All that skill, all those furies at her command, all the good she could do—and she spends her time plotting how to take the throne, instead."

"You don't approve."

"I don't *understand*," Bernard corrected her. "For years, I would have given anything for a strong talent at windcrafting."

"Everyone would like to fly," Amara said.

"Maybe. But I just wanted to be able to do something about the crowbegotten furystorms that come down on my stead-holt," Bernard said. "Every time Thana and Garados sent one down, it threatened my holders, damaged crops, injured or killed livestock, destroyed game—and did the same for the rest of the steadholts in the valley. We tried for years to attract a strong enough windcrafter, but they're expensive, and we couldn't find one willing to work for what we could pay."

"So," Amara said, giving him a coy little glance, "your hidden motives are at last revealed."

Bernard smiled. She loved the way his eyes looked when he smiled. "Perhaps you could consider it for your retirement." He looked into her eyes, and said, "You're wanted there, Amara. I want you there. With me."

"I know," she said quietly. She tried to smile, but it didn't feel as if it had made it all the way to her face. "Perhaps one day."

He moved his arm, brushing the back of his hand unobtrusively against the side of her stomach. "Perhaps one day soon."

"Bernard," she said quietly.

"Yes."

She met his eyes. "Take me," she said. "For a walk."

His eyelids lowered a little, and his eyes smoldered, though he kept the rest of his face impassive and bowed his head politely. "As you wish, my lady."

Max blinked at Tavi and then said, incredulously, "*You* took it?"

Tavi grinned at him and tossed a heavy grain sack up into the bed of the supply wagon.

"She's been going insane about her purse. She hasn't stopped complaining to Cyril since she lost it." Max hit his forehead with the heel of his hand. "Of course. You took it and bribed Foss and Valiar Marcus to let you ride."

"Just Foss. I think he handled Marcus's cut on his own."

"You're a crowbegotten thief," Max said, not without a certain amount of admiration.

Tavi threw another sack into the supply wagon. There was room for only a few more sacks, and the timbers of the wagon groaned and creaked under the weight of the load. "I prefer to think of myself as a man who turns liabilities into assets."

Max snorted. "True enough." He gave Tavi an oblique glance. "How much did she have?"

"About a year's worth of my pay."

Max pursed his lips. "Quite a windfall. You have any plans for what's left?"

Tavi grunted and heaved the last sack into the wagon. His leg twinged, but the pain was hardly noticeable. "I'm not loaning you money, Max."

Max sighed. "Bah. That everything?"

Tavi slammed the wagon's gate closed. "That should do it."

"Got enough to feed the Legion for a month there."

Tavi grunted. "This is enough for the mounts of one *alae*. For a week."

Max whistled quietly. "I never did any work in logistics," he said.

"Obviously."

Max snorted. "How much money is left?"

Tavi reached into a pocket and tossed the silk purse to Max. Max caught it and shook it soundlessly. "Not much," Tavi said in a dry tone. "Not many Antillan-made crowns are floating around the Legion, so I've been getting rid of them a little at a time."

He walked back through the dark to the steadholt's large barn and traded grips with a gregarious Steadholder who had agreed to sell his surplus grain to the Legion—especially since Tavi was offering twenty percent over standard Legion rates, courtesy of Lady Antillus's purse. He paid the man their agreed-upon price, and returned to the wagon. Max held up the silk purse and gave it a last, forlorn little shake before tossing it back to Tavi. Tavi caught the purse.

And something clicked against his breastplate.

Tavi threw up a hand, frowning, and Max froze in place. "What?"

"I think there was something else in the purse," Tavi said. "I heard it hit my armor. Give me some light?"

Max shrugged and tore a bit of cloth from a knotted-closed sack in the wagon. He rubbed the cloth between his fingers a few times, and a low flame licked its way to life. Seemingly impervious to the heat, he lowered the burning cloth and held it a few feet over the ground.

Tavi bent over, squinting, and saw a reflection of the improvised candle's light shine off of a smooth surface. He picked up a small stone, about the size of a child's smallest fingernail, and held it closer to the light. Though it was not faceted, the stone was translucent, like a gem, and was such a brilliant color of red that it almost seemed to be wet. It reminded Tavi of a large, fresh-shed droplet of blood.

"Ruby?" Max asked, peering, bringing the flame closer.

"No," Tavi said, frowning.

"Incarnadine?"

"No, Max," Tavi said, frowning at the stone. "Your shirt is on fire," he said absently.

Max blinked, then scowled at the fire, which had spread

from the strip of sackcloth to his shirt. He flicked his wrist in irritation, and the flame abruptly died. Tavi could smell the curls of smoke coming up from the cloth in the sudden darkness.

"Have you ever seen a gem like that, Max? Maybe your stepmother crafts them."

"Not that I know of," Max said. "That's new to me."

"I've got the feeling I've seen this before," Tavi murmured. "But crows take me if I can remember where."

"Maybe it's worth something," Max said.

"Maybe," Tavi agreed. He slipped the scarlet stone back into the silk purse and tied it firmly shut. "Let's go."

Max clambered up onto the wagon, took the reins, and brought the team into motion. Tavi swung up beside him, and the slow-moving cart began its ten-mile trek back to the First Aleran's camp at Elinarch.

The march had taken them seven long, strenuous days from the training camp to the bridge over the vast, slow-moving Tiber River. Foss, once honestly bribed, had kept Tavi "under observation" while his leg healed. Lady Antillus clearly hadn't liked the idea, but since she'd dumped the responsibility into his hands, she could hardly take it away again without displaying her animosity for Tavi in an unacceptably flagrant lack of the impartiality expected in a Legion officer.

Even so, Foss had kept Tavi busy. Bardis, the wounded Knight who had been saved by Lady Antillus, required constant attention and care. Twice, during the march, Bardis had simply stopped breathing. Foss had saved the young Knight, but only because Tavi had noticed what was happening. The young Knight hadn't regained more than vague consciousness during the march, and had to be fed, cleaned, and watered like a baby.

As he first sat beside the wounded Bardis, Tavi was struck by how *young* the Knight looked. Surely, an Aleran Knight should have been taller, thicker in the shoulders and chest and neck, with a heavier growth of beard and more muscle than the wounded Knight possessed. Bardis looked like . . . an injured, not yet fully grown child. And it inspired an immediate and unexpected surge of protectiveness in the young Cursor. To his own surprise, he set about the task of tending Bardis without complaint or regret.

Later, he realized that Bardis wasn't too young to be a Knight. Tavi was simply five years older. He knew far more of the world than the boy, had seen a great deal more of life's horrors, and had gained inches and pounds of physical size that he had, for most of his life, lacked. All of that made the wounded Knight seem much smaller and far younger. It was a matter of perspective.

Tavi realized, bemused, that he was no longer the child, unconsciously expecting those stronger and older than he to assist and protect him. Now he was the stronger, the elder, and so it fell to him to accept and discharge his responsibilities rather than to seek ways to avoid or circumvent them.

He did not know when this shift in perspective had happened, and though it might have seemed small in some ways, it was far deeper and more significant than he had at first realized. It meant that he could never again be that child, the one deserving of protection and comfort. It was time for him to provide it for others, as it had been provided for him.

So he cared for poor Bardis and spent much of that march in reflection.

"You've been moody," Max said, breaking the silence as the wagon bumped steadily down the trail—a path worn by use, not furycraft. "This whole march, you've been quiet."

"Thinking," Tavi said, "and avoiding attention."

"How's the fish?"

"Bardis," Tavi corrected him. "Foss says he'll be all right, now that we've stopped and he can be cared for more properly." He shook his head. "But he might not ever walk again. And I don't know if he'll be able to use his right arm. He's given his body in service to the Realm, Max. Don't call him a fish."

Sullen red fire played within the bone-dry storm clouds overhead, and one of the horses danced nervously. Tavi saw Max nod. "True enough," he agreed, a quiet gravity in his own voice. After a moment, Max said, "Magnus says Kalarus is making his move. That he came up with at least four extra Legions somewhere. That if they take Ceres, they'll roll right over Alera Imperia. Which doesn't make much sense to me. Placidus's Legions are going to pin them against the city walls and cut them to pieces."

"Placidus isn't moving," Tavi said.

"The crows he isn't. I know the man. He doesn't care much about getting involved with the rest of the Realm, but he doesn't care for treason, either. He'll fight."

"He isn't," Tavi said. "At least, according to the last—the only—dispatch that got through from the First Lord, though it didn't say why."

"That was a week ago," Max said.

Tavi nodded up at the sky. "Wherever this storm came from, it's pretty well prevented the use of Knights Aeris as messengers. The First Lord and the High Lords can communicate through the rivers, but they know there's nothing to stop others from listening to everything they send that way."

"Or worse," Max said. "Altering the message en route."

"They can do that?" Tavi asked.

"It can be done," Max said. "I can't manage it yet. It's too delicate. But my lord father could. So could my stepmother."

Tavi stored the fact in memory for future reference. "Do you think Ceres will hold?"

Max was quiet for a moment before admitting, "No. Cereus is no soldier, he's getting long in the tooth, and he doesn't have a male heir to help with any of the fighting." His voice took on the note of a scowl. "His daughter Veradis has got talent, but it's mostly in healing. And she's a real cold fish."

Tavi found himself smiling. "She pretty?"

"Very."

"Turned you down, huh?"

"About a hundred times." Max's tone turned somber again. "Kalarus is a powerhouse. Even my lord father thinks so. And that twisty little bastard Brencis had me fooled about how strong he was, too. Cereus can't beat them. And if the First Lord takes them on, he'll be turning his back on Aquitainus. He's pinned down."

Silence fell. Tavi watched the lightning play through the clouds. "I suppose I should be used to this."

"What's that?"

"Feeling very small," Tavi said.

Max snorted out a laugh. "Small? Crows, Tavi. You've foiled coups orchestrated by the two most powerful High Lords in the realm. *Twice.* I don't know anyone less small than you."

"Luck," Tavi said. "Mostly luck."

"Some of it," Max allowed. "But not all. Hell, man, if you had furies of your own . . ."

Max's teeth suddenly clicked together as he choked the sentence to a halt, but Tavi still felt the familiar old stabs of frustration and longing.

"Sorry," Max said a moment later.

"Forget it."

"Yeah."

"I just wish we could do something," Tavi said. "*Something.* We're stuck out here in the back end of nowhere while the Realm is fighting for its life." He waved a hand. "I understand that this Legion isn't ready to fight yet. That no one is sure it could be trusted, with troops from all sides in the ranks and officers. But I wish we could do something other than sit out here and drill and"—he tilted his head at the back at the wagon—"shop for groceries."

"Me, too," Max said. "But I can't say we'd be enjoying the fight if we were there. This Legion wouldn't last long. Garrison duty on the bridge is dull, but at least it won't get us killed."

Tavi grunted and fell quiet again. The furylights of the town of Elinarch, as well as the vast, lit span of the bridge itself, came into sight at last. A few hundred yards later, the hairs on the back of Tavi's neck tried to crawl up into his eyebrows.

Max wasn't a terribly skilled watercrafter, but he had raw talent, Tavi knew, and would have felt Tavi's sudden surge of unease. He sensed Max tensing beside him.

"What?" Max whispered.

"Not sure," Tavi said. "Thought I heard something."

"I do not see how, Aleran," said a voice from not a yard behind Tavi's head. "Stones and fish hear better than you."

Tavi spun, drawing the dagger from his belt. Max reacted even more swiftly, turning at the waist and sweeping an arm back in a blow of fury-born power.

Red lightning bathed the landscape for a pair of breaths, and Tavi saw Kitai smile as Max's flailing arm missed her by perhaps half of an inch. She sat crouched atop the sacks of grain, the pale skin of her face all but glowing within her cloak's hood. She wore the same ragged clothes Tavi had seen her in before, though her blindfold had been pulled down to hang loosely around her throat. Mercifully, she did not also wear the same odor.

"Blood and crows," Max spat. The horses danced nervously, making the cart lurch, and he had to bring them under control. *"Ambassador?"*

"Kitai," Tavi said, now understanding the odd, instinctive reaction he'd felt. "What are you doing here?"

"Looking for you," she said, arching a brow. "Obviously."

Tavi gave her a level look. Kitai smiled, leaned forward, and gave him a firm and deliberate kiss on the mouth. Tavi's heart abruptly raced, and he felt short of breath. He didn't really intend to reach up and grip the front of her cloak to pull her momentarily closer, but Kitai let out a pleased sound a moment later and slowly drew away. Tavi stared into her exotic, gorgeous eyes and tried to ignore the sudden flames of need that raged through his flesh.

"No justice in the world," Max sighed. "Middle of the night, middle of crowbegotten nowhere, and you're the one with a woman." He drew the horses to a halt. "I'll walk in from here. See you in the morning."

Kitai let out a quiet, wicked laugh. "Your friend is wise." Then her smile vanished. "But I have not come here for us to pleasure one another, Aleran."

Tavi struggled to ignore the hunger that rose in the wake of the kiss and drew his thoughts into order. Kitai might be able to switch her thoughts gracefully from one trail to another, but Tavi didn't share that talent—and though he could see the obvious concern in her expression, it took him a heartbeat or three to ask, "What's happened?"

"Someone came to the camp," Kitai told him. "He claimed to

have a message for your Captain Cyril, but the guards on watch sent him away, to return in the morning. He told them it was important, to wake the captain, but they did not believe him and—"

"So?" Max interrupted. He looked at Tavi. "Happens all the time. Practically every messenger anyone sends thinks the world will end if he isn't seen at once. A Legion captain needs to sleep, too. No one wants to be the one that gets him out of bed."

Tavi frowned. "In peacetime," he said quietly. "There's a war on, Max. Captains need all the information they can get, and we're practically blind out here. Cyril's left standing orders for any messengers to be taken to him immediately." Tavi frowned at Max. "So the question is, why wouldn't they obey those orders?"

"There is more," Kitai said. "When the messenger left, the guards set out after him, and—"

"*What?*" Tavi demanded, thoughts racing. "Max. Who is on duty at the gate tonight?"

"Erasmus's century. Eighth spear, I think."

"Bloody crows," Tavi said, his voice grim. "They're Kalarans. They're going to kill him and intercept the message."

Kitai snarled in frustration and clamped a pale, slender, strong hand over Tavi's mouth and another over Max's. "By the One, Aleran, will you shut your mouth for a single instant and let me finish?" She leaned forward, eyes almost glowing with intensity. "The messenger. It was Ehren."

ᴏᴄᴏᴄᴏ Chapter 26

"Wait," Max said. "Ehren? *Our* Ehren?"

Before he had finished the sentence, Tavi had already leapt down from the wagon and unhooked one of the horses from its harness a heartbeat later. As he did, Kitai freed the other horse in the team. Tavi grasped the mane of the first horse and leapt up to its bare back, pulling hard against the weight of his armor with his arms as he did. Kitai flicked the long reins of the second horse at Max, then took Tavi's outstretched hand and mounted behind him.

"Our Ehren," Max said, heavily. "Right." The big Antillan shook his head as he clambered down from the wagon, then hauled himself up onto the draft horse, who snorted and shook his head. "Stop complaining," Max told him, and nodded at Tavi.

Tavi grinned and kicked his mount into a heavy-footed run. He could feel one of Kitai's slender, fever-hot arms wrap around his waist. Tavi held on to the horse's mane carefully. He had learned a good deal of riding in the capital, but very little of it had been done bareback, and he knew his limits. "Which gate was he at?" he asked Kitai.

"North side of the river, west side of the city," Kitai called back.

Beside them, Max rode with the casual skill with which he did almost everything. Max, Tavi knew, had been riding since he could walk. "Did he know he was followed?"

"Ehren knew," Tavi said firmly.

"So I'm Ehren," Max said, "with an unknown number of unknowns following me. Where do I go?" Max frowned. "Wait. What the crows am I doing all the way out here in the first place? I thought Ehren got sent to Phrygia."

"Did you notice that he packed those peppermints he kept around?" Tavi asked.

"Yes. I thought he liked peppermints."

"No. He gets seasick."

Max frowned. "But Phrygia's thousands of miles from the sea and—oh."

Tavi nodded. "I assume he was under orders to keep it secret, but I suspect he was sent out to the islands."

Max grunted. "So, I'm Ehren, who is a sneaky little git like Tavi, in from the islands, followed by bad men who want to do bad things. Where do I go?"

"Somewhere that presents you more options," Tavi called

back. "Where you can deal with them appropriately and as discreetly as possible." He paused for a moment, then he and Max said together, "The docks."

They pressed on, Tavi in the lead. Dry red lightning lit their way in flickers of dim fire that only made the shadows deeper and more treacherous. Tavi could navigate by the furylights in the town and upon the Elinarch, but he could barely see what was five feet in front of him. Haste was necessary, but they would do Ehren no good if they all brained themselves on low branches or broke the legs of their mounts in potholes in the trail, and Tavi began to slow the pace.

"No," Kitai said in his ear. The arm around his waist shifted, and she clasped the hand in which Tavi held the reins. She pulled his hand to the right, and the horse altered course, Max's mount following suit. Lightning flashed, and Tavi saw the black maw of a sharp-edged pothole flash by, narrowly avoided.

Kitai leaned forward, and he felt her cheek against his as she smiled. "I will be your eyes, blind Aleran."

Tavi felt his own mouth stretch into a grin to match hers, and he shouted to his mount, coaxing all the speed he could from the draft horse.

They entered the town through the eastern gate, shouting passwords to the *legionares* on duty there, thundering over the stone streets, the heavy steel-shod hooves of their horses striking sparks from the stone. The western gate of the town had been left unguarded and slightly ajar. As they approached, Max crafted a miniature cyclone that hammered it the rest of the way open, and they swept through, altering course to follow the city's wall down to the riverside.

The town of Elinarch had been founded as little more than a standard Legion camp anchoring either end of the bridge. In the century since, its rising population had spread beyond the original walls, building homes and business around the wall's outskirts and, especially, constructing extensive docking facilities for the river traffic that supported the town. The wooden wharves and piers had spread hundreds of yards upon either side of the original town's boundaries on both banks of the river.

Piers brought ships and boats, which brought a steady and large number of sailing men, which gave birth to an inevitable, if modest, industry of graft and vice. Wine clubs, gambling halls, and pleasure houses were built upon both the wharves and permanently anchored barges. There was a paucity of furylamps throughout the docks—partly because no one wanted even a tiny fire fury that close to so much aged wood, and partly because the darkness suited the clandestine nature of the businesses there.

Tavi swung down from the horse and flicked the reins around the nearest wooden post. "Knowing Ehren, where do we look?"

"Little guy liked to plan ahead," Max said. "Be early for lecture. Set aside time to study."

Tavi nodded. "He'd have prepared a spot in case he had to run or fight. A distraction, to keep people from noticing while he slipped away." Tavi nodded toward a number of large, roomy buildings built directly beneath the soaring stone Elinarch. "Warehouses."

The three of them started out at a hard pace, and though Tavi's leg ached from the effort, it supported his weight easily enough. The first warehouse was open and lit as Legion teamsters unloaded the wagons of foodstuffs the Subtribunes Logistica had scrounged—like the one they'd left back on the road. Haradae, the seniormost Subtribune Logistica, a watery-eyed young man from Rhodes, looked up from a ledger book and frowned at Tavi. "Scipio? Where is your wagon?"

"On the way," Tavi called back, slowing. "Have you seen any of Erasmus's eighth spear out tonight?"

"Just went by, not five minutes ago, chasing some thief," he said, hooking a thumb. "But I thought they were on gate duty, not night watch."

"Erasmus thought that, too," Tavi improvised. "No one's·at the gate."

Haradae shook his head and checked his list. "Here. Bandages. I'll have some set out for Erasmus after he's done lashing them."

Max growled under his breath, "Think he has any coffins?"

"Come on," Tavi said, and picked up the pace again.

They found the body in the shadows beside the fifth warehouse in the row, and Tavi's heart leapt into his throat as he peered at the empty black shape in the darkness. "Is it . . . ?"

"No," Kitai said. "A *legionare*. He is older than Ehren and has a beard." She bent and casually tugged at the corpse. Light gleamed on steel for a second. "Knife in the neck. Well thrown."

"Shhhh," Tavi said, and held up a hand. They were quiet for a moment. The lazy river whispered now and then beneath them. The wooden wharves creaked and groaned. Tavi heard a pair of men arguing in tight, tense voices meant not to carry. Then there was a heavy thud.

Tavi drew his sword as silently as he could and nodded to Max. The pair of them started down the walkway in a hurried prowl. They were able to slip up behind a group of seven *legionares*. One of them held a single, dim furylamp while two others spoke and the rest stood in a loose half circle around a weather-beaten wooden storage shed, perhaps five feet high and wide and ten deep. One of the men held a wounded arm in close to his body, a kerchief wrapped around his hand in a crude bandage.

Max narrowed his eyes and crouched, but Tavi lifted a hand, silently signaling him to halt. A second gesture told Max to follow his lead, and Tavi walked boldly into the dim light of the lamp.

"And just what the crows do you men think you're doing?" he demanded.

The *legionares* whirled to face him. The two men arguing froze, startled expressions of guilt on their faces. Tavi recognized them, though he did not know them by name—apart from the wounded man. It was Nonus, the *legionare* who had given Tavi trouble his first day in the camp. His companion Bortus stood uneasily beside him. Though no one had ever commented on it, Tavi suspected that a quiet word from Max had convinced Valiar Marcus to transfer them to Erasmus's century—a less-senior century within his cohort, which had doubtless resulted in a reduction in pay.

"Well?" Tavi demanded. "Who is the file leader of this sorry bunch?"

"Sir," mumbled one of two debaters. He wore his helmet sloppily unfastened, cheek flaps loose. His voice had a Kalaran accent. "I am, Subtribune Scipio."

Tavi tilted his head and kept his face fixed in a steadily darkening scowl. "Name, soldier?"

The man glanced about uneasily. "Yanar, sir."

"Yanar. You want to tell me why one of your men is dead in that alley and you've another wounded, *instead* of being at your crowbegotten *post*?"

"Sir, Creso was *murdered*, sir!"

"I assumed that from the way a knife was sticking out of his neck," Tavi said in a quietly acidic tone. "But that is hardly important. Why was he murdered *there* and not at his *post*?"

"We were pursuing a criminal, sir!" Yanar stammered. "He fled."

"Yes, file leader. I did manage to deduce that if you were *pursuing* him, he most probably had *fled*. But why are you *here* instead of at your *post*?"

"Yanar," growled one of the *legionares*. He was a man of medium size, slender in build, dark of hair and eye. Tavi did not know his name. "He's just one prating little subbie." He jerked his head at the storage shed. "Maybe he tries to help us. We tell him not to, but maybe he goes in first. Maybe our boy killed him and Creso both."

Yanar turned back to Tavi, a look of ugly speculation in his eyes.

"Careful, Yanar," Tavi said in a quiet voice. "You're getting near to treason."

"It's only treason," said the dark man, "if you get caught."

Yanar narrowed his eyes at Tavi and said, "K—"

Tavi presumed the man was going to say "kill·him," but he decided not to waste a perfectly good second in listening. He took a bounding step forward and struck straight down with his *gladius*. The blow landed on the crown of Yanar's untied helmet, slamming it forward and down, breaking the *legionare's* nose and roughly gouging at one cheek. Tavi slammed his armored shoulder into Yanar's chest, knocking him down, ducked the swing of another sword, and kicked against the dark man's knee, crushing the joint, sending him to the wharf with a cry of pain.

Tavi parried another sword strike, and attacked, forcing the *legionare* to react with a textbook-perfect return stroke—one that would have been excellent in the press of battle. It wasn't a street-fighting move. Tavi disengaged his blade from his foe's, took a step forward to the diagonal, and slammed his armored fist into the man's nose with all of his own strength plus his opponent's momentum, stunning him for an instant. Tavi drove the pommel of his sword into the man's armored temple, sending him crashing to the ground. Max came rushing up to Tavi's side, but the *legionares* around him had fallen back in shock at the sudden, vicious assault.

"Not bad," Max observed.

Tavi shrugged.

"All right, gentlemen," Tavi snarled at the rest of them. "So far, you've only deserted your post, presumably at the orders of this idiot." Tavi pointed his sword at the unconscious Yanar. "The consequences for that aren't pleasant, but they aren't too terrible. Everyone who wishes to add insubordination, failure to obey an officer, and attempted murder to his list of offenses should keep his weapon in hand and give me an instant of trouble."

There was a short silence. Then Nonus swallowed, drew his sword, and dropped it to the wharf. Bortus followed, as did the other *legionares*.

"Return to your posts," Tavi said, voice cold. "Wait there to be relieved while I get your centurion out of his cot and send him to deal with you."

The men winced.

"Sir?" Nonus said. "What about the thief, sir? He killed a *legionare*. He's dangerous."

Tavi glared at them, then said, "You, in the shed. I'm placing you under arrest and binding you by Crown law. Come out now, unarmed, and I'll see to it that you are treated in accord with the Crown's justice."

A moment later, Ehren appeared in the doorway of the shed. He had more muscle than Tavi remembered, and his skin was dark brown from time in the sun that had washed most of the color from his hair. He was dressed in simple if somewhat ragged clothes, and had his hands held up, empty. His eyes widened when he saw Tavi and Max, and he drew in a sudden breath.

"Keep your crowbegotten mouth shut," Tavi told him bluntly. "Centurion. Take him into custody."

Max went to Ehren and casually twisted the smaller man's arm behind him in a common come-along hold, then marched him out of the alley. "You, you, you," Tavi said, pointing at *legionares*. "Carry these idiots on the ground." He walked around, picking up their surrendered weapons as they did, stacking them in the circle of one arm, like cordwood. "You," Tavi said, as Nonus picked up the dark man. "What is your name?"

The man narrowed his eyes, but said nothing.

"Suit yourself," Tavi said, and turned to lead the men from the alley.

A sudden sensation of panic hit him like a shock of cold water.

"Aleran!" Kitai's voice called.

Tavi dropped the swords and dived forward, over them, turning in place. The dark man had broken free from Nonus, and now held a curved, vicious-looking knife. He swept it hard at Tavi's throat. Tavi rolled in the direction of the strike. The knife missed him by a hair. Tavi managed to grab on to the man's arm as he missed, and a hard tug sent him stumbling, so that his crushed knee gave out on him.

He cried out and fell, but started to push himself up again, knife still in hand.

Kitai dropped from the roof of the warehouse and landed on his back, slamming him to the wharf. She seized the crown of his helm with one hand, the neck of his tunic with the other, and with a snarl slammed his head completely *through* the flooring, shattering the wooden planks beneath his face, trapping his head there.

Then the Marat woman seized his shoulders and twisted.

The dark man's neck broke with an ugly crack.

"Crows," Tavi swore. He scrambled to the man's side and

felt for the pulse in his wrist. He was, however, quite dead. "I wanted him to talk," he told Kitai.

Her feline green eyes almost seemed to glow in the shadows. "He meant to kill you."

"Of course he did," Tavi said. "But now we can't find out who he was."

Kitai shrugged and bent to pick up the curved knife, now lying under the man's limp hand. She held it up, and said, "Bloodcrow."

Tavi peered at the knife, then nodded. "Looks like."

"Subtribune Scipio?" Max called.

"Coming," Tavi called back. He glanced at Nonus and the other *legionares*, who were staring openly at him.

"Who *are* you?" Nonus asked in a quiet voice.

"A smart soldier," Tavi replied quietly, "knows when to keep his mouth shut. You've screwed up enough for one day already."

Nonus swallowed and saluted.

"Move it, people," Tavi said, raising his voice. He recovered the swords as the *legionares* marched out, and tucked the curved Kalaran knife through his belt.

"What now?" Kitai asked him quietly.

"Now we take everything to Cyril," Tavi said quietly. "Ehren, Yanar, all of it. The captain will know what to do." More red lightning played overhead, and Tavi shivered. "Come on. I've got a feeling we don't have any time to lose."

⊲⊲⊲⊲⊲ CHAPTER 27

"Isana," Giraldi rumbled. "Steadholder, I'm sorry, but there's no more time. You need to wake."

Isana tried for a moment to remain in the blissful darkness of sleep, but then forced herself to open her eyes and sit up.

She felt thoroughly wretched, exhausted, and wanted nothing more than lie down once more.

But that was not an option.

Isana blinked whatever exhaustion she could from her eyes. "Thank you, centurion."

"Ma'am," Giraldi said, with a nod, and stepped back from the bed.

Veradis looked up from where she sat beside Fade and the healing tub, holding the unconscious slave's hand. "Apologies, Steadholder," the healer murmured with a weak smile. "I have no more than an hour to give today."

"It's all right, Veradis," Isana replied. "If you hadn't given me a chance to get some sleep, I'd never have lasted this far. May I have a moment to . . ."

Veradis nodded with another faint smile. "Of course."

Isana availed herself of the facilities and returned to kneel beside Veradis, slipping her own hand between hers and Fade's, and reassuming control of the steady effort of furycraft required to fight the man's infection. The first time she had handed the crafting off to Veradis, it had been a difficult, delicate maneuver—one only possible because of an unusual degree of similarity in their styles of furycraft, in fact. Repetition had made the extraordinary feat commonplace over the past twenty days.

Or was it twenty-one, Isana thought wearily. *Or nineteen.* The days began blurring together once the low, heavy storm clouds above the city had rolled in. Even now, they roiled restlessly above them, flickering with sullen thunder and crimson light but withholding the rain that should have come with it. The storm cast the world into continual twilight and darkness, and she had no way to measure the passing of time.

Even so, Isana had managed, barely, to hang on to the furycrafting that was Fade's only hope. Without Veradis giving her the odd hour or two to sleep, now and then, Fade would long since have died.

"How is he?" Isana asked. She settled down in the seat Veradis rose from.

The young healer once more bound Isana's hand to Fade's with soft rope. "The rot has lost some ground," Veradis said quietly. "But he's been in the tub too long, and he hasn't kept enough food down. His skin is developing a number of sores, which . . ." She shook her head, took a breath and began again. "You know what happens then."

Isana nodded. "Other sicknesses are pressing in."

"He's getting weaker, Steadholder," Veradis said. "If he doesn't rally soon—"

They were interrupted as the room's door banged opened. "Lady *Veradis*," said an armed *legionare* in a strained, urgent voice. "You must hurry. He's dying."

Veradis grimaced, her eyes sunken and weary. Then she rose, and said to Isana, "I don't know if I shall be able to return again," she said quietly.

Isana nodded once. Veradis turned and walked from the room, her steps swift, calm, and certain. "Describe the injury," she said. The *legionare's* description of the blow of a heavy mallet faded as the pair walked down the hall.

Giraldi watched them go, then rumbled, "Steadholder? You should eat. I'll bring you some broth."

"Thank you, Giraldi," Isana said quietly. The old soldier left the room, and she turned her attention to the crafting within Fade.

The pain of exposing herself to the substances within Fade had not lessened in the least. It had, however, become something familiar, something she knew and could account for—and as she had grown more weary, day by day, as she grew less able to distinguish it as a separate entity from her body's exhaustion, it had become increasingly unimportant.

She settled herself comfortably in the seat, her eyes open but unfocused. The infection now existed as a solid image in her mind that represented its presence within Fade. She pictured it as a mound of rounded stones, each solid and heavy, but also eminently moveable. She waited for a moment, until the beating of her heart and the slow cadences of her breath matched those of the wounded man. Then, in her mind's eye, she picked up the nearest stone and lifted it, carrying it aside and tossing it into a featureless imaginary stream. Then she repeated the action, deliberate, resolute, one stone after another.

She did not know how much time passed as she focused on helping Fade's body fight the contagion, but she suddenly felt a presence beside her at the imagined mound of rock.

Fade stood there, frowning up at the mound of rocks. He did not look as he did in the healing tub, worn and wan and wasted. Instead, he appeared to her as a young man—thin with youth and a body not yet done filling out. His hair was cut Legion style, his face bore no scar of a coward's brand, and he wore the simple breeches and tunic of an off-duty soldier. "Hello," he said. "What are you doing here?"

"You're sick," Isana told the image. "You need to rest, Fade, and let me help you."

At the mention of his name, the image figure frowned. His features changed for a moment, aged, the scar of the coward's brand emerging from his skin. He reached up to touch his face, frowning. "Fade . . ." he murmured. Then his eyes widened. He looked up at Isana, and his features abruptly aged, hair growing longer, scars reappearing. "Isana?"

"Yes," she murmured.

"I was wounded," he said. He blinked his eyes as if trying to focus. "Aren't we in Ceres?"

"Yes," she said. "You're unconscious. I'm attempting to craft you well."

Fade shook his head. "I don't understand what's happening. Is this a dream?"

An interesting thought. Isana paused to consider him. "It might be. I'm in a state of mind somewhere close to sleep. You've had a fever for days, and I've been in close contact with you, through Rill, almost the whole time. I've felt the edges of some of your dreams—but you've been in a fever the whole while. It was mostly just confusion."

Fade smiled a little. "This must be your dream, then."

"In a manner of speaking," she said.

"Days . . ." He frowned. "Isana, isn't that sort of crafting very dangerous?"

"Not as dangerous as doing nothing, I'm afraid," she said. Fade shook his head. "I meant for you."

"I'm prepared for it," Isana said.

"No," Fade said, abruptly. "No, Isana. You aren't to take this kind of risk for me. Someone else must."

"There is no one else," Isana said quietly.

"Then you must stop," Fade said. "You cannot come to harm on my account."

Back in the physical world, Isana dimly felt Fade begin to move, the first such motion in days. He tried, weakly, to pull his hand from hers.

"No," Isana said firmly. She went to fetch the next stone and resume her steady labor. "Stop this, Fade. You must rest."

"I can't," Fade said. "I can't be responsible for more harm to you. Bloody crows, Isana." His voice became thick with anguished grief. "I've failed him more than enough already."

"No. No you haven't."

"I swore to protect him," Fade said. "And when he needed me most, I left him to die."

"No," Isana said quietly. "He ordered you to see us clear of the Valley. To keep us safe."

"I shouldn't have followed the order," Fade said, his voice suddenly vicious with self-hatred. "My duty was to protect him. Preserve him. He had already lost two of his *singulares* because of *me*. I'm the one who lamed Miles. Who drove Aldrick from his service." His hands clenched into fists. "I should never have left him. No matter what he said."

"Fade," Isana said quietly. "Whatever killed Septimus must have been too much for anyone to stop. He was the son of the First Lord, and every bit as powerful as his father. Perhaps more so. Do you really think you could have made a difference?"

"I might have," Fade said. "Whatever killed Septimus, I might have been able to stop it. Or at least slow it down enough to allow him to handle it. Even if I only managed to preserve him a single second, and even if I'd died doing it, it might have been all he needed."

"Or it might not," Isana said quietly. "You might have died

senselessly with him. You know he wouldn't have wanted that."

Fade clenched his teeth, the tightened muscles of his jaw distorting the lines of his face. "I should have died with them. I wish I *had*." He shook his head. "Part of me died that day, Isana. Araris Valerian. Araris the brave. I ran from the fight. I left the side of the man I swore to protect."

Isana stopped and touched the brand upon his face. "This was only a disguise, Araris. A costume. A mask. They had to think you were dead if you were to be able to protect Tavi."

"It was a disguise," Araris said, bitter. "It was also the truth."

Isana sighed. "No, Fade. You are the most courageous man I've ever known."

"I left him," he said. "I left him."

"Because he wished you to protect us."

"And I failed him in that, as well. I let your sister die."

Isana felt a dart of remembered pain strike her chest. "There was nothing you could have done. That was not your fault."

"It was. I should have seen that Marat. Should have stopped him b-before—" Fade held his hands up to his ears and shook his head. "I can't do this anymore, I can't see him, see you, be there anymore, my lady please, just leave me, let me go to him, to my lord, left him, coward mark, coward heart . . ."

He trailed off into incoherent babbling, and when his body thrashed weakly in the healing tub, trying to take his hand from hers, the image-Fade vanished again, leaving Isana alone with the mound of imaginary stones.

She went back to work.

Later, she blinked her eyes, forcing her thoughts back to the chamber in Cereus's citadel for a moment, looking around the room. Fade lay in the tub, muscles quivering in random little twitches. She reached across him to touch his forehead with her free hand, and confirmed what she already knew.

Fade had given up the fight. He did not want to recover.

His fever had grown worse.

He was dying.

The door opened and Giraldi paced quietly into the room, a mug of broth in his hand. "Steadholder?"

She gave him a faint smile as he passed her the mug. It was difficult for her to eat and keep food down, given the constant pain the crafting required, but it was vital that she do so. "Thank you, centurion."

"Course." He stumped over to the window and stared out. "Crows, Steadholder. I always hated getting into a battle. But I think standing around like this is worse." The fingers of his sword hand opened and closed rhythmically upon his cane.

Isana took a slow sip of broth. "How fares the battle?"

"Kalare's taken the upper hand," Giraldi responded. "He worked out how to draw out Cereus's Knights so that he could eliminate them."

Isana closed her eyes and shook her head. "What happened?"

"He ordered his Knights to attack a residential district," Giraldi replied. "Including the city's largest orphanage and a number of streets where retired *legionares* were living out their pensions."

Isana grimaced. "Great furies. The man is a monster."

Giraldi grunted. "Worked, though." His voice became something distant, impersonal. "There's only so many times you can see an elder getting cut down. Only so many times you can hear a child screaming. Then you have to do something. Even if it's stupid."

"How bad were the losses?"

"Kalare and his son were personally involved in the attack. Cereus lost half his Knights. Mostly Knights Aeris. If Captain Miles and the Crown Legion's Knights hadn't intervened, they'd have died to a man. Cereus himself was injured, getting them out of the trap. He and Captain Miles went up against Kalarus and his son in the front hall of the orphanage. From what I've heard, it was an amazing battle."

"In my experience, rumors rarely bother to get the details correct," said a gentle voice at the door.

Isana turned to find Captain Miles standing in the doorway, still in full battle armor, his helmet under his left arm. The armor and helm were both dented and scratched in too many places to count. The right arm of his tunic was soaked in blood to the elbow, and his hand rested on the hilt of his *gladius*. His hair was Legion-cropped, greying, and he smelled of sweat and rust and blood. He was not a particularly large man, and he had plain features that gave Isana an immediate sense of fidelity and loyalty. He moved with a detectable limp as he stepped into the room, but though he spoke to Isana and Giraldi, his eyes were on the man in the healing tub.

"Cereus played the wounded bird and lured them in. They came in to take him down, and I was hiding in the rafters. I hit the boy from behind and wounded him badly enough to make Kalarus panic and pull him out."

"Captain," Giraldi said with a nod. "I heard Kalarus tried to roast you for it, sir."

Miles shrugged. "I wasn't in the mood for roast. I ran away." He nodded to Isana. "Steadholder. Do you know who I am?"

Isana glanced at Fade and back to Miles. They were brothers, though Miles, like the rest of Alera, had thought Araris dead for nearly twenty years. "I know you," she said quietly.

"I would ask a favor of you." He glanced at Giraldi, including him in the sentiment. "A few private moments of your time, Steadholder?"

"She's working," Giraldi said, and though his tone was not disrespectful, neither was it prepared to compromise. "She doesn't need any distractions."

Miles hovered for a moment, as though uncertain of which way to move. Then he said, "I spoke to Lady Veradis. She said that there might not be much more time."

Isana glanced away. Despair washed through her for a moment, her weariness lending it tremendous potency. She pushed the tide of it away, then said, "It's all right, Giraldi."

The centurion grunted. Then he nodded to Isana and

limped to the door on his cane. "A moment," he said to Miles. "I'll hold you to it, sir."

Miles nodded, and waited for Giraldi to depart the room. Then he went to Fade's side, knelt, and laid a hand on the unconscious slave's head. "He's on fire," Miles said quietly.

"I know," Isana replied. "I'm doing all that I can."

"I should have come sooner," Miles said, his voice bitter. "Should have been here every day."

From outside, there came the loud, hollow cough of thunder that accompanied a firecrafter's assault, when fire would suddenly blossom from nothing into a white-hot sphere. The fire-thunder was answered, seconds later, by an almost-continuous rumbling from the glowering storm.

"You've been somewhat busy," Isana said, tired amusement in her voice.

Miles shook his head. "It wasn't that. It was . . ." He frowned. "My big brother. He always won. He's been in fights that should have killed him time and time again. And even when he *did* die, he managed to come back. It may have taken him twenty years, but he did it." Miles shook his head. "Invincible. Maybe part of me didn't want to admit that he might not be. That I might . . ."

Lose him, Isana thought, finishing his thought.

"Can he hear me?" Miles asked.

Isana shook her head. "I don't know. He's been in and out of consciousness, but he's grown more incoherent each day."

Miles bit his lip and nodded, and Isana felt the depth of his grief, pain, and regret. He looked up at her, his eyes frightened, almost like a child's. "Is what Veradis said true?" he asked. "Is he going to die?"

Isana knew what Miles wanted to hear. His emotions and his eyes were begging her for hope.

She met Miles's eyes, and said quietly, "Probably. But I'm not going to give up on him."

Miles blinked his eyes several times and moved his right hand as though brushing sweat from his forehead. It left his face smeared with thin streaks of the blood on his sleeve. "All right," he said quietly. Then he leaned down closer to Fade. "Rari. It's Miles. I'm . . ." He bowed his head, at a loss for words. "I'm here, Rari. I'm here."

He looked up at Isana. "Is there anything I can do help you?"

Isana shook her head. "He's . . . he's very tired. And very sick. And he isn't fighting it. He isn't trying to recover."

Miles frowned. "That doesn't sound like him. Why not?"

Isana let out a sigh. "I don't know. He's only been lucid enough to speak for a few moments. And even then, he wasn't making much sense. Guilt, perhaps. Or perhaps he's just too tired."

Miles stared down at Fade for a moment. He was about to speak when boots thumped up to the door.

"Captain!" called a young man's warbling voice. One of the citadel's pages, then. "My lord requests your immediate presence."

Miles looked up at Isana, and called, "On my way." Then he bent down and leaned his forehead against Fade's for a second. Then he rose. "Should he come around again before . . . Please tell him I came to see him."

"Of course," Isana said.

"Thank you," Miles said.

Miles left the room. Giraldi stuck his head back in, glanced around once, then went back out. He shut the door and leaned his back against it to prevent any more disturbances, Isana supposed.

Miles had been right. Fade was not the sort of man simply to surrender. He had lived with the guilt of Septimus's death for twenty years, yet never attempted to end his life, never gave in to despair.

It had to be something else. Something more.

Bloody crows, Isana thought. If only he could speak to her. Even if just for a moment. She ground her teeth in frustration.

Outside, fire-thunder boomed and cracked. Trumpets blared. Drums rattled. Beneath them, the roar of angry armies. The sullen sky flickered with spiteful thunder.

Isana finished the broth, forced all such distractions from her mind, and went back to work.

CHAPTER 28

Captain Cyril stared at Ehren for a long moment. Then his mouth turned down into a thoughtful frown. He studied the almost-too-bright silver of one of Gaius's personal coins, given to the Cursors as tokens of their authority. A full minute passed before he asked, "Are you sure?"

"Yes, sir," Ehren said, his tone grim and calm.

They stood inside the captain's command tent, flaps down, lit by a pair of soft yellow furylamps. When they arrived, Cyril had been awake, armored, and waiting for them without a trace of sleep lingering in his eyes. His bedroll was neatly stored atop the standard trunk in the corner. The soldier who led by example.

A brief silence followed Ehren's reply, and Magnus used the time to refresh the captain's cup of tea. Max waggled his own empty cup at Magnus. Magnus arched an eyebrow at him, then passed him the carafe. Max smiled and poured his own, then refilled Tavi's as well.

"Marcus?" Max asked.

Valiar Marcus shook his head, declining. The ugly old centurion stood beside the captain, scratching at his head. "Sir, I have to wonder if this isn't a hoax of some kind. The Canim have never come to Alera's shores in such numbers."

Ehren looked ragged and tired, but he bristled at the First Spear's words. "Are you calling me a liar, centurion?"

"No," the First Spear said, meeting Ehren's eyes. "But a man may speak the truth and still be incorrect."

Ehren clenched his hands into fists, but Cyril stopped him with a hard look. "The First Spear is right to be cautious, sir Cursor," he said to Ehren.

"Why?" Ehren demanded.

"Because of the timing," Cyril said. "Kalarus's Legions have marched upon the forces of the First Lord."

Ehren stared at him for a moment. "What?"

Cyril nodded. "Ceres is under siege. Kalarus's forces have cut off the eastern High Lords for the time being. Placida and Attica stand neutral. If Kalarus could manage to create a false threat from the Canim and force Aleran Legions to respond, it could spread Gaius's supporters out more thinly, rob them of the advantage of numbers."

Ehren shook his head. "I saw them, Captain, with my own eyes. Hundreds of ships, driven before the storm that has made it all but impossible for us to fly, to carry word swiftly, to outmaneuver them. This is no mere raid."

The First Spear grunted. "How come this didn't come through official channels of intelligence?"

"Because I made landfall at the harbor in Redstone to find that my contact in the Cursors had been murdered the previous week. I didn't dare reveal myself for fear that his murderers would be watching for other Cursors."

"A plausible explanation," Cyril said. "But one that does not readily lend itself to confirmation. My orders are to hold the bridge, Sir Ehren, not to mount expeditions against an incursion. I am willing to send out a party to verify—"

"*Captain,*" Ehren said, voice rising in alarm. "There's no time for that. My ship outran the Canim armada, but not by much. If they've kept their pace, they'll make landfall in the harbor at Founderport in the next few hours. There aren't many harbors along this coast. It's obvious that they must control the Elinarch or risk being attacked from several directions." He pointed to the south. "They're coming *here*, Captain. By this time tomorrow, you'll have the largest Canim battlepack in the history of Alera coming over that hill."

Cyril frowned at Ehren for a moment, then looked at the First Spear.

"Crows," Marcus muttered, running a finger down the

lumpy bridge of his often-broken nose. "Why?" he asked. "Why here? Why now?"

It came to Tavi in a flash. "Wrong question, centurion." Tavi looked at Cyril and said, "Not 'why,' sir. Who."

"Who?" Cyril asked.

"Who are they working with," Tavi said quietly.

Silence fell.

"No," Max said after a moment. "No Aleran Citizen would have traffic with the Canim. Not even Kalarus. It's . . . no, it's unthinkable."

"And," Tavi said, "it is the most likely explanation. This storm has blinded us and severely harms our ability to coordinate."

"It does the same to Kalarus," the First Spear pointed out.

"But he *knew* when it was coming. Where his targets were. Where he would strike. His forces were already coordinated and in motion." Tavi glanced at Cyril. "That storm does far more to harm Gaius than Kalarus. The only problem is how the Canim told Kalarus that it was about to begin." Tavi chewed his lip. "They'd need a signal of some kind."

"Like red stars?" the First Spear snarled in disgust. He spat a vile oath, hand coming to rest on his sword. "Kalarus's attack began the night of the red stars. So did the Canim's."

"Bloody crows," Max said. He shook his head in disbelief. "Bloody crows."

Cyril looked at the First Spear, and said, "If they take the Elinarch, they'll run right through Placida's heartlands on the north side, and with the river protecting their flank, they'll be able to lay waste to Ceres' lands on the south."

"There's not another full Legion within eight or nine hundred miles, sir," the First Spear said. "And we can't send any requests for reinforcement by air. No one could reach us in time to make any difference." He set his jaw in a grim line, and said, "We're alone out here."

"No," Cyril corrected quietly. "We are a Legion. If we do not fight, the holders in the towns and steadholts the Canim will attack will be alone."

"The fish aren't ready, sir," Valiar Marcus warned. "Neither are the defenses of the town."

"Be that as it may. They are what we have. And by the great furies, they are Aleran *legionares*." Cyril nodded once. "We fight."

The First Spear's eyes glittered, and his teeth showed in a wolfish smile. "Yes, sir."

"Centurion, summon my officers here at once. All of them. Go."

"Sir," Marcus said. He saluted and strode from the tent.

"Antillar, you are to carry word to the cavalry and auxiliaries to prepare for immediate deployment. I'm sending Fantus and Cadius Hadrian over the bridge tonight, to slow any advance elements of the enemy forces, gather what intelligence they can, and to give our holders a chance to run, if need be."

"Sir," Max said. He saluted, nodded at Tavi, and strode out.

"Magnus. Go into town and contact Councilman Vogel. Give him my compliments and ask him to send any boats that can manage it up the river to spread the word of a Canim incursion. Then ask him to open the town's armory. I want as many militiamen as we can equip armed and ready to fight."

Maestro Magnus saluted the captain, nodded to Tavi, and slipped out.

"And you, Scipio," Cyril said, fixing a speculative stare on Tavi. "You seem to have a talent for finding trouble."

"I'd prefer to think that it finds me, sir."

The captain gave him a humorless smile. "Do you understand the wider implications of a relationship between Kalarus and the Canim, and the attempt to prevent Sir Ehren, here, from reaching us?"

"Yes, sir," Tavi said. "It means that Kalarus probably has further intelligence assets within the Legion, and that they may well take other actions to leave us more vulnerable to the Canim."

"A distinct possibility," Cyril said, nodding. "Keep your eyes open. Carry word to Mistress Cymnea that the followers should ready to retreat to the town's walls, should battle be joined."

"Sir," Tavi said, saluting. "Shall I return here for the officers' meeting?"

"Yes. We'll begin in twenty minutes." Cyril paused and glanced from Tavi to Ehren. "Good work, you two."

"Thank you, sir," Tavi said, inclining his head to Cyril in acknowledgment of the captain's deduction. Then he traded a nod with Ehren and ducked out of the tent. He hurried through the lightning-strobed darkness as the camp began to waken from its late-night torpor to the sounds of shouted orders, nervous horses, and clanking armor.

ᴄᴏᴄ CHAPTER 29

The Legion followers' camp lay farther from the actual Legion camp than was the norm: While the Legions had inhabited the standard-format fortifications built into the town itself, there was not room enough for townsfolk, Legion, and followers alike. The newer portions of the town had been built outside the protection of the walls, and the followers had pitched their tents on the common land surrounding the city, on the downriver side of the town.

It wasn't a pleasant camp, by any means. The ground was soft and too easily churned into mud by passing feet. Footprints filled with water that oozed into them, which in turn gave birthplaces to uncounted midges, mites, and buzzing annoyances. When the wind blew from the river or the city, it carried a distinct odor in one or more of several unpleasant varieties.

But for all that, the followers' camp had been set up in roughly the same order as it had been at the training grounds, and Tavi picked out the flutes and drums of Mistress Cymnea's Pavilion without trouble. He wound his way there through the darkened camp. The sharp smell of amaranthium incense, burned at each fire to ward off insects, made his nose itch and his eyes water slightly.

Tavi glimpsed a shadow ahead of him and came to a stop beneath a single lonely furylamp hung beside the entrance to the Pavilion. Tavi unfastened and removed his helmet and held up a hand in greeting. Bors, lurking near the entrance as always, lifted his chin a fraction of an inch by way of reply, then held up a hand, indicating that Tavi should wait.

He did, and after a moment, a tall, slender shadow replaced Bors, and walked with swaying grace to him.

"Mistress Cymnea," Tavi said, bowing his head. "I hardly expected to see you up this late."

Cymnea smiled from within her cloak's hood, and said, "I've been following Legions since I was a little girl, Subtribune. Shouts and signal drums in the middle of the night mean one of two things: fire or battle."

Tavi nodded. "Canim," he said, and his voice sounded grim, even to him. "We aren't sure how many. It would appear to be a major incursion."

Cymnea drew in a sharp breath. "I see."

"Captain Cyril's compliments, Mistress, and he wants the camp followers to be ready to withdraw into the city's walls should it become necessary."

"Of course," she said. "I'll see to it that the word is spread."

"Thank you." Tavi paused. "The captain didn't say anything about it, Mistress, but if you're entertaining any Legion personnel . . ."

She gave him a brief smile. "I know the drill. I'll get them sober and send them home."

"Thank you," Tavi said, with another bow.

"Subtribune," she said, "I know that you have your duties, but have you seen Gerta this evening?"

"Ah," Tavi said. "I saw her in town earlier this evening."

Cymnea frowned. "I worry about slavers, her running off alone in a strange town. She's such a fragile little thing. And not quite right in the head."

Tavi worked very hard to hold back both a bark of laughter and a wide smile. "I'll grant that's true, but I'm sure she's all right, Mistress," he said seriously. "Elinarch is a law-abiding town, and the captain won't tolerate any nonsense from the men."

"No," Cymnea said. "The best of them never do."

"You know the trumpet call to flee to the city?"

She nodded and bowed her head to him. "Good luck, Sub-tribune. And thank you for the warning."

"Good luck, Mistress," he said, returning her bow. He nodded to the silent presence of Bors, then headed back to town at a steady if uncomfortable jog.

In the outbuildings before the town's walls, Tavi heard a movement to his right a fraction of an instant too late to allow him to evade. Something hit his side in midstride, and sent him to the ground on his face. Before he could rise, what felt like steel bars wrapped around one of Tavi's wrists and pinned the wrist high up on his back. The fury-assisted pressure was painful in its own right, and one of the banded plates of Tavi's armor ground against his ribs.

"All right, Scipio," hissed a voice. "Or whatever your name really is. Hand over my mother's purse."

"Crassus," Tavi growled. "Get off me."

"Give me her purse, you thief!" Crassus shouted back.

Tavi clenched his teeth against the pain. "You're making me late for an officers' meeting. We're mobilizing."

"Liar," Crassus said.

"Get *off* me, Sir Knight. That is an *order*."

Crassus's grip tightened. "You're a fool as well as a liar. You've merely annoyed her, and you think what she's done so far is bad? You haven't *seen* what she can do when she's angry."

"The crows I haven't," Tavi spat. "I've seen Max's back when he changes his tunic."

For whatever reason, the words hit Crassus hard, and Tavi felt him rock back from them, almost as if they'd been a phys-ical blow. The pressure on his wrist eased just enough that Tavi had room to move—and he was in a position to make a real fight of it. The incredible strength offered by the use of an earth fury was enormous, but earthcrafters often forgot its limitations. It did not make its user any heavier; and one's feet had to be on the ground.

Tavi got a knee under his body and slithered out of Crassus's loosened grip. He seized the Knight's tunic at the throat, twisted with the weight of his whole body, and used arms and legs both to throw him up onto the wooden porch of a nearby shop. Crassus hit hard, but rolled back up onto his feet, his face dark with rage.

Tavi had followed Crassus onto the porch, and when Crassus lifted his head to glare at him, Tavi's kick was already halfway to the young man's head. His boot struck Crassus on the mouth, a stunning blow, and he reeled back.

Tavi slipped aside a clumsy counterblow with one hand and struck Crassus with closed fists, nose and mouth, followed by a hard push that slammed the back of Crassus's head against the shop's wall. The young man wobbled and fell. When he growled and started getting up, Tavi struck him again.

Crassus staggered up again.

Tavi sent him crashing to the wooden floor again with precise, heavy blows.

All in all, he had to beat Crassus back to the ground four times before the young Knight let out his breath in a groan, blood all over his face and nose, and lay on his back.

Tavi's hands hurt terribly. He hadn't been wearing his heavy fighting gloves, and he'd ripped several knuckles open on Crassus's head. Though he supposed he shouldn't have been surprised that it was at least as thick as Max's.

"We through?" Tavi panted.

"Thief," Crassus said. Or so Tavi supposed. The word came out mushy and barely understandable. Which was the expected result if one's lips were split and swollen, one's nose broken, and when several teeth had gone missing.

"Maybe. But I'd die before I lifted a hand against my own blood."

Crassus looked up and glared, but Tavi saw a flicker of shame in the young man's eyes.

"I take it this is about the red stone?" Tavi asked.

"Don't know what you're talking about," Crassus said sullenly.

"Then I don't know anything about a purse," Tavi said, frowning at the beaten young man. Tavi didn't have the advantages of a skilled watercrafter, but he was as good as anyone without that advantage could be, when it came to reading people. Crassus wasn't lying to Tavi about the stone. He was sure of it.

"You'll get what you want now," Crassus said quietly. "You'll report me to the captain, won't you. Have me cast from the Legion. Sent home in shame."

Tavi regarded Crassus for a moment. Then he said, "You don't get dishonorably discharged for falling down a flight of stairs."

Crassus blinked at him. "What?"

"Sir Knight, just what the crows do you think those drums are for? Lulling the fish to sleep? We're mobilizing, and I'm not going to do anything that robs the Legion of a capable Knight and our Tribune Medica." Tavi extended his hand. "As far as I'm concerned, you fell down some stairs, and that's the end of it. Come on."

The young man stared at Tavi's hand for a moment, blinking in confusion, but then hesitantly reached out and let Tavi help him to his feet. He looked frightful, and while Tavi knew the injuries were painful, they weren't serious.

"I take it your mother sent you to speak to me?" Tavi asked him.

"No," Crassus said.

Tavi arched a skeptical eyebrow.

Crassus's eyes flashed with anger. "I'm not her valet. Or her dog."

"If she didn't tell you to do it, why are you here?"

"She's my mother," Crassus said, and spat blood from his mouth. "Trying to look out for her."

Tavi felt his eyes widen, as he suddenly realized the young man's motivation. "You didn't do it to protect her," he said quietly. "You were trying to protect *me*."

Crassus froze for a second, staring at Tavi, then looked away.

"That's why you didn't draw a sword on me," Tavi said quietly. "You never intended for me to be hurt."

Crassus wiped at his mouth with a corner of his sleeve. "She's . . . got a temper. She's reached the end of it. She left earlier tonight. I thought to find you and return the purse to her. Tell her I found it on the ground." He shook his head. "I didn't want her to do anything rash. Sometimes her anger gets the better of her."

"Like with Max," Tavi said.

Crassus grimaced. "Yes." He looked back toward the camp. "Maximus . . . some of those scars he took for me. Confessed to things I had done, trying to protect me." He glanced at Tavi. "I don't like you, Scipio. But Max does. And I owe him. That's why I came here. I wanted to reconcile us somehow. I thought if we could . . ." He shrugged. "Spend some time together, and not back at Antillus. Mother told me she was going to offer him an apology for how she has treated him."

Tavi felt a surge of anger for Max's stepmother. She'd offered him something, all right. She'd tried to kill him again. But Tavi had a strong suspicion that Crassus's opinion of her was anything but objective. He felt sure that the young knight would never allow himself to believe that his mother had Max's murder in mind.

Tavi reached into his pocket and withdrew the silk purse, shaking the small red stone out of it as he did, so that the stone remained in his pocket. He offered the purse to Crassus.

Crassus took it, and then said quietly, "I could report this to the captain."

"And I could suddenly remember that there are no stairs around here," Tavi replied without rancor. "But I think we've both wasted enough effort for tonight."

Crassus bounced the empty purse on his palm a few times, then pocketed it. "Maybe I should have just asked you for it."

Tavi grimaced, and said, "Sorry about your, uh, your face."

Crassus shook his head. "My own fault. I jumped you. Hit you first." He touched his nose lightly and winced. "Where'd you learn that throw?"

"From a Marat," Tavi replied. "Come on. I'm already late. And we'll both be needed tonight."

Crassus nodded, and they started walking.

They hadn't gone twenty paces when the brightest dance of scarlet fire Tavi had yet seen in the glowering overcast rushed from one horizon to the other and back again, rippling back and forth like some vast and unthinkably swift wave.

"Crows," Tavi said softly, staring up at the display.

And then the night was torn with blinding white light and a wall of thunder that smashed against Tavi in a sonic tsunami, staggering him, almost robbing him of his balance. He managed to steady Crassus when the young man began to fall. It lasted for a bare heartbeat, then the thunderous sound vanished into a high-pitched ringing tone in his ears, while the flashing streak of light remained burned into his blinded eyes, shifting colors slowly against the blackness.

It took several moments for his eyes to readjust to the night, and even longer for his ears to stop ringing. His instincts screaming, he hurried forward as fast as he could, to return to the town and the legion's fortification there. Sir Crassus, his expression somewhat dazed, followed along.

Fires burned in the fortifications. Tavi could hear the screams of wounded men and terrified horses. There were shouts and cries all around them, and confusion ran rampant.

Tavi reached the captain's command tent and stopped in his tracks, stunned.

Where Cyril's command had been, there was now a great, gaping hole torn in the blackened earth. Fires burned in patches all around it. Bodies—and pieces of bodies—lay scattered in the ruins.

Overhead, the thunder from the unnatural storm rumbled in what sounded to Tavi like hungry anticipation.

"Scipio!" shouted a frantic voice, and Tavi turned to find Max running forward through the chaos.

"What happened?" Tavi asked, his voice shocked.

"Lightning." Max panted. He had lost half of one eyebrow, singed away by the head, and there were blisters on the skin of his forehead and along one cheekbone. "A crowbegotten *wall*

of lightning. Came down like a hammer, not twenty feet away."
Max stared at the ruins. "Right on top of the captain's meeting."

"Great furies," Tavi breathed.

"Foss and the healers are with some survivors, but it
doesn't look good for them." He swallowed. "As far as we can
tell, you're the only officer able to serve."

Tavi stared at Max. "What do you mean?"

Max looked at the results of the lightning strike grimly and
said, "I mean that you are now in command of the First
Aleran, Captain Scipio."

◦◦◦◦◦ CHAPTER 30

Tavi threw down his bedroll and his regulation trunk in the
smoldering ruins where Captain Cyril's command tent had
been. "All right," he said to Foss, sitting down on the trunk.
"Let's hear it."

"Captain's alive," Foss said. The veteran healer looked exhausted, and the grey in his hair and beard stood out more
sharply than they had the day before. "Barely. Don't know if
he'll ever wake up. Don't know how much use he's gonna
have of his legs if he does."

Tavi grunted and worked on keeping his expression calm
and remote. He wasn't sure how well he was doing it. Telling
a lie to his aunt wasn't the same thing as pretending to be
competent and confident when all he really wanted to do was
run screaming and hide somewhere.

Around him, the Legion continued preparing to fight.

Screaming and hiding was not an option.

"First Spear should be on his feet in an hour or two," Foss
continued. "Old Marcus got lucky. He was out getting more
mugs for tea when it came down. Maximus was able to get to

him, pull him out of the fire. He's got a few more scars from it."

"Who'd notice," Tavi said.

Foss showed his teeth. "True." He was silent for a second, then cleared his throat, and said, "We've got two more survivors so far."

"Who?" Tavi asked.

"That's the thing," Foss said. "I can't tell."

Tavi winced.

"They'll have to tell us if they wake up. Burns are too bad. Look like they got skinned. Some of it was so hot, pieces of their armor melted." Foss let out a shaking breath. "I've seen bad. But never bad like that."

"Tell me," Tavi said. "Have you seen Lady Antillus this evening?"

Foss was quiet for a long time until he said, "No, sir."

"Would it have made any difference, if she'd been there?"

Foss grunted. "Probably. Maybe. Hard to say for sure, sir."

Tavi nodded and glanced up as Max came striding up. "First Spear made it through."

Max began to smile, then shook himself, came to attention, and saluted. Tavi stiffened uncomfortably at the formality, but returned it. "That's something, at least, sir," Max said. "The auxiliaries are ready to move out. Four hundred cavalry and eighty scouts."

"What about the horses?" Tavi asked.

Max grimaced. "We're missing a pair of our courier mounts."

"We're missing two of our fastest horses. We're missing Lady Antillus." Tavi shook his head. "I'm tempted to draw unkind conclusions."

"I'm tempted to . . ." Max's voice dropped off into a low, muttering growl.

Foss grunted. "You think she had something to do with what hit the captain, sir?"

Tavi grimaced. Actually speaking of his suspicions aloud, in the course of his duties to one of his officers, would have the legal weight of a lawful accusation. "I don't have any way of knowing, centurion. But I've got a lot of questions that I'd like to have answered."

Max scowled. "Make me a list, sir. I'll think of some creative ways to ask them."

"While you're doing that," Tavi said, "saddle up. You're acting Tribune Auxiliarus. I want you with them when they find the Canim."

Max grunted. "What about my fish, sir?"

"Tell Schultz he's an acting centurion."

"He isn't ready," Max said.

"He'll fit right in around here," Tavi said. "I don't want to break up century structures and surround the fish with new faces now."

Max nodded. "I'll get my horse."

"Get me one, too," Tavi said. "I'm coming."

Foss and Max traded a look. "Um," Max said. "Captain . . ."

Tavi held up a hand. "I've got to get a look at what we're up against, Max. I don't know a damned thing about the terrain out there, and I need to see it if we're going to be fighting in it. I want to see the Canim for the same reason."

"They're big, sir," Max said. "They have teeth. They're strong as bulls and they run real fast. Pretty much all you need to know."

"Or maybe it isn't," Tavi said, voice harder. "Get me a horse, Tribune."

Max's objection was clear in his expression, but he saluted, and said, "Yes, sir." Then spun cleanly on a heel and marched off.

"Thank you, Foss," Tavi said. "I think we can assume our first healing station should be on the south side of the bridge. We'll need a second one on this side, in case we get pushed back. Set them up, centurion."

"Understood, Captain," Foss said, saluting.

Tavi lifted a hand, and said, "No, wait. Set them up, Tribune Medica."

Foss grimaced, though there was a defiant light in his eyes as he saluted again. "A fight with Canim and a promotion. Today isn't going to get much worse."

Ehren drifted in on soundless feet as Foss left. The young Cursor sat down cross-legged next to Tavi and watched the camp activity with a weary expression. A moment later, a squat, bulky-looking centurion rolled up at a quick march and saluted Tavi. "Captain."

"Centurion Erasmus," Tavi said. "This is Sir Ehren ex Cursori, the agent who brought us word of the Canim incursion."

Erasmus stiffened. "The man eighth spear is accused of assaulting."

"The charges are dereliction of duty in time of war, attempted murder, and treason," Tavi said quietly.

Erasmus's face reddened. And well it should, Tavi thought. Those crimes carried lethal consequences. No centurion wanted to see his own men tried and executed, for all kinds of reasons.

"Frankly, centurion," Tavi said, "I have no intention of killing any *legionare*, especially veterans, whatever the reason, so long as I have any alternative. If this incursion is as large as it would seem to be, we'll need every sword."

Erasmus frowned at Tavi, and said, cautiously, "Yes, sir."

"I'm assigning Sir Ehren to question your *legionares*. Frankly, I suspect they're more stupid than treasonous, but . . ." He gestured at the ruined ground around them. "We obviously can't afford to take any chances with our security. *Someone* told the Canim where to strike. Sir Ehren, find out what the prisoners know." He paused, fighting down a sick little feeling in his stomach, then said, "Use whatever means necessary."

Ehren didn't even blink. He nodded calmly to Tavi, as if he tortured prisoners often enough to expect the order to do so.

"Centurion Erasmus," Tavi said. "Go with him. I'll give you a chance to convince your men to cooperate, but we don't have much time, and I *will* know if there are any more turncloaks waiting to stab us in the back. Understood?"

Erasmus saluted. "Yes, sir."

"Good," Tavi said. "Go."

They did, and Magnus appeared from the darkness. He passed Tavi a cup of tea in a plain tin mug. Tavi accepted it gratefully. "You heard everything?"

"Yes," Magnus said quietly. "I don't think you should leave the town."

"Cyril would have," Tavi said.

Magnus said nothing, though Tavi fancied he could hear disapproval in his silence.

Tavi took a sip of bitter, bracing tea. "Foss says Valiar Marcus will be on his feet soon. He's acting Tribune Tactica. Make sure he knows I want him to take charge of the town's defenses and get any unarmed civilians over the bridge and onto the north side of the river."

"Yes, sir," Magnus said quietly.

Tavi frowned and looked at him. "I'm still not sure we shouldn't hand the Legion to Marcus."

"You're the next in the chain of command," Magnus replied quietly. "The First Spear is the senior centurion, and career soldier, but he isn't an officer."

"Neither am I," Tavi said wryly.

Magnus paused for a reflective moment, then said, "I'm not sure I trust him."

Tavi paused with the cup near his lips. "Why not?"

Magnus shrugged. "All those officers, many of them powerful furycrafters, dead. He just happened to live through it?"

"He happened to be outside the tent at the time."

"Quite fortunate," Magnus said. "Don't you think?"

Tavi glanced at his torn knuckles. He hadn't had time to clean them or bandage them properly. "So was I."

Magnus shook his head. "Luck isn't usually so common. Valiar Marcus was meant to die at that meeting. But he survived."

"So did I," Tavi said quietly. And after a moment, he added, in a neutral voice, "And so did you."

Magnus blinked at him. "I was still talking to the town's militia tribune."

"Quite fortunate," Tavi said. "Don't you think?"

Magnus stared for a second, then gave Tavi an approving smile. "That's a smart way to think, sir. It's what you need in this business."

Tavi grunted. "I'm still not sure I'm ready."

"You're as ready as any Third Subtribune Logistica would be," Magnus said. "And better able than most, believe me. The

Legion has enough veterans to know its business. You just need to look calm, confident, and intelligent and try not to lead anyone into any ambushes."

Tavi glanced around him, at the ruins of the tent. His mouth twisted bitterly. It was just then that the crows flooded by overhead, a raucously cawing mass of the carrion birds, thousands of them, sweeping over the Tiber and the Elinarch toward the southwest. They flew by for a solid two minutes, at least, and when a ripple of scarlet lightning went through the clouds overhead, Tavi could see them, wings and beaks and tail feathers of solid black against the red, moving together in a nearly solid mass that almost seemed to be a creature in its own right.

Then they were gone, and neither one of the Cursors on the storm-wracked ground spoke. The crows always knew when a battle was brewing. They knew how to find and feast upon those who would fall.

Magnus sighed after a few seconds more. "You need to shave, sir."

"I'm busy," Tavi said.

"Did you ever see Captain Miles unshaven?" Magnus asked quietly. "Or Cyril? It's what *legionares* will expect. It's reassuring. You need to give them that. Take care of your hands, too."

Tavi stared at him for a second, then let out a slow breath. "All right."

"For the record, I strongly disagree with your decision regarding Antillus Crassus. He should be imprisoned with the other suspects."

"You weren't there," Tavi said. "You didn't see his eyes."

"Everyone can be lied to. Even you."

"Yes," Tavi said. "But he wasn't lying to me tonight." Tavi shook his head. "Had he been into some kind of plot with his mother, he'd have left with her. He stayed. Confronted me directly. I'm not sure how intelligent he is, but he isn't a traitor, Magnus."

"All the same, until we know what further damage his mother might wreak—"

"We don't know for certain she was involved," Tavi said quietly. "Until we do, we should be careful with our words." Magnus didn't look happy about it, but he nodded. "Besides. Crassus is likely the most powerful furycrafter we have left in the Legion, apart from Maximus, and he's the one who has been training with the Knights Pisces. He's the only choice to lead them."

"He'll be in a position to ruin anything this Legion attempts to accomplish if you're wrong, sir."

"I'm not."

Magnus pressed his lips together, then shook his head and sighed. He drew a small case out from behind a mound of lightning-tortured earth, and opened it, revealing a small shaving kit and a covered bowl. He opened it to reveal steaming water. "Maximus should be back shortly. You clean up," he said. "I'll find you a proper cavalry weapon."

"I'm going to look, not fight," Tavi said.

"Of course, sir," Magnus said, handing him the kit. "I assume you prefer a sword to a mace."

"Yes," Tavi said, taking the kit.

Magnus paused, and said, "Sir. I think you should consider appointing a small number of *singulares*."

"Captain Cyril didn't use any bodyguards."

"No," Magnus said, his tone pointed. "He didn't."

CHAPTER 31

Tavi knew that the enemy was near when he saw the first massive, wheeling flights of crows, circling and swooping around columns of black smoke.

The sun rose behind them as they followed the Tiber toward the harbor town of Founderport, almost twenty miles from the Elinarch. Tavi rode with Max at the head of an alae of cavalry, two hundred strong, while the second alae, mostly made up of the more experienced troops, had been broken into eight-man divisions that moved in a loose line through the hills south of the Tiber, marking terrain and, together with the swift-moving scouts, searching for the enemy.

As the sun rose, it lit the gloomy and unnatural cloud cover overhead, and as the ruddy light finally fell through the low, undulating hills around the river, it revealed points of black smoke rolling up in the broad river valley. Tavi nodded to Max, who ordered the column to a halt. He and Tavi walked forward, to the crest of the next hill, and looked down. Max lifted his hands, bending the air between them, and let out a low, pained grunt.

"You should see this," Max said quietly.

Tavi leaned over as Max held the windcrafting for him to look through. Tavi had never seen it working from so close, and the crafting made the image far more clear and intense than his little curved piece of Romanic glass. He had to force himself not to take a moment simply to admire the marvel of the apparently close view the crafting offered. A few seconds later, as he realized what he was looking at, he had no need to feign an officer's calm, analytical distance for the sake of his troops. He had to do it to keep his stomach from emptying itself.

Max's crafting let Tavi see the corpses of steadholts—dozens of them, throughout the fertile valley. Black smoke rose from solid shapes that had once been houses and barns and halls like the ones Tavi grew up in, each inhabited by scores of families. If the Canim had taken them by surprise, there would be few, if any, survivors.

Here and there, Tavi saw small groups on the move, most of them coming toward him. Some were small, slow-moving masses in the distance. Others were larger and moved much more quickly. As he watched, one such swift group fell upon a smaller one, in the distance. It was too far away to make out any real details, even with Max's windcrafting to help him, but Tavi knew what he had to be looking at.

A Canim raiding party had just slaughtered a group of refugees, fleeing without hope of salvation from the destruction behind them.

A surge of pure, white-hot rage went through him at the sight, a primal fury that brought stars to his eyes and tinged everything he saw with red—and at the same time, it washed through him, coursed through his veins like a river of molten steel while leaving his thoughts sharp, harsh, perfectly clear in a way that had happened only once before: deep in the caverns beneath Alera Imperia, where a mindless agent of the creatures known as the Vord had come to murder his friends and his liege.

He heard leather creaking and noted, in passing, that his fists had closed tightly enough to torture the leather of his gloves, hard enough to tear open the injuries on his knuckles. The fact did not strike him as particularly important, and the sensation came from so far away that he could barely tell it was his own.

"Crows," Max breathed, his rough-hewn face stony.

"I don't see their main body," Tavi said quietly. "No concentration at all."

Max nodded. "Raiding packs. Usually fifty or threescore Canim in each."

Tavi nodded, and said, "That means we're only looking at maybe a thousand of them here." He frowned. "What kind of numbers advantage do we need to ensure victory?"

"Best if we can catch them in the open. They're big, and strong, but horses are bigger and stronger. Cavalry can stand up to them in the open. Infantry can take them on one-to-one on an open field, if they can keep their momentum and have decent support from Knights. It's when you fight them in enclosed areas or bad terrain or you stalemate them and grind to a halt that their advantages start mounting up."

Tavi nodded. "Just look at them. Moving every which way. They don't look like advance forces at all. There's no coordination."

Max grunted. "You think Ehren was wrong?"

"No," Tavi said quietly.

"Then where is their army?" Max said.

"Exactly."

Max suddenly stiffened as, in the valley below them, the

morning light and the lay of the ground revealed a group of refugees not a full mile away. They moved sluggishly down the road, obviously trying to hurry, obviously weary beyond haste. The road through the valley was not one of the major furycrafted causeways that supported the Realm—the expense of such a creation made the use of the broad, slow waters of the Tiber far more practical for shipping and travel.

Economics had left the folk of the valley at the mercy of the Canim.

Moments after they spotted the refugees, a marauding pack of Canim loped into view, hard on the heels of their helpless prey.

Though Tavi had seen Alera's ancient foes before, he had never seen them like this—moving together in the open, swift and lean and bloodthirsty. Each Cane was far larger than a human being, the smallest of them standing well over seven feet tall—though the way their lean bodies hunched at the shoulders meant they would have been another foot taller standing straight. The Canim in the raiding party were tawny of fur, dressed in leathers of some hide Tavi did not recognize. They bore their odd, sickle-shaped swords, axes with oddly bent handles, and needle-pointed battle spears with bladed crescents at the base of their steel heads. Their muzzles were long, narrow, gaping open to show teeth already stained with blood as they sighted their quarry.

The refugees, mostly children and elderly men and women, together with one cart drawn by a single workhorse, spotted the foe and panicked, trying to increase their pace though they knew it was hopeless. Death, violent and horrible, had come for them.

The fury seared through Tavi, and his own voice sounded hard and calm to him as he spoke. "Tribune," he said to Max. "Divide the column. I'll take the north side of the road. You'll take the south. We'll hit them from both sides."

"Yes, sir," Max said, his voice grim, and he began to turn.

Tavi stopped him with a hand on his friend's shoulder. "Max," he said quietly. "We're going to send the Canim a message. Their raiders don't escape from this. Not one."

Max's eyes hardened, and he nodded, then whirled to face the cavalry, bellowing orders. A trumpet blasted a short series of notes, and the column divided and drew from a long line into a more compact battle formation.

Tavi mounted and drew his sword.

The sound of two hundred swords being drawn from their sheaths behind him was startlingly loud, but he kept himself from reacting. Then he lifted the sword and lowered it to point forward, the signal to move, and within seconds he found himself leading the cavalry down the road. His horse broke into a nervous trot, then quickened its pace to a smoother canter, then at Tavi's urging shifted into a full run. He could hear and feel the presence of the other *legionares* upon their steeds behind him, and the deafening thunder of their running horses rose around him, pounded through him, rang on his armor and beat a wild rhythm against his heart.

They closed on the refugees faster than Tavi would have believed, and when they saw Aleran cavalry riding down upon them, the refugees' expressions of terror and despair filled with sudden hope. Arms lifted in sudden shouts and cheers and breathless cries of encouragement. Tavi lifted his sword and pointed to the right, and half of the alae flowed off the road, to circle around the refugees. Max, his sword mirroring Tavi's, led his hundred men to the left.

They rounded the refugees and found the Canim not fifty yards beyond. Tavi led his men in an arch that would let them charge straight down into the Canim's flanks, and as he did he realized something.

Fifty Canim seen from a mile away looked alien and dangerous.

Fifty Canim seen from a rapidly vanishing distance looked enormous, hungry, and *terrifying*.

Tavi suddenly became very aware that he had never fought a true Canim before, never led men into battle, never fought a live enemy from horseback. He could not remember ever being so frightened.

Then the rising columns of black smoke, the cries of the holders behind him brought new life to the furious fire in his veins, and he heard his shout ring out over the thunder of the cavalry charge.

"Alera!" he howled.

"Alera!" cried a hundred mounted *legionares*, in answer.

Tavi saw the first Cane, an enormous, stringy beast with mange in its dun-colored fur and an axe grasped in one paw-like hand. The Cane whipped the axe at him in an odd, underhand throw, and red metal glinted as it spun toward him.

Tavi never made a conscious choice of what to do. His arm moved, his sword struck something, and something slammed against his armored chest, barely registering on his senses. He leaned to the right, sword sweeping back, and as his horse thundered past the lead Cane, he struck in the smooth, graceful, effortless strike of a mounted swordsman, focused on precision and letting the weight of the charging horse give the blow both power and speed. His sword flew true and struck with a vicious force that surged up his arm in a tingling wave.

There was no time to see the results. Tavi's horse was still running, and he recovered his weapon, flicking another strike to a Cane on the left side of his path. There was a flash of bloody Canim teeth in the corner of one eye, and his horse screamed. A spear thrust at his face, and he swatted it aside with his sword. Something else slammed into his helmet, and then he was plunging past Aleran cavalry surging in the opposite direction—Maximus and his men.

Tavi led his men clear, while they maintained only a very ragged line. They wheeled about, never slowing, and once again swept forward into the now-scattered Canim on the road. This time, he seemed to be thinking more clearly. He struck down a Cane attempting to throw a spear at one of Max's men, guided the plunging hooves of his horse into the back of another Cane, and leaned far down to deliver a finishing blow to a wounded Cane struggling to rise. Then he swept past elements of Max's group, and clear once more.

Only a handful of Canim were still capable of fighting, and they threw themselves forward with mad, almost frenzied howls of rage.

Tavi found himself answering their howls with his own, and kicked his horse forward until he could slip aside from the blow of a sickle-sword and drive his own blade in a straight, heavy thrust through the neck of the Cane who had swung at him. The Cane wrenched and contorted viciously as Tavi's blade struck, tearing it from his hand.

Tavi let the horse take him by, and drew his short sword, though it was a weapon ill suited to mounted use, and turned, looking for more of the foe.

But it was over.

The Aleran cavalry had taken the Canim by surprise, and not one had escaped the swift mounts and blades of the First Aleran. Even as Tavi watched, the last living Cane, the one he had left his sword in, clutched at the weapon, spat out a blood-flecked snarl of defiance, and collapsed to the earth.

Tavi dismounted and walked across the bloodied ground amidst a sudden and total silence. He reached down and took the hilt of his sword, planted a boot on the chest of the Cane, and heaved the weapon free. Then he turned to sweep his gaze around the young cavalrymen and lifted his weapon to them in a salute.

The *legionares* broke out into cheers that shook the earth, while horses danced nervously. Tavi recovered his mount, while spear leaders and centurions bellowed their men back into position.

Tavi was back on his horse for all of ten seconds before a wave of exhaustion hit like a physical blow. His arm and shoulder ached horribly, and his throat burned with thirst. One of his wrists had blood on it, where it looked like it had trickled out from the torn knuckles beneath his gauntlets. There was a dent as deep as the first joint of his finger in his breastplate, and what looked like the score marks of teeth on one boot that Tavi did not remember ever feeling.

He wanted to sit down somewhere and sleep. But there was work to do. He rode over to the refugees, and was met by a grizzled old holder who still had the general bearing of the military—perhaps a retired career *legionare* himself. He saluted Tavi, and said, "My name's Vernick, milord." He squinted at the insignia on Tavi's armor. "You aren't one of Lord Cereus's Legions."

"Captain Rufus Scipio," Tavi replied, returning the salute. "First Aleran Legion."

Vernick grunted in surprise and peered at Tavi's face for a moment. "Whoever you are, we're mighty glad to see you, Captain."

Tavi could all but hear the old man's thoughts. *Looks too young for his rank. Must be a strong crafter from the upper ranks of the Citizenry.* Tavi felt no need to disabuse him of the notion—not when the truth was considerably more frightening. "I wish I could give you better news, sir, but we're preparing to defend the Elinarch. You'll have to get your people behind the town walls to make them safe."

Vernick heaved out a tired sigh, but nodded. "Aye, milord. I figured it was the most defensible spot hereabouts."

"We'd not seen any Canim until we got here," Tavi replied. "You should be all right—but you need to hurry. If the incursion is as large as we suspect, we'll need every *legionare* defending the town of Elinarch's walls. Once the gates close, anyone on this side might not get in."

"I understand, milord," the holder said. "Don't you worry, sir. We'll manage."

Tavi nodded and saluted him again, then rode back to the column. Max rode out to meet him and tossed Tavi a water flask.

Tavi caught it, nodded his thanks to Max. "Well?" Tavi asked, then drank deeply from the flask.

"This was as close to ideal as we could ever expect. Caught them on flat, open ground between two forces," Max said quietly. "Fifty-three dead Canim. Two Aleran dead, three wounded, all of them fish. We lost two horses."

Tavi nodded. "Pass the spare mounts off to those holders. They'll make better speed if they can put some of their little ones on the horses' backs. See if they have room in the wagon for our wounded. Speak to a holder named Vernick."

Max grimaced and nodded. "Yes, sir. You mind if I ask our next step?"

"For now, we keep moving down the valley. We kill Canim and help refugees and see if we can spot their main force. I want to send word to the alae in the hills to concentrate again. I don't want bands of eight taking runs at any Canim battlepacks."

Tavi found himself staring at two riderless horses in his own formation, and he fell silent.

"I'll see to it," Max said. He took a breath, and asked, very quietly, "You all right?"

Tavi felt like screaming. Or running and hiding. Or sleeping. Or possibly a combination of the first several, followed by the last. He was not a trained leader of *legionares*. He had never asked to be in a position of command such as this, never sought to be. That it had happened to him was a simple and enormous fact that was so stunning that he still had not come to grips with its implications. He was accustomed to taking chances—but here, he would take them with lives other than his own. Young men would die—already *had* died—based upon his decisions.

He felt disoriented, lost somehow, and he almost welcomed the desperation and haste the situation had forced on them, because it gave him something clear and immediate to sink his energy into. Reorganize the command. Decide on a strategy. Deal with a threat. If he kept going forward through the problems without slowing down, he could keep his head on his shoulders. He wouldn't have to think about the pain and death it was his duty, as captain of the Legion, to prevent.

He did not want to pretend that nothing was wrong and project an aura of authority and calm to the young *legionares* around them. But their confidence and steadiness was critical to their ability to fight and would ultimately improve their chances of survival. So he ignored the parts of himself that wanted to scream in bewildered frustration and focused on the most immediate crisis.

"I'm fine," he told Max, his voice steady. "I don't want to

push things too far. If we move too far down the valley and the horses play out, the Canim will run us down before we can get back to Elinarch. But we've got to do everything we can for the holders who are still alive."

Max nodded. "Agreed."

"Max. I'll need you to tell me when you think we're hitting our limits," Tavi said quietly. "And I don't want you pulling any craftings if you don't absolutely need to. You're my hole card, if it comes to that. And you're the closest thing we have to a real healer."

"Got it," Max said, just as quietly. He gave Tavi half a smile. "I've seen officers on their third hitch that didn't handle themselves that well in action. You're a natural."

Tavi grimaced. "Tell that to the two who aren't coming back."

"This is a Legion," Max said quietly. "We're going to lose more before the day's out. They knew that there were risks when they volunteered."

"They volunteered to be trained to handle themselves and led by experienced officers," Tavi said quietly. "Not for this."

"Life isn't certain or fair. That isn't anyone's fault. Even yours."

Tavi glanced at Max and nodded grudgingly. He turned his horse, staring farther down the valley, where more helpless holders tried to run for safety. It felt like the day must have been nearly over, but the cloud-veiled sun couldn't have been halfway to its peak. "What were their names, Max? The men who died."

"I don't know," Max confessed. "There hasn't been time."

"Find out for me?"

"Of course."

"Thank you." Tavi squared his shoulders and nodded to himself. "I'm going to speak to our wounded before they go, but more holders will need our help. I want to be moving again in five minutes, Tribune."

Max met Tavi's eyes when he saluted, and said, quietly, fiercely, "Yes, Captain."

"Bloody crows," Tavi swore, frustrated. "It doesn't make any crowbegotten *sense*, Max."

The sun was vanishing beyond the horizon, and Tavi's alae of cavalry had clashed with the Canim raiders in no less than six swift, bitter engagements that day, all against smaller packs than the first. Three more *legionares* died. Another nine were wounded in action, and one broke his arm when his weary horse stumbled on the trail and threw him from the saddle.

"You worry too much," Max told him, and leaned idly against the trunk of a tree. The pair were the only two *legionares* standing, other than the half dozen men spread around the group, on watch. The rest lay on the ground in silent, hard sleep, exhausted after the day of marching and fighting. "Look, the Canim don't always do things that make sense."

"You're wrong," Tavi said, his tone firm. "It always makes sense to *them*, Max. They think differently than we do, but they aren't insane or stupid." He waved his hand at the countryside. "All those loose packs. No organization, no direction. No cohesive force. This is a major move. I've got to figure out what they're doing."

"We could just keep on riding until we got to the harbor. I'll bet you we'd figure it out then."

"For about five minutes. Then our horses would collapse from exhaustion, and the Canim would rip our faces off."

"But we'd know," Max said.

"We'd know." Tavi sighed. He shook his head. "Where is he?"

"Messengers are sort of funny about wanting to get where

they're going in one piece and breathing. This is hostile territory. Give him time."

"We might not *have* time."

"Yes," Max drawled. "And worrying about it won't get him here any faster." Max opened a sling bag and dug out a round, flat loaf of bread. He broke it in half and tossed one to Tavi. "Eat, while you have a chance. Sleep, if you like."

"Sleep," Tavi said, faint scorn in his voice.

Max grunted, and the two of them ate. After a moment, he said, "Notice anything?"

"Like?"

"Every one of your *legionares* is either on his back or wishing he was there."

Tavi frowned at the shadowed forms of recumbent soldiers. Even the sentries sagged wearily. "You aren't sleeping," Tavi pointed out.

"I've got the metalcraft to go without for days if I have to." Tavi grimaced at him.

"You're missing my point. You aren't sleeping, either," Max said. "But you aren't stumbling around. Your mouth is running faster than any horse in Alera."

Tavi stopped chewing for a second, frowning. "You don't mean that I'm using metalcraft?"

"You *aren't*," Max said. "I could tell. But you're rolling along just fine."

Tavi took a deep breath. Then he said, "Kitai."

"Granted, she'd put a bounce in any man's step," Max said. "But I'm serious. Whatever herb you're using . . ."

"No, Max," Tavi said. "It's . . . I can do without sleep a lot better than I used to. Since Kitai and I have been—"

"Plowing furrows in the mattress?"

It was dark enough for Max not to be able to see Tavi's sudden blush, thank the great furies. "I was going to say *together*. You ass."

Max chortled and swigged from a skin. He passed it to Tavi.

Tavi drank and grimaced at the weak, watered wine. "I haven't needed as much sleep. Sometimes I think I can see more clearly. Hear better. I don't know."

"Bloody odd," Max said, thoughtfully. "If handy."

"I'd rather you didn't talk about it," Tavi said quietly.

"Course," Max said, taking the skin back. "Surprised the crows out of me, to see her here. Figured she'd stay in the palace. She liked the toys."

Tavi grunted. "She's of her own mind about such things."

"Least she's safe back at Elinarch now," Max said.

Tavi gave him a level look.

"She's not?" Max asked. "How do you know?"

"I don't. I haven't seen her since she led us into town last night. But I know her." He shook his head. "She's out here somewhere."

"Captain!" called one of the sentries.

Tavi turned and found his sword in his hand, a split second after Max's weapon leapt from its own sheath. They eased back as the sentry called an all's-well signal, then they heard hooves approaching.

A battered-looking, gaunt *legionare* appeared from the darkness, his age marking him as a veteran. His helmet had a smear of what looked like dark red Canim blood on it. He swung down from his horse, gave Tavi a weary salute, and nodded to Max.

"Captain," Maximus said. "This is *Legionare* Hagar. I served with him on the Wall."

"Legionare," Tavi said, nodding. "Good to see you. Report."

"Sir," Hagar said. "Centurion Flavis sends his compliments, and advises you that his alae has encountered and dispatched fifty-four Canim raiders. Seventy-four refugees were given what assistance he could, and he directed them to seek refuge in the town of Elinarch. Two *legionares* were slain and eight wounded. The wounded are en route back to Elinarch."

Tavi frowned. "Did you encounter any enemy regulars?"

Hagar shook his head. "No, sir, but Centurion Flavis suffered both of his fatalities and the majority of his unit's injuries fighting three Canim garbed and equipped differently than the standard raiders."

"Three?" Max burst out.

Hagar grimaced. "It wasn't long ago, Antillar, the light was starting to go grey on us. And these things . . . I've never seen anything that fast, and I saw Aldrick ex Gladius fight Araris Valerian when I was a boy."

"They went down hard, eh?"

"Two of them didn't go down at all. They got away, and Flavis let them go. It would have been suicide to send anyone out into the dark after them."

Tavi felt a sensation almost akin to that of his mouth watering at the scent of a fine meal. "Wait. Differently garbed? How so?"

Hagar turned to his horse, and said, "I've got it here, sir. Flavis said you might want to see it."

"Flavis was right," Tavi said. "Tribune, a lamp please."

"It will give away our position, sir," Max said.

"So will the scent of a hundred horses," Tavi said drily. "I need to see this."

Max nodded and fetched a lamp. He draped his cloak over it, then murmured, "Light." Very little of the golden glow of the furylamp emerged from beneath the cloak, and the three of them hunkered down to examine the gear Hagar had brought.

A hooded black cloak big enough to make a small tent was first, wrapped around the rest. Within the cloak lay a pair of short fighting blades—or what would have been so, for a Cane. The blades of the weapons were three feet long, curved, and made of the tempered, scarlet bloodsteel from which the Canim forged their best equipment. The spines of the knives bore teeth like those of a wood saw, and the pommel of one was made in the shape of a wolf skull, complete with tiny scarlet gems for eyes. Half a dozen heavy, metal spikes were next, as long as Tavi's forearm and as thick as his thumb. A Cane's enormous arm could throw them entirely through a human target, or crack a man's skull through a good helmet. Finally, the equipment included a matte black chain of some strange and enormously heavy metal that made almost no sound when link brushed against link.

Tavi stared down at them for a moment, thinking.

"Looks more like a Cursor's gear," Max said quietly.

"Smaller than their normal stuff. Light. Perfect to disable a target and make an escape."

"Mmm," Tavi said. "Which is exactly what they used it to do. Add in how well they fought, and it indicates that they might be elite soldiers of some kind. Certainly scouts."

"Either way, they've got regulars behind them somewhere."

Tavi nodded grimly. "And now they know where we are."

Max frowned and fell silent.

"Sir," Hagar said, "I should also tell you that the scouts may have taken heavy losses."

Tavi grunted and frowned. "How so?"

"Only about forty-five of the eighty that went out this morning made the rendezvous. Scouts are an independent bunch, and they can get pinned down in a hiding place for days, sometimes. No one saw any bodies, but a couple of them found signs that some of their companions had been attacked."

"They want to keep us blind," Tavi said, nodding. "Hold on." Tavi rose and walked over to one of the horses they'd used to carry supplies. He unloaded a heavy square of leather wrapped around a bundle, untied the cord holding it closed, and drew out a pair of Canim sickle-swords and one of their axes. He brought them over and tossed them down beside the other gear. He squinted down at them for a long moment, tracking an elusive thought that danced about just beneath the surface of realization.

"If they know we're out here," Max said quietly, "we'd best not linger. We don't want to get hit by a squad of their regulars in the dark."

Hagar nodded. "Flavis is already on the way back to the Elinarch."

Tavi stared at the weapons. There was something there. An answer. He knew it.

"Sir?" Max said. "We might need to get a move on. Whatever they're doing or however many they are, they aren't going to be able to sneak up on the town."

Suddenly, realization hit Tavi in a flash, and he slammed a fist against his palm. "Crows, that's *it*."

Hagar blinked at him.

Tavi pointed at the sickle-swords and the Canim axe. "Max. What do you see."

"Canim weapons?"

"Look closer," Tavi said.

Max pursed his lips and frowned. "Um. Bloodstain on that one. Edges are nicked up pretty bad on those sickle-swords. And there's rust on . . ." Max paused and frowned. "What are those stains on the sickles and the axe?"

"Exactly," Tavi said. He pointed at the bloodsteel gear. "Look. Edges in excellent shape. High quality craftsman-ship." He pointed at the gear taken from the slain raiders. "Rust. Much lower quality manufacture. More damage on them. Less care taken of them—and those stains are green and brown, Max."

Max raised his eyebrows. "Meaning?"

"Meaning that I grew up on a steadholt," Tavi said. "Those are stains you get from scything crops," he said, pointing at the sickles, then tapped the axe, "and from chopping wood. These aren't *weapons*. They're *tools*."

"No disrespect intended, but that's the beauty of an axe, sir. It's both."

"Not within the context of what we know," Tavi said.

"Um?" Max said. "What?"

Tavi held up a hand and said, "Look, we know that the Canim landed in great numbers, but we haven't seen any reg-ular troops. The raiders we've seen have been running around a like a rogue gargant, without any coordination or plan. None of them carried quality weapons, and none of them wore steel armor."

"Which means?"

"They're *levies*, Max. Untrained conscripts. Farmers, out-laws, servants. Whoever they could push out in front of them armed with something sharp."

Max's face twisted into a pensive scowl. "But all they're doing is throwing them away, sending them out in random groups like this."

"But they're causing all kinds of chaos by doing it. I think the Canim intentionally brought expendable troops with them,"

Tavi said. "They aren't here to fight us. They're here to provide a distraction. We're supposed to focus on them, just like we have been all day. I'll bet you they hoped to draw the First Aleran out onto open ground so that they could swamp us."

"Crows," Max spat. "Bastard dogs don't need us to make a mistake that big. More likely they did it so that the Canim scouts can move around freely in the chaos. They can find the best route for their regulars while they're taking out our scouts."

Tavi blinked and snapped his fingers. Then he dug into his pockets and withdrew the bloody little gem he'd taken from Lady Antillus. He held it up next to the gems in the pommel of the jeweled bloodsteel sword.

They were identical.

"That's where I'd seen that gem before," Tavi said quietly. "Varg wore a ring and an earring with the same kind."

Max let out a low whistle. "Crows," he said quietly. "I guess my stepmother's had it now."

"Yes, she has," Tavi growled.

Max nodded slowly. "So. What do we do now, sir?"

Tavi glanced up at the *legionare*. "Hagar."

The veteran saluted. "Captain." Then he withdrew, quietly leading his mount away.

"Recommendation?" Tavi asked quietly.

"Get back to the Elinarch and fort up," Max said promptly. "The Canim wouldn't have gone to all this trouble if they weren't planning to come this way."

Tavi shook his head. "Once we do that, we lose any chance we might have had of gaining any more intelligence about their capabilities. If they can repeat that stunt with the lightning, or if Lady Antillus really has pitched in with them, they could blast the gates down and swamp us in an hour."

"If regulars catch us out here in the open, we won't have to worry about that problem. But it's your call, sir."

Tavi chewed the question over for a moment. "Fall back," he said quietly. "We'll leave a line of pickets behind us to warn us when they're in sight. Wake the men and ask for volunteers."

"Sir," Max said, saluting. He immediately rose, barking commands, and the weary *legionares* began to stir.

The column was forming—a much more difficult prospect in the dark, Tavi noted—when a rippling chill flickered down Tavi's spine and made the hairs on his arms stand up. He glanced around him in the evening gloom, then headed for the darkest patch of shadows on the west side of the camp.

When he got close, he saw a flicker of pale skin within a dark hood, and Kitai whispered, "Aleran. There is something you must see."

There was something very odd, very alien in her voice, and Tavi realized that Kitai sounded . . . afraid.

Kitai glanced about, drew back her hood, and met Tavi's eyes with hers, poised in perfect, graceful suspension of motion, like a hidden doe ready to flee from a grass lion. "Aleran, you *must* see this."

Tavi met her gaze for a moment, then nodded once. He went to Max and murmured, "Take them back to town. Leave two horses here."

Max blinked. "What? Where are you going?"

"Kitai's found something I need to see."

Max lowered his voice to a fierce whisper. "Tavi. You're the captain of this Legion."

Tavi answered just as quietly, and just as fiercely. "I am a *Cursor*, Max. It is my duty to acquire information for the defense of the Realm. And I'm not about to order *anyone* else to go out there tonight. I've gotten enough people killed today."

Max's expression became pained, but then a centurion called out that the column was ready.

"Go," Tavi said. "I'll catch up to you."

Max exhaled slowly. Then he squared his shoulders and offered Tavi his hand. Tavi shook it. "Good luck," Max said.

"And to you."

Max nodded, mounted, and called the column into motion. Within a moment, they were out of sight. A moment more, and the sound of their passage faded as well, leaving Tavi suddenly alone, in the dark, in a strange part of the country filled with enemies only too glad to kill him in as painful and horrible a fashion as possible.

Tavi shook his head. Then he started stripping out of his armor. A beat later, Kitai was at his side, pale, nimble fingers flying over straps and buckles, helping him remove it. He drew his dark brown traveling cloak from his saddlebags, donned it, and made sure that both horses would be ready to move when he and Kitai returned.

Then, without a word, Kitai headed out into the night at a vulpine lope, and Tavi fell into pace behind her. They ran through the night and the occasional flicker of bloody lightning, and Kitai led him up into the rolling hills that framed that stretch of the Tiber valley.

His legs and chest were burning by the time they reached the top of what seemed like the hundredth hill, nearly two hours later, then Kitai's pace began to slow. She led him over the next few hundred yards at a slow, perfectly silent walk, and Tavi emulated her. It took them only a moment more to reach the lip of the hill.

Light glowed in the distance, bright and golden and steady. For a moment, Tavi thought he was looking at the burning city of Founderport—until he saw that the light of the tremendous fire was actually *behind* the city, from his perspective, its light making the city walls stand out as sharp, clear silhouettes.

It took him a moment longer to recognize what he was seeing.

Founderport wasn't burning.

The Canim *fleet* was.

The fire roared so loudly that he could actually, faintly hear it, as a far-distant moaning sound. He could see, amidst smoke and fire, the shapes of masts and decks of sailing vessels being consumed by flame.

"They're burning their own *ships* behind them," Tavi whispered.

"Yes, Aleran," Kitai said. "Your people would not have believed it, from the lips of a Marat. Your eyes had to see."

"This isn't a raid. It isn't an incursion." Tavi suddenly felt very cold. "That's why there are so many of the Canim this time. That's why they're willing to sacrifice a thousand troops just to keep us occupied."

He swallowed.

"They mean to *stay*."

◦◦◦◦◦ CHAPTER 33

Tavi stared out at the burning ships, so far away, and thought about all the implications their presence would mean. It meant that whatever the Canim had done in the past, matters had altered, and drastically.

For all of Alera's history, conflict with the Canim had been for control of the various islands between Alera and the Canim homeland—harsh, pitched fights for seaside fortifications, mostly, usually with a naval battle or two mixed in. Every few years, Canim raiding ships would hurtle from the deep seas to Alera's shores, burning and looting towns where they could, carrying away the valuables to be had there, and occasionally seizing Alerans and dragging them off to a fate no one had ever been able to ascertain. Whether they wound up as slaves or food, it was certainly an unpleasant ending.

More infrequent were larger Canim incursions, some of which had curled around the coastline to the seafaring cities like Parcia, and dozens of ships swept down together in a much larger attack. The Canim had burned Parcia to the ground some four hundred years before and had leveled the city of Rhodes no fewer than three times.

But Ehren had said that this invasion force was infinitely larger than any previously seen. And they had no intention of striking at Alera and returning to their homeland. The Canim, for whatever reason, were there to stay, and the implications of *that* were terrifying.

For the Canim, their attack upon Alera was literally a do-or-die situation. They had nothing to lose, everything to gain, and they would be certain that the only way to ensure their own safety would be to destroy the folk of Alera, *legionare* and holder, city and steadholt alike. They were trapped, desperate, and Tavi well knew the kind of berserk, fearless ferocity any trapped creature could display.

He watched the fires for a moment more, then said to Kitai, "This is the first time I've ever seen the sea. I wish it hadn't been like this."

She did not answer him—but her warm hand slipped to his, and their fingers intertwined.

"How did you see the fires in the first place?" Tavi asked Kitai. "What were you doing all the way out here?"

"Hunting," she said quietly.

Tavi frowned. "Hunting what?"

"Answers."

"Why?"

"Because I killed the man you wished to make talk. I thought it proper to make amends for that discourtesy." She looked from the distant pyres to Tavi. "When you were returning to your camp with the prisoners, I saw the High Lady of Antillus ride from the city by the great bridge. Since then, I have tracked her. She has gone to ground nearby. I can show you where. Perhaps she will have the answers you wanted to find."

Tavi frowned and stared at Kitai for a moment. "Do you have any idea how dangerous she is?"

Kitai shrugged. "She did not see me."

Tavi gritted his teeth for a moment, then said, "She's too much for us to handle."

"Why?" Kitai said.

"She's a High Lady," Tavi said. "If you had any idea all the things she could do . . ."

"She is a coward," Kitai said, contempt in her tone. "She lets others do all her killing for her. She arranges accidents. Things in which she will never be found and blamed."

"Which does not mean that she couldn't burn us to cinders with a flick of her hand," Tavi said. "It can't be done."

"Like taking Max from the Grey Tower could not be done, Aleran?"

Tavi opened his mouth to argue. Then he closed it again and scowled at Kitai. "This is different." He narrowed his eyes. "But . . . why in the world would she be all the way out *here*? You say she's camped?"

Kitai nodded. "A narrow gulch not far from here."

Tavi's legs ached terribly, and his belly was going to be screaming for food once he got the long run out of his system. Lady Antillus was a deadly opponent, and with no witnesses, out here in the wilderness, she would almost certainly kill them both if she became aware of them—but the chance to learn more about any arrangements the traitorous Citizen might have made with the enemy was irreplaceable. "Show me," he told Kitai.

She rose and led him farther into the night, over the crest of the hill and down its far side, where the ground rose to the rocky bones of ancient mountains that had been worn down to rounded hills, broken here and there by jagged fissures. There, the heavy, low foliage and large trees of the river valley gave way to lower scrub brush, scrawny evergreens, and patches of brambles that, in some places, had grown into thickets several feet tall.

Kitai tensed slightly, as she began to walk along a thicket, and she slowed down to stalk forward in careful, perfect silence. Tavi emulated her, and she led him through a narrow opening in the thicket. After a few feet, they were forced to drop to a crawl. Small thorns jabbed at Tavi, no matter how carefully or slowly he moved, and he had to clench his teeth and strangle his own painful exhalations before they could give him away.

Ten apparently endless yards later, they emerged from the thicket into a comparatively heavy growth of evergreens, and Kitai prowled slowly forward in the relatively open, pine-needle-covered spaces beneath the trees, until she came to a halt and beckoned to Tavi. He eased up next to her, lying on his stomach beside her and staring out and down through the tree's branches, into a small, semicircular area located within one of the larger fissures in the stone hills. Water trickled down a rock face, into a pool barely larger than a steadholt cook's mixing bowl, then continued on its way down through the stone.

The low campfire, sunken into its own little pit to hide its light better, was not more than twenty feet from where they lay. Lady Antillus sat beside the pool, evidently in the midst of a conversation with a small and vaguely human-shaped water-sculpture that stood on the surface of the tiny pool.

"You don't understand, brother mine," Lady Antillus said, her tone agitated. "They aren't here with an overly large raiding force. They came in *hundreds* of ships, Brencis. Which they then burned behind them."

A tinny, petulant voice came from the water-sculpted figure. "Don't use my name, foolish child. These communications may be intercepted."

Or eavesdropped upon, Lord Kalarus, Tavi mused.

Lady Antillus let out an exasperated sound. "You're right. If we're overheard, someone might suspect you of treason. If all the Legions and killings and abductions haven't managed it already."

"Rising up against Gaius is one thing," the water figure said. "Being found in collusion with the raiding Canim is something else. It could motivate the neutral High Lords to come out against me. It might even draw a rebuke from the northern Lords—including your own dear husband, and I have worked far too hard to allow that now." The figure's voice became quiet and dangerous. "So guard. Your. Tongue."

Lady Antillus's back straightened in subtle, frightened tension, and her face turned pale. "As you wish, my lord. But you have yet to see my point. The Canim haven't come here merely to create this cloud cover to slow down the First Lord's troops. They haven't come here simply to raid and provide a distraction to divide his forces. They intend to *stay.*"

"Impossible," Kalarus responded. "Preposterous. They'd be swept back into the sea before the summer is out. They must know that."

"Unless they don't," Lady Antillus said.

Kalarus snarled something incoherent. "Are you at the meeting point?"

"To conclude the bargain. Yes."

"Impress upon Sarl the futility of his position."

Lady Antillus hesitated before saying, "He's powerful, my lord. More so than I would have been willing to believe. His attack upon the command of the First Aleran was . . . much more intense than I would have thought possible. And came more swiftly than we had believed. I was forced to . . . to leave several minor matters unattended."

"All the more reason to give the dog a pointed reminder of that with which he must contend. You need not fear his breed's power, and you know it. Give him my warning, then return to Kalare."

"What of your nephew, my lord?"

"Crassus is welcome, too, of course."

Lady Antillus shook her head. "He remains with the Legion."

"Then he takes his chances."

"He isn't ready for war."

"He's grown. Old enough to make his own choices. If he hasn't been thoroughly prepared to survive those choices, that is neither fault nor concern of mine. Take it up with his parents."

Her voice took on the barest hint of heat. "But my lord—"

"Enough," the figure of Kalarus snarled. "I have work to do. You will obey me in this."

Lady Antillus stared for a second, then shivered. She bowed her head. "Yes, my lord."

"Courage, little one," Kalarus's image said, tone softer. "We are near the end of the race. Just a little longer."

Then the image slid back down into the tiny pool, and Lady Antillus sagged. Tavi saw her hands clenched into fists so tight that her nails had cut into her palms. Tiny droplets of blood fell to the stone floor of the fissure, sparkling in the light of the small fire.

Then she rose abruptly, and flicked a hand at the stone of the fissure wall. It stirred, pulsed, then writhed into a bas-relief image of a young man. In fact . . .

It was a life-sized image of Tavi, carefully and chillingly detailed.

Lady Antillus spat upon it, then struck out at it with one fist, furycraft infusing the blow with such power that it literally tore the stone head from the fissure wall and sent out a cloud of stone fragments that rattled to the ground. Her next blow struck the figure in the heart, her fist driving halfway to her elbow in the stone. Cracks sprang out from the point of impact, and more pieces of the statue broke off and fell to the ground. She whirled, took two long paces back from the image, then howled and drove her open palm toward the remnants of Tavi's likeness. Fire split the darkness and the quiet night with a blaze of sudden light and thunder, and the stones shrieked protest.

A cloud of dust and smoke covered everything. Stone clattered on stone. When the haze cleared, there was an enormous, glass-smooth hollow fully five feet deep where the stone image had been.

Tavi gulped.

Beside him, Kitai did, too.

He forced himself to breathe slowly and evenly, to control the fearful trembling of his limbs. He could feel Kitai shivering against him. They crept away from the High Lady's little camp as silently as they came.

It took most of forever to crawl back out of the painful thicket without making noise, and Tavi wanted to break into an immediate sprint as soon as he was upright again. It would have been a mistake, so close to Lady Antillus—possibly a fatal one. So he and Kitai prowled slowly and carefully for nearly half a mile before Tavi finally stopped beside a brook and let out a shaking breath.

He and Kitai crouched down together by the brook, cupping water with their hands and drinking. Tavi noticed, as they did, that Kitai's hands were trembling. Though she struggled to remain calm, behind her exotic eyes he could see the fear she held tightly leashed.

After they drank, they crouched together in silence for a moment. Tavi found Kitai's hand in the darkness and squeezed it tight. She squeezed back and leaned into him, her shoulder against his, and both of them stared at the reflections of occasional crimson lightning in the water.

Far in the distance, Tavi heard the low, alien, blaring call of a Canim war horn.

Kitai's fingers squeezed tighter. "They're coming," she whispered.

"Yes," he said. He lifted his eyes to the west, from where the horn call had come.

There was a terrible sense of helplessness in the moment, a sudden and crushing realization that in the face of all that was happening, he was very, very small. Vast forces were in motion, and he could do nothing to stop them, and almost nothing to influence them. He felt like a *legionare* piece on a *ludus* board—small, slow, and of very little value or ability. Other hands were directing the pieces, while like a *ludus legionare*, he had little to say about those moves and precious little ability to change the outcome of the game, even if he made them himself.

It was terrifying, frustrating, unfair, and he leaned back against Kitai, taking solace in her presence, her scent, her touch.

"They're coming," he murmured. "It won't be long now."

Kitai looked up at him, her eyes searching his face. "If it is true, if they are a great host, can your Legion destroy them?"

"No," Tavi said quietly. He closed his eyes for a moment, helpless as a *ludus* piece, and every bit as likely to be destroyed with the killing came and hurtled them into a grim endgame.

Endgame.

The wolfish Canim war horns sounded again.

Ludus.

Tavi took a sudden deep breath and rose to his feet, mind racing. He stared out at the light of the burning ships in Founderport's harbor, reflecting against the low clouds overhead.

"We can't destroy them," he said. "But I think I know how we can stop them."

She tilted her head. "How?"

He narrowed his eyes, and said, very quietly, "Discipline."

CHAPTER 34

Isana, exhausted, did not lift her head to ask, "What day is it, Giraldi?"

"The twenty-ninth day of the siege. Dawn's in a few hours more."

Isana forced herself to churn thoughts through her weary brain. "The battle. Is Lady Veradis likely to be free today?"

Giraldi was silent for a long minute. Then he dragged a stool across the floor to Isana and sat down on it in front of her. He leaned down and lifted her chin with callused, gentle fingers, so that she had to look up at him.

"No," he said quietly. "She won't, Isana."

Isana struggled to process the thought. Not today, then. She must hold another day. Another eternal, merciless day. She licked her dried, cracked lips, and said, "Gaius will come soon."

"No," Giraldi said. "There's something about this storm that keeps Knights Aeris from flying more than a few yards off the ground. The First Lord could not send rapid response troops to lift the siege, and Kalarus has disrupted the causeways between Ceres and the capital. It will take them another week to march here."

A week. To Isana, a week almost seemed like a mythical amount of time. Perhaps that was a mercy. A single day was a torment. Just as well that she could not clearly remember how many days were in a week. "I'm staying."

Giraldi leaned forward. "Kalarus's forces have breached the city walls. Cereus and Miles managed to collapse enough buildings to contain them for a time, but it's only a matter of hours, probably less than a day, before he's forced back to the citadel here. The fighting is worse every hour. Cereus and Miles have lost more Knights, and now the enemy takes a greater and greater toll on the rank-and-file *legionares*. Veradis and her healers work to save lives until they drop. Then they get up and do it again. None of them can come to help you."

She stared at him dully.

Giraldi leaned forward and turned her head toward Fade. "Look at him, Isana. *Look* at him."

She did not wish to. She could not quite remember why, but she knew that she did not want to look at Araris. But she could not summon up the means to deny the centurion's command. She looked.

Araris, Fade, her husband's closest friend, lay pale and still. He'd coughed weakly for several days, though that had ceased sometime in the blurry, recent past. His chest barely rose and fell, and it made wet sounds as it did. His skin had taken on an unhealthy, yellowish tinge in patches around his torso and neck. He had cracks in his skin, angry sores swollen and red. His hair hung limp, and every feature of his body looked softened, more indistinct somehow, as if he'd been a still-damp clay statue slowly melting in the rain.

Two things stood out clearly.

The brand on his face, which looked as hideous and sharp as ever.

The mostly dried blood beneath his nostrils, and the accompanying flecks of ugly, dark scarlet on his lips.

"You remember what Lady Veradis said," Giraldi told her. "It's over."

Isana stared at the blood and remembered what it meant. She didn't have strength enough to shake her head, but she managed to murmur, "No."

Giraldi turned her face back to his. "Crows take it, Isana," he said, his voice frustrated. "Some fights can't be won."

Fire-thunder erupted nearby outside, rattling the room's furniture and sending ripples across the glassy surface of the water in the healing tub.

Giraldi looked at the window, then back to Isana. "It's time, Steadholder. You haven't slept in days. You tried. Great furies know you tried. But he's going to die. Soon. If you don't withdraw, you'll die with him."

"No," Isana said again. She heard the unsteady quaver of her voice as she did.

"Bloody crows," Giraldi said, his tone at once gentle and anguished. "Steadholder. Isana. Crows and ashes, girl. Fade wouldn't want you to throw your life away for no reason."

"The decision is mine." So many words took a noticeable effort, and she felt short of breath. "I will not leave him."

"You *will*," Giraldi said, his voice heavy and hard. "I promised Bernard I'd watch over you. If it comes to that, Isana, I'll cut you loose of him and drag you out of this room."

A quiet and very distant surge of defiance whispered through Isana's thoughts, and it gave her voice a barely audible growl of determination. "Bernard would never abandon one of his own." She took a breath. "You know that. Fade is mine. I will not leave him."

Giraldi said nothing. Then he shook his head and drew the knife from his belt. He reached for the rope that kept her hand in contact with Fade's.

The defiance returned, stronger, and Isana caught the centurion's wrist in her fingers. Joints crackled with tension. Her knuckles turned white. Then she lifted her head and glared into the centurion's eyes. "Touch us," she said, "and I'll kill you. Or die trying."

Giraldi's head rocked back—not from the grip of Isana's weakened fingers, she knew, and not from the feebly voiced threat. It had been her eyes.

"Crows," he whispered. "You mean it."

"Yes."

"Why?" he demanded. "Why, Isana? Don't tell me Fade is just a simpleton slave that took a liking to following your nephew around. Who is he?"

Isana struggled to think clearly, to remember who knew and who was supposed to know and who absolutely could not know. But she was so tired, and there had been so many years—and so many lies. She was sick to death of the lies and the secrets.

"Araris," she whispered. "Araris Valerian."

Giraldi mouthed the word to himself, his eyes visibly widening. Then he looked from the wounded man to Isana and back, and his face went absolutely white. The old soldier bit his lip and looked away. His features sagged visibly, as if he'd suddenly aged another ten years. "Well," he said, his voice shaking. "A few things make more sense."

Isana released his wrist.

He looked down at the knife for a moment, then returned it to its sheath on his belt. "If I can't stop you . . . I may as well help you. What do you need, my lady?"

Isana's eyes widened suddenly as she stared at Giraldi, and she suddenly saw how to get through to Fade. Her heart labored, sudden hope spreading through her exhausted mind in a wave of sudden, tingling heat.

"That's it," she said.

The old soldier blinked and looked behind him. "It is? What is it?"

"Giraldi, bring me tea. Something strong. And find me his sword."

⋙ CHAPTER 35

It was a long and weary march back to the horses, and an even wearier ride all the way back to the Legion fortifications at the Elinarch. Tavi arrived in the coldest, heaviest hours of the night. It still seemed odd to him that despite the blazing heat of late summer in the southwest of the Realm, the night managed to be just as uncomfortably cool as in the Calderon Valley.

They were challenged by mounted pickets in two lines as they approached, and as they crossed the final open ground to the town, Tavi took note of silent shapes in the tree lines— local archers and woodsmen, most likely, always moving west with steady caution. The First Spear must have sent them out to watch and harass the incoming Canim army, and to attempt to take the foe's scouts as they advanced. It was a measure Tavi should have thought of himself—but then, that's why he'd left Valiar Marcus in charge of the defenses.

Tavi and Kitai rode into the half of the town on the southern end of the Elinarch, then across the great bridge, their footsteps ringing on the stone. The water-mud-fish scent of the great Tiber River rose up to them. They were better than a hundred feet off the water, at the top of the bridge's arch, and Tavi closed his weary eyes and enjoyed the cool breeze that flowed over him.

Word of his return went ahead of him, called from one sentry to the next. Magnus, as the captain's senior valet, was there to meet him and accompanied them to the command tent—a general-issue Legion tent now instead of Cyril's larger model. Several people entered and left as they approached, all moving at a brisk trot. They had to dance around each other as they did.

All in all, that tent looked grossly undersized and inadequate, in the center of the circle of lightning-blasted earth. That was appropriate, Tavi supposed. He was feeling somewhat undersized and inadequate himself.

"No, crows take it," snarled Valiar Marcus's voice from within the tent. "If our food supplies are on the south bank, and the dogs take it, we'll be eating our boots when we fall back to the north."

"But I just had my whole century toting supplies over there like pack mules," protested a second voice.

"Good," Marcus snapped. "They'll know the exact route to return them."

"Marcus, those storage houses are on the docks, not behind the city walls. We can't leave them unsecured, and our own storage buildings haven't been completed."

"Then dump them somewhere. Or commandeer a house."

Tavi slid off his horse, stiffened muscles complaining. He beckoned Kitai, and she leaned down toward him. Tavi muttered a quiet request, and she nodded before turning her horse and kicking it into a run toward the followers' camp.

Magnus watched her go, frowning. The darkness and her hood would have hidden her features from the old Cursor, but she was still obviously a woman. "Who is that, sir?" he asked Tavi.

"Later," Tavi said. He flicked his eyes at the tent. Magnus frowned, but then nodded.

Tavi took a moment to order his thoughts, tried to project all the authority he could fabricate, and entered the tent "Don't commandeer a house," he said, "ask for a volunteer. You won't have any trouble finding residents willing to sacrifice for the good of the only thing standing between them and a horde of Canim."

The tent bore two tables made of empty water barrels and planks. Paper, much of it half-consumed by flame, lay scattered in complete disarray over all of them. Two fish sat at each table, attempting to sort out the surviving papers in the light of a single furylamp.

The First Spear and the argumentative centurion snapped to attention and saluted. "Sir," Marcus said.

The fish were a beat behind the centurions, and began to rise. Tavi felt certain that if they did, they'd knock the crude tables over and undo whatever they had accomplished.

"As you were," Tavi told them. "Get back to work." He nodded at Marcus. "First Spear. And Centurion . . . ?"

"Cletus, sir."

"Centurion Cletus. I know your men are tired. We're all tired. We're going to get more tired. But crows take me if I let the Legion be tired *and* hungry. So find a storage building and secure the food."

Cletus clearly did not like the notion. No centurion would want his men to be forced into action while bone-tired from physical labor if he could possibly avoid it. But he was Legion to the core and nodded at once. "Yes, sir." He turned to leave.

Tavi nodded in approval. "Take one of the fish centuries to help you haul. Grains and dried meat first, the perishables after."

Cletus paused and bowed his head to Tavi in silent thanks, then departed.

The stocky First Spear had lost most of the short-cropped hair from one side of his head due to the fire, and the fresh-healed skin, where the healers had been able to help him most, was pink and shiny and slightly swollen. It made his scowl no less ferocious, his ugly, craggy face even uglier and craggier.

"Captain," Marcus growled. "Glad to see you back in one piece. Antillar said something about you scouting out the Canim."

"Not quite," Tavi said. "A scout picked up on a trail and tracked it back to . . ." Tavi glanced at the fish sitting at the tables.

"Right," Marcus said. "Boys, get out. Get some food and report back to your century."

"Magnus, send for Tribunes Antillar and Antillus, please," Tavi said. "I want them here for this."

"Right away, sir," Magnus said, and slipped out of the tent, leaving Tavi alone with the First Spear.

"You look like something the crows have been at, Marcus," Tavi said.

The First Spear narrowed his eyes at Tavi, then grunted out a muted chuckle. "Since I was a boy, sir."

Tavi grinned and sat down on one of the stools. "What's our status?"

The First Spear waved an irritated hand at the parchment-covered tables. "Difficult to say. Gracchus was a good Tribune Logistica, but his records were organized about as well as your average forest fire. We're still trying to sort out where every-thing is stored, and it's making it hard to get anything done."

Tavi sighed. "My fault. I forgot to appoint a replacement Tribune Logistica to coordinate before I left."

"To be fair, they wouldn't have gotten much done yet in any case."

"I'll take care of it. What about the militia?"

The First Spear scowled. "This is a major smuggling town, sir."

Tavi grunted. "Graft, I take it?"

"They have the best council money can buy," he confirmed. "There weren't two hundred full suits of armor, and they hadn't been maintained very well. I think odds are pretty good that some of Kalarus's outlaw *legionares* are wearing the rest of the town's stores. Little bit better on swords, but not much. There are a lot of privately owned swords here, though. Placida sends them home with his *legionares* when they finish their service, and there are a lot of Placidan freemen that move out this way."

"What about the steadholts?" Tavi asked.

"Word's been sent, but it's going to take a while for any volunteers to arrive. So far, only men from the nearest circle of steadholts have showed up."

Tavi nodded. "The defenses?"

"In the same shape as the armory, pretty much. Give us two days and we'll have them up to code."

"We won't get them," Tavi said. "Plan on fighting before afternoon."

Marcus's expression became more grim, and he nodded. "Then I recommend we focus the engineering cohort on the southern wall. The Legion may be able to hold it long enough for the engineers to finish the other positions."

Tavi shook his head. "No. I want fortifications on the bridge. Stone, sandbags, palisades, whatever you can get that will hold up. I want five lines of defense on the bridge itself. Then put the engineers on our last redoubt at the northern end of the bridge and tell them to make it as big and nasty as they possibly can."

The First Spear stared hard at him for a moment. Then he said, "Sir, there are a lot of reasons why that isn't a very good plan."

"And more reasons why it is. Make it happen."

A heavy silence fell, and Tavi looked up sharply. "Did you hear me, First Spear?"

Marcus's jaw clenched, and he stepped close to Tavi, dropping into a loose crouch to look him in the face. "Kid," he said, in a voice that would never have carried from the tent. "I might be old. And ugly. But I ain't blind or stupid." His whisper turned suddenly harsh and fierce. "You are *not* Legion."

Tavi narrowed his eyes, silent.

"I'm willing to let you play captain, because the Legion needs one. But you ain't no captain. And this ain't no game. Men will die."

Tavi met the First Spear's eyes and thought furiously. Valiar Marcus, he knew, was perfectly capable of taking command of the Legion from him. He was well-known among the veteran *legionares*, respected by his fellow centurions, and as the senior centurion present was, rightfully, next in the chain of command since no actual officers of the Legion were capable of exercising authority. Short of simply killing him, Tavi had no way to prevent him from seizing Legion command if he chose to do it.

Worse, the First Spear was a man of principle. If he genuinely thought Tavi was going to do something uselessly idiotic and kill *legionares* who didn't have to die, Marcus *would* take command. If that happened, he would not be prepared to face the threat that was coming. He would fight with courage and honor, Tavi was sure, but if he tried to apply standard Legion battle doctrine, the Legion would not live to see another sunset.

All of which meant that the next battle Tavi had to fight was right here, right now, in the mind and heart of the veteran First Spear. If he had Marcus's support, most of the rest of the centurions would follow. Tavi had to convince Valiar Marcus so thoroughly that he actively supported Tavi's course of action instead of merely accepting it as one more distasteful order he had to obey. The tacit, indirect resistance of unwilling obedience to orders perceived as foolish could kill them just as thoroughly as the Canim.

Tavi closed his eyes for a moment. Then he said, "I asked Max once how you won your honor name. Valiar. The Crown's House of the Valiant. Max told me that when he was six years old, Icemen came down and took the women and children from a woodcutter's camp. He told me that you tracked them for two days through one of the worst winter storms in living memory and assaulted the entire Iceman raiding party. Alone. That you took the captives from them and led them home. That Antillus Raucus gave you his own sword. That he appointed you to the House of Valiar himself, and told Gaius to honor it or he'd call him to *juris macto*."

The First Spear nodded without saying anything.

"It was stupid of you to do that," Tavi said. "To go into the storm. Alone, no less. To attack what? Twenty-five Icemen on your own?"

"Twenty-three," he said quietly.

"Would you send Cletus there out to do that?" Tavi asked. "Would you send me? One of the fish?"

Marcus shrugged. "No one sent me. I did what I had to do. Truth be told, I waited until most of the Icemen were asleep and cut the throats of half of them before they could wake up."

"I figured it was something like that. But before you left, you didn't know how many of them there were. Or that you'd have a chance to take them while they were asleep. You didn't know if the weather would worsen and kill you. There, at that time, it was an act of insanity."

"It wasn't insane," Marcus said. "I knew them. I knew what I could do. I had advantages."

Tavi nodded. "So do I."

The old soldier's eyes narrowed. "This isn't a gang of angry Marat we're talking about, kid. This isn't a Lord's personal soldiery, or an outlaw Legion. We're going up against the Canim. You don't know them. You've never seen anything like them."

"You're wrong," Tavi said.

The First Spear lifted a lip from his teeth in a sneer. "You think you know them? You trying to tell me you've fought them, kid?"

Tavi met his gaze steadily. "Fought them, side by side with *legionares* and alone. I've seen them kill *legionares* I knew by name, and felt their blood hit my face. I've seen Canim killed. I killed one alone."

Marcus narrowed his eyes in suspicion.

"More than that," Tavi said. "I've spoken to Canim. I learned to play *ludus* from a Cane. Learned about their society. I even speak a little of their language, First Spear. Do you understand any Canish, Valiar Marcus? Do you know any-thing about their homeland? Their leaders?"

Marcus was silent for a moment before he said, "No. Every Cane I ever saw was too busy trying to kill me to give me any schooling."

"They aren't monsters. They aren't anything like us, but they aren't mindless killing machines, either. You know the difference between their raiders and their regulars, I take it?"

The First Spear grunted. "Raiders are bad enough. I never faced their regulars, but I know men who have. They're worse. Bigger, stronger, better fighters. You don't take them down without Knights and casualties."

"The raiders are their conscripts. They're not even their ac-tive military. The regulars you've heard about are their sol-diery. Specifically, they come from an entire social class of hereditary soldiering bloodlines. Their warrior caste."

He grunted. "Like our Citizens?"

"Something like," Tavi agreed. "But there's another caste that's usually at odds with them. The ritualists. Like the ones who called this cloud cover down. Like the ones who struck the captain."

"Hngh," Marcus said. "They have furycraft?"

"I don't think so," Tavi said. "Or at least, not like Alerans use it. But they have some kind of power that lets them do similar things. Three years ago, they threw a series of storms at the coasts. The First Lord himself had to assist in stopping them. Fantus told Cyril that these clouds overhead were defi-nitely not a windcrafting. However they do it, it works."

The First Spear pursed his lips. "Sounds like these ritualist dogs are dangerous. Kalarus would never have made a bargain with them if he didn't think he could crush them later."

"I think the Canim betrayed him."

"Why?"

"Because the scout I followed found Lady Antillus's trail," Tavi said. "We found her camp. The two of us couldn't have captured her alone. I'd have gone for the kill, but what I learned was too important to chance losing."

Marcus shook his head and blew out a breath. "All right, kid. I'm listening."

"I got close enough to listen in on a watercrafted conversation she was having with her brother. It turns out that he made a pact with the Canim."

"What?" Marcus snarled.

"Kalarus offered a Cane named Sarl, a ritualist, a bargain. Kalarus wanted this cloud cover, to help paralyze the Crown's communications and Legions. Then he wanted the Canim to hit the coastline and draw off Aleran troops from the theater between Ceres and Kalare. He thought they would cripple Ceresian crops and prevent the local militias from being called up to help the Crown against him."

The First Spear scowled in thought. "Might have worked."

"Except instead of several hundred Canim, Sarl showed up with tens of thousands."

"How's he going to *feed* that many mouths?" Marcus said. "Armies march on their stomachs, and landing here, they can't possibly reach one of the major cities before they start starving. He couldn't have brought more than a few weeks' supplies with him on the ships, and we won't let him seize enough to feed an army that large. They'll have to fall back to the ships before summer is out."

"No," Tavi said. "They won't."

"Why?"

"Because when I scouted out the Canim, I got close enough to Founderport to see their ships in the harbor."

"At night?" Marcus said. "You expect me to believe you waltzed into an occupied town?"

"Didn't have to," Tavi said, "what with how the whole harbor was lit up. They'd set their ships on fire. I could see them from maybe six miles out."

Marcus blinked. "That's crazy. How do they expect to leave?"

"I don't think they do," Tavi said quietly. "I think they mean to take land and keep it."

"An invasion," Marcus said quietly.

"The timing for it is fairly good, you have to admit," Tavi said. "Right when we're at one another's throats."

Marcus grunted. "That idiot Kalarus told them just when to arrive, didn't he."

Tavi nodded. "He showed Sarl a weakness, and Sarl came after it."

"Sounds like you know him."

"I do," Tavi said. "Some. He's a backstabbing little slive. Cowardly, ambitious, clever."

"Dangerous."

"Very. And he doesn't like the warrior caste."

"Seems like that'd be something of a failing in a military leader."

Tavi nodded. "Not just a failing. A weakness. Something we can exploit."

Marcus folded his arms, listening.

"If there are as many of them as Ehren said, we can't beat them," Tavi said. "We both know that."

Marcus's face turned grim, and he nodded.

"But I don't think they're going to be very cohesive. The warriors with him know that Sarl would cheerfully throw their lives away for no purpose. They're cut off from the support of the rest of their caste, and if I'm guessing correctly, they're probably only there because Sarl threatened them into it. He'd never surround himself with that many warriors if he didn't have the means to control them. I think they'd rather be anywhere but here under Sarl's leadership."

"Why do you think that?" the First Spear asked.

"Because it explains the burning ships. Sarl knew that if he came ashore with the warriors, he'd never be able to stop them from abandoning him and sailing back home. He burned the ships because he wanted to trap the warriors here. He wanted them to have no options *except* to fight, and win."

Marcus frowned and chewed over the thought. "That's one crow of a motivation," he finally admitted. "But I don't see how that plays to us."

"Because they aren't a united force," he said. "They're not

used to operating against us in numbers this large. They don't trust their leaders. They don't like the current chain of command. They're bound to be angry at Sarl for trapping them here. With that many fractures in the foundation, anything they build on it will be unstable. I think that if we can force them to react to a series of things, quickly, they're going to have real trouble maintaining solid positions."

Marcus narrowed his eyes. "Draw them out. Then we hit them in concentration."

"That's the core of it, yes."

"You might have noticed we have plenty of fish in this bunch. Nothing says we'll be able to maintain the kind of discipline we'd need to do it."

"Maybe not," Tavi said. "But we aren't exactly spoiled for choice."

The First Spear grunted. "Assuming we pull it off, we'll cut them up pretty good. But it won't kill them all."

"No. But if we can break Sarl's hold on them, we might be able to convince the rest to turn away."

"Break his hold. You mean kill him?"

Tavi shook his head. "That won't be enough. If we kill Sarl, one of his lieutenants will step up in his place. We've got to see his power broken, prove he was wrong to come here, that there's nothing but death where he's trying to lead his army—and we have to do it in front of the warriors."

"To what end?"

"Canim warriors respect fidelity, skill, and courage," Tavi said. "If we break Sarl, it might force them to withdraw, at least temporarily. They might go looking for an easier target. But even if they don't, it could at least buy us time to prepare better, maybe get reinforcements."

Marcus exhaled slowly, and looked around the interior of the too-small tent with tired eyes. "If it doesn't work?"

"I think it's our only chance."

"But if it doesn't work?"

Tavi frowned at him and said, "Then we destroy the Elinarch."

Marcus grunted. "First Lord isn't going to like that."

"But he isn't here, is he," Tavi said. "I'll take full responsibility."

"Engineers already looked at it," Marcus said. "The bridge is as furycrafted as any causeway. It's strong, almost impossible to crack, and the stone repairs damage to itself. We don't have enough earthcrafters to do the job quickly. It will take days to tear it down."

"Let me worry about the earthcrafters," Tavi said. "I know where we can get some."

The First Spear squinted at Tavi. "Are you sure, kid?"

"I'm sure that if Sarl isn't stopped here, he'll run rampant over every steadholt between here and Ceres just to get enough food to survive."

Marcus tilted his head to one side. "And you think you're the best one to stop him?"

Tavi rose and met his eyes. "I honestly don't know. But I'll promise you this, Marcus. I'll be at the front and in the center the whole way. I won't ask any *legionare* to do what I won't."

The First Spear stared at him, and his eyes suddenly went very wide. "Bloody *crows*," he whispered.

"There's not much time, First Spear, and we can't afford confusion or delays." Tavi offered him his hand. "So I need to know, right now. Are you with me?"

Footsteps approached the tent.

The First Spear stared at Tavi's outstretched hand. Then he nodded once, sharply, and lifted his fist to his heart. His voice came out hoarse, low. "All right, sir. I'm with you."

Tavi nodded at the First Spear and returned the salute.

Magnus entered the tent with Crassus and Max in tow. They saluted Tavi, and Tavi nodded to them. "We don't have much time," he began without preamble.

He was interrupted when the tent flap opened again, and Mistress Cymnea entered, tall and calm, her hair and dress flawless, as though she hadn't been dragged from her bed to rush to the fortifications.

"I'm sorry, Mistress," Magnus said at once. "I'm afraid you can't be here for security reasons."

"It's all right, Magnus," Tavi said. "I asked her to be here."

The old Maestro glanced at Tavi, frowning. "Why?"

Cymnea bowed politely to Tavi. "My thoughts precisely, Captain."

"I need you to do something for me," Tavi said. "I wouldn't ask for your help if it wasn't important."

"Of course, Captain. I will do whatever service I may."

"Thank you," Tavi said. "Gentlemen, when we're finished, you'll need to coordinate with our new Tribune Logistica, here."

Max's jaw dropped open. *"What?"*

Cymnea's eyes grew very wide. *"What?"*

Tavi arched a brow at Max. "Which word didn't you understand?"

"Sir," Magnus began, tone heavy with disapproval.

"We need a Tribune Logistica," Tavi said.

"But she's just—" Max began. He broke off, cheeks flushing, and muttered under his breath.

Cymnea turned a steady and unamused gaze upon Max. "Yes, Tribune. She's just a . . . what? Which word did you have in mind? Whore, perhaps? Madam? Woman?"

Max met her eyes. "Civilian," he said quietly.

Cymnea narrowed her eyes for a second, then nodded in accession, somehow conveying a mild apology with the gesture.

"Not anymore, she's not," Tavi said. "We need someone who knows what the Legion will require and who is familiar with our people. Someone with experience, leadership skills, organizational ability, and who knows how to exercise authority. If we appoint any centurion in the Legion to the post, it's going to disrupt the century we draw him from, and we need every sword and every century." He glanced around the room. "Does anyone have a better suggestion?"

Max sighed, but no one spoke.

"Then let's get to work," Tavi said. "This is what we're going to do . . ."

CHAPTER 36

Purposeful strides approached, and by the time the tent's flap was thrown aside, Tavi had his sword in his hand and half-drawn from its scabbard.

"Whoah," Ehren said, holding up open hands. The tanned, sandy-haired little Cursor looked more amused than threatened, backlit by the cloudy light of full day. "I surrender, Captain Scipio."

Tavi blinked his eyes several times, glanced blearily around, then put his sword away. "Right. Sorry."

Ehren closed the tent flap, darkening it again.

Tavi sighed. "On the trunk to your left."

"Oh," Ehren said. "Sorry. I forgot. Light." The little fury-lamp on the trunk flickered to life.

"You didn't forget," Tavi said, half-smiling. "You wanted to see if I'd developed any crafting of my own yet. No."

Ehren put on an innocent look. "I hardly recognized you with your hair cut so short."

"I hardly recognized you with a tan," Tavi replied. "I'm sorry we haven't been able to talk yet, but . . ."

"We're working," Ehren said. "I get it."

Tavi had slept in his trousers and with his boots on. He rose, slipped on a tunic, and turned to greet Ehren with a rough hug.

"Good to see you," Tavi said.

"Likewise," Ehren replied. He drew back and looked suspiciously at Tavi, up and down. "Crows, you've gotten taller. You're supposed to stop growing after age twenty or so, Ta—" He shook his head. "Ahem. Scipio. At the Academy, we started off the same height. Now you're as tall as Max."

"Making up for lost time, I suppose," Tavi said. "How are you?"

"Glad to be rid of the islands," Ehren said. He frowned and glanced away. "Though I wish I'd come back with better news. And given it to someone else."

"Did you speak to the prisoners?"

Ehren nodded. "They cooperated. I'm fairly sure that the dead man was Kalarus' agent, and was the brains of the operation. The rest were just . . . well. There's always shady business for a *legionare* to involve himself in."

"Especially troublemakers."

"Especially troublemaking veterans," Ehren agreed.

"Fine," Tavi said. "Release them and send them back to their century."

Ehren blinked. "What?"

"That's an entire spear of veteran *legionares*, Ehren. I need them."

"But . . . Captain . . ."

Tavi met the Cursor's eyes, and said, quietly, "This is my decision. Do it."

Ehren nodded. "All right," he said quietly. "The First Spear asked me to tell you that the Canim are moving through the second picket line now, and they're making no effort to conceal their presence. He estimates that they'll be here in an hour or so."

Tavi scowled. "I told him to wake me when the *first* pickets reported contact."

"He said you'd need your sleep more than he in the next day or two. Tribune Antillus agreed."

Tavi scowled. Max, of course, could rely upon his furycrafting to go for days and days without sleeping. Odds were excellent that Valiar Marcus could do it as well, but Tavi had no such resource—and though he'd needed less sleep and less time to rest in the past two or three years, he had no idea exactly to what extent he could rely upon the nebulous endurance.

Max and the First Spear had probably been correct to let

him get as much rest as possible. Great furies knew, he'd need his wits about him today.

"All right," he said quietly. "Ehren, I know I don't have any authority to give you a command, but . . ."

Ehren quirked an eyebrow. "Since when have you let niceties like the law slow you down?"

Tavi grinned. "I don't mind law. Provided it doesn't get in the way."

Ehren snorted. "Seems like yesterday we were dodging bullies in the Academy courtyard. Now it's an army of Canim." He gave Tavi a long-suffering look and sighed. "All right. I'm in."

Tavi nodded. "Thank you."

Ehren nodded back.

"Tell Magnus to get you a courier's horse," Tavi said. "Armor, too. I want you close to me. I may need a messenger today, and I want it to be someone I trust."

"Of course," Ehren said.

"And . . ." Tavi frowned. "If things don't go well here, Ehren, I want you to go. Take word back to Gaius, yourself."

Ehren was silent for a minute. Then he said, in a whisper, "You're a Cursor, Tavi. It's your duty to go yourself, if it comes to that."

Tavi reached up and ran his hand over the short, bristling hairs on his head. "Today," he said quietly, "I'm a *legionare*."

Tavi stood atop the city walls on the southern half of the town, on the battlements over the gate. The defenses were neither as tall as those of the fortress of Garrison, back in his home in the Calderon Valley, nor were they built as thick, but for all of that they were obdurate Aleran siege walls, grounded in the bones of the earth itself and all but impervious to any damage not supported by massive furycraft.

Of course, he had no idea if they would withstand whatever strange powers the Canim ritualists seemed to possess. He kept his face calm and confident and his mouth shut. Victory, today, depended far more upon the courage of his men than upon their raw strength, and he would not allow himself to weaken their morale. So though he was acutely afraid of a second bolt of crimson lightning, which might come down precisely where he was standing, he stood there without moving, his breathing steady, hopefully looking utterly indifferent to the oncoming danger.

Around him stood the veterans of the First Spear's century. Their brother centuries within their cohort waited along the length of the walls, ready to defend them or lend support to their cohort-brothers. In the courtyard behind them waited two more entire cohorts, one with a mixed level of experience, the second composed almost entirely of fish—including what had been Max's century. In total, nearly a thousand *legionares* stood in arms and armor, at the ready.

Tavi knew that behind them, placed at key defensive positions, ready to move in to support the defenders of the gate, were another thousand men, and behind *that*, at the base of the bridge, were three thousand more. The rest maintained a watch on the northern side, while the remaining cavalry waited at the apex of the bridge, ready to respond to any enemy thrust from unexpected quarters.

When the Canim came, the first thing Tavi saw was the crows.

At first, he thought it was a column of black smoke rising from the hills southwest of the town. But instead of drifting with the wind, the darkness rose, widening, stretching out into a line, then Tavi could see that it was the crows he'd been looking at, spinning over the heads of the Canim host like a wagon wheel on its side. He half expected to see the Canim only a moment later, but nearly a quarter of an hour went by while the vast disc of wheeling crows grew larger.

Tavi understood. He had underestimated the number of crows. Four or five times as many of the carrion birds as he guessed whirled over the Canim. Which meant that this was the largest murder of crows he had ever seen—including those that had descended upon the carnage of the Second Battle of Calderon.

A mutter went up and down the wall among the *legionares*. Tavi got the sense that they had never seen that many of the scavenger birds, either.

Then they heard the drums and droning war horns. The sound of the drums began as a low rumble, hardly audible, but rose quickly to a distant, steady, pulsing crash. The horns screamed mournfully through the din, and the whole was like listening to the cries of some unimaginably vast wolf loping through a thunderstorm.

Tavi could feel the men growing restless behind him, expressed in a thousand uncomfortable shiftings of stance, in mutters, in the rasp of metal on metal as *legionares* fought their own anxiety by checking and rechecking their arms and armor.

On the open ground nearest the town, horsemen and infantry alike appeared, moving toward the town—the pickets and skirmishers who had been watching for the Canim and harassing them on their way in. They had gathered into groups as they retreated, and came toward the town at a weary trot after a full day and more in the field. Not all of the skirmishers would return. Some had undoubtedly fallen. Others, the most woodcrafty auxiliaries and local volunteers, would remain in the field, hiding from the enemy host, watching its movements, and striking its flanks and rear in hit-and-run missions.

At least, that was the plan. Tavi was well aware of how quickly and lethally reality could deviate from his intentions.

The last of the returning troops reached the shelter of the city's walls, and the gates rumbled shut behind them. The drums and horns drew nearer, and Tavi wanted to scream with the sheer frustration of waiting. He longed to fight, to kill, to run, to do *anything* at all, really.

But it was not yet time to act, and his men had to be feeling much the same as he. So Tavi stood facing the enemy, apparently calm, apparently bored, and waited.

The first of the Canim finally stalked into sight over the top of the last hill to hide them from his view. Raiders, spread out before the army, crested the hills in a skirmish line half a mile across. Upon sighting the city, and the Aleran defenders upon its walls, they tilted back their heads and let out long, ululating howls. The warbling cries sent the hairs on the back of Tavi's neck to standing.

A burst of chatter rose up from the cohort of fish in the

courtyard behind them, and Tavi heard Schultz telling them to pipe down.

"All right, Marcus," Tavi said. He was surprised at how calm his own voice sounded. "Raise the standard here."

Marcus had opposed any move that would identify the captain's position to the enemy, but Tavi had overruled him, and one of his men lifted the banner of the First Aleran, with its red-and-blue eagle, to fly in the wind at the tip of the wooden shaft from a long battle lance. As the banner first flew into the breeze, Tavi stepped up onto the battlements, where the *legionares* could all see him. He drew his sword and raised it over his head, and this time a thousand swords did the same, a chorus of steely chimes that rose in defiance of the eerie howls and savage drums.

Tavi threw back his head and let out his own cry of challenge, wordless, throwing all of his impatience and fear and rage into it, and he was instantly followed by a thousand *legionares*, a furious storm of sound that shook the walls of the town.

As the full numbers of the Canim host crested the rise, they were met with the sight of a thousand steel-clad *legionares*, bright swords in hand, standing to battle and casting screams of defiance into their enemy's teeth. Unafraid, furious, and spoiling for a fight, the First Aleran stood behind their captain, ready—and more than ready—to meet the Canim host. Though outnumbered, strong position, furycraft, and sheer will would make them a dangerous foe.

Or so Tavi wanted the Canim to believe. Uncle Bernard had taught him a great deal about successfully facing down a predator threatening a flock. First impressions were important.

Tavi leapt back down from atop the stone merlon, as the cheers died, and the First Spear began roaring out an old Legion marching song. It had more to do with wanton maids and mugs of ale than war and battle, but every *legionare* knew it, and it had a seemingly inexhaustible number of verses. The First Spear bellowed out the opening call, and the refrain came as a rumbling, rhythmic shout from the rest of the *legionares*.

It was part of Tavi's plan to keep his men occupied with their singing as the Canim host came over the hill—Canim in armor of lacquered black, oddly ornate, here and there touched with various colors in what was probably some sort of system of denoting personal honors won. Many thousands of them, every one of them large, lean, enormous—and, if what Varg had told him about their life spans was true, each of them probably possessed much more personal experience and knowledge than even his veteran *legionares*.

The men kept the song up while Tavi counted enemy numbers, eventually coming to a grim estimate—twenty thousand Canim regulars, at the least, and twice that many raiders, roving in loose packs of fifty or so ahead of the main body of the army, loping along its flanks, ranging out behind it, following the way lean wild dogs would follow a herd of grass lions, waiting to scavenge from the larger predators' kills.

The Canim outnumbered them ten to one, and facing regulars toe-to-toe would not yield the decisive successes of the cavalry assaults upon isolated packs of raiders. Men now singing around him would die. Tavi himself might die. The fear that came with those thoughts made Ehren's statement that he was a Cursor, and that his duty was to report to the First Lord, a poisonously seductive one. He could be on a horse and riding away from the Canim and the Legion alike in moments, should he wish it.

But Tavi had also made a promise to Captain Cyril, to serve the Legion as well as the Crown. He could not abandon that promise. Nor could he leave his friend behind him, and Max would never leave fellow *legionares* in danger, not if ordered to do so by Gaius himself.

Tavi desperately wished he could leave. But then, so would anyone born with brains enough to walk and talk. So did every man there with him on the wall and waiting behind.

He would stay. Regardless of the outcome, he would see it through to the end.

With that decision, the fear faded, replaced with a sense of quiet purpose. He did not quit feeling afraid—it simply became a part of the situation, of the day before him. He had accepted it, the possibility of death, and in so doing it had lost some of its power over him. He found himself able to focus, to think more clearly, and felt certain that this was the best thing he could have done for himself, and for the men now following him. That confidence in turn reassured him about his own plans, that they gave the Legion, if not a certain victory, at least a fighting chance to survive.

And so he faced the enemy as the skirmish packs of raiders parted, scarlet lightning flashed madly in the clouds, and, with an earthshaking roar, the Canim regulars washed over the earth toward the city like a tide of howling shadow.

◦◦◦◦◦ CHAPTER 37

Tavi was sure that his voice would sound every bit as weak and thready as he felt, but it came out smooth and strong. "All right, Marcus. Let's open negotiations."

"Ready!" bellowed the First Spear, and along the walls, *legionares* snapped into their standard defense formation—one man bearing a shield stepping up to his crennel, while his partner, armed with a bow, stepped up close to the shieldman's flank. At a nudge from the archer's hip, the shieldman would swiftly step aside as his partner took his place, loosed a shot, and reversed the process, letting the shield move back to cover both men, providing but a bare second for the enemy to hit a living target.

Though all *legionares* were given basic training in the use of a bow, they were hardly a substitute for Knights Flora. The *legionares* had the reach on their foe, but the Canim were swift, difficult targets, and well armored. Several Aleran arrows found their marks, and some of the enemy went down—but not many, especially when compared to the number of Canim still remaining.

The Canim covered the distance to the walls with unnerving speed—not so swiftly as horsemen, perhaps, but far more quickly than a man could run. Once they were within perhaps sixty or seventy yards, the oncoming Canim hurled a shower of javelins thicker and heavier than an Aleran battle spear.

The weapons hit hard. Beside Tavi, there was a heavy, crunching sound and a grunt of surprise as one of the javelins smashed into a veteran's shield. The Canim weapon shattered, but threw the *legionare* to the ground and left an enormous dent in the shield's surface.

Down the wall, one of the archers stepped up for a shot, just as the missiles flew. A spear slammed completely through one biceps, its red steel tip passing all the way through, to half the length of the weapon's haft. The hit *legionare* cried out and fell.

"Medico!" Tavi shouted, and the waiting healers rushed to the man.

"Sir!" Marcus shouted, and Tavi felt something hard hit him between the shoulder blades an instant before something else hit the back of his helmet. Thunderous sound filled his ears, and he fell to one knee. In the corner of his eye, he saw a Canim javelin arc away from him on a skewed, wobbling line of flight.

"Keep your eyes open, sir!" bellowed Marcus as he hauled Tavi back to his feet. "The men know what to do."

"Ram!" screamed a grizzled *legionare* farther down the wall. "Here comes their ram!"

"Ready over the gate!" Marcus roared.

Tavi took a quick look around the sheltering merlon. Below, the Canim surged for the wall. Perhaps twenty feet behind the leading Canim came a tightly packed group bearing a rough wooden ram nearly three feet in diameter between them. Around them, new ranks of Canim hurled their javelins as the whole of the body charged the walls, and more of the creatures came within range, so that there was a continual stream of deadly shafts arching through the air. Tavi barely jerked his head back in time to avoid one such javelin, and it flew past him to bury itself to the base of its head in the wooden beam of a two-story building behind him.

"Lines!" called another *legionare*, just as the shapes of several enormous iron hooks the size of boat anchors attached to lengths of steel chain flew up from the ground outside the wall.

The hooks landed with heavy clanks, and their chains were drawn tight. *Legionares* seized and threw down most of them before they could settle into position, but a few caught solidly, and their chains rattled as Canim began swarming up them.

Tavi suddenly heard and felt an enormous boom, an impact that made the walls tremble beneath his boots, the sound loud enough to drown even the howling chaos of the battle for a moment. The ram had reached the gate, and it seemed inconceivable that it could withstand the terrible power driving its weight for long.

"Ready!" shouted the First Spear, leaning out to look down despite the deadly javelins still hurtling through the air. He flicked his head to one side to idly dodge an incoming missile, then growled, "Now!"

The bowmen over the gate had already dropped their bows. Now they lifted large wooden buckets of hot pitch, grunting and straining with the effort, and poured them down to splash over the area before the gate, eliciting shrieks of surprise and agony from the Canim beneath them—and liberally spattering the wooden ram with the material, as well.

Marcus got back under cover, and shouted to Tavi. "Ready!"

Tavi nodded and lifted his fist, glancing back over his shoulder at the courtyard.

At the signal, Crassus and a dozen of his Knights Pisces, as the Legion had generally dubbed them during the march, suddenly shot up out of the courtyard on columns of wind. They shot out over the river, dodging and weaving in a flight pattern meant to make it difficult to target any single Knight in the air, banked around to face the city again, and streaked by no more than sixty feet over the earth, scattering hundreds of startled, circling crows as they did.

More missiles flew up at the flight of Knights, but none found their mark, and as Crassus flashed past the gates, Tavi saw him point a finger and cry out. A flickering bead of white-hot fire appeared before him and screamed earthward, striking the pitch-soaked wooden ram and bursting into a sudden cloud of angry fire.

The flame seared and burned, and Canim screamed. The

deadly hot pitch took fire as well, dooming anything already soaked in it to a swift and terrible demise.

Atop the walls, Tavi saw one of the Canim reach the wall above his scaling chain, but hard-faced *legionares* were waiting. Swords and spears lashed out, and the Cane fell out of sight. Other *legionares* used captured javelins as pry bars, levering the heavy grappling hooks out of position and sending more Canim to the earth.

Tavi could not have said precisely what it was that let him understand it, but he sensed the sudden hesitation in the Canim charge. He turned to Crassus and whirled his arm in a circle over his head.

The Knight Tribune had blackened eyes since Tavi had broken his nose, but they were sharp, and the flight of Knights banked and hurtled along the walls again upon a furycrafted gale, casting dirt and dust into the Canim's eyes and noses while Crassus hurled half a dozen more blazing spheres down into the Canim, tiny beads of light blossoming into explosions of flame.

Before Crassus and his Knights could make another pass, the low horns of the Canim sounded in rapid rhythm, a signal to the attacking troops, and the armored regulars below began a swift and orderly withdrawal. They were back out of bow range within two minutes, though the Alerans on the walls sent as many arrows as they could into the departing ranks.

Crassus began to lead his Knights into a harrying action, but Tavi saw the movement, and lifted his spread hand straight over his head, clenched it into a fist, and drew it back down to shoulder level. Crassus saw the signal, acknowledged it with a raised fist, and he and the other Knights returned to the fortifications.

Around him, *legionares* let out cheers and rained defiant insults on the backs of the departing Canim. Every man there knew that the battle was far from over, but for the time being, at least, they were alive and unbeaten, and Tavi did nothing to discourage the jubilation given them by the small victory in the opening moments of the battle. He sheathed his sword and watched the retreating Canim, breathing hard though he had barely been physically involved. He leaned out over the battlements and looked down. Still, broken forms lay below, totaling perhaps seven- or eightscore dead. None of the Canim left behind were wounded—only the dead lay there. The regulars had taken their wounded with them.

"Well," Ehren panted behind him. "That was bracing."

"Medico!" Tavi called to a nearby healer. "What's the count?"

"Three casualties, two moderate, one mild. No dead, sir."

That drew another round of shouts from the *legionares*, and even the First Spear almost smiled. "Good work!" Tavi shouted to them. Then he turned and headed for the stairs down to the courtyard.

"So," Ehren said, following. The little spy was hardly able to wear the armor Magnus had procured for him. "Now what happens?"

"That was just a probe," Tavi replied. "And I'll give fair odds that their leader wanted it to fail."

"Fail? Why?"

"Because Sarl is a ritualist, but he's got a bunch of warriors to control," Tavi said. "To do that, he has to convince them that he's strong enough and worthy enough to lead them. He let the warriors take the first swing at us, knowing we'd hit them hard enough to let them know they'd been kissed. His next move is going to be to prove how worthy a leader he is, when he uses whatever powers he has to help them take the walls. He saves lives. Gets to be the hero. Proves his strength."

Ehren nodded, as he and Tavi reached the courtyard, and Tavi walked toward a horse being held there. "I see. So what are you doing now?"

"Cutting Sarl's drama out from under him," Tavi replied. He sheathed his sword and mounted the horse. "If I move now, I can steal his thunder."

Ehren blinked. "How are you going to do that?"

Tavi nodded to the *legionares* at the gate, and they swung it wide open. He whistled up at the First Spear, over the gate, and Marcus tossed him the Legion's standard on its wooden haft. Tavi grounded it next to his boot on the stirrup.

"I'm going to ride out there and make him look like an idiot," Tavi said.

Ehren's eyes widened. "Out there?"

"Yes."

"By *yourself*?"

"Yes."

Ehren stared at Tavi for a second, then turned and looked out the gates, to where the Canim host waited less than a mile away. "Well, Captain," he said after a beat. "Whatever happens, I suppose *someone's* going to look awfully foolish."

Tavi flashed Ehren a smile and winked, though on the inside he felt more like screaming and running to a very small, very dark hiding place. It was possible that his whole plan was little more than a fantasy—but after spending so much time with Ambassador Varg, Tavi thought that his knowledge of the enemy might be the only effective weapon against them. If he was right, he could cripple Sarl's support, and if extremely lucky, he might even divorce Sarl from his regulars altogether.

Of course, if he was wrong, he probably wouldn't live to ride back into the shelter of the town's walls.

He closed his eyes for a second and fought against his fear, forcing himself to tightly controlled calm. Fear, now, would quite literally kill him.

Then he kicked his horse lightly and rode forward out of the protection of the First Aleran Legion and the safety of the town's walls, toward sixty thousand savage Canim.

◇◇◇◇◇◇ CHAPTER 38

Tavi rode out past the crackling bonfire his *legionares* had made of the Canim's ram. The scent of burnt wood and of something astringent and bitter filled his nose. The fire popped, and his mount's hooves struck the ground in the three-beat of a slow canter. Crow calls had become a constant, low background noise, like the crashing of the surf in a seaside town. Otherwise, the gloomy afternoon in the space between armies was freakishly silent.

That was fine by Tavi. The farther he could stay from the Canim host and still be heard, the better.

The ride took forever, and as he drew closer to the Canim host, they seemed larger and larger. Tavi was familiar with the enormous, dangerous presence of the Canim, but even so the sight of the monstrous warriors roused a kind of primitive, instinctive alarm that threatened to undermine his self-control far more powerfully than he would have believed. They crouched down on their haunches on the earth in organized ranks, their own version of standing at ease, tongues lolling out of open mouths as they rested after the attack.

A moment later, the odd, acrid scent of Cane filled his nose. Seconds after, his horse balked, alarmed at the smell. Tavi moved swiftly, hands tight on the reins to turn the horse's flinch into a sharp turn without breaking the animal's pace. Not even his steed could be allowed to show fear, regardless of how well justified it might have been.

Tavi cantered down the line, perhaps a hundred yards from the Canim host. During the attack of the regulars, the raider troops had dispersed, spreading out into an enormous half circle around the town, hemming in the Alerans between superior numbers and the river. He wheeled his horse and rode down the lines in the other direction, finally stopping in the center of the Canim lines, before the black-armored ranks of their warriors. His horse screamed and shook its head, half-rearing, but Tavi kept the animal under control, and stared at the Canim with his chin lifted, the First Aleran's standard in his right hand.

Tavi took a deep breath. "Sarl!" he cried. His voice cut through the silence, ringing out clearly. "Sarl! I know you are there! I know you lead these warriors! Come out and face me! Come forth that I may speak to you!"

There was no response. Only thousands of blood-colored Canim eyes and tens of thousands of fangs.

"Sarl!" he called. "I am captain of the Legion you now face! I come to you alone, to have words with you!" He took

the standard into his left hand for a moment and drew his
sword, holding it up for the Canim to see. Then, with a gesture
of contempt, he cast it aside. "I, an Aleran! Alone! Unarmed!
I bid you come to me, scavenger!" His voice turned mocking.
"I will guarantee your safety if my presence terrifies you so
badly that you fear for your pathetic life!"

A low, almost-subsonic murmur went through the black-
armored warriors. It was a wordless expression, a muted
growl, but it came from ten thousand throats, and Tavi could
feel the sound vibrating the breastplate of his armor.

And then a single Cane rose to his feet. He was a big one,
nearly as tall as Varg, and like the Ambassador, his coal black
fur was broken by a maze of old scars. His lacquered black armor was intricately patterned with stripes of bright red. The
Cane stared intently at Tavi. Then he moved his head very
slightly, casting an oblique glance over his shoulder.

"Scavenger!" Tavi shouted again. "Sarl! Come forth,
coward!"

Then a rumbling horn blared. From the rear of the host,
there appeared two rows of Canim in long black half capes and
cowls with mantles of pale leather. The leader in each row carried a bronze censer suspended from dark, braided strands of
rope. Viscous-looking clouds of grey-green incense oozed over
the sides of the censers. The cowled Canim paced slowly to the
front line of troops, then divided, spreading out in a straight
line ten yards ahead of the rest of the host. They faced Tavi,
then, in a single movement, settled slowly to their haunches.

Then Sarl appeared from the ranks.

The Cane looked precisely as Tavi remembered him—
dirty, wiry, reddish fur, where it wasn't covered, sharp features
and beady, malicious eyes. Instead of his scribe's dress,
though, he wore the dark cape and cowl of the Canim who had
preceded him, and he wore lacquered armor of solid bloodred.
A heavy satchel the same color as his mantle rode at his side.

The ritualist walked out to meet Tavi, steps slow and deliberate, and stopped ten feet away. The Cane's eyes burned with
bloody fury. It was plain to Tavi that Sarl had not wished to

come forth—but Tavi's phrasing, and especially his accusations of cowardice, had left Sarl with little choice. He was far more likely to survive facing a single Aleran in the open than his own warriors—and the Canim, Tavi knew, had little patience for cowardice.

Tavi returned the Cane's stare, then made a slight, deliberate motion of his head, a fraction to one side, then back, a Canim gesture of greeting and respect.

Sarl did not return it.

Tavi couldn't be sure, but over the ritualist's shoulder, he thought he saw the eyes of the warrior leader narrow.

"These are not your lands, Sarl," Tavi said, letting his voice carry, his gaze never wavering from the Cane's. "Take your kindred and depart now, while you still have a chance to escape. Remain here, and you will find nothing but your death and the death of those you lead."

Sarl let out a choking, snarling sound that passed for laughter among the Canim. "Bold words," he said, his throat and fangs mangling the words almost beyond recognition. "But empty words. Flee that hovel you defend, and we may decide to kill you on another day."

Tavi laughed, a sound full of arrogance and scorn. "You are not in your home territory. This is Alera, Sarl. Are all ritualists so ignorant of lands outside their own? Or is it just you?"

"You do not face expeditions from a handful of ships this time, Aleran," Sarl replied. "Never have you fought a host of our folk. Never will you defeat them. You will die."

"One day," Tavi replied. "But even if you slay me and every man under my command, others will take our place. Perhaps not today. Nor tomorrow. But it will happen, Sarl. They'll keep on coming. They will destroy you. When you burned your ships, you turned any chance of survival you might have had into ashes and smoke."

Sarl bared his teeth and began to speak.

"You will not pass," Tavi snarled, interrupting the Cane. "I will not yield you the bridge. I will destroy it before it can fall into your hands, if need be. You will throw away the lives of your warriors for *nothing*. And when the lords of Alera come to wipe our land clean of your kind, there will be no one to sing the blood songs of the fallen. No one to bear their names up through the dark sea to the blood lands. Turn away, Sarl. And live a little longer."

"*Nhar-fek,*" the Cane snarled. "You will suffer for this arrogance."

"You talk a lot," Tavi said. "Don't you?"

Sarl's eyes blazed. He thrust a hand up, a dark claw pointing at sullen, cloud-covered sky. "Look up, Aleran. Your very skies are already ours. I will take you. I will make you watch. And when you and the other *nhar-fek* have been hunted down, to the last female, the last squalling spawn, only then will I rip out your throat, so that you can see that the earth has been purged of your unnatural kind." One of the Cane's hands shot toward his satchel.

Tavi had been waiting for just such a thing. He had known that, whatever happened, Sarl couldn't afford to be so openly challenged. If Tavi walked away from this confrontation, it would display weakness to Sarl's fellow Canim—and among their kind, it would be a lethal mistake. Sarl could not afford to let Tavi go free, and Tavi knew that it had only been a matter of time until Sarl made a move.

Tavi lifted a finger into a dramatic point toward the Cane, and his voice crackled with sudden tension and menace. "Don't try it."

Sarl froze, fangs bared in hate.

Tavi faced him steadily, finger pointing, his mount dancing restlessly in place. "You have some power," he said, more quietly. "But you know what Aleran furycraft can do. Move your hand another inch, and I'll roast you and leave you for the crows."

"Even if you succeed," Sarl growled, "my acolytes will tear you to pieces."

Tavi shrugged. "Maybe." He smiled. "But you'll be just as dead."

The two faced one another, and the moment stretched on and on. Tavi fought to remain calm, confident, as a powerful furycrafter would be. The fact of the matter was that if Sarl tried to rip him apart, his only choice would be to trust to his mount's speed and flee. If Sarl tried some kind of sorcery, it would kill him. He was, by any reasonable standard, helpless against the Cane.

But Sarl didn't know that.

And when push came to shove, Sarl was a coward.

"We are speaking under truce," he growled, as though he hated the fact, and that it was the only thing keeping Tavi alive. "Go, Aleran," he said, hand lowering to his side. "We will meet again shortly."

"Now we agree on something," Tavi said. The bluff had worked. His anxiety began to give way to giddy relief, and it was almost as difficult to contain as the fear had been.

He began to turn his mount, then paused, looked at the standing Canim warrior behind the line of Sarl's ritualists, and called out, "Should you wish to recover the remains of your fallen, I will permit unarmed Canim to retrieve them provided they do so in the next hour."

The Cane did not respond. But after a few pensive seconds, he tilted his head, very slightly, to one side. Tavi mirrored the gesture, then began to withdraw, turning his face into a mild breeze.

Sarl suddenly sniffed, a snuffling sound nearly identical to any canine investigating a scent.

Tavi froze, and the relief he'd begun feeling transformed itself in an instant to an almost-hysterical terror. He looked over his shoulder in time to see Sarl's eyes widening in shock and recognition.

"I know you," the Cane breathed. "*You.* The freak. The *messenger* boy!"

Sarl's hand flashed to his satchel and flicked it open, and Tavi suddenly realized that the pale leather case, like the ritualist's mantles, was made of human skin. Sarl withdrew his hand, flinging it straight up over his head. His hand was covered in fresh, scarlet blood, and the droplets flew into the air, scattering, vanishing. He howled something in Canish, and the acolytes behind him joined in.

Tavi turned his horse, desperate to flee, but everything moved with nightmarish deliberation. Before he could give the beast its head, the clouds above them lit up with an inferno of scarlet lightning. Tavi looked up in time to see an enormous wheel of streaming lightning suddenly condense into a single, white-hot point overhead.

Tavi tried to kick the horse into a run, but he was moving too *slowly*, and he could not tear his eyes from the gathering stroke of power—the same power that had massacred the First Aleran's officers, none of whom were as helpless as Tavi.

The point of fire suddenly expanded into a blinding white light and an avalanche of furious noise, and Tavi opened his mouth and screamed in terror and disbelief. He never heard it.

ᐅᐅᐅᐅᐅ CHAPTER 39

Blinding light stole Tavi's sight. A sudden pressure became a single, enormous pain against either side of his head, and there was no longer any sound. He lost all sense of direction, and for a moment everything whirled around him, leaving him with no point of reference, no sense of position.

Then his sight returned in shadows that deepened into colors, and he was able to sort out his perceptions.

First—he was alive. Which came as something of a surprise to him.

Second, he was still mounted, though his horse was staggering in jerking little jumps, as though it couldn't decide whether to run or to buck him off. There was an overwhelming scent of ozone, clean and sharp.

Tavi looked down blearily. There was smoke everywhere, and he felt himself coughing though he could not hear it. The ground beneath him was burned black, the grass charred to ash. More grass burned in a twenty-foot circle around him—an area almost precisely the size of the blasted earth of the command tent.

His clothes were singed. His armor was blackened, but not hot. He still held both the reins of his mount and the lance staff that bore the Legion's standard. The standard's pole was burned along one side, but whole. The flag's eagle had been wrought of a different thread than the rest, and that thread had charred, so that instead of the azure-and-scarlet emblem, the whole of the war bird was black.

Tavi stared dully up at the black bird, while overhead thousands of crows swirled and danced in hungry excitement. The breeze pressed silently against one cheek, and the smoke began to clear. As it did, Tavi began to gather his wits about him again, to realize where he was, and he somehow managed to get the horse to stop trying to throw him off, though it still danced restlessly.

The smoke lifted, and Tavi found himself standing not ten yards from Sarl.

The Canim ritualist was stretched to his full height, head tilted back in a pose of bizarre ecstasy, jaws gaping, his bloody hand still raised to the sky. Then he flinched, evidently at some sound, and his eyes dropped to settle on Tavi. The Cane's eyes widened, his nostrils flared, and his ears quivered and flicked about. His jaws opened and closed twice, faltering motions, though Tavi could not hear any sound Sarl made, if any.

Tavi was still stunned, trying to sort out what had happened, and he never gave any real thought to what he did. It flowed out of him on raw instinct as his emotions coalesced into a single incandescent fire of rage and he dug his heels into the near-panicked horse's flanks.

The terrified horse shot forward, seemingly attaining a full run within the space of a single surge of power, directly at Sarl. Tavi felt himself screaming, felt the pounding of the horse's hooves striking the earth, and felt the banner drag at the air as he swung the standard down upon Sarl with all of his strength and in total silence.

Tavi's aim was true. The heavy haft of the lance came

down at an angle upon Sarl's muzzle, and struck with such force that the Cane's jaws clamped shut on his lolling tongue and drove the ritualist to the ground.

Tavi whipped his head around in time to see one of Sarl's acolytes leaping for him. Tavi pulled his mount around to face the Cane, and the warhorse's hooves lashed out and struck with terrible force. A second Cane ran at Tavi, and he jabbed the lower end of the standard pole squarely into his attacker's face, striking with such force that he clearly saw the yellow shards of shattered fangs fly into the air.

His wits returned to him in full in a sudden flash, and he knew the other acolytes would be charging as well—and that there were another sixty thousand Canim behind them. He'd fought off the first two, but even without help, they would kill him if he stayed to give them battle. He looked around wildly, got his bearings, then turned the horse for the town and gave the beast its head.

The animal needed no encouragement, and it fled for the shelter of the town.

Fast as the beast was, it wasn't fast enough to avoid another Canim that threw itself at the horse in a frenzy, clawed hands ripping at the horse's withers, drawing a splatter of blood. The horse's body shook with a scream of pain Tavi could not hear, and the animal veered wildly, ripping the reins from Tavi's hands.

A glance over his shoulder showed him more acolytes rushing forward, and others sprinting through the ranks of squatting warriors—though the warriors themselves did not rise. One of them threw a dart of some kind. Tavi could not see if it struck, but the horse bucked in pain and nearly faltered before thundering on.

Tavi reached for the reins, but his head was still whirling, and the horse was pounding over open ground as fast as it could move. It was difficult enough simply to stay seated, and by the time Tavi recovered the reins, he looked up to see the broad waters of the Tiber not fifty feet ahead.

Tavi looked around wildly to find the walls of the city several hundred yards to the east. He checked over his shoulder.

Behind him, dozens of ritualists were not ten seconds away. The beast's injuries must have slowed its pace. Tavi turned the horse toward the town, but its feet slipped on the loose earth and shale near the river, and the mount fell, taking Tavi with it.

The water of the river slapped him hard in the face, and there was a brief and terrible pressure on one of his legs. The horse thrashed wildly, and Tavi knew that the panicked animal could easily kill him in its frenzy. Then the horse's weight was gone, and Tavi tried to rise.

He couldn't. The leg that had been pinned beneath the horse had sunk into the clay of the river's bottom. He was trapped there, with the surface less than a foot away.

He almost laughed. It was inconceivable that he had escaped an entire army of Canim, survived that deadly, bloody lightning, only to drown.

He forced himself not to thrash in panic and instead reached down, digging his fingers into the clay. It had been softened by the water, or the task would have been hopeless, but Tavi was able to work his knee lose, and from there to pull the rest of his leg from the cold grasp of the river's bottom.

Tavi rose from the river, looked wildly around him, and saw the standard lying half out of the water. He sloshed to the river shore and seized it up, taking it in a fighting grip, and looking up to face twenty or more of the ritualist acolytes, in their black cloaks and mantles of human skin. They had fallen upon the horse as it came from the water, and now their claws and fangs were scarlet with new blood.

Tavi looked back to his left, and saw that the Aleran cavalry was already on the move over the Elinarch. It would be a futile gesture. By the time they arrived, there would be nothing of Tavi *left* to rescue.

Strange, that it was so quiet, Tavi thought. He saw his death in the eyes of the bloody Canim. It seemed that such a thing should have been a great deal noisier. But he heard nothing. Not his enemy's snarls, nor the cries from the city. Not the gurgle of water as the Tiber flowed around his knees. Not even the sound of his own labored breath or the beating of his heart. It was perfectly silent. Almost peaceful.

Tavi gripped the standard and faced the oncoming Canim without moving. If he was to die, it would be on his feet, against them, and he would take as many of the things with him as he possibly could.

Today, he thought, *I am a* legionare.

The fear vanished, and Tavi abruptly threw back his head and laughed. "Come on!" he shouted to them. "What are you waiting for? The water's fine!"

The Canim rushed at him—and then suddenly slid to a halt in their tracks with two dozen panicked, inhuman stares.

Tavi blinked, entirely confused. Then he looked behind him.

On either side of him, the waters of the Tiber had flowed into solid form, into water-sculptures similar to those he had seen before.

Similar, but not the same.

Two lions, lions the size of horses, stood at his sides, their eyes flickering with green-blue fox fire. Though formed of water, every detail was perfect, down to the fur, down to the battle scars upon their powerful chests and shoulders. Stunned, Tavi lifted a hand and touched one of the beasts on its flank, and though its substance appeared to be liquid, it was as hard as stone beneath Tavi's fingers.

Tavi turned to face the Canim again, and as he did so both lions opened their mouths and let out roars. Tavi could not hear it, but it set his armor to buzzing, and the surface of the waters rippled and jumped in place for a hundred feet in every direction.

The Canim flinched away from the river, and their stance changed, becoming wary, their eyes apprehensive. And then, almost as one, they turned and fled over the grass, back toward the Canim host.

Tavi watched them go, then slogged up out of the river and planted the standard's butt on the ground. He leaned wearily against it and turned his head to consider the enormous furies that had risen to his defense.

A faint tremble in the earth warned him of approaching horses, and he looked up to find Max and Crassus thundering up to him on horses of their own. Each of the young *le-*

gionares dismounted and came toward him. Max's mouth started moving, but Tavi shook his head, and said, "I can't hear anything."

Max scowled at him. Then he turned to the larger of the two water furies. The great old lion greeted Max and nuzzled his hand as affectionately as a pet cat. Max placed his hand on the fury's muzzle and nodded, the gesture both grateful and dismissive, and the fury sank back into the river.

Beside him, Crassus went through almost precisely the same routine, and the second water lion also sank from sight. The half brothers stood in their place for a moment, staring at one another. Neither of them spoke. Then Crassus flushed and shrugged. Max opened his mouth and let out a bark of the laughter Tavi was familiar with, then shook his had, punched his brother lightly on the shoulder, and turned to Tavi.

Max faced him and mouthed words exaggerated so that Tavi could read them, *That was not in the plan.*

"He read my bluff," Tavi said. "But I made him look pretty bad. It might have worked."

Max mouthed, *This it what it looks like when it works? You are insane.*

"Thank you," Tavi said. He tried to sound dry.

Max nodded. *How bad is your leg?*

Tavi frowned at him, puzzled, and looked down. He felt startled to find, high on his left thigh, a wide, wet stain of fresh blood on his breeks. He touched his leg tentatively, but felt no pain. He hadn't been injured there. The fabric wasn't even torn.

Then an inspiration hit him, and he reached into his pocket. At the very bottom, precisely at the top of the bloodstain, Tavi found it—the scarlet stone he'd stolen from Lady Antillus. It felt oddly warm, almost uncomfortably so.

"I'm fine," Tavi said. "I don't think that's mine." He frowned down, and then peered out at the Canim host, and then at the scarlet clouds overhead.

You need not fear his breed's power, and you know it, Kalarus had told Lady Antillus. And then immediately after, he had ordered her to fly to Kalare. But if she could have flown, why would she steal horses?

Because the stone would have protected her from the Canim ritual sorcery that blanketed the skies.

Just as it had protected Tavi from the same power.

His heart beat faster. He tried to think of another explanation, but it was the only thing that made sense. How else could he have survived a blast of the same power that had slain the Legion's officers?

Of course. The Canim had known precisely where to strike. Legion commanders kept their tents in the same location in any camp, no matter where they went. No one was supposed to have survived that blast—no one but Lady Antillus, who would have had the stone with her had not Tavi stolen it when he took her purse.

The original treason became clear to Tavi. After assuming command of the Legion according to the proper chain of command, Lady Antillus was probably supposed to lead the union in a retreat, so that the Canim could control the bridge, thereby preventing any sort of Aleran incursion from the north that could march through to Kalarus's lands.

Of course, that had been before she knew the Canim were arriving in such enormous numbers. Kalarus had tried to use them as a weapon, but they had turned and sliced into his own hand.

Hey, Max mouthed, sticking his face into Tavi's. *Are you all right?*

Max and Crassus suddenly whipped their heads toward the Canim host, then they both started back for their horses. Max mouthed to Tavi, *They're coming. We need to go.*

Tavi grimaced, nodded, then took the standard and mounted behind Max. The three of them rode for the town as the Canim host began to stir once more. Out of sheer defiance, Tavi raised the standard and let the wind of their passage send the blackened eagle flying where anyone with eyes could see.

Tavi couldn't hear it as they rode back through the town's gates, but as they closed behind them he looked up at the battlements and around the courtyard in surprise. Every man in sight, fish and veteran alike, pale-eyed northmen and dark-eyed southerners, old, young, Knight, centurion, and *legionare* all stood facing Tavi, slamming their steel-cased fists to their breastplates in what had to be a deafening thunder as together they shouted and cheered their captain's return.

ᗅᗅᗅᗅᗅ᙮CHAPTER 40

Pain flashed through Tavi's head again, sudden, harsh, and every bit as painful as the lightning blast that had deafened him. Someone started screaming sulfurous expletives with great volume and sincerity.

A second later, Tavi realized that the cursing was his own, and he came to an abrupt stop. He could suddenly hear the battle he knew was raging at the gates, the deafening howls of a sea of Canim punctuated in surges by the shouting and cheering of the town's defenders.

"There you go, sir," Foss rumbled. "Your eardrums were broken. Happens to young Knights Aeris a lot when they're showing off. Eardrums can heal up on their own, but it can take a while, which we don't have, and keeping sickness out of them isn't any fun." The big healer crouched down at the head of the healing tub and snapped his fingers on either side of Tavi's head. "Hear that? Both sides?"

The snaps had an odd reverberation to them that Tavi had never heard before, but he could *hear* them. "Good enough. You shouldn't be wasting energy on me in any case."

"Deaf Captain won't be much help to us, sir," Foss disagreed. "And we're staying ahead of the wounded so far."

Tavi grunted and pushed himself up out of the tub. His muscles and joints screamed protest. Sarl's thunderbolt may not have killed him, but the fall from the horse had done him no favors. He started climbing back into his clothing. "Help me armor up?"

"Yes, sir," Foss drawled, and stood by, helping with the buckles on Tavi's armor.

"What's the count?" Tavi asked quietly as he worked.

"Seventy-two injured," Foss said at once. "All but eleven are back in the fight. Nine dead."

"Thank you, Foss. Again."

The veteran grunted and slapped a hand on Tavi's breast-plate. "You're set."

Tavi put on his sword belt and slipped a replacement *gladius* Magnus had dug up into the scabbard. Outside, a fresh round of singing broke out of the troops waiting in the court-yard to reinforce the walls or gate. The verses now contained a great many disparaging references to the men currently on the walls, complemented by enthusiastic boasting of the men waiting for the alleged incompetents to step out of their way.

Magnus entered the tent and nodded. "Sir," he said. "Crassus asked me to tell you that Jens is finished."

"Jens?" Tavi asked.

"Our only Knight Ignus, sir."

"That's right," Tavi said. "Good. Thank you, Magnus." He beckoned and strode out of the tent, back toward the fighting on the wall. As he left the tent, Ehren appeared at his side and kept pace on Tavi's left, and Tavi nodded to him.

"What's happening?" Tavi asked Magnus.

"The Canim sent about a third of their raiders forward. Valiar Marcus says that the regulars have shifted their position, and that they're ready to move forward fairly quickly."

Tavi grimaced. "Crows take it."

Magnus lowered his voice. "It was worth a try. It may be that the Canim's loyalties are not so fractured as we hoped."

"Looks that way." Tavi sighed. "They're using their raiders to wear us down. They'll send the regulars in once they've softened us up."

"Quite probably," Magnus said.

"What about Tribune Cymnea's project?" Tavi asked.

"Let's just say it's a good thing you weren't in the river for very long, Captain."

"Good," Tavi said. "Come nightfall, the Canim will try to get some troops across. They'll want to hit us in the rear and send the regulars through the front door." He paused as a thought struck him. He squinted up at the dim outline of the lowering sun behind the bloody clouds. "Two hours?"

"A little less," Magnus said.

They had to pause as Crassus and his half dozen Knights Aeris swept overhead to strafe the enemy lines with howling winds and bursts of flame. The miniature gale supporting them temporarily precluded conversation.

"What about the bridge?" Tavi asked, when he could be heard again.

"The engineers say they'd like more time to strengthen it, but they always say that. They've got it up to what you asked for." Magnus paused. "Did you want to give the order now?"

Tavi bit his lip. "Not yet. We hold the gate until sundown."

"You don't know that the regulars will come then," Magnus said. "And it's going to be hard on the men at the gate to stay there. Not to mention the fact that it's going to be difficult for them to maneuver and retreat in the dark."

"Send for fresh troops from the north side of the river then," Tavi said, glancing at Ehren. The Cursor nodded. "Then tell the First Spear to increase the rotation on the walls and keep our men as rested as possible."

"If we do that, we'll have to start using the fish."

"I know," Tavi said. "But they've got to get into the mud sometime. At least this way, they'll have the veterans to back them up."

Magnus grimaced. "Sir, the plan isn't going to be easy, even if we move right now. If we wait another two hours . . ." He shook his head. "I don't see what there is to be gained by the wait."

"Without more Knights Ignus, we've only got one really big punch to throw. It's got to count. The regulars are their backbone and this may be our only chance to break it." He glanced back at Ehren and nodded, and the spy set out at a swift jog to deliver Tavi's orders.

"How long has Marcus been on the wall?"

"Since it started. Call it almost two hours."

Tavi nodded. "We'll need him fresh and in charge when we fall back, wouldn't you say?"

"Definitely," Magnus said. "The First Spear has more experience than anyone on the field."

"Anyone on our side of it, anyway," Tavi muttered.

"Eh? What's that?"

"Nothing," Tavi sighed. "All right. I'm going to order him down. Get some food into him and make sure he's ready for nightfall."

Magnus gave Tavi a wary look. "Can you handle them up there on your own?"

"I've got to get in the mud, too," Tavi replied. He squinted up at the wall. "Where's the standard?"

Magnus glanced up at the walls. "It had been burned and muddied pretty thoroughly. I'm having a new one made, but it won't be ready for a few more hours."

"The burned one is just fine," Tavi said. "Get it for me."

"I'll put it on a new pole, at least."

"No," Tavi said. "Sarl's blood is on the old one. That will do."

Magnus shot Tavi a sudden grin. "Bloodied, dirty but unbroken."

"Just like us," Tavi agreed.

"Very good, sir. I'll send it up with Sir Ehren."

"Thank you," Tavi said. Then he stopped and put a hand on Magnus's shoulder, and said, more quietly. "Thank you, Maestro. I don't think I've said it yet. But I enjoyed our time at the ruins. Thank you for sharing it with me."

Magnus smiled at Tavi and nodded. "It's a shame you're showing an aptitude for military command, lad. You'd have been a fine scholar."

Tavi laughed.

Then Magnus saluted, turned, and hurried off.

Tavi made sure his helmet was seated snugly and hurried

up onto the battlements, making his way down the lines of crouched *legionares*, bearing shields, bows, and buckets of everything from more pitch to simple, scalding water. He deftly made his way through the fighting, not jostling or interfering with any of the men, and found the First Spear, bellowing orders ten yards down the wall from the gates, where the Canim were attempting to get more climbing lines—these of braided leather and rope, not chain—while their companions below showered the walls with rough spears and simple, if enormous, stones.

"Crows take it!" Marcus bellowed. "You don't have to stick your fool head up to cut a line. Use your knife, not your sword."

Tavi crouched and, while he waited for Marcus to finish bellowing, drew his knife and sawed swiftly through a braided line attached to a hook that landed near him. "Let's keep the hooks, too, Tribune," Tavi added. "Not throw them back out to be reused against us." Tavi checked the courtyard below, then tossed the hook down.

"Captain!" shouted one of the *legionares*, and a round of shouts of greeting went up and down the walls.

Valiar Marcus checked over his shoulder and saw Tavi there. He gave him a brisk nod and banged a gauntlet to his breastplate in salute. "You all right, sir?"

"Our Tribune Medica set me right," Tavi said. "How's the weather?"

A thrown stone from below clipped the crest of the First Spear's helmet, and the steel rang for a second. Marcus shook his head and crouched a little lower. "If the sun was out, we'd still be fighting in the shade," he said a moment later, teeth flashing in a swift, fighting grin. "Two or three of them gained the wall once, but we pushed them back down. We burned down six more rams. They aren't trying that one anymore."

"Not until it gets dark," Tavi said.

The First Spear gave him a shrewd look, and nodded. "By then, it shouldn't matter."

"We hold," Tavi said. "Until they bring the regulars in."

Valiar Marcus stared· at him for a moment, then made a sour face and nodded. "Aye. It'll cost us, sir."

"If we can break their regulars, it could be worth it."

The grizzled soldier nodded. "True enough. We'll see to it, then, Captain."

"Not you," Tavi said. "You've been here long enough. I want you to sit down, get a meal in you, some drink. I need you fresh for sundown."

The First Spear's jaw set, and for a second Tavi thought he was going to argue.

Then a shout went up down the wall, and Tavi looked to see Ehren hurrying toward them down the wall—and though the little Cursor kept his head down, he bore the blackened standard upright, and the men cheered to see it.

The First Spear looked from the men to the standard to Tavi and nodded. "Use your head," he said. "Trust your centurions. Don't take any chances. We got another veteran cohort coming in five minutes to relieve this one."

"I will," Tavi said. "See Magnus. He's got something ready for you."

Marcus nodded, and the pair exchanged a salute before the old soldier made his way back down the wall, keeping his head down. Ehren hurried to Tavi's side, keeping the standard high.

The attack continued without slacking, and Tavi checked in with each of the two centurions on the wall—both veterans, both worried about their men. Tavi saw a number of *legionares* breathing hard. A man went down, struck on the helmet by a stone almost as large as Tavi's head. The cry for a medico went up. Tavi seized the man's shield and blocked the crennel with it, hiding the medico as he hurried to the fallen man. A spear struck against the shield, and a moment later another stone struck it so hard that it slammed back into Tavi's helmeted head hard enough to make him see stars, but then another *legionare* stepped into position with his own shield, and the fight went on.

It was terrifying, but at the same time it had become an experience oddly akin to an afternoon of heavy labor back at his old home on the steadholt. Tavi moved steadily along the wall, from position to position, encouraging the men and watching for any change in behavior from their foes. After what seemed almost an hour, fresh troops arrived to relieve the *legionares*, and the men on the wall switched out smoothly, one crennel at a time, with their replacements. And the battle went on.

Twice, the Canim raiders managed to get a number of hooks up into locations where a barrage of stones had disrupted the defenses, but both times Tavi was able to signal Crassus and his Knights Aeris to deliver a burst of pain and confusion to the enemy, delaying them in turn until the Aleran defense could solidify again.

Against the raiders, the *legionares'* archery had considerably greater effect. The wild troops were not nearly as disciplined as the regulars, which slowed them down substantially as they struggled to work together. Their armor was also much lighter, where they had any at all, and arrows that struck and inflicted injuries were almost more useful to the defense than outright kills. Wounded Canim thrashed and screamed and had to be carried away from the fighting by a pair of their comrades, vastly slowing the pace of whatever operation they'd been attempting, whereas the dead were simply left where they fell.

The Canim dead numbered in the hundreds, and in places the corpses lay so thick that the Canim had been forced to stack them in piles, like cordwood—piles that they then used for shelter from enemy arrows. Even so, Tavi knew, they could afford the losses far more easily than the Alerans. As far as Sarl was concerned, Tavi thought, their deaths would simply reduce the number of hungry mouths to feed. If they could kill any Alerans while they died, so much the better.

And then it happened. The *legionares* on station began switching out with the next unit in the rotation, one with a much higher concentration of green recruits. A particularly thick shower of rocks was thrown up from the base of the wall, lobbed up on a high arc to come almost straight down upon the defenders. The stones wouldn't hit with the same killing force as those hurled directly at a target, but they were so large that they hardly needed more than a few feet to fall to attain enough speed to be dangerous to even an armored *legionare*.

Tavi was about twenty feet away when it happened, and he clearly heard a bone snapping, just before the injured men began screaming.

There was a sudden, furious wave of Canim howls and war cries, and more ropes and hooks were thrown up along the whole length of the wall, just as another group of Canim appeared from their rear areas and charged forward, bearing another heavy ram.

Tavi stared for a second, trying to understand everything that was happening, knowing full well that he had to act, and quickly, or risk being overrun. He had to direct the force of his Knights to where they would do the most good. If the Canim gained the walls, they would still be contained to one degree or another. Hampered by being forced to climb a rope, they could pour in added numbers, but only in a trickle. If the gates were breached, their entire force could pour through as quickly as they could fit. Whatever else happened, the gates had to hold.

Tavi let out a sharp whistle and signaled Crassus to attack the enemy center—he had to trust that the young Knight Tribune would see the ram and correctly identify it as the largest threat to the town's defenses. There was little more he could do about the oncoming ram, because the only *legionares* not fully occupied fending off the assault were the men directly over the gate. Tavi pointed at half of the men there. "You, you, you, you two. Follow me."

Legionares seized shields and weapons, and Tavi led them down the wall, to the first point of attack, where two Canim had already gained the walls while more came behind them. A green recruit screamed and attacked the nearest Cane, forgetting the founding principle of Legion combat—teamwork. The Cane was armed with nothing but a heavy wooden club, but before the young *legionare* could close to within range of his Legion-issue *gladius*, the Cane took a two-handed swing that slammed the heavy club into the *legionare's* shield, sending him sailing into the air to fall to the stone courtyard below, where he landed with bone-shattering force.

"Ehren," Tavi shouted, as he drew his own sword. The

Cane took club in hand again, raising it to strike at Tavi before he could close the range.

But just as the Cane began to swing, there was a flash of steel in the air, and Ehren's skillfully thrown knife struck the Cane's muzzle. The blade's point missed by an inch or so, and it only drew a single, short cut across the Cane's black nose, but even so, the knife was deadly. The Cane flinched from the sudden pain in such a sensitive area, and it threw off the timing and power of its attack. Tavi slipped aside from the heavy club, drove in hard, and struck with a single slash that opened the Cane's throat clear to the bones of its neck.

The mortally wounded Cane dropped its club and tried to seize Tavi, teeth bared, but Tavi kept driving forward, inside the Cane's easy reach, and the *legionare* coming along behind Tavi added his own weight to Tavi's rush, as did the man behind him, so that their weight drove the Cane back against the battlements, where the *legionares* dispatched the raider with ruthless savagery.

Tavi hacked down at a heavy rope on the battlements, but the tough stuff refused to part despite several blows, and another Cane gripped the top of the wall, to haul himself up. Tavi slashed at the Cane's hand, drawing a cry of pain, before the raider fell back, and Tavi finished the job on the rope.

He looked up in time to see his *legionares* chopping their way down the wall, dispatching the second Cane, though the creature's sickle-sword took one veteran's hand from his arm before it fell. *Legionares* hacked at the remaining climbing lines. There was a howl of wind, then a roar and a blossom of fire at the gate, and all the while, more of those high-arcing stones rained down on Aleran heads and shoulders.

"Buckets!" Tavi shouted. "Now!"

Legionares seized the buckets of pitch, scalding water, and heated sand, and hurled them down upon the Canim at the base of the walls, eliciting more screams. It gave some of the defenders precious seconds to throw down the remaining lines, while archers had the opportunity to send arrows slicing down into the foe, inflicting even more injury, even before Crassus and his Knights made a second run along the wall, blinding and deafening the foe with the gale of their passing.

The morale of the attackers broke, and they began fleeing from the walls, at first hesitant, then in an enormous wave. The archers sent arrows flying after them as swiftly as they could loose them, wounding still more, while *legionares* began to whoop and cheer again.

Tavi ignored the Canim, looking up and down the wall. The attack had been repulsed, but it had cost the defenders, badly. The high-arced stones had been distressingly effective, and the medicos rushing to assist the injured were far outnumbered by the casualties. The green troops coming up to the walls weren't moving with the swift certainty of the veterans, and the rushing medicos and *legionares* attempting to carry the wounded to help weren't improving matters. The *legionares* had barely held the wall before, and if they did not reorganize and restore discipline to the defensive positions on the battlements, the Canim might well overwhelm them. Or at least, they might have, had they not broken instead of maintaining the attack.

The deep Canim horns blared and jerked Tavi's gaze to the host outside the walls.

The black-armored regulars had risen to their feet, and were moving with terrible, casual speed for the walls of the town.

⬦⬦⬦⬦⬦ CHAPTER 41

Tavi drew in a sharp breath as the regulars approached. He'd been certain that they would strike at sundown—but that was an hour away, and Marcus was not on the wall. If the trap was to be successfully sprung, the Canim would need something to occupy their attention, and the plan had been for the Alerans to fall back in a fighting retreat, forcing the Canim to keep the pressure on the withdrawing troops.

The problem with that sort of ploy was that it would be all too easy for the false panic to become perfectly genuine and for the situation to spin totally out of anyone's control. Given that their discipline and training were the only things that gave the Legion anything like a fighting chance against a foe like the Canim, putting it at risk was the maneuver of a foolish or desperate commander.

Tavi supposed he could well be both.

"I need Max at once," Tavi told Ehren, and the young Cursor immediately leapt from the wall to the bed of a wagon parked beneath, then sprinted off across the courtyard.

"Centurions, finish the rotation and clear these walls of noncombatants!" Tavi shouted. "Medicos, use those wagons and get the wounded back to the secondary aid station!" Then he turned and flashed another hand sign to the rooftop several streets away where Crassus and his Knights Aeris waited. Tavi drew his hand in a wave, right to left, and then drew it in a sharp, slashing motion across his throat. Crassus turned to one of his Knights, and they descended from the rooftop.

Tavi whirled to check on the Canim and found the raiders pulling back, leaving the regulars plenty of room in which to work. For the first time, at the crest of the hill, Tavi made out the outlines of several black-cloaked, pale-mantled Canim. Sarl, or at least some of his ritualist acolytes, were apparently intent on observing the regulars' assault.

"Move!" Tavi shouted, as the regulars marched closer. "Reserves, withdraw to your secondary positions near the bridge!" Tavi whirled, spotted the nearest centurion, and growled, "Get those men's shields strapped on tighter. One of those hurled stones will spin the bloody things on their arms and smash their brains out."

The young centurion turned to face Tavi, his face pale, saluted, and began bellowing at the indicated *legionares*.

The centurion was Schultz. Tavi took a look left and right, and found few faces as old as his own. Only the centurions were veterans at all, and even they looked like young men serving in their first term of service in that rank.

Crows, he shouldn't have ordered the veterans off the wall, but it was too late to change it now. After the pounding they'd just received, after brutal and exhausting battle on the wall, they might not have held up against a tide of armored Canim. It was possible that the fish would be better suited to the maneuver than the veterans—if only because they were too inexperienced to realize just how much danger they were about to face.

Tavi bit on his lip and silently, savagely berated himself. That was no way to think about young men who were about to put their lives on the line for their Realm, their fellow *legionares*—and for him. He was about to order these young men into a storm of violence and blood.

And yet the cold fact was that if the ploy worked, it could cripple the Canim army, perhaps beyond its will to fight. If Tavi had to sacrifice a hundred *legionares*—or a thousand—to contain the Canim invasion, it would be his duty to do precisely that.

The walls were finally cleared, the wounded headed back to the next aid station, the reserve cohort coming up behind the fish on the wall marching for the fallback point. Tavi looked up and down the walls one more time—and saw quietly terrified young men, all of them pale, all of them standing ready.

Boots pounded down the battlements, and Max arrived at Tavi's side, along with Ehren. Crassus was a dozen steps behind, and Tavi glanced over his shoulder to find most of the Knights Aeris not yet judged ready to fly in combat rushing into positions opposite the gate.

"Great bloody crows," Max panted as the Canim came on.

"Ready, Captain," Crassus added. "Jens is all set."

"This is one bloody big throw of the dice, sir," Max said. "I never heard of such a thing being used."

"How much time have you spent working within a steadholt's woodshop, Max?" Tavi asked him.

He scowled. "I know, I know. I just never heard of it before."

"Trust me," Tavi said. "Sawdust is more dangerous than

you know. And if the grain storehouse was on this side of the town, it would have been even better." He watched as the regulars closed, and said, "All right. You two get back and be ready to cover us."

Crassus saluted and turned to go, but Max remained in place, frowning out at the Canim.

"Hey," Max said. "Why'd they stop?"

Tavi blinked and turned around.

The Canim regulars had, indeed, stopped in their tracks, several dozen yards out of arrow range. To Tavi's increased surprise, they all settled down onto their haunches again, and they were so many that even that sounded like a rumble of distant thunder.

"That," Ehren said quietly, "is a whole lot of Canim."

At the front and center of the regulars, a single figure remained standing—the same Cane Tavi had addressed earlier in the day. He swept his gaze around the armored Canim, nodded, then took a long, curved war sword from his side. He held the weapon up, facing the town, then deliberately laid it aside. Then he strode out onto corpse-strewn killing ground between and stopped halfway to the wall.

"Aleran Captain!" the Cane called, his deep, growling voice enormous and unsettling. "I am Battlemaster Nasaug! I have words for you! Come forth!"

Max let out a grunt of surprise.

"Well," Ehren murmured, beside Tavi. "Well, well, well. *That* is interesting."

"What do you think, Max?" Tavi murmured.

"They think we're stupid," Max said. "They've already broken faith with us once. They tried to murder you the last time you went to them, Captain. I say we return the favor. Call up our Knights Flora, shoot him full of arrows, and let's get on with it."

Tavi snorted out a low laugh. "Probably the smart thing."

"But you're going to go talk to him," Max said.

"Thinking about it."

Max scowled. "Bad idea. Better let me go. He gets frisky, I'll show him how we do things up north."

"He's already seen me, Max," Tavi said. "It has to be me. If he makes a move first, take him down. Otherwise, leave him alone. Make sure everyone else knows it, too. And get Marcus back up here, meanwhile."

"You think you've driven a spike between their leader and the warriors?" Ehren asked.

"Possibly," Tavi said. "If this Nasaug had hit us instead of stopping out there, it could have been bad. Now we're getting a chance to breathe and reorganize. I can't imagine Sarl's terribly pleased about that."

Ehren shook his head. "I don't like it. Why would he do that?"

Tavi took a deep breath, and replied, "Let me go ask him."

Tavi did not ride out to meet the Canim this time. Instead, he went to the gates, which opened just enough to let him step outside the protection of the walls. The ground beneath the walls stank of blood and fear, fire and offal. Canim bodies lay piled in windrows, and since the fighting had ceased, thousands of crows descended to begin feasting upon the dead.

Tavi fought to keep his stomach under control as he walked out to meet the Battlemaster—a rank akin to an Aleran captain, a commander in charge of an entire force. Twenty yards from the Cane, he drew out his sword and laid it down on the ground beside him. With or without it, he stood little chance against an armored and experienced Cane afoot—but he could all but feel the watching eyes of his fellow Alerans behind him. They would be of greater protection than any horse or suit of armor. In all, Tavi had the position of greater strength, for Nasaug was in the reach of Tavi's companions. Tavi was far from Nasaug's.

Nonetheless, as Tavi approached the Cane, he had to admit that Nasaug's sheer size was more than frightening enough to protect him from Tavi, personally. Not to mention that his natural weaponry was considerably more fearsome than Tavi's. It was not a situation of perfect balance, but it was as close to one as they were likely to get.

Tavi stopped ten feet from Nasaug, and said, "I am Rufus Scipio, Captain of the First Aleran."

The Cane watched him with dark and bloody eyes. "Battlemaster Nasaug."

Tavi wasn't sure who moved first, and he didn't remember consciously deciding to make the gesture, but both of them tilted their heads very slightly to one side in greeting.

"Speak," Tavi said.

The Cane's lips peeled back from his fangs, a gesture that could indicate either amusement or a subtle threat. "The situation prevented me from recovering my fallen within the time limit you granted me," he said. "I wish your permission to recover them now."

Tavi felt his eyebrows lift. "Given how matters transpired before, my men may be nervous about yours so near the walls."

"They will approach unarmed," Nasaug replied. "And I will remain here, within range of your Knights Flora, as a pledge of their conduct."

Tavi stared at Nasaug for a long moment and thought he saw a certain amount of smug amusement in the Cane's eyes. Tavi smiled, a baring of his own teeth, and said, "Do you play *ludus*, Nasaug?"

The Cane lifted his helmet from his head, ears twitching and flicking as they came out from beneath the steel. "At times."

"Allow me to call out a messenger to send word to my men while you send for your own. Your men, unarmed, may approach until the sun is set. I will remain here with you until that time, in order to help avoid any unfortunate misunderstandings."

A burbling growl came from Nasaug's throat—quite possibly the most threatening chuckle Tavi had ever heard in his life. "Very well."

And so, in the next five minutes Tavi faced Nasaug across a traveling *ludus* set, a case whose legs unfolded to support it as a small, portable table. Plain discs of stone were carved on one side with piece designations, rather than being the full miniature statuettes of a conventional board. Tavi and Nasaug began playing, while eighty Canim, armored but unarmed, trooped forward, digging through the carnage at the base of the walls to locate the black-armored corpses of their fallen brothers in arms. None of them passed within a twenty-foot circle of the two commanders.

Tavi watched the Cane as the game began, and he opened with what seemed to be a reckless attack.

Nasaug, for his part, narrowed his eyes in thought as the game progressed. "Nothing wrong with your courage," he said, several moves in. "But it does not secure a victory alone."

A few moves later, Tavi replied, "Your defense isn't as strong as it might be. Pushing it hard enough might shatter it."

Nasaug began to move in earnest then, exchanging the first few pieces, while more moved into position, gathering for the cascade of exchanges that would follow. Tavi lost a piece to the Cane, then another, as his attack began to slow.

Footsteps suddenly approached, and a Cane in the accoutrements of one of Sarl's acolytes stalked up to them. He bared his teeth at Tavi, then turned to Nasaug and snarled, *"Hrrrshk naghr lak trrrng kasrrrash."*

Tavi understood it: *You were ordered to attack. Why have you not done so?*

Nasaug did not respond.

The acolyte snarled and stepped up to Nasaug, put a hand on the Battlemaster's shoulder, and began to repeat the question.

Nasaug turned his head to one side, jaws flashing, and in a single, vicious snap tore the hand from the end of the acolyte's arm, following it with a vicious kick that sent the other Cane sprawling, screaming in pain.

Nasaug reached up and took the acolyte's severed hand from his mouth and idly threw it at him without looking up from the board. "Do not interrupt your betters," he growled, also in Canish. Tavi could make out most of it. "You may tell Sarl that had he wished an immediate attack, he should have given me time to recover my fallen from the Alerans. Tell him that I will attack when and where it suits me." The Battlemaster glanced at the acolyte, and snarled, "Move. Before you bleed to death."

The wounded Cane clutched the bleeding stump of his arm to his belly and retreated, making high-pitched whimpering noises in his throat.

"Apologies," Nasaug then said to Tavi. "For the distraction."

"No offense was given," Tavi replied, his tone thoughtful. "You have little love for the ritualists."

"Your eyes can see the sun at midday, Captain," Nasaug replied. He studied the board a moment later, and said, "Your strategy was sound. You know much of us."

"Some," Tavi replied.

"It took courage and intelligence to attempt it. For this, you have earned respect." Nasaug looked up at Tavi for the first time since the game began. "But however much I may despise Sarl and those like him, my duty is clear. Sarl and his ritualists are few, but they have the faith of the maker caste." He tilted an ear in a vague gesture at the enormous number of raiders. "They may be fools to believe in the ritualists, but I will not turn upon the makers or desert them. I have studied your forces. You cannot stop us."

"Perhaps," Tavi said. "Perhaps not."

Nasaug bared his teeth again. "Your men are half-trained. Your officers were slain, your Knights far weaker than they should be. There is little help to be had from the Alerans of the city." He pushed a *ludus* Lord forward, beginning his own attack. "You have not seen our caste in battle, but for the probe this morning. You will not repulse us again, Aleran. Before to-morrow's sunset, it will be over."

Tavi frowned. Nasaug wasn't posturing. There was neither threat nor anger nor enjoyment in the tone of his voice. He was simply stating a fact, attaching no emotion to it, no menace. It was far more disturbing than anything else he could have said.

But Nasaug was a warrior Cane. If he was anything like Varg, his words were like blood—never loosed unless necessary. And then as little as possible. "I wonder why you bother to speak of it."

"To offer you an alternative. Retreat and leave the bridge sound. Take your warriors, your people, your young. I will give you two days to travel, in which I will make sure no forces are sent after you."

Tavi regarded the board for a silent moment and altered the position of a single piece. "Generous. Why offer it?"

"I do not say we will destroy you without loss, Captain. It will save lives of my warriors and your own."

"Until we fight again another day?"

"Yes."

Tavi shook his head. "I cannot give you the bridge. It is my duty to hold it or destroy it."

Nasaug nodded once. "Your gesture to allow us to take back our fallen was a generous one. Especially given how Sarl dealt with you. For that, I offered you what I could." The Cane began moving his pieces in earnest, and the rapid exchange began. It took him only three moves to see what Tavi had done, and he stopped, staring at the board.

Tavi's reckless assault had been nothing of the kind. He had spent a great deal of time thinking about Ambassador Varg's stratagem in their last game together, and he had adapted it to his own strengths as a player. The sacrifice of some of his lesser pieces earlier in the game had given the greater pieces a far more dominant position, and within the next two moves he would control the skyboard completely and have the positioning and power he would need to strike down Nasaug's First Lord. His pieces would take terrible losses to do it, but Nasaug had seen the trap a bare move too late, and he could not possibly escape it.

"Things," Tavi said quietly, "are not always as they seem."

The last of the fallen Canim had been found and borne back to the Canim camp by their unarmed fellows. A grizzled Cane nodded to Nasaug in passing.

Nasaug stared at Tavi, then tilted his head very slightly to one side in acknowledgment of the defeat. "No. Which is why my warriors will not be the first to enter the town."

Tavi's heart all but stopped in his chest.

Nasaug had figured out the trap. He might not yet know the details, but he knew it was there. Tavi kept all expression from his face and stared impassively at the Battlemaster.

Nasaug let out another rumbling chuckle and nodded at the board. "Where did you learn that strategy?"

Tavi regarded the Cane, then shrugged. "Varg."

Nasaug froze.

His ears came to quivering attention, pricked forward at Tavi. "Varg," he growled, very low. "Varg lives?"

"Yes," Tavi replied. "Prisoner in Alera Imperia."

Nasaug narrowed his eyes, his ears twitching. Then he lifted a hand and beckoned.

The grizzled Cane returned, bearing a cloth bundle held upon his upraised palms. At a nod from Nasaug, the Cane set the bundle down on the *ludus* board and unfolded it. Tavi's *gladius*, the one he had cast aside that morning, lay within.

"You are dangerous, Aleran," Nasaug said.

Instinct told Tavi that the words were a high compliment. He kept his eyes steady, and said, "I thank you."

"Respect changes nothing. I will destroy you."

"Duty," Tavi said.

"Duty." The Battlemaster gestured at the sword. "This is yours."

"It is," Tavi replied. "You have my thanks."

"Die well, Aleran."

"Die well, Cane."

Nasaug and Tavi fractionally bared their throats to each other once more. Then Nasaug backed away several paces before turning and striding back toward his army. Tavi folded up the *ludus* board back into its case, recovered both of his blades, and made his own way back to the city. He slipped in through the gates just as deep drums began to rumble and Canim war horns began to blare.

Tavi spotted Valiar Marcus and called to him. "First Spear, get the men into position! This is it!"

◇◇◇◇◇ CHAPTER 42

"Very well," Lady Aquitaine said. She nodded to Odiana, and said, "Time we got into costume."

Odiana promptly opened a backpack and handed Amara her disguise.

Amara stared down at the scarlet silk in her hands, and said, "Where is the rest of it?"

Aldrick stood at the hostel's window, watching the street outside. The big swordsman glanced back at Amara, made a choking sound in his throat, and turned away.

Odiana exercised no such restraint. The lovely water witch threw back her head and let out a peal of laughter, a sound too loud for the room they had rented from a surly Kalaran innkeeper. "Oh, oh, my lord. She's blushing. Isn't she fetching?"

To her horror, Amara realized that Odiana was right. Her cheeks felt as though she could have heated water on them, and she had absolutely no idea what to do about it. It was not the sort of situation she had been trained to handle. She turned away from Lady Aquitaine and her retainers and held up her disguise.

It consisted of a simple sheath of red silk, held up by a pair of tiny silk straps. Neckline, such as it was, was alarmingly low—and in back, the garment would leave her naked almost to the waist. The little shift's hem would fall to the tops of her thighs if she was lucky.

"Now, now," Lady Aquitaine chided Odiana. "Show her the rest of it."

"Yes, Your Grace," Odiana said with a little curtsey. Then she drew out a pair of light sandals with straps that would wrap the leg to the knee, a pair of slender silver armbands wrought in the shapes of ivy vines, a beaded headdress that faintly resembled a chain coif and a plain, smooth metal band.

A discipline collar.

It was a slaver's device, furywrought to give control of whoever wore it to the slaver. It could incapacitate its wearer with pain—and, more insidiously, it could, at the slaver's option, provide the inverse of that sensation, and just as intensely. Discipline collars were sometimes used to restrain particularly dangerous furycrafters being held for trial in the legal system, though such cases were historically rare.

But in the past century or so, their manufacture and use had become far more widespread, as the institution of slavery deepened and darkened. Prolonged exposure to the collars could shatter the mind and will. Continually forced through agonies of torment and euphoria, victims were compelled to obey the slaver and forced to experience pleasure as they did so. Over time, often years, many such slaves were reduced to little more than animals, their humanity torn from them and replaced with the simple, irresistible compulsion of the collar. Chillingly, they were often deliriously happy to be that way.

More independent-minded individuals could often resist the extremes of dehumanization others faced—for a time, at least. But none of them survived it unscathed. Most went hopelessly mad.

"Blushing," Odiana singsonged, and spun on her toes in a little dance step. Her silk dress changed colors, shifting from pale blue to pink. "Just *this* color, Cursor."

"I'm not wearing a collar," Amara said quietly.

Lady Aquitaine arched an eyebrow. "Why on earth not?"

"I'm aware of how dangerous they can be, Your Grace," Amara said. "And I have certain reservations about the notion of closing one around my neck."

Odiana covered a titter with one hand, dark eyes shining as she stared at Amara. "You needn't be so afraid, Countess," she murmured. "Honestly. Once the collar is on, it's quite difficult to imagine living without it." She shivered, and licked her lips. "You scream all the time, but it's the inside kind. You scream and scream, but you can only hear it when you're asleep. Otherwise it's quite lovely." She gave Aldrick a somewhat petulant look. "My lord won't collar me. No matter how naughty I am."

"Peace, love," Aldrick rumbled. "It isn't good for you." He glanced at Amara and said, "the collars aren't genuine, Countess. I made them out of table knives this morning."

"It isn't the sort of pretend I like to play," Odiana sniffed. "He never lets me have my favorites." She turned away from Aldrick, passing a second costume like Amara's to Lady Aquitaine, and took a third for herself.

Lady Aquitaine regarded Amara thoughtfully, and said, "I've some cosmetics that should make your eyes look lovely, dear."

"That won't be necessary," Amara said stiffly.

"Yes it will, Countess," Rook said quietly. The plain-looking young woman sat in a chair in the corner farthest from Aldrick and Odiana. Her eyes were sunken, strained, and worry lines crisscrossed her brow. "The pleasure slaves Kalarus imports for his retainers and personal guard in the citadel are a common sight. Kalarus's favored slave traders are always in competition with one another and spare no expense. The clothing, the cosmetics, the perfume. To do anything else will draw unwanted attention."

"Speaking of perfume," Lady Aquitaine murmured, "where is the good Count Calderon? We all smell like folk who have been traveling for days."

A beat later, the room's door opened, and Bernard came in. "Bath's ready," he said quietly. "Other side of the hall, two doors down. There's only two tubs."

"I suppose it was too much to hope for a proper bath," Lady Aquitaine said. "We'll just have to go in turn. Amara, Rook, by all means go first."

Rook rose, gathering up her clothing—the same dark colors she'd been wearing when Amara had captured her. Amara pressed her lips into a firm line as she took her own costume and turned to the door.

Bernard leaned casually against the door and held up a hand. "I don't think so," he said. "I don't want you alone with her."

Amara arched a brow at him. "Why not?"

"Regardless of what she might or might not have to lose, she's the master assassin for a rebel High Lord. I'd prefer it if you weren't alone in the bath with her."

"Or perhaps," Odiana offered, "he wants to see what Mistress Bloodcrow looks like beneath her clothes."

Bernard's nostrils flared, and he glared at Odiana. But instead of speaking he turned the look on Aldrick.

The big swordsman did nothing for several seconds. Then he exhaled slowly and said, to Odiana, "Love, hush now. Let them work this out in peace."

"I only want to help," Odiana said piously, moving to stand beside Aldrick. "It is hardly my fault if he is so—"

Aldrick slid an arm around Odiana, and placed one broad,

scarred hand over her mouth, pulling her gently against him. The water witch subsided immediately, and Amara thought that there was something smug and self-satisfied in her eyes.

"I think," Amara said to Bernard, "that it would be wise to have a pair of eyes watching the hall in any case. Wait outside the door?"

"Thank you, Countess," Lady Aquitaine said. "Thank goodness someone in this room can be reasonable."

"I'll go first, Countess," Rook said quietly. She walked to the door, eyes lowered, and waited until Bernard grudgingly moved aside. "Thank you."

Amara slipped out after her, and Bernard followed close behind her. Rook went into the bathing room, and Amara began to follow her, when she felt Bernard's hand on her shoulder.

She stopped and glanced back at him.

"Crows take it, woman," he said quietly. "Is it so wrong for me to want to protect you?"

"Of course not," Amara said, though she couldn't keep a small smile off her face.

Bernard frowned down at her for a moment, then glanced back at the hotel room and rolled his eyes. "Bloody crows." He sighed. "You got me out of that room to protect *me*."

Amara patted his cheek with one hand, and said, "At least one person in that room is mad, Bernard. One has already run you through once. The other could kill you, have the body gone, and make up any tale she wanted by the time I got back from the bath."

Bernard scowled and shook his head. "Aldrick wouldn't do it. And he wouldn't hurt you."

Amara tilted her head, frowning. "Why do you say that?"

"Because I won't shoot him in the back or hurt Odiana."

"Talked about this, have the two of you?"

"Don't need to," Bernard said.

Amara shook her head. Then she lowered her voice, and said quietly, "You're too noble for this kind of work, Bernard. Too romantic. Aldrick is a professional killer, and he's loyal to the Aquitaines. If she pointed her finger, he'd kill you. Don't let yourself believe otherwise."

Bernard studied her face quietly for a moment. Then he smiled, and said, "Amara. Not everyone is like Gaius. Or the Aquitaines."

Amara sighed, frustrated, and at the same time felt a flush of warmth run through her at her husband's . . . faith, she supposed, that there was something noble in his fellow human beings—even those as cold-blooded and violent as the mercenary swordsman. At one time, she knew, she would have thought the same thing. But that time was a considerable distance behind her. It had ended the moment her mentor had betrayed her to the same man and woman now in the room with Lady Aquitaine.

"Promise me," she said quietly, "that you'll be careful. Understanding with Aldrick or no, be careful of turning your back on him. All right?"

Bernard grimaced, but gave her a reluctant nod and bent to place a light kiss on her mouth. He looked like he was about to say something else, but Amara's little scarlet shift caught his eye and he raised his eyebrows at her. "What's that?"

"My costume," Amara said.

Bernard's grin was not—quite—a leer. "Where's the rest of it?"

Amara gave him a very level look as she felt her cheeks warming, and she turned and walked firmly into the bathing room, shutting the door behind her.

Rook was already sitting in one of the small tubs, bathing briskly. She folded a modest arm across her breasts until the door was closed. Then she went back to bathing, while watching Amara obliquely.

"What are you looking at?" Amara asked quietly. The words came out far more belligerently than she had intended.

"A master assassin of the High Lord currently on the throne," Rook replied, her tone laced with only the barest trace of irony. "I'd prefer I wasn't alone in the bath with her."

Amara lifted her chin and gave Rook a cool look. "I am no assassin."

"Perspective, Countess. Can you say you have never killed in service to your lord?"

"Never with an arrow fired from ambush," Amara said.

Rook smiled, very slightly. "That's very noble." Then she frowned and tilted her head to one side. "But . . . no. Your training was unlike mine. Or you'd not blush quite so easily."

Amara frowned at Rook, and took a deep breath. There was no profit in bickering with the former bloodcrow. It would accomplish nothing but to waste time. Instead of replying sharply, thoughtlessly, she began to undress and to bathe herself briskly. "My education as a Cursor did not include . . . that sort of technique, no."

"There are no bedchamber spies among the Cursors?" Rook asked, her tone skeptical.

"There are some," Amara said. "But every Cursor is evaluated and trained a bit differently. They intend us to play to our strengths. For some, it includes an education in seduction. My training was focused in other areas."

"Interesting," Rook said, her tone detached, professionally clinical.

Amara tried to match her tone. "I take it your own training included how to seduce men?"

"To seduce and pleasure, men and women alike."

Amara dropped her soap into the bath in surprise.

Rook allowed herself the hint of a chuckle, but it died quickly as she frowned down at the bathwater. "Relax, Countess. None of it was by my choice. I . . . I don't think I would care to revisit that sort of situation at all if there was any way I could possibly avoid it."

Amara drew in a breath. "I see. Your daughter."

"A by-product of my training," Rook said quietly.

"Her father?"

"Could be one of ten or twelve men," Rook said, her voice cool. "The training was . . . intensive."

Amara shook her head. "I can't even imagine."

"No one should be able to imagine it," Rook said. "But Kalarus strongly favored that sort of training for his female agents."

"It gives him greater control over them," Amara said.

"Without resorting to the use of collars," Rook agreed, her

voice bitter. She scrubbed at herself with a cloth, harshly, almost viciously. "Leaves their wits intact. Better able to serve him."

Amara shook her head again. Her experience as a lover was hardly extensive, consisting of a single young man at the Academy who had dazzled her for three glorious months before dying in the fires that had first brought her to the attention of the First Lord—and Bernard. Who made her feel glorious and beautiful—and loved.

She couldn't even conceive what it might be like for such an act to be undertaken coldly, without the fires of love and desire to heat it. To be simply . . . used.

"I'm sorry," Amara said quietly.

"Nothing you did," Rook replied. She closed her eyes for a moment, then her facial features began to change. The alteration was neither swift nor dramatic, but when she looked up again, Amara would never have recognized her as the same person. She got out of the tub, dried, and began to dress in her dark clothing. "We're as safe here as anywhere in the city, Countess. The owner knows who I work for, and he's proven himself adept at being blind and deaf when necessary, but the sooner we can leave the better."

Amara nodded and finished bathing quickly, rising to dry off and take up her scarlet "clothing."

"Easier to step into it than draw it down," Rook provided. "I'd better help you with the sandals."

She did so, and when Amara had slipped the armbands around her biceps she looked down at herself and felt more than mildly ridiculous.

"All right," Rook said. "Let me see you walk."

"Excuse me?" Amara said.

"Walk," the spy said. "You've got to move correctly if I'm to pass you off as a new pleasure slave."

"Ah," Amara said. She paced to one side of the room and back.

Rook shook her head. "Again. Try to relax this time."

Amara did, growing more self-conscious by the step.

"Countess," Rook said, her tone frank, "you've got to

move your hips. Your back. You've got to look like a slave so conditioned to her uses that she anticipates and enjoys them. You look like you're walking to market." Rook shook her head. "Watch me."

And with that, the spy paused, her stance shifting subtly. Then she slunk forward, eyes half-closed, mouth curled into a tiny, lazy smile. Her hips swayed languidly with each step, her shoulders drawn back, and her back arched slightly, her whole manner daring—or inviting—any man looking on to keep looking.

Rook turned on a heel, and said to Amara, "Like that."

The change in the woman was startling. One moment she'd looked like a courtesan in her private chambers with a young lord after half a bottle of aphrodin-laced wine. The next, she was a plainly attractive, businesslike young woman with serious eyes. "It's all about what you expect. Expect to draw every man's eye as you pass him, and you will."

Amara shook her head. "Even in"—she gestured vaguely—"this, I'm not the kind of woman men like to look at."

Rook rolled her eyes. "Men like to look at the kind who breathes and wears little. You'll qualify." She tilted her head to one side. "Pretend they're Bernard."

Amara blinked. "What?"

"Walk for them as you would for him," Rook said calmly. "On a night you have no intentions of allowing him to go anywhere else."

Amara found herself blushing again. But she steeled herself, closed her eyes, and tried to imagine it. Without opening her eyes, she walked across the room, picturing Bernard's chambers at the Calderon garrison.

"Better," Rook approved. "Again."

She practiced several more times before Rook was satisfied.

"Are you sure this is going to work?" Amara asked her quietly. "Your way in?"

"It isn't even a question," Rook replied. "I'll get you in there. I'll find where your prisoners are. The difficult part will be leaving afterward. With Kalarus, it always is."

Bernard knocked on the door, and said politely, "Are you almost ready, ladies?"

Amara traded a glance with Rook and nodded. Then she slipped the headdress onto her hair and fit the false steel collar around her neck. "Yes," she said. "We're ready."

·ᴏᴏᴏᴏᴏ·CHAPTER 43

One would think that sneaking into the citadel of a High Lord of Alera, the single most secure bastion of his power, would be a nigh-impossible task, Amara mused. And yet, when guided by that same High Lord's master spy, the task was evidently quite simple.

After all, Fidelias had demonstrated the same principle only a few years before, when he led Lady Aquitaine into the First Lord's citadel in Alera Imperia on a desperate mission to save the First Lord—so that she and her traitorous husband could be assured that they, not Kalarus, would be the ones to replace him.

Politics, Amara decided, really did make strange bedfellows. An idea that acquired an uncomfortable spin, given its proximity to the focus of thought demanded by her current role.

Amara swayed sleepily along the streets of Kalare in her slave costume, holding herself with a loose-limbed air of decadence, her lips constantly parted, her eyes always half-lidded. There was a peculiar sensuality to the movement, and though some part of her was fully cognizant that they were in mortal danger simply moving openly through the city, she had forced the reasoning, analytical aspects of herself to the rearmost areas of her mind. Walking, then, became an activity that carried a sensuous, almost wicked sense of indulgence, in equal parts sweetly feminine and sinfully titillating. For the first time in her life, she drew long, silently speculative looks from the men she passed.

That was good. It meant that her disguise was more complete than if it hadn't happened. And, though she could barely admit it to herself, it gave her an almost-childish sense of pleasure, simply to be stared at and desired.

Besides, Bernard, dressed in the plain garments and equipment of a travelling mercenary, walked only an arm's length behind her, and she knew from the occasional glance over her shoulder that he was staring at her far more intently than any of the men passing by.

Lady Aquitaine walked in front of Amara. She had altered her appearance via watercrafting, darkening her skin tone to the deep red-brown of the inhabitants of the city of Rhodes and changing her hair to waves of exotic, coppery red curls. Her shift was emerald green, but other than that her outfit was a match for Amara's. The High Lady moved with the same half-conscious air of wanton sensuality, and if anything, was better at it than Amara. At the front of the slave line was Odiana, in azure silk, all dark hair and pale skin and sweet curves. Aldrick paced along in front of her, and the big swordsman carried such an aura of menace that even in the teeming streets of Kalare, they were never slowed by foot traffic. Rook walked beside him, her expression bored, her manner businesslike as she guided the party toward the citadel.

Even as she concentrated on her role, though, Amara noticed details of the city and extrapolated on her observations. The city itself was, for lack of a more accurate term, a squalid cesspool. It was not as large as the other major cities of the Realm—though it housed a larger population than any but Alera Imperia herself. It was hideously crowded. Much of the city was in savage disrepair, and impoverished shanties had replaced more solid construction, in addition to engulfing the land around the city's walls for several hundred yards in every direction. The city's waste disposal was abysmal, likely because it had been designed for a much smaller population and never updated as the city overflowed with inhabitants, and the entire place reeked of odors that turned her stomach.

The inhabitants of the city were, as a group, the most miserable-looking human beings she had ever seen. Their clothing was mostly rough homespun, and mostly in disrepair. They went about their business with the kind of listless deliberation that screamed of generations of deprivation and despair. Vendors hawked shabby goods from blankets spread beside the street. One man whose clothes proclaimed him a Citizen or a wealthy merchant passed by surrounded by a dozen hard-eyed, brawny men, obviously professional bruisers.

There were slaves everywhere, even more beaten down than the city's free inhabitants. Amara had never seen so many of them. In fact, from what she could see, there were very nearly as many slaves as freemen walking the streets of Kalare. And at every crossroads and marching along at regular intervals, there were soldiers in Kalare's green-and-grey livery. Or at least, there were armed and armored men wearing Kalare's colors. From the slovenly way in which they maintained themselves and their equipment, Amara was sure that they were not true *legionares*. There were, however, a great many of them, and the automatic deference and fear they generated in the body language of those passing nearby them made it clear that Kalarus's rule was one of terror more than of law.

It also explained how the High Lords of Kalare had managed to put together a fortune larger than that of every other High Lord in the Realm, rivaling that of the Crown itself—by systematically and methodically stripping everything from the people of Kalare and its lands. Likely, it had been going on for hundreds of years.

The last section of the city before the citadel itself was where the most powerful lords of Kalare kept their homes. That level of the city was at least as lovely as those she had seen in Riva, Parcia, and Alera Imperia—and the contrast of the elegant white marble, furylit fountains, and exquisitely artistic architecture made such a stark contrast to the rest of the city that it literally made her feel physically ill to see it.

The injustice proclaimed by even a simple stroll through Kalare stirred a deep anger in Amara, one that threatened to undermine her concentration. She fought to divorce her feelings from thoughts, but it proved to be nearly impossible, especially after she saw how richly the elite of Kalare lived at the expense of its non-Citizenry.

But then they were past the Citizens' Quarter, and Rook led them up a far less crowded road—a long, straight lane sloping up to the gates of the innermost fortress of Kalare. The guards at the base of the road, perhaps slightly less shoddy-looking than their counterparts in the city below, nodded at Rook and waved her and her party of slaves by them without bothering to rise from their seats on a nearby bench.

After that, they had only to walk up a long hill, which led to the main gate of the citadel. Kalare's colors flew on the battlements, but the scarlet and blue of the House of Gaius were conspicuous by their absence.

Amara sensed immediately that the guards at the gate were nothing like those they had seen at the bottom of the hill or in the town below. They were young men in superb physical condition, one and all. Their armor was ornate and immaculately kept, their stance and bearing as suspicious and watchful as any Royal Guardsman. As they drew nearer, Amara saw something else—the metallic gleam of a collar at their throats. By the time they had ordered Rook and her company to halt, she was close enough to see the etching on the steel: *Immortalis*. More of Kalarus's Immortals.

"Mistress Rook," said one of them, evidently the leader of the guards on station. "Welcome back. I received no word of your coming."

"Centurion Orus," Rook replied, her tone polite but distant. "I am certain that His Grace feels little need to inform you of the comings and goings of his personal retainers."

"Of course not, Mistress," the young centurion replied. "Though I confess that it surprises me to see you enter here, rather than by air coach upon the tower."

"I am come ahead of His Grace and his captains," Rook replied. "I was ordered to make ready the citadel for a celebration."

Orus's eyes gleamed, as did those of the other Immortals

there. Amara did not see much in the way of thought in those eyes. "His Grace is victorious in the field?"

Rook gave him a cool look. "Did you have doubts?"

Orus snapped to attention. "No, Mistress Rook."

"Excellent," Rook said. "Who is on duty as Watch Tribune?"

"His Excellency the Count Eraegus, Mistress," Orus said. "Shall I send a runner ahead of you?"

"Unnecessary," Rook replied, brushing past him. "I know where his office is."

"Yes, Mistress Rook. But regulations prohibit armed retainers from entering the citadel." He nodded at Aldrick and Bernard and gave Rook an apologetic glance. "I'm afraid I'll have to ask them to leave their arms here."

"Absolutely not," Rook said. "His Grace charged me with the particular protection of these slaves until such time as he permits liberties with them."

Orus frowned. "I understand. Then I will be pleased to assign a pair of my own guardsmen to you for such a duty."

Amara struggled to remain in her drowsy, languidly sensual stance. It was difficult, given that she was quite certain that Aldrick had just shuffled his feet slightly in order to have them already in position for when he drew steel.

"Are they eunuchs?" Rook asked, her tone dry.

Orus blinked. "No, Mistress."

"Then I'm afraid they don't qualify, centurion." Rook dropped the mildest emphasis on the pronunciation of the rank. "I'll be sure to clear this with Count Eraegus at once, but for the time being I have my orders. Here are yours. Remain at your post."

The young centurion looked more than a little relieved. He saluted her with perfect precision and stepped back to his post.

"You," she snapped, looking at Aldrick. "This way."

The guards stood aside as Amara's group calmly walked in through the citadel's front door.

"Quickly," Rook said quietly, once they were past the guards and in the small courtyard on the other side. "Until we reach the upper levels, there's too much chance someone might see me and start asking questions."

"Someone just did," Bernard murmured.

"Someone with a mind," Rook clarified. "Kalarus controls the Immortals completely, but the collars have damaged their ability to ask questions or take the initiative in exchange for providing perfect obedience. The Immortals won't question me or act against me unless ordered to—but Kalarus's staff and officers might. They're the ones we have to avoid." She picked up the pace to a more brisk walk, led them down a side hallway, then to a wide, spiraling staircase that wound up through the heart of the tower.

Amara counted one hundred and eighteen stairs before they heard a footstep ahead of them, and an overweight, sallow man in overly fine livery stained with wine appeared four steps above them. His jowls were pocked with scars, his hair thick and uncombed, his face unshaven. He drew up to a halt and squinted at them.

"Rook?" he said.

Amara saw Rook's spine tighten with tension, but she gave no other sign of nervousness. She bowed her head, and murmured, "Milord Eraegus. Good morrow."

Eraegus grunted, and eyed the other women. His mouth spread into an appreciative leer. "Bringing in some fresh toys for us?"

"Yes," Rook said.

"Pretty bunch," Eraegus said. "When did you get in?"

"Late last night."

"Didn't expect you back this soon," he said.

Amara could see the curve of Rook's cheek as she gave Eraegus a disarming smile. "We were fortunate on the road."

Eraegus grunted. "Not what I meant. There were reports that you might have been capt—"

He broke off and stared, just for an instant. His eyes flicked from Rook to Aldrick, and then down to the big man's sword, and everyone there froze. For an agonizing second, Eraegus's eyes darted around, then he licked his lips and took a sudden, deep breath.

The stiffened edge of Rook's hand slammed into his throat before he could cry out an alarm. Eraegus shoved at her with vicious strength that could only have been the result of furycraft, and turned to go.

Before he could move, Aldrick was on his back, knife in hand.

"Stop!" Rook hissed. "Wait!"

Before she'd finished the first word, Aldrick had opened Eraegus's throat with his knife. The pockmarked man twitched and twisted, and managed to slam Aldrick's back against the stone wall beside the staircase. But the mercenary rode out the blow, and within seconds Eraegus collapsed, and Aldrick let his corpse fall to the stairs.

"Idiot!" snarled Rook in a furious whisper.

"He would have sounded an alarm," Aldrick growled.

"You should have broken his crowbegotten *neck*," Rook snarled. "We could have put him in his office, splashed some wine on him, and no one would notice anything unusual until he started to bloat." She slashed a hand at the bloodstains. "The next sweep will be through here in no more than a quarter hour. They'll see this. And the bloody alarm will go up anyway."

Aldrick frowned at Rook, then gave Odiana a glance. "She can clean it up."

"And sound the alarm," Rook said, furious. "Were you even listening when I told you about the security measures? Anyone in the tower who uses any furies Kalarus hasn't permitted rouses the gargoyles. I've seen the bodies of twenty-three different morons who did so despite being warned not to."

"Then you do it," Aldrick said. "You're a watercrafter, and one of Kalarus's own. Surely you have been cleared."

Rook's eyes narrowed. "Kalarus is arrogant, sir, but not so arrogant that he trusts his assassins with full access to their crafting in his own home." Rook paused, then added, heavy with vitriol, "Obviously."

"Obviously?" Aldrick asked, his voice rising in anger. "Then it should be equally obvious that our friend there was using earthcrafted strength. I physically *couldn't* have broken his neck, but he'd have broken mine if I hadn't put him down at once."

Amara stepped forward between them. "Silence, both of

you," she said. They fell quiet. She nodded at them, and said, "We don't have much time. And none to waste on argument and blame." She nodded at Rook. "So move."

Rook nodded once and half ran up the stairs, boots laboring noisily on the stone. She stepped out into a hallway and across it to an open door. She went inside, and Amara followed her into a small office.

"Eraegus's office," Rook said, voice terse. She started raking her eyes over the papers on his desk. "Help me out. There should be a record here of where they're keeping your Citizens. Look for anything that might indicate their location."

Amara joined her, swiftly going over page after page of reports, accounting statements, and other records of all kinds. "Here," Amara said. "What's this, about sending blankets to the aviary?"

Rook hissed. "It's at the top of the tower. An iron cage on the roof. We'll have to reach it through Kalarus's personal chambers. Come."

They hurried back to the stairs and started up them, following Rook to the top of the tower, passing the occasional window slit in the wall.

"Wait," Bernard growled. "Quiet."

Everyone there froze in place. Amara closed her eyes and heard a sound, though the tiny openings that passed for windows obscured most of what she could only describe as distant tones of some kind.

"What's that?" Bernard wondered aloud.

Rook's face suddenly went bloodless. "Oh," she said, and the young woman's voice was thready with panic. "Oh, oh crows and bloody furies. *Hurry.*"

"Why?" Amara demanded, following hard on Rook's heels. "What is that?"

"It's the fanfare," Rook stammered, terrified. "High Lord Kalarus has just returned to the citadel."

"Bloody crows," Amara snarled.

And then there was a cry from somewhere far below on the staircase, and the alarm bells of the citadel of Kalare began to ring.

CHAPTER 44

"Guards," Amara snapped.

"Six on the top floor," Rook said. "They'll come down the stairs and hold the only way to the roof."

"Where the prisoners are," Amara said. "We have to go through them."

"Right," Aldrick growled, and drew his sword. "Calderon."

Bernard already had his bow untied from the quiver on his shoulder. The weapon was already strung, since he would have had to use earthcraft to give himself enough strength to do so. He set an arrow to the string, then he and Aldrick started up the stairs.

Amara turned to Lady Aquitaine. "Can you counter Kalarus?"

"This is his house," Lady Aquitaine said in a cool voice. "A confrontation with him here would be unwise."

"Then we should hurry," Odiana said. "To the roof, free the prisoners, and leave immediately."

"My daughter!" Rook snarled. "She's on the level below the guard station."

"There's no time!" Odiana insisted. "They're coming, now!"

"He'll *kill* her," Rook cried.

The thud of heavy boots on the stairs below them began to grow steadily nearer.

"She isn't important!" Odiana shot back. "The prisoners are what matter. We have what we needed from the spy, Countess, and it is clearly your duty to—"

Amara slapped Odiana across the face, cupping her hand as she did, to make the blow sting and startle.

Odiana stared at Amara, utter shock on her face, which then immediately darkened with fury.

"Shut. Your. Mouth," Amara said in a quiet, cold voice, each word carrying acidic emphasis. Then she turned to Lady Aquitaine. "Take Odiana and go to the roof. Help them clear the way—but for goodness' sake, don't employ any overt crafting unless you must. If we don't have a clear path of retreat when the gargoyles waken, none of us are getting out."

Lady Aquitaine nodded once, gave Odiana a firm push to get her moving, and the two of them started up the stairs after Aldrick and Bernard.

Amara turned back to Rook to find the spy staring at her, eyes wide.

The Cursor put an arm on the woman's shoulder, and said, quietly, "There's no time to waste. Let's go get your daughter."

Rook blinked tears out of her eyes, then something steely slid into her features, and she led Amara up the stairs at a run.

Rook opened a door and hurried through it, though Amara lingered for a moment as steel rang on steel up the stairway. Aldrick had engaged the guards, it would seem. He was likely one of the three or four deadliest men in the world with a blade, a former *singulare* of the Princeps Septimus, which was doubtless why the Aquitaines had retained his service to begin with. But even so, the difference between an excellent swordsman and a world-class swordsman like Aldrick was very fine—and six excellent swordsmen might well be able to overwhelm even Aldrick ex Gladius.

Shouts came from above. They were answered from below, though they bounced around the stone stairway too badly for Amara to understand them. A moment later, she didn't need to understand—more guards were racing up the stairs, and they were not far away.

Amara cursed. She should have taken the fallen officer's blade while she had the opportunity, once their chances of a completely covert entry had gone to the crows. "Bernard!" she shouted.

Her husband came leaping down the stairs, bow in hand. "They're Immortal Knights Ferrous!" he called to her. "Aldrick's in trouble, and I can't get a clean shot!"

"He'll be in more trouble if the rest of the guards come up

the stairs behind," Amara said. "You've got to hold them off."

Bernard nodded once, never slowing his pace, feet moving swiftly and silently down the stairs. A beat later, she heard the heavy, bass thrumming of his bow, and a cry of pain.

Amara wanted to scream with fear, for her husband and for herself and for all the people who were counting on the success of this mission. She ground her teeth instead and flung herself after Rook.

This level of the tower was a richly appointed apartment, the entry room a large study and library rolled into one. The woven carpets, the tapestries, a dozen paintings and several sculptures were all lovely enough—but they were put together with no sense of style, theme, or commonality of any kind. It was an insight into Kalarus's character, Amara decided. He knew what beauty was, but he did not understand what made it valuable. His collection was expensive, expansive, all of undeniable masterpieces—and that was all he cared about; the shell, the price, the proclamation of his wealth and power, not beauty for its own sake.

Kalarus did not love beauty. He merely had use for it. And the fool probably had no idea that there was a distinction between the two.

Amara saw why Rook had chosen their method of entry, their disguises as she had. It was a blind spot in his thinking, and since his control over affairs in his household certainly ran far deeper than any other High Lord Amara had seen, his own prejudices and idiocies could only be reflected and multiplied throughout it, including his tendency to assign value based purely upon external appearance. Everyone there was used to the sight of new slaves brought in to amuse the staff. Such a group of new slaves would be quickly dismissed and even more quickly forgotten.

Or would have been, at least, if Aldrick hadn't cut Eraegus's throat.

Rook frowned as she walked to the door to the next room. It opened at a touch, and she looked around a small sitting room or antechamber. Like the larger area they'd just come through, it was expensive and absent of the kind of warmth that would make it more than simply a room.

Rook paced to a plain section of expensive hardwood paneling and struck the heel of her hand firmly against it. A crack split through the panel, and Rook drew aside a wooden section that concealed a storage area behind it. She promptly withdrew a pair of swords, a longer duelist's blade and a standard, plain-looking *gladius*. She offered their hilts to Amara. Amara took the shorter blade, and said, "Keep that one."

Rook looked at her. "You wish me to be armed, Countess?"

"If you'd had it in mind to betray us, Rook, I think you've had ample opportunity. Keep it."

Rook nodded and carried the scabbarded blade in her left hand. "This way, Countess. There's only his boudoir and bath left on this level."

The next door opened onto a bedchamber at least as large as the study had been, and the bed was the size of a small sailing vessel. Hand-carved hardwood wardrobes were left carelessly open, revealing row after row of the finest clothing Alera had to offer.

The prisoners had been secured by chains attached to the stone fireplace.

Lady Placida sat on the floor, hands folded calmly in her lap, her expression regal and defiant as the door opened. She wore only a slender white undergown, and a rough ring of iron circled her throat, and was attached to a heavy chain, which was in turn fastened to the stones of the fireplace. She faced the door as it opened, eyes hard and hot, and then blinked in utter surprise as Amara and Rook entered.

"Mama!" came a small, glad cry, and a girl of perhaps five or six years of age flung herself across the room. Rook stooped to gather her up with a low cry and held the little girl tight against her.

"Countess Amara?" Lady Placida said. The red-haired High Lady came to her feet—only to be jerked up short by the chain, which was set at such a length as to make it impossible for her to stand fully upright.

"Your Grace," Amara murmured, nodding once at Lady Placida. "I've come to—"

"Countess, the door!" Lady Placida cried.

But before she had finished, the heavy door to the chamber slammed shut behind them with a power and a finality that could only be the result of furycraft. Amara spun to the door and tried to open it, but the handle would not turn, and she could not so much as rattle the door in its frame.

"It's trapped." Lady Placida sighed. "Anyone can open it from the other side, but . . ."

Amara turned back to the High Lady. "I've come to—"

"Rescue me, obviously," Lady Placida said, nodding. "And none too soon. The pig is returning sometime today."

"He arrived but moments ago," Amara said, crossing to Lady Placida. "We have little time, Your Grace."

"Amara, anyone who rescues me from this idiot's soulless little bower should feel free to call me Aria," Lady Placida said. "But we have a problem." She gestured up the chain fastened to the ring on her neck. "It's not a lock. The chain's been crafted into place. It has to be broken, and if you'll look up . . ."

Amara did, and found four stone figures glaring down at her, carved shapes of hideous beasts that rested atop the stone pillars at each corner of the room. The gargoyles had to have weighed several hundred pounds each, and Amara knew that even though they would not move with speed any greater than that of a human being, they were so much heavier and more powerful than any human that it would make them altogether deadly to anyone who got in their way. One could not block the unthinkably powerful blow of a gargoyle's fist. One could get out of its way or be crushed by it. There was no middle ground.

"According to my host," Lady Placida said, "the gargoyles are set to animate if they detect my furycrafting." Her mouth twisted bitterly and she glanced significantly at Rook and the little girl. "Moreover, he assured me that I would not be their first victim."

Amara's mouth firmed into a hard line. "The bastard." More screams and shouts came to them from the central stairwell, muffled a low mutter by the thick door. "He's on his way up, by the sound of things."

"Then your team does not have much time," Lady Placida said. "He'll pull out his men and pour fire up the stairwell. He won't mind sacrificing a few of those poor fools in the collars if it means he gets to incinerate a team of the Crown's Cursors."

Amara coughed. "Actually, I'm the only Cursor. This is Rook, lately the head of Kalarus's bloodcrows. She helped us get this far."

Lady Placida's fine, red-gold eyebrows arched sharply, but she looked from Rook to the child, and an expression of comprehension came over her. "I see. And who else?"

"Count Calderon, Aquitainus Invidia, and two of her retainers."

Lady Placida's eyes widened. "Invidia? You're kidding."

"I'm afraid not, my lady."

The High Lady frowned, eyes calculating. "There's little chance that she intends to play this through entirely in good faith, Countess."

"I know," Amara said. "Could you handle the gargoyles if the child wasn't part of the equation?"

"I assume there's at least a chance I could," Lady Placida said, "or Kalarus wouldn't have needed to take the additional measure." She glanced at the child again, tilted her head at each of the statues, and said, "Yes. I can deal with them. But these are close quarters. There won't be much time for me to act—and I can hardly fight them if I am chained to the floor."

Amara nodded, thinking furiously. "Then what we must do," she said, "is determine exactly what your first furycrafting will be."

"One that will free me, put me in a position to destroy the gargoyles quickly, *and* allow you to leave the chamber so that I don't kill you both while I do so," Lady Placida said. "And let us not forget that Kalarus will come for me with blood in his eyes if he realizes I'm free."

"It is my hope that you and Lady Aquitaine will be able to neutralize his crafting until we can escape."

"Gaius always did favor optimists in the ranks of the Cursors," Lady Placida said in a dry tone. "I assume you have a brilliant idea of some sort?"

"Well. *An* idea, at least," Amara said. She glanced back at Rook to make sure she was listening as well. "There's little time, and I'm going to have to ask you both to extend some trust to me. This is what I want to do."

⬦⬦⬦⬦ CHAPTER 45

The night fell, dark and thick beneath the ritualists' shroud of storm clouds. The night made the Canim battle cries even more terrifying, and Tavi could feel the primal, inescapable dread of fangs and hungry mouths rising in the back of his thoughts. No furylamps lit the walls as he ran to his position above the gate, and the orange band of a fading sunset was the only light. He couldn't see the men on the wall well enough to make out expressions, but as he walked past them he could hear restless movement among them—and noted that they were uniformly far more slender than most of the more mature ranks of veterans. The First Spear had kept the cohort of fish on the wall.

"Marcus?" Tavi asked as he reached the center wall.

"Sir," growled a dark form near him.

"Everything set?"

"Yes, sir," the First Spear said. "We're ready."

"Men know the signal?"

"Yes. Sir," Marcus growled, tone tight. "That's what I mean when I say we're ready, sir."

Tavi started to snap a reply but held his tongue. He stood on the wall in silence as the light continued to fade. Drums rattled outside. Horns blared. Night fell, blackness only broken by flashes of scarlet lightning.

Then there was a sudden silence.

"Here they come," Tavi breathed.

Howls rose into the air, louder and louder. The ground began to shake.

"Stand by furylamps," Tavi barked. The order was repeated by spear leaders up and down the wall. A flash of lightning showed Tavi a mass of black-armored Canim closing on the gates, and he called, "Furylamps now!"

A dozen large furylamps, suspended by chains to be hung five feet down the outside of the walls, flared into light. They cast a cold blue light out over the ground before the walls, illuminating the ground for the Aleran defenders while glaring into the eyes of the attacking Canim.

"Engage!" Tavi cried, and *legionares* snapped into two-man teams, shieldman and archer. Arrows darted down into the heavily armored Canim warriors, but this time, many of the warriors carried heavy shields of scarlet steel, and arrows struck with small effect. The deadly, heavy javelins came next, striking *legionares* standing between the merlons. One archer took an instant too long to aim, and a spear struck him, its tip exploding from his back, while the force of the impact threw him from the battlements entirely to land on the stones of the courtyard. Another *legionare* had not properly secured his shield to his arm, and when a spear struck it, the top edge of the shield spun back, striking him in the face and wrenching his arm from its socket in a burst of crackling pops.

"There," Tavi said, pointing at a tight group of Canim approaching in two rows. "Their first ram. Ready pitch."

"Ready pitch!" bellowed Marcus.

The ram closed on the gate and slammed against it once. Then the men over the gate dumped pitch down upon the attackers—but something went wrong, for no howls of pain came up. Tavi risked a deadly second leaning out over the battlements to peer down. A long section of wood, no thicker than Tavi's leg, lay smoldering beneath the splashed pitch, but it was far too light to have been an actual ram. The Canim must have abandoned it after a single strike against the gates for the sake of showmanship.

It had been a decoy, Tavi realized.

A second group surged forward, several Canim beneath

some kind of portable canopy constructed from overlapping shields, and made for the gates. Tavi clenched his teeth. Even if they'd had more pitch ready, it might have been useless against the ram's canopy.

Excellent.

The ram slammed into the gates, hard enough to rattle the battlements beneath Tavi's boots. Again, in half the time it would have taken a team of Alerans wielding a ram to swing again. Boom, boom, boom, then, with the next strike, there was a single, sharp *crack* as one of the timbers of the gate gave way.

"That's it!" Tavi called. "Courtyard!"

The *legionares* waiting in the courtyard turned and double-timed away from the gates, toward the bridge, following a single row of widely spaced furylamps. As they did, more hooks flew up over the wall, attached to steel chains, and as the gate began to give way, more armored warriors gained the walls beneath the cover of hurtling spears.

"They're through!" Marcus snapped.

Outside, Canim horns began blaring a charge, and many of the black-armored warriors parted to allow the raiders an un-obstructed charge at the gates. Thousands of the inhuman raiders surged forward in a massive wave of fangs and muscle.

"Fall back! Frying pan!" Tavi bellowed. "Fall back! Frying pan!"

The gate gave way, and the Canim let out a roar. Tavi and the *legionares* on the wall rushed down in frantic, terrified haste. One young *legionare* stumbled and fell down several stairs and sprawled on the courtyard. There was a sharp, hissing sound, and he cried out in sudden agony. Two of his fellows seized him and began dragging him between them.

"Go!" Tavi shouted, half-pushing *legionares* past him and down the stairs, while he swept his gaze through the confusion and darkness to make sure none had been left behind. "Go, go, go!"

"That's all of them!" Marcus shouted.

Together, the pair of them hurried down to the courtyard and sprinted across it. Tavi could feel uncomfortable heat through the soles of his hobnailed boots after half a dozen strides. He could hear the gate fall behind him, and the Canim howled in triumph.

Marcus let out a cry beside him, and Tavi saw the First Spear fall. A Canim javelin had struck his lower leg, sinking into his calf just below the bend of his knee.

Marcus managed to fall on his shield, preventing his flesh from striking the stones and sizzling like a slab of bacon, like the poor *legionare* who had fallen a few seconds before. He tried to wrench the javelin from his leg, but the tip must have struck bone. He couldn't pull it free.

Tavi slid to a stop and went back for the First Spear. A javelin struck sparks from the stones a few feet away. Tavi grabbed Marcus's arm and hauled him almost entirely off his feet. The First Spear let out a cry of pain between his clenched teeth, and hobbled along as quickly as he could, until in desperation, Tavi lifted him clear onto one of his shoulders and ran.

Then he reached the edge of the courtyard, and he saw the shapes of Knights Aeris crouched on rooftops. A sudden wind began sweeping down, blowing in a gale at the gates, foiling the accuracy of any further missiles. Tavi looked over his shoulder, to see raiders plunging through the gates the warriors had opened, breaking into sudden howls of agony as their bare feet struck the heated stones of the courtyard. They could no more have turned back against the tide of their own assault than they could have swum up a waterfall. Thousands of their frenzied fellows poured through the breached gates, and their screams split the air.

Canim desperately tried to find escape from the heated stones, leaping up onto houses, shops, and other buildings around the courtyard. Still, more poured through, and in seconds there *were* no more such places to go. Canim fell, succumbing to agony, only to have it doubled and redoubled as their flesh fell fully onto the courtyard stone. The gale winds blew into Canim eyes, ears, and noses, and the confusion changed the assault into a madhouse of the dead and dying.

And *still* more Canim poured in, the raiders now maddened and howling, thirsting for blood, walking on the burned and burning bodies of their dead and dying fellows to find respite from the sizzling stone of the courtyard. They oriented on the bridge, and Tavi saw them begin charging toward it. He put his head down and ran, flanked by Knights Aeris, who moved from roof to roof and kept the nearest Canim blind to Tavi and the stragglers from the walls.

It seemed to take forever to run the few hundred yards to the Elinarch—and to the defenses the engineers had constructed upon it. Using clay from the riverbed, they had constructed a series of five walls spaced evenly over the bridge, earthcrafted into shape, and then blasted with firecrafting until the clay had baked into a consistency almost as tough and hard as stone, leaving an opening scarcely wide enough for two men. At the southern end of the bridge was another such barrier, this one fully as large as the city's walls themselves.

Tavi and the covering Knights Aeris rushed through the newly created defenses while the Canim, goaded to fury by the heated stones, rushed forward.

"Medico!" Tavi shouted. Foss appeared, and Tavi all but dumped the First Spear into the healer's arms. Then he ran for the wall and pounded up the crude steps built into it to the improvised battlements there. Max and Crassus, together with the First Aleran's cohort prime, waited, already in position with the other Knights Aeris spread along the wall. The last of the Knights Aeris followed Tavi up to the walls.

Max and Crassus both looked exhausted, and Tavi knew that the firecrafting they'd used to heat the stones had been intensely fatiguing. But if they looked bad, the skinny young redheaded Knight Ignus beside them looked nine-tenths dead. He sat with his back against the battlements, his eyes focused elsewhere, shivering in the cool of the evening. Ehren appeared out of the night's shadows, still bearing the Legion's standard. Tavi nodded at him, and Ehren planted the blackened eagle standard in a socket in the adobe battlements the engineers had prepared for it.

Enough furylamps remained in the town to let Tavi see the raiders charging through the town, bounding over rooftops with inhuman grace, and their eyes gleamed red in the near darkness. Their cries and howls grew louder and louder.

Tavi watched them impassively, until the nearest one he could see was no more than fifty yards from the bridge. "Ready," he said quietly, to Max.

Max nodded, and put a hand on Jens's shoulder.

Tavi tried to count the oncoming Canim, but the shifting light—now only furylamps, now dancing red lightning strobes—made it impossible. More than a thousand of them, maybe even two or three times that many. He waited a few instants more, to give the Canim as much time as possible to pour more troops into the city.

"All right," he said quietly, "Frying pan's done. Time for fire."

"Bring up the wind!" Crassus commanded, and he and his Knights Aeris faced the oncoming foe and brought up a strong, steady wind.

"Jens," Max said to the young Knight. "You can let it go."

Jens let out a gasp and sagged like a man suddenly rendered unconscious by a blow to the neck.

And the entire southern half of the town became a sudden and enormous bonfire. Tavi could see, in his mind's eye, the boxes and barrels that had been filled with fine sawdust, intentionally manufactured by volunteers through the town and the followers' camp for the past several days, and stored in whatever containers they could find—then scattered still more sawdust liberally throughout each building. In each container was a furylamp, put in place by Jens, each tiny fire fury leashed to his will, restrained from flickering to life within the fine, volatile sawdust.

When Jens released them, hundreds of tiny furies had suddenly been free to run amok, and the barrels and barrels of sawdust all but exploded into flame. The dust-strewn buildings went up like torches, and the strong winds commanded by Crassus's Knights both fed the fires more air, making them hotter and hotter, and blew them back toward the onrushing enemy.

Tavi watched as Canim died, horribly, consumed by the flames, trapped within the city's stone walls. Some of them might have survived, he supposed. But even with the wind keeping the conflagration away from the bridge, the heat of it was uncomfortable on Tavi's face. The fire made an enormous roaring sound, drowning out the occasional thunder of the lightning overhead, the cries of the dying Canim, and the cheers of the Alerans watching their terrifying foes fall.

Tavi let it go on for five or ten minutes. Then he signaled Crassus with a wave of one hand, and the Knight Tribune and his Knights Aeris sagged in relief, ceasing their efforts. There was a long silence on the walls, broken only by the low roar of flames, and the occasional shriek of tortured wood as burning buildings fell in upon themselves.

Tavi closed his eyes. He could, quite faintly, make out another sound beneath the fire—the long, mournful, angry howls of grieving Canim.

"At ease, people," Tavi said to no one in particular. "Maximus, Crassus, get yourselves and your people some food and some rest. It will be a couple of hours before those fires die down enough to let them through. But when they come, they're going to be angry."

Crassus frowned at Tavi, and his voice sounded heavy. "You don't think this will convince them to go somewhere else?"

"We cost them plenty," Tavi said. "But not from their best. They can afford it."

Crassus frowned and nodded. "What's next, then?"

"Next, you get some food and rest. We've still got a bridge to defend. Send something up for the prime cohort, too."

"Yes, sir," Crassus said. He saluted, then began giving orders to his men, and they descended from the wall. Moments later, several fish arrived carrying pots of spiced tea and fresh bread, and at a nod from Tavi, the veterans on the walls went to collect food and drink. Tavi took advantage of the moment to walk down to the far end of the wall. He slipped up onto the wall itself, hung his feet over the side, and sat with his head leaning against a merlon.

Tavi heard Max's footsteps approach.

"You all right?" Max asked.

"Go get some food," Tavi said.

"Balls. Talk to me."

Tavi was quiet for a second, then said, "Can't. Not yet."

"Calderon . . ."

Tavi shook his head. "Let it be, Max. We still have work to do."

Maximus grunted. "When we're done, we'll go get drunk. Talk then."

Tavi made an effort to smile. "Only if you're buying. I know how much you can drink, Max."

His friend snorted, then made his way from the wall, leaving Tavi alone with this thoughts.

Tavi's stratagem had lured maybe half a Legion of Canim to their deaths in the inferno, but the burning buildings lit up the countryside beyond the walls and the enormous numbers of Canim moving toward the river. He couldn't tell, at a glance, that the enemy had taken any losses at all.

The cold, leaden reality of mathematics pressed relentlessly into his thoughts. He'd known that the Canim army outnumbered the Alerans, but numbers mentioned on paper, on a tactical map, or in a planning session were entirely different than numbers applied to a real, physical, murderous enemy you could see marching toward you. Looking out at thousands of Canim, all in view and moving for the first time, Tavi gained an entirely new perspective on the magnitude of the task they faced.

It made him feel bitterly, poisonously weary.

At least he'd gained a few hours of respite for the men. For whatever it was worth. Except for those who had already died, of course. They now had all the time in the world to rest.

He sat for a moment, watching half of the town he was defending burn. He wondered how many homes and businesses he'd just destroyed. How many hard-earned generations of wealth and knowledge he'd sacrificed. How many irreplaceable family heirlooms and artifacts he'd burned to ashes.

He wasn't sure precisely when he fell asleep, but something cold on his face woke him. He jerked his head upright, wincing as he found his neck had stiffened as he leaned it against the adobe merlon, and muscles tied themselves into knots. He rubbed at his neck with one hand, blinked his eyes a few times, and heard a little plinking sound. Then again. Cold water struck one cheek.

Raindrops.

Tavi looked up at the sullen clouds, and more rain began to fall—first lightly, but it rapidly built up to a torrent, a storm that brought the pent-up rain from the clouds in sheets so thick that Tavi had to spit water from his mouth every few breaths. His heart lurched in panic, and he hurried to rise to his feet.

"To arms!" he bellowed. "All cohorts to their positions!"

The sheeting rain hammered down onto the burning town and began strangling the flames. Clouds of steam and smoke billowed up, and, together with the rain, they hid the view of the enemy entirely.

Once more, the Canim horns began to blare.

Shouts sounded through the downpour, muffled by the rain. Boots thudded on stone. Tavi ground his teeth and slammed his fist against the merlon. The veterans on the wall snapped into motion, strapping on shields, stringing bows that would be rendered largely ineffective by the rain. As the fires died, the forms of the men on the wall grew murky.

"Lights!" Tavi shouted down at the men on the bridge below. "Get some lights up here, quick!"

One of the *legionares* on the wall shouted, and Tavi spun to see black-armored forms, almost invisible against the darkness, rushing forward with incredible speed. Tavi turned to order more men into the makeshift "gate" in the wall, a simple arch barely wide enough for two men to walk through upright—and a tiny fit indeed for a Cane. As he did, he bumped into a veteran hurrying into position with his bow, and both men slipped on the water-slicked adobe battlements.

Otherwise, they would have died with the others.

Even as *legionares* moved to battle positions, there was a humming sound and then a series of miniature thunderclaps. A spray of blood erupted from a veteran three feet from Tavi, and the man dropped without a sound. Down the wall, the same happened to others. Something slammed through a shield and killed the veteran behind it. One of the archers jerked, then collapsed. Another's head snapped back so sharply that Tavi clearly heard his neck break. The corpse fell near him, head lolling to one side, eyes open and unblinking. A vaned metal shaft as thick as the circle of Tavi's thumb and forefinger protruded from the helmet. As Tavi stared, a trickle of blood slithered down over one of the *legionare's* sightless eyes, and was almost instantly thinned and washed away by the rain.

Seconds later, Tavi heard that humming, thrumming sound again, and there were screams from the bridge below. Then a horrible bellowing roar, and Nasaug burst through the tiny opening with terrifying ease and agility, curved war sword in his hand. The Cane Battlemaster killed three *legionares* before any of them had time to react, the massive sword shattering bone even through steel armor, and slicing through exposed flesh with terrible efficiency. He parried another *legionare's* thrusting sword, seized the rim of the man's shield with one paw, and with a simple, clean motion threw the man twenty feet through the air, over the side of the bridge, to fall screaming to the river below.

Nasaug batted another pair of *legionares* aside, then shattered the furylamps being brought up to the wall with several swift kicks, plunging the entire area into darkness. By the increasingly frequent bursts of red lightning, Tavi saw more Canim enter behind Nasaug, their long, lean bodies almost seeming to fold in upon themselves as they came through the opening.

The veteran beside Tavi rose and lifted his bow to aim at Nasaug.

"No!" Tavi shouted. "Stay down!"

A buzzing thrum sounded, and another steel bolt ripped through the *legionare's* lower back, straight through his armor, until an inch of the bolt's tip showed through the veteran's breastplate. The man gasped and fell—and a second later screamed in pure, feeble terror as the savage snarling of Canim rose from the darkness. *Legionares* fought warriors in the nightmarish murk, broken by flashes of bloody light. Men and Canim screamed in rage, defiance, terror, and pain.

Tavi lay frozen. If he rose, whatever marksmen were releasing those deadly steel bolts would kill him—but the Cane assault had come so swiftly and terribly that Tavi was already cut off from the *legionares* below. If he descended to the bridge, he'd be facing the Canim alone, with nothing but his *gladius*.

Tavi didn't remember drawing his sword, but his fingers ached from how hard he squeezed the hilt as he desperately tried to think of a way out.

And then the shadowy shape of a black-armored Cane, its eyes reflecting bits of red light in the dimness, started up the steps to the wall. Tavi knew it would spot him in mere seconds.

He had just run out of time.

◁◻◻◻◻▷ CHAPTER 46

Tavi had nowhere to run, nowhere to hide, and if he did nothing he would simply be killed.

So as the Cane mounted the stairs, Tavi let out a howl of terror and rage and threw himself into the armored body of the Cane with every ounce of strength and reckless violence he could summon.

He hit the Cane hard and high on its chest. Though the Cane was far larger, Tavi's armored weight and momentum were more than enough to overcome the surprised Cane, and then Tavi drove the Cane back and down the stairs to crash heavily to the stone surface of the bridge. Before the Cane could recover, Tavi slammed his helmet repeatedly into the creature's sensitive nose and muzzle, then raised his sword, gripping the hilt with one hand and halfway up the blade with the other, and rammed it with all his strength down into the Cane's throat.

Either he missed anything vital or the Cane was simply too

tough to know when it should die. It seized Tavi with one desperate arm and flung him away. Tavi slammed against the raised side of the bridge, but his armor took the brunt of the impact, and he came back to his feet as the wounded Cane rose, teeth bared in a horrible snarl.

"Captain!" shouted a voice, and fire blossomed in the night, a sudden sheet of it rising from the stone between Tavi and the wounded Cane. In the light, Tavi just had time to make out the features of his opponent—the grizzled Cane who had brought Tavi the very sword he had just employed—and then Knights Aeris descended around him.

They landed roughly, and before they hit the ground, Nasaug turned and flung one of the steel bars Tavi had examined the previous day. It struck one of the young Knights in a knee with crippling force, throwing his leg out from beneath him so that he fell to the ground.

Crassus landed beside Tavi, and with a grunt of effort flung a streamer of flame at the nearest Cane. It licked out weakly in the heavy rain, but sufficed to force the Cane to pause, and that was enough. Knights Aeris seized Tavi's arms, and under Crassus's direction, they rose from the bridge into the night sky. A flash of lightning showed Nasaug, throwing another bar at Crassus, but the young Knight Tribune flicked it deftly aside with his blade, before leading the Knights Aeris up and out of range of hurled weapons.

But not out of range of those deadly steel quarrels.

More thrums sounded from below, and one of the Knights Aeris holding Tavi grunted and fell from the sky, vanishing into the dark below. The single Knight remaining almost dropped him, and everything spun around wildly. Then Crassus was there, taking the place of the fallen Knight, and the weary band of fliers descended to the second defensive position, a hundred yards from the south end of the bridge.

The next few hours came as one enormous blur of darkness, cold, and desperation. Two entire cohorts had been all but annihilated in the first, stunning assault. The prime cohort had been slain to a man, cut to shreds by the steel quarrels and overwhelmed by the Canim warriors led by Nasaug. Ninth co-

hort had tried to rush forward in the confusion and stem the
breakthrough at the end of the bridge, only to be cut down in
the near-total darkness by Nasaug's troops. Most of a single
century had managed to fall back to the next defensive position, but eight in ten of the cohort perished on the bridge.
Even the wounded who made it back to the suddenly overwhelmed healers found little help. There were simply not
enough hands, and men who would have survived the wounds
in other circumstances died waiting their turns.

Nearly six hundred Alerans fell.

It had taken all of seven or eight minutes.

Tavi remembered shouting orders, frantic questions and
answers from the First Spear. There was never enough light.
The Canim destroyed every lamp they or their marksmen
could reach—and furylamps were in short enough supply already, thanks to the trap Tavi had laid on the south side of the
village. Twice more, Tavi found himself facing hulking Canim
warriors in almost-total darkness, and fought simply to retreat
and survive.

The Canim overran the next two defensive positions on the
bridge, and it became a race to see who could reach the center
arch of the bridge first—the Canim or the Aleran engineers
who made a desperate attempt to collapse the bridge.

In the darkness and confusion, the Canim won the race.
Tavi watched with helpless frustration and terror as Nasaug
himself vaulted over the much lower fortifications at the apex
of the bridge, slew half a dozen Alerans attempting to defend
the wall, and began cutting down fleeing *legionares*.

Tavi knew that if the Canim were not stopped at that point,
they would use the "downhill" momentum on the far side of
the bridge to simply smash through the remaining defensive
lines and into the town at the north end of the bridge—and
into the civilians huddled there for protection.

Somehow, he and the First Spear managed to get a solid
block of men together in front of the last wall upon the bridge
itself, while Crassus's exhausted Knights Aeris lined the low
city wall behind them. Tavi had furniture taken from the town
behind them piled into two massive mounds, doused them in

liquor, and had Max set them aflame to provide light for the *legionares*—and to *keep* it burning with firecrafting. The Knights sent a gale of wind into the faces of the Canim, both shielding the fires and blinding their enemies in the down-pouring rain, and a roaring charge led by the First Spear hammered into the Canim advance. Tavi watched from the wall as *legionares* and warriors locked in desperate, grinding battle, but in the close confines of the bridge, once the Canim's momentum was checked and the darkness broken by the bonfires, the advantage fell to the tightly coordinated, disciplined—and desperate—*legionares*. Step by bloody step, they drove the Canim back, until the inhuman foe leapt back over the wall to take up defensive positions of their own.

Tavi ordered the *legionares* back to the last wall on the bridge, fearing that they would be cut down by Canim marksmen if they remained in the open.

And for the space of an hour, the battle ceased.

Tavi sagged to the ground behind their last wall and sat there for a moment. He stripped off his helmet and tilted his head up to the sky to drink falling rain. The rainfall had been growing slowly if steadily lighter over the past hours. It made the cool evening positively uncomfortable, and spasms of shivering came and went every minute or so.

"Captain?" Ehren said quietly. Tavi hadn't heard him approach. "You all right?"

"Tired, is all," Tavi replied.

"You should get out of the rain. Get some hot food into you."

"No time," Tavi said. "They can see in the dark. We can't. They'll hit us again before dawn. I need Tribune Cymnea to round up every furylamp she can find, any wood that will burn, and every drop of liquor in the whole town. We'll need it to start fires so that the men can see. Valiar Marcus is taking a head count. Ask Foss for the count on deaths and casualties, and relay it to the First Spear."

Ehren frowned, but nodded. "All right. But after that . . ."

"After that," Tavi said, "take the two fastest horses you can find and get out."

Ehren fell silent.

"It's your duty," Tavi said quietly. "The First Lord needs to know about what the ritualists can do. And about those bolt throwers the Canim are using. And . . ." He shook his head. "Tell him that we're going to find a way to take down the bridge. Somehow. Convey my apologies that I couldn't keep it intact."

There was another silent moment. Then Ehren said, "I can't just walk away from my friends."

"Don't walk. Run. As fast as you can." Tavi rose and slipped his helmet back on. Then he put a hand on Ehren's shoulder and met his eyes. "If Gaius doesn't at least hear about it, it was all for nothing. Don't let that happen."

Rain plastered the little Cursor's hair to his scalp. Then he bowed his head and nodded. "All right."

Tavi squeezed his shoulder, grateful. At least he'd get one friend out of this mess alive. "Get a move on."

Ehren gave him a weak smile and a sloppy salute, then turned and hurried away.

Max said quietly, from the darkness nearby, "He's right, you know."

Tavi jumped, startled, and glared in the direction of Max's voice. "Crows, Max. You just scared me out of ten years of life."

Max snorted and said, "Sounds to me like you don't think you'll be using it anyway."

"You should get food," Tavi said. "Rest. We'll need your crafting soon."

In answer, Max took a ceramic bowl from beneath his cloak, and passed it to Tavi. It was so warm that he could feel it through his gloves, but as the scent of the thick stew reached his nose, a sudden demand from his belly overruled his caution, and he gulped down the stew, barely pausing to chew the meat. Max had a second bowl, and kept Tavi company.

"All right," Tavi said. "I should probably—"

"Marcus is organizing," Max said. "Said you should eat. Sit down for a minute. So relax."

Tavi began to shake his head and deny him, but his aching body prevented him from doing more than leaning up against the wall.

"This is pretty bad," Tavi said quietly. "Isn't it?"

Max nodded. "Worst I've seen."

From startlingly nearby, there was the frantic snarl of an enraged Cane and the violent thrashing of water. Max had his sword out of his sheath before the sound died away, and his gaze flickered around them. "What the crows . . ."

Tavi hadn't moved. "It's in the river below us."

Max arched an eyebrow. "Shouldn't it concern us if they're sending troops across?"

"Not particularly. It's been happening since nightfall. They haven't made it to this side yet."

Max frowned. "Water furies?"

"You think I'd let the healers waste their time on something like that?" Tavi asked.

"You're too clever for your own good, Calderon," Max growled.

"Sharks," Tavi said.

"What?"

"Sharks. Big fish with big teeth."

Max lifted his eyebrows. "Fish?"

"Mmmm. Attracted to blood in the water. Tribune Cymnea's been collecting from everyone butchering animals in the camp and the town, and dumping the blood into the river. The sharks followed the blood trail up from the sea. Hundreds of them. Now they're hitting everything that goes for a swim." Tavi made a vague gesture at the water. "Old fisherman who works this river told me it even attracted a baby leviathan. Little one, about forty feet long."

Max grunted. "Fish. Sooner or later they're going to get full, and the Canim are going to have an assault team on this side of the river. You should let me send some of my riders out to patrol the shore."

"No need," Tavi said. "Kitai will spot any Cane that gets through."

"Yeah?" Max said. "There's only one of her, Calderon. What can she do that fifty of my men can't?"

"See in the dark," Tavi said.

Max opened his mouth, then shut it again. "Oh."

"Besides," Tavi said, "if she wasn't there, she'd be here."

Max blew out a breath. "Yeah. Always clever."

"Not always," Tavi said. He could hear the bitterness in his voice. "Nasaug made a fool out of me."

"How?"

"I thought he was delaying his attack just to tweak Sarl's nose. That wasn't what he was doing at all. Sarl was stupid enough to order a major attack against the walls with an hour of daylight left. Nasaug managed to stall that attack until night fell, when the Canim would have a major advantage. He broke the gates, then he fixed it so their most expendable troops would soak up the losses from the fire trap." Tavi shook his head. "I should have realized what he was doing."

"Even if you had," Max said, "it wouldn't have made any difference."

"And those bolt throwers." Tavi's stomach fluttered as he thought of the men they had slain. "Why did I sit around thinking that they would only have hand-thrown weapons for ranged combat."

"Because that's all they ever *have* used," Max said. "No one could have seen that coming. This is the first time I've heard of it."

"All the same," Tavi said.

"No," Max said. "Crows take it, Calderon. You've done a sight more than anyone expected you to do. Probably more than you should have been able to do. Stop blaming yourself. You didn't send the Canim here."

In the dark, another Cane's scream came up from the river.

Tavi let out a tired laugh. "You know what bothers me the most?"

"What?"

"When I was at the riverbank, and those Canim were coming for me, and those lions came up, for just a second . . ." He shook his head. "I thought that maybe it was something I'd done. Maybe they were my furies. Maybe I wasn't . . ." His throat tightened and closed almost shut.

Max spoke quietly from the darkness. "Father never let me

manifest a fury. A creature, you know? Like your uncle's stone hound, or Lady Placida's fire falcon. But he never taught me anything about water, and in the library there was this old book of stories. There was a water lion like that in there. So . . . I pretty much taught myself all my watercraft. And since he wasn't around, it came out like that lion. Named him Androcles." Tavi couldn't be sure in the dimness, but he thought he might have seen Max blush. "It was kind of lonely for me, when my mother died."

"Crassus must have read the same book," Tavi said.

"Yeah. Funny. Never thought I'd have anything in common with him." He shifted his weight restlessly. "I'm sorry. That it wasn't what you'd hoped."

Tavi shrugged a shoulder. "It's all right, Max. Maybe it's time I stopped dreaming of having my own furies and got on with living. I've wanted them for so long, but . . . your furies don't make things different, do they."

"Not where it matters," Max said. "Not on the inside. My father always told me that a man's furycraft just makes him more of what he already is. A fool with furies is still a fool. A good man with furies is still a good man."

"Old Killian tried to tell me something like that," Tavi said. "The day of our combat final. The more I think about it, the more I think maybe he was trying to make me understand that there's more to the world than furies. More to life than what I can do with them."

"He was no fool," Max said. "Calderon. I know what you've done. I owe you my life, despite all my furycrafting. You were the one who stood at the end. And that goes double for Gaius. You've killed assassins and monsters all by yourself. You faced down a Canim warlord without arms or furycraft to protect you, and I don't know anyone else who would do that. That trap south of the bridge killed more Canim in an hour than the Legions have in the last ten years. And I still have no idea how you managed to stop their charge—I thought we were finished. And you did all of that without a single fury of your own." Max's fist lightly struck

Tavi's armored shoulder. "You're a crowbegotten *hero*, Calderon. Furies or not. And you're a born captain. The men believe in you."

Tavi shook his head. "Believe what?"

"Plenty," Max said. "They think you must be hiding some major furycraft to have survived that lightning strike. And not many of them really understood the whole plan with the sawdust and furylamps. They just saw you wave your hand, and the whole southern half of the town went up. You fought your way clear of the attack that killed the whole prime cohort—and some of those veterans were near Knight-level metalcrafters themselves." Another Cane screamed in the river, more distantly. "I guarantee you that right now, rumors are going around that you've got furies in the river killing Canim."

"I didn't do any of that, Max," Tavi said. "They're believing a lie."

"Balls," Max said, his voice serious. "You've done those things, Tavi. Sometimes you had help. Some of them took a whole lot of work. None of it involved furycraft—but you've done them." Max tilted his head toward the town. "They know what's over there. Any sane man would be running for the hills. But instead, they're angry. Their blood is up for a fight. You've been right there beside them in the battle. Struck blows against the Canim running on pure guts, and you've bloodied their slimy noses. The men think you can do it again. They'll follow you, Calderon."

"You've seen that force, Max. You know what's still over there. And we're tired, out of room, and out of tricks."

"Heh," Max said. "That's how belief works. The worse the situation is, the more a man's belief can do to sustain him. You've given them something to believe in."

Tavi felt a little nauseous at the statement. "We have to take down the bridge, Max. We've got to get our engineers out to the top of the arch so that they can collapse it."

"I thought we didn't have enough bodies who could earthcraft," Max said.

"If you will remember," Tavi said, "the Pavilion has a

rather large number of employees who are quite practiced at earthcraft."

Max blinked. "But those are *dancers*, Calderon. Professional, ah, courtesans."

"Who have practiced earthcrafting every day of their professional lives," Tavi said. "I know, stonework isn't the same thing, but you've always told me that any application of one area of furycraft carries over toward different uses of the same gift."

"Well," Max said. "Yes, but . . ."

Tavi arched an eyebrow. "But?"

"Crafting a room full of *legionares* into a frenzy is one thing. Altering heavy stonework is another."

"I've had them practicing," Tavi said. "They aren't exactly engineers, but this isn't a complicated crafting. It's a demolition. All the engineers really need to get it done is earthcrafting muscle, and the dancers have got that. If we can get them and our engineers to the top of the bridge, they can take it apart."

"Big if," Max said quietly.

"Yes."

Max lowered his voice in realization. "Someone will have to hold the Canim back while they work. Whoever does that will either go into the river or be trapped on the southern half of the bridge, when it goes."

Tavi nodded. "I know. But there's no way around it. It's going to cost us to get it done, Max. We've got to hold through the night. If we can do that, we're still going to take heavy losses pushing the Canim back through our own defenses. Maybe enough to break us."

"Give the men some credit," Max said. "Like I told you. They believe. Especially the fish. They'll bloody well fight."

"Even if they do," Tavi said, "we might not be able to win through. It might not be possible."

"Only one way to know for sure."

"And if it is possible," Tavi said, "whoever holds the Canim off is going to die." He was quiet for a moment, then said, "I'll lead it. I'll ask for volunteers."

"It's suicide," Max said quietly.

Tavi nodded. Then he shivered again. "Any chance you could do something about this rain?"

Max squinted up. "It isn't crafted. I think a strong enough crafter could change some things. But to do that, you have to be up inside it, and with those things floating around . . ."

"Right," Tavi said. "Crows take this rain. Without it, they'd still be waiting for the town to burn down. Without it, we could build a massive fire on the bridge and let *it* hold them off until daylight."

Max grunted. "What I wouldn't give for twenty or thirty Knights Ignus right now, instead of all those Aeris. Thousands of Canim, all trapped on that narrow bridge. With a solid bunch of Knights Ignus, we could turn those dogs into kindling."

An idea hit Tavi, so hard that the bowl tumbled from his suddenly numb fingers and shattered on the stone of the bridge.

"Calderon?" Max asked.

Tavi held up a hand, thinking furiously, forcing his weary mind to quicken and consider the notion, the possibilities.

It could work.

By crows and thunder, it could *work*.

"He told me," Tavi heard himself say in amazement. "He bloody well *told* me exactly where to hit them."

"Who did?" Max asked.

"Nasaug," Tavi said. He felt a sudden, wide grin stretch across his mouth. "Max, I've got to speak to the men," he said. "I want you to get your brother and every Knight Aeris we have to meet me outside the town gates. They'll need time to practice."

Max blinked. "Practice what?"

Tavi glared up at the heavy storm clouds with their chilling rain and scarlet lightning, while Canim howls drifted toward him from the enemy positions on the Elinarch. "An old Romanic trick."

CHAPTER 47

"Are you sure this will work, Steadholder?" Giraldi asked quietly. The centurion had hauled the room's bed over to the side of the healing tub, and Isana now lay on it, her hand still bound to Fade's. His sword lay in its sheath along the length of her body.

Isana tightened the fingers of her other hand on the sword's hilt. "Yes."

"Furycrafting in your sleep," Giraldi said. He didn't sound happy. "Sounds dangerous."

"Fade was able to make contact with me when I was in a state of near sleep," she said. "If I am asleep, as he is, I might reach him again."

"He isn't taking a nap, Steadholder," Giraldi said. "He's dying."

"All the more reason to make the attempt."

"Even if you do it," Giraldi said, "is it going to make a difference now? Even if he decides he wants to live, there's only so much that it can do for him."

"You don't know him like I do," Isana replied quietly. "He has more will than any man I've ever known. Save one, perhaps."

"And if his will is to die?" Giraldi pressed. "I can't let that happen to you, Isana."

Isana felt her voice crackle with sudden fire. "Neither can he. He simply needs to be reminded of the fact." She turned to the centurion. "No interruptions."

Giraldi clenched his jaw and nodded once. "Luck."

Isana laid her head back down on the pillow and closed her eyes, all the while still focused upon the crafting. She held on to that focus as hard as she could. Her exhaustion made war upon her concentration, but only for a brief, dizzying moment. And then . . .

And then she was back at Calderon. Back twenty years. Back at that terrible night.

This time, though, the dream was not her own.

She saw her younger self, hurrying through the night, rounded with pregnancy, gasping with pain. Her little sister Alia walked beside her, holding one of Isana's arms to steady her as they stumbled along. Araris walked with them, first before, then beside, then behind, his eyes sharp and glittering and everywhere.

In the distance, flashes of light against the night sky painted the outline of trees and hills upon Isana's vision, darkly dazzling. From here, the roar of clashing armies sounded like the sea crashing upon the shore at high tide, back where the Crown Legion pitted itself against the Marat horde.

She followed the images of the dream, a silent and invisible witness to them, but the awareness of things she could not possibly know flowed through her thoughts. She was impressed that her younger self had maintained such a pace, and certain that it was not enough to have outpaced any barbarian trackers. Already, they had circled two enemy positions—a shock to Isana, who had known nothing of it at the time—and on one of his heartbeat-long forays out of sight of Isana and her sister, Araris had silently slain a Marat lying in ambush, never making mention of it.

Isana saw her younger self abruptly lose her balance and fall, crying out and clasping at her swollen belly. *"Crows,"* the younger Isana swore, breathless. "Bloody crows. I think the baby is coming."

Alia was at her side immediately, helping her up, and the younger woman traded an uncertain look with Araris.

Araris pressed forward. "Are you sure?"

Isana watched as another spasm wrenched her younger self, and she spewed a stream of profanity worthy of a veteran centurion. It took her a moment to catch her breath, then she gasped, "Reasonably so, yes."

Araris nodded once and looked around him. "Then we must

go to ground. There's a cave not far from here." He looked around him for a moment, clearly evaluating his choices.

The dream froze in place.

"This was my first mistake," said a voice from beside Isana. Fade stood there, ragged, scarred, dressed in rags, a figure utterly beaten down by hardship and time.

"Fade?" Isana asked quietly.

He shook his head, his eyes bitter. "I never should have left you there."

The dream resumed. Araris vanished into the night. He moved like a shadow through the woods, casting about for perhaps three or four minutes, until he found the dark outline of the cave's entrance. Then he spun and ran back toward Alia and Isana.

As he approached, he suddenly became aware of another Marat hunter, not ten feet from the two young women, unseen in the shadows. He moved at once, his hand darting to his belt, to the knife there, but it seemed to Isana to happen very slowly. The Marat arose from his hiding place, bow in hand, an obsidian-tipped arrow already upon the string. Isana realized, through Fade's recollection of the scene, that the Marat had seen Alia's golden hair, an incongruous bit of lighter shadow. He had aimed at her because he could more easily see her.

Fade threw the knife.

The Marat released the arrow.

Fade's knife buried itself to the hilt in the Marat's eye. The hunter pitched over, dead before his body struck the ground.

But the arrow he'd released struck Alia with a simple, heavy thump. The girl let out an explosive breath and fell to her hands and knees.

"Crows," Fade snarled, and closed the distance to them. He stood there for a moment, torn.

"I'm all right," Alia said. Her voice shook, but she rose, blood staining her dress, several inches below one arm. "Just a cut." She picked up a shard of a shattered wooden shaft, black crow feathers marking the Marat missile. "The arrow broke. It must have been flawed."

"Let me see," Araris said, and peered at the wound. He

cursed himself for not knowing more of the healing arts, but there was not a great deal of blood, not enough to threaten the girl with unconsciousness.

"Araris?" Isana asked, her voice tight with pain.

"She was lucky," he said shortly. "But we must get out of sight now, my lady."

"I'm not your lady," Isana responded, by reflex.

"She's hopeless," Alia sighed, her voice carrying a tone of forced good cheer. "Come on, then. Let's get out of sight."

Araris and Alia helped Isana to the cave. It took them far longer than Araris would have liked, but Isana could barely keep her feet. At last, though, they reached the cave, one of several such sites Septimus's scouts had prepared in the event that elements of the Legion might need a refuge from one of the violent local furystorms, or from the harsh winter squalls that came howling down out of the Sea of Ice.

Its entrance hidden by thick brush, the cave bent around a little S-shaped tunnel that would trap any light from giving away its location. Then it opened up into a small chamber, perhaps twice the size of the standard *legionare's* tent. A small fire pit lay ready, complete with fuel. A quiet little stream had been diverted to run through the back corner of the cave, murmuring down the rock wall to a small, shallow pool before continuing on its way beneath the stone.

Alia helped Isana to the ground beside the fire, and Araris lit it with a routine effort of minor furycraft. He spoke the furylamps to life as well, and they burned with a low, scarlet flame. "No bedrolls, I'm afraid," he said. He stripped out of his scarlet cloak and rolled it into a pillow, which he slipped beneath Isana's head.

The younger Isana's eyes were glazed with pain. Her back contorted with another contraction, and she clenched her teeth over an agonized scream.

Time went by as it does in dreams, infinitely slowly while passing in dizzying haste. Isana remembered little of that night herself, beyond the steady, endless cycles of pain and terror. She had no clear idea of how long she lay in that cave all those years ago, but except for a brief trip outside to obscure signs of their passing, Araris had watched over her for every moment of every hour. Alia sat with her, bathing her brow with a damp kerchief and giving her water between bouts of pain.

"Sir Knight," Alia said finally. "Something is wrong."

Araris ground his teeth and looked at her. "What is it?"

The true Isana drew in a sharp breath. She had no memory of the words. Her last memory of her sister was of seeing her through a haze of tears as Alia used the wet cloth to wipe tears and sweat from Isana's eyes.

"The baby," Alia said. The girl bit her lip. "I think it's turned wrong."

Araris stared helplessly at Isana. "What can we do?"

"She needs assistance. A midwife or a trained healer."

Araris shook his head. "There's not a steadholt in the whole of the Calderon Valley—not until the new Steadholders arrive next year."

"The Legion healers, then?"

Araris stared steadily at her. Then he said, "If any of them lived, they would have been here already."

Alia blinked at him in surprise, and her brow furrowed in confusion. "My lord?"

"Nothing but death would have kept my lord from your sister's side," Araris said quietly. "And if he died, it means that the Marat forces were overwhelming, and the Legion died with him."

Alia just stared at him, and her lower lip began to tremble. "B-but . . ."

"For now, the Marat control the valley," Araris said quietly. "Reinforcements from Riva and Alera Imperia will arrive, probably before the day is out. But for now, it would be suicide to leave this place. We have to stay until we're sure it's safe."

Another contraction hit the young Isana, and she gasped through it, biting down on a twisted length of leather cut from the *singulare's* belt, even though she was too weakened by the hours of labor to manage a very loud scream. Alia bit her lip, and Araris's eyes were haunted as he watched, unable to help.

"Then . . ." Alia straightened her shoulders and lifted her chin. It was a heartrending gesture for Isana to see now, a child's obvious effort to put steel into her own spine—and almost as obviously failing. "We're on our own then."

"Yes," Araris said quietly.

Alia nodded slowly. "Then . . . with your assistance, I think I can help her."

He lifted his eyebrows. "Watercrafting? Do you have that kind of skill?"

"Sir?" Alia said hesitantly. "Are we spoiled for choice?"

Araris's mouth twitched at one corner in a fleeting smile. "I suppose not. Have you ever served as a midwife before?"

"Twice," Alia said. She swallowed. "Um. With horses."

"Horses," Araris said.

Alia nodded, her eyes deep with shadows, worried. "Well. Father actually did it. But I helped him."

The younger Isana screamed again.

Araris nodded once the contraction had passed. "Get her other arm."

The ragged image of Fade, standing beside Isana, said, "This was the second mistake. Fool. I was such a fool."

Together, the pair dragged Isana into the shallow pool. Araris stripped out of his armor with hurried motions and knelt behind Isana, supporting her upper body against his chest while Alia knelt before her.

Isana stared at the entire thing, fascinated by Fade's memories. She remembered none of this. She had never been told of this.

Araris gave the young Isana his hands, and she squeezed them bloodless through each contraction. Alia knelt before her sister, hands framing her belly, her eyes closed in a frown of concentration. The scene acquired a timeless quality, somehow removed from everything else that was happening, existing in its own, private world.

Alia suddenly fell to her side in the pool, splashing water. Araris's gaze snapped up to her. "Are you all right?"

The girl trembled for a moment before closing her eyes and rising again. Her face had gone very pale. "Fine," she said. "Just cold."

"Fool," Fade mumbled from beside Isana. "Fool."

Isana's belly twisted in sudden, horrible understanding of what was coming.

An hour passed, Alia encouraging her sister, growing more unsteady and more pale, while Araris focused the whole of his concentration on supporting Isana.

In time, there was a tiny, choked little cry. Alia gently took a tiny form in her arms, and wrapped it in the cloak that lay nearby and ready. The baby continued to cry, a desperate, horribly lonely little sound.

Alia, moving very slowly, reached out and passed the baby to the young Isana. She saw a fine down of dark hair. The miserable little infant began to quiet as his dazed mother pressed her against him, and he blinked up at her with Septimus's grass green eyes.

"Hail, Octavian," Alia whispered.

Then she slid down to the ground, into the pool, suddenly motionless.

Araris saw it and panicked. With a cry, he drew Isana and the baby from the pool. Then he returned for Alia. She did not move. Did not breathe.

Fade tore her dress from the wound and there found an ugly sight. The broken end of an arrow pressed up from the wound like some obscene splinter, and Araris realized with a shock that several inches of arrow, tipped with the head of volcanic glass, had pierced her deeply.

Darkness fell.

"She lied," Fade said quietly to Isana. "She was more worried about you than she was herself. She didn't want to distract me from helping you and the baby."

Tears blurred her vision, and her heart felt a fresh stab of pain at witnessing Alia's death—and then a horrible, crushing mountain of guilt that her little sister had died to save *her* fell upon Isana's shoulders.

"I never should have left you both alone," Fade said. "Not even for a moment. I should have seen what was happening to her. And Tavi . . ." Fade swallowed. "He never found his furies. It had to have happened during the birthing. The cold maybe. Sometimes a difficult birth can damage the child, impair his mind. If I had only remembered my duty. Used my head. I betrayed him—and you, and Alia and Tavi."

"Why, Fade?" Isana whispered. "Why do you say that?"

"I can't," he whispered. "He was like a brother. It should never have happened. *Never*."

And then, suddenly, the scene shifted again. Isana and Fade stood back at the Legion camp, just before the attack. Septimus stood before them in his command tent, eyes hard and calculating. A steady stream of orders flowed from his lips, giving commands to his Tribunes as Araris helped him into his armor.

He finished, and the tent emptied as the camp stirred itself to battle. Araris finished the last lacing on the armor and banged hard on Septimus's armored shoulder, then seized the Princeps's helm from its stand and tossed it underhand to Septimus.

"I'll help ready the command position," Araris said. "See you there."

"Rari," Septimus said. "Wait."

Araris paused, frowning back at the Princeps.

"I need you to do something."

Araris smiled. "I'll see to it. We're sending the noncombatants out already."

"No," Septimus said. He put a hand on Araris's shoulder. "I need you to take her out of here yourself."

Araris stiffened. "What?"

"I want you to take Isana and her sister out."

"My place is beside you."

Septimus hesitated for a moment, and glanced to the east with haunted eyes. Then he said, "No. Not tonight it isn't."

Araris frowned. "Your Highness? Are you all right?"

Septimus shook himself like a dog shedding water, and the uncertainty vanished from his expression. "Yes. But I think I finally understand what's been happening since Seven Hills."

"What do you mean?" Araris asked.

Septimus shook his head and lifted his hand. "There's no time. I want you to take them to safety."

"Your Highness, I can assign a mounted unit to escort them out."

"No. It's got to be you."

"Crows, Septimus," Araris said. "Why?"

Septimus met his eyes directly, and said quietly, "Because I know you'll take care of her."

Araris's eyes widened, and his face went pale. He shook his head. "Sep, no. No, it isn't like that. I would *never* want that. Not for my lord. Not for my friend."

The Princeps's face suddenly lit in a smile, and he threw back his head in a belly laugh. "Crows. I know that, Rari, you fool. I know you wouldn't."

Araris ducked his head, frowning. "Still. I shouldn't. It isn't right."

Septimus thumped a fist down on Araris's shoulder. "Bah, man. I can't very well throw stones at anyone who falls in love with her. I did, after all." He glanced in the direction of the tent he shared with Isana. "She's something special."

"She is," Araris agreed quietly.

Septimus's face sobered. "It's got to be you."

"All right," Araris said.

"If something happens to me—"

"It won't," Araris said firmly.

"We can't know that," Septimus said. "No one ever can. It's got to be you. If something happens to me, I want her to be taken care of." He glanced back at Araris. "I can't stand the thought of her and the child being alone. Promise me, Araris."

Araris shook his head. "You're being ridiculous."

"Maybe," Septimus agreed. "I hope so. But promise me."

Araris frowned at the Princeps for a moment. Then he jerked his chin in a quick nod. "I'll watch over her."

Septimus clapped his arm gently, his tone warm. "Thank you."

The dream froze, locked into that image.

Fade, beside Isana, stared at the image of Septimus. "I failed him," he said. Tears rolled down his cheeks, over the burn scars. "I should have stood with him. But when push came to shove . . . all I wanted was to get you away from the battle. To make sure you were safe." He bowed his head. "I let my heart guide my head. I let it blind me to my duties. Blind me to possible dangers. Blind me to your sister's injuries. Blind me to what might happen to the baby."

He looked up at her, his eyes miserable. "I loved you, Isana. The wife of my best friend, my sword brother. I loved you. And I am ashamed."

Isana stared at Septimus's image for a long moment, though dream-tears blurred her dream-vision. "Fade . . ."

"I can't make amends for my mistakes," Fade said. "The blood won't ever be washed from my hands. Let me go. There's nothing left for me here."

Isana turned to face Fade and reached out to cup his face between her pale, slender hands. She could feel his anguished guilt, feel the pain, the self-recrimination, the bottomless well of regret.

"What happened," she said quietly, "was not of your making. It was horrible. I hate that it happened. But you didn't cause it to be so."

"Isana . . ." Fade whispered.

"You're only human," Isana said over him. "We make mistakes."

"But mine . . ." Araris shook his head. "I had a hand in this war, as well. Had Septimus lived, he would have been the greatest First Lord Alera has ever known. He'd have a strongly gifted heir. A gracious, compassionate wife at his side. And none of this would be happening."

"Perhaps," Isana said gently. "Perhaps not. But you can't hold the actions of thousands and thousands of other people against yourself. You've got to let it go."

"I can't."

"You can," Isana said. "It wasn't your fault."

"Tavi," Fade said.

"That isn't your fault either, Fade." Isana drew a breath. "It's mine."

Fade blinked at her for a moment. "What?"

"I did it to him," Isana said quietly. "When he was still a baby. Whenever I bathed him, I would think about what it would mean if he showed his father's talents. How it would draw attention to him. How it would mark him as Gaius's heir. As a target for the power-hungry maniacs of the Realm intent on seizing the throne. At first, I didn't realize what I was doing to him." She met his eyes steadily. "But when I did . . . I didn't stop, Fade. I pushed harder. I stunted his growth so that he would look younger than his age, so that it would seem to be impossible that he was Septimus's child. And in doing it, I stunted his mind, somehow. I prevented his talents from ever emerging, until the water furies around the steadholt were so used to it that I hardly needed to think about it at all.

"Unlike you," she said, "I knew precisely what I was doing. And so in that, I am as much to blame for this war as you are."

"No, Isana," Fade said.

"I *am*," Isana replied quietly. "Which is why I'm staying here. With you. When you go, I will go with you."

Fade's eyes widened. "No. Isana, no, please. Just leave me."

She took both her hands in his. "Never. I will not allow you to fade away, Araris. And by crows and thunder, your *duty* is not complete. You swore yourself to Septimus." She squeezed his hands, staring hard into his eyes. "He was your friend. You *promised* him."

Araris stared back at her, trembling and silent.

"I know how badly your soul has been wounded—but you can't surrender. You can't abandon your duty now, Araris. You do not have that right. I need you." She lifted her chin. "Octavian needs you. You *will* return to duty. Or you will make your treachery true by allowing yourself to die—and taking me with you."

He began to weep.

"Araris," Isana said in a low, compassionate voice. She touched his chin and lifted it until his eyes met her. Then, very gently, she said, "Choose."

Amara tried to smile at the little girl and held out her arms to her.

"Masha," Rook said quietly. "This is Countess Amara. She's going to take you out of here."

The little girl frowned and clung more tightly to Rook. "But I wanna leave with you this time."

Rook blinked her eyes rapidly for a few seconds, then said, "We are leaving this time, baby. I'll meet you outside."

"No," the little girl said, and clung tighter.

"But don't you want to go flying with Amara?"

The little girl looked up. "Flying?"

"I'll meet you on the roof."

"And then we leave and get ponies?" Masha asked.

Rook smiled and nodded. "Yes."

Masha beamed at her mother and didn't object as Rook lifted her to Amara's back. The little girl wrapped her legs around Amara's waist and her arms around Amara's throat. "All right, Masha," she said, tensing her throat muscles against the child's grip. "Hold on tight."

Rook turned to the great bed and tore off a quilted silk sheet large enough to serve as a pavilion. She hurried to one of the large wardrobes, flicked a corner of the sheet around one of its legs, and tied it with brisk, efficient motions. "Ready."

"Your Grace?" Amara asked. "Are you ready?"

Lady Placida looked up, her face blank and remote with concentration. She knelt on the floor facing the opposite wall, her hands folded calmly into her lap. At Amara's words, she shifted her stance into something resembling a sprinter's crouch, and said, "I am."

Amara's heart began to race, and she felt her legs trembling with incipient panic. She looked up at the four gargoyles on their perches, then walked across the room to stand beside Rook against one wall. She focused her eyes on the center of the ceiling, where she would be able to see any of the gargoyles when they began to move. "Very well," she said quietly. "Begin."

Lady Placida focused her defiant eyes on the opposite wall and growled, "Lithia!"

Nothing happened.

Lady Placida growled, raising a clenched fist, and cried, "Lithia!"

And at that, the floor of the chamber heaved and bucked, and the stone formed into the shape of a horse, head and shoulders rising from the ground as it rushed at the opposite wall.

Simultaneously, Amara called out to Cirrus. Locked in the stone room as they were, she was far from the open air the fury loved, and Cirrus responded to her call sluggishly, weakly. She had expected nothing more—for the moment— and simply drew upon the fury's native swiftness to quicken her own movements.

So when the four gargoyles simultaneously exploded into abrupt life, she saw the sudden reaction abruptly slow, as her own senses became distorted through her communion with her fury.

The gargoyles opened their eyes, revealing glittering green emeralds that glinted with their own faint light. Shaped into the rough form of lions, their heads were a monstrous mix of a man, a lion, and a bear. Sharp horns curled out from the sides of their broad heads, pointing directly forward from their eyes in deadly prongs, and their forefeet bore oversized talons like those of a bird of prey.

As Kalarus had warned Lady Placida, the gargoyles focused immediately upon the child.

Amara saw the gargoyle nearest her as it leapt from its perch, drifting down toward her like a falling leaf. She pushed off from the wall, dancing away from its pounce, and felt the floor shudder at the impact, then heard an enormous booming sound from somewhere behind her.

Masha wailed as her grip on Amara's neck began to slip.

As tightly as the little girl clung, Amara's speed of reaction had nearly pulled her clear of the child entirely. She seized one of Masha's arms with one hand, a leg with the other, and had to reverse her momentum as the second gargoyle slammed to the floor across the chamber and flung itself at her.

She only just evaded it, dived, and fell to the floor rolling as the third earth fury leapt at her and passed through the space her head had occupied an instant before. She came to her feet a beat more slowly than she should have. The child on her back had altered her center of gravity, forcing her to struggle to keep her movements balanced and fluid. She leapt up onto the bed, bounced once to cross it, and ripped down the bed's canopy, dropping the heavy drapes over the head of the fourth gargoyle as she leapt away from its pursuit.

But her opponents seemed to be moving more and more quickly, and pure terror rolled through Amara as she realized that Cirrus, enclosed in stone as he was, had begun to falter. She only had seconds.

Then Lady Placida cried out again, and Amara whipped her head around in time to see the High Lady's earth fury smash into the outer wall of the tower. Stone shattered and screamed its torment, and the earth fury ripped a hole the size of a *legionare's* shield in the hardened siege-stone of the citadel's outer wall.

Panic gave way to exaltation as Amara felt Cirrus abruptly strengthen again, and she bounded forward, planted a sandaled foot on the head of one of the lunging gargoyles, and leapt for the opening. She flung herself through it just as Lady Placida seized her heavy chain in one hand, and pulled it from the wall with a single contemptuous jerk, taking a block of stone the size of a man's head with it.

Amara fell.

Masha screamed again as they plummeted, and Amara called desperately to Cirrus. It was a race against gravity. Though the fury could support her and Masha without difficulty, it took precious time to establish a windstream, and the fall from the tower was not a long one.

Unless, of course, she should fail to arrest their descent, in which case it would be more than long enough.

The wind suddenly howled around her, eerily like the defiant scream of a warhorse, and the cloudy, nebulous equine shape became visible around her as Cirrus turned the fall into a forward-rushing glide no more than two feet above the ground. Amara altered course, using her momentum to slingshot herself into a vertical climb.

As she did, the little girl's scream of terror became one of excitement and exhilaration, which Amara could hardly fault her for feeling. But she also knew that it was a near certainty that Kalarus's citadel was protected by a miniature legion of wind furies whose only purpose would be to interfere with the flight of unwelcome windcrafters. Cirrus could probably bull through them, at least for the moment, but Amara knew that it was only a matter of time before she would be driven from the air.

She turned anxious eyes up at the tower, and saw Rook come sliding feetfirst out of the hole in the wall. She shot off the edge. For a second, Amara thought she would fall. Instead, the former bloodcrow held a double handful of the silk sheets she'd tied to the wardrobe. Rook turned as she fell and swung toward the wall, absorbing the shock with her feet and legs with the skill of an experienced mountain climber.

Now that Rook was out of the chamber, Lady Placida was free to deal with the gargoyles without harming her allies. Horrible crashing sounds and billows of dust came from Kalarus's upper chamber. More alarm bells began to ring. Amara heard screams from within the tower, terrible, terrible sounds of men and women in mortal agony, and she realized with horror that the tower must have held many more gargoyles than the four in the bedchamber. She heard someone blowing a signal horn, the notes crisply precise—the Immortals, she supposed, immediately reacting to the alarm and organizing their efforts.

Amara shot back up to the chamber, hovering at a distance she hoped was out of the leaping distance of any of the gargoyles. "Lady Placida!"

Ten feet down the wall from the first hole, the stone ex-

ploded outward again, this time creating a much larger opening, and one of the gargoyles flew out with the debris. It fell,
thrashing wildly, all the way down to the ground below, where
it shattered into shards and pebbles.

Amara jerked her head back up again just in time to see
one of the gargoyles leap to the first opening in the wall, green
eyes glinting, and crouch to fling itself at Masha.

Amara bobbed to one side in an effort to evade the gargoyle's pounce—but before the fury could attack, an enormous block of stone attached to a heavy chain slammed into
its posterior, flinging it out of the tower to fall to the stones
and share the fate of its companion.

Lady Placida appeared in the opening, the chain still attached to her collar. She held it about two feet above the section of stone attached to its end, as if it were a flail. She gave
Amara a curt nod, set the heavy stone down, and snapped the
chain with all the effort a seamstress might use to snap thread.
"Done! Get to the roof!"

"See you there!" Amara shouted. She soared upward while
Lady Placida drew Rook back up into the bedchamber. Amara
heard another crash a moment later, presumably the sound of
the bedchamber's locked door being smashed down, and she
landed on the roof of the citadel, eyes searching for the presence of any further gargoyles or guards, but the roof was devoid of them—at least for the moment.

The tower's roof was quite plain, its surface broken only by
two distinct features. The first was a square opening in the
floor in its center, where stairs led down into the tower. Amara
heard steel ringing on steel inside the opening.

Not far from the stairway down was Kalarus's aviary—a
simple dome of steel bars perhaps five feet across and only
waist high to Amara. Inside it was a young woman who could
not have been more than fifteen or sixteen years old. Like
Lady Placida, she wore nothing more than a white muslin un-
derdress, and her dark hair was straight and listless in the heat
and humidity atop the tower. There were blankets strewn
about on one side of the cage, the subject of the letter she and
Rook had found, no doubt.

The girl crouched in the center of the cage, eyes wide—and Amara was somewhat startled by her resemblance to Gaius Caria, the First Lord's second, quasi-estranged wife; though this child did not have the sense of bitter petulance to her features that Amara had generally seen in Caria's. The girl stared at her with a mixed expression of despair, worry, and confusion.

"Atticus Minora?" Amara asked quietly.

"Call me E-Elania," the girl said. "W-who are you?"

"Amara ex Cursori," Amara said, simultaneously holding a finger to her lips, urging the girl to silence. "I'm here to take you from this place."

"Thank the furies," the girl breathed, keeping her voice down. "Lady Placida is inside. I don't know where."

"I know," Amara said.

The clash of steel nearby was suddenly drowned out by an enormous hissing sound, and Amara turned her head to see the head and shoulders of an armored Immortal emerge from the hole in the floor, still facing down the stairs. But before he could emerge fully, there was another chorus of hissing sounds, and what Amara could only describe as white-hot raindrops shot up from the tower's interior in a cloud that pierced the doomed Immortal soldier wherever they struck his armored body, streaking through him as easily as needles piercing cloth, leaving small, glowing holes in the steel of his armor. The man staggered, but grimly kept his feet, thrusting his blade down at someone below him.

A woman's voice rang out in an imperious tone, then a second swarm of streaking firedrops flashed through the doomed Immortal. This time, the attack left half a dozen red-hot holes in his helmet, and the man fell.

"Hurry!" called Lady Aquitaine's voice. Aldrick emerged from the stairway first, hard-eyed gaze sweeping the tower's roof. His eyes widened a bit at the sight of Amara, and the Cursor found herself unconsciously tugging down the hem of her tunic.

"Move!" insisted Lady Aquitaine. "Kalarus is about to—"

Then Amara heard a man speak in an impossibly loud,

roaring voice that literally shook the stones of the tower beneath her feet.

"No man makes a fool of me in my own house!" boomed the fury-enhanced voice.

Then a woman's voice answered, every bit as loud, nowhere near so melodramatic, and drily amused. "While the rest of us hardly need *try*. Tell me, Brencis," Lady Placida taunted. "Do you still have that little problem bedding women, the way you did in the Academy?"

Kalarus's answer was a roar of pure rage that shook the tower, raising dust in a choking cloud.

"Move, move!" Lady Aquitaine shouted from below, then Odiana appeared, shoving frantically at Aldrick's back. The big swordsman stumbled onto the roof, while Odiana and Lady Aquitaine hurried frantically up the stairs, diving to either side of the opening.

Less than a second later, a titanic roar shook the tower again, and a column of white-hot fire exploded from the tower below, roaring up from the stones and rising for hundreds of feet into the sky above Kalare. The air turned hot and dry in an instant, and Amara had to throw her arms across her face to shield her eyes from the blinding light of the flame Kalarus had crafted into being.

The fire passed swiftly, though the bloom of heat from so much flame had parched the air and left several of the bars in the domed cage glowing with sullen fire. Amara looked up at Odiana, Aldrick, and Lady Aquitaine. "Bernard?" she cried, hearing her own voice shaking with panic. "Where is he? Bernard?"

"No time!" Odiana spat.

Lady Aquitaine pointed at the cage. "Aldrick."

The big swordsman crossed to the cage, set his feet, and swung his blade in three swift strokes. Sparks rose from the steel bars, and Aldrick stepped back. A beat later, a dozen sections of iron bar fell to the stones with a metallic clatter, their ends glowing with the heat of parting, leaving an entire triangular section of the dome-shaped cage missing.

Aldrick extended his hand politely to Atticus Elania, and said, "This way, lady, if you please."

Lady Aquitaine gave the girl a narrow look, then turned to Odiana, and said, voice sharp, "Fire crystals."

Odiana's hand dipped into the low neckline of her slave's tunic and she tore at the lining, one hand cupped. She caught something as it tumbled from the neckline and passed it to Lady Aquitaine—three small crystals, two scarlet and one black, glittered in the palm of her hand. "Here, Your Grace," Odiana said. "They are ready."

Lady Aquitaine snatched them from Odiana's hand, muttered something under her breath, and cast them down onto the far side of the tower's roof, where they promptly began to billow with smoke—two plumes of brilliant scarlet and one of deepest black, the colors of Aquitaine.

"Wh-what's happening?" Elania asked, her voice shaking.

"The smoke is a signal," Aldrick told the girl, his tone briskly polite. "Our coach should be here in a moment."

"Lady Aquitaine!" Amara snapped. After pausing a deliberate beat, the High Lady turned to Amara, one eyebrow raised. "Yes, Countess?"

"Where is Bernard?"

Lady Aquitaine gave an elegant shrug. "I've no idea, dear. Aldrick?"

"He was holding the stairs below us," Aldrick said, his tone short. "I didn't see what happened to him."

"He couldn't possibly have survived that firestorm," Lady Aquitaine said, her voice practical and dismissive.

The words drew a spike of anger such as Amara had never felt before, and she found herself standing with her hands balled into fists, her jaws clenched while tiny spangles of light danced in her vision. Her first instinct was to hurl herself bodily at Lady Aquitaine, but at the last instant, she remembered the child still clinging to her back, and she forced herself to stand in place. Amara took a second to control her voice, so that it would not come out as an incoherent snarl. "You don't *know* that."

"You saw it," Lady Aquitaine said. "You were there, just as I was."

"My lady," Odiana said, her voice hesitant, even cringing.

"Here they come," Aldrick called, and Amara looked up to see their Knights Aeris arrowing swiftly for the top of the tower, bearing the coach between them.

Lady Aquitaine glared back at Amara. Then she closed her eyes for a moment, lips pressed together, shook her head tightly, and said, "It doesn't matter at this point, Countess. With the alarm raised, we must leave immediately if we are to leave at all." She glanced at Amara, and added, in a quieter tone, "I'm sorry, Countess. Anyone left behind is on his own."

"It's so nice to feel cared for," called Lady Placida. She padded up the stairs, still holding her chain and stone in one hand. Her white muslin undergown showed half a dozen rips and any number of scorch marks. Her right hand was raised, bent at the elbow and wrist, and a small falcon of pure fire rested upon her wrist like a tiny, winged sun.

"Given how fashionably late you generally are, Invidia," she said, "I would expect you to have more tolerance for others."

She hurried onto the roof, turning immediately to offer a hand down to Rook. The young spy looked disoriented, her balance unsteady, and if Lady Placida hadn't been helping her when her balance wavered, Rook would have fallen.

Amara felt her heart stop for a single, terrible, seemingly eternal moment, then Bernard came up behind Rook, his bow in hand, his face pale and nauseated. He had one hand on the small of the spy's back and was pushing her up more or less by main strength. Relief flooded through her, and she clasped her hands tightly together and bowed her head until she could blink sudden tears from her eyes. "What happened?"

"Kalarus tried to burn us out," Bernard said, his voice hoarse. "Lady Placida countered him. Sheltered us from the flame, then sealed the stairway in stone."

"He meant to say, 'Lady Placida and I' sealed the stairway in stone," Lady Placida said firmly. "Though your friend there was struck on the head by some debris. I've exhausted myself, and it won't take Kalarus long to open a passage through the stone we put in his way. Best we hurry."

No sooner had she spoken than the wind rose to the familiar roar of a shared windstream, and Lady Aquitaine's mercenary Knights Aeris swept down and landed heavily, clumsily on the roof, the coach slamming down onto the stone.

Amara reached out to Cirrus, preparing to raise a windstream of her own, and found that her connection to the fury had grown fainter, more tenuous. She swore and shouted, "Hurry! I think Kalarus has his wind furies interfering with ours to prevent our escape!"

"Just be thankful that doing it is keeping him downstairs," Lady Aquitaine said. "I'll try to counter him until we can get farther away. Into the coach!" She flung herself inside, followed by Odiana, Aldrick, and Atticus Elania.

While Bernard covered the doorway with his bow, Amara shrugged the bewildered child from her shoulders and into Lady Placida's arms. She helped the dazed Rook into the coach, which was rapidly growing quite crowded. Then another tremble in the stone beneath her feet made her look up and around in time to see two gargoyles, much like those Lady Placida had dispatched, as they clawed their way up the outside of the tower, talons sinking into stone as if it was mud, and over its battlements.

"Bernard!" Amara screamed, pointing.

Her husband spun, drawing the bowstring to his cheek as he did, and let an arrow fly at the nearest gargoyle out of sheer reflex.

Amara thought the shot would be utterly ineffective, given that the gargoyles were made of stone and that the wind the Knights Aeris were summoning would have made such things impossible for all but the best of archers.

But Bernard *was* one of the best, and Amara had reckoned without the deadly combination of an earthcrafter's superhuman strength working together with the sheer, deadly expertise of a woodcrafting archer. Bernard was fully powerful and skilled enough to have qualified as a Knight Terra or Flora in any Legion in the Realm, and his war bow was one of the weapons borne by the hunters and holders of Alera's northernmost reaches—a weapon designed to put down predators that outweighed the holders by hundreds of pounds and powerful enough to punch through breastplates of Aleran steel.

Too, Bernard was using a heavy, stiletto-headed arrow, one designed for piercing armor, and the experienced earthcrafter knew stone as few other Alerans could ever understand it.

All of which combined to mean that, as a rule, when the Count of Calderon released an arrow at the target, he expected it to go down. The fact that his target was living stone rather than soft flesh was only a minor detail—and certainly did not qualify as an exception to the rule.

Bernard's first arrow struck the nearest gargoyle just to the left of the center of its chest. There was an enormous cracking sound, a shower of white sparks, and a network of fine cracks spread over the gargoyle's stone chest. It leapt from the battlements to the tower's roof—and fell into half a dozen still-thrashing pieces upon impact.

Before the first gargoyle fell, Bernard had drawn again, and his second arrow shattered the left forelimb of the second gargoyle, sending it into a sprawl on its side. Another arrow cracked into the gargoyle's head as it tried to rise a beat later, and the impact sheared off a quarter of the gargoyle's misshapen head, knocking it down again and evidently disorienting it as it tried to scramble upright again with futile energy.

Bernard leapt for the coach just as the windcrafters began to lift off. He caught the running board along its side with one hand, slung his bow over his neck, and used both hands to struggle to pull himself up as the coach rose away from Kalare, steadily gathering speed.

Amara called to Cirrus and found the fury more responsive, if still more sluggish than normal, presumably thanks to Lady Aquitaine countercrafting against Kalarus's wind furies. She soared up to the coach, landed with her feet on the running board, twined her left arm through the coach window, and reached down to Bernard with her right.

Her husband looked up, glanced at all the leg she was showing in her scarlet slave tunic, and leered cheerfully at her as he grasped her hand. She found herself both laughing and blushing—again—as she helped him up to the running board, then into the coach.

"Are you all right?" he shouted to her.

"No!" she called back. "You scared me to death!"

He burst out into a rolling laugh, and Amara stepped off the coach's running board and into Cirrus's embrace, stabilizing herself before darting ahead of the coach and slightly above. She looked back over her shoulder, cursing that she hadn't been able to braid her hair for the disguise, and hadn't thought to bring along something to tie it back with. Now it whipped around her face wildly, in her eyes whenever it wasn't in her mouth, and it took her a moment to get enough of it out of the way to see behind them.

She almost wished she hadn't done it.

The gleaming figures of Knights Aeris were rising from Kalare. Rook had warned them of the twenty or so who had remained in the city's garrison. Amara looked at the four mercenary Knights Aeris struggling to keep the overloaded coach in the air. They did not have the speed to evade a pursuit, and the terrain below them offered them few opportunities to play hide-and-seek with Kalarus's forces. Without being able to rise to the higher winds, they could not use the clouds as cover, the other favored tactic for evading airborne pursuit, and the only one their slower group might have successfully employed.

Which meant, Amara thought, that they would have to fight.

It was not a ridiculous prospect for them to fend off a score of enemy Knights or so—not with Amara and no less than two High Ladies of Alera there.

But as Amara watched, more Knights Aeris rose from the city. Twenty more. Forty. Sixty. And still more.

With a sinking heart, Amara realized that when Kalarus returned to his citadel, he must have come by air—and that he must have brought his personal escorts, the most capable and experienced of his Knights Aeris.

Against twenty Knights, they would have had a chance. But against five times that number—and, she felt certain, Kalarus himself . . .

Impossible.

Her throat went dry as she signaled the coach's bearers that they were being pursued.

CHAPTER 49

Amara thought furiously, struggling to find alternative courses of action. She forced herself to look at the situation in dispassionate, emotionless terms. No foe was invincible, no situation utterly insoluble. There had to be something they could do to at least improve their chances, and that meant that she needed to make some kind of assessment of their foe's capabilities and resources.

And at once, she saw that things might not be entirely hopeless.

True, there were scores of Knights Aeris on the way, but only twenty had been in Kalare on their regular post. The rest had returned to Kalare with their master—and *that* meant that they'd already been traveling, probably since before first light, which meant that they might not have the endurance for a protracted chase—particularly if they were forced to pursue through the energy-sapping lower winds.

And then another thought came to her. There had been no slowly approaching roar of such a large group of fliers coming in at low altitude. They'd clearly heard Lady Aquitaine's Knights approaching minutes before they'd reached the tower. They should have heard a group with twenty times as many windcrafters coming for three or four times as long as that, before they'd actually entered the citadel. Which meant . . .

In fact, now that she thought about it, it could hardly have been anything else. Kalarus had most certainly not spent the previous ten or eleven days flying along the nape of the earth as Amara's party had. His presence would have been absolutely necessary with one or more of his Legions—he could not simply throw away days and days in travel. While he might be sadistic, ruthless, and inhumanly ambitious, he was not stupid.

Which meant that Kalarus and his Knights had come through the upper air in a far more conventional approach, after either half a day or a day and a half of travel. The former would give him time to fly from Ceres back to Kalare—the latter would be about right for him to be returning from the forces put in place to stymie Lord Parcia's Legions.

And if Kalarus could carry groups through the upper air when the rest of the Realm was grounded by the Canim's unnatural cloud cover, it would give him an enormous advantage in the campaign.

It also meant, she realized with a cold ripple of nausea, that if he had overcome the Canim's interdiction of the upper air when even Gaius could not, it was because Kalarus was meant to be able to do so. It meant coordination with the most bitter foe of the whole Realm.

Kalarus had made a bargain with the Canim.

The fool. Could he possibly have found a better way to declare to Alera's enemies that she was vulnerable to attack? Or a way more certain to alienate him from any of Alera's Citizenry who might otherwise remain neutral?

Not that their lack of neutrality would be of any use to Amara. She and the rest of her company would be long-dead by then if Kalarus truly could use the upper air while their party was reduced to low-level flight.

But flight at the upper levels would be both totally concealed and totally blind. Kalarus could no more easily see through the clouds than anyone else. Though he might be able to travel farther, faster, leaping ahead of them if they pulled away, all they would have to do to confound such a leapfrog pursuit would be to alter their course.

A sprint, then, was their best option—a straight bid to outpace the pursuing Knights Aeris, who were bound to be weary after their travel. That should at the very least thin out the numbers of their pursuers. And it was not impossible that the High Ladies might, between them, make it more difficult for their pursuers to continue the chase. Ladies Placida and Aquitaine were already weary from their efforts, true—but then, so was Kalarus.

Amara nodded once, decided. She idly noted that bare seconds had passed since she'd first spotted the pursuit, but she felt sure her reasoning was sound. They might even have a real chance of escape.

She sideslipped into view of the coach's bearers and signaled for them to flee at their best speed. The flight leader signaled in the affirmative, and the winds rose as he passed signals to his men, and they gathered their furies and ran for it. Amara nodded once at them, and darted down to fly beside the coach's window.

"We're under pursuit!" she called. "Kalarus and four- to fivescore Knights Aeris. But his escort has to be tired if they flew in today. We're going to try to outpace them."

"The coach is overloaded!" Aldrick shouted back. "The men can't hold a hard pace for long!"

"Your Graces," Amara called to Ladies Placida and Aquitaine. "I hope you might be able to help our fliers or discourage our pursuers somewhat? If we're able to outrun them, we might not have to fight."

Lady Aquitaine gave Amara a cool little smile. Then she glanced at Lady Placida, and said, "I think I'm more of a mind to discourage Kalarus and company."

"As you wish," Lady Placida said, with a bleak nod, supporting the wilting form of Rook. Then she leaned across the coach and offered Amara the hilt of the longer blade she'd carried with her from Kalarus's tower chamber. "In case you're of a similar mind to Lady Aquitaine, Countess."

Amara took the sword with a nod of thanks and traded a look with Bernard. Then she flicked over to the other side of the coach, long enough to lean her face in the window and press her mouth to his.

"My turn," she breathed.

"Careful," he said, voice rough.

She kissed him again, hard, then called to Cirrus and rose above the coach, sword in hand.

What followed was little different than any other day of flying—except for the small details. The wind sang and shrieked all around them. The landscape rolled by, hundreds of feet below, so slowly that one would be led to believe that they hardly moved at all.

Little things gave the lie to the routine appearance. The coach swayed and shimmied as the bearers took advantage of the flowing winds, cutting to one side or another, jockeying up or down by several feet, eking every extra bit of speed they could from their efforts. Amara felt the winds shifting around her, sometimes easing Cirrus's labor, sometimes making it fractionally more difficult, as wills and talents greater than her own contended for the sky. Lady Placida's skill certainly gave them more speed with less effort than they would have otherwise had, but Amara felt sure that Kalarus's furies struggled against them—and so close to the heart of his domain, he would have an enormous advantage against strangers to it.

Lady Aquitaine's power was a sullen whisper that fled swiftly past Amara and the other Knights Aeris, interfering with the windstreams of the pursuing Knights, degrading their efforts, forcing them to work harder to maintain the pace. Within moments, Amara saw the first overwearied Knight suddenly descend, exhausted past the ability to continue pursuit. Others fell by the wayside as the miles rolled by, but not swiftly, and not in the numbers Amara had hoped for.

Worst of all was one last small, simple detail.

Kalarus and his Knights were slowly, surely closing the distance.

The coach's bearers saw it as well, but there was little they could do about it, regardless of how unnerving it was to watch happen. Amara drove them relentlessly, repeatedly answering their frantic signals with orders to continue on their course with all possible speed, and over the course of the next hour she was rewarded for it with the sight of another twenty-six enemy Knights dropping out of the pursuit.

Some instinct warned her to keep an eye on the skies above them, and as the enemy Knights closed to within perhaps fifty yards, she saw a stirring in the heavy grey clouds above them, strands of mist drawn down into swirling spirals, pulled out of place as if by the passage of more Knights Aeris, though none were visible.

She realized what she was seeing at the last second, and screamed a frantic signal to the bearers. Only those on the left side of the coach saw her, but they realized what her panicked gestures meant, and they twisted in their harnesses, throwing the whole power of their furies in against the coach. Their efforts pushed the coach sharply to one side, and the loss of lift sent them into a steep and sudden descent, as the men on the far side of the coach struggled to prevent the coach from sliding into a deadly spin.

Amara rolled to the other side only a second before she saw through the wavering form of a rapidly approaching veil, and saw five figures flying in a classic V-shaped attack formation dive down between her and the evading coach. She saw the gleaming collars on the throats of the Knights Aeris—*more of those crowbegotten Immortal madmen,* she thought—then she met gazes with High Lord Kalarus himself. His already-thin features were stretched to vulpine proportions by strain, desperate ambition, and rage, and his eyes burned with pure hatred as he swept past, his diving attack foiled by Amara's warning.

But though Kalarus's attack had been hidden by the veil he'd crafted over it until almost too late, it had succeeded in one sense. The coach had been slowed, and the swiftest Knights Aeris behind the coach swept down on it, swords gleaming.

Amara sliced through the air down to the Knights Aeris, and shouted, "Lower! As close to the ground as you can!" The frantically weary men responded at once, the dive giving them enough speed to stay ahead of their attackers for a few more moments, while Amara maneuvered, rolling out widely to one side—then abruptly reversing the motion with every ounce of speed Cirrus could bring her, slicing into the wake of those Knights nearest the coach, who in their excited rush had drawn just a bit too far ahead of their comrades.

Amara didn't even attempt to use her sword. Instead, she ground her teeth and angled her arms, wrists turned in such a way to set her spinning in a tight, corkscrewing circle. Then she cried out to Cirrus and poured on the speed, rushing up on the wearied Knight's backs.

Amara's windstream, by the time she blew past them, was

a swirling vortex set on its side to their plane of movement, and scattered the half dozen Knights Aeris like dry leaves before an autumn gale. The tactic was hardly an original one, and every Knight Aeris had gone through a great deal of training that would enable him to recover from a windstream suddenly disrupted in such a fashion. However, that training had never been intended to counter the tactic while flying only ten or fifteen feet above the treetops, while High Lords and Ladies battled for influence of the broader winds, at the ends of exhausting chases that had already whittled their numbers down to less than half of their original company.

The near-exhausted Knights Aeris would have recovered and flown on within a handful of seconds.

But Amara had not left them that much time.

Men tumbled wildly out of her wake. She heard a sickly-sharp crunching sound as one of them slammed bodily into the solid trunk of a particularly tall oak. Of the other five, four of them dropped down into the branches, and even the fragile uppermost parts of the trees spun and tumbled them, given how swiftly they were flying when they struck. If they avoided solid impacts with the central trunks of the trees, they might survive the fall, so long as they were very, very lucky.

The last of the Knights Aeris, like Amara, found himself thrown a bit higher by the collision of wildly contradicting windstreams—but he was still slower to recover his equilibrium than the Cursor. By the time he had, Amara streaked across his flight path again, blade striking down at his back. The blade was a fine one, and links of shattered mail flew up from the blow. The wound she inflicted wasn't deep—but the shock and pain were enough to distract the Knight, and he joined his companions in vanishing through the branches of the waiting forest and disappearing from sight.

Her eyes lingered on the spot in the trees where the men had gone down, just for a moment. She couldn't feel it now, remorse and nausea and a hypocritical empathy for the men she'd maimed and killed. She refused to. But she'd just murdered six men. Granted, it was in service to the Realm and in self-defense—but it hadn't even been a fight. As tired as they'd been, they could not possibly have survived the vortex a fury as powerful as Cirrus had thrown into them, except by accident, as the last man had. Even he had never seen her sword coming. It was one thing to kill an enemy in battle, but it hadn't been one. Not really. It was an execution.

It was frightening. Frightening that she could make herself do such a thing, and even more frightening because she knew that if she made a similar mistake, she could be killed just as easily. There was at least one windcrafter among their enemies who could swat her from the skies just as ably as she had the wearied Knights. She was every bit as vulnerable, as mortal, as they were—more so, in fact, given that all she wore was the ridiculously brief red silk tunic. Should she tumble into the trees, at her rate of speed, totally unarmored, she would be crushed and slashed to ribbons all at the same time.

Crows, as it was, thanks to her costume, she was going to be windburned and chapped in places human beings rarely suffered such things. Assuming she managed to survive at all.

Amara jerked her eyes from the trees and pulled her thoughts back into focus, back to her duty. She looked up to find that the coach had managed to draw a bit away from her, and checking around her revealed that a dozen vengeful brothers of the Knights she had downed were closing on her, using the speed gained from their own dive to bring her within reach of their charge.

Amara waited until they were nearly on top of her, banked to one side, then shot upward with all the speed she could muster, hoping to draw them all into a climb—in their condition, the effort might prove too taxing for them to sustain and take them from the chase entirely.

It didn't work out the way Amara had hoped it would. These knights were flying in tight, triangular wings of three men each—a formation that was difficult to maintain without long practice in cooperative flying effort. While the lead man would find it no easier to fly, those on his flanks had a much steadier and more easily maintained windstream. The net result was a formation that let two men effectively rest while the third did the lion's share of the work, cycling through with each of the three taking turns in the lead. It was excellent for long-distance flight, and a sign that these men knew their trade.

The faster Knights she'd cast from the sky must have been younger, less experienced, probably some of the Knights who had been left behind in Kalare when Lord Kalarus began his campaign. These men, though, were clearly veterans. One wing followed her with patient caution, close enough to make her work to stay ahead of them, but clearly not attempting to overrun her. Another wing began a slow, shallow climb, while the others swept out to her flanks and shot ahead.

She was in trouble, and she knew it. The enemy Knights Aeris were employing the patient, ruthless tactics of a wolf pack. The slowly climbing wing would eventually rise to whatever altitude she did, though without spending nearly so much effort. The nearest group would stay on her heels and force her to keep maneuvering, taxing her own endurance while the enemy switched out with relatively rested Knights always ready to step into the lead. The two wings on the flanks would keep her boxed in, until either she faltered and was taken down by the immediate pursuers, or until the higher-flying wing could be in a position to dive and overtake her, probably in order to fling salt at Cirrus and send her tumbling to her death far below.

She had drawn off a considerable portion of the remaining Knights Aeris, at least. But while they were running her down, Kalarus and his Immortals would assault the coach.

And Bernard.

Amara ground her teeth, struggling to think of what else she could do. Scarlet lightning rolled through the clouds overhead, and the thunder that followed shook against her stomach and chest and pressed painfully on her ears. Amara suddenly stared up at the clouds.

"Oh," she told herself out loud. "That is an awful idea." She took a deep breath. "Though I suppose I'm not wildly spoiled for choice."

She decided, nodding firmly.

Then she called to Cirrus again and shot up into the rumbling thunder and blood-colored lightning of the Canim storm clouds.

CHAPTER 50

Amara plunged into the fine mist and found it shockingly cold. She had flown through cloud cover before, of course, but never while wearing so little. The lands below were as uncomfortably sultry as anywhere in the Realm, this time of the year, but the sun seemed to have denied the unnatural clouds its warmth, somehow bypassing them to reach the land below. She could see no more than a few dozen yards in the mist, and at the speed she was flying she might as well have been blind.

Which did not bode well considering what dwelt in the sorcerous clouds.

Amara began to tremble, and she did not bother trying to tell herself it was because of the change in temperature.

It was eerily quiet for a time, with only the constant rush of wind to drown out her swift, panting breaths. And then she heard high-pitched, thready sounds, something like the howl of one of the small desert wolves of the dry mountains east of Parcia. The cries were immediately echoed from every direction, and though Amara could not see the creatures that voiced them, they grew swiftly louder and nearer.

She saw a flicker of motion in the corner of her eye and instantly changed course, banking into a slewing turn that sent the mist to swirling. Something tangible brushed against her hip, and she felt a sudden, sharp burn like the sting of red ants. Then she began to emerge from the mist, to find all four wings of Knights Aeris who pursued her cruising along the underside of the clouds, strung out in a search line—and coming straight at her.

Once more, Amara poured on the speed, even as the mist behind her suddenly exploded with howls and motion. The tentacle-waving horrors the Canim had placed in the mist rushed after her. The Knights Aeris saw them coming and struggled to evade the nightmarish mass—but again, Amara had timed things too well, and there was nothing they could do as they plunged into a forest of burning, writhing vines.

Men screamed, and died, and suddenly there was no one pursuing her.

Her heart pounded with terror and exaltation that she had survived—and at the same time, she fought down a nauseating shame and loathing of the death and pain she'd been responsible for. Some of the Knights might fight through the creatures, but none who did would be in any condition to pursue the coach. They were, if not dead, certainly out of the chase.

Amara dived and swept back toward the still-fleeing coach with all the speed she could muster, and found it under attack.

More Knights Aeris must have dropped out of the race, and perhaps a dozen of them had closed the distance and reached the coach. Flying above and ahead of the coach was a five-man wing—Lord Kalarus and his Immortals. Amara could not see why they hadn't attacked and downed the coach already. They appeared to be waiting for an opening of some kind.

Half a dozen Knights swept in on either side of the coach, below the level of its occupants, to strike at the bearers. Someone must have shouted a warning, because the coach abruptly dropped perhaps six feet and veered to one side, almost directly into the attackers on that flank.

The Knights Aeris dived in to thrust spears through the coach windows, but the coach's door suddenly flew open, and Aldrick ex Gladius appeared in the door, legs bent, one hand hanging on to something inside the coach, his long blade in the other. A pair of swift cuts shattered two spears, inflicted a wound on one Knight's thigh that erupted in a deadly fountain of blood, and opened a long slash on a second Knight's scalp, so that blood flew into his face and eyes and fanned out into a mist behind him.

Lady Aquitaine slipped up beneath Aldrick's arm and raised a hand in an imperious gesture. Wisps of white cloud gathered at her fingertips roiling like a miniature thunderstorm, then she hurled it out and away from her, where it expanded into an enormous bank of nearly opaque mist. From her position above and behind them, Amara saw the coach juke to one side and the other again, and the attacking Knights Aeris had to break off, blinded and unable to support one another—not to mention the fact that if they made a mistake or simply got unlucky, they might be slammed by the full weight of the dodging coach, an event likely to prove gruesomely fatal so close to the treetops below.

Then that explained it. Kalarus knew Lady Aquitaine was there, and employing only minor uses of watercrafting, saving her strength for when he, personally, assaulted the coach. Kalarus was hardly a courageous soul, spending his Knights' lives in an effort to tire—or if they were lucky, perhaps even wound or kill—Lady Aquitaine. But the tactic would give him the maximum advantage he could possibly attain in this situation, and he was playing it ruthlessly. Amara could tell just by watching the bearers at work that they were beginning to falter. Dodging and maneuvering with that much weight was exhausting them.

The enemy Knights were waiting when the coach soared out of Lady Aquitaine's cloud bank, and they immediately pressed the attack again. This time, they were ready when they closed to one side and the coach door slammed open, and as Aldrick struck at one Knight, a second's arm blurred in a furycrafted speed, hurling his spear at the big swordsman.

Aldrick's arm swept into a perfect parry—perhaps a tenth of a second too late, and the downward-cast spear drove into his right thigh and out the back of his leg.

The swordsman faltered and nearly fell, and though Amara knew that Aldrick could, at need, simply ignore pain great enough to drive a strong man unconscious, that talent would not serve to make his leg function and support weight if it had been damaged. Lady Aquitaine seized him by the collar and hauled him back into the coach, and the Knights Aeris swarmed in closer, spears and swords ready to strike.

One reeled back and fell, spinning wildly out of control as he vanished into the trees, perhaps struck by a blow or weapon. Another got *too* close, was hauled head-and-shoulders deep into the coach, then dropped like a stone, head lolling loosely on a broken neck. Another explosion of white mist hid everything from Amara, but she could hear cries and shouts as the enemy Knights stayed close, pressing the attack instead of withdrawing.

Kalarus led his wing a bit closer to the action and drew his sword with an anticipatory-seeming motion akin to a wolf licking its chops. He gestured with the sword, focused entirely on the coach, shouting to his escorts and . . .

. . . and, Amara realized, utterly failing to notice her presence.

Amara's mouth went completely dry, and for a second she thought her hands would lose their grip on her sword. Kalarus Brencis, High Lord of Kalare. One of the titans of furycraft, a man who had worn Ladies Placida and Aquitaine near to exhaustion, who had assaulted them and maintained a battle for control of the skies while holding up a veil, keeping himself aloft, and coordinating his men's attack. Reputed to be a swordsman of the highest caliber, his talent for firecrafting had once snuffed out an entire forest fire when a range of his expensive, exported hardwoods had nearly been consumed. Further stories claimed that he had once slain a leviathan that had haunted his coastline outright, and he wielded power and authority with consummate, calculated skill, so much so that he was threatening to topple Gaius from his throne.

Worse, Amara had seen some of what he had created in his city, for the people beholden to him, and she knew what he truly was: a monster, in every sense of the word that mattered, an odious murderer who had enslaved *children* with discipline collars, reared them into the mad Immortals who served him, whose agents had slain Cursors all over the face of Alera; Amara's compatriots. Some, her friends. The man had no regard for anyone's life but his own. If he turned upon Amara, he could swat her as easily as a man could an ant, and with the same amount of concern.

But if he never knew she was there—not until it was too late—then she had a chance. He was only a man. Dangerous, powerful, skilled, but he was still mortal. It might not even take a deadly blow. They were perhaps two hundred feet above the coach, but if she could drive him down, knock him out of control even for a few seconds, the forest would give him no more special treatment than it had his fallen men.

The least mistake would mean her death. Amara knew it.

If she did nothing, he would almost certainly send the coach down and kill everyone inside.

That made her choice a great deal easier than she had thought it would be. And though she began to shake harder, as she swam in a nauseating flood of her own terror, she also surged ahead, tightening her windstream down as much as she possibly could to prevent Kalarus or one of his Knights from sensing it. She flung herself out ahead of them, leading the group, judging as best she could where their course would take them.

And then she gripped her sword so hard that pain flared up and down her right arm, and dismissed Cirrus, and with the fury, her windstream.

Amara plummeted down toward the small shape of the coach far below, falling in total silence, without the use of the furycraft that might betray her presence to someone of Kalarus's skill and power. She knew how to guide her fall, arms and legs splayed out, as she rushed down with greater and greater speed, focused completely upon her target, the High Lord of Kalare's bare neck, a strip of pale skin showing above the streaming cloth of his grey-and-green cloak.

Suddenly he rushed closer, in one breath several hundred feet away, and then suddenly beneath her, still flying on course, watching for the coach to emerge from the furycrafted fog. She raised the sword, both hands on the hilt, point down as she fell.

Amara screamed and struck, calling out to Cirrus as she did.

Wind rose in a massive, chaotic gale as Cirrus disrupted the windstreams of Kalarus and his escort.

At the last possible second, one of the Immortals flying beside Kalarus looked up, and snapped into an immediate roll, placing his own body between Amara's sword and Kalarus's back.

Amara struck the Immortal with bone-breaking power. The sword slammed through his mail as if it did not exist, plunged through him clear to the hilt. The impact came to her as a single hammerblow that somehow struck the whole of her body, all at once. She heard a snap, and her left arm dissolved into white-hot agony. The world spun in dizzying circles, and she could barely feel Cirrus's presence through the pain.

Something hit her lower leg, and she felt the straps of the sandal on that leg fall away, taking the sandal with them. The shock of it let her see that she had struck the thinnest branches of a particularly tall tree, and her shin had been laid open as sharply and cleanly as if struck by a knife. She called desperately to Cirrus, unable to sort out the haze of sensation, pain, color, and sound. Somehow, she managed to keep from vanishing into the trees, and found herself cruising along beside the coach, her course swaying like a drunkard, her left arm dangling uselessly, her sword no longer in her hand.

"Countess!" called Lady Placida. "Watch out!"

Amara blinked at her for a second, then turned and saw one of the Knights Aeris sweep down at her, spear in hand. She began to dodge, but knew that it was useless. She was too slow.

The enemy Knight drew back his sword to strike.

And an arrow struck him in the throat, drawing a sudden geyser of blood, and the Knight spun helplessly into the trees.

Amara blinked and looked back at the coach.

The Count of Calderon stood in a low crouch atop the coach, his war bow in hand, his legs spread and braced against the howling wind. He stood atop the coach simply *balanced* there, without any kind of safety strap, without so much as a rope to belay him. Bernard had cast off his cloak, and his expression held all the distant, cool indifference of a professional archer. Moving with unhurried precision, he drew another arrow, eyes focused above Amara and behind her, and the arrow flashed out.

She turned to see it strike another enemy Knight, though the shaft flew wide in the wind, slamming through the man's right arm rather than his heart. He screamed and slowed, carefully controlling his flight to let the enemy pull ahead.

"Amara!" Bernard called. He took one end of his bow in hand and held the other out to her.

Still dazed, it took her a second to understand what she was to do, but she grabbed the bow and let Bernard pull her to a landing on the coach's roof. She sat there for a moment, and Bernard shot twice more—both misses. Without being able to touch the earth and call upon his fury's strength, he could only draw the bow part of the way back, which would both make aiming more difficult and change the dynamics of the arrow's flight. And regardless of anyone's skill, the turbulence of flight made it enormously difficult to hit anything more than a few yards away, and the Knights Aeris were keeping their distance for the moment, dodging and weaving in and out to provoke Bernard into shooting—and expending his arrows on shots unlikely to strike his foes. They could see, just as Amara could, that only a handful of arrows remained in his quiver, but by the time Bernard realized what they were doing, only three remained.

Amara's wits unscrambled in a sudden rush. The pain was still there in her arm and left shoulder, but it was distant and of minimal importance. A glance down at the nearby treetops told her that though the coach was moving swiftly, it was weaving about, dangerously unbalanced as the bearers' strength waned.

"What are you doing, you fool?" she called to Bernard.

"No room to shoot inside, love," Bernard answered.

"If we survive this, I'll kill you with my bare hands," she snarled at him. She leaned over the side and called, "Lady Aquitaine! We've got to move faster!"

"She can't hear you!" Aldrick called back, voice tight with pain. "It's all the both of them can do to keep the coach in the air!"

Red lightning flashed, and a shadow fell across the back of the coach.

Amara looked back to see Kalarus descending toward them. His cloak had been torn in a dozen places by the same tree branches that had slashed the left side of his face to bloody, swollen meat. His teeth were gnashed in hate and rage, and when he met Amara's eyes, the blade of his sword suddenly began to glow like iron on the forge, red, then orange, then white-hot. The metal shrieked in anguished protest.

Bernard moved, hands blurring, and let fly two arrows as Kalarus closed in. The High Lord of Kalare flicked them aside with his burning blade, shattering them with armor-piercing heads. Kalarus came on, murder in his eyes. Amara hurled Cirrus against him, but she might as well have tried to stop a charging gargant with a silk thread. The High Lord powered through Cirrus as though the fury had not been there.

She wanted to scream in frustration and terror, in helpless protest that this scum, this, this . . . *creature* was going to kill her, kill her husband, kill everyone in the coach, and drag Alera into total chaos. She turned to Bernard, eyes searching for his. She wanted to be looking at him when Kalare's blade took her life. Not at the animal who had killed her.

Bernard's face was pale, but his eyes held no trace of defeat, no hint of surrender. He looked down at Amara, a single, fleeting glance—and winked at her.

Then he set his last arrow to string and loosed it as Kalare closed to within ten feet of the coach. Once more, Kalare sneered, blade moving with sinuous grace to strike the arrow before it could reach him. Its shaft shattered into splinters.

But the arrow's head, a shaped, translucent crystal of rock salt like the ones he'd loosed against the windmanes in Calderon, exploded into *powder*.

It tore into Kalarus's wind furies, blanketing him, ripping his windstream to shreds, murdering the power that kept him aloft.

Kalarus had time for one brief, mystified expression of shock and disbelief.

And then he screamed as he fell like a stone into the trees below.

Then there was silence, but for the surf-thunder of steady wind.

Bernard lowered his bow slowly and let out a long breath. He nodded his head pensively, and said, "I think I'll write Tavi and thank him for that idea."

Amara stared at her husband, speechless.

She needed to tell the bearers to keep going for as long as they could before setting down to rest beneath the canopy of the forest, somewhere near a large stream or small river, so that she could send word to the First Lord. But that could come in a moment. For now, the need to look at his face, to realize that they were alive, that they were together, was far more important than mere realms.

Bernard slung his bow over his shoulder and knelt beside Amara, reaching gently for her arm. "Easy. Let's see what you've done to it."

"One of your salt arrows," she said quietly, shaking her head.

He smiled at her, his eyes alight with green, brown, and flecks of gold; colors of life and growth and warmth. "It's always the little things that are important," he said. "Isn't it."

"Yes," she said, and kissed him gently on the mouth.

"Excellent," said the water figure of Gaius, a translucent form that lacked the solid-color enhancement the First Lord used to favor. "Well done, Countess. What is the status of the rescuees?"

She stood beside a large, swift stream that rolled down from the hills many miles from Kalare. The forest here was particularly thick, and they'd barely managed to get the coach down through it in one piece. The bearers had all but collapsed into sleep, without even unhooking their flight harnesses. Bernard went around to each man, gently freeing them from the coach and letting them stretch out on the ground. The High Ladies were in a similar state, though Lady Aquitaine managed to seat herself primly at the base of a tree before leaning her head back against it and watching Odiana help Aldrick to the stream to tend to his wound.

Lady Placida hardly seemed strong enough to keep her head held up, but she insisted on staying with Atticus Elania, who had been injured during the flight—not by a weapon, but when the wounded Aldrick had half fallen back into the coach. He'd fallen hard against one of the crowded seats and broken the girl's ankle. Lady Placida had managed to ease Elania's pain, then promptly fallen back onto the grass to sleep.

Rook stepped out of the coach with her eyes closed, holding her daughter's hand. She found a patch of ground near the stream bank, where the sunlight reached the warm earth. She sat in the light, holding her daughter, her face weary and sagging with something rather like shock.

"Countess?" prodded Gaius gently.

Amara looked back to the water-image. "My apologies, sire." She took a deep breath, and said, "Atticus Elania Minora was injured during the escape, but not seriously. A broken ankle. We'll have it crafted well again soon."

Gaius nodded. "And Lady Placida?"

"Exhausted but otherwise well, sire."

Gaius raised an inquisitive eyebrow.

Amara explained. "She and Lady Aquitaine spent themselves in an effort to speed our escape and hinder the pursuit. Only a bit more than a score of nearly a hundred Knights Aeris managed to catch up to us, and without the ladies' efforts I am certain we would have been overpowered and killed."

"Where are you now?" Gaius asked. Then immediately raised a hand. "No, best not say. This communication could be observed by others. In general, what is your situation?"

"We pressed on for as long as we could after Kalarus fell, sire, but we didn't make it terribly far. It's possible that a follow-up search could find us, so we'll only rest here for an hour or two, then move on."

Gaius lifted both eyebrows. "Kalarus fell?"

Amara smiled and inclined her head. "Courtesy of the good Count Calderon, sire. I am not certain he is dead, but if he did survive it, I doubt he will be in any condition to run a revolution."

Gaius's teeth showed in a sudden, wolfish smile. "I'll want details in person as soon as you can manage it, Countess. Please convey my thanks to His Excellency of Calderon," the First Lord said, "and to the Ladies and their retainers as well."

"I'll try to keep a straight face when I do, sire."

Gaius threw back his head and laughed, and when he did the water-image changed. For a moment, there was color in it, greater detail, and more animation. Then he shook his head, and said, "I will leave you to your rest and travel then, Cursor."

"Sire?" Amara asked, "Were we in time?"

Gaius nodded once. "I think so. But I must move quickly." The image met Amara's eyes, then Gaius bowed, ever so slightly, to her. "Well done, Amara."

Amara drew in a deep breath as she felt a flash of ferocious pride and satisfaction. "Thank you, sire."

The image descended back into the stream, and Amara slumped wearily down onto its banks, her arm throbbing dully, but with slowly increasing discomfort. She glanced aside at Bernard, who stood near Lady Aquitaine, in the shade of the same tree, his eyes distant as, through his connections with furies of earth and wood, he kept watch for anyone approaching.

"Hello, Amara," said Odiana cheerfully.

Despite her weariness and discomfort, Amara twitched in surprise, and pain shot in burning silver lines from her shoulder to the base of her neck. The water witch had approached in total silence and spoken to her from a foot away.

"I'm sorry," Odiana said, a quiet laugh hidden in the words. "I didn't mean to scare you that way. That must have hurt awfully, jumping like that, poor darling."

"What do you want?" Amara said quietly.

Her dark eyes glittered. "Why, to repair your poor shoulder, little peregrine. You'll be as useful to your lord as a falcon with one wing. We can't have that."

"I'm fine," Amara said quietly. "Thank you anyway."

"Tsk, tsk," Odiana said, waggling a finger. "Lying that way. I promise you that I'll make it stop hurting."

"That's enough teasing," Lady Aquitaine said smoothly.

Odiana scowled at Lady Aquitaine, stuck her tongue out at her, then got up to wander idly down the stream bank.

Lady Aquitaine rose from the base of the tree and said, "We have now reached a crossroads, Cursor. There are difficult decisions that must be made."

"Concerning what?" Amara asked.

"The future," Lady Aquitaine replied. "For instance, I must decide whether or not allowing you to live is likely to prove helpful or inconvenient. You are, after all, a quite capable agent of the Crown. Given the political climate, you could be a small but significant obstacle to my plans should you turn your hand against me." She gave Amara a thoughtful look. "But you could be in a position to be very helpful indeed if we can reach some sort of arrangement."

Amara drew in a slow, deep breath, steadying herself. "I suppose it was too much to hope for that you would act in good faith, once you had what you wanted," she said quietly.

"We aren't playing the game for copper rams, Cursor. You know that as well as I do."

"Yes. But I've heard this offer before. I think you know what my answer was."

"The last time the offer was made," Lady Aquitaine said, "you weren't married."

Amara narrowed her eyes, and said in a cold voice, "Do you really think you'll get away with it?"

"If I take that path?" Lady Aquitaine shrugged. "I can simply explain how we were found by one of Kalarus's search parties, which came on us by night, and that there were few survivors."

"And you think people will believe that tripe?"

"Why on earth not, dear?" said Lady Aquitaine in a cold voice. "You just told Gaius yourself that the party was still in danger of discovery, after all." She narrowed her own gaze, her pale face bleak as stone. "And there will be no one to gainsay me. Not only will I get away with it, Countess. They'll most likely award me another medal."

"My answer is no," Amara said quietly.

Lady Aquitaine arched an eyebrow. "Principle is well and good, Countess. But in this particular instance, your options are quite limited. You can either agree to work for me . . . or Aldrick can take Aria's head, at which point I will ask again."

Amara shot a hard look over her shoulder, where the still-limping swordsman stood over Lady Placida's recumbent form, sword held in a high guard.

"Right now," Lady Aquitaine said, "Gaius is likely contacting Placida, telling him that his wife is safe. But if she should die now, the furies she restrains will be freed with catastrophic results to Placida's lands and holders. From where he stands, he will have little choice but to draw the conclusion that Gaius betrayed him."

"Assuming," Amara said, "that you can make good on your threat. I don't think you'd kill another member of the League in cold blood."

"No, Countess?" Lady Aquitaine said, her voice cold. "You know I am perfectly willing to kill every one of you rather than risk having you in my way. You know it."

Amara glanced at Rook, who held Masha tight by the stream bank and had her head bowed, attempting to go unnoticed. "Even the little girl?"

"Children of murdered parents often grow up to seek revenge, Countess. That's a bitter life with a terrible ending. I'd be doing her a kindness."

Bernard placed the tip of his dagger lightly against the back of Lady Aquitaine's neck, seized a fistful of her lustrous dark hair to hold her steady, and said, "You will kindly tell Aldrick to sheathe his sword, Your Grace."

Aldrick bared his teeth in a snarl.

Lady Aquitaine's lip lifted in a contemptuous sneer. "Odiana, dear?"

Water suddenly surged up out of the stream in a set of writhing tentacles not too terribly unlike those of the Canim cloud beasts. They whipped up around Rook and Masha like constrictor serpents, twining around them. For a sickening second, one of the water tendrils covered their noses and mouths, strangling them, before Odiana gestured and they were allowed to breathe again.

Lady Aquitaine glanced at Amara and tilted her head, her expression daring Amara to respond.

"There's a flaw in your reasoning, Your Grace," Amara said quietly. "Even if your pet mercenaries kill them both, you will still be dead."

Lady Aquitaine's smile grew even more smug. "Actually, there's something you haven't accounted for, Countess."

"And that is?"

Lady Aquitaine threw back her head and laughed, her body rippling through changes, her face contorting into different features—and by the time she lowered her head again, Odiana stood where Lady Aquitaine had been. "I'm not Lady Aquitaine."

Lady Aquitaine's voice said, from behind Amara, "Really, Countess. I'm somewhat disappointed in you. I gave you even odds of seeing through the switch."

Amara looked over her shoulder to find Lady Aquitaine,

not Odiana, holding the watercrafting that held Rook and Masha in its grasp.

"Can you grasp the situation now, Cursor?" Lady Aquitaine continued. "This game is over. You lost."

"Perhaps." Amara felt her mouth curl up into a slow smile, and she nodded at Rook. "Perhaps not."

Rook gave a hard, unpleasant smile—and then there was a flash of light, a sudden cloud of steam, and the burning shape of a falcon, Lady Placida's fire fury. It shattered the water-bonds and streaked at Lady Aquitaine like a miniature comet.

At the same instant, Lady Placida's unconscious figure swept Aldrick's good leg out from under him, and the wounded one buckled, pitching him to the ground. Before he could recover, Lady Placida was on his back with a knee between his shoulder blades and a heavy strangling cord around his neck.

Lady Aquitaine threw her hands up to ward off the charging fire fury. She stumbled and slipped down the bank and into the stream.

Rook rose—then she, too, changed, growing taller, more slender, until Placidus Aria stood in her place, the bewildered child held on one hip. She lifted her other hand and the fire fury streaked back to her wrist, perching there, while she faced Lady Aquitaine.

At the same time, the figure atop Aldrick blurred as well, until it was Rook that held him down.

"I confess," Amara drawled to Lady Aquitaine, "I'm somewhat disappointed in you. I gave you even odds of seeing through the switch." She showed Lady Aquitaine her teeth. "You didn't really think I was unaware of your listening in on my conversations with Bernard, did you?"

Lady Aquitaine's face began to flush an angry red.

"Did you believe it when I said I had no idea what you might do, no idea what I could do to prepare, no idea whether or not you'd turn on us?" Amara shook her head. "I never prevented you from listening in because I wanted you to hear it, Your Grace. I wanted you to think you would be dealing with a helpless little lamb. But to be honest, I didn't think you'd be quite so egocentrically stupid as to fall for it."

Lady Aquitaine bared her teeth, furious, and began to rise from the stream.

"Invidia," warned Lady Placida, gesturing slightly with the wrist where the fire fury perched. "I've had a bad week."

"Can you grasp the situation now?" Amara said, her tone hard. "This game is over. You lost."

Lady Aquitaine inhaled slowly, making a visible effort to rein in her temper. "Very well," she said in a quiet, dangerous voice. "What are your terms?"

Amara said, "Nonnegotiable."

"May I ask you a question?" Bernard asked.

"Certainly," Amara said.

"How did you know that those two were going to be trading faces during the rescue?"

"Because Odiana was there," Amara said. "Honestly, why else would she be? Lady Aquitaine certainly didn't need to bring an extra healer, and I can't imagine that she would let a madwoman like her come along on an operation like this just to keep Aldrick company. She didn't need any of that. She needed someone who could look like her and serve as her double, her stalking horse. It seemed reasonable that Lady Aquitaine would want to hide her true identity during the rescue attempt. That way, if things went sour, or if in the long run Kalarus wound up with the throne, she'd be in a position to deny any involvement."

Bernard shook his head. "I can't think in circles that twisty. And you got Lady Placida and Rook to do the same thing? Switch identities?"

"Yes. So that in the confrontation, Lady Aquitaine would take action against the wrong targets and give us a chance to get the drop on her entirely."

"Some people," Bernard said quietly, "might argue that we should have killed them."

Amara shrugged. "Lady Aquitaine and her retainers could quite possibly have taken several of us with them, had they been sure that they were to die. Terms let us all walk away in one piece. And given Lady Aquitaine's contacts and influence, arresting her for trial would be a pointless exercise."

"Some people might not be happy with that answer," Bernard rumbled. "They'll say you could have killed them with impunity once they'd surrendered."

"People like Gaius?" Amara suggested.

"He's one," Bernard said, nodding.

Amara turned to her husband and met his eyes steadily. "I swore to uphold and defend the Crown, my lord. And that means that I am bound by the law. One does not arrest, judge, sentence, and execute prisoners without due course of law." She lifted her chin. "Neither does an agent of the Crown betray her word, once given. Besides, the First Lord still needs Aquitaine's support, until Kalare's Legions are put down. Murdering his wife might reduce the enthusiasm of his support."

Bernard studied her face, his features unreadable. "Those people are dangerous, Amara. To me, to my family, to you. We're in the wilderness, amidst the chaos of a war. Who would know?"

Amara met his gaze calmly. "I would. Decent people don't *murder* their fellow human beings if it is not necessary. And Invidia did, after all, do a great service to the realm."

"Right up until it went a little sour at the end," Bernard growled.

Amara put her hands on either side of his face. "Let her have her world. It's cold there, and empty. For us, it isn't enough to win, my lord. It isn't enough to simply survive. I will not live in a realm where calculations of power supersede justice and law—regardless of how inconvenient that may be to the Crown."

Bernard's teeth showed in another white, fierce smile. He kissed her gently. "You," he said, "are more than that old man deserves."

She smiled at him, warmly. "Be careful, my lord husband. If you say too much, I may have to report your seditious remarks to the First Lord."

"Do that. How long do you think it will take them to get out of there?"

They sat beside one another in the coach, Rook, reunited

with her daughter, had fallen asleep while holding her, her cheek resting on Masha's curls. The little girl's cheeks were pink with the warmth of a young child's deep sleep. Lady Placida and Elania were likewise drowsing.

"Ten minutes, perhaps," Amara said. "Once Lady Aquitaine's had a little rest, she'll snap those ropes and free the others. But without transportation for her retainers, she'd have to pursue us on her own. She wouldn't do that, even if Lady Placida wasn't in a position to destroy her public image and her support in the Dianic League with damning testimony about conspiracy to commit murder."

Bernard nodded. "I see," he said. "And what's stopping the bearers from just dumping us out on the ground and going back for her?"

"They're mercenaries, my love. We offered them money. Lots and lots of money."

"Right," Bernard said. "We're good for it. Though I feel I must ask . . . why did we leave them naked? To slow them down?"

"No," Amara sniffed. "Because the poisonous bitch deserved it."

Bernard's eyes wrinkled at the corners, and he turned to place a slow, gentle kiss upon her mouth, and one upon each eyelid. Amara found that once closed, her eyes simply refused to open, and she leaned into Bernard's delicious warmth and was asleep before she'd finished letting out a contented sigh.

ᐅᐅᐅᐅᐅCHAPTER 51

Tavi shivered in the rain, struggling to hide it from the men around him, and wanted nothing in the world so much as to be warm and asleep.

The Alerans had made ready to meet the next assault in

less than an hour. Torches and furylamps beat back the darkness far more effectively than they had under the first withering assault, and the *legionares* themselves were more organized, more determined.

At least Tavi hoped they were.

Tavi stood atop the last adobe wall with Valiar Marcus. The First Spear moved with a noticeable limp thanks to the Canim javelin. His leg was tied off with a bloodstained bandage, the wound closed with needle and thread, evidence that Foss's healers were badly overworked. Under most circumstances, a wound like Marcus's would have been closed, treated, and the First Spear returned to action virtually whole. The healers had been treating so many light injuries—and closing off far worse ones in order to keep more badly wounded men alive until they could be seen to later—that the First Spear had, by all reports, asked a wounded veteran to withdraw the javelin, then cleaned and stitched the wound himself, covered it with a bandage, and stumped back to his post.

Rain continued to fall, cold and steady. The occasional flashes of scarlet lightning showed little more than sheeting rain. Tavi had been able to make out occasional movement in the darkness, but the Aleran-built defensive wall across the bridge prevented him from making out any details.

However, the simple fact that Tavi *could* stand on the wall and observe told him one thing: the Canim bolt throwers had ceased their deadly thrumming.

"I thought you were listed as out of action, First Spear," Tavi said.

Marcus glanced at the nearest *legionare* and lowered his voice so the man would not overhear. "I never held much with reading, sir."

"You able?" Tavi asked.

"Yes, sir," Marcus said. "I won't be running any races, but I can stand on a wall."

"Good," Tavi said quietly. "We'll need you."

"Sir," Marcus said. "There's no way to know if their warriors have pulled back."

"No. But it makes sense," Tavi replied. "The warriors are

their nutcracker. Then the raiders come in and mop up. It saves casualties among their most effective troops and gives their raiders experience."

"It doesn't make sense," Marcus growled. "Another hard push, and they'd have finished us."

"I know that," Tavi said. "You know that. Assume that Sarl and the ritualists know it as well. I don't think they want Battlemaster Nasaug to have the glory of a victory that looks too much like his own. Sarl has to be the one to finish us to stay in the good opinion of the maker caste. It gives him the glory and lets him share it out to the makers. The makers have first call on the loot if they're the first ones to overrun us. Nasaug gets upstaged. Sarl gets to stay popular with the makers."

"If you're right," Marcus said.

"If I'm wrong," Tavi said, "we'll probably catch some of those steel bolts before much longer."

The First Spear grunted. "At least it'll be quick." There was uncharacteristic bitterness in his voice.

Tavi looked at Marcus's stocky, lumpy profile for a moment. Then he said, "I'm sorry. About the prime cohort. The men of your century."

"Should have been there with them," Marcus said.

"You were wounded," Tavi said.

"I know."

"And I stood with them for you," Tavi said.

Marcus's rigid stance eased a bit, and he looked at Tavi. "I heard. After you carried me out like a lamed sheep."

Tavi snorted. "The sheep I worked with were twice your size. Rams were even bigger."

Marcus grunted. "You were a holder?"

Tavi clenched his jaw. He'd forgotten his role, again. He could blame it on his weariness, but all the same, Rufus Scipio had never been near a steadholt. "Worked with them for a while. My folks told me it was a learning experience."

"Worse trades you could learn if you mean to lead men, sir."

Tavi laughed. "I didn't plan it to happen like this."

"Wars and plans can't coexist, sir. One of them kills the other."

"I believe you," Tavi said. He stared up the long, empty stretch of bridge, rising toward its center, two hundred yards of sloping stone thirty feet across, littered with fallen Alerans and Canim alike. "We've got to last until daylight, Marcus."

"You want to push them at first light?"

"No," Tavi said. "Noon."

Marcus grunted in surprise. "We aren't going to get any stronger. The longer this fight goes on, the less likely it is that we'll be able to push them back."

"Noon," Tavi said. "You'll have to trust me on this one."

"Why?"

"Because I'm not sure that we don't have more spies in the camp. Need to know only, First Spear."

Marcus stared at him for a moment, then nodded. "Yes, sir."

"Thank you," Tavi said quietly. "When we push through to the center of the bridge, I'm going to drive forward with one cohort, while the engineers work."

"One cohort?" Marcus asked.

Tavi nodded. "If the plan works, one cohort will be enough. If it doesn't, we should be able to hold the Canim off long enough for the engineers to finish."

Marcus took a slow breath. The First Spear understood the implications.

"I'm going to ask for volunteers," Tavi said quietly.

"You'll get them," Marcus said. "But I don't see why we shouldn't hit them at first light, cut the bridge, and call it a day."

"If we lose the bridge, they'll be able to secure their entire northern front with just a few of their troops, and the rest of them will be free to kill Alerans elsewhere. As long as the bridge is up, we'll be able to put Legions into the territory south of the bridge, and they won't dare divide their forces." Tavi narrowed his eyes. "This is our job, Marcus. It isn't a pretty one, but I can't just hand it to someone else."

There was a quality of frustration to Marcus's grunt of acknowledgment.

"I'll hold the volunteers back to rest until we push. The rest of First Aleran is at your disposal, as are our Knights Flora."

"All six of them." Marcus sighed.

"Tell them to keep their heads down. If those marksmen start up again, they're going to be your only chance to counter them."

"Teach your grandmother to suck eggs, sir," Marcus muttered.

Tavi snorted and turned to the First Spear. "You've got to hold them, Marcus. At any cost."

Marcus let out a slow breath. "Yes, sir." He stared at the night for a moment before he said, "Offer you a suggestion, sir?"

"Go ahead," Tavi said.

"Don't split up a cohort when you get your volunteers. These men know each other. Trained together. It makes a difference."

Tavi frowned. "I won't take anyone with me who doesn't want to go."

"Then make sure men who are willing to die for you have every chance to survive. You owe them that."

Tavi arched an eyebrow. "Three hundred and twenty men, all volunteering together? How likely is that?"

Marcus gave him a sidelong look, and said, "Sir. It's the infantry."

Three cohorts volunteered to spearhead the attack.

Tavi had them draw lots. By the time the Canim renewed their assault, he stood at the north end of the Elinarch with the winners. *Or,* he thought, *the losers.* Depending on whether or not his idea worked.

His heart skipped a few beats, but he sternly ordered it back to work.

"Sir," Schultz said, "when Antillar Maximus was our centurion, he was senior centurion in this cohort, and his century was first century. But I'm only an acting centurion, sir. I don't have the seniority to command first century, much less the cohort."

Tavi glanced at the fish. "I've spoken to the other centurions. They agree that you know what you're doing, Schultz, and that your century is still the best disciplined. So you're senior centurion until I tell you you're not. Do you hear me, soldier?"

"Yes, sir," Schultz responded at once.

"Good," Tavi said.

A roar went up from the *legionares* on the last wall, and

every man in the spearhead cohort looked suddenly tense. Canim horns blared, and heavy drums rolled, and the screaming roar of combat came down to the town as the rest of the Legion battled the Canim on the bridge.

Tavi listened for two minutes before seeing the signal on the wall, a blue banner lifted beside the Legion's standard.

"Good call, Captain," Max observed, his voice amused. He walked forward from the rear of the cohort, buckling on the much-longer sword preferred by duelists and mounted *legionares*. "They did what you thought they would. They're hitting us with their raiders."

Tavi exhaled very slowly, and nodded. "You ready?"

"Born ready," Max replied cheerfully, drawing a round of quiet chuckles from the waiting Legion. The only three Knights Terra in the Legion came with him, their armor clanking, their vicious, oversized weapons weighing heavy on their shoulders.

Tavi nodded to the Knights and raised his voice. "Tribune Antillus?"

"Ready when you give the word, sir," called Crassus from the rear of the cohort, where he waited with his Knights Aeris—and the Legions' engineers, including their new recruits, the dancers from the Pavilion, now dressed in the armor of slain or incapacitated *legionares*.

"All right, then," Tavi said. "Keep the men in this courtyard, but let them get some food and rest. Once we start pushing, there won't be time for anything else."

Maximus nodded to Schultz, who began giving orders for his inexperienced cohort to fall out for food and remain nearby.

"Captain," Max said, under the cover of the noise. "Sit down. We have some time to wait through, and you haven't rested."

"No," Tavi said. "I need to be on the wall with the First Spear until it's time to move. I'll come back and get you then."

"Captain," Max said, in exactly the same tone of voice. This time, though, he put a hand on Tavi's shoulder, and his fingers clamped down on it like steel bands. "You aren't going to do anything up there that he can't. You let yourself get too tired, and it will slow down your wits. And since we're betting it all on your wits, sir, I think it best that you make sure they're ready to perform." Max met his eyes. "Please, Calderon."

Tavi closed his eyes for a second, and that horrible fatigue threatened him again. Part of him wanted to snarl at Max to shut up and follow orders. The rest realized that the big Antillan was right. He was asking these men to risk their lives carrying out a course of action he had planned. He owed it to them to give them his very best effort when they put everything on the line.

"All right," Tavi said. "I'll sit down. But just for a minute."

"A minute," Max said, nodding. "That's fine."

Tavi slipped out of his helmet, sat down with his back against the stone columns at the base of the Elinarch, and closed his eyes. He'd never be able to get any sleep, but at least he could take a few moments of quiet to order his thoughts, to go over the possibilities, all the things that could go wrong with his plan.

Try as he might, he couldn't think of anything else he might do, and after a few moments of effort, he shook his head and opened his eyes.

Gloomy daylight greeted his gaze, the veiled sun barely visible through the overcast above the land. Tavi blinked up at it in confusion for a second. A muscle cramp seized his neck and set off a series of similar painful contractions in the muscles between his shoulder blades. He labored to his feet and bent, trying to stretch the muscles, until the cramps eased.

"Sir," said Schultz from behind him.

"Centurion," Tavi mumbled, turning. "How long was I asleep?"

"Hours, sir," Schultz replied. "Tribune Antillar said to leave you be."

Tavi muttered something about Max—under his breath. It wouldn't do for a Legion's captain to call one of his Tribunes names in front of the men, after all.

"Oh," Schultz said. He swallowed, then hurried to one side and picked up a plate covered with a soft napkin and a tankard that lay nearby. "He told me to give you these first thing, sir."

Tavi ground his teeth, but managed to keep from snatching the plates from Schultz's hands. "Thank you."

"Welcome, sir," Schultz said. Then he hastily backed away as though he expected Tavi to rip his head off.

Tavi suffocated a grumpy snarl, wolfed down the food, and drank the water in the tankard. By the time he finished, the lingering after-spasms of the muscle cramps had vanished.

"Can you form words yet, sir?" Max asked, striding up to Tavi. He nodded to Schultz, and the acting centurion bellowed for the cohort to fall in. *Legionares* began to rise from where they'd dropped into sleep on the ground or sat awaiting their turn to fight.

"Don't make me hurt you, Max," Tavi said. He cocked his head, frowning up the slope of the bridge, where the sound of battle continued. "Our status?"

"Valiar Marcus did it," Max said. "He held them."

Tavi gave Max a look.

"But you knew that," Max said. "Since we're all standing here."

"Max . . ."

Max gave him an easy grin. "Just trying to lighten things up a little, sir. You're always so grumpy in the morning." He nodded toward the walls. "The raiders have been attacking all morning. Our Knights Flora started going through arrows like water, and the First Spear caught them flat-footed between assaults and pushed them back to the second wall about an hour ago."

"Losses?" Tavi asked.

"Heavy," Max said, his expression sobering. "Without proper gates, someone has to meet the Canim on foot as they come through, and even their raiders are hard to kill for any *legionare*. And those ritualists came up a while ago, started throwing these smoking censers at our people. The smoke was poison. Killed a lot of men. Not quick."

"What happened?" Tavi asked.

"Our Knights Flora started dropping any ritualist that stuck his nose out, and the wind changed after sunrise. It would blow back onto the Canim if they tried it now. No smoke since then."

A cart rumbled up, drawn by a pair of harried horses led by a young boy. He turned the cart around, and Tavi could see light shining on the blood that lay inside. The boy called out, and *legionares* came running from the bridge, bearing their injured comrades to the cart. They were clearly desperate, and loaded men as swiftly as they possibly could. When the cart was filled, the boy called to the horses, leading them back to the healers as fast as they could run.

Tavi watched, sickened, as another cart passed the first. There were more, coming along behind them, to pick up wounded and bring them back to the healers.

Tavi tried to swallow. "How many?"

"Uh. Around eleven hundred dead, I think," Max said, his tone quiet, neutral. "About the same number of men out of action. Foss and his boys look like something the crows have been at. It's all they can do just to save men who are bleeding out."

Tavi watched as more of the *legionares* following his orders were loaded onto the half dozen carts for the wounded.

The dead were stacked like cordwood into the last of the carts. It was the largest of the carts in service, with a high-railed bed, and it required the patient, enormous strength of a team of oxen to pull.

"The First Spear has his men ready for the push," Max said. "But they're tired, and barely holding together. He says if we don't hit them soon, we won't be able to."

Tavi took a deep breath, nodded once, then put on his helmet. "Our Knights?"

"On the way, sir," Max said.

Tavi laced his helmet into position and stalked over to the waiting cohort of fish. Max kept pace beside him, and the armored figures of the Knights Terra with him followed him. Before Tavi had reached the fish, Crassus and his Knights Pisces marched double time into position beside the volunteer cohort. Crassus called the halt, and the Knights stopped with commendable discipline, given how little time they'd spent in marching drill. The engineers, meanwhile, hurried into position at the rear of the other two forces.

Tavi stopped before them all, looking the men over, trying to think of what to say to them at a time like this. Then he stopped and blinked at the armor of the two groups of men.

The *legionares'* armor had changed. Instead of the blue-and-red eagle of the First Aleran, the insignia over their hearts had become the perfect black silhouette of, not an eagle, but a flying crow.

Beside them, the Knights Pisces' armor had changed as well. Again, the original insignia of the Legion had been replaced—this time with the finned, solid black shape of a shark, jaws opened wide.

Tavi arched an eyebrow and glanced at Crassus. "Tribune. Was this your doing?"

Crassus saluted Tavi, and said, "We watched the Canim trying to swim the river this morning, sir. Apparently, they never realized how bad a bunch of fish could hurt them." Crassus straightened his spine. "It seemed appropriate, sir."

"Hngh," Tavi said. He glanced at Schultz. "And what about you, acting centurion? Did you men also take it upon yourselves to change your uniforms?"

"Sir," Schultz said with a crisp salute. "We just wanted to match the standard, sir!" Schultz glanced aside at Tavi. "And to let the Canim know that this time the crows are coming for them, sir!"

"I see," Tavi said. He turned to speak to Max, and found Ehren standing beside Max, dressed in an ill-fitting breastplate. The little Cursor carried Tavi's standard in his right hand, and the armor and helmet made him look a great deal more formidable than Tavi would have expected.

Standing beside Ehren was Kitai. The Marat girl wore another set of armor which, while clearly not her own, fit her tall, athletic form perfectly adequately. She'd slung a Legion-issue *gladius* from either hip. Her mouth was curled up into a small, excited smile, and her exotic green eyes burned with the intensity of her anticipation.

"What are you two doing here?" Tavi asked.

"It occurred to me, Captain," Ehren said, "that since the First Lord already has messages on the way about the Elinarch, he and his captains will be here within a week or two at the most, and it would take me nearly four weeks to ride it. The fastest way to get him that message was to stay here, Captain."

Kitai snorted, and said, "Aleran, did you really expect us to allow you to order us to stay away from danger while you faced it alone?"

Tavi met Kitai's eyes for a long and silent moment. Then he glanced at Ehren. "I don't have time to argue with you both," he said quietly. "But if we survive this, I'm going to take it out of your hides."

"That," Kitai murmured, "could prove interesting."

Tavi felt his cheeks heat up, and he turned back to the men.

"All right, people," Tavi said, loudly enough to be heard by all. "The Canim did what we expected. Their raiders tried to finish what the warriors started. First Spear Valiar Marcus and your Legion-brothers didn't let them do it. So now that we're all rested, it's our turn. We're going to push them over the center wall at the bridge apex. You and I, along with Tribune Antillar, all of our Knights, and our fellow *legionares* are going to hit the Canim hard enough to knock their teeth all the way back across the crowbegotten ocean."

The cohort rumbled with a low, growling laugh.

"If this goes well," Tavi said, "we'll carry the day, and the beer's on me." He paused at another laugh. "But no matter what happens, once we've gotten the engineers into place to destroy the bridge, we've got to hold. No matter what else happens, that bridge has got to come down. You knew that, and you're here anyway."

Tavi drew his blade, snapped to attention, and saluted the ranks of crow-signed young men in front of him.

"First Aleran, Battlecrow Cohort!" Tavi bellowed. "First Aleran, Knights Pisces! Are you with me?"

They answered him with a roaring crash of voices and drawn steel. Max, Ehren, Kitai, and the Knights Terra fell into position around him as Tavi turned and led his Battlecrows and Knights Pisces onto the Elinarch.

◦◦◦◦◦CHAPTER 52

The Elinarch was a marvel of Aleran engineering. It arched over the waters of the Tiber for a distance of more than half a mile, a span of solid granite drawn from the bones of the world. Infused with furies of its own, the bridge was very nearly a living creature, healing damage inflicted upon it, shifting its structure to compensate for the heat of summer, the cold depths of winter. The same crafting that allowed the roads to support and strengthen Aleran travelers also surged in unbroken power throughout the length of the bridge. It could alter its surface to shed excess water and ice, and smooth grooves collected rainwater in small channels at either side of the bridge during rainstorms.

During this storm, though, those channels ran with blood.

Tavi led his men at a quick march up the bridge. Twenty feet after they started, Tavi saw the trickles of blood in the channels. At first, he thought that the reddish overcast was simply shining on water, runoff rain. But the rain had stopped hours before, and the gloomy day drained color from the world, rather than tinting it. He didn't really, truly realize it was blood until he smelled it—sharp, metallic, unsettling.

They were not large streams—only as deep, perhaps, as the cupped palm of an adult man, only as wide as his spread fingers. Or rather, they would not have been large streams of rainwater. But Tavi knew that the blood running down the slope of the bridge had carried the lives of many, many men out onto the unforgiving, uncaring stone of the bridge.

Tavi turned his eyes away from it, forcing them to focus ahead, on the uphill march that still remained before him. He heard someone retch in the ranks behind him, as the *legionares* realized what they were seeing.

"Eyes forward!" Tavi called back to the *legionares*. "We have a job, gentlemen! Stay focused!"

They reached the final defensive wall, which was now manned by perhaps half a cohort of *legionares*—all of them wounded but capable of bearing arms. They saluted Tavi as he and his volunteers approached.

"Go get those bastards, boys!" bellowed one grizzled centurion.

"Send 'em to the crows, Captain!" called a wounded fish with a bloodied bandage around his head.

"Give it to 'em!"

"Take 'em down!"

"First Aleran!"

"Kick their furry—"

"Assault formation!" Tavi called.

On the move, the cohort's formation changed, shifting into a column two *legionares* wide. Their pace slowed somewhat as the column squeezed through the opening in the northern-most defensive wall, and Tavi kept them in the slender formation as they double-timed to the next defensive wall. The din of battle grew louder.

The bulk of the Legion was there, at the next wall. Tavi could see Valiar Marcus's short, stocky form on the wall, bellowing orders. *Legionares* stood at the wall, then in two long lines at either side of the bridge, where the rough steps up to the improvised battlements awaited them. As defending *legionares* on the wall were cut down, the next men in line took their places. Tavi shuddered, imagining a nightmare wait in a line to pain and death with little to do but watch the blood of your brothers in arms flow past you in the gutter.

A larger force was positioned to block the opening in the center of the wall. The *legionares* nearest the opening fought with shield and short blade, but those behind them plied spears, reaching over and around the shieldmen to wound and distract the constant stream of Canim raiders trying to batter their way in by main strength. Canim bodies lay in piles that had become makeshift barricades. Alerans lay unmoving among them, their fellows unable to drag them free in the furious press of melee.

A cry went up, and the weary *legionares* of the First Aleran roared in sudden hope.

"Max!" Tavi called. "Crassus!"

"Boys!" Max called. Then he grinned at Crassus and flashed his half brother a wink. Crassus returned it as a pale, ghastly parody of a smile. Max and Crassus took over the head of the column, with the Knights Terra filling the next two ranks, then Tavi with Ehren. Kitai, perhaps inevitably, did not run in formation but out to one side of the column, green eyes bright, her pace light and effortless despite the weight of the borrowed armor.

"Alera!" Tavi cried, raising his sword to signal the charge. The column picked up speed. His heart was beating so hard that he thought it might break his ribs.

Valiar Marcus's head whipped around, and he screamed orders. At the very last moment, the force on the ground split, ducking to either side. With a triumphant howl, several Canim poured through the opening.

They were met by the sons of Antillus Raucus, bright steel in their hands.

To Tavi, Max and Crassus's attack was a glittering blur. Max took a bare step ahead and hit them first, all speed and violence and deadly timing, his blade lashing out high. He struck the nearest Cane and laid open its weapon arm to the bone at the shoulder, then pivoted to one side, blade passing through a second Cane's throat. He lashed out again, another strike that hammered aside an incoming sickle-sword.

Crassus fought with such flawless coordination with Max's attack that he might have been his brother's own shadow. He dispatched the disarmed Cane with a thrust that went through the roof of its mouth, blocked a desperate, frenzied attack from the Cane whose throat was already gushing out its life onto the bridge, and struck the third Cane's weapon hand from its arm while Max struck its blade, throwing open its defenses.

The brothers went through the leading Canim and hit the opening in the wall without even slowing down. Canim screams and cries came from the opening, then the Knights

Terra were through and spreading out to either side. Tavi and Ehren were next, and the stinking metal-sewer smell of the dead was suffocating, the small passage terrifyingly confining. They emerged from it in the space of a breath, though it had seemed much longer to Tavi, and he found himself staring at an enormous length of sloping bridge rising toward the improvised walls built at the Elinarch's apex.

Momentum was everything. Max and Crassus began slashing a way through the Canim as if they were Rhodesian scouts chopping a clear trail through the jungles of their home. Once the Knights Terra were able to fan out to either side of them, they brought their enormous weapons into play. Tavi watched as a sword swung with fury-born strength tore a Cane in half at the waist, to let it fall to the ground in two confused, bleeding, dying pieces. A great hammer rose and fell, crushing another Cane with such force that the tips of broken bones in its rib cage and spine ripped their way out through its skin.

Tavi saw a flash of movement in the corner of his eye, and turned to see one Cane bound entirely over the Knights and land on the stones before him. It swept an enormous cudgel at his head. Tavi ducked it, faked to one side, then darted in close before the Cane could recover its balance. He slashed hard in an upward stroke, laying open the huge arteries in the Cane's inner thigh, spun from its way as the Cane fell, and used the momentum of the spin to strike the back of the Cane's neck. The blow was not strong enough to cut through the Cane's thickly furred and muscled neck entirely, but it was more than sufficient to split open its spine at the back of the neck, and dropped it at once to the ground, helpless as it bled to death.

A second Cane bounded over the line, landing outside of Tavi's sword reach. It whirled on Ehren.

The little Cursor flicked the standard pole out, the Legion's blackened eagle—crow now, Tavi supposed in some detached corner of his mind—standard lashing out and snapping like a whip into the Cane's nose. The blow did nothing more than startle the Cane for the space of a second. Tavi could have struck in that second, but he didn't. Instinct warned him not to, and Tavi recognized and trusted the intuition.

Kitai's armored figure descended from the wall behind them, swords in either hand sweeping down, opening horrible wounds on the Cane. The Marat girl had bounded up the stairs while they labored through the tunnel, and she had hurled herself from the battlements a beat after they emerged. Kitai rolled forward, under the blind, furious swipes of the Cane's sickle-sword, came to her feet behind the raider, and cut it down in a short, vicious flurry of slashing blades.

Kitai flicked blood from her swords and circled to continue forward on Tavi's right, while Ehren took his left. They pressed ahead, furious sound and violence all around them, and behind them the Battlecrows began to emerge from the passage through the wall, led by acting centurion Schultz, the shaft of the spear behind Max and Crassus's deadly point.

The Canim had not been prepared to defend themselves against an attack, Tavi realized. The enemy must have known that the Aleran's ability to fight was faltering, must have known that time and wounds were taking their toll. The Canim, Tavi somehow knew, had spent the last hour or more in eager anticipation of the final, deadly fall of the Aleran defenders, and when the defenders had abandoned the opening in the wall, the Canim had known that the time for the final, killing rush had come at last. They had pressed forward, hungry for the killing blow that would destroy their enemies.

Instead, they found themselves faced with the deadliest swordsman in the Legion and the superhuman power of the Knights Terra, followed by the blackened, bloody banner of the captain who had defied Sarl and his ritualists, shamed him before the host, and lived to tell the tale despite the terrible powers the ritualists had sent after him.

Battles are fought in muddy fields, in burning towns, in treacherous forests, in unforgiving mountains, and on the blood-spattered stones of contested bridges, Tavi realized. But battles are *won* within the minds and hearts of the soldiers fighting them. No force was defeated in battle until it *believed* that it was defeated. No force could be victorious unless it *believed* it could be victorious.

The First Aleran *believed*.

The Canim raiders weren't sure.

At that time, on that bridge, before the terrible swords of the sons of Antillus, before the crushing power of the Knights Terra, before the blackened banner of the First Aleran and the reckless, frenzied charge of the Battlecrows, those two facts were what mattered.

It was as simple as that.

The resistance of the Canim forces on the bridge did not simply waver—it abruptly vanished, as panic descended on them. Max and Crassus pressed the assault, and Tavi led the Battlecrows after them. On the walls behind them, trumpets rang. Valiar Marcus had seen the Canim break, and the rest of the weary Legion began rushing forward to lend their strength and momentum to the advance.

The advance had to cover most of five hundred yards, all uphill to the defenses at the bridge's apex—which had not, after all, been designed to defend against an assault from the *Aleran* side of the bridge. Without battlements, the only real protection they offered the Canim was the simple impediment of movement caused by the walls themselves and the relatively small opening in them.

That opening, however, also slowed the Canim now attempting to *flee*. The *legionares* were slower on foot than their opponents, but caught up to them as the choke point in the wall stranded them on the northern side.

Tavi was barely able to get his cohort into a more conventional fighting front, incorporating the Knights in its center, before the vengeful Alerans fell on the Canim. Canim screamed. *Legionares* went down. Tavi fought to keep the lines stable, to get the wounded clear of the fighting before they were trampled. The desperate Canim rushed up onto the improvised battlements and threw themselves over, perfectly willing to fall rather than face the juggernaut of the First Aleran's advance. A few even cast themselves off the bridge. It was a long, dangerous fall to the water from there, the maximum height of the bridge from its surface.

Dangerous as it might have been, the waiting sharks were a far more serious threat—and after two days of constant blood-taint in the water and relatively little food, they were hungry. Nothing that fell into the river came out alive again.

Tavi was the first *legionare* to mount up onto the battlements at the bridge's center. Ehren was close behind him, and a roar went up from the Alerans as the black eagle/crow banner gained the wall.

Tavi watched as Max and his Knights plunged through the opening in the wall to make sure the Canim had a reason to continue their retreat. They were followed by a number of excited Battlecrows who should have been taking defensive positions, but who had allowed the heat of battle to control their movements. Max, Crassus, and the Knights Terra settled for crippling blows upon the fleeing Canim where they had to, and the following *legionares* finished up the gruesome work the Knights had begun.

Tavi had no idea whether Max realized how far past the wall the assault had actually rolled, and he signaled the Battlecrows' trumpeter to sound the halt. The clarion call rolled out over the downhill slope of the far side of the bridge, and at its signal Max looked around him, and even a hundred yards away, Tavi could see the expression of dismay on Max's face as he saw how far forward he'd come.

Beside Tavi, Kitai sighed and rolled her eyes. "Alerans."

Max got the Knights and *legionares* stopped and began an orderly withdrawal back to the wall at the bridge's center.

Tavi glanced over his shoulder, then turned and started back down to the surface of the bridge, barking out orders. "Bring up the engineers! Knights Aeris to the wall! Battlecrows, with me!"

Ehren followed hard on his heels. "Uh, sir? Shouldn't we be preparing to, uh, you know. Defend against a counterattack?"

"That's what we're doing," Tavi said. He stalked through the opening in the wall and out onto the surface of the bridge. Tavi stared down the Elinarch's slope, to where the Canim were already rallying, down at the next defensive wall. "Schultz! Bring them up!"

"Right," Ehren said. His voice sounded distinctly nervous. "It's just that it seems a shame that the engineers went to all this trouble to build us a real nice wall, and here we are out in front of it. Not using it. I'm just worried that it might hurt their feelings."

"The Knights need the space on the walls and the engineers can't afford to be interrupted by a breakthrough. We have to buy them all room to work in," Tavi said.

"Us," Ehren said. "And one cohort." He stared down the bridge. "Against the next best thing to sixty thousand Canim."

"No," Kitai put in quietly. "Us against one."

Tavi nodded. "Sarl."

Ehren said, "Ah." He glanced back as the Battlecrows filed into place around them. "You don't think there's a chance he might bring a friend or two?"

"That's the idea," Tavi said. "Make sure they can see the standard."

Ehren swallowed and adjusted the standard against the wind. "So they know exactly where you are."

"Right," Tavi said.

Down the slope of the bridge, brassy horns began to blare once more—this time in a different sequence than used before. Tavi watched as Canim began to emerge from the opening in the next wall, and his heart sped up as he did.

Every single one of them wore the mantles and hoods of the ritualists. They fell into rows, clouds of greenish smoke dribbling from censers, many of them clutching long bars of iron, each end ribbed with dozens of fang-shaped steel blades. They formed the spearhead of a column of raiders, pouring out onto the bridge by the dozens. The hundreds. The thousands.

"Oh, my," Ehren said quietly.

"There," Tavi said to Kitai, barely suppressing a surge of excitement. "Coming up from the back. See the bright red armor?"

"That is he?" she asked. "Sarl?"

"That's him."

Ehren said, "Signal your Knights Flora. Have them kill him when he advances. They could almost do it from here."

"Not good enough," Tavi said. "We can't simply kill him. The next ritualist down the ladder will just step into his place. We've got to discredit him, break his power, prove that whatever he promised the rest of his people, he isn't able to deliver."

"He can't deliver if there's an arrow stuck through his gizzard," Ehren pointed out. But he sighed. "You always seem to do things the hard way."

"Habit," Tavi said.

"How are you going to discredit him?"

Tavi turned and beckoned. Crassus leapt lightly down from the wall, as if the ten-foot drop did not exist. He made his way to Tavi's side through the troops and saluted him. "Captain."

Tavi walked a bit ahead of the troops, out of easy earshot. "Ready?"

"Yes, sir," Crassus said.

Tavi drew a small cloth bag from his pocket and passed it over to Crassus. The Knight Tribune opened the pouch and dumped the little red bloodstone into his hand. He stared at it for a moment, then put the gem back and pocketed it. "Sir," he said quietly. "You're sure this was in my mother's pouch."

Tavi knew he wouldn't accomplish anything by repeating himself. "I'm sorry," he told Crassus.

"It was the only such gem she had?"

"As far as I know," Tavi said.

"She's . . . she's ambitious," Crassus said quietly. "I know that. But I just can't believe she'd . . ."

Tavi grimaced. "It's possible we don't know the whole story. Maybe we're misinterpreting her actions." Tavi did not believe it for a second. But he needed Crassus to be confident, not gnawed by guilt and self-doubt.

"I just can't believe it," Crassus repeated. "Do you think she's all right?"

Tavi put a hand on Crassus' shoulder. "Tribune," he said quietly, "we can't afford to divide our focus right now. There will be plenty of time for questions after, and I swear to you that if I'm alive, we'll find her and answer them. But for now, I need you to set this aside."

Crassus closed his eyes for a moment, then shivered, a motion that reminded Tavi of a dog shaking off water. Then he opened his eyes and saluted sharply. "Yes, sir."

Tavi returned the salute. "On your way. Good luck."

Crassus gave Tavi a forced smile, traded nods with Max, who stood with the Knights on the wall, then shot up into the sky on a sudden column of wind.

Tavi shielded his eyes from blowing droplets of water and blood and watched Crassus soar upward. Then he went back to his place in the ranks.

"I thought that those clouds were full of some kind of creature," Ehren said. "That's why we couldn't fly."

"They are," Tavi told him. "But the bloodstone is some kind of counter to the ritualists' power. It should protect him."

"Should?"

"Protected me," Tavi said. "From that lightning."

"That's not the same thing as clouds full of creatures," Ehren said. "Are you sure?"

Tavi took his eyes from the dwindling figure of the young Knight and stared down the slope. "No. He knows it's my best guess."

"A guess," Ehren said quietly.

"Mmmhmm."

The Canim host's drums began, and the Canim began marching toward them, their pace steady and deliberate. The sound of hundreds of growling voices chanting together rose like a dark and terrible wind.

"What happens if you're wrong?"

"Crassus dies, most likely. Then the engineers and our Knights Terra take down the bridge while we hold the Canim."

Ehren nodded, chewing his lip. "Um. I hate to say this, but if Crassus has the gem, what's going to stop Sarl from blasting you to bits with lightning as soon as he sees you?"

Tavi turned as Schultz passed him a shield. He started strapping it tightly to his left arm. "Ignorance. Sarl won't know I don't have it."

Ehren squinted. "Why does that sound so much like another guess?"

Tavi grinned, watching the oncoming assault. "Tell you in a minute."

And then Sarl threw back his head in an eerie howl, and his entire host answered it with a deafening, painful gale of battle cries. Tavi's newly healed ears twinged again, and the surface of the bridge shuddered.

"Ready!" Tavi screamed, though his voice was lost in the tumult. He drew his sword and raised it overhead, and all around him the Battlecrows did the same. At the same signal, the Knights Flora on the wall behind him began sleeting arrows into the oncoming Canim, aiming to wound in an effort to force the Canim charge to slow for its wounded.

Sarl, though, would permit no wavering in the advance, and the Canim marched past the wounded, leaving them to bleed on the ground, hardly slowing.

Tavi muttered a curse. It had been worth a try.

"Shieldwall!" Tavi screamed, and the Battlecrows shifted formation, pressing closer to their fellow *legionares* and overlapping the steel of their shields. Kitai and Ehren could not join the wall without shields of their own, and they slipped back several rows in the formation. Tavi felt his shield rattling against those of the men beside him, and he gritted his teeth, trying to will away the terror-inspired trembling.

Then Sarl howled again, lifting his own fangstaff, and the Canim, led by the mad-eyed ritualists, charged the Battlecrows.

Stark terror reduced Tavi's vision to a tunnel. He felt himself screaming along with every man in the cohort. He closed even more tightly with the men beside him, and their armored forms pressed together while the ranks behind closed as tightly as they could, leaning against the men in front of them to lend their own weight and resistance to the shieldwall.

The Canim host smashed into the Aleran shieldwall like a living, frenzied battering ram. Swords flashed. Blood flew.

Tavi found himself fighting desperately simply to see, to understand what was happening around him—but the noise, the screams, and the confusion of close battle blinded him to anything beyond the instant. He ducked behind his shield, then barely jerked his head to one side as a sickle-sword came straight down at him, the tip of the curved weapon threatening to hook over the shield and drive into his helmet. He struck out blindly with the strokes Max and Magnus had drilled into him a lifetime before. He couldn't tell whether or not most of them scored, much less inflicted wounds, but he planted his feet and stood his ground, bolstered by the support of the rear ranks.

Others were not so lucky. A ritualist's fangstaff struck and ripped through the neck of a nearby *legionare* like some kind of hideous saw. Another ducked behind his shield, only to have the hooked tip of a sickle-sword pierce his helmet and skull alike. Still another *legionare* was seized by the shield and dragged out of the wall, to be torn apart by a trio of screaming ritualists in their human-leather mantles.

The Battlecrows stood their ground despite the losses, and the Canim assault crashed to a savage halt against them, roaring like tide from a bloody sea as it pounded fruitlessly on a stone cliffside.

As men fell, their cohort brothers pushed up, straining forward with all the power and coordination and battlecraft they possessed.

It was hopeless. Tavi knew it was. The cliff might stand against the ocean for a time, but little by little the ocean would grind it away—it was simply a matter of time. The Battlecrows might have stopped the opening charge, but Tavi knew that they couldn't hold the vast numbers of Canim on the bridge for more than a few moments.

Tavi found himself fighting beside Schultz. The young centurion dealt swift, savage, powerful blows with his *gladius*, downing a ritualist and two raiders with four precisely timed strokes—until he paid the price for his prowess, and slipped on the blood of his foes, twisting forward and out of the wall. A Cane drove a spear down at Schultz's exposed neck.

Tavi never hesitated. He turned and chopped through the thrusting spear's haft in a single, hard stroke, though it left his entire left flank open to the fangstaff of the foaming-mouthed ritualist facing him. He saw the Cane strike in the corner of his eye and knew that he would never be able to block or avoid the deadly weapon.

He didn't have to.

The *legionare* on Tavi's left pivoted forward, slamming the fangstaff aside with his shield, and flicked a menacing blow at the ritualist's head, forcing him to jerk back to avoid it. It wasn't much of a delay, but it was enough for Schultz to recover his balance. He and Tavi snapped back into formation, and the fight went on.

And on.

And on.

Tavi's arms burned from the effort of using shield and sword, and his entire body trembled with the exhausting effort of holding against the overwhelming foe. He had no idea how long the fight lasted. Seconds, minutes, hours. It could have been any of them. All he knew for certain was that they had to hold their ground until it was over. One way or the other.

More men died. Tavi felt a flash of heat upon one cheek as a Canim sickle-sword passed near. Canim fell, but their numbers never seemed to lessen, and bit by bit, Tavi felt the supporting pressure of the rear ranks waning. The inevitable collapse would come soon. Tavi ground his teeth in raw frustration—and saw a flash of red only a few feet away. Sarl was there, in his scarlet armor, and Tavi saw the ritualist's fangstaff smash down onto an already-wounded *legionare*, slamming him to the bridge's surface.

Grimly, Tavi began to give the order to advance. A single, hard push might bring Sarl within the reach of his blade—and he was determined that no matter what happened, Sarl would not leave the bridge alive.

As he was about to scream the order, golden sunlight suddenly washed over the bridge.

For the space of a breath, confusion turned the combat into a spastic, inexpert affair, as virtually everyone involved turned their gazes to the sky in shock. For the first time in nearly a month, the golden sun shone down upon the Elinarch, the blazingly hot sun of a late-summer noon.

Though he knew he would never be heard, Tavi screamed, "Max!"

On the wall behind them, the Knights let out a sudden cry of mass effort and unleashed upon the Canim a weapon such as no Aleran had ever seen.

Though not all of the Knights Aeris could fly well, their lack of ability was more an issue of inexperience than it was of strength. Every Knight Aeris there had considerable power for other applications of windcrafting—and given how basic this one was, they were more than up to the task.

Tavi could only imagine what was happening now, behind him and up on the walls and in the skies over the Elinarch. Thirty Knights, all together, raised a far-viewing crafting of the kind normally used to observe objects at distance. Instead of forming only between their own hands, however, *this* crafting was massive, all their furies working in tandem to form a disk-shaped crafting a quarter of a mile across, directly above the wall where they stood. It gathered in all of that sudden sunlight, shaping it, focusing it into a fiery stream of energy only a few inches across that bore down directly upon Max.

Tavi heard Max bellow, and his mind's eye provided him with another image—Max, raising up his own far-view crafting in a series of individual disks that curved and bent that light to flash down the length of the bridge's slope.

To shape it into a weapon. Precisely as Tavi had used his bit of curved Romanic glass to start a fire, only . . . larger.

The searing point of sunlight flashed across the bridge, and where it touched, raiders and ritualists screamed as skin blackened and clothing and fur instantly burst into flame. Tavi glanced over his shoulder, and saw Max on the wall, arms lifted high, his expression one of strain—and rage. He cried out and that terrible light began sweeping over the Canim, felling them as a scythe fells wheat. A horrible stench—and an cacophony of infinitely hideous shrieks—filled the air.

Back and forth flicked the light, deadly, precise, and there was nowhere for the Canim to hide. Dozens died with every single one of Tavi's labored heartbeats—and suddenly the tide of battle began to change. The rift in the clouds widened, more light poured down, and Tavi thought he could see the shadow of a single person high in the air, at the center of the clear area of sky.

And, as the Canim attack came to a shocked halt, Tavi saw Sarl again, not twenty feet away. The ritualist stared upward for a second, then whirled to see his army dying, burned to death before his very eyes. He whirled around, naked terror on his face, as his final assault became a desperate rout. The panicked raiders ran for their lives, trampled their fellows, and threw themselves from the bridge in their effort to avoid the horrible, unexpected Aleran sorcery. Those nearest the next wall managed to scramble through it in time.

The rest died. They died by fire, at the hands of their comrades, or in the jaws of the hungry sea-beasts in the river below. By the hundreds, by the thousands, they died.

In seconds, only those Canim nearest the Aleran shieldwall, and therefore too close to the Alerans to be targeted, were still alive. Those who attempted to flee were cut down by Antillar Maximus's deadly sunbeam. The rest, almost entirely ritualists, flew into an even greater frenzy born of their despair and the death they knew had come for them.

Tavi grimly dodged the wild backswing of a fangstaff, and when he looked back at Sarl, he saw the Cane staring at him—then up at the sky overhead.

Sarl's eyes turned calculating, burning with rage and madness, and then he suddenly howled, body arching up precisely as it had the day before.

Sarl had to know that his life was over, and Tavi knew that Sarl had plenty of time to call down the lightning once more—and Tavi was surrounded by his fellow Alerans. Though the blast would be meant for him, anyone near him would die as well, just as they had when Sarl's lightning struck Captain Cyril's command tent.

He'd given Lady Antillus's bloodstone to Crassus, so Tavi made the only choice he could.

He sprinted forward, out of the wall, and charged Sarl.

Once more the power crackled in the air. Once more, lights blazed along the ritualist's body. Once more the scarlet lightning filtered through the clouds all around the single shaft of clear blue sky Crassus had opened.

Once more blinding, white light and thunderous noise hammered down upon Tavi.

And once more it did *nothing*.

Chips of hot stone flew up from the bridge. A ritualist, accidentally standing too close, was charred to smoking meat.

But Tavi never slowed. He crossed the remaining space in a single leap, sword raised.

Sarl had a single instant in which he stared at Tavi, eyes wide with shock. He fumbled for a defensive grip on his fangstaff.

Before he could get it, Tavi rammed his sword into Sarl's throat. He stared at the Cane's startled eyes for a single second—then he twisted the blade, jerking it free, ripping wide the ritualist's throat.

Blood sheeted down over Sarl's scarlet armor, and he sank limply to the bridge, to die with a surprised look still on his face.

There was a horrified cry from the ritualists as their master fell.

"Battlecrows!" Tavi howled, signaling them forward with his sword. "Take them!"

The Battlecrows charged the Canim with a roar.

And a moment later, the Battle of the Elinarch was over.

◁◦◦◦◦◦ CHAPTER 53

Max came running up to Tavi after the last of the ritualists had been slain. The maddened Canim had neither given nor asked for quarter, which Tavi supposed was just as well. He wasn't at all sure that he could have restrained his *legionares* after the losses they'd suffered.

"Calderon," Max demanded. "He tried the lightning on you. *Again.*" Max was sweating from the effort of his crafting and looked pale. "How the crows did you survive it?"

Tavi reached to his belt and drew the Canim knife they'd captured while engaging the raiding parties the day before the battle. He held up the skull-shaped pommel. A bloodstone glimmered wetly in one of the eyes. Wet, red blood dribbled down from the jewel and over the handle. "We had another gem, remember?"

"Oh," Max said. "Right." He frowned. "So how come you can hear me?"

"Opened my mouth and had some lining in my helmet," Tavi said. "Foss said it made a difference. Something about air pressure."

Max scowled at Tavi, and said, "Gave me a heart attack. Thought you were dead, and you just had another gem the whole time." He shook his head. "Why didn't you just give that one to Crassus?"

"Wasn't sure it would work," Tavi said. "I knew the one I gave him would. He was more important than me for this."

The young Knight in question descended wearily from the sky and landed on the bridge to the cheers of the Knights Pisces. Crassus walked slowly over to Tavi and saluted. "Sir."

"Well done, Tribune," Tavi said, his voice warm. "Well done."

Crassus smiled a bit, and Max clapped him roughly on the shoulder. "Not bad."

Ehren, still bearing the standard, also offered his congratulations, though Kitai only gave Crassus a speculative glance.

Tavi looked around him, struggling to order his thoughts. It was more difficult than he had thought it would be. Too many emotions were rushing back and forth through him. Elation that his plan had succeeded. Crushing guilt, that so many had died for that success. Fury at the Canim, at Kalarus, at the treacherous Lady Antillus, and fury, too, for Sarl and his like, whose lust for power had killed so many Alerans and Canim alike. Sickness, nauseous sickness at the sight and scent of so much blood, so many corpses, cut down with steel or charred by the savage sunfire he'd had his Knights unleash on the enemy. Giddiness that he had, against difficult odds, survived the past several days. And . . . realization.

His work was not yet done.

"All right," he said, raising his voice. "Schultz, get the wounded to the healers and fall back to the wall. Tell the First Spear I want him to consolidate units with too many losses into functioning cohorts and take up defensive positions until we're sure the enemy has withdrawn from the town and is on his way back to Founderport. Get everyone a meal, some rest, especially the healers, and tell him . . ." Tavi paused, took a breath, and shook his head. "He'll know what to do. Tell him to shore up defenses and see to our people."

Schultz gave him a weary salute. "Yes, sir."

"Max," Tavi said. "Go get our horses."

Max lifted his eyebrows. "We going for a ride?"

"Mmmm. Bring one alae of cavalry. We're going to follow the Canim withdrawal and make sure they want to keep moving away."

"Yes, sir," Max said, saluting. He gave a sharp whistle and a hand signal to someone on the wall and marched away.

"Sir Ehren, if you would, find Magnus and make sure he knows what has happened."

"Right," Ehren said. He nodded to Tavi and passed over his standard. "I don't get along very well with horses, anyway."

Tavi issued several more orders to other members of the Legion, but after that he found himself standing over Sarl's fallen form. The Cane looked far smaller now, broken like a toy at Tavi's feet. His skinny body and mangy fur were only partly concealed by the scarlet armor, and his yellowed teeth were worn.

Tavi tried to find some sense of satisfaction that he had taken the life of an enemy of the Realm, of a murderous slive whose plans had nearly killed his friends and his patron at Wintersend, years ago. But he couldn't. Sarl had been a threat. Now he was dead. There was no rancor in that thought, for Tavi—nor pride. Nor shame. But perhaps a twinge of regret. Sarl might have been a murdering traitor, but Tavi doubted that every Cane who had followed him was the same kind of monster. And his orders had slain thousands of them. They, too, had been dangerous, but not in the same, malicious way. Or not entirely in that way. Regardless, he'd had little choice. But he wished he could have found a way that didn't involve so much blood. So much death.

He felt Kitai's presence behind him and glanced over his shoulder at her. They were now alone upon the bridge, though the wall behind them was manned by *legionares*. Tavi wondered how long he'd been staring at the dead.

Kitai stepped up to stand beside him, also regarding the fallen.

"You had to," she said quietly. "They would have killed you. Killed everyone."

"I know," Tavi said. "But . . ."

Kitai looked up and regarded him for a moment, a faint frown marring her brow. "You are mad, Aleran," she said, her tone gentle. "You can be strong. Hard." She laid her fingertips on Tavi's breastplate. "But beneath that, you bleed for the fallen. Even those who are not your own folk."

"I doubt there's another Aleran alive who has spent more time talking to Canim than I," Tavi said. "My people usually skip straight to the killing. So do theirs."

"You think this wrong?"

"I think . . ." Tavi said, frowning. "I think that it's been going on for so long, neither of us can consider the possibility of stopping it. There's too much history. Too much blood."

"In your place, they would not bleed for you."

"Doesn't matter," Tavi said. "It isn't about being fair and equal. It's about the difference between right and wrong." He stared out at the bloody Elinarch. "And this was wrong." His vision blurred with sudden tears, but his voice stayed steady. "Necessary. And wrong."

"You are mad, Aleran," Kitai said quietly. But her fingers found his, and they stood with clasped hands for a time. Rolling storm clouds still lay overhead, but now they were in motion, restless, and between heavy showers, there were frequently breaks in the clouds to let more sunlight in.

Tavi suddenly snorted out a little laugh.

Kitai tilted her head and waited.

"My *ludus* game with Nasaug. I was giving him a warning. Showing him that he should fear us. Or trying to, at least. But the whole time, he was playing me like one of the pieces. Pushing me where he wished me to be."

"In what way?" Kitai asked.

"He used me to kill Sarl," Tavi said. "He couldn't abandon his countrymen with him. Nor could he permit Sarl to lead them to disaster. Nor could he actually enlist my aid, the way

Sarl conspired with Kalarus. He saw me trying to call Sarl out of their host, and he led that night assault and made sure that if Sarl didn't step in at once, Nasaug would carry the day. Then, instead of backing Sarl up, he stood back and watched. And we killed Sarl for him. Just like he wanted."

Kitai shook her head. "The Canim are more like your people than mine, I think," Kitai said. "Only the mad would handle things in such a manner. When my father disagreed with Atsurak leading my people, he challenged him and killed him. It was over in minutes."

Tavi smiled. "Not all of us can be as wise as the Marat." He felt the smile fade. "I did what he wanted. But I may have made a mistake, in the long term."

Kitai nodded. "Nasaug may not have Sarl's powers, but he will lead his people much more ably than Sarl ever could have."

"Yes. Inspire loyalty. Courage. Nasaug is cut off from his home, from help. But he could turn every single Cane with him into the equals of his warriors. We dealt with the raiders fairly well, but we barely gave the warriors a bloody nose. Imagine if he'd had fifty thousand of them, instead of ten. He would have taken the bridge in a day."

"I will imagine it when it is before me," Kitai said firmly. "You beg fate to make your fears into reality, Aleran. But for the moment, they are only fears. They may come. If so, then face them and overcome them. Until then, pay them no mind. You have enough to think on."

Tavi took a deep breath and nodded. "You're probably right. I'll try."

Behind him, Tavi heard the makeshift walls groan and squeal. He looked over his shoulder, to where the engineers were raising the opening in the walls so that horses could slip through. Moments later, Max and his cavalry rode toward them.

"You go to watch the Canim retreat?" Kitai asked.

"Yes. Nasaug might rally them and hit us again, before we can recover. I don't think we could stop him, but as long as we keep them in sight, we can always take the bridge down before they reach it."

"I will go with you," Kitai said. Her tone brooked no dissent.

Tavi gave her part of a smile. "Once people have time to catch their breath, they're going to realize that you aren't Aleran."

Kitai's teeth flashed in a smile. "That will be interesting."

Tavi felt like ten miles of bad road, but he and Kitai mounted up and rode forth with Max and the cavalry. They trailed the main body of the Canim host at a distance as they marched back to Founderport. Twice during the ride, they were attacked by wounded Canim, stragglers who had fallen behind the column. The attacks were swift, brutal, and ended quickly, and the cavalry advanced in a loose line, finishing off any Canim who could not keep pace with the retreat.

At the end of the day, Tavi watched, exhausted, as a team of eight horsemen entered the occupied ruins of a barn in one of the burned-out steadholts. Tavi followed behind as they swept the ruins, and snarls and the ringing chimes of weaponplay sang out into the dusk.

Tavi watched as a single large, shadowy form leapt a ruined wall and ran. The Cane was slower than most, its gait unsteady, and in its panic it fled directly toward the Aleran cavalry outside the ruins. A second team spurred forward to intercept the lone Cane.

Then Kitai let out a harsh, sudden breath from her horse, beside Tavi's, and hissed, "Stop them. Do it now."

Tavi blinked at her, but then immediately barked, "Second spear, halt!"

The horsemen hauled their mounts to a stop, looking over their shoulders in confusion.

"Come, Aleran," Kitai said, and set out after the lone Cane.

"Wait here," Tavi told Max. "We'll be back in a minute."

"Uh. Sir?" Max said.

Tavi ignored him and followed Kitai. She led him into the twilight, until they found the fleeing Cane, crouched in the feeble shelter offered by a half-collapsed earthen overhang beside a stream.

She stared at them with wide, frightened eyes, and gathered a number of small, piteously mewling forms to her breast.

She.

She.

Tavi stared at her, speechless. A female Cane, with young. Newly born from the look of it. She must have been giving birth while the Canim retreat began. No Aleran had ever actually *seen* a female Cane, and over the centuries it had given rise to a number of unsavory rumors about how the Canim perpetuated themselves. The truth was simpler, more obvious, and an embodiment of it shivered in the rain before him, clutching her young to her, as desperate and as frightened as any Aleran mother would be in her place.

Tavi stepped forward, toward the female Cane. He lowered his chin toward his chest and bared his teeth.

The female's eyes flashed with desperate anger, waging against even more desperate fear, and then her ears flattened, and she tilted her head far to one side, her body bending to bare her throat in abject surrender.

Tavi relaxed his own stance and nodded at the Canim female. Then he tilted his head slightly to one side, and moved a hand at her in a brushing-away gesture.

The female lifted her head and stared at him, ears twitching.

"Go," Tavi told her. He struggled to remember the proper Canish word, and settled for the one Varg would occasionally use when he thought Tavi was taking too long to move a piece on the *ludus* board, while making the same gesture. *"Marrg."*

The female stared at him for a moment. Then she bared her throat again, rose, never taking her eyes from him, and vanished into the dark.

Tavi watched her go, thinking furiously.

The Canim had come to Alera—and brought their mates and offspring, their *families* with them, something that had never happened before.

Which meant . . .

"Great furies," Tavi breathed. "I am not afraid of Nasaug anymore."

Kitai stared after the female Cane and nodded grimly.

"I'm afraid," Tavi whispered, "of what drove him from his home."

Isana woke to the sound of distant trumpets and a clamor in the hallway outside her room. She sat up, disoriented. She was in her bed. Someone had bathed her, and she wore a soft, white nightgown that was not her own. On the table next to the bed were three bowls and a simple mug. Two of the bowls were empty. The third was about half-filled with some kind of broth.

She sat up, a shockingly difficult task, and pushed her hair back out of her face.

Then she remembered. The healing tub.

Fade.

The tub was gone, and the maimed slave was not in sight.

If she hadn't been so tired, her heart would have been racing with fear for the man's fate. As it was, her worries were merely galvanizing. Isana got out of bed, though it became an act of sheer will, so weak did she feel. One of her simple grey dresses hung over the back of a chair, and she pulled it on over the nightgown, and walked carefully to the door.

There was shouting in the hallway outside, and the thud of running footsteps. She opened the door, and found Giraldi standing in the hall outside, facing the half-open door of the chamber across the hall from hers.

"That's as may be," the old soldier growled, "but you aren't the one who gets to decide whether you're well again or not." He paused as a trio of youths, probably pages, went sprinting by. "Lady Veradis says you're lucky to be alive. You stay in bed until she says otherwise."

"I don't see Lady Veradis anywhere," said a man in a *legionare's* tunic and boots. He stood in the doorway, looking down the hallway so that Isana saw him in profile. He was handsome, if weathered, his brown hair flecked with grey, and shorn in a standard Legion cut. He was thin, but built of whipcord and sinew, and he carried himself with relaxed confidence, the heel of one hand resting in unconscious familiarity on the hilt of the *gladius* at his hip. He had a deep, soft voice. "So obviously, she can't say otherwise. Why don't we go and ask her?"

The man turned back to Giraldi, and Isana saw that the other side of his face was horribly maimed with burn scars, seared into the skin in the Legion mark of a coward.

Isana felt her mouth drop open.

"Araris," she said quietly.

Giraldi grunted in surprise and turned to her. "Steadholder. I didn't know you were awake . . ."

Isana met Araris's steady gaze. She tried to say something, but the only thing that came out of her mouth was, "Araris."

He smiled and gave her a small, formal bow. "I thank you for my life, my lady."

And she felt it. She felt it in him now, felt it as she met his eyes. She had never sensed it in the past, never in all the years he'd served her brother and then her. It was his eyes, she thought. In all those years, with his hair grown long and unkempt, she had never, never *once* seen his entire face, seen both of his eyes at once. He'd never been willing to let her see him. Never been willing to let her know what he felt for·her.

Love.

Selfless, quiet, strong.

It was love that had sustained him through years of labor and isolation, love that had prompted him to surrender his identity, brand himself, disguise himself, even though it cost him his position, his pride, his career as a soldier—and his family. He had willingly murdered everything he was in the name of that love, and not only that which he felt for Isana. She could feel that in him as well, the bittersweet, bone-deep sorrow and love for his friend and lord, Septimus, and by extension to his friend's wife and son.

For his love, he had fought to protect Septimus's family, endured a life of difficult labor in a steadholt smithy. For his love, he had destroyed his life, and if he was called upon to do so, he would spend his last breath, shed his last drop of blood to protect them without an instant's hesitation. His love would accept nothing less. .

Isana's eyes blurred with sudden tears, as the warmth and power of that love washed over her, a silent ocean whose waves rippled in time with the beating of his heart. Isana was awed—and humbled—by it. And something stirred in her in answer. For twenty years, she had felt it only in dreams. Now, something broke inside her, shattering like a block of ice beneath a hammer, and her heart soared in exaltation, in the sheer, golden, bubbling laughter she thought was gone forever.

That was why she had never sensed it in him. She had never felt it growing in herself, over the long years of work and grief and regret. She'd never allowed herself to understand the seed had taken root and begun to grow. It had lain quietly, patiently, waiting for the end of the winter of mourning and grief and worry that had frozen her heart. Waiting for a new warmth. Waiting for spring.

His love had slain Araris Valerian.

Hers brought him back to life.

She didn't trust her legs to walk, so she held out one hand to him.

Araris moved carefully, evidently still recuperating himself. She couldn't see anything but a blur, but his hand touched hers, warm and gentle, and their fingers twined together. She began to laugh, through the tears, and she heard him join her. His arms wrapped around her, and they held one another, choking on laughter and tears.

They said nothing.

They didn't need to.

Amara wearily looked up from her book as the knob to the door to their chambers in the guest quarters of Lord Cereus twisted. The door opened and Bernard came in, carrying a tray laden with various foods. He smiled at her, and said, "How are you feeling?"

Amara sighed. "You'd think I'd be used to cramps by now. I've had them every month since I was a girl." She shook her head. "I'm not curled up and whimpering anymore, at least."

"That's good," Bernard said quietly. "Here. Mint tea, your favorite. And some roast chicken . . ." He crossed to where she sat curled up in a chair in front of the fireplace. Despite the summer's heat, the interior of the thick stone walls of Cereus's citadel made it cool enough to be uncomfortable for her, particularly during her cramps. Between the exhaustion of travel, the bangs and scrapes and abrasions she'd acquired, the shoulder she'd dislocated, and the horrible new memories of violence and death, the disappointment as her cycle continued unabated had assumed monstrous proportions. So much so, in fact, that she'd accepted Bernard's offer to attend the debriefing with the First Lord and High Lords Cereus and Placidus in her place.

Perhaps that had been unprofessional of her. But then, it would hardly have been professional to break down weeping from the weight of so many different flavors of agony. No doubt, she would look back at that decision and berate herself for it in the future, when the memories of pain had softened—but where she was now, still in the shadow of some of the worst physical and emotional torment she'd ever felt, she did not begrudge herself the time to recuperate.

"How was the meeting?" she asked.

Bernard settled the tray on her lap, uncovered the chicken, and poured a few drops of cream into the tea. "Eat. Drink."

"I'm not a child, Bernard," Amara said. She certainly didn't mean for her voice to sound quite so petulant. It drew a smile from Bernard as he read her expression. "Don't say it," she told him.

"I wouldn't dream of it." He got the other chair and settled into it. "Now. Eat your dinner and drink your tea, and I'll tell you all about it."

Amara gave him another glowering glance and picked up the tea. It was the perfect temperature, just barely cool enough to drink without scalding herself, and she savored the warmth as it spread down her throat to her belly.

Bernard waited until she took the first bite of chicken to begin. "The long and short of it is that Kalarus's forces are in retreat. Which is good, because they're no longer coming here—and bad because there are still Legions *able* to retreat and fight another day.

"Aquitaine crushed both Legions holding the passes from the Blackhills, though they were able to retreat in reasonably good order."

Amara smirked. "He's probably negotiating with their officers, trying to bribe them away from Kalarus. Why destroy when he can recruit?"

"You've spent too much time with Lady Aquitaine," Bernard said. "Finish your chicken, and I'll do something nice for you."

Amara arched a brow at him, then gave a diffident shrug and went back to eating.

"Once Atticus's daughter was freed," Bernard continued, "and he was certain that Kalarus wasn't going to bushwhack him the minute he revealed himself, Atticus froze the bloody floodplain into one enormous sheet of ice. Then he marched his Legions right over it to cut off the easternmost of Kalare's Legions and trap them in the fortress they'd taken. He's got *them* under siege now, and Gaius is sending Second Imperian to aid them."

"What about the clouds?" she asked.

"Apparently they started breaking up over the cities farthest inland the day before we reached Kalare. After two or three days they fell apart completely."

Amara sipped tea thoughtfully. "Do we know how the Canim did it?"

"Not yet."

She nodded. "How did Placida's Legions arrive at Ceres so quickly? They got there before *we* did, and we were windborne. I thought he'd have to march them all the way from his home city."

"I suspect everyone was supposed to think that," Bernard replied. "But instead he marched all three of them down to the very edge of his territory the day after Kalarus took his wife. The second Gaius told him Aria was safe, he force-marched all the way to Ceres. Got there in less than a day by highway."

Amara arched an eyebrow. "All three of his Legions?"

Bernard nodded. "Said he figured either Aria would be freed, in which case he'd be able to aid Ceres at the earliest opportunity, or else she'd be killed, in which case he was taking every soldier he had and going after the crowspawn who had done it." Bernard shook his head. "He doesn't strike me as the kind of man to live and let live with someone who touches his wife."

"No," Amara said quietly. "He isn't. But there will always be fools who believe that if a man dislikes violence and goes to great lengths to avoid it, it is a sign of weakness and vulnerability."

Bernard shook his head. "There's an unlimited supply of fools in general. Take, for instance, Lord Kalarus. You remember you told me you thought he must have been in cahoots with the Canim?"

"I'm fairly sure he never used the word *cahoots* to describe it," murmured Amara.

"Hush and eat," Bernard scolded. "Gaius asked me to make sure you knew that there has, apparently, been a significant Canim incursion, which began at approximately the same time as Kalarus's rebellion."

Amara sucked in a breath. "Indeed? What has happened?"

"Details are still sketchy," Bernard said. "The Cursors in the area were under attack from Kalarus's Bloodcrows. Several are dead, many more missing and presumed underground. But apparently Gaius has some way of seeing things that are happening out there once the clouds were out of his way. The Canim came ashore near . . ." He frowned, brow furrowing. "It's a big bridge over the Tiber. I can't remember the name, I hadn't heard of it before."

"The Elinarch," Amara said. "It's the only place a sizeable force can cross the river securely."

"That's it," he agreed. "He sent the First Aleran Legion to hold the bridge."

"First Aleran? That . . . dog and pony Legion? There's a pool on in the Cursors as to how many years it will be before that circus actually sees combat."

"Mmm?" Bernard said. "I hope you bet low."

Amara's eyebrows lifted.

"Apparently, they managed to stand off about sixty thousand Canim."

She nearly choked on the bite of chicken. "What?"

Bernard nodded. "They landed near the bridge, but they've moved south, and they're securing several fortified towns in the area and along the coast."

"The Canim have never done anything like that before," Amara said. "Or come in numbers like this." She fretted her lower lip. "Sixty thousand . . ."

"The next best thing to ten Legions of their own, yes," Bernard said.

There was a knock at the door. Bernard rose and went to it. His deep voice rumbled quietly as Amara finished her meal, and he returned with Placidus Aria in tow.

Lady Placida was once again regal, calm, and immaculately dressed in green silk. Her deep auburn hair was worn loose and flowing, and she smiled warmly at Amara as she approached and bowed her head. "Count, Countess."

Amara started to set her tea aside and rise, but Lady Placida lifted a hand. "No, Amara, please. I know you've been injured. Please, rest."

Bernard gave Lady Placida an approving glance and offered her his chair.

"No thank you, Count," she said. "I shan't keep you long. I only wanted to see you both, so that I could thank you for taking me out of that awful place. I consider myself to be deeply indebted to you both."

"Your Grace," Amara said, shaking her head. "There is no need to—"

"Thank you," Lady Placida cut in, "because you were only doing your duty and my thanks should rightfully go to the First Lord, yes, yes. Save yourself the trouble of making the speech, Amara. What you did was more than simply a job. Especially given the murky group dynamic of your associates. Which was, by the way, very well handled." Her eyes flashed, wickedly merry. "Especially the bit where you took their clothes."

Amara shook her head, and said, "It probably would have been better not to do that."

"Never fear, dear," Lady Placida said. "You're too decent to court her favor, too smart to believe everything she tells you, and too loyal to the Realm to involve yourself in her little games. You could never have been anything but Invidia's enemy." She smiled. "You just . . . started it a bit early. With style."

Amara felt a little laugh escape her.

Lady Placida's expression sobered. "You went beyond the call of duty." She turned her head to Bernard and bowed again. "Both of you did. I and my lord husband are in your debt. If you are ever in need, you have only to ask."

Amara frowned at her, and then glanced at Bernard. "Is Rook . . . ?"

"I spoke to Gaius on her behalf," Bernard said quietly. "Pardoned and free to go."

Amara smiled, somewhat surprised at the sense of satisfaction his words brought her. "Then, Lady Placida, there *is* something I wish to ask of you."

"Only," she said sternly, "if you stop Ladying me. I have a name, dear."

Amara's smiled widened. "Aria," she said.

"Name it."

"Rook and her daughter have nowhere to go, and don't even own the clothes on their backs. She doesn't want to remain involved in the game—not with her daughter to care for. If it isn't too much to ask, perhaps you know a steadholt where she might fit in. Somewhere quiet. Safe."

Aria pursed her lips, looking thoughtfully at Amara. "I might know such a place."

"And . . ." Amara smiled at Bernard. "One other thing."

"What?" Bernard said. Then his expression changed to one of understanding, and he smiled. "Oh, right."

Amara looked back at Aria and said, "She'll also need a pony. Her daughter, you see. Rook had promised her, and I want her to be able to make good on it."

"She'll need two," Bernard said, smiling at Amara. He glanced at Aria, and said, "My favor can be the other pony."

Lady Placida looked at both of them, then shook her head, a smile growing over her mouth. "I think I'm going to like you both very much," she said quietly. Then she bowed to them again, more deeply this time, and said. "I'll see to it. If you will excuse me?"

"Of course," Amara said, bowing her head. "And thank you."

Bernard walked Lady Placida to the door, and returned to Amara. He stopped to regard her for a moment, pride in his eyes. Then he leaned down and kissed her on the forehead, on both eyes, on her lips. "I love you very much, you know."

Amara smiled back at him. "I love you, too."

"Time for something nice," he said, and slipped his arms beneath her. He picked her up lightly, carrying her to the bed.

"Bernard . . ." Amara began. "You drive me mad with lust, but today isn't the best time . . ."

"Wouldn't dream of it," Bernard replied. "But all that flying around in that little red silk number wasn't good for your skin." He laid her down on the bed and gently removed her clothes. Then he took a small jar from the nightstand drawer and opened it. A warm scent, something like cinnamon, rose into the air. Bernard settled down on the bed beside her, and poured some of the jar's contents, some sort of scented oil, onto his palms. He rubbed his hands together for a moment and murmured, "The healer said this would be best to help your skin mend itself. Your legs first, I think."

Then his strong, warm hands began to slide over her legs, spreading oil over irritated, tender, dry skin. Amara felt herself melt into a puddle of contented exhaustion, and for the next hour or so, she just lay beneath his hands. He would move her limbs from time to time, and then he turned her over to take care of that side, too. The warmth of the oil, the sensation of his gentle hands on her worn muscles, the satisfying, heavy heat of the meal in her belly combined to keep her warm and send her into a languid torpor. She shamelessly reveled in it.

Amara woke up later with his arms around her, and she laid her cheek against his shoulder. It was dark. The only light came from the last embers of the fire.

"Bernard?" she whispered.

"I'm here," he said.

Her throat swelled up, tightened, and she whispered, "I'm so sorry. I haven't ever been late before." She squeezed her eyes shut. "I didn't mean to disappoint you."

"Disappoint me?" Bernard murmured. "This just means that we'll have to try harder." His finger traced the line of her throat, and the touch sent a pleased little shiver through her. "And more often. I can't say I'm disappointed about that."

"But . . ."

He turned to her and kissed her mouth very gently. "Hush. There's nothing to forgive. And nothing has changed."

She sighed, closed her eyes, and rubbed her cheek against his warm skin. The various pains had eased, and she could feel drowsiness filling the void they left in her.

A thought occurred to her, just at the border of dreams and consciousness, and she heard herself sleepily murmur, "Something's missing."

"Hmmm?"

"Lady Aquitaine. She took Aldrick and Odiana to assist her."

"You're right. I was there."

"So why didn't she take Fidelias? He's her most experienced retainer, and he's done this kind of rescue mission a dozen times."

"Mmmm," Bernard said, his own voice thick with sleep. "Maybe she sent him somewhere else."

Maybe, Amara thought. *But where?*

The hour was late, and Valiar Marcus stood alone at the center of the Elinarch, staring quietly out over the river.

It had been ten days since the battle ended. The town's southern walls had been built into a far more formidable defense in anticipation of a fresh Canim assault that never came. The work had gone swiftly, once they'd cleaned out the charred remains of the buildings that the captain had burned down, and the engineers were rebuilding that portion of the town from stone, designing the streets into a hardened defensive network that would make for a nightmarish defense, should the walls ever be breached again.

The unnatural clouds had emptied themselves into several days of steady rain, and the river's level had risen more than three feet. The waters below were still thick with sharks that had feasted on the remains of fallen Canim, dumped there over the course of more than a week.

Few furylamps had survived the battle, and funeral pyres for fallen Alerans provided the only dim lights Marcus could see. The last of the pyres still burned in the burial yards north of the bridge—there had simply been too many bodies for proper, individual burials, the rain had complicated burials and pyres alike, and Marcus was glad that the most difficult work, laying the fallen to rest, was finally done. Dreams of faces dead and gone for days or decades haunted his sleep, but they didn't disturb his rest as they might have three years ago.

Marcus felt sorrow for them, regret for their sacrifice—but also drew strength from their memories. Those men might be dead, but they were still *legionares*, part of a tradition that stretched back and vanished into the mists of Aleran history. They had lived and died Legion, part of something that was greater than the sum of its parts.

Just as Marcus was. Just as he always had been. Even if, for a time, he had forgotten.

He sighed, looking up at the stars, enjoying the seclusion and privacy of the darkness at the peak of the bridge, where the evening breezes swept away the last stench of the battle. As difficult and dangerous as the action had been, Marcus had found himself deeply contented to be in uniform again.

To be fighting a good fight, in a worthy cause.

He shook his head and chuckled at himself. Ridiculous. Those were notions that rightfully belonged in far younger, far less bitter hearts than his own. He knew that. It did not, however, lessen their power.

He heard nothing but a faint rustle of sound behind him, cloth stirred by wind.

"Good," he said quietly. "I was wondering when you'd get here."

A tall man in a simple, grey traveling cloak and hood stepped up beside Marcus and also leaned his elbows on the stone siding of the bridge, staring down at the river. "Well?"

"Pay up," Marcus said quietly.

Gaius glanced aside at him. "Really?"

"I've always told you, Gaius. A good disguise isn't about looking different. It's about *being* someone else." He shook his head. "Watercrafting is the beginning, but it isn't enough."

The First Lord said, "Perhaps so." He watched the river for a time, then said, "Well?"

Marcus exhaled heavily. "Bloody crows, Sextus. When I saw him in uniform, giving orders on the wall, I thought for a moment I'd gone senile. He could have *been* Septimus. The same look, the same style of command, the same . . ."

"Courage?" the First Lord suggested.

"Integrity," Marcus said. "Courage was just a part of it. And the way he played his cards—crows. He's smarter than Septimus was. Wilier. More resourceful." He glanced aside at the First Lord. "You could have just told me."

"No. You had to see it for yourself. You always do."

Marcus grunted out a short laugh. "I suppose you're right." He turned to face Gaius more fully. "Why haven't you acknowledged him?"

"You know why," Gaius said, voice quiet and pained. "Without furycraft, I might as well cut his throat myself as make him a target to men and women against whom he couldn't possibly defend himself."

Marcus considered that for a moment, then said, "Sextus. Don't be stupid."

There was a shocked little silence, then the First Lord said, "Excuse me."

"Don't be stupid," Marcus repeated obligingly. "That young man just manipulated his enemies into disarray and cut down a ritualist with fifty thousand fanatic followers. He didn't just defeat him, Sextus. He destroyed him. Personally. He stood to battle shoulder to shoulder with *legionares*, survived a Canim sorcery that killed ninety percent of the officers of this Legion—twice—and employed his Knights furycrafting with devastating effect." Marcus turned and waved a hand toward the Legion camp on the south side of the bridge. "He earned the respect of the men, and you know how rare that is. If he told this Legion to get on their feet, right now, and start marching out to take on the Canim, they'd do it. They'd follow him."

Gaius was silent for a long moment.

"It isn't about furycraft, Gaius," he said quietly. "It never has been. It's about personal courage and will. He has it. It's about the ability to lead. He can. It's about inspiring loyalty. He does."

"Loyalty," Gaius said, light irony in the word. "Even in you?"

"He saved my life," Marcus said. "Didn't have to. Nearly got himself killed doing it. He cares."

"Are you saying you'll be willing to work for him?"

Marcus was quiet for a moment. Then he said, "I'm saying that only a fool will discount him simply because he's furyless. Crows, he's already checked a Canim invasion, helped forge an alliance with the Marat, and personally prevented your assassination at Wintersend. How much more bloody qualified does he need to *be*?"

Gaius absorbed that in silence for a moment. Then he said, "You like being Valiar Marcus."

Marcus snorted. "After I got done with him and he retired from the Shieldwall Legions . . . I forgot how much I'd liked being him."

"How long did it take you to do the face?"

"Three weeks, give or take, several hours each day. I've never been particularly strong at watercraft." They both fell quiet again. Then Marcus sighed. "Crows take it, Sextus. If only I'd known."

Gaius chuckled without much humor. "If only *I'd* known."

"But we can't go back."

"No," the First Lord agreed. "We can't." He turned to Marcus, and said, "But perhaps we can go forward."

Marcus frowned. "What?"

"You recognized him, when you finally got a good look at him. Don't you think anyone else who ever served with Septimus might do the same?" Gaius shook his head. "He's grown into a man. He won't go overlooked for much longer."

"No," Marcus said. "What would you have me do?"

Gaius looked at him and said, "Nothing. Marcus."

Valiar Marcus frowned. "She'll find out soon enough, whether or not I say anything."

"Perhaps," Gaius said. "But perhaps not. In either case, there's no reason it couldn't slip your notice as it has everyone else's. And I hardly think she'd be displeased to have an agent as Octavian's trusted right hand."

Marcus sighed. "True. And I suppose if I refuse, you'll take the standard measures."

"Yes," the First Lord said, gentle regret in his voice. "I don't wish to. But you know how the game is played."

"Mmmm," Marcus said. Both were quiet for perhaps ten minutes. Then Marcus said, "Do you know what the boy is?"

"What?"

Marcus heard the faint, quiet wonder in his own voice when he spoke. "Hope."

"Yes," Gaius said. "Remarkable." He reached out a hand and put several golden coins on the stone siding, next to Marcus's hand. Then he took another one, an ancient silver bull, the coin worn with age, and placed it beside them.

Marcus took up the gold. He stared at the silver coin for a long moment, the token of a Cursor's authority. "You and I can never be made right again."

"No," Gaius said. "But perhaps you and Octavian can."

Marcus stared at the silver coin, the token of a Cursor's allegiance to the Crown. Then he picked it up and put it in his pocket. "How old was Septimus when he started crafting?"

Gaius shrugged. "About five, I think. He set the nursery on fire. Why?"

"Five." Marcus shook his head. "Just curious."

The man in the grey cloak turned to walk away.

"You didn't have to show me this," Marcus said to his back.

"No," he answered.

"Thank you, Sextus."

The First Lord turned and inclined his head to the other man. "You are welcome, Fidelias."

Marcus watched him go. Then he drew out the old silver

coin and held it up to let the distant fires shine on its surface. "Five," he mused.

"How long have we known one another, Aleran?" Kitai asked.

"Five years this autumn," Tavi said.

Kitai walked beside Tavi as he left the hospital—the first building Tavi had ordered the Legion's engineers to reconstruct. A clean, dry place to nurse the injured and sick had been badly needed, given the numbers of wounded and the exhaustion of Foss and his healers, particularly during the final hours of the battle, when the healers had barely been able to so much as stabilize the dying, much less return them to action.

Tavi had spent his evening visiting the wounded. Whenever he'd been able to find a few moments, he would visit a few more of his men, asking about them, giving them whatever encouragement he could. It was exhausting, to see one mangled *legionare* after another, every one of them wounded while obeying orders he had given.

He brought Kitai with him whenever he visited—in fact, he brought her nearly everywhere he went, including staff meetings. He introduced her as Ambassador Kitai, and offered no other explanation whatsoever for her presence, his entire manner suggesting that she belonged there and that anyone with questions or comments about her had best keep them to himself. He wanted the men to get used to seeing her, to speaking her, until they got the idea that she was not a threat. It was a method adapted from his uncle's lessons in shepherding, Tavi had thought, amused. It was the same way he would train sheep to accept the presence of a new shepherd or dog.

She had discarded her beggar's outfit to wear one of Tavi's uniform tunics, leather riding breeches, and high riding boots. She had shorn her long hair Legion style, and what remained was her natural color, silver-white.

She nodded as they walked. "Five years. In that time," she said, "have I ever attempted to deceive you?"

Tavi put a finger on the fine, white scar he had on one cheek. "The first night I met you, you gave me that with one of those stone knives. And I thought you were a boy."

"You are slow and stupid. We both know this. But have I ever deceived you?"

"No," he said. "Never."

She nodded. "Then I have an idea you should present to the First Lord."

"Oh?"

She nodded. "We will be facing Nasaug and his people for a time, yes?"

Tavi nodded. "Until the First Lord can put down Kalarus's forces, we'll have to be here to contain them and harass them—hopefully to keep as many of them as possible pinned down here, not helping Kalarus, while avoiding another pitched battle."

"You will need many scouts, then. Forces for small group action."

Tavi grimaced and nodded. "Yes. Which isn't going to be fun."

"Why not?"

"Because of their speed, for one thing," Tavi said. "It's too easy for scouts to be seen or tracked, then run down—especially at night. But there just aren't enough horses to mount them all. If I can't find some way around it, we're going to lose a lot of good people."

Kitai tilted her head. "Are you to remain the captain, then?"

"For now," Tavi said, nodding. "Foss says that Cyril's going to lose his left leg. Crown law forbids any Legion officer who cannot march and fight beside his men. But I'm almost certain he's going to be added to the Legion as an attaché from the Crown or made into a regional Consul Strategica."

Kitai arched an eyebrow. "What does that mean?"

"That he'll give me orders and advice, in how and where to move. But I'll be the one making the calls in action."

"Ah," Kitai said. "A war-master and a camp-master, is what my people call it. One makes decisions outside of battle. The other inside."

"Sounds about right," Tavi said.

Kitai frowned, and said, "But are you not subject to the

same law? You cannot march with the men. Not using the furycraft of your people's roads."

"True," Tavi said, smiling. "But they don't know that."

Kitai's eyebrows shot up in sudden surprise.

"What?" Tavi asked her.

"You . . . you aren't . . ." She frowned. "Bitter. Sad. Always, when you spoke of your own lack of sorcery, it caused you pain."

"I know," Tavi said, and he was somewhat surprised to hear himself say it calmly, without the familiar little ache of frustration and sadness at the unfairness of it all. "I suppose now, it isn't as important to me. I know what I can do now, even without furycrafting. I've spent my whole life waiting for it to happen. But if it never happens, so be it. I can't sit around holding my breath. It's time let it go. To get on with living."

Kitai looked at him steadily, then she leaned up on her toes and kissed his cheek.

Tavi smiled. "What was that for?"

"For forging your own wisdom," she said, and smiled. "There may yet be hope for you, *chala*."

Tavi snorted as they approached the second stone building the engineers had constructed—a command center. They had built it out of the heaviest stone they could draw from the earth, and set most of the building so far into the ground that its lowest chambers, including its command room, were actually below the level of the river. Tavi hadn't wanted that building to get priority, but Magnus and the rest of his officers had quietly ignored his authority and done it anyway. It would take more than one of the Canim's vicious bolts of lightning to threaten the building, the engineers had assured him.

Tavi had to admit that it had been extremely helpful all around to have a solid location for organizing the Legion. The rest of the Legion had laid their tents around the command building and hospital in standard order, and though the fallen and injured were sorely missed, a sense of normality, of continuity had returned to the First Aleran. He solved problems as they arose, though most days he felt like some kind of madman beating out random brush fires with a blanket before sprinting for the next source of smoke.

If he'd known that they were going to build an apartment, complete with private bath, into the command building, he'd have told them not to do it. But they'd simply walked him there at the end of the tour. He had a small sitting room, a bathing room, and a bedroom that would have been of distinctly modest size in any setting other than a Legion camp. As it was, he could have fit a standard tent into it without trouble, and his bed was wide enough to sprawl carelessly on, a distinct difference from the standard Legion-issue folding cot and bedroll.

Guards stood outside the command building, and saluted as Tavi came walking up with Kitai beside him. He nodded to the men, both of them Battlecrows. "Milias, Jonus. Carry on."

The young cohort had taken the duty for guarding the captain's quarters upon themselves with quiet determination, and the men on duty were always careful that their uniforms were immaculate, and that the crow sigil the cohort had taken as their own was obvious upon their breastplates and, in more stylized detail, upon their helmets and shields. The burned standard had been duplicated many times, always with the black crow and not the Crown's eagle, and one such standard hung on the door to the command building.

He passed inside and headed for the rear area on the first floor—his apartment. It was plainly, sensibly furnished with sturdy, functional furniture. He had dropped off several things there earlier in the day, but this would be the first time he had stayed the night. "So what is this idea?"

"To me," Kitai said, "it seems that you have a problem. Your scouts are not swift enough to evade the foe if discovered. Nor can they see in the dark, while your foe can."

"I just said that."

"Then you need swift scouts who can see in the dark."

Tavi shrugged out of his cloak and tossed it onto a chair. "That would be nice, yes."

"It happens," Kitai said, "that my mother's sister is just

such a person. In fact, I believe she knows some few others who share those qualities."

Tavi's eyebrows shot up. Kitai's aunt was Hashat, leader of the Horse Clan of Marat, and likely the second most influential of the Marat clan-heads.

"Bring a Marat force *here*?" he asked.

"Evidence suggests it may be possible for them to survive," she said, her tone dry.

Tavi snorted. "I thought Doroga needed Hashat to keep things in order at home."

"Perhaps," Kitai said. "But you would not require the whole of the clan. A herd or two of riders would be adequate for your needs. That much strength could be spared, if needed to ensure the stability of your mad Realm, Aleran. The order of Alera means as much to the Marat as our stability means to you."

"True enough."

"And cooperation between your folk and mine, even on a small scale, could be an important step in solidifying our friendship."

"It could," he agreed. "Let me think about it. And I'll have to speak to the First Lord."

"And it will save lives you would otherwise be forced to sacrifice."

It would do that, Tavi thought. But then a notion struck him, and he arched a brow and tilted his head at Kitai, grinning. "You're just doing this so you get to ride around on horses more often."

Kitai gave him a haughty glance. "I *wanted* a horse. But I got you, Aleran. I must make the best of it."

Tavi went to her, pushed her against a wall with a certain amount of careless strength, then pinned her there with his body and kissed her. The Marat girl's breath sped up, and she melted into the kiss, hands lifting to touch, body moving in slow, sinuous tension against his.

Tavi let out a low growl as the kiss made him burn for her. He lifted the hem of the tunic and slid his hands over the soft, feverish skin of her waist and lower back. "Shall we try the bath?"

She broke the kiss long enough to say, "Here. Now. Bath later." Then she took the front of his tunic in both hands, her canted green eyes intense and feral, and started pulling him to the bedroom.

Tavi paused in the doorway and let out a groan. "Wait."

The look in Kitai's eyes made Tavi think of a hungry lioness about to pounce, and her hips swayed toward his, but she stopped, waiting.

"The furylamp," Tavi sighed. "As long as it's on, the sentries know I'm available and receiving visitors."

Kitai's eyes narrowed. "And?"

"And there's not a lot I can do about it. I'm going to have to go find Max or someone."

"Why?"

"Because it's not as if I can just tell the light to go out."

Blackness fell on the room.

Tavi fell to the floor on his rump in pure shock.

He sat there feeling an odd, fluttery sensation in his belly, and his scalp felt as if something with many sharp little legs was running over it. He felt the hairs on his arms stand on end.

"Aleran?" Kitai whispered, her voice low, even awed.

"I . . ." Tavi said. "I just said . . . I wanted it to go out. And . . ."

The enormity of that fact hit him, hard and all at once. He found himself wheezing, unable to get a full breath.

He'd told the furylamp to go out.

And it had.

He had *made* it go out.

He had *crafted* it out.

He had *furycrafted*.

"Light," he managed to whisper a moment later. "I need it to turn on."

And it did.

Tavi stared at Kitai with wide eyes, and she returned the same incredulous look.

"Kitai. I did that. *Me!*"

She only stared at him.

"Light, off!" Tavi said. It flickered out, and he immediately said, "Light, on!" And it was so. "Bloody crows!" Tavi swore, laughter bubbling through his voice. "Off! On! Off! On! Off! Did you *see* it, Kitai?"

"Yes, Aleran," she said, her tone that of one who has been abruptly and deeply offended. "I saw."

Tavi laughed again and drummed his heels on the stone floor. "On!"

The light came on again, to reveal Kitai standing over him, hands on her hips, scowling.

"What?" Tavi asked her.

"All this time," she said. "You moping around. Sad about it. Sure it was so awful. For *this*?"

"Well. Yes. Off!"

Kitai sighed. "Typical." Cloth rustled.

"What do you mean?" Tavi asked. "On!"

When the lamp came up again, she stood before him, naked and beautiful, and Tavi nearly exploded with wanting her as a surge of lust and joy and love and triumph blazed through him.

"What I mean, Aleran," she said quietly, "is that all this time you were acting as if it was some kind of monumental task. When it is so *simple*." She turned her head enough to regard the furylamp and said, firmly, "Off."

The lamp went out.

And before Tavi's utter shock could really register, Kitai pressed him down to the floor and stopped his mouth with a kiss.

Tavi decided the crowbegotten lamp could wait.

There were more important things.

Tavi's story continues in the
fourth book of the Codex Alera . . .

CAPTAIN'S FURY
by Jim Butcher

Now available from Ace Books

"My ass hurts," said Antillar Maximus, Tribune Auxiliarus of the First Aleran.

"My ass hurts, *sir*," Tavi corrected him.

"Hey. Sacred right."

Tavi grunted where he lay prone and peered steadily through the yellow-and-brown winter grass of the Vale at the valley beneath them. "Just imagine if you'd marched here instead of riding."

"No thank you, sir," Max replied. "I'm too busy imagining I decided to take a few more terms at the Academy so that I could practice my earthcrafting with wealthy and beautiful Citizen girls, sir, instead of riding around the back of beyond looking to pick a fight with big, scary monsters."

The two of them lay low, and Max's voice was pitched barely louder than a whisper, for all that it never stopped running. As long as they didn't stand up and present the enemy force marching through the valley below with a beautiful silhouette, they were far enough above them to avoid being seen. Probably.

"I make that four thousand," Tavi murmured after a moment. "You?"

"Forty-two hundred," Max replied promptly. For all his complaining, the big Antillan was every bit the trained observer Tavi was. In fact, Tavi trusted his friend's estimate over his own.

Tavi frowned, thinking. "Figure one cohort for camp security . . ."

". . . and one more for scouting ahead and behind as they march," Max continued the thought.

"Bloody crows." Tavi sighed. "A full Legion."

Max let out a grim sound of agreement. "Looks that way."

Tavi felt a cold little shiver run along his belly.

In the valley below, an army of Canim marched steadily through the dry grass. The wolf-headed warriors moved with steady purpose, a good three thousand of them spread in a loose, horseshoe-shaped arrangement around a core of solid, heavily armored troops marching in ranks. Three thousand raiders shifting position would not have stirred Tavi to launch any kind of assault. Conscripted Canim, with a minimum of military discipline, the raiders were dangerous only by virtue of their numbers and their tremendous size and strength. The average Cane stood between seven and eight feet tall, and that was in their standard, half-crouched posture. Standing erect, they would have been a foot taller than that, and the sheer speed and power held within those lean frames was terrifying.

Still, the Canim army now occupying much of the territory of the cities of Ceres and Kalare could afford to lose three thousand of their dregs. It was the core of disciplined troops marching at their center, members of the elite Canim warrior caste, that had drawn Tavi from the fortifications.

A thousand of those hardened, disciplined, supremely dangerous troops represented a tithe of the Canim's total number of heavy infantry. In all their clashes with the Canim, the First Aleran had killed a relatively limited number of the warrior caste. Canim losses had been almost universally drawn from among their raiders. Nasaug, the leader of the Canim forces, never used his best troops except in devastatingly well-timed assaults, and the vast majority of Aleran losses had been at the hands of the Canim warrior caste.

Ehren's report of a thousand of them shifting position had represented an opportunity to inflict serious harm upon Nasaug's troops. A thousand were not so many as to be undefeatable, but more than enough to represent a significant loss to the enemy's prize corps of troops. When Tavi had learned which territory they were moving through, he had ordered his most mobile and dangerous units into the field at once.

The Canim warriors were walking through a death trap.

This particular valley had remarkably steep walls, and the lattice of tiny streams that ran through it provided enough water to ensure a growth of luxuriant grass—which had not yet flushed into the lush, verdant sea of green it would become within a few more weeks. For now, it was a ten-mile-long, one-mile-wide box filled with kindling and a thousand of Nasaug's finest.

The First Aleran's Knights Ignus were already in position, with the far more numerous Knights Aeris beside them. At Tavi's signal, the Knights Ignus would set the valley ablaze while the Knights Aeris used their furies to call forth a gale and send a sudden riptide of fire and fury over the foe. The Battlecrows stood at the head of the valley, ready to set a backfire and blockade the valley's only means of egress, while Max's cavalry stood ready to sweep down from the other end of the valley and crush any Canim who managed to escape immolation.

Which was why the *second* Legion marching beside the Canim company was a problem.

They were Alerans.

Better than four thousand Alerans in full Legion regalia marched beside the most dangerous historic foes of the Realm, under banners that did not correspond to any of the great cities of Alera. Worse, they were moving in good order. Two years ago, Tavi would never have understood how difficult such an apparently simple maneuver actually *was*. It took serious discipline to achieve such uniform movement, and was evidence of a disturbing amount of competence on behalf of whoever was training those troops.

"Give me a lens, please," Tavi said quietly.

The big Antillan rose a little, leaned over Tavi, and held his hands out on either side of Tavi's face, fingers spread. The air between Max's palms blurred, and suddenly the force below them seemed to rush hundreds of yards closer, as Max's furies bent the air, magnifying Tavi's view.

"Those aren't Kalaran banners," Tavi murmured after a moment's study.

Max let out a skeptical grunt. "Maybe Kalare didn't want to be openly associated with them."

"He's already attacked his neighbors without warning, kidnapped several family members of his fellow High Lords, and had dozens and dozens of Citizens murdered by his pet maniacs," Tavi pointed out. "You really think he's worried about covering up his involvement with the Canim at this point?"

"Put that way," Max said. "No."

Tavi let out a little snort of a breath. "Take a look at their gear."

Max moved his hands up to hold before his own face. A moment later, he reported, "It's old. I mean, everything looks to be in pretty good shape, but the armor is of a design that went out of use years ago. There are lots of missing pieces, too. Mismatched greaves, nonstandard-length spears, that kind of thing." Max grunted.

"Never seen any banners like that, either. Brown and green? Who uses brown and green for *banners*? They're supposed to be *visible*. That's the *point* of banners."

"Exactly," Tavi said quietly, watching the enemy column's progress.

"They're almost in position," Max said, lowering his hands. "Once their leading elements hit that old streambed, there's no way they're getting out in time."

"I see them," Tavi said.

Max nodded and said nothing for a minute. Tavi watched the disciplined but partially equipped Legion march steadily in step with the far larger Canim.

"Sir," Max said, "they're in position. It's time to signal Crassus, sir."

"It doesn't make *sense*, Max," Tavi said. "This has got to be a Legion of volunteers from within the occupied territory. Why would they be fighting *beside* an army of invaders?"

"Who knows. Maybe Nasaug is forcing them into it. Holding their families prisoner or something."

"No," Tavi said. "Nasaug is too smart for that. You don't take a man's home and family away, demand that he serve and obey you, and then put a weapon in his hand and give him four thousand friends just as angry and well armed as he is."

"Sir," Max said, "at this point, the longer we delay the attack, the more the Canim vanguard is going to be able to pressure the Battlecrows at the head of the valley."

"Why?" Tavi demanded to no one in particular. "Why are they *down* there?"

Max's voice gained a tense edge. "Captain, at this point it's academic. Should I order the attack?"

Tavi stared at the valley below. Fighting the Canim was one thing. He'd been doing that for a while. He respected them enough to regret the necessity of killing them though he knew he had little real choice in the matter. It was war. If Alerans didn't kill the Canim, the Canim would promptly kill Alerans, and it was as simple as that.

Except that the cobbled-together Legion below was not made up of Canim. They were Alerans. They were people Tavi had sworn to safeguard and protect.

But they were also the enemy. Two years had taught him that no matter how experienced the army or how skilled the commander, the calculus of war had a single, unalterable constant: death.

More than four thousand Alerans were about to die, and die horribly, and they shouldn't have been there at *all*. Tavi could not afford to let such a tempting target as the vulnerable column of Canim regulars get past—even if the only way to get them was to destroy the strange Legion with them, whoever they were.

His duty was clear.

Four thousand Alerans. He was about to murder more than four *thousand* fellow Alerans.

"Bloody crows," he whispered.

Tavi fought the sudden urge to throw up as he raised his hand and began to flash the signal that would travel down the relay line, ordering his men to begin the attack.

Before he could lift his arm enough to give the signal, Tavi felt an odd, sourceless, faint sensation of shock and surprise. He puzzled over it an instant before he realized that the emotions had not been his own. He had sensed them, if only dimly, coming from another source nearby, and Tavi whipped his head around in a sudden panic.

The enemy scout wore loose clothing of plain homespun that had been intentionally stained with earth and plant juices. He was a blocky little brick of a man, not tall, but with grotesquely overdeveloped shoulders and a neck that was literally thicker than the base of his skull. Despite his ragged clothing, he wore genuine *legionare's* boots, and though his leather sword belt shone with age, it bore a genuine *gladius* at his hip—and there was nothing old or ragged about the short, powerfully curved hunting bow in his hands. He had emerged from the tall grass and scrub on the ridge not ten feet away.

Tavi got his legs underneath him and whipped his knife from his belt, releasing the heavy blade into a throw almost directly from its sheath. There was no time to grip the knife properly, to set himself to throw or to aim. The knife tumbled through the air, and Tavi noted that even if it had hit point on, instead of landing almost flat against the enemy scout's upper arm, it wouldn't have inflicted anything more than a scratch.

But that hadn't been the point of the throw. The scout released the arrow strung to his bow in an instinctive snap shot, but flinched away from the whirling knife, and his arrow flew wide.

Tavi charged after his knife, put his head down, and plowed an armored shoulder into the scout's belly. The shock of impact jarred his shoulder and neck, and the scout let out a sickly sounding croak as he fell. Tavi came down on top of the scout, seized the man's homespun tunic in both hands, and slammed his helmeted forehead against the scout's face. Tavi felt the shock of the blow through the steel, and heard the scout's nose break with a squishy crunch.

The scout reacted by lifting one iron-strong hand and clamping it down on Tavi's throat. Tavi felt the fury-assisted strength of the scout's arm, and knew that if he didn't do something, the earthcrafter would snap his neck.

Tavi brought his armored knee up in a savage blow that struck home between the scout's legs, and, for a single instant, the power in that deadly arm faltered. Tavi slammed his helmet against the scout's face again, then again, and the man sagged limply back to the ground.

The entire fight had taken all of three or four seconds.

Tavi fell back from the man, his throat on fire. It was hard to suck air in through his mouth, and for a second he feared that the enemy scout had managed to crush his windpipe, but after a few seconds more he was able to gulp down great breaths of air.

Max had his sword out and had been on the way, but Tavi's reaction had been the swifter, and the big Antillan's face was pale. "Bloody crows," he hissed. "Captain?"

"I'm all right," Tavi choked out. "Did they see? Did they hear anything?"

Max rose to a low crouch and looked slowly around, then dropped down again. "There'd have been some noise by now." He met Tavi's eyes. "Captain. You have to signal the attack *now*."

Tavi stared at the senseless young man lying limp in the grass. He reached up to touch the front rim of his helmet, and his fingers came away wet with blood.

"I know," Max said, his voice low and hard. "I know you don't like killing. I know that they're our own people. I know this is hard and horrible. But that's what war *is*, Captain. You've *got* to order the attack."

"Signal Crassus," Tavi said quietly.

Max let out a low breath of relief and nodded, beginning to rise.

"Do not engage. Fall back to the rally point and meet us there."

Max stared at Tavi, his eyes widening.

Tavi continued, wiping his hands clean of blood on the dry grass. "Get word to the Battlecrows to abandon their position and fall back."

Max remained still for a moment. "Captain," he said quietly. "We aren't going to get another opportunity like this one."

Tavi narrowed his eyes as he looked up at his friend. "We're leaving, Tribune. You have your orders."

"Yes, sir," Max said at once, and very quietly. Then he paced off through the grass where he would, Tavi knew, begin flashing hand signals down the line of riders.

Max returned a moment later and watched the enemy

forces below begin to march out of the ambush area and beyond their reach. "Bloody crows, Calderon. Why?"

"Why not burn four thousand of our own people to death?" Tavi asked. He gestured at the downed scout. "Look at him, Max. What do you see?"

Max stared down at the unconscious man for a moment. Then he frowned, leaned closer, and tugged aside the man's tunic a bit before he rose again. "Muscles are all lopsided, misshapen. He's been chained to a wheel or a plow, for them to develop like that," he said quietly. "He's got lash scars." His right cheek twitched in a tic that Tavi thought Max didn't know he had. "Curling over his shoulders. More on his belly. Collar scars on his neck, too. He's a slave."

"He *was* a slave," Tavi replied quietly. "No collar now." He nodded down at the army below. "We wanted to know what could make an Aleran fight beside a Cane, Max."

Max grimaced, and said, "They're freeing slaves."

Tavi nodded slowly.

"How many?" Max asked. "How many do you think they have?"

"Can't be too many," Tavi said. "They don't have a lot of gear, if this man's equipment is any indication. And if they were raising really large numbers, Ehren's spies would have heard something about them. Which makes sense."

"How?" Max said.

Tavi nodded at the slave Legion below. "Those men know that if they lose, they're dead men, Max. Some slaves have it bad, but a lot of them don't. My guess is that the ones willing to fight are a lot less common than the ones who just want to stay low and quiet until the fighting is over."

"But those are going to fight like the crows are coming for them," Max said, his voice grim.

"Yes," Tavi said quietly.

Max was silent for a minute. Then he said, "All the more reason to order the attack. I know why you didn't do it. Great furies know I agree with your principles. But a lot of men are going to have to die to stop them now. You could have have done that without a loss. It's going to cost us."

"It won't cost as much as creating a Legion of martyrs," Tavi said quietly. "If I'm right, then right now, four thousand slaves have taken up arms. If we'd wiped them out, Max, if we'd proven to every slave in the occupied territory that Alera didn't give a crow's feather about their lives, Nasaug wouldn't have four thousand fresh troops ready to fight. He'd have forty thousand terrified, outraged volunteers. Read history, Max. The Canim have." Tavi shook his head. "Men fight hardest for their lives—and for their freedom."

Max drew in a slow breath, his rough, appealing features drawn into a pensive frown. "This was a trap," he said quietly. "We were offered those warriors as bait."

"This could have been a trap," Tavi said, nodding. "But Nasaug doesn't plan operations with only one purpose if he can possibly help it. I think this was something else, too."

"What?" Max said.

"A message." Tavi rose, nodding to the downed scout. "Come on. We'd better clear out before his friends notice that he's missing and come looking for him." Tavi leaned down and rolled the limp man onto his side.

"What are you doing?"

"Making sure he doesn't choke on his own blood," Tavi said. "Let's move."

They moved at a crouch out to where they'd left the horses, hidden in a thick copse of evergreens. "Tavi?" Max asked.

"Yes?"

"Is that really why you didn't order the attack? Did you really think it was a trap?"

Tavi regarded his friend steadily. "You think I felt sympathy for them."

"No," Max said. "I bloody well know you did, Calderon. I know you. But we're at war. I'm not sure you can afford that. I'm not sure the men can afford it."

Tavi paused beside Acteon, one hand on the saddle, one on the reins, and stared at nothing in particular. "I think," he said quietly, "that I have a duty to Alera, Max. All Alerans." He took a deep breath and mounted. Then he said, his voice distant and very calm, "And yes. That's why I didn't kill them all."

Max mounted a moment later and rode up beside Tavi as they moved back toward the rally point. "That works for me." He glanced back at the ridge behind them and let out a low chortle.

"What?" Tavi asked.

"Your *singulare* has been walking around in your shadow for almost two years now. The first day he's not here, you charge out into the field and get yourself half-choked to death. He's going to be furious. So's Kitai."

Tavi let out a rough-sounding chuckle. It grated painfully in his throat. "Don't worry, Max. I'll deal with them."

Max's smile faded. "Senator Arnos was hoping to put a big new feather in his cap for this conference with the First Lord. He and the War Committee are not going to be happy about you letting those regulars get away."

Tavi felt his eyes narrow as his smile turned into a simple baring of his teeth. "Don't worry, Max," he said. "I'll deal with them, too."

THE DRESDEN FILES

Wizards are cool.

I mean, come on. When it comes to fantasy, you can't swing a cat without hitting a wizard somewhere, striding through the shadows and wars of epic battles of light and darkness, uncovering lost knowledge, protecting, inspiring, and guiding others toward the future. Merlin, Gandalf, Allannon, Dalben, Belgarath, Raistlin, Goblin, and One-Eye—and their darker counterparts like Morgana, Arawn, Soulcatcher, and Saruman. Wizards wield secrets as warriors do swords, driven by a vision that lets them see and know more than mere mortals, gifted with a power that makes them treasured allies—and terrifying foes. Throughout fantasy fiction, when the need is most dire it is the wizard who stands to face balrogs and dragons, dark spirits and fearsome beasts, natural catastrophes and dark gods.

Harry Blackstone Copperfield Dresden, wizard for hire, is happy if he manages to pay the rent for another month. He's in the Chicago Yellow Pages, under "Wizards." He's the only entry there. Most people think he is some kind of harmless nutball at best, and a charlatan-psychic at worst.

But then, most people haven't seen what Harry's seen. Most people don't know the truth: that the supernatural is perfectly real, existing quietly side by side with most of humanity's perceptions of reality. Trolls lurk under bridges, and faeries swoop down to kidnap children. Vampires prowl the shadows by night, restless ghosts rise up from the darkness of the grave, and demons and monsters to boggle the mind lurk in the shadows, ready to devour, maim, and destroy.

A few people know the truth, of course. Wizards such as Harry know. So do a few of the cops, like Lt. Karrin Murphy, head of Chicago P.D.'s Special Investigations division, who knows the touch of the supernatural when she sees it and who hires Chicago's only professional wizard to come in as a consultant when an investigation begins to look like an episode of *The X-Files*.

And other people learn the truth the hard way, when something out of a bad dream shows up at the front door. For those poor mortals, the supernatural becomes a sudden, impossible, terrifying nightmare come true—a nightmare no one can help them wake up from.

No one but Harry Dresden, that is. Hauntings, disappearances, missing persons, murders, curses, monsters—you name it, and Harry knows something about it. More than that, he shares the convictions of his literary ancestors—a deep and genuine commitment to use his power to protect those who cannot protect themselves, to stand between the darkest beings of the supernatural and his fellow man.

When the need is most dire, when the night is most deadly, when no one else can help you, give Harry Dresden a call.

He's in the book.

Jim Butcher's newest Harry Dresden novel, *White Night*, is now available in hardcover from Roc Books.